THE MODERN LIBRARY
of the World's Best Books

49 STORIES

49 STORIES

by

JOHN O'HARA

The Modern Library · New York

THE MODERN LIBRARY

is published by

RANDOM HOUSE, INC.

BENNETT CERF • DONALD S. KLOPFER

Manufactured in the United States of America

Several of the stories in this volume originally were published in *The New Yorker*.

INTRODUCTION

They toss that word "master" around pretty easily these days, awarding it with equal generosity to people who commit small, secret chunks of poetry in misty magazines and large, empty novels calculated to sell by the pound. What is the word, then, for a writer who, knowing just what he is doing, and doing it with precision, authority and ever increasing range and insight, has created through the years a body of fiction not equaled by any fellow countryman of his now living?

The word, I venture to say, is still "master," but restored to its old dignity and worth, with all that that says about a writer's dedication to his art—dedication, that is to say, in the sense of his duty to himself, to his materials, and to those readers (by no means *all* readers) whom he most wants to reach. That John O'Hara is such a writer it seems to me impossible to doubt, although there are those who, for curious reasons, do doubt it.

Do they actually read him, one sometimes wonders, or do they merely resent him? If there is something preposterous about the necessity to defend excellence, it is because the success of a writer who is both excellent and popular has a way of imposing a penalty upon him. As often as not the penalty is, in sum, his contemporaries' envy.

There is indeed something enviable, minus envy's ill will, about the O'Hara mastery as you will find it in the forty-nine stories assembled here; enviable, but not surprising. Even before the novel that made his reputation, *Appoint-*

ment in Samarra (1934), he was on his way to becoming a modern master of the short story—a place later confirmed by *The Doctor's Son and Other Stories, Files on Parade, Pal Joey, Pipe Night, Hellbox*. However, in life as in his fiction, a storyteller can create suspense, and so a certain expectancy was in the air when in 1960 it was known that O'Hara was returning to the short story after eleven years in which he had largely devoted himself to the novel. Would the old touch for the shorter form, as in "The Doctor's Son," "Do You Like It Here?" and "The Lieutenant," still be there? After all, for better and worse, good writers do not stand still.

The old touch was emphatically still there, as *The New Yorker*'s readers realized who had first view of ten of the stories later gathered, along with sixteen others, in *Assembly* (1961). It continued to be there in *The Cape Cod Lighter* (1962), whose twenty-three stories, with those in *Assembly*, make up the present volume.

There was the old touch, and more. Together with what was long and happily familiar about the O'Hara talent in this form he brought, upon this return, a new delicacy of suggestion, a further depth of feeling. To be sure, he never was the hard-boiled artisan his more myopic critics deemed him. He never has written cruelly. He has described cruelty with the objectivity of one who despises it. He now does so again in certain of these stories, and we see once more—as in "The Weakness" and "The Free"—how much more forceful is the compassion of the artist who does not wear the heart on the sleeve. Without slipping into middle age's autumnal sentiment, the further depth of feeling in the later O'Hara seems to me to lie in the subtlety with which—still letting character, scene and event speak for themselves—he reveals aspects of the basic sadness of life; and with it his unspoken but manifest sympathy for the victims of wayward fate and a world they never made.

Consider, for instance, the wife in "The High Point" remembering her first love; the small-town jazz singer in "The Pioneer Hep-Cat" who might have been another Bing Crosby if only . . . ; and the man who, in "The Father," has a sudden and terrible vision of the years awaiting his doomed daughter. And if there is violence as abrupt and extreme as that in "In a Grove," there is a tenderness as affecting as that in "The Lighter When Needed" and "Winter Dance."

The "hard-boiled" O'Hara?

What it comes to is simply that the content of an O'Hara story dictates its tone, form, length, and that in no O'Hara story I can think of would one have it other than as it is: nothing to be added, altered, removed. It is not every writer's kind of craftsmanship, but it is his. "I don't feel myself a stylist," he told a newspaper interviewer in 1955, "but I have a presentation." Because the heart of this "presentation" is economy, with an absence of personal flourish, a single, un-signed page of O'Hara could easily be taken for a page by some other writer. But never an entire O'Hara story—and not merely because that story might have for its setting O'Hara's Gibbsville, Pa., a town now as recognizable to his readers as their own.

A number of other and less specific things would tell you that a given story was unmistakably his. Among them, I suggest, is that splendid base for any writer, a genuine au-thority, the assurance that he knows absolutely what he is talking about. It follows, does it not, that the more he knows, the more varied and interesting his performance will be? And who, among current American writers of fiction, writes from such a variety of experience as O'Hara does?

The sources of that experience are all around you in the forty-nine stories in this book. Having grown up in and absorbed a medium-size Pennsylvania city—street by street, "Gibbsville" is his native Pottsville—he knew the gin mill on one side of the tracks, the social structure of the country club on the other side. (Observe how they meet, so to speak, in the long story "Pat Collins.") In "Claude Emerson, Reporter" is the corruption of the press in an industrial city as only one who has been a newspaperman there can know it. In "Mary and Norma" is the casually squalid sexuality that, as any small-town person knows, originates as much in boredom as in anything else. As a physician's son, O'Hara must always have had a special sense of the doctor's private and professional worlds. Somewhere along the way he stored up a knowledge of pool and football. What he learned as a big-city reporter in the 1920's and early 1930's—in the New York of hoodlum-haunted speakeasies, big- and small-time show business, prize fighting—is put to wonderfully graphic use in "The Sun-Dodgers," "First Day in Town" and "The Weakness." Only a man who has observed New York club life could have written "The Trip," and only a working student of the Hollywood character could have written "The Girl from California." Yes, it is well for a writer to get around.

In a society in which money or the lack of it is extremely important, and to a large degree determines social position, attitudes and opportunities, O'Hara recognizes and dramatizes this fact whose existence the devotees of pure democracy prefer to sweep under the rug. People get away with a good deal, various stories of his declare, if they are in a position to afford it, as witness the doctor in "A Case History," the dissipated son in "Mrs. Stratton of Oak Knoll." About this O'Hara is neither approving nor morally censorious. To the extent that he is a moralist at all, he is a nondidactic one, letting the moral point itself, as in "Justice," where a smug philanderer finally gets what he has been asking for.

Considered as a whole, his novels and stories are a massive social document of the time in which he has been alive: how Americans behave, speak and spend their money, what they value and wear, in areas ranging from brothel to Broadway, from Hollywood to suburbia. It is a design not without its dangers. Given O'Hara's all but incredible memory, and his Balzacian passion for fact, another kind of writer—a naturalistic one—might well fall back on a process of mere cataloguing. O'Hara more often than not summons up a whole place or time with a single evocative word or term— the name of an automobile long gone, a song they were playing at house parties in 1926, an old bit of slang. You may be sure that in this field, too, he knows what he is talking about, and it is important, because this kind of detail is correspondingly as vital to him as it is to a painter, and for the same reason.

And so it is also with the O'Hara ear for the exactly recorded inflection and intonation that distinguish the speech of one person from another. It has been said, and truly so, I believe, that among American writers within living memory none save Mark Twain and Ring Lardner have listened so discerningly. Like his pictorial detail, this plays a positive, creative role in his work. "Some evening you and your wife might like to have dinner with my wife and I," says a Los Angeles real estate tycoon and Rolls-Royce owner in "Sterling Silver"; you can see the road he traveled before he came to the Rolls-Royce. "It starda rain out," says the hatcheck girl in "It's Mental Work"; at once you can hear her New York voice as surely as if you were in the same room with it.

All this—the range of experience, the scenes and occupations and voices precisely observed and remembered— surely explains much of O'Hara's popular appeal. Instinctively the reader must have a sense of confidence in him. It's a small thing, you say, that a writer should inevitably write Grand Central *Terminal* instead of Grand Central *Station,* give correctly the lyrics of an ancient song hit, not confuse a Pierce-Arrow with a Locomobile? But it is not small at all. It means that by temperament he is incapable of faking, and that in his storytelling company you will be undeceived, no matter how far from your own world the storytelling takes you. And could it be, I have sometimes wondered, that the other side of that coin reveals something—that no little of the antagonism felt for O'Hara by cloistered academics reflects their suspicion of one who knows life as they have never had the will or chance to? (This could make for a nice irony sometime in the future—namely, that the cloistered parties' successors may one day be studying him with the grave respect now accorded such forerunners of his, startling in their own time, as Stephen Crane, Frank Norris, Theodore Dreiser.)

But above all, of course, O'Hara has won public favor for the reason that other storytellers of the first order have enjoyed it since time out of mind. His narratives move, swiftly and without contrivance. His people are interesting, in many and diverse ways, and always alive. Together the narratives and the people pass brilliantly that most demanding and satisfying of tests, the kind of return visit you are invited to pay in the pages that follow.

JOHN K. HUTCHENS

CONTENTS

ASSEMBLY

THE CAPE COD LIGHTER

ASSEMBLY

My task, which I am trying to achieve, is, by the power of the written word, to make you feel—it is, before all, to make you see. That—and no more. And it is everything. JOSEPH CONRAD

Mrs. Stratton of Oak Knoll

As was their nightly custom, Evan Reese and his wife Georgia finished their small chores and took their seats to watch the eleven o'clock news program on the television. Evan Reese's chore was to put the backgammon men in place for the next night's game; Georgia's was to remove the coffee tray to the kitchen. Evan Reese now lit his pipe, Georgia lit a cigarette, and they sat patiently through the preliminary commercial announcements. "And now the news," said the announcer.

"Do tell," said Georgia, stroking the head of their Airedale.

Evan Reese smiled. His wife had given up her letters of protest to the newspaper editorial pages against the length and number of commercials, but she always made some small audible comment when the man said, "And now the news."

"Quiet, please," said Evan Reese.

"A four-engine bomber on a routine training flight over the Rocky—" the announcer began. At that moment the dog growled and the Reeses' doorbell rang.

Evan Reese frowned and looked at his wife, and they said, together: "Who could that be?" and Georgia Reese added, "At this hour?"

"You pay attention to the news, I'll see who it is," said Evan Reese. He switched on the carriage lamps at the front door and the floodlight that illuminated the driveway. He peeked through the draperies and saw, in the driveway, a large black limousine. He held the dog by the collar and opened the door.

A middle-aged man in chauffeur's livery raised his hand in a semi-military salute. "Stratton residence?" he said.

"No, this isn't the Stratton residence. You have the wrong house."

"This is Ridge Road and West Branch Lane, isn't it?" said the chauffeur.

"Yes it is, but if you'll notice there's a driveway across the road, with a sign that says Oak Knoll. That's the entrance to Mrs. Stratton's place."

"Sorry, I didn't see no sign."

"It's there in plain sight," said Evan Reese.

"What the hell's the delay?" The voice came from inside the limousine, and Evan Reese could make out a man's hatless head but little more. The Airedale barked once.

"I'll leave the floodlight on and you can turn around—and you can tell your employer to mind his manners."

"I'll tell him a lot more when I get my tip," said the chauffeur. "I don't work for him, I work for the rental company. He only hired this car, and believe me, I'll never drive him again."

"Is he drunk? He sounds it."

"Drunk? He was drunk when I called for him. The Racquet Club."

"New York, or Philadelphia?"

"New York. Well, sorry to trouble you, Mister."

"That's all right. Hope you get a big tip. Goodnight."

"Goodnight, sir, and thanks again." The chauffeur saluted, and Evan Reese closed the door, watching through the draperies until the limousine was out of his driveway.

"A drunken man calling on Mrs. Stratton. Obviously with the intention of spending the night, since it's a hired car. Now we have something on her."

"I guess it must be that son."

"No, I'd rather think it was some gigolo she sent for."

"She's a little old for that. Did you get a look at him?"

"I can give you a perfect description. Black patent leather hair, waxed moustache, and a gold bracelet . . . No, I didn't really see him. Would her son belong to the Racquet Club?"

"Oh, at least. You can look him up in the Social Register."

"Where is it?"

"It's in my sewing-room, by the telephone."

"Too much trouble," said Evan Reese. "Anything in the news?"

"I wasn't listening very carefully, I was overcome with curiosity about who'd call on us at eleven o'clock at night."

"Mrs. Stratton's drunken son, I guess. Now the next time she writes us one of her neighborly notes about our dog, we can come back at her."

"Oh, Ev, that was ten years ago."

"Well, it's still the only time we ever heard from her. Ten years and she never came to call on you. I think I *will* look up the son. By the telephone?"

"On the lower shelf of the little table."

Evan Reese obtained the book and returned to the library. "Now then," he said. "Stratton, there *she* is. Mrs. Francis, Oak Knoll, High Ridge, New Jersey. Phone number 7-1415. Ah, yes, here he is. Francis A., Junior, 640 East Eighty-third. R for Racquet, B for Brook, K for Knickerbocker, H-37. Harvard, '37. That would make him about forty-five years old. Oh, and here's one. Stratton, Mrs. Virginia C., Virginia Daniels, and under her name another Virginia, at Foxcroft, and another Francis, at St. Mark's. There we have the whole story, the whole tragic story of the drunken mama's-boy, coming home to see mama because the boys at the club were mean to him."

"It may not be that at all."

"I'll bet it's close to it. Now let's see if he's in *Who's Who?*" said Evan Reese. He took down a volume and opened it. "Nope. I didn't think he would be. I formed my impression of him when he barked at the driver of that car. Driver was a polite, decent-looking fellow. Probably very efficient, too, except for not seeing the Oak Knoll sign. *Say*, that's interesting."

"Why?"

"Wouldn't you think that Stratton would know where his mother lived? Maybe he was asleep, or so drunk—no, he wasn't that drunk. And he wasn't asleep. Maybe it isn't her son after all. But I think it is. Do you know what I think, Georgia?"

"What?"

"I think we have a mystery on our hands."

"Well, you puzzle it out, I'm retiring. I have all sorts of things to do tomorrow, and don't forget. We have Bob and Jennie for dinner tomorrow night."

"God, is tomorrow Wednesday? Well, at least they're coming here. We don't have to go out."

"If you stay up reading, don't fall asleep in your chair or your arm'll get stiff again and you won't be able to work."

This was a bit of caution she gave him about once a week. He was miserable when his arm hurt and he could not paint, especially when he was painting well, and more especially when he was finishing the last of his pictures for a one-man show in the spring. It was not only his habit of falling asleep in his chair that made his arm sore, nor was he telling the truth when he blamed the weather. He had bursitis, he knew it and she knew it, but they pretended he was in perfect health. He—they—would not admit that he was sixty years old and already a victim of the painter's occupational disease. He refused to see a doctor, to confirm what he had long suspected, to submit to treatment that was never wholly successful. "The minute I hear myself snoring, I'll come to bed," he said.

"Goodnight, dear," she said.

"Goodnight, Pussycat," he said. He put her hand to his cheek and kissed it, and she left him. The dog stretched out on the rug and dozed.

Evan Reese turned the television to a different channel and for an hour or so watched a lovely British movie that he knew by heart, having seen it at least ten times. He did not have to follow the plot, which was nothing much to begin with and concerned the refusal of some Scotsmen in a remote village to pay their taxes until the government promised them a new road. Evan Reese could share the Scotsmen's feelings toward London; he could sing "Men of Harlech" in the Welsh, although he had never been to the land of his fathers; but he knew the movie so well that he could pick up the story anywhere along the way, and there was no suspense in it for him. The charm of it was in the characters and the acting and in the verisimilitude of the exteriors and interiors—the laird had a forty-year-old

Rolls-Royce station wagon instead of the 1960 Cadillac that Hollywood would have considered suitable for a laird. The house in which the laird lived was not too unlike Evan Reese's; built to last, furnished for comfort, a warm shelter whether the winds came down from Canada or from the North Sea.

The movie came to its happy ending and Evan Reese turned off the television. At the cessation of the sound, Mike, the Airedale, raised his head, expecting to be let out. "Just you hold it now till I finish my pipe," said Evan Reese. The dog wagged his tail to indicate that he knew he was being addressed, and Evan Reese reached down and scratched the animal's head. "I think you must be getting old, too," said Evan Reese. "You're not the watchdog you used to be. You never heard Mr. Stratton's car."

The dog again wagged his tail.

"Well, you're twelve years old," said Evan Reese. "And that's supposed to be the equivalent of eighty-four human years. You're a good boy."

At the words "good boy" the dog got to his feet and began to back out of the room, keeping his eyes on the master.

"All right," said Evan Reese, and opened the front door and let the dog run into the darkness. It was not his custom to turn on the floodlights for Mike, and in the moonless, starless night he noticed that Mrs. Stratton's house was lit up on two stories. The shades were drawn, but there was light behind them, and he could not recall ever having seen light in the house at such a late hour. It was past midnight. As his eyes became accustomed to the darkness he began to see smoke issuing forth from one of the chimneys on the Stratton roof, and he wondered what could be going on, what scene was taking place between the widow and her son. A happy reunion? He thought not.

Evan Reese whistled softly for his dog, which responded to the signal, and man and dog returned to the warm house. "Snow tomorrow, for sure," said Evan Reese. "I can feel it in my bones." He saw that the dog was curling up on his piece of carpet in the library, and he now retired for his own rest.

Bob and Jennie Hewitt were fourth-generation residents of High Ridge. She as an amateur painter and he as president of the local bank had been the Reeses' first acquaintances in the town and the friendship between the two couples had become a pleasant one. The men were the same age, the women were only two years apart, and when Bob Hewitt got over the first shock of discovering that he was somewhat less conservative than a man who earned a good living as a painter, the weekly dinner-and-bridge was instituted and had continued. A running score was kept, and at the end of their October-through-May season never more than $50 changed hands.

"Bob, get Evan to tell you about the visitor he had last night," said Jennie Hewitt. "Go on, Evan. He'd be interested. I think it's fascinating."

"Well, with that build-up, who was it, Ev? Brigitte Bardot?" said Bob Hewitt.

"Not quite," said Evan Reese, and related the events of the previous night.

Bob Hewitt was a good listener, and at the end of Evan's report he said: "Well, you have him pegged about right. Frank Stratton is a mama's-boy and a heavy drinker. Did you see him around today?"

"No. I looked for him, but there was no sign of him."

"The last time he did this, came home to mama, was before you moved to High Ridge. It was when his wife left him. He came home then, under almost the same circumstances. Drunk, and in a hired car. But the next day the old lady sent him packing. Banished him. She didn't want him around, or that was the story. Jennie, you tell that part."

"I'm dying to," said Jennie Hewitt. "And I'm dying to know if she lets him stay this time. What happened before was that Mrs. Stratton was furious because Frank did what everybody always said he'd do. Come home to mother at the first sign of trouble. And there *was* trouble. It even got in the papers, a little bit. You see, Frank is—well it was *in* the *papers,* so I might as well say it. Frank is a fairy."

"Well, don't say it that positively, Jennie. After all, he did

marry and he had two children." Bob Hewitt spoke sardoni-
cally.

"But what was he arrested for?"

"He wasn't arrested. The other fellow was arrested for beating him up and stealing money and stuff. You've got it all
mixed up."

"Well then you tell it," said Jennie Hewitt.

"There isn't much else to tell. He was beaten up by a young
serviceman that he met in a bar, and the police found Frank's
wallet and cigarette case on him. Stupid. You'd think he'd have
got rid of such incriminating evidence, but as I recall it the
soldier tried to sell the cigarette case in some bar on Eighth
Avenue and the bartender tipped off the military police. Then
the New York cops went to Frank's apartment and found him
lying in a pool of blood, and that was how the story got out.
You had to read between the lines—"

"Oh, Bob. Between the lines. They couldn't have been more
explicit."

"No, maybe not, but there was no charge preferred against
Frank. That's where you're giving the Reeses the wrong impression."

"I was trying to give them the right impression. Ev, Georgia,
what would you think if you read that story in the newspapers?"

"I'd be inclined to think that Mr. Stratton was very indis-
creet, not to say impulsive," said Evan Reese.

"I'd say he got what was coming to him," said Georgia
Reese. "Picking up soldiers in a bar."

"And you'd be right, and his mother was furious," said
Jennie Hewitt. "She told him to go right back to New York and
face it out. Brazen it out, I'd call it. But she was right, as it
turned out. He did go back to New York, and went right on
seeing people and of course nobody could come up and say to
him point-blank, 'Were you a fairy with that soldier?' And
after while people began to say well maybe the soldier *did*
follow him to his apartment and try to rob him. In other words,
people sort of gave him the benefit of the doubt. That was his
version to the police."

"Maybe it was true," said Evan Reese. "When I was a young man living in Greenwich Village there were certain reprehensible characters who made a living by blackmailing older men. They'd see a man getting drunk in a speakeasy and they'd get in a taxi with him or follow him home, and then threaten to expose him if he didn't shell out. Some of those men were certainly guilty, or at least vulnerable, but I wonder how many were innocent. I knew a sculptor who paid blackmail for years because he got drunk with a male model and he could never actually remember whether he'd made passes at him or not. My friend, the sculptor, was of course vulnerable. He was bisexual. He said to me more than once, 'Reese, I honestly don't know. Maybe I did.' "

"What ever happened to him?" said Jennie Hewitt.

"My friend? He gave up. He became very successful, made a lot of money, and one day when the young bum came around for his cheque, my friend told him to go to hell. 'You can't blackmail me any more,' he said. 'I've stopped denying it or pretending I'm anything else, so get out.' "

"How delightful," said Jennie Hewitt.

"Not really," said Georgia Reese. "He later hanged himself. He was genuinely in love with a girl, and she wouldn't have him."

"I guess the old Greenwich Village must have been quite a place, Ev?" said Bob Hewitt.

"It doesn't sound much different today, only worse," said Georgia.

"We had some gifted people," said Evan Reese. "Real talent. Once in a while a genius, or very close to it. Anyway, real artists. First-rate writers, some of the best. But now all I ever hear about is an occasional saxophone player. You see, we worked. We did a lot of talking, and a great deal of drinking and sleeping around, but we also worked. Now we don't hear much about work down there. Talk, yes. Drinking and sleeping around, and dope. But they don't seem to know how to paint or write."

"I never liked the Village," said Georgia. "You never did anything really good till you got out of it."

"Oh, yes, I did some good things, but I never did anything first-rate till I was past forty anyhow, so the Village did me no harm. And I did work."

"Well, this isn't very interesting to the Hewitts. We were talking about this Stratton man."

"And I wouldn't waste any pity on him," said Jennie. "Unfortunately, Bob and I weren't surprised when that happened, the beating and so on."

"No, it's one of those small-town secrets that only a few people think they're in on, but it was pretty generally known, I guess," said Bob Hewitt. "When did we first hear about it?"

"When did we first hear about it? Why, that time—"

"That time he had that friend home from college. You're right. The maid quit because Frank brought a friend home from college and—"

"Lorna. Lorna Parton."

"Lorna walked in to clean the drawing-room and there was the friend sitting at the piano, stark naked at nine o'clock in the morning. Went right on playing, too."

"Where was Stratton?" said Evan Reese.

"Oh, I don't know where he was, probably upstairs sleeping off a hangover," said Bob Hewitt. "But the friend went right on playing, even when Mrs. Stratton came in to remonstrate with him. What was it he said to her?"

"He was the boldest thing I ever heard of. He finished playing whatever it was, regardless of her saying *Mister* Jones, or whatever his name was. He came to the end of the piece and then he turned to her and said: 'Do you play?' You know, as though he expected her to join him in a duet."

"No more friends home from Harvard," said Bob Hewitt.

"What do you *mean?* No more *Frank*. She told him she didn't want him to come home at all," said Jennie Hewitt.

"That's right," said her husband. "She wouldn't have him in the house, not even at Christmas."

"Till he announced his engagement. And even then she wouldn't go to the wedding. She stayed home on some pretext or other. She never actually met Frank's wife till the first grandchild was born, and then she couldn't do enough for them. She adored the grandchildren, and they used to all four of them come visit her."

"The money," said Bob Hewitt.

"Oh, yes. She gave Frank's wife a hundred thousand dollars when each grandchild was born, *and* a trust fund for the children."

"And changed her will."

"And changed her will so that Frank gets nothing, not a penny. He gets what is it?"

"A thousand a month while she's alive. Twelve thousand a year. Then when she dies, nothing. It all goes into a trust fund for the grandchildren."

"And the ex-wife gets the income as long as she doesn't remarry. If she remarries, it all goes into the children's trusts."

"And that's our neighbor?" said Evan Reese. "I had no idea she was so rich."

"*Rich?* At one time she owned this whole mountain, or her husband did. You've never been in that house, have you?" said Bob Hewitt.

"I've never even had a good look at it from the outside. The trees and the hedges," said Evan Reese.

"Tell them about the downstairs," said Bob Hewitt.

"Tell us about the whole house," said Georgia Reese.

"Well, you knew that Frank had an older sister," said Jennie. "Bernice. She was my age."

"No, we never heard about a sister," said Georgia Reese.

"Oh, yes. Bernice, about twelve years older than Frank. I went there a lot when we were children and until Bernice eloped, at seventeen. Mrs. Stratton would send the car to my house—"

"A Rolls, needless to say," said Bob Hewitt. "Limousine when the weather was bad, and a touring car when it was good."

"I was one of the girls that Bernice was allowed to play

with, but she never came to my house except to things like birthday parties. I always had to go to her house, but of course I didn't mind."

"The house, the house," said Bob Hewitt.

"But later I want to know about the daughter," said Georgia Reese.

"So do I," said her husband.

"First let her describe the house," said Bob Hewitt.

"Well, it's so long since I've been inside it that now it's almost unbelievable, although I'm told it hasn't been changed much. The main hall was two stories high, with at one end stained glass windows, imported from Italy, and they went all the way up to the second floor. On the right as you went in, a small reception room, then next to that, the drawing-room, where Frank's friend played the piano, and off that the music-room, as it was called. That was all done in white and gold and those two rooms were where we danced when they had their big parties. On the other side of the hall, the big dining room, easily room enough for, oh, sixty people. The library, lined with books all the way up to the ceiling with one of those ladders on a track like the old-time shoe stores. Two huge fireplaces. When I was little I could stand erect in the fireplaces. And a smaller room that had been Mr. Stratton's office, although they called it a study. I remember he had a stock ticker in that room, although I didn't know what it was then. They changed it after he died. On that side of the house was an enclosed porch, and on the other side, opening off the drawing-room, the conservatory. And I wouldn't attempt to describe the furniture. The dining-room chairs, high-back armchairs, brocaded, of course, and I'll bet the table weighed a ton. The paintings, you *must* have a look at them somehow, Ev. There's a Gainsborough in the main hall. A Van Dyke, a Rubens—"

"Yes, yes," said Bob Hewitt. "But don't start telling all about the paintings. Just give them the general idea. For instance, the pipe organ."

"They had a pipe organ, that was in the main hall, with the console on the first landing. They used to have an organist from Philadelphia with the wonderful name of Thunder, he'd come and give recitals once a year. Henry Thunder, a famous organist he was. And on Easter they always had a big crowd for lunch and then they'd have one of the local organists play."

"The only house in this part of the State with a pipe organ. And I'll bet no other house had something else they had. A barber chair. A real barber chair in Mr. Stratton's dressing-room."

"Sunken bathtubs?" said Georgia Reese.

"No, I guess the house was built too early for that. The tubs were iron, but had wood all around them. Encased in wood with mother-of-pearl inlaid. I remember when they added an elevator. We were absolutely forbidden to ride in it, probably because of several experiences when we got stuck in the dumb-waiter."

"Ev, this will impress you," said Bob Hewitt. "They had their own road-roller. A steam road-roller, with a little whistle. They used to lend it to the township, but it belonged to them. I suppose at one time they had around eight hundred acres. Now it's dwindled down to, oh, I think she has no more than twenty acres now, but I think I remember the figure eight hundred. This house that you're in, this used to be occupied by a cousin of Old Man Stratton's."

"Yes, I heard that when I bought it," said Evan Reese.

"They owned all these houses on Ridge Road and rented them out to relatives and retired couples for practically nothing. I don't think there was a house within a mile of the Strattons' that they didn't own. Not that there were so many houses in those days. This section wasn't started to be built up till the Thirties," said Bob Hewitt.

"Where did Stratton's money come from?" said Evan Reese.

"In two words, Wall Street. Railroad stocks, land out west, coal mines in Pennsylvania and West Virginia. He didn't make it all himself, by any means. His father was in with Jim Fisk and Dan Drew and Gould, that crowd, but not as a very big operator. Enough to leave old Frank Senior a nice fortune, and Frank had brains. He may not have been the most honest man in the world, by present-day standards, but he stayed out of trouble. He married late in life. The present Mrs. Stratton, the old lady, was about nineteen or twenty and he was in his forties when they got married. He was well in his fifties when the present Frank was born."

"Who was she?" said Georgia Reese.

"She was a High Ridge girl, born here. She was a Crowder. The Crowders weren't immensely wealthy, but they were well fixed and got around in New York society. Oh, she had plenty to offer. She was a good-looking girl."

"She was a handsome young woman," said Jennie Hewitt. "I can remember her very well. Beautiful bone structure and quite sexy-looking."

"When did he die?" said Evan Reese.

"Let me see now, in the late Twenties. He was eighty or close to it when he died," said Bob Hewitt.

"And that was when she became a recluse?" said Georgia Reese.

"Before that. Mr. Stratton was paralyzed and they practically never left Oak Knoll after that."

"Just lived there in solitary splendor?" said Evan Reese.

"Solitary splendor!" said Jennie Hewitt. "Splendor, but not solitary. They had Phillips, the majordomo. Pierre, the chauffeur. Tripp, the coachman, and a colored groom. A head gardener whose name I forget, and as many as five or six other gardeners. Mrs. Phillips, the cook. A full-time waitress. Three or four chambermaids. Mrs. Stratton's personal maid, Alice. A tweeny."

"What's a tweeny?" said Georgia Reese.

"A tweeny is a sort of a cook's helper and not quite a regular maid. In-between."

"I never heard of it," said Georgia Reese.

"It's English, and I understand that the butler has certain privileges there. *Droit de seigneur,* you know, although I don't think Phillips claimed his. How many is that?"

"About seventeen or eighteen," said Bob Hewitt. "And you didn't include the handyman-carpenter, the night watchman, or people like the old boy's secretary, O'Neill, or nurses for the children."

"Well, twenty or so. So it was splendor, Ev, but not solitary," said Jennie Hewitt.

"No, and you left out Madigan, the superintendent, and a lot of these people had husbands and wives living on the place, but not what you might call staff," said Bob Hewitt.

"Where did they put them all?" said Georgia Reese.

"Oh, some lived in the big house, some over the garage and the carriage-house," said Jennie Hewitt.

"I had no idea we were so close to such grandeur," said Evan Reese.

"Grandeur is right," said Bob Hewitt. "They even had their own buttons for the servants' livery. An oak, of course, and if you looked carefully, the letter 'S' in the foliage."

"No coat of arms?" said Georgia Reese.

"I never saw one," said Bob Hewitt. "In spite of everything we've told you, the old boy wasn't much for show. He had the very best of everything, mind you. Cars and horses, and paintings by famous artists. But when he took the train to New York, he rode in the day coach. He had a pass, of course. And when he got to Jersey City, his private car was probably sitting there on a siding. For a man as rich as he was, he lived very inconspicuously. Take for instance, living here. This was never like Tuxedo or one of your Long Island communities. Nothing fashionable about High Ridge."

"That's true," said his wife. "And they never had a yacht or a racing stable or any of those things."

"Don't disillusion me," said Evan Reese. "I was beginning to feel that some of the grandeur would rub off on me."

"I'm afraid there isn't much of it left," said Bob Hewitt. "My father told me one time how much it cost Stratton to whitewash all the post-and-rail at Oak Knoll. You know, my father was in the building supply business. Brick and lumber, cement and paint. So he knew pretty well what Stratton spent. Stratton was my Dad's best customer, year in, year out. We—

my Dad, that is—supplied the trap rock for Stratton's roads. Stratton put me through college, if you want to look at it that way. But I'll tell you one thing. Madigan, the superintendent, never had any chance to knock down a little graft. You'd always see that 'S' on the upper right-hand corner of every bill, which meant that Stratton had seen it before okaying payment. If Stratton caught a man stealing or even cheating a little bit, the fellow'd be on the next train out of here, bag and baggage, with orders to never return to High Ridge."

"The result was there was very little cheating," said Jennie Hewitt. "And they all knew they had a good thing. They were well paid, and they didn't have to eat slop or live in broken-down shacks."

"Yes, the Strattons paid their help a little more than the going rate because this was such an out-of-the-way place," said Bob Hewitt. "And he was a great believer in education. For instance, Phillips's son graduated from Johns Hopkins with an M.D. degree, and practices medicine out in California somewhere. Quite a few of the kids on the place went to college with Stratton's help."

"Anybody that wanted to, if his mother or father had been with the Strattons long enough. Ten years, I think it was," said Jennie Hewitt.

"The boy that wanted to go to Harvard," said Bob Hewitt.

"Oh, yes. Pierre, the chauffeur, had a son that was the same age as Frank Stratton, and the boy decided he wanted to go to Harvard. So Pierre told Mrs. Stratton his son wanted to go to college and would she lend him—"

"Four thousand dollars," said Bob Hewitt.

"Four thousand dollars," said his wife. "Pierre didn't want to touch his savings account, and Mrs. Stratton could take the money out of his salary. 'Why of course,' she said. She'd be *glad* to help. And what college was Joseph going to? 'Harvard,' said Pierre."

"That cooked it," said Bob Hewitt.

"She said no. 'But Madame is sending her own son to Harvard,' said Pierre. 'Precisely,' said Madame. Then of course Pierre, being a Frenchman, caught on. So Joseph went to Dartmouth."

"She was no fool," said Bob Hewitt. "Frank and his naked piano-players, classmates of her chauffeur's son."

"I'm dying to know about Bernice, the sister," said Georgia Reese.

"Shall we forget about bridge tonight?" said Evan Reese. "I'd rather hear about my neighbors. Ten years. Might as well have been living in an apartment house in New York. There you don't expect to know your neighbors."

"I'm perfectly willing, if you'd care to hear about them," said Jennie Hewitt. "You never heard of Bunnie Stratton?"

"I don't think so," said Georgia Reese.

"Madcap Bunnie Stratton? That's what she was called by the newspapers. Madcap Bunnie Stratton."

"She made up for all the publicity her father didn't get," said Bob Hewitt.

"Notoriety, you mean. Not just publicity. She was a regular F. Scott Fitzgerald heroine," said Jennie Hewitt.

"Which one?" said Evan Reese.

"Which one?" said Jennie Hewitt. "Why—I don't know which *one.*"

"The reason I asked, Fitzgerald's heroines weren't madcaps," said Evan Reese.

"Well, I always thought they were," said Jennie Hewitt.

"No. Here's another example of the picture versus the printed word. People tend to think of John Held's girls when they hear Fitzgerald's name. But Fitzgerald's heroines, at least the ones I remember, were totally unlike the Held girls. Do you remember Daisy, in *The Great Gatsby*? She wasn't a Held girl. And Nicole, in *Tender Is the Night*. The very thought of John Held doing a picture of that tragic figure is repellent to me."

"Ev, I'm afraid you're a little too literal-minded. When I said an F. Scott Fitzgerald heroine I might as well admit I never read a word he wrote. And I *was* thinking of the John Held Junior drawings."

"Then call her a John Held Junior girl, but don't call her a Fitzgerald heroine. Give the artist his due, and don't distort what the author wrote."

"Oh, come on, Ev," said Bob Hewitt.

"No, now don't you protest before you think," said Evan Reese. "If I came into your bank and tried to tell you that a share of stock was a bond, you'd correct me damn quickly. Well, this happens to be something *I* know about. For years I've been hearing and reading people talking about John Held's girls and Fitzgerald's, as though they were one and the same thing. They just simply weren't. From the literary point of view, one of the worst things that ever happened to Fitzgerald was the simultaneous popularity of John Held's drawings. Those damn editorial writers were largely to blame. Who would want to take Fitzgerald seriously if all they ever knew about him was that he wrote about those John Held girls? Held was a very good satirist, and he didn't *want* his girls to be taken seriously. Of course Fitzgerald was partly to blame. He called one book *Flappers and Philosophers,* and in the public mind the flapper was the John Held girl. Actually, of course, Fitzgerald and Held and the editorial writers were all misusing the word flapper. A flapper was English slang, and it meant a society girl who had made her debut and hadn't found a husband. On the shelf, they used to say. It wasn't an eighteen-year-old girl with flopping galoshes."

"Well, according to your definition, Ev, Bernice was never a flapper, but according to mine she was," said Jennie Hewitt. "She was a sort of a John Held girl. One of the first to bob her hair and smoke in public and all the rest of it. And she didn't even make her debut."

"And *that* was a party we were looking forward to," said Bob Hewitt. "The plans."

"They started planning that party I don't know how many years ahead," said Jennie. "She was to have a New York party, but her real party was going to be here, June 1921, it was supposed to be. A thousand invitations. Mrs. Stratton hired a secretary just for that party, and she came to work over a year ahead of time. Special trains were going to leave Jersey City and Philadelphia."

"Art Hickman," said her husband.

"Art Hickman, Ted Lewis, and Markel's orchestra."

"The club," said Bob Hewitt.

"They engaged the whole club for the weekend, a year in advance, and every available hotel room for miles around. Not including families like my family and Bob's that offered to put up guests."

"Sherry. Louis Sherry."

"You can imagine the preparations Sherry's would have had to make. A thousand guests, extra servants and musicians. Supper and breakfast. Dinner before the party and luncheon at the club the next day."

"What about liquor?" said Evan Reese. "We had Prohibition by that time."

"I don't know what they were going to do about liquor. We had Prohibition, but not much enforcement then. They wouldn't have had any trouble. The stuff was coming in from Rum Row and Canada, and you can be sure Stratton would have had the best, not just Jersey Lightning."

"What was Jersey Lightning?" said Georgia Reese.

"Applejack. What we drank instead of corn liquor. They served it over the bar in every country hotel, and it wasn't bad. It had the desired effect."

"But they never had this party?" said Georgia Reese.

"No," said Jennie Hewitt. "Bunnie eloped. Don't either of you remember that? Bunnie Stratton and Jack Boyle?"

"Oh, hell," said Evan Reese. "Of course I remember now. Jack Boyle, the baseball player. Played first base for the New York Giants, and one of the first All-Americans Fordham ever had. But I'd forgotten *her* name. How did they ever get together?"

"They weren't together very long," said Jennie Hewitt. "Less than a year. Jack was a lifeguard at Belmar."

"Belmar?" said Georgia Reese.

"Belmar-by-the-Sea. A summer resort we used to go to in

those days. Bob's family went there and so did mine, and quite a few of the *nicer* Irish."

"Which didn't include Jack's family. Jack was a hell of a good athlete and a handsome son of a gun, but let's face it, they weren't the lace-curtain Irish. Jack was from Jersey City, and his father was a watch repairman for the Jersey Central. White-collar, but not lace-curtain."

"We'll come to that," said Jennie Hewitt. "Anyway, Bunnie was allowed to spend a whole week with me at Belmar, the summer of 1919. She'd never swam in the ocean before, in spite of all their money, and I can't give you any better proof of how strictly *I* was brought up than by telling you that the Strattons allowed Bunnie to visit me. And a whole *week*. Six days too long."

"She took one look at Jack Boyle," said Bob Hewitt.

"And he at her. One day was too long. Love at first sight if there ever was a case of it," said Jennie Hewitt.

"Your father," said her husband.

"My father told Jack that if he didn't stop hanging around our house he'd have him fired, and Jack told my father to go straight to hell and he *was* fired. So then he had nothing to lose, and he saw Bunnie every day and every night."

"She was sixteen then?" said Georgia Reese.

"Sixteen. Jack was about twenty-one."

"Older than that, Jennie," said Bob Hewitt. "He'd been overseas in the war. He was a good twenty-three or four."

"Well, whatever. My parents were afraid to tell Mr. and Mrs. Stratton, and hoped it would blow over, but Jack went back to Fordham and that year Bunnie was at Spence and they managed to see each other."

"Then Boyle quit Fordham and went with the Giants," said Bob Hewitt.

"Now I remember. Sure. Boyle eloped, and McGraw fired him," said Evan Reese.

"But *I* don't know any of this, so go on, Jennie," said Georgia Reese.

"Well, her family of course were outraged, but so were his.

They were Catholic and Bunnie and Jack had been married by a justice of the peace, in Greenwich, Connecticut. So the Boyles wouldn't have anything to do with Jack. Wouldn't let him in the house. And the only thing Jack could do was play baseball."

"But as I remember it, he did," said Evan Reese. "He played for some team in the International League, Binghamton or one of those teams."

"It *was* Binghamton," said Bob Hewitt.

"But they didn't pay him much, and Bunnie was pregnant. Mr. Stratton sent a lawyer to talk to Bunnie, but Jack wouldn't let him see her."

"Wouldn't let him *see* her?" said Bob Hewitt. "He was arrested for giving the lawyer a punch in the nose, and he told him that was what Mr. Stratton could expect, too, if he ever came around."

"Bunnie adored her father," said Jennie Hewitt. "And he did come to see her in Binghamton, while Jack was away, and he persuaded her to come home with him, knowing that Jack would follow her."

"*Thinking* that Jack would follow her. Mr. Stratton *wanted* Jack to follow her. I know that. And he wanted to give Jack a job. But he didn't know Jack Boyle. That fierce Irish pride, I guess. When Boyle got back to Binghamton and read Bunnie's letter, he quit baseball and Bunnie never heard from him again. Never. Not a word, not a line."

"What happened to him?" said Georgia Reese.

"He drifted around for a while, and then joined the Army. He'd been a lieutenant, but he enlisted as a private. I think you had to enlist for seven years then. Anyway, when he got out he became a bootlegger with some of his old friends in Jersey City. He's still alive. Frank Hague got him a job on the Hudson County payroll. Inspector of something or other. The last I heard he was a sort of an organizer for one of the labor unions."

"And what happened to her?" said Georgia Reese.

"Oh, plenty," said Jennie Hewitt. "She didn't have the baby.

Whether she lost it or they got her an abortion, I don't know. The latter, I suspect, because after she divorced Jack and married the Englishman she had two children, one of which the Englishman refused to take the credit for."

"When you say the Englishman, you mean the first Englishman," said Bob Hewitt. "She married two Englishmen. The Army officer, and the writer."

"Yes, but the writer was an Australian, and if he was a writer, nobody ever heard of anything he wrote," said Jennie Hewitt. "Except bad cheques. I always understood that the first Englishman, the *English*man, was quite attractive and very much in love with Bunnie. He resigned from the Army to marry her, and I guess he took all he could stand."

"What happened to her two children?" said Georgia Reese.

"The first was killed in the war, North Africa. The second was a girl," said Jennie Hewitt. "I heard that she got married during the war, but what's happened to her since I have no idea."

"And where is Bunnie herself?" said Georgia Reese.

"Majorca, surrounded by pansies and Lesbians of all nationalities. She has enough to live on and supply wine and gin for her hangers-on. She's a countess. She picked up an Italian along the way. There's some doubt about the title, or not so much about the title as her right to it. She married her Italian on a steamship, or so she says. But if she wants to call herself countess, none of her present friends are going to object. The count is over seventy and feeble-minded. I haven't seen or heard from Bunnie in over twenty years. We saw her once, briefly, in London before the war. But a friend of ours looked her up in Majorca and she said Bunnie refuses to speak English because all her little boys and girls are Italian or Spanish or French. When we saw her in London we could hardly understand her, she was so English. But not any more. She's had her face lifted a couple of times and she wears oversize sunglasses and big floppy hats, never goes out in the daylight, and her house is lit by candles. I wonder what she thinks."

"Yes," said Georgia Reese.

"You know. People like you and I, Georgia. Let's face it, we live a lot on our memories. We love our grandchildren and these two nice old things that we're stuck with—"

"Oh, thanks," said Bob Hewitt.

"But my life would be very empty without my memories, the good times we had, *and* the bad, and the old sentimental recollections. Think of what our life would be like without them. And yet I don't suppose Bunnie ever gives a thought to Jack Boyle and those days."

"Probably not," said Georgia Reese.

"Or the Englishman, or the Australian. Or the dear-knows how many lovers she had. I imagine she shuts all that out and just goes on from day to day, as though one part of her brain had been removed."

"Let me give you the other side of the coin," said Evan Reese.

"All right, Ev," said Jennie Hewitt.

"What about Mrs. Stratton, who has nothing *but* memories?"

Jennie Hewitt nodded. "Yes, that's a pretty horrible thought, too."

They were all silent for a moment, then Georgia Reese spoke. "They must suffocate her, her memories."

"Yes, who has it worse? The mother remembering everything, or the daughter remembering nothing?" said Bob Hewitt.

"Why, Robert Morris Hewitt, you're almost poetic tonight," said his wife.

"I have my moments," said Bob Hewitt. "I get in the same rut everybody gets in, and I take the old lady for granted. But every once in a while I have to talk to her on the phone, about bank business, and when she calls me Robert, I feel as though I were just starting out and she was old Queen Mary. The most personal she ever gets is to say 'Good morning, Robert,' and 'Thank you, Robert.' She never asks about Jennie or our children or grandchildren. These are business calls. But she's quite an old gal, to be able to make me feel like a fumbling assistant paying teller at my age. I don't really give a damn what Bunnie thinks, if she thinks anything. But I often wonder about the old lady in that house, the money going, the place shrinking a little every year. From eight hundred acres to twenty in a little over one generation. And the God damn futile mess that her two children have made of their lives. That was a beautiful woman once, Mrs. Stratton. I remember one time twenty-five or thirty years ago, I happened to be walking up Fifth Avenue and she was twenty or thirty feet ahead of me. She was alone. But as I followed her I couldn't help noticing how the people coming in her direction would automatically fall out of the way. Just looking at her, they'd make way for her. I never forgot that."

"I wish she hadn't written that letter about the dog," said Evan Reese. "The only communication we ever had from her."

"What did the letter say?" said Jennie Hewitt.

"Well, it was ten years ago, and I can't quote it verbatim, but to the effect that Airedales were known as one-man dogs and ours had snapped at somebody on her place."

"I know why she sent that letter," said Jennie Hewitt. "Ten years ago? Ten years ago her grandchildren used to come here a lot."

"Then why didn't she say so?" said Evan Reese.

"Oh, that wasn't her way," said Jennie Hewitt. "Nothing dramatic or appealing to your better nature. Or sentimental about children. She was simply stating the facts about Airedales, impersonally. She wouldn't dream of mentioning her grandchildren. That would be a show of weakness on her part, inviting familiarity."

"That's true, Ev," said Bob Hewitt. "She approved of you, or you never would have got this house. She probably knew your work, and for all I know, she may even own one of your paintings."

"No, I know where all my paintings are."

"In any event, you were okayed as a purchaser and a neighbor, but that's as far as she'd ever go. Like she wouldn't call on Georgia, not because she wanted to be rude to Georgia, but because she didn't want Georgia to return the call. I see her household bills, you know, and as far as I know, she hasn't had anyone for dinner in at least ten years. At least. She buys a lot of books, and she has four television sets in the house. But for instance, she hasn't bought a bottle of liquor or wine since before Pearl Harbor. She smokes a lot of cigarettes. Camels. That was the only thing she asked for during the war, was a regular supply of Camels. And I got them for her because she never cheated on gas rationing, or shoe coupons or any of those things, and it would have been easy for her to. Technically, Oak Knoll was a farm, and there was a lot of funny business by so-called farmers then."

"I'm going to have to see this woman. That's all there is to it," said Evan Reese.

"Make it accidental," said Bob Hewitt. "Don't let her see you coming up the driveway, or she'll hide in the closet."

"Not hide," said Jennie Hewitt. "She just won't be at home."

"Well, that's what I meant. Ev knows that. And it's nothing personal. I've known her all my life, and I handle a lot of her business and talk to her over the phone, but I never go to her house, even when there are papers to sign. I send my secretary, who happens to be a notary public."

"Oh, I'll make it accidental," said Evan Reese.

"And make it soon," said Jennie Hewitt. "She's over eighty."

"Yes, and *I'm* over sixty," said Evan Reese.

The Hewitts' car was covered with snow when the time came for them to depart. "I missed the weather report," said Bob Hewitt. "Was this expected?"

"Ev expected it," said Georgia Reese.

"Look at Mike," said Bob Hewitt. "He doesn't want to go out in it. Come on, Jen. Goodnight, Reeses, thanks for a pleasant evening. And I didn't lose any money."

"Have you got snow tires?" said Georgia Reese.

"We'll be all right. Bob's careful."

"I'd feel better if you'd call us when you get home," said Georgia Reese.

"All right, as soon as we get home, but don't worry. It hasn't had a chance to freeze," said Jennie Hewitt.

For a little while Evan Reese stood at the window, looking out at the new winter scene under the floodlight. "I can think of three men that I'd like to see do that. Maxfield Parrish. George Luks, and Charles Sheeler. And Salvador Dali, that makes four. Each of them had his own special blue, and none of them would see it the way I do."

"How are you going to do it?" said his wife.

"I'm not going to attempt it. When I finish this picture I'm not going to paint anything for at least six months."

"I wasn't talking about your painting. How are you going about meeting Mrs. Stratton?"

"Is that what I was thinking about, Georgie?"

"That's my guess. Whenever you're really thinking about painting, you don't talk about it."

"It must be fun to guess. Well, you're right, this time. I'm not always thinking about something else when I talk about painting, but this time I was. With that son staying there she's not going to be very receptive, less so than usual. But then isn't that just the time to make a sortie, when she's least prepared for it?"

"Sounds mean."

"I am above meanness. However, I'm not above curiosity, and believe me, I'm damn curious. Instead of a rather dull, cranky, faceless old woman, our neighbor turns out to be— well, Jack Boyle's first mother-in-law. Boyle to me was one of the really interesting baseball players. Much more interesting really than if he'd stayed in the game and been as good as your fellow Georgian, Mr. Tyrus Raymond Cobb. And he might have been almost as good as Cobb. Potentially he was, they all said. Maybe he'd have been better. But I've always been interested in the near-misses. Understandably. I'm one myself."

"Now, now," said his wife.

"Well, you know how I feel about my work, so the hell with that. But Boyle was a near-miss, and in her way, so is Mrs. Stratton. She was never one of the famous hostesses, or mistresses, or philanthropists, and yet she could have been any

of those things. Or all three. Or any two. I never even heard
of her as a great beauty."

"You never heard of her husband, either."

"Yes, I did. He was a well-known millionaire, but I forgot
all about him many years ago, and never connected him with
the woman we bought this house from. When I was young
and living in Paris and the Village, I knew the names of the
millionaires. If a millionaire bought one of our pictures our
prices went way up, overnight. If one of us sold a picture to
Jules Bache for a thousand dollars, that was ever so much better than getting a thousand dollars from someone with less
money. The inconspicuous fellow, the art-lover that happened
to like your picture, and happened to have a thousand dollars—that was nice. But that kind of a sale was usually considered a lucky accident. On the other hand, if someone like
Bache shelled out a thousand bucks, we never sold another
picture for that little. We didn't have to. Writers have the same
experience. I'm sure that William Faulkner and Ernest Heming-
way got big prices for pieces that they would have sold for
fifty dollars when they first wrote them. And that's as it should
be. Faulkner is a great artist, and all his work is extremely
valuable, whether it's his best work or his worst. The mere fact
that he wrote it makes it valuable, because there is only one
Faulkner. Fortunately, people believe that about painters. Look
at Pablo Picasso."

"Look at Evan Reese," said his wife.

"Yes. You'll never starve, as long as you have enough of
my pictures lying around," he said. "A snowscape! Tomorrow
morning. I shall take my little camp stool and some of the tools
of my trade, and do some sketches."

"No."

"I'll bundle up good and warm. I'll go up West Branch
Road, where I can be seen from the big house. We'll *try* that
anyway."

"So that's what you were thinking?" said Georgia Reese.

"Well—yes," said her husband. Bob Hewitt telephoned,
and the Reeses retired for the night.

In the morning Evan Reese put on hunting socks, heavy shoes and six-buckle arctics; tweed suit and sweaters; sheepskin reefer and cap with earlaps. He carried his camp stool, large sketch pad, and a vacuum bottle of coffee, and established a vantage point in the middle of the West Branch Road, which had not yet been visited by the township snow-plow. He made several quick sketches of the valley, then paused to take a few sips of the coffee. He screwed the cap back on the bottle and resumed sketching, aware that he was about to have company.

"Do you mind if I watch?" said his visitor. Evan Reese recognized the voice from the limousine, the same harshness but now without petulance. The harshness was of the kind that is usually attributed to whiskey-drinking.

"Why, no," said Evan Reese. "If you'd like to see what effect cold weather has on fingers. My name is Reese."

"Oh, I know. My name is Frank Stratton. My mother's a neighbor of yours."

"Of course."

"I won't talk any more. Don't let me interrupt."

Evan Reese quickly finished the sketch he had begun, turned over the page and started another. "Do you know anything about this kind of work?"

"Not a thing."

"Well, then I'll explain what I'm doing. This is what I call my shorthand. My notes. As you see, I didn't try to do that barn or that farmhouse in any detail. The silo. The pigpen. I've lived here ten years and I know all that. But as I sketch—now here for instance, I'll do this clump of trees. Ten years from now, twenty years from now, if I'm alive, I'll be able to look at this sketch and remember what I don't want to forget, which is the metallic white of the snowdrifts over there to the right, as it looks at half past ten, Eastern Standard Time. There. That's enough. My fingers are getting clumsy with the cold. Would you like a spot of coffee?"

"I was going to suggest that you come back to the house and have a cup with me."

"Thank you very much, but I think I've done enough walking. I'm headed for home. But you're obviously out for exercise. Would you like to come down with me and have a cup of coffee at my house? Do you like hot cinnamon buns? That's what I'm going to have."

"I haven't had one since I was ten years old. Sure, if it's all right?"

"Of course it is. Here, you're a young fellow. I'll give you this stool to carry, and you'll feel as if you earned your cinnamon bun."

"Fine."

"I'm not going to do this again, till I get one of those electric hand-warmers. You know the ones I mean, in the Abercrombie catalog?"

"Let me send you one when I go back to New York."

"All right. I'll trade you. One of these sketches for a hand-warmer."

"Oh, no, Mr. Reese. I get much too much the best of that deal."

"I suggested it, so it's satisfactory to me."

"Well—okay. But if you're going to be generous, will you put your initials on it?"

"When we get to my house," said Evan Reese. "You know, it's God damn cold up here. That kitchen's going to feel good."

They entered the house through the kitchen door, unbuckling their arctics and leaving them inside the storm door. "Georgia, I have a customer for a hot cinnamon bun. This is Mr. Stratton, our neighbor's son. Mr. Stratton, my wife."

"How do you do, Mr. Stratton. Come in and get warm. Just put your things any old place. It's nice to have a visitor. You take coffee?"

"I'd love some coffee."

"And I dunk," said Evan Reese. "The molasses sticks to my teeth if I don't dunk. A good cold slice of butter, dunk just a little so the butter doesn't melt, and then enjoy yourself. And don't count the calories."

"I never count the calories," said Stratton. "I'm glad to see you've kept this kitchen just the way it used to be. I used to come here when I was a boy. My cousins lived in this house, and they had a cook that made apple butter."

"Apple butter," said Evan Reese. "Let's get some, Georgia?"

"All right. I'll put it down."

"Did you ever eat apple butter on fried scrapple?" said Stratton.

"Never heard of it, but I don't know why it wouldn't be delicious," said Evan Reese. "But scrapple is no good any more. We tried it, and it isn't the same. I'm a Pennsylvanian, and I got some to introduce it to my wife, but it just wasn't right."

"No, I didn't care for it," said Georgia Reese.

"It's a long time since I've had scrapple. Or fried mush with molasses."

"I had that for breakfast every morning before I went to school," said Evan Reese. "Or mush-milk. Corn meal mush in a soup dish, with milk and sugar."

"That's why children are so nervous these days. They go to school without breakfast, half the time," said Georgia Reese. "They might as well start the day with a cigarette and a Coke, the kind of breakfasts they eat nowadays. Have you got children, Mr. Stratton?"

"I have two. A boy and a girl, and I know what you mean." Stratton looked about him. "You *have* made some changes. Do you use the big range at all?"

"Hardly ever from about the first of April to November," said Georgia Reese. "But beginning around Thanksgiving I use it. I like to cook on it, and there's nothing like it for heating the kitchen."

"Please don't ever get rid of it. You have bottled gas, I suppose? Oh, now I see. You have all the new things in what used to be the laundry. Your electric icebox. This is the dishwasher? Electric iron. *That's* how you did it. You have the old kitchen, but you have the modern conveniences. You see, we didn't have bottled gas in my day, and I can remember when we had our own electricity. We had a Delco plant, for Oak Knoll and the nearest houses like this one." He got up and went to a cabinet and opened a drawer. "Oh, look. You still have it." He took from the drawer a removable hand-grip for the laundry irons. "Where are the irons? Have you still got them?"

"Where they always were. Keep looking," said Georgia Reese.

"They should be—*there* they are." On a brick ledge beside the coal range were half a dozen laundry irons. He clamped the grip on one of them. "See, I remember how it works. My sister used to love to iron. I have an older sister. She lives abroad now, but I can remember coming down here with her when I was just a small boy, and she loved to help my cousin in the kitchen. Have you ever been to Majorca, Mr. Reese?"

"No."

"That's where my sister lives. She's a good deal older than I am. But she loved this house. She was very domestic, considering. I mean she's been married a lot and lives an odd sort of life. Oh, well . . . You have all those wonderful canisters. The spices and coffee and sugar. This table used to be covered with blue-and-white checkered oilcloth. I see you like it better without the cover."

He asked to see the rest of the house, and they showed him around. He enjoyed himself in simple fashion, admiring the Reeses' possessions, exclaiming delightedly on recognizing items that had been in the house when he knew it. His delight was strange, coming from a man of middle age who carried the scars of dissipation in face and figure. His sweater and tweed jacket fitted him tightly; the jacket sleeves were a little short, indicating that he had put on weight in shoulders and arms since the jacket was made. The fat sloped down from his temples and his original features were hidden in the puffy veined cheeks. He was just under six feet tall, the same height as Evan Reese, but beside Reese he appeared chubby. Reese, mentally carving away the excess flesh, saw a sensitive man enlarded in the person Stratton had made of himself. And yet as Stratton's visit extended to an hour, Evan Reese found that he was liking the man, pitying him, and hoping that he would remain as he now saw him. No matter what his intelligence told him—which was that Frank Stratton was a committed voluptuary, beyond redemption—Evan Reese wanted to postpone the reversion, and to do so he prolonged Stratton's visit.

"I'm having an exhibition in February," said Evan Reese. "How would you like to have a preview?"

"I'd be delighted, on condition that you won't hold it against me if I say anything stupid," said Stratton. "Where do you work?"

"You remember the potting-shed your cousin used to have? I turned it into a studio. It looks small, but it has as much space as some studios I've had in New York. I'm very pleased with it. I put in skylights and a linoleum floor, and that's about all I had to do. We won't be there very long, however. The only heat is from two electric heaters, and they're so murderously expensive, I never turn them on except when I'm working. So put your coat on."

Evan Reese put on his reefer, Stratton put on his trench coat and they went to the studio. It was a strictly utilitarian one-room house, containing canvases of various sizes in profusion; easels and paint tubes, brushes, knives and palettes and paint-stained rags; one damaged leather chair, several camp chairs and stools, and a bridge table on which lay a couple of large metal ash trays and a half-filled pipe rack. There were two naked electric bulbs hanging from the ceiling. "You see what I mean by cold," said Evan Reese. He turned one of the two spigots of a kitchen sink, and water came forth. "Not frozen," said Evan Reese. "But I'm going to have to get that snow shoveled off the skylight."

"Maybe I can do it. Have you got a ladder?"

"Thanks, but there'll be a fellow along some time today. A sort of a handy man. He'll be out to put the chains on my tires and maybe he might even clear the driveway, if he's in the mood. One of those local characters. I don't like to make suggestions to him, because he always says, 'Mr. Reese, I got it all planned out, now you just let me do it my way.' And he's usually right. He wants to make sure that I understand, you see, that he knows this property better than I do."

"Oh, I guess that's Charley Cooper."

"That's who it is, all right. But he's Mr. Cooper to me. Well, here are thirty-nine pictures, and on the big easel is the fortieth. All sizes. They're the ones I'm going to show in February. My last exhibition was six years ago, and these are all pictures I've done since about—well, since I chose the ones for my 1954 show. These aren't all I've done, of course. I often have three going at a time, and always two. Now for instance, here is a house in Rhode Island, Saunderstown. While I was painting this I was also painting—where is it, now? Here it is, this young lady. Pretty, isn't she?"

"Lovely."

"She talked a blue streak and smoked one cigarette after another. She was very stimulating company, and a very relaxing change from the job of doing that house. This is Spithead, Bermuda. This is a still life done right here in two days, actually in about six hours. But this son of a bitch, this took me three months before I got it right. Same size picture, and apparently just another still life. Same number of objects, just about. But why do you suppose this one took six hours, and this one three months?"

"Just answering for myself, you probably felt like painting when you did the quick one, and were getting fed up when you did the other."

"You've hit it on the nose. My wife and I'd been abroad and I hadn't had a brush in my hand for over two weeks, and we got home and I came right here and started painting without even taking my hat off. Literally. But this one, the one that took me three months, it wasn't because I was fed up with painting. No. You see, I'd seen a picture I didn't like, in Dublin. Had a quick glance at it and dismissed it from my mind, or so I thought. Then one day I arranged some fruit in a bowl and set a table for two. Plates, knives and forks, and began to paint. I worked on that damn thing, I thought about it, I had dreams about it. And then one morning, just before I woke up, I had a dream that I was painting this picture and someone kept getting in my way, standing in front of the table and obstructing my view. And do you know what I decided it was? It was the artist who had painted that picture in Dublin. I didn't know the artist's name or whether it was a man or a woman, but I was unconsciously plagiarizing him, or her. So I went right on and deliberately plagiarized, as much as I could remember of that ugly picture in Dublin, and when I finished it it was about as unlike the original as a picture could be. If you look on the back, I don't always give names to my pictures, but this is one called Plagiarism."

"Fascinating," said Stratton. "And they're not at all alike?"

"Yes, they are alike. A layman would say right away that the two pictures had been painted by the same man, but an expert, another painter or a first-rate dealer or an art historian, would know right away that the two pictures couldn't possibly have been painted by the same man. If I get a good price for this picture I'm going to track down the Dublin picture and buy it. It was a terrible, terrible picture, but it was that artist's masterpiece. The son of a bitch got something in there, in his picture, that offended and irritated me, and it was good. And *he* wouldn't be able to tell me what it was. He wouldn't know it was there. I'm sure of that, because he was such a bad, mediocre painter for the rest of the picture, that he couldn't possibly know what was good. Now that, of course, poses a problem in ethics."

"How so?"

"Well, I could buy his picture, pay a good price for it if he still owns it, which I don't doubt. But then what do I do? Do I tell him that I, a pretty well-known painter, have bought his picture and thereby encourage him? Or do I keep quiet? Or do I buy it and tell him the truth, that he's a bad painter and try to discourage him? Tell him to quit while he's ahead?"

"I really don't know."

"There's still another alternative. I can destroy *my* picture. But I can't, because I know it's good."

"Maybe you ought to find out all about the painter before you decide."

"That's the humanitarian approach, and I've rejected it. I

don't want to know about this painter. If it's a he or a she, a dilettante, a half-taught amateur, a poor struggling bog-trotter. Art is cruel, and in this problem I represent art. This painter will never do anything good. Never."

"He did once, Mr. Reese."

Evan Reese laughed. "Damn it, Stratton, you've touched me where I'm vulnerable. I can't *be* art, with a capital A. A genius would be ruthless. A genius would do what it's only my inclination to do."

"A man that makes a mistake usually gets a second chance. I think a man that does something good ought to, too."

"Well, apparently that's what I've decided. I had all this out with myself a dozen times, and never done a thing. So I probably won't do anything."

"And the Dublin artist did inspire a good picture."

"Oh, naturally I keep telling myself that," said Evan Reese. "Hello, dear?" Georgia Reese entered the studio.

"Mr. Stratton is wanted on the telephone," said Georgia Reese.

"Wanted on the telephone?" said Stratton.

"I'll show you," said Georgia Reese. "And you come in, Ev. You've been out here long enough."

Evan and Georgia Reese waited in noncommittal silence in the kitchen while Stratton was answering the telephone in the library. He returned shortly, smiling. "That was my mother. She was afraid I might have fallen in the snow and broken my leg."

"How did she know you were here?" said Georgia Reese.

"That's funny. How did she? I never thought to ask her."

"I imagine she was going to try every house in the neighborhood before sending out a scouting expedition," said Evan Reese.

"That's probably it. Well, it's been a very interesting morning, at least for me," said Stratton. "Thank you very much for the coffee and the cinnamon buns, Mrs. Reese. And, Mr. Reese, may I remind you that we made a deal?" He obviously was about to leave.

"Here's your sketch. I'll expect the hand-warmer any day now." Evan Reese had written: "To Frank Stratton, Oak Knoll, November 1960. Faithfully, Evan Reese."

"I'll have it framed. Maybe I'll become an art collector."

"I'm all for that, if you have the money," said Evan Reese.

"That's very dubious, but many thanks. Goodbye."

"Nice to've seen you," said Evan Reese.

The Reeses watched him trudging up the hill in the snow.

"That's going to take it out of him," said Evan Reese. "He's in terrible physical condition."

"His manners aren't any too good, either," said Georgia Reese. "Not even a mention of our coming to his mother's."

"How did she seem over the phone?"

"She didn't ask for him. It was a maid with an Irish brogue."

"We'll be invited, don't think we won't," he said.

"Why are you so sure all of a sudden?"

"Why am I so sure? Because he's going to want to come back here, and he can't very well do that without inviting us to his house *sometime*."

"And why is he going to be so anxious to come back here? Were you at your most fascinating?"

"Yes, I was at my most fascinating, and you were nice to him, and he likes this house. He isn't very bright, and he isn't much of a man. But he isn't the pig I thought he was. He *has* good manners, and when I told him about the Dublin still life I liked his reactions. Decent. Honorable. Also, he isn't an art-phony. People with a bit of pansy in them are apt to be art-phonies. One thing you've got to say for the Zuleika Dobson school, they aren't art-phonies."

"That's my school."

"I know it is. Someone brought up as rich as Stratton was shouldn't have to be phony about anything, but unfortunately you get just as much bullshit about art from the rich as you do from everybody else. I wish I knew something about the ballet. I'd try this fellow out on the ballet and see if he goes phony there. Why don't *you* know something about the ballet?"

"Because for thirty-one years I've been your cook and mis-

tress, and nursemaid and mother of your children, and haven't
had time to get culture."

"Well, I'll accept that excuse. But don't let it happen again.
Telephone. Probably Joel Channing wanting to know when he
can see the pictures. Tell him I've gone skiing." He followed
her slowly to the library and listened to her side of the conversation.

"Yes it is," she said. "Oh, yes . . . This afternoon? Well,
I'd have to ask my husband and call you back. He's working
and I can't disturb him, but he'll be in for lunch any minute
. . . I hope so, too. And thank you for calling."

"The old lady?" said Evan Reese.

"Could we come in for tea this afternoon about five. So
bland. You might think we'd moved here yesterday."

"Maybe from her viewpoint it *was* yesterday."

"Do you want me to say we'll go?"

"Yes, what's the use of pretending? She'd see through that,"
said Evan Reese. "And as Jennie pointed out, the time is
getting short."

A few minutes before five that afternoon the Reeses' door-
bell rang. Evan Reese recognized the man at the door, Elwood
Blawen, who had a farm on West Branch Road. "Hello, Mr.
Blawen. Come in."

"No thanks. I came to fetch you to Mrs. Stratton's," said
Blawen. He pointed to an old jeep with a winter top.

"How did that happen?"

"How did that happen? Why, she just called me up and said
I was to go fetch you at five o'clock in my jeep. Wasn't any
more to it than that. But I *imagine* she figured'd take a jeep to
get you there, and she's pretty near right. You'd never get up
the hill in your car, 'specially without chains. No Charley
Cooper, I see."

"No, he must be counting on all this to melt away."

"Charley's all right once he gets working, but I never saw
such a man for putting things off. Deliberating, he always
calls it. But there's other names for it, too. Good afternoon,
Mizz Reese."

"Mr. Blawen. You going to be our transportation?"

"Looks that way. She's all cleaned out inside," said Blawen.
"I even got a heater in there for you."

"Not just for us, I hope," said Georgia Reese.

"Oh, no. If you mean did I put it in special." He smiled.
"Oh, no. Those days are gone forever. But mind you, I seen the
day when the Stratton family *would* do a thing like that. Why,
they tell me she used to have a man come all the way from
Philadelphia just to play a few tunes on the organ." He
lowered his voice. "Paid him five—hundred—dollars." They
got in the jeep. "Five hundred dollars, just to play a few tunes
on the pipe organ. One time they had Woodrow Wilson here
for Sunday dinner. The President of the United States. And
old Stratton wasn't even a Democrat. But him and Wilson
were acquainted with one another outside of politics. Oh, yes,
there was always something going on around here in those
days. Twenty-eight people on the payroll, sometimes more."

"You don't work for Mrs. Stratton, do you?" said Evan
Reese.

"Only when she has something special and I can spare the
time. Like today, she knows I have my jeep, so she phoned and
said would I call for you and Mizz Reese. I always try to accommodate her if I can. Never been here before, have you?"

"No, but how did you know that?" said Evan Reese.

"How did I know that? Just took a good guess. She don't
have many visitors. She only got twenty acres left out of what
used to be eight hundred, and I guess she feels hemmed in.
Here we are."

"Thank you very much," said Evan Reese.

"Oh, I'll be here when you come out," said Blawen.

"How long will *we* be here?" said Evan Reese.

"Well, maybe that's not for me to say, but not more'n a
half an hour."

Frank Stratton came out to greet them. "I heard the jeep,"
he said. "I'm so glad you could come."

A maid took their things and Frank Stratton showed the way
to the library. Mrs. Stratton turned from gazing into the fire-

place, but she did not rise. Her left hand clutched the silver mounting of a highly polished walnut walking stick. She was obviously very feeble.

"Mother, this is Mr. and Mrs. Reese."

"Good afternoon. I'm glad you could come," said Mrs. Stratton. "Did you have a nice ride in Elwood Blawen's hideous conveyance? But it does do the trick, doesn't it?"

"My first ride in a jeep," said Georgia Reese.

"And you, Mr. Reese? Your first ride in a jeep too?" said the old lady.

"Oh, no. I did some painting for the Navy during the war, and I rode in a lot of jeeps."

"What kind of painting? Camouflage?" said Mrs. Stratton.

"No. I did some pictures of the landings at Iwo Jima, in 1945."

"Photography?"

"No. Paintings."

"*Painting?*" she said. "But wouldn't photography be much more accurate? I don't understand."

"There's no lens wide enough to take in the whole scene, so we did some sketches and the painting came later."

"And weren't you frightened?"

"I was on a big ship. It was noisy, but you don't mind it so much if you have something to do."

"How far away were you?"

"Three or four miles, most of the time."

"But that's close enough to be dangerous, isn't it?"

"Yes. But not much more dangerous than it is around here during the deer season."

"Oh, come now, Mr. Reese," said the old lady. "Did you approve of this undertaking, Mrs. Reese?"

"Yes. My husband wanted to do it very much," said Georgia Reese.

"Frank, will you ring, please?" said the old lady. "And you believe in supporting your husband in such matters? Well, I must say so do I. Division of authority only leads to confusion." She pronounced her words so slowly that they seemed to be shaking during utterance, but plainly her speech was not keeping up with her thought. "My son tells me you are preparing for an exhibition. February, did he say?"

"The last week in February," said Evan Reese.

"We'll have some tea and then Frank can show you some of my husband's purchases. They should all be in museums, but I can't bear to part with them. Not because I appreciate their merit. I don't. But I'd miss them. They're all spoken for, or I'd give one or two of them to private people. I'm not at all sure that a museum is the right place for a painting. How do you feel about that, Mr. Reese?"

"Most good pictures should be in museums," said Evan Reese.

"Then we don't agree. Do you paint to have your pictures in museums?"

"No one ever asked me that before. In fact, I never asked myself. Do I paint to have my pictures in museums? No. I paint to satisfy my need to paint, and in the hope that one person will see a picture and like it well enough to buy it. Preferably somone who can afford to pay a lot."

"I got an original Evan Reese for the price of a hand-warmer."

"What's that about a hand-warmer, my dear?"

"Mr. Reese and I made a trade. He gave me a sketch, and I'm giving him an electric hand-warmer."

"That isn't why I'm giving you the sketch, Mr. Stratton. I'm giving you the sketch because you impulsively offered to give me the hand-warmer."

"Mrs. Reese, would you with your steady young hands . . ." The old lady directed the maid with the tea things to place them in front of Georgia Reese. "Not very strong for me, please. One lump. No cream or lemon. Frank, will you take Mr. Reese on a very brief tour, but don't be gone long, as I have to leave our guests."

Evan Reese followed Stratton into the great hall and inspected the Gainsborough, the Van Dyke, and the Rubens, devoting about one minute to each picture, but making no comment. After each picture he looked at Stratton, and after the Rubens he said: "Very interesting. Now I think we ought to go back."

"Yes. You can come again and have a longer look," said Stratton.

In the library the old lady looked at Evan Reese. "Very interesting, don't you think, Mr. Reese?" she said.

"Very."

"I thought you'd find them so. Now, I'm afraid you'll have to excuse me." She got to her feet. "Thank you for coming, and now you understand why I haven't been more hospitable before. Mr. Reese, I'm sure *you* understand?"

"I do indeed, Madam," said Evan Reese. "Perfectly."

The old lady took the maid's arm and left them.

"Would you have time to see some more of the house?" said Stratton.

"Oh, I'd—" Georgia Reese began.

"Not today, thanks," said Evan Reese, quickly and emphatically. "But ask us again, will you? Or come in for a cup of coffee tomorrow. I'll have some heat in the studio, and we can have our coffee there."

The Reeses were returned to their house, and Evan Reese, taking his accustomed chair in the library, lit his pipe and stretched out his legs.

"Why did you rush us away? I wanted to see the rest of the house."

"We'll be seeing the rest of the house. And why am I sure? Well, I was sure before and I'm just as sure now. I also know why the old lady never invited us before."

"Obviously because she's so helpless and didn't want to be seen," said Georgia Reese.

Evan Reese shook his head. "You didn't get that little by-play between her and me, at the end."

"No. I thought she was being old-lady flirtatious. A by-play?"

"Yes. She and I understood each other. Do you know why we were never invited to her house? I'll tell you. Because I'm a painter. And there isn't a painter in the world over twenty-five years old that wouldn't know right away that the Rubens, the Van Dyke and the Gainsborough are all fakes. And the son doesn't know it. The Gainsborough is in Pasadena, California. The Rubens is owned by a man named Lee, in Chicago. And the Van Dyke is owned by the Spencer family, in Newport. Mrs. Stratton hasn't owned either of the originals since long before the war. I wonder if she has any jewelry that her heirs presumptive are counting on. If so, I'll bet it's all paste."

"But how do you get rid of three old masters without any publicity?"

"You do it through a dealer, who arranges a private sale, and you make sure that the picture isn't bought for a museum. You sell to people who have the money and want the pictures, but don't want the publicity. There are still a few people in this country who can pay a hundred and fifty thousand for a picture for their own private enjoyment. I imagine that a condition of the sales was that there should be no public announcement, and a reputable dealer would keep quiet."

"But Bob Hewitt knows all about her financial condition."

"No he doesn't. He talks big, but Bob only knows about her account in his bank. She probably deals with some firm like the United States Trust, in New York. Bob handles the grocery bills, but I'll bet you he's never had anything to do with her securities."

"I wonder what made her change her mind, and let you in the house?"

"Well, she knows what we're like after ten years, and I think she trusts us. But of course it also has something to do with her son's visit. We'll know when she gets ready to tell us."

"She's very feeble."

"But she's a fighter."

In the morning Evan Reese was in his studio, intent on his painting, and he was irritated when Stratton knocked on the door. "Come—in," said Evan Reese. He had his pipe in his clenched teeth and he knew he sounded fierce, but Stratton's interruption was unwelcome.

"Is it too early for a cinnamon bun?" said Stratton. "I can come back, or maybe you'd like to be left alone."

"Oh, that's all right," said Evan Reese. Stratton was almost pathetic in his desire for company. "Have a seat and I'll be with you in about two minutes."

"I'll be perfectly quiet."

"You can talk. I don't mind, if you don't mind getting delayed answers."

"You've got it nice and warm in here today."

"Yes, the electric heaters."

"With the heat on it's a very pleasant room. Cozy," said Stratton. "You must like it here."

"I do," said Evan Reese. "I can work any place, but I've done more work in this little shack than anywhere else. And I've become attached to it. Probably in more ways than one."

Stratton was silent for a moment, and Evan Reese glanced at him quickly.

"What was I thinking?" said Stratton. "I was thinking about how you can hold the pipe in your mouth and go on talking and painting. The English do that. You see them riding along on bicycles, both hands on the handlebars and never taking their pipes out of their mouths."

"But I'm not English. I'm Welsh."

"Of course. Of course," said Stratton apologetically. Then, as though to make up for his mistake, he said: "You made a great hit with my mother."

"She made a great hit with me."

"You know, Mother knows a lot more about you than you might think."

"There isn't a hell of a lot to know," said Evan Reese. "Unless you want to argue that there's a hell of a lot to know about everybody. But there's nothing very spectacular about me. I've never had much personal publicity."

"That isn't the kind of thing I meant anyway. Mother doesn't care for that sort of thing, either. But she's studied you."

"Has she? I don't see how. I never met her before yesterday."

"I'll show you how," said Stratton. He stood up and went to a window. "Would you like to see how?"

"Just one second," said Evan Reese. He pressed his thumb on the canvas, put down his brush and palette, wiped his hands with a rag, and took his pipe out of his mouth. "Okay. Through for the morning."

"Well, you see the bay window on the second floor of Mother's house?"

"Indeed I do. I've often envied her that view."

"That's where she sits. And do you know what she has there? A telescope."

"I would too, if I had that bay window. And that's how she studies me?"

Stratton nodded. "You, and Mrs. Reese, and God knows how many others. People think of Mother as an old lady all alone in her mountain fastness. Actually she's an old busybody."

"In Pennsylvania a busybody is an arrangement of mirrors. You see them on second-story window-sills. You can see who's walking on the sidewalk to the right or left of your house, or ringing the doorbell, without opening the window."

"I've heard of them. At least I've seen them mentioned in novels without quite knowing what they were. But Mother's the other kind. The human kind."

"Oh, indeed she is. Very human. That's why I like her."

"Oh, you like her? I'm glad you like her. She's had a very tough life, at least the second half of it. My father was ill, and between me and my sister, we didn't give her much to be thankful for. I suppose you may have read about my sister, or heard about her."

"A little."

"A little is enough, and that goes for me, too, if you know anything about me, and I'm sure you do. People talk. People gossip."

"Yes. They do," said Evan Reese. "Shall we go over to the kitchen?"

"You'd rather I didn't talk about myself?"

"Oh, you're wrong. But there's coffee in the kitchen, and a place to sit."

"You don't *mind* if I talk?"

"Not a bit. I just thought we'd be more comfortable in the house."

"Oh, fine. You see, Mr. Reese, I know what people say about me, and they have every right to. But I always think that artistic people and writers take a different point of view. More tolerant, if you know what I mean."

"I don't know that they're really more tolerant, but they have to pretend to be."

"Well, that's almost as good. It's better than being avoided. I'm not going to be a pest, honestly I'm not. But I felt right away that you were someone I could talk to. I could tell that you'd heard about me. I always can. But you didn't try to get rid of me first thing, the way so many do."

"Let's have some coffee, and a cinnamon bun."

Stratton's face was transformed, from middle-aged voluptuary's to trusting boy's. "Yes, let's," he said.

Georgia and Evan Reese, jointly present, restrained Stratton from further candor, if that had been his inclination; but he stayed an hour and the conversation was easy and obviously enjoyable to him. "I hate to leave you two," he said. "But Mother likes me to be prompt. By the way, Mr. Reese, it's perfectly all right to tell Mrs. Reese about the telescope."

"Oh, I'd have told her without your permission."

"I know you would. I was just kidding," said Stratton. "Thank you both, I had *such* a good time."

Georgia Reese said to her husband: "Watch out, Ev. You may be taking on a responsibility that you didn't ask for."

"I've thought of that," said Evan Reese. "But the poor son of a bitch."

"Yes," said Georgia Reese. "We were lucky with ours."

"It wasn't all luck."

"No, it wasn't."

"Any more than what's happened to this fellow was all bad luck. Or what's happened to his sister. That old lady with her telescope, and her fake paintings. I must find out more about her. And the father, her husband."

"Well, you'll find out more from people like Elwood Blawen and Charley Cooper. Bob and Jennie Hewitt want us to think they knew the Strattons better than they really did."

"Frank Stratton? You mean the old man?" said Charley Cooper. "I don't know's I could tell you anything about him, beyond that he loved the almighty dollar. I aint saying he was a stingy man, not by any manner or means. He got rid of it, but he knew where every penny went and he made sure he always got value received. Take for instance when we voted to get rid of the horses and buy motorized equipment down't the hose company. We went to Mr. Stratton and asked how much we could count on from him. And he said, and I remember because I was there, he said if we went about it the usual way, not a penny. He said he wasn't going to give any money for a fire truck, knowing that some slick salesman would arrange to take care of certain parties on the committee. Well, now how did Francis A. Stratton, a mul-tie-millionaire, know that that was the usual way? But he knew it, and that's the way it was going to be done, till he spoke up. Embarrassed hell out of the committee, and I was tickled pink, because I didn't figure to get a red cent out of it. So what Francis A. Stratton did, he bought the fire truck through one of the big corporations he was interested in. Through a regular purchasing agent. And then he *do*nated it to the borough. But he wouldn't let a few fellows have their little graft.

"Same thing with other opportunities for a bit of hanky-panky. Like one time he bought fifty dollars' worth of chances for some prize the Legion was auctioning off. By golly, the night they had the drawing, there was Francis A. Stratton, with all his stubs, in case one of his numbers won. That was kind of embarrassing, too. Because some of the Legion boys had it all arranged that one of their wives was going to get the prize. But when Francis A. Stratton showed up they had to quick dump a lot of his tickets in the bowl, and of course

he won. A Victrola, I think it was. Yes. A Vic. And as soon
as he won, he said he was donating it to the children's ward at
the hospital. Made a certain friend of mine's wife sore as all
hell. But that's the way he was, old Stratton. He you might say
kept us honest. On the other hand, like donating land for a
playground, he done that without the least hesitation. I guess
you'd say, about honesty, he carried it to an extreme."

"Tell me about his appearance. What did he look like?"

"What did he look like? Oh-ho. If you was a stranger in
town and you saw Francis A. Stratton, you'd know right away
who was the big noise around these parts. If he wasn't riding
in one of his Rolls-Royce English cars, if you happened to see
him before he took sick, he was a regular country squire.
Derby hat, checkered riding pants and polished-up boots, one
of them there white collar-and-tie affairs only the tie and the
collar are the same piece of cloth. They had a name for them."

"Stock."

"Stock is right. Stocks and bonds. I ought to be able to
remember that, talking about Francis A. Stratton. Well, once
in a while he'd take a notion to come down to town on horseback. He usually rode a white horse, although he had
every color of horse there was, and every kind of carriage
and buggy. But he'd ride down and leave the horse at the
livery stable and do his errands, carrying one of them riding
whips. And if he didn't look like he owned the town, nobody did. Polite and all. But he was Francis A. Stratton and
nobody knew it better than he did. The time he fell off his
horse, he lay there because nobody had the nerve to touch
him. They didn't. They stood around and looked at him lying
there, unconscious, till somebody had sense enough to send for
Doc Frelinghuysen."

"He fell off his horse? Was he drunk?"

"Well now that's where you won't get any two agreeing,
on whether he was drunk or sober. If he was drunk, it was
the only time any town people ever seen him in that condition, and some didn't believe he was a drinker. But for
others it was a pretty well-known fact that Francis A. Stratton

sometimes would come home from New York and more or less lock himself up with a bottle and stay out of sight for a week at a time. He had a stock ticker in his house. You know, one of those stock tickers? And he had a fellow worked for him as secretary, O'Neill, that they used to say knew as much about Stratton's business as Stratton did. And maybe more than business. Never liked that O'Neill. He was honest, but the people in town never trusted him. Everybody always shut up when O'Neill was around, for fear he'd carry tales back to Stratton. But he was faithful to Stratton, no doubt about that, and I always heard that O'Neill was a bitterly disappointed man when Stratton didn't leave him anything in his will. Must of been some reason, but I never knew what it was."

"So Stratton was a secret drinker?"

"Well, I don't know's you'd call him secret. The way he lived, as far as the town people knew, he was a secret eater. By that I mean, he didn't drink with town people, but he didn't eat with them neither."

"How old was he when he fell off the horse?"

"Along. Fifties. Maybe more. I understand he got some kind of a clot in the brain from it, but maybe that was just talk. It didn't stop him from working. Or riding horseback. He was out again in a couple months."

"He was quite a handsome man, wasn't he? Or was he?"

"Well, yes. Yes, he was handsome, for a man. Bald-headed, and he had a little black moustache. Not as big a moustache as most men wore in those days. I don't know whether you'd call him handsome or not. If you're thinking of a movie actor's looks, no. Had a nice set of teeth, I remember. In fact, you could have taken him for an Eye-talian, in the summer. Sunburned from being outdoors so much. She used to play tennis with him. They had two tennis courts, one inside and one outside, and they were the first ones around here to have a swimming pool. That was considered the height of luxury then, to have a swimming pool. But I considered the height of luxury having an inside tennis court. It's the ways they think of to spend their money that makes one rich man different than another. I used to think, who would want to play tennis in the winter? Who'd ever think of it? Would you? Maybe now you would, but not that long ago. Tennis wouldn't of been my game in the middle of the summer, let alone spend a wad of money to play it inside in the winter. But Francis A. Stratton wanted to play tennis, so he built himself a house for it, and a lot of famous players used to come there and practice."

"Who, for instance?"

"Oh, don't ask me. I never cared for tennis that much. My sport was cycling. Frank Kramer was my man, the *Iron* Man, they used to call him. I used to go over to Newark, to the Velodrome, just to watch him. If I could of been anybody else I'd have been Frank Kramer. The Iron Man."

"I don't think I ever heard of him."

"Well, that's the same way I was with your tennis players."

"To each his own, as they say."

"Yes, as far as I know, Francis A. Stratton never rode a wheel, so we didn't have much to talk about, him and I."

"What was he like, to talk to?"

"Well, as I said before, polite. There was men in town that he could buy and sell, that they wouldn't treat you as polite as Mr. Stratton. The help all liked him, too. I only ever heard of one quitting on their own accord, but she didn't quit on account of Mr. Stratton." Charley Cooper giggled. "That was a funny one, but it happened long after Francis A. Stratton passed on. You know Lorna Disney, works in the post office?"

"Know her to say hello to," said Evan Reese.

Cooper giggled again. "A fine hello she got one day. Lorna was Lorna Parton then, a hired girl working for Mrs. Stratton, and one day young Frank was home from school and had a friend visiting him. Lorna walks in to do her dusting and there sat Frank's friend in his bare skin, not a thing on him, and playing the piano. Must of been quite a shock to Lorna. She quit then and there. Did her some good, though. She got married soon after. Left an impression, you might say. Oh, there was always something to talk about going on up at the Strattons', but they had so many foreigners working for them and they didn't mix. Lorna could tell you a thing or two, but don't ask her about the piano player. She don't like to have that brought up. *I* can joke with her about it, but she wouldn't like *you* to."

"No, I guess not."

"Everybody has some story about the Strattons, everybody that was living here forty-fifty years ago, what you might call their heyday. Since then you don't hear so much about them. Young Frank—well, I don't know. And Bunnie, now that she's an Italian princess. But they're a different generation, gone to pot. And they moved away. Just as well they did move away. Young Frank, he liked the boys. And Bunnie, she liked the boys, too. If they'd of stayed around here there'd have been trouble, for certain. The old lady was right in kicking them out."

"She kicked them out?"

"As good as. Wouldn't let them hang around here. If they were gonna make damn fools of themselves and get into scrapes, she didn't want it to happen here. And don't forget, it wasn't as easy to buy their way out of trouble. Mrs. Stratton, the widow, didn't carry as much weight as Francis A. when he was alive. I doubt if she's worth a tenth as much as when Mister passed on."

"Where did it all go?"

"You tell me. A fellow like myself, an ordinary working man, I been making money and saving it all these years. But I don't know what happens to a big fortune. Taxes, but that don't explain it. I think she must of got hold of some bad advice in the stock market. I don't know *where* it went. But it's a shame and a disgrace to let a big fortune like that get all pissed away. They could of done a lot for this town if they'd of held on to it, but I'll bet you when she dies there won't be enough to pay the inheritance taxes, and nowadays you can't *give* away a house like that. They used to have thirty people working up there, but the last couple years she only has me there two days a week, and two women in the house, and Elwood Blawen helps out. You know, when she married Francis A. Stratton and got him to build that house and all, it looked like High Ridge was safe and sound. But the last twenty-five-thirty years she's been selling land, and school taxes went up four or five times and this town, I'm predicting, this town inside of another couple years will be so changed nobody will recognize it. I don't want to be living here when *that* happens, and my folks have lived here since the 1700's. No matter what you say about Francis A. Stratton, he was pretty fond of this town. And I guess when you come right down to it, we were pretty fond of him."

"That's what I wanted to hear you say."

"Well, I never would of thought to say it if it wasn't for getting started talking this way. But it's a fair statement. He didn't suck up to nobody. He wasn't natured that way. But he was polite to people, and he didn't infringe on anybody's rights. He wasn't so different from any the rest of us, except richer, and nobody minded him marching around in his riding pants. What the hell? We wouldn't of trusted a man that rich that went around wearing overhalls."

"All in all, you liked Mr. Stratton, then?" said Evan Reese.

"That's what I been trying to tell you, Mr. Reese. You wanted to know some facts, and I's willing to give them to you. You're entitled to any facts I have—"

"Why? How am I?" said Evan Reese, vaguely complimented.

"How are you entitled? Well, facts is the truth, and the truth will out, and everybody's entitled to the truth. But there's different ways of telling facts, so one person telling the same facts could give a different impression. 'S far as we know, you're a reliable man and that entitles you to the facts the way I see them."

"What if I hadn't been a reliable man, Mr. Cooper?"

Cooper smiled. "You'd be surprised how little you'd find out."

"Oh."

"Newspaper reporters been around here two-three times. Once when Bunnie run away and got married. Once when Francis A. Stratton died. And a scandal sheet when Frank

Junior got into trouble. They all went back and wrote up High Ridge people like we was afraid to talk about the Strattons. Afraid? Not afraid, Mr. Reese. One thing we never was was afraid. There was Coopers buried here two hundred years before any Stratton ever set foot in High Ridge. And plenty of Crowders in the same churchyard. She was a Crowder."

"Ah, now I see. She belongs to High Ridge, too."

"Sure does."

"So it wasn't so much that you liked Mr. Stratton that made you protect him, as much as her being a Crowder?"

"I thought you knew that, Mr. Reese."

"Well, it's a little hard to follow, unless you bear in mind that Mrs. Stratton was a Crowder."

"That's the whole thing. If she was just some stranger."

"But your real loyalty was to her, to Mrs. Stratton."

"To High Ridge, put it that way. Take Lorna Disney, for instance. Lorna wouldn't have no difficulty proving kinship to Mrs. Stratton. She might not be as close as the Coopers, but the Partons go back, and Lorna was a Parton."

"What about the Hewitts, for instance?"

Charley Cooper shook his head. "Not High Ridge. They come up from South Jersey, an altogether different breed of cat, you might say. There was some Coopers and some Hewitts got together in New York, but these weren't the same Hewitts. These here in town came from South Jersey."

"Then I take it Mrs. Stratton is a cousin of yours?"

"Yes indeed. The Crowders and the Coopers married over and over again. You take a walk through the churchyard and you'll wonder if they ever married anybody else. Didn't always draw the line at first cousins, either. Back in those days, I guess they didn't always know for sure, when it was mostly farms. Twenty miles away'd be a good strong young woman, and a young farmer had to have a wife. A young fellow tried to run a farm without a wife, he couldn't *do* it. You had to have a wife. And not only for the work, either, if you know what I mean. Come a certain age, and a young fellow had to have a *woman*."

"To go to bed with?" said Evan Reese.

"To, right, go to bed with. It was that or start buggerin' the sheep. Or one another. And when that happened it wasn't long before everybody'd know it. A farmer that didn't have a woman, first he'd go to pot. Usually he'd stink so that nobody'd want to go near him. And pretty soon the farm would go to hell."

"Was this in your lifetime?"

"Sure was in my lifetime. I remember one Crowder had a piece of land he tried to farm without a woman. Him and his brother, the two of them. Jack'd never bring the brother to town with him, just come by himself. Stink? That fellow you could smell him a hundred yards off, and he grew his hair long and a beard. He couldn't read or write and to tell the truth, his vocabulary was pretty small. Just enough to ask for what he wanted in the store, like salt, molasses, shells for his gun. Children used to yell at him and he'd throw stones at them. Hit them, too. But he never run after them. He was the slowest-moving white man I ever saw."

"And what happened to *him?*"

"The brother run away one day, and Jack shot himself with the shotgun."

"And what happened to the brother?"

"They found him living in a cave, couple of miles from the farm. They put him away, he was an idiot. And he died of some sickness a couple months after they locked him up. The sheriff accidentally on purpose set fire to the shack they lived in. He told my father no self-respecting pig would live in it. Slaughtered the stock, a couple of cows, and the court awarded the land to the next of kin. That was an uncle, and the uncle was a cousin of Mrs. Stratton's father. So you see?"

"Mm-hmm." Evan Reese nodded. He was not sure whether he was supposed to see that a farm could not be run without a wife, or that Mrs. Stratton had some odd relatives.

"We had just as bad among the Coopers, I guess. They hung a Cooper when I was a young boy, and the sheriff that sprung the trap was a Cooper. How's that for family relations?"

"Well, where I come from in Pennsylvania there were over a dozen Evan Reeses in the same town, and five Reese Evanses. Originally r, h, y, s, but pronounced Reese. And Billy Williamses and Tommy Thomases and Johnny Johnses."

"Then you ought to know," said Charley Cooper. "But here it's been like that for close to three hundred years."

"I guess it was a good thing Mrs. Stratton married a stranger."

"Why?"

"New blood," said Evan Reese.

"New blood? Take a look at Frank Junior. Take a look at Bunnie. If that's all new blood can do for you, you're no better off than as if you married your first cousin. You can't go by that with people."

"You have a point," said Evan Reese. "But maybe Frank's grandchildren will be all right, or Bunnie's."

"Well, I doubt if I'll be around to see it, so I don't intend to let it worry me. I got one of my own grandchildren the brightest boy in his class at Rutgers, and another, his sister, in a mental institution. They had new blood, too. You figure it out, Mr. Reese."

"All right, Mr. Cooper, and if I do I'll call you up."

Cooper smiled. "No hurry, Mr. Reese. They're gonna make babies no matter what you tell them. That we won't be able to stop. Nobody could of stopped *me* when *I* was the right age." He jabbed a thumb in Reese's rib. "Didn't wait till it was legal, either."

"I'll bet you didn't."

"There's a few extra Coopers in addition to them that have the name. Know what I mean?"

"A few extra Coopers, eh?"

"One or two, must be. And I often think to myself, I wasn't the only one after nooky. Consequently, if I's getting mine, other parties were getting theirs, and the old saying, it's a wise child that knows his own father."

"True the world over, I suppose," said Evan Reese.

"I don't know about the world over, Mr. Reese. I only know

about High Ridge, but I sure know my High Ridge. An education in itself."

The conversation was taking place in Evan Reese's studio, to which Cooper had gone to report on some trees that had been overburdened in the snowfall. In cold weather it was never difficult to get Charley Cooper to talk, if the studio was warm. "Well, if you let me have your saw, I think I'll trim off some of them limbs," said Cooper, reluctantly.

"Hanging in the closet," said Evan Reese.

"Always used to rub a little ham fat on a saw," said Cooper. "As good as anything I know to keep the rust out. I never put a saw away without rubbing a little ham fat, but I guess oil's all right if it does the trick. How you coming along with your picture-painting?"

"Slow but sure," said Evan Reese.

"These here pictures, they look as good to me as some the Strattons paid thousands of dollars for."

"Thank you. They bought some very valuable paintings," said Evan Reese.

"So they did," said Cooper.

Evan Reese waited. He knew that Cooper was on the verge of saying something about the Stratton pictures.

"That puts me in mind of a question I wanted to ask you, Mr. Reese. What do they do when they *clean* a picture? Supposing you had an expensive picture. Would you send it away to have it cleaned?"

"I might, yes."

"Oh, you would?"

"Oh, yes. To have an expert job done."

"Put it in a crate and send it off to New York, eh?"

"Yes, that's done all the time, with valuable paintings. Why?"

"Costs a lot of money, I'll bet."

"It's not cheap, but it's worth it for a good picture."

"Mrs. Stratton used to do it. Anyway, she did it some years ago and I wondered why anybody'd want to go to all that trouble. She had me up there building crates for two or three pictures, oh, back before the war. That is, a fellow came from New York and told me how he wanted the crates built. That was carpentry, so I had to charge her extra, but she didn't complain. I made her a price of $15 a crate, labor and materials. Well, that's one of the ways the rich have of spending their money."

"In this case, protecting an investment."

"Very likely," said Cooper, unsatisfied. "Fifteen dollars apiece to me, and then whatever the cleaner charged. What *would* he charge?"

"That depends on the value of the painting."

"Say a painting by Van Dyke?"

"Oh, probably a thousand dollars. I don't know. Maybe more."

"Then I didn't overcharge her for my crates."

"I think that was a fair price."

"I wondered. 'S far as I know, she never sent any more away, and I wondered if she thought I overcharged her."

"The Van Dyke is the one that's hanging in the hall?" said Evan Reese.

Cooper nodded. "I wouldn't of remembered Van Dyke, except there's a whole family of Van Dykes living around here."

"Did they do a good cleaning job?"

"I don't know. I didn't unpack it for her, and I don't get in the hall very often. My work don't take me but to the cellar and the kitchen, generally speaking." He paused. "Supposing she wanted to sell a picture like that. What would she get for it?"

"Oh, Lord. Fifty, a hundred, a hundred and fifty thousand. Possibly more. The market changes, and some paintings are worth much more than others by the same man."

"What if, supposing a fellow come to you with a picture and wanted to sell it to you. Would you know right away if it was genuine?"

"That depends. If I knew the painter's work very well I

think I could tell. And of course you realize that some individual paintings are famous. The Mona Lisa, for instance. Everybody knows where that is."

"I don't. I heard of it, but I don't know where it is."

"It's in the Louvre, in Paris. And to a certain extent that's true of a great many famous paintings."

"Then if you took a look at a painting by Van Dyke, you'd know right away if it was genuine?"

"If I had occasion to study it, probably. Why? Have you been wondering about Mrs. Stratton's Van Dyke?"

"Oh, I wouldn't want you to say that," said Cooper. "No, sir, I wouldn't want that at all, Mr. Reese. Don't put words in my mouth."

"I wouldn't think of doing that, Mr. Cooper."

"Hope not," said Cooper. "Well, this aint getting my work done, much as I enjoyed talking with you."

"I enjoyed it too. Come in any time."

"And everything I said this morning—?"

"Oh, absolutely between the two of us."

"She never liked anybody talking about her. Starting with marrying a man twice her age."

"I imagine."

The expected call from Mrs. Stratton came later in the day. "I'd like your advice on something, if you have five minutes," she said. It was an invitation that unmistakably excluded Georgia Reese. "My son's gone over to Princeton for lunch, so it'll be just you and I."

Evan Reese was led by the maid to the study-office.

"Some coffee, Mr. Reese?" said Mrs. Stratton.

"No thanks."

"Do have some? It's here, and it's hot, and I always feel more like a hostess if my guests take *something*. Sugar?"

"One lump, please." He accepted the demitasse and took a chair facing hers.

"Mrs. Reese isn't going to say anything about those frauds, is she?"

"Of course not."

"No. She's a lady. I knew that. I sold the pictures quite a long while ago. It was the only way I knew to provide for my grandchildren. Even so, I didn't get a very good price for them. The dealer took a larger commission than usual. *He* said because he wasn't getting any publicity, but what he meant was that *I* wasn't getting any publicity. In other *words,* he'd keep his mouth shut for a price. Well, I had no choice but to pay him."

"I think I ought to warn you that Charley Cooper is suspicious." He reported some of his conversation with Cooper, and she listened in silence until he finished.

"Yes," she said. "Charley Cooper would like somehow to collect a little money from me for *his* silence. But first he has to have someone to back up his suspicions. He'll try you, later, when he's decided you can be trusted. Not that that will be a very high compliment, Mr. Reese."

"No, it won't be, will it?"

"I know Charley so well because he's my cousin, or has he told you that?"

"Yes, he's told me that."

"The question on Charley's mind would be whether to risk losing the few dollars I pay him fifty-two weeks a year. When he was younger he was more trustworthy. Not more honest, but more trustworthy. He was satisfied with ten or twenty dollars a week. But he's old now, and why is it that the old like money so much? Is it because that's all there is? As a young man Charley was quite dashing. The girls in High Ridge swooned over him, if that doesn't tax your imagination. He was a handsome young man, scorching about on his bicycle. My husband used to give him a lot of his clothes, and Charley cut quite a figure. But then he married and settled down. His wife made him refuse my husband's old suits, and he became very straitlaced. Always had two or three jobs at the same time and brought up his children with an iron hand. Isn't it always that way with reformed rakes? Were you a rake when you were a younger man, Mr. Reese?"

"I did some raking, but I don't think I was a rake."

"Charley was a rake, by High Bridge standards. He's supposed to have been the father of at least two children by other men's wives. Luckily for him, though, the mothers were the kind that couldn't be sure. There was more of that here than we like to admit."

"There is, no matter where you go."

"I daresay. But I didn't ask you here to discuss my cousin Charley Cooper. I want to know what you think of my son. Is there any hope for him?"

"In what way?"

"In any way. You may not think it's fair of me to ask you such a question. You don't know me very well, and I haven't been very cordial to you and Mrs. Reese. But I'm a very old woman, and we haven't got time to get acquainted by easy stages. The nice thing about being old is that I can dispense with those easy stages, dinner twice a year for ten years, tea four times a year, and so forth. You and I can make up our minds about each other much more quickly. And I knew from the way you acted after you saw those fake pictures that I could tell you anything and ask you anything. If I had known you all my life I couldn't be surer."

"Thank you."

"You're welcome. And so—what about my son? I'd hoped that when he was divorced he'd be able to face his problem squarely. In plain language, stop torturing himself with this pretense of being like other men. He never has been. He loved the girl he married, and he loves his children. But he forced that girl to marry him by convincing her that she would be his salvation. Salvation! He very nearly ruined her life as well as his own. And he knew what a dreadful thing he was doing to her, and that was what made him take to drinking. As to the children—they're exactly like dolls, animated dolls. When he speaks of them that's the way he sounds, as though he were talking about dolls. And he loved dolls when he was a little boy. But only too well I remember that for no reason at all he would smash a doll, and I sided with his wife on the question of custody of the children."

"Well, aside from his drinking, what's the matter with him now?"

"You say *aside* from his drinking? There *is* nothing *aside* from his drinking, Mr. Reese."

"But he hasn't been drinking since's he's been here."

"He doesn't drink here because I won't have it. But in New York he drinks all day long, every day."

"What do you mean when you say you won't have it? Do you lock up the whiskey supply?"

"Nothing as easy as that. He simply knows that if he takes more than a few cocktails before meals, I'll send him away. I won't have him in my house. And he understands that."

"So he complies?"

"He has no alternative," she said.

Evan Reese stood up and went to the window.

"You seem to me to want to light your pipe," said Mrs. Stratton. "Go right ahead."

"How sensitive you are. That's exactly what I want to do," said Evan Reese.

"I like the smell of pipe tobacco. I don't like the smell of pipes, but the tobacco burning is very pleasant."

"Well, I'll light up as quickly as I can," said Evan Reese. He filled his pipe and lit it, and remained standing. "Mrs. Stratton, I agree with you that we can dispense with the early stages."

"That's good."

"But even if I'd known you, we'd known each other, all our lives, that wouldn't necessarily mean that complete candor existed between us."

"No, that's true. What are you getting at, Mr. Reese?"

"This. Whether we've known each other a couple of days, or forty or fifty years, the question is how well do we know each other? In other words, what things can we say, and what things must we not say?"

"There's nothing we can't say, when I've asked you such a terribly inside-of-me, intimate question about my son. I should think that such a question would make you feel free to answer me with complete candor. In fact, Mr. Reese, as a gentleman you *have* to reply to my question with the same candor. That's the only courteous thing you can do."

"I wonder."

"Oh, don't *wonder*. It *is*. It cost me something in pride and humility to be so frank with you."

"But I don't want to be equally frank with you. It won't cost me any humility or pride, but it might cost me your friendship. I have that, haven't I?"

"You have indeed. In fact, you may be my only friend. I can't think of any other, so I guess you are."

"Madam, I *am* your friend," said Evan Reese. "Will you believe that?"

"Yes. I promise."

"Then I'll say what I think, but I hope you'll forgive me."

"Please go on."

Evan Reese emptied his pipe in the fireplace and again seated himself, facing her. "First of all, I'm what I am, a painter, and not a psychiatrist."

"I don't want a psychiatrist."

"Your son has made a failure of his marriage. He has affection and I suppose admiration for his wife. He has a great fondness for his children, his dolls. He got out of his marriage, with its heterosexual obligations. But getting out of his marriage didn't make him happy, or give him any release. You tell me that he drinks heavily all the time."

"Morning, noon and night," she said.

"*Except!* Except when he comes here, Mrs. Stratton. Except when he's here with you. The only time he's at all happy, the only time he doesn't need to drink—"

"He knows I won't have it in my house—"

"Mrs. Stratton, he doesn't drink here because he doesn't *want* to drink here. This is where he wants to be, with you."

"Do you know what you're saying?" she said.

"Of course I do. Of course I know what I'm saying."

"Then stop saying it. You know it isn't true."

"What isn't true, Mrs. Stratton?"

"What you're thinking. It was never true, never in my life."

"I believe you."

"Then why must you say these things?"

"I believe *you*, Mrs. Stratton. *You*. But I don't disbelieve what your son feels."

"He feels nothing. He's past all feeling."

"Then let him be happy, here with you."

She shook her head. "I'm too old. I don't want him here," she said.

"My dear lady, you sent him away once before. Twice before. What happens when you send him away?"

"Oh, you know these things?"

"Yes," said Evan Reese. "And now you're old, Mrs. Stratton, but even so you'll probably outlive him."

"I'm sure I will."

"Then let him stay, the more reason."

"I *am* old, you know. But he is my son. The poor, bloated, miserable boy. I hardly know him any more. Tell me, Mr. Reese, so wise and kind you are, why does *this* last?" She held her hand to her bosom.

"Something must," he said.

The Weakness

Bob Buzzell had about seventy-five thousand dollars left out of
the money he had made in the ring; seventy-five thousand dollars and his senses, he was fond of saying; seventy-five thousand dollars and a lot of memories, recognition, respect, and a
clear conscience by the standards of the racket. He had thrown
two fights in the beginning of his career, and he had carried one
fighter whom he could have knocked out after becoming champion. At thirty-three he had all his marbles, and enough money
to open a cigar store–poolroom, with the half promise of
backing for a bowling alley if the cigar store–poolroom
caught on. He was thirty-three years old, had a wife and two
children, a house on the edge of town, fourteen suits of clothes,
a four-year-old Cadillac, and all those memories of luxury-
travel, association with the famous in show business and politics, two nights in bed with one of the all-time greats of the
movies, and a roomful of statuettes and scrolls and belts and
photographs. He would never again have to dry out to make
the weight, like a goddam jockey; or stay away from women,
like a goddam priest; or go through that dreary routine of bag-
punching and road work and leg exercises, like a goddam college football player. And he would never again have to listen
to Marty Carroll, who the boxing writers said had managed, or
piloted, him into the championship but didn't have a mark on
his face and did have a lot more than seventy-five thousand dollars to show for their nine years together. He would never again
have to listen to Marty Carroll referring to him as "my guy" or
how "we" had won twenty-two straight without a knockdown.

"One more," Marty Carroll had said, when Bob Buzzell
told him he was quitting.

"No, no more," said Buzzell.

"Don't be stupid. I can get you Rubinello."

"I don't want Rubinello. I don't want nobody."

"Now listen, wise guy, I said I can get you Rubinello, and then if you ever want to come out of retirement you'll be a light heavyweight."

"You talk like I was going to lose to Rubinello."

"Rubinello right now would have a hard time making you last five rounds. Five rounds is the most he could stretch it, if you stayed away from him the first two rounds. Right now Rubinello could drop you in Round One if he took the notion."

"This is suppose to boog me, hey, Marty? Well, it don't. It shows I'm right, wanting to quit."

"All right, quit. I always knew there was some mouse in you. Just a bit of kayoodle. I seen it come out the first time when you fought the Frenchman."

"Yeah, he had me scared. So did Burns."

"Burns, you weren't scared. The Frenchman, you were. You give the Frenchman everything you had, and when he didn't go down you got the lump, but big. You butted the Frenchman and you should of lost that one. You're what I call a desperation dirty fighter. A front runner. All right, I could of got you Rubinello, insurance for the future. But you walk out on me now and you got nothin'. A big fat nothin', now or any other time. Wuddia plan to do? Get a job teaching philosophy? You got the mind for it. That's a great brain you got there, you know. Go on, get the hell out of my office."

"Rubinello must want me pretty bad. You thought you had it made, eh, Marty?"

"Oh, I got it made without the like of you. I got a little put away, don't you worry. And I had it when you were still fighting for fifty-dollar watches."

"Only now you got more."

"Yeah, I got more." Marty Carroll picked up the newspaper and opened it wide, and Buzzell walked out of the office for the last time.

At the end of the first year the cigar store–poolroom had

lost some money. The early curiosity trade had been profitable, but after six months it dwindled down to the regulars, and Bob Buzzell could tell from week to week how much they would spend. The soft drink and candy vending machines and the pool tables were profitable as were the pay telephones, but there was no money in cigars and the patrons bought their cigarettes cut-rate at the chain drug store. He had some visitors from the numbers racket and a salesman wanted to install a machine that dispensed contraceptives, but currently there was a local campaign against juvenile delinquency and he was quite aware that the numbers and contraceptive people needed him more than he needed them, and he put them off. He was also anxious to close a deal with the bowling alley people, and this more than any moral consideration influenced his stand. He was lucky. The district manager of the bowling alley concern appeared one morning and said he liked the way Buzzell was running his business. "We had to see if you'd go for the fast buck. No offense, Bob, but you could of got tied up with the numbers racket and one thing another, and then you wouldn't of been worth a dime to us. The bowling alley is the biggest thing in the U.S. today, and it got that way because the whole family bowls. The women, and the school kids. And with the automatic pin-spotter, a bowling alley is a big investment. I mean big. You start in six figures, you know. Well, you passed the test. You lost a little this year, but you're clean. No numbers. No dope pushers. No trouble with the law, so we have a proposition."

They used his name, they required his presence five nights a week, and they paid him a salary and a small percentage of the gross income. They kept the books and did the hiring and firing. The contract was for one year, with renewals annually at increases in salary so long as the grosses were maintained at the first year level, and larger salary increases if business warranted additional lanes. They encouraged his participation in community activities, but he was not allowed to run for public office. In spite of their reluctance to have him face the electorate the bowling entrepreneurs made no objection when the grand opening of the Bob Buzzell Bowling Alleys was attended by the mayor, the sheriff, the State assemblyman, the district Congressman, and the chief of police; as well as clergymen of several denominations, the president of the chamber of commerce, the commanders of the Legion and V.F.W. posts, the coaches of nearby town and consolidated high school teams, the sports editors of the local daily and the county weeklies and other such dignitaries. The radio station covered the event for half an hour, and music was provided by the high school orchestra. The mayor, bowling the first official ball, completed a split on his second try, and Mrs. Dora Ringgold, vice-president of the school board, received a canvas carrying case for bowling the first strike.

"You got time now for a little home life," said Betty, his wife, after the bowling alley had been in business a few weeks.

"How do you mean, home life? I gotta be there five nights a week."

"Yeah, but with the poolroom you were there from ten o'clock in the morning to past midnight. I mean like gardening. I don't mean you ought to take up gardening, and I'm not complaining, Bob. Don't think that. I was just thinking we have the daytime we could do things together."

"Like what, for instance?"

"Well, like little trips in the car. The kids are off to school by ha' past eight in the morning, and don't get home till near four. That would give us time to take a *lot* of trips."

"Yeah, but like where?"

"Well, take for instance, we been to Los Angeles and Montreal, Canada. But I'd like to go to Gettysburg."

"Gettysburg? You mean where they had the battle? What the hell's the attraction to Gettysburg?"

"Well, it's historical. My great-grandfather's name is on the Pennsylvania Monument."

"You want to drive over a hundred miles to see your great-grandfather's name on a monument?"

"I would. For all you know, maybe you have some ancestors that their names are on the Monument."

"I got my name on the roll of honor in front of the Legion post. I can see that any time without driving a hundred miles to see my great-grandfather's name. How do you know your great-grandfather is on a monument?"

"I seen it when I was a little girl. My parents took me."

"All right, you seen it once. Wuddia wanta see it again for?"

"Oh, you don't understand. Anyway, I don't care about Gettysburg. It's just the idea of you don't have to be at the bowling alley till six o'clock. That gives us nearly the whole day we could be doing something."

"I thought you had plenty to do, the housework."

"I do, but once in a while we could take a trip. I could arrange my housework."

"I'll take you on a trip, but Gettysburg. Jesus! I just as soon go back to Guadal. At least on Guadal I could show you where your husband knocked off a couple Japs, not some great-grandfather's name on a monument. What is this, anyway, Betty?"

"Well—you're a real businessman now. All those big wheels when they opened the bowling alley. You aren't just a retired fighter with a poolroom. You're a big man in town."

"A big man in town. What was I before? Just a bum?"

"I didn't say that. I didn't even hint at it. But you got to admit it yourself, you're better off now than fighting. You don't have to be afraid somebody's gonna put your eye out."

"I was never afraid anybody would put my eye out."

"You were so. And you didn't want to end up punchy. You told me that a hundred times."

"I was never afraid of anybody."

"You say that now, Bob, but you used to be."

"Ah, shut up. Don't tell *me* what I was."

"Wuddia wanta argue with *me* for? I'm trying to tell you you're better off. You don't have them things worr'ing you. You can sleep nights and you don't have to go around with those no-good gangsters and creeps. And *I* can go places without people thinking I'm one of those tramps."

"What tramps?"

"Oh, what tramps? Those women. I used to feel ashamed of myself to sit in a night club with those women. As if I was one of them. If you'd of thought more of me you wouldn't of made me sit with them."

"I didn't make you sit with them. You wanted to be there, and I never saw you break no cameras when the photographers came around."

"Yeah, and that time my picture was in the paper, only it said I was one of them tramps and the tramp was Mrs. Bob Buzzell."

"Oh, God, you never got over that."

"No, I never got over it, because that's what they were all thinking. I go all the way to Los Angeles and they don't know I'm your wife. Well, now it's time I got some enjoyment out of life. You're out of that racket and I wanta live respectable. I did it your way for nine years, but now it's your turn to take into consideration me and the children. I don't care if you don't take me to Gettysburg, but from now on I want to live decent for a change."

"I didn't hear no beefs all the time you were staying at them big hotels."

"No, and I didn't beef when I didn't see you for three months at a time, either. But I didn't beef when you were in the Marines, either."

"Well, that was damn nice of you."

"Well, it was. Listen, I know you. That's why I was willing to overlook certain things, because I know your weakness. But you got some things to make up for, Bob Buzzell."

"Wuddia trying to tell me, Betty?"

"All right, I'll tell you. I was a good wife and mother and everybody in town knows it. I went to church and brought up the children neat and clean, and polite. And I'm entitled to some credit."

"All right, I give you credit. I never said I didn't."

"I got more to say."

"I just bet you have."

"And you better listen. I just happen to know that before

they'd put up all that money for the bowling alley, those men investigated me, your family life."

"Oh, I get it. You're declaring yourself in."

"Not for money. Don't think I'm trying to get money out of you. But if I was one of those tramps that hang around prize-fighters, you wouldn't of had a prayer to have your name on that bowling alley. You ask Reverend Buchholtz. You ask the mayor. So don't think you got the bowling alley just because you won twenty-two straight fights. *I* had something to do with it, too. And when I ask you to show a little gratitude, I'm only asking for what I'm entitled to."

"Yeah, but what if I thought you were entitled to a poke in the nose?"

"Only once you'd have to do that, Bob. I'd never take it from you. I seen enough of that when I was little. Once a woman lets a man beat her, if she don't get out right away he'll do it again. I seen it with my aunt, and some others, too. There aint a man that's worth it."

"Well, then don't aggravate me. Because if I'm only gonna get one crack at you, believe me, kid, it'll be a good one."

"My advice to you is you better stop thinking along those lines."

"And my advice to you is just don't aggravate me," he said.

She had waited nine years, and she had learned patience. For the time being it was enough that she had stated her wishes, and she did not soon again ask him to take her anywhere. He had arrived at his decision to quit prizefighting without any discussion with her. It was what she wanted but had not dared to speak of. Now, with a little prodding, he might proceed from the bowling alley to something else, like a store, or real estate, a garage, or insurance salesman—some business in which he could stop calling himself Bob, and she would become Mrs. Robert Buzzell, or Mrs. Robert W. Buzzell. She hated the sign on the roof of the bowling alley, with the phony signature, Bob Buzzell in neon tubing. She hated their name on their mailbox. All the other mailboxes in the neighborhood were William J., John H., or F. J., or

B. F. Nobody had nicknames on their mailboxes. Bob Buzzell on their mailbox seemed like an invitation to tramps and strangers, and in nine years she had seen enough tramps and strangers to do her for the rest of her life. She wanted to be like other wives, with a husband like other husbands, and to have people gradually forget that she was the wife of a man who was most often photographed with his body bare from the waist up, who had made his living by punching other half-naked men into insensibility. He was the masculine version of the beauty pageant girls, revealing himself as much as possible, and with his physical measurements printed all over the world. She had seen the letters he got from foolish women and from men who were not really men, letters that sometimes enclosed photographs of themselves. They had made him laugh, but they had never struck her as funny, and she had destroyed letters and photographs before anyone else could see them. But she knew that he had only stopped showing her the letters. The letters had not just suddenly stopped coming; he had simply stopped showing them to her. And once in New York she had seen a message asking him to call a famous movie actress at the Savoy-Plaza.

Marty Carroll had never wanted Betty around while Bob was training for a fight, but he was equally insistent on her being present at ringside when the fight took place; and of all the people at the parties after Bob's fights, the only one she had any use for was Marty. He had a mean face; cold, blue little eyes and a thin nose that was more like a beak; almost invisible lips; and a dead-white, closely shaved skin as white as his brushed-down hair. She did not like Marty Carroll, but there was something about his coldness and his extreme personal cleanliness that set him apart from the rest of Bob's paid and unpaid hangers-on. In nine years she had never seen him laugh, and when he smiled it was always because of some little triumph over somebody. And yet Betty was more comfortable with him than with any of the others. She never called him anything but Mr. Carroll, and he never in nine years suggested that she call him Marty; but when other people—including Bob Buzzell—called him Marty she had the feeling that they were taking liberties and that in so doing they cheapened themselves without getting any closer to him. All sorts of people called him Marty, but he called no one by a first name or a nickname. Betty was Mrs. Buzzell; Mrs. Marty Carroll lived in New Jersey and not even Bob Buzzell had ever laid eyes on her. All Bob knew about her was that she lived in New Jersey and had a kennel where she bred Kerry Blues, and that when Mrs. Carroll spent the night in New York, she and Marty stayed at a hotel on the other side of town. No one connected with prizefighting had ever been invited to the Carrolls' farm. Sometimes Betty had envied Mrs. Carroll, but she had never been able to ask Marty about her. He plainly considered Betty one of the people who would never be invited to the farm and with whom any discussion of his wife would be a waste of time.

Two things she had come to understand about herself and the Marty Carrolls: she had wished that Bob could be like Marty, making the money that was in prizefighting, but remaining aloof from the people in it; and she had wished that she could be like Mrs. Marty Carroll, who derived all the benefits and still remained even more aloof than her husband. The sums of money that Bob was supposed to be making while fighting were exaggerated and came to fractions of the originals by the time Bob put the money in the bank; but even what was left after taxes and expenses and Marty Carroll's cut and the honest truth had reduced the size of the purses was still more than a Bob Buzzell had a right to expect. He had no education, no trade, no business ability. He happened to have been born quick and strong, naturally left-handed, and able to remember to do what he was told while receiving punches. The boxing writers refused to put him among the great, but they called him tough, aggressive, and a crowd-pleaser, who gave the fans their money's worth and never dogged it. Possibly because it was so obvious, they refrained from commenting that in the ring as well as in the negotiational stages he was master-minded by the old fox, Marty Carroll. Obvious or not, it was a fact that Betty Buzzell discovered for herself, and from the moment of her husband's retirement she was determined to emulate Marty Carroll in his guidance of Bob Buzzell. Marty Carroll knew all about prizefighting, but Betty Buzzell considered herself an authority on home life, the kind of home life she wanted for herself and her husband and children. They had the money and the first respectable job of Bob's new career, and the rest was up to her. She was not quite sure what a Kerry Blue was, but she had earned her right to have a kennelful of them just as much as the remote Mrs. Marty Carroll. She did not resent Mrs. Carroll's having Kerry Blues with money that Bob Buzzell had made. That was life. Brains did it, and the brains belonged to Marty Carroll. But Betty had had a lot of time to think, and if Bob Buzzell could be managed into a world's championship, he could be made into something more important than proprietor of a bowling alley in a third-class city in Pennsylvania. In this situation his weakness was her strength, and she had certain advantages. No matter how many women Bob may have slept with, he always came back to her. She could be as indispensable as Marty Carroll had been, and from observing Bob Buzzell's dependence on Marty Carroll she had learned that her husband had to have someone to think for him.

Betty Buzzell had never been to bed with any man but her husband, but there was a whole world of sexual knowledge in the experience of ten years with him. Not the love that he avowed or the admiration of her body that he displayed was the strength of her hold on him. It was shame. He laughed about sex, he liked to talk dirty in front of people and to make fun of peculiarities. Betty, limiting her actual experience to this one man, had come to understand the subject universally. He lied about the other women, and she never believed the lies. He wanted every pretty woman he saw, and some who were far from pretty, but none of them lasted; he always came back to her, and she knew why. He was proud of his strength, of his masculinity, and she knew he took women to bed with him. She could often guess which women; she could always guess when. He needed women as he needed kids with auto-graph books and instant recognition by taxi drivers, and this need was covered by the all-embracing term, his weakness. Her use of the term included women without specifying them as it included the taxi drivers' recognition without mentioning it. The weakness was adulation and the public flexing of muscles, showing off and being admired. But Betty always knew when he had gone to bed with one of those easily available women. He would come to her with his unfulfilled desire to be hurt, his basic need to have love-making accompanied by the infliction of physical pain. There was his shame. As the public symbol of masculinity he could not in private reveal his special peculiarity, and he would quickly drop a woman for fear that in a continued affair she would find him out. Always there had to be pain, and he was most grateful when Betty would surprise him with a new way of inflicting it. "Why is that?" she once asked him.

"I don't know. I just can't help it. But don't talk about it no more." He was ashamed of the peculiarity and doubly ashamed of her knowledge of it, and notwithstanding his momentary gratitude there was anger in his command for silence. All at once she knew that some day he might kill her, but he would never leave her, and she was not afraid of him.

The bowling alley stayed open till two in the morning. As though to discourage such things as excursions to Gettysburg he formed the habit of waiting at the bowling alley until closing time, and stopping for a hamburger at an all-night diner, although his contract did not require his presence after midnight and he did not have to pay for hamburgers at the alley. He got home nearer four o'clock than three, was careful not to wake her, and slept seven or eight hours. She would make his breakfast and have her lunch with him. The arrangement left them with at most four hours together before the children were let out of school, and every day, depending upon the season of the year, he would go to a driving range and hit golf balls, or go for a swim, or go ice-skating. When the weather was bad he would go to the Legion and play pool. He would get home at five o'clock and have early supper with Betty and the children. Thus, and almost without deviation, they passed a year. For two weeks in the summer they placed the children on her father's farm while they drove to Canada on a vacation trip.

Everywhere they went people would ask him when he was going to come out of retirement, was it true he was going to fight Rubinello as a light heavyweight, what did he think of this new Swede. It was two years since he had been away from home, and the still lively interest of filling station attendants and motel proprietors and highway patrolmen—even a Mountie asked about the punch that had knocked out a promising Canadian five years earlier—was just what he needed to enjoy the vacation. In Montreal he called up some prizefighting friends who invited him and Betty to lunch, but she told him to go without her. She did not want to see them. He did not return to the hotel until after seven that evening, and she knew immediately that he had been with a woman.

"What you do all afternoon?" she said.

"Oh, they broke out the wine and Jules made his load and we got to talking."

"You didn't have any wine, did you?"

"You know anything makes me sick. Why'd you ask me that? I aint had a drink of anything since I got out of the Marines, and you know it."

"Then you did a lot of talking. Nearly seven hours." She had no desire to make an accusation, but she wanted him to feel guilt through her unspoken suspicion.

"Well, there was a whole gang of us. Some of them I didn't see since five years ago. You want to go out and eat?"

"Sure, I been ready since six o'clock."

"All right, put your dress on and we'll go out and eat."

She removed her wrapper, and in her pantie-girdle and brassiere she took her time deciding which dress to wear. As

she expected, he postponed their departure and made love to
her, and she gave him pleasure. When it was over he lay on
the bed, smoking a cigarette and staring at the ceiling.

"Aren't you gonna take me out and eat?" she said.

"I been thinking, maybe I ought to get a match with Rubinello."

"You go back in the ring and that's the end of you and
me," she said.

"Why? I'm in good condition. You notice I take exercise
every day. It'd be six months before Rubinello could fight me,
maybe a year. He has a return match with Munson he gotta
take care of first, so maybe it'd be a year. By then I'd be ready
and I could take him."

"And he'd have it in the contract that *you* had to give *him*
a return match," she said. "So it wouldn't be one fight, it'd be
two."

"And all that loot. Jules would guarantee me eighty-five
gees for my end. Stage the first fight here in Montreal."

"Give me a hundred dollars," she said.

"What for? I give you a hundred dollars the day before
yesterday."

"I spent it. I want a hundred dollars to go home. I don't
want to be in the same room with you till you get some sense
into you."

"That's the way you feel about it, take a hundred dollars
out of my wallet."

"I will, but don't you come home till you get some sense.
Stay here with Jules *and those friends of his.*"

"I'll do that. That's exactly what I will do. And you better
not start hangin' by your thumbs till I come home. In other
words, Betty, don't hold your breath that long."

By plane and bus she made her way home, was there before midnight and spent the night alone in their house. To the
people she saw in the next few days she explained that Bob
was working on a business proposition in Montreal, and she
was so elaborately secretive that her story was accepted.

She knew his weakness. The woman in Montreal would

last him two or three nights and then there would be another, and then he would come home. But she would take him back only on her terms, and for a week she planned what the terms would be. He would have to start going to church. Church was very important in her plans for him. He would have to do more at the Legion than just shoot pool. He would take an active part in Little League baseball. And she decided that his contacts could be used to best advantage in the insurance business. Inside of a year, two years at the most, he would be able to give up the bowling alley and demand a partnership, a name partnership, in one of the insurance agencies. In a way she was grateful for the week alone; it gave her time to think.

On the night of the seventh day of their separation she went to bed early. She had heard nothing from him, but she was not alarmed when she was awakened by the sound of the garage door rolling up, then rolling down; the familiar kick of his foot against the bottom of the kitchen door, his heavy tread on the way upstairs. She already had the bedroom light on when he opened the door.

He needed a shave badly. He was wearing slacks and a sport shirt and he put his suitcase down gently. "Hello," he said.

"Hello," she said.

"You're not surprise to see me?"

"No."

"You been listeninga the radio?"

"No, why? Is there something on the radio about you?"

"Could be," he said.

"Could be? You mean there is. What are you, in some kind of trouble?"

"Uh-huh. Yeah, I guess you could say that."

"What did you do?"

"Oh, I got in a jam in Montreal. I'll tell you about it tomorrow. It's too long a story."

"Not too long for me. What did you do?"

"Betty, I drove all the way from Montreal. I been thinking about you all the way."

"It's near time you thought about me. A week you didn't phone."

"That's because you walked out on me," he said. "That's what got me in the jam."

"What jam are you in, Bob? Are the police in it?"

"I wanta get in bed with you and stop asking me questions."

"No. You're in trouble with the police, aren't you?"

"If I'd of stayed in Canada. But I aint in Canada. I'm in Pennsylvania."

"Will it be on the eleven o'clock radio?"

"Maybe it will and maybe it won't."

"It's some kind of trouble over a woman. Did you kill her?"

"I didn't kill nobody. I give her a beating."

"Oh, God," she said wearily.

"Well, you walked out on me and what did you expect? A wife walks out on her husband, she got no claim on him if he gets another woman. And you walked out on me, you got to admit that. Wud you tell them in town?"

"I said you were staying there on business."

"Well, that's what I was."

"And beating up one of those tramps. You were with her the day I walked out."

"No."

"Yes you were."

"Well, all right, so I was. But I didn't start it. She started it."

"How bad did you beat her up?"

"I hit her a couple times."

"And what?"

"I broke her jaw. That's what I heard on the radio. The radio from Albany, New York. I was in the car, and I had the radio going and I heard it, that she was in the hospital and the Montreal cops were looking for me. But by that time I was over the border."

"God in heaven," she said.

"Didn't nobody phone you? The papers or nobody?"

"I was next door till ha' past nine, and then I come home and went to bed." She looked about her, at the furniture, the draperies, the pictures on the walls. "The kids are still with Mom."

He forced a smile. "Well, it's lucky you didn't have some guy here."

"Yeah. Judging other people by yourself."

"I was thinking of you go to the bank tomorrow and get the money out and I'd go somewhere till this blows over."

"And then what? You come back and manage the bowling alley again?"

"When this blows over."

"Are you crazy? I bet if you look tomorrow night they won't even have your name lit up."

"So what? I'll get a fight."

"Who with? Some whore?"

"Hey, now, don't *you* aggravate me. That aint what I come home for," he said.

The Man with the Broken Arm

Anna Lyman's rudeness to Charles Weston was so deliberate and thorough that hardly anyone among the passengers failed to notice it and comment on it. She was so careful and cruel that I did not expect to see Weston again during the rest of the voyage. But on the morning after the ship's concert, where the rudeness had occurred, Weston was up and about, taking his jaunty walk past the rows of steamer chairs, nodding and smiling to this one and that one, tipping his cap in semi-military salute, and seeming to spring up from each step in his rubber-soled brown suèdes. It was a courageous performance, and I felt like telling him so when we met in the smoke-room before lunch, but he had anticipated me.

I had met Weston several times through the years, but until this trip we had never sat down together for a meal or conversation. Now, two men traveling alone, we usually had a drink together before going to the dining-room. From the first day out we had started, of course, with a mutual acquaintance of a thousand men and women in the theater and films, and conversation was easy for us.

"Annie certainly gave it to me last night," he said, as he took his seat. "Were you there?"

"Yes, I was there," I said. "Why did she do it?"

"She had her reasons," he said. "And this was her chance. She wanted to show me up in front of that kind of an audience. The big wheels in television. Two English managers. The picture people. The English duke. And all these millionaires." The jauntiness faded as he recalled the audience. His clothes were perfect; a reddish tweed jacket, sleeveless sweater, tan slacks, Tattersall shirt, knitted necktie. But for the moment his costume seemed to be sitting there unoccupied by a living man, while the living man consisted of head and hands. The wrinkles and lines stood out, now that he was sitting quietly; the carefully brushed hair showed more grey. His lips moved although he was not speaking, and he had to hold his head up to maintain a chin line. In one spotted hand he held a cigarette, which he smoked busily, and in the other hand he kept turning a gold Zippo lighter. "It's just as bad to know something about somebody as it is to do them a dirty trick. In fact, it's a dirty trick to remember things. At least Annie thinks so. How long have you known her?"

"I can't say that I know her at all," I said. "About as well as I knew you, and about as long, I guess."

"That's another dirty trick. I shouldn't be around to remind her of her exact age. Fifty-six. Annie's fifty-six. There must be a lot of people on this boat that can guess at her age, but I'm the one that knows it exactly. Do you know something? Last night was the first time she spoke to me since we left New York. She saw me the first day out, even before they printed the passenger list, and she refused to speak to me. Well, I thought, if that was the way she wanted it, what the hell? But I didn't think I'd spoil her trip just by being aboard. However, I found out last night. You knew I was once married to her?"

"Yes, I knew that," I said.

"I just wanted to make sure you knew that. A lot of people *don't* know it. She'd rather forget it, but she can't. She's been married three times since she was married to me, but I'm the only one she hates. The only one that was nice to her, never gave her a bit of trouble, never took her for any money, never traded on her reputation. And probably the only one that ever really loved her. Loved her at the time, and never got over it, even though I've been happily married since Annie divorced me. I only thank God my wife and two boys weren't there last night. I have a boy at Lawrenceville and another at Princeton, and if they'd seen what happened last night I really think I'd have gone over the side. You see, Jim, the reason why I'm not more upset about last night is that years ago I took everything a man can take from that woman. She can embarrass me, as she did last night, but the only way she could ever really do me any more damage would be if she made a fool of me in front of my boys."

"What about your wife?"

"My wife knows the whole story, and she regards Anna Lyman as something cheap and evil. No, not cheap. Stupid and evil. Unintelligent and evil. No man could ever have the same contempt for Anna that my wife has. You know how we feel about some guys that women like? That's the way my wife feels about Anna Lyman. To her there's no attractiveness about Anna. Anna is the kind of mistake men make because they're men." He smiled a little. "You know how women see right through other women? It gives them a great sense of superiority over men when they see what kind of women we sometimes fall for. And of course a woman judging another woman isn't befuddled by sex, the hay department. Jonesey, my wife, isn't a bit jealous of Anna Lyman. She considers Anna as something like whooping cough. Maybe a form of whooping cough that I got when I was in my twenties, but still one of those ailments that you get and then get over. Unfortunately I never did completely recover. I did, in a way. But I still remember the illness, the way you remember an illness you actually had in childhood. Or a broken arm. When I was a boy I broke my arm, falling off an ice wagon, and I remember all the attention I got. Privileges. Presents from my grandparents and so on. Broken arm." He lifted a hand and with his forefinger pointed to our nearly empty glasses. The steward nodded.

"If you knew I was married to Anna Lyman, then you must remember about her and L. M. Zeeman. You knew she was his girl friend?"

"I heard that, yes."

"Well, you see, I didn't. I didn't know a damn thing about her and Zeeman. I was a Broadway actor, not a movie actor. I was the thitta, old boy, not feelms. I don't suppose it would have made a damn bit of difference if I had known. I was so stuck on Annie that if someone'd told me she was working in a house in Port Said, I still would have married her. Two months after we were married Zeeman sent for her to do a picture, and *I* didn't know she was going back to her old boy friend. I was in a play, and she was in a picture, and that was show business. The fact of the matter is that she only married me because Zeeman wouldn't get a divorce, and she was punishing him. Two months' punishment, and he was going crazy. That was our married life. Two months. We were married longer than that, but that was all we lived together. I was the chump of all time. When she finished her picture I expected her to come back to New York, but she stalled around and I finally got some sense in my head and my brother told me what was going on. So I called her up and issued an ultimatum—and I can still hear her laughing over the phone. I was crushed. I thought the world had come to an end. I began hitting this stuff and I finally went to George Chisolm and asked him as a friend to release me from my contract, which he did. The play was about ready to fold anyway, and so I went out to the coast and little Annie wouldn't even let me spend the night at her house. Out there she was honest enough. She told me why she'd married me and all the rest of it, but even then I wanted her back. 'You must be crazy,' she said. 'I'm Zeeman's girl.' She told me to go ahead and get a divorce. Zeeman would pay for it, or she'd pay for it. She even hinted that Zeeman might hold still for some extra money if I wanted it. Have you ever felt that way about a woman? You know she's sleeping with another guy, crazy about him, and still you want her back?"

"No, I don't think I have," I said. "I've had affairs with married women, but that's not the same thing. If I were married and my wife slept with another guy, that would end it for me."

"Then you must think I was a real chump, and I was. I said I'd go back to New York and let her think it over, and she said there was nothing *to* think over. She'd promised Zeeman never to sleep with me again and what the hell did I get out of staying married to her? Why not get a divorce? Well, back in New York I carried a torch, as we used to say, and I chased around and drank a lot, but even *I* couldn't go on like that forever and one day Zeeman's lawyer offered me $50,000 for a divorce and that was too much for me. I didn't take the money, but I played one hell of a big scene to an audience consisting of Zeeman's lawyer and my lawyer, and I must say I gave myself some very good lines. Cliché stuff, but damn good. Both lawyers said I was magnificent. Well, how often does an actor give up fifty thousand bucks to play a scene? I wouldn't have played it nearly as well if I'd been *paid* that much."

Charles Weston finished his drink and put the glass on the table with a decisively audible click. "Let's go to lunch," he said.

We were at different tables in the dining-room and our conversation was thus interrupted but, I knew, would continue. I could not believe in Weston's sudden characterization of himself as an actor playing a scene in a lawyer's office. The man who had been telling me the story of the marriage to Anna Lyman was not a wisecracking youth; he was very nearly an old man, permanently injured a long time ago, and badly wounded again in the past twenty-four hours. It had cost him an effort to circle the ship and face the witnesses to Anna Lyman's rudeness, and in so doing he had behaved admirably, with courage and grace. There was even some grace toward Anna Lyman; as though by pretending he had not been affected by her rudeness he was assuring her public that she had not really been rude, that it was intra-professional badinage, or rough kidding, as it was oftener called. But no one was deceived. She had been brutal.

The concert had consisted of two solos by an operatic baritone; some rather good feats of magic by an amateur, one of the television executives; two tap dances by the wife of another television executive, a former musical comedy star; and a dramatic reading by Anna Lyman, who was the only big star aboard the ship. Charles Weston was master of ceremonies. Anna Lyman's dramatic reading was a scene from *Perihelion,* a play in which she had made one of her biggest hits, and her first small rudeness was in asking the magician to play the tiny part of the clergyman whose questions cued her into her two long speeches. The magician literally read his lines from a play-script, and he was not good. Everyone wondered why Mr. Weston, a professional, had not been chosen instead. This snub was followed by another: when Weston moved the standing microphone out of the way, obviously implying that as a good actress she did not need mechanical help, she said, so all could hear: "Really, Mr. Weston? Don't you want them to hear me?" I had no doubt that if he had moved the microphone in front of her she would have told him to take it away. He could not win either way. Then, as she was taking her bow after playing the scene, Weston reached out his hand in courtly fashion, to lead her onstage. She ignored him and left him standing with outstretched hand. Her final rudeness was at the end of the concert, when all the performers were taking a company bow. Anna Lyman placed herself between the baritone and the magician, linking arms with them and during the applause presenting her cheek for each of them to kiss. Weston and the tap-dancing woman stood to the right of the arm-in-arm trio, but unmistakably out of the position of prominence. It remained for Weston to thank the audience and to announce that dancing would take place in the lounge in fifteen minutes. In the middle of his announcement Anna Lyman burst into laughter at some private joke between her and the baritone, and she gathered together the baritone, the magician, and the tap-dancing woman and they marched off before Weston had quite finished. As I went to my room I saw Weston, uncomprehending, and alone for a few seconds until the purser, fully comprehending, went to him and shook his hand.

The purser was having one of his cocktail parties on the afternoon following the concert, and I was the first to arrive. "Have I got my facts all mixed up, or weren't Miss Lyman and Mr. Weston once husband and wife?" said the purser.

"They were, a long time ago," I said.

"Quite a show last night, wasn't it?"

"A show of bad manners, yes," I said.

"Well, yes it was, wasn't it?" he said. "Tell me, that is if you don't mind, was he terribly upset?"

I knew this purser, a man named Breckenridge, from voyages I had made in this and other ships of the line, and between us there was the friendliness of old acquaintance if not real friendship. He always provided those small extra courtesies that added to the pleasure of my trips, and he noticed things. He was a subtle, unobtrusive, humorous man, and I liked him.

"Yes, he was upset," I said.

"I was afraid so," said Breckenridge. "I'd like to do something to—you know—restore his morale. He's leaving the ship at Cherbourg, and I won't get much chance to see him in the morning. Miss Lyman is staying aboard till Southampton. Can you think of anything I might do, that would buck him up?"

"Offhand, I can't."

"I've even looked up the date of his birth on the off chance that his birthday might be close. But it's months away, so that's out. Naturally I'll see that the French press make a fuss over him, but I'd like to do something tonight to make up for last night's disaster. The same people, you know."

"We could throw her overboard," I said.

"Oh, that occurred to me," said Breckenridge. "But that's an impulse I've learned to control after so many years in this job."

"I imagine so," I said.

"And it isn't so much that I'd like to do something *against* her as wanting to do something *for* him, although the end result may be the same. But she mustn't have cause for complaint, you know. It very definitely isn't part of my job to provide cause for complaint. Well, let's see if we can think of something between now and dinner-time. And here is Mrs. McMurray. How nice. Mrs. McMurray, may I present Mr. Malloy, Mr. James Malloy, the author?"

Mrs. McMurray and then Mr. and Mrs. Fishbein and Father Kelly and Sir John and Lady Pancoast and Professor Ropes and Charles Weston and the Countess di Palacci and Mr. Howe crowded into the purser's reception room, and I left to finish my packing before dinner, or so I said in making my departure. Actually I had finished my packing some hours earlier, and I left because Mrs. McMurray was most anxious to have me read the war letters of her son, which she did not have with her, but had apparently memorized. She was sure that in the right hands, the letters could be processed into another *Mr. Roberts*.

I wandered about and inevitably stopped at my usual table in the lounge and ordered an Americano. The room was almost deserted except for a group at a large table across the dance floor. There were about a dozen men and women at the table, and it seemed to me that I had seen precisely the same group when I had stopped in for coffee after lunch. I did not have to eavesdrop very closely to realize that they had all been drinking all afternoon. One of the men was drunk, and kept getting up from his chair to circle about, kissing the back of the women's necks. "Harry is a kissing bug," said one of the women.

"Harry is a kissing bug, Harry is a kissing bug," said Harry.

"Harry, sit down before you fall down," said his wife.

"That's what I'm trying to do, sit down before I fall down," said Harry.

"Does anybody know what time it is?" said one woman.

"Where?" said a man.

"Well, what the hell? If it's five o'clock it's five o'clock. Oh, no, that's right. We do something funny—" said the woman.

"You do something funny," said the man.

"I meant we do something funny with the clocks. Twenty minutes ahead, or forty minutes behind."

"Oh, *that's* what you meant," said the man. "You're either twenty minutes ahead or forty minutes behind."

"Oh, go to hell," said the woman. "Whatter you two whispering about? Anna Lyman, what are you whispering? Jack, what's she whispering?"

"You're too young to know," said Jack.

"I'll bet it was dirty," said the woman.

"It's ha' past six," said a man. "It's twenty-five of seven. It's the cocktail hour."

"Well then what are we waiting for?"

"Anna Lyman, I asked you a question. What were you two *whispering?*"

"When?" said Anna Lyman.

"A minute ago."

"A minute ago? I wasn't whispering—oh, when I was whispering to Jack? Oh, well I don't think I'll tell you."

"All right, then don't. But it isn't polite."

"Believe you me, it wouldn't be polite if I *didn't* whisper it," said Anna Lyman.

"What was it? We're all friends," said a man.

"We're not that good friends," said Anna Lyman. "At least not *yet.*"

"Oho, that sounds promising," said a man.

"Hey, who has some French money?" said another man.

"Every French whore," said another man.

"Hey, that's pretty good."

"No, now seriously, has anybody got any French money?" said the man. "Is the purser's office open?"

"Are you getting off at Cherbourg? I thought you were going to Southampton."

"You got me mixed up with somebody else. I'm getting off at Cherbourg."

"Let's everybody get mixed up with somebody else," said a woman.

"I think some already have," said another woman.

"Not me. I'm fancy-free," said Anna Lyman.

"You may be fancy, but I'll bet you're not free," said the woman.

"Just how did you mean that? Explain that remark," said Anna Lyman.

"I don't have to if I don't want to," said the woman.

"Well then get away from this table and take your kissing-bug with you. Go on, scram. I didn't invite you anyway, you and your kissing-bug. Kissing-bug. I'll bet." Anna Lyman whispered to Jack and Jack laughed.

"Come on, Harry. We won't stay where we aren't wanted."

"Too bad you didn't think of that hours ago," said Anna Lyman.

"I don't want to go," said Harry. "Anna, I think you're the greatest actress in the American theater."

"And I think you're the biggest pest on the Atlantic Ocean. And I wish you were at the bottom of it. So scram," said Anna Lyman.

"Huh?" said Harry.

"Come on, Harry. Come on, now."

There was a silence while Harry and wife made their departure, then Anna Lyman spoke. "Who *are* they, anyway? Does anybody here know them? I never saw them before this afternoon."

"Oh, what difference it make who they are? We'll never see them again," said Jack.

"Well, as far as that goes, I never expect to see any of you again," said Anna Lyman.

"I thought we were all having lunch in London the day after tomorrow. Quaglino's," said a man.

"I changed my mind," said Anna Lyman. "Look at Nosey over there, all by himself, taking notes for his next book. Hey, Nosey, did you get a good earful?"

"Yes, I got a pretty good earful, Anna," I said.

"Well, come on over and I'll really give you an earful," said Anna Lyman.

"No thanks," I said.

"I'll give you an earful about your friend Mr. Charles Weston," she said.

"Anna, why don't you shut up?" I said. I left some money on the table and started to go. Anna Lyman picked up a small club soda bottle and threw it at me, missing me by yards. "Close, but no cigar," I said.

"That's for you and your friend Mr. Charles Weston. I know you've been gabbing about me. Why don't you two go steady?"

I went out and walked around the promenade deck, in my first anger unable to think clearly. And then I remembered Breckenridge's eagerness to do something for Weston and I went to his room. The last of his guests, Father Kelly and Mr. Howe, were just leaving, and when they had gone I said: "I've thought of something."

"Good, let's have it," said Breckenridge.

"It's a bastard, but it'll make Weston look better than Anna Lyman."

"That's what we want," said Breckenridge.

"All right. All you have to do is get her on her feet and in front of a microphone. You won't have to do another damn thing. She'll do the rest."

At about eleven o'clock that evening the bingo game ended and Breckenridge spoke into the microphone. "That about does it, ladies and gentlemen, and now the next announcement will be made by that pre-eminent star of stage, screen and the telly, Miss Anna Lyman. Miss—Anna—Lyman, ladies and gentlemen. A *nice* hand for this great star."

Anna Lyman got up from her table, very drunk, and made her way to the microphone. "Good evening, ladies and jella-men, thizz your old friend Singing Sam," she said. "I forget what the hell I'm suppose to say. Oh, yes. There will be dancing until one o'clock. Where is the dancing gonna be?"

"The Little Lounge," said Breckenridge.

"The Little Lounge, that's right. Until one o'clock, so all you dear, lovely, stupid people—"

"Attaboy, Anna," the man named Jack shouted.

"Oh, you shut up. You bore me."

There was some laughter among the passengers, but it was nervous and unpleasant.

"What do I get for this, anyway?" said Anna Lyman. "I been playing one benefit after another, ever since I been on this God damn old tub."

Again there was laughter, tentative, as though the passengers were anticipating a big joke. Charles Weston, who was sitting at my table, said: "She'd better think of an exit line quick."

"I would like to say that I enjoyed every minute, every second of this trip, but if I did I'd be the biggest God damn liar that ever sailed the ocean blue."

Laughter again. This was more like it.

"We will now have the orchestra play 'Nearer My God to Thee' and all you jerks remember. women and children first. Personally, I like men first."

More laughter, then silence awaiting her next utterance. But her mind had stopped, and she stood unsteadily, looking slowly from right to left.

"She doesn't know how to get off," said Weston. "She's stoned." Then suddenly he rose and threaded his way among the passengers and took her by the arm. She looked at him gratefully, and without resisting she allowed him to steer her out of the room. All the way out, and for a few seconds after they had gone, the passengers applauded.

"It didn't work out quite as we'd expected," said Breckenridge, sitting at my table.

"What does?" I said.

The Lighter When Needed

The girl was having a good time. The orchestra was playing "From This Moment On," a dear old tune that dated back to dances before she had officially come out, before love, before second love and marriage and first baby, and a century-and-a-half before the besetting problems that for the moment she could forget. Dear old "From This Moment On." Dear old society bounce. Dear old Lester Lanin hat.

The young man she was dancing with was from the dinner party she had been to. He had been in the golf tournament that day and had won something and was feeling pretty good about it. "I don't often tie one on," he was saying, "but I've been trying to win one of those tournaments since I was seventeen years old."

"Goodness," said the girl.

"You mean did they have golf when I was seventeen years old? Sure. They had it when I was fifteen. We go back a long way together, golf and I. You don't play, do you?"

"Yes, I play."

"I'll bet you play pretty well, too, the way you said that. Have you ever played here? I don't think you ever made this scene before, did you, Mary? I've never seen you here."

"I've been here, but when I was very little. We came here one summer when my father was in the Navy. My mother used to come here, though."

"What do you shoot in? The low eighties, for instance?"

"I've been in the high eighties. Once I had an eighty-four, at home."

"That's good. That's not bad. If you can shoot consistently

around eighty-four you'll win most ladies' tournaments. Home. Where is home?"

"Pittsburgh."

"Oh, sure. *There's* a Pittsburgh man, a fellow townsman of yours. At least originally. I guess he doesn't live there any more."

"Who?"

"Arnold Abbott."

"Where? Where is Arnold Abbott? Point him out to me."

"Sitting at that table on the way out. Talking to Mrs. Rhodes. Or *not* talking to Mrs. Rhodes. The somewhat aging couple at that table. That's Arnold Abbott, and with him is Mrs. Llewellyn Rhodes. Why the interest in Arnold Abbott? Don't you know him?"

"No, I don't."

"Come from Pittsburgh and don't know Arnold Abbott? Mary, you must be one of the poor people. Or else you're one of those that don't approve of Arnold Abbott."

"Neither one. He's just a bit old for me. He was a bit old for my mother, as a matter of fact."

"I guess so. Boy, the stories they used to tell about him. And they must be true. You don't get a reputation for spending money like that unless you had the money. And spent it."

"I never heard about spending the money. I just heard he was the charm boy."

"Arnold Abbott? Are you sure? He and Mrs. Rhodes have been a thing ever since I can remember."

"Is there a Mr. Rhodes?"

"Would you like to touch him? You're only two people away from Lew Rhodes. The heavy man. Plaid dinner coat."

"Oh. Let's dance over toward Mr. Abbott. I want to get a closer look at him."

"Listen, I'll introduce you to the old boy if you like."

"No, I just want to see him close to."

Arnold Abbott sat straight up, watching the dancers. Once in a while Mrs. Rhodes would say something to him and he would nod, sometimes but not always adding a word or two of his own. She too sat up straight, holding her chin up, gazing at the dancers, now and then breaking her impassivity with a surprisingly bright smile of greeting to a couple dancing by, but as soon as the greeting was over a curtain seemed to come down over her face. An invisible curtain, that as it rolled down erased all animation from her expression. It was like that gesture of children, pretending to "wipe that smile off" their faces.

Mrs. Rhodes chain-smoked, and Arnold Abbott sat with his lighter in his hand, flicking it on when she needed it for a fresh cigarette, turning it over in the palm of his hand until it was needed again.

"Mary, they're going to get wise if you keep staring at them. Let's sit down with them for a minute?"

"Do you think they'd mind?"

"Mind? Nobody pays any attention to them. They'll sit that way all night."

"They seem perfectly content—but I would like to meet him, just to say hello to."

They danced over to Arnold Abbott's table, and Abbott rose. "Hello, Jack," he said.

"Hello, Jack," said Mrs. Rhodes.

"This is Mrs.—oh, Mary, what *is* your name?"

"Mrs. Elliott," she said.

"This is Mrs. Elliott, and Mary, this is Mr. Abbott. May we sit down a minute?"

"Do, please," said Mrs. Rhodes.

"Champagne, or Scotch, Mrs. Elliott?" said Arnold Abbott. "It's one or the other, I'm afraid. Or ginger ale. Somebody seems to be drinking ginger ale."

"She doesn't drink, so give her ginger ale. I'll personally have Scotch and just a little spoiler. Just a touch of plain water. You don't know each other, you two Pittsburghers?"

"Are you a Pittsburgher, Mrs. Elliott?" said Abbott.

"Well, I'm not, and Mrs. Rhodes isn't, so that more or less automatically leaves you two," said Jack. "I think it just about cancels us out, Mrs. Rhodes and I. Mrs. Rhodes, care to dance?"

"Oh, no thanks, Jack. I hardly ever."

"Are you a native Pittsburgher, or one by marriage?" said Abbott.

"Both. My maiden name was Husted."

"Oh, yes. Schenley Park district. I knew your father. He was younger, but I knew him. Doug Husted?"

"That's right."

"And your mother was a Pittsburgh girl? What was her name?"

"Jean Buckingham."

He nodded. "Mm-hmm. Knew her, too. They didn't live right in Pittsburgh, did they? The Buckinghams, I mean. Didn't they live out toward Rolling Rock?"

"*Then* they did."

"Are you down for the summer, Mrs. Elliott?" said Abbott.

"No, just for a long weekend. I'm staying at Frank and Mollie Holt's."

"Oh, yes. *They* had the big party tonight. Is your husband here?"

"No. He couldn't make it, unfortunately."

"I haven't asked you to dance, but I hope you'll forgive me. I don't like these crushes, do you? Do you remember those pictures of Eisenhower in India? And Kennedy? And those were friendly crowds. That's why I'm never late for the theatre. That last-minute pushing and shoving before the curtain goes up."

"I hate it, too," said the girl.

"Do you? You see what I mean, then? It doesn't mean that we have an aversion to people, does it? It's just that we don't like to be mauled, don't you think?"

"Really hate it," said the girl.

"Now isn't that interesting? We could have known each other for ten years and never known that we had that in common. What else do you feel that way about? How are you on, for instance—well, sudden noises? I could fall sound asleep in the very middle of that orchestra. But if I'm at home reading in the evening, and there's an unusual sudden noise, I can't concentrate again until I've found out what it was."

"I don't think that bothers me so much. We live in an apartment in town, and there are a lot of sudden, unusual noises."

"Oh, yes. But you do object to being moved along by a crowd?"

"Hate it."

His hair was almost all grey, brushed down smoothly, and she noticed that he had a habit of running his hand over it gently to keep it smooth. His eyelids were heavy, and the lower lids especially made her think that they were full of tears of sadness. When he smiled, the last muscles to move were those that controlled the area about his eyes, and the smile was over before it was quite complete.

Now, without seeming to have noticed that Mrs. Rhodes had taken a fresh cigarette from a square gold box, he held out his lighter for her. Mrs. Rhodes, in conversation with the younger man, muttered her thanks to Abbott without interrupting what she was saying to Jack. And yet, the girl noticed, the lighting of the cigarette maintained the closeness between Arnold Abbott and Mrs. Rhodes, in spite of the separate conversations in which they were taking part.

"I've heard a lot about you, Mr. Abbott," said the girl.

"You've heard a lot about me, my dear?" He smiled. "There *was* a *time,* I must admit. But I thought I'd stopped giving people anything to talk about—oh, before you were born. What on earth would people say about me in your lifetime?"

"It was nice."

"Oh? Well, that's a comfort. It wasn't always, you know. I, I, uh, supplied food for conversation. Uh, food for conversation. Those little sandwiches that they serve at tea-time. That kind of, uh, food for conversation." He was not altogether satisfied, and he went on: "That kind of food for that kind of conversation. That's what I wanted to say. But that was before you were born."

"That isn't what I meant, though."

"Not the parties I used to give? That's chiefly what I'm remembered for."

"Not by everybody. I never heard about the parties—well, till tonight. But I did hear about the charm."

His face went blank. "In connection with me? Charm? My dear, I'm afraid you've got me mixed with my brother, Stuart Abbott. He was the one that had the charm. But there again, before you were born. He was killed in World War One."

"*Arnold* Abbott. I've never *heard* of *Stuart* Abbott."

"Oh, I'm afraid there's been a mistake somewhere. Much as I'd like to appropriate some of it for myself, I'm afraid—"

"What are *you* two talking about?" said Mrs. Rhodes.

Abbott smiled faintly. "Will you tell her, Mrs. Elliott?"

"I'd love to. I was just telling Mr. Abbott that I'd always heard of his great charm."

Mrs. Rhodes gave a little laugh. "Ho! He's the most charming man I've ever known in all my life. I'm sorry, Jack, but that's a flat statement. Hope for you when you get older, but this is the most charming man I've ever known."

"Me?"

"Why, yes, of course, Arnold."

"I don't see it," said Abbott.

Mrs. Rhodes looked at the girl. "He doesn't see it," she said. "Arnold, you're a fool. Here is by all odds the most attractive young woman at this party, and she hasn't looked at another man since she sat down at this table. Was your mother in love with this man, Mrs. Elliott?"

"I think she must have been."

"You can see why she would have been," said Mrs. Rhodes.

"Oh, yes."

"But I didn't know your mother, not really. She must have been—I don't know—probably in pigtails, when I still lived in Pittsburgh."

"What difference does that make?" said Mrs. Rhodes. "If you have it, it works on females of all ages. Isn't that true, Mrs. Elliott?"

"Absolutely true."

"As long as I've known you, you've never given me the slightest hint of this," said Abbott.

"Too cagey for that, my love."

The music stopped, and Llewellyn Rhodes and a youngish woman came to the table. "Oh, now who is this? I'm Llewellyn Rhodes. What's your name? Another worshiper at the shrine of A. Abbott?"

"Yes. I'm Mary Elliott."

"Well, Mary, you're barking up the wrong tree. Hello, Jack. Hear you finally won one. What did you do? Bribe your caddy? Who was your partner?"

"Frank Holt, and I carried him all the way."

"The hell you say. Oh, Mrs. Elliott, this is Mrs. Corbin."

"We've got to get back to our party," said Jack.

"You go, and leave Mrs. Elliott. I'll see if I can't seduce her away from A. Abbott."

"I'd love to have you try, but I'm afraid we must go back," said the girl.

"Come to lunch tomorrow," said Mrs. Rhodes. "Jack, you come, too."

"Not on that kind of an invitation, I won't," said Jack.

"Well, that's the best you'll get. Mrs. Elliott, I invite you, too," said Llewellyn Rhodes. "Arnold, you'll be there, as always?"

"Yes, thank you, I'll be there," said Arnold Abbott.

"I think my hostess is having some people, but could I come after lunch?" said the girl.

"Any time. It's buffet, and starts at two," said Mrs. Rhodes. "Come for lunch if you can, and if not, drop in and have coffee with us. Bring anyone you like."

It was easy to get away from Mollie Hunt's Sunday lunch; the hung-over wanted to take naps or stay close to the bar, the athletic were off to the golf links and the tennis courts. Mary Elliott borrowed Mollie's car and drove alone to the Rhodeses' beach house, which was a fair distance from their main house.

Approaching the beach house from the parking area Mary Elliott saw with relief that only Mrs. Rhodes and Arnold Abbott were there, and sitting as they had sat the night before, with the difference that now they were in beach clothes, watching the ocean and two bathers instead of the crush of dancers. She regretted that her sponge-rubber soles gave them no warning of her approach, but she was not ungrateful for the opportunity to see them this way, so close, so quiet, so—resigned.

She had to walk around and in front of them before they were aware of her presence, and Arnold Abbott immediately got to his feet. He was wearing yellow slacks and a club blazer, with a Paisley neckerchief. He had on sun glasses. Mrs. Rhodes, likewise wearing sun glasses, had on a pajama suit that buttoned to the neck. "Oh, there you are," said Mrs. Rhodes. "How nice of you to come."

"Good morning, Mrs. Elliott. Some coffee? Large or small?"

"Good morning, Mrs. Rhodes. Mr. Abbott. Could I have a small coffee?"

"It's right here. Sugar? Cream?"

"One sugar, please, and black. Have you been in?" said Mary Elliott.

"Oh, yes. Hours ago. We were in and out before you were awake, I daresay," said Mrs. Rhodes. There was not the slightest doubt that "we" referred to Abbott and herself.

"I don't expose my shanks to the public view any more than I have to."

"You have good legs, so hush," said Mrs. Rhodes.

"Mrs. Elliott, your visit has brought on a rush of compliments. Mrs. Rhodes isn't always this kind."

"No I'm not, am I? But how else can I hope to compete with someone as pretty as this young woman. Did you stay long at the dance?"

"Forever," said Mary Elliott.

"So did Lew, my husband. I hear that there was another skinny-dipping party."

"Nude bathing," said Arnold Abbott.

"Yes, I got it."

"Oh, dear. Do you remember the first one, Arnold? At least the first one I ever went to."

"I'd be very damn ungallant if I said I didn't. Of course I remember."

"That was on a Saturday night too. Sunday afternoon I was packed off to my uncle's camp in the Adirondacks, to spend the rest of that summer in the woods. Mollie Hunt's mother was sent abroad. And at least one other girl was put in a private hospital in Westchester. Physical examinations that I assure you were totally unnecessary. The whole thing couldn't have been more innocent."

"May I correct you? Sinless. Not innocent," said Abbott.

"I stand corrected. Sinless. Forty years ago, almost. I sometimes think that we'd all have been better off if we'd been allowed to run riot that night. Let nature take its course, man and his mate. I'm the only one of those girls that hasn't been divorced at least once. And . . ." She could not have said more plainly in words: "And look at me."

"The same is true of the men, except me. All the men have been through the mill once or twice."

"Do you think that's the answer, Mrs. Rhodes?" said Mary Elliott. "Throw the girls and boys together, and let nature take its course?"

"Oh—I wouldn't say that. I wouldn't say it to you, because I don't know anything about your marital status."

"I have a husband and two children."

Mrs. Rhodes looked at her quickly, sharply, and Mary Elliott nodded. "Yes, I'm temporarily separated from my husband. We hope it's temporary—or do we? I don't know."

"Well, I guess that's not so unusual these days," said Mrs. Rhodes. "Isn't that a perfectly innocuous comment?"

"Yes, perfectly. In this case I'm the problem one. I'm the one that wants out."

"What years are you thinking about, Mrs. Elliott?" said Mrs. Rhodes.

"What years am I thinking about? Oh, you mean am I thinking about the present, or the future. Why, the present. I *have* thought about the future, of course."

"Tell her, Arnold. That's why she came. Isn't it, Mrs. Elliott? You wanted the advice of two aging lovebirds, Arnold and I."

"You embarrass her," said Abbott.

"Not really, a young woman who's had two children. I don't embarrass you, do I, my dear?"

"I guess not. Except I didn't think it was written all over me. I thought I was more subtle."

"Subtlety is much more embarrassing in the long run," said Mrs. Rhodes. "And what you want is help. It's a great compliment to us, your wanting to talk to us, but Arnold is the better talker. You talk, Arnold."

"I'll answer any questions," said Abbott.

"Mrs. Rhodes said what years was I thinking of, and my immediate response was the present. But you and Mrs. Rhodes, you must have been in love all these years. I don't know when I've seen two people of any age so much in love. And yet you never got married. *Have* you been in love all these years?"

"Well, over thirty of them," said Abbott.

"I'll help," said Mrs. Rhodes. "Why didn't we marry? Because I was married when we fell in love, and loving Arnold wasn't a good enough reason to divorce my husband. Does that shock you?"

"Yes it does, a little. It's so old-fashioned that it's almost super-modern. And coming from you."

"Call me old-fashioned. I don't mind. But I hate divorce. I hated it as much as I hated what I was doing to Arnold. You heard of the Arnold Abbott parties and Arnold Abbott the playboy. Now you know why he gave those parties, why he— all those movie actresses and English ladies of title. Those were the bad years, Mrs. Elliott. That's why I asked you what years you were thinking about. Now we have our good years. I see him every day, every day of my life. We don't happen to sleep in the same house together every night, but except for those hours we're together more than most husbands and wives. And will be, as long as we're both alive. The bad years are over for us."

"I know what the next question is going to be—or would be if Mrs. Elliott weren't so nice," said Abbott.

"Of course," said Mrs. Rhodes. "But she may ask it if she wants to."

"I do ask it, because I must. What happens when one of you dies?"

Mrs. Rhodes put her hand on Arnold Abbott's hand, the hand that continually turned his cigarette lighter over and over. "We have a solution to that, haven't we, my love?"

Arnold Abbott smiled.

The Pioneer Hep-Cat

Every time I come here you all seem to want to hear some more about Red Watson. I declare, if I ever thought there would have been such a demand for stories about Red Watson I would have sat down and written a book about him. I've told you story after story about people that I thought were much more interesting than Reds. Big people. People that made something of themselves instead of a man that nobody ever heard of outside of two or three counties in Pennsylvania, and even here the name Red Watson never meant a thing to the people generally considered worthwhile. You young people nowadays, I'd much rather tell you about a mine-boy, a young lad that worked in a breaker but was rescued from that and went away to a seminary and became a cardinal. We had one young fellow in this town that most of you don't even know he was born here, but he was. I'm talking about General Henry T. Corrigan. Lieutenant-General Corrigan was born right here in this town and sold papers here till his family moved away. I used to play ball with Henny Corrigan, out at the old Fourteenth Street schoolyard. He caught, and I played shortstop on a team we used to have, called the Athletics. I guess *some* of you would be able to guess where we got that name. Those of you that can't guess, we didn't get the name from Kansas City, if that's any hint. And I might mention that a few years ago, when I was attending the newspaper editors' convention in New York City, the principal speaker was none other than Lieutenant-General Henry T. Corrigan, all decorated with a chestful of ribbons and surrounded by famous editors and publishers from all over the country, all wanting to ask him questions about the Strategic Air Command. And there I was, not a very important person I must admit, but when it came my turn to meet the general he looked at me and then he looked at my name on the convention badge we were all wearing and he burst into a big smile. "Winky Breslin!" he said. That was my nickname when I was young. "Winky, you old son of a gun," and with that he took me by the arm and the two of us went over and sat down and you'd be surprised how many local people he remembered, some now dead and gone, but quite a few still living. Some of them the parents and grandparents of you here today. I ran a little story about it at the time, but I guess not many of you saw it. In any case, that's the kind of man I'd rather talk about, but every time I'm asked to speak at one of your Press Club suppers your representative either asks me outright or gives me a strong hint to the effect that the person you'd like me to talk about is Red Watson. I don't understand it.

I'd understand it a lot better if Reds were still alive, and some rock-and-roll idol. But he passed away before you even had swing, let alone rock-and-roll. And it isn't as if there were any of his old records floating around. Reds never made a record in his life. I don't say he wouldn't have been good, or popular. He would have been. If they'd ever heard of him outside of this section of the country, he might have been, well, not as popular as Gene Austin, or the early Crosby. He had a totally different style. As I've told you before, or your predecessors, there's nobody around today to compare him with. The styles of singing have changed so much from when Reds was around. Beginning I'd say with Rudy Vallee and then on to Russ Columbo and Bing, the crooners came in. All toned down as far as the volume was concerned and running ahead of or behind the beat. Not Reds. When Red Watson let go, he belted out a song in a way that you'd think was going to break every window in the place. And on the beat. Perfectly on the beat. And he was a tenor. The singers nowadays, if you can classify them at all, you'd have to call them baritones. But Reds was a tenor, a high tenor.

I was thinking the other evening, I happened to be watching a show on TV and one of your Tommy Sandses or Bobby Darins came on and those squealing girls, that I suspect are paid, began screeching. And I thought to myself, Red Watson hit a higher note than any of those bobby-soxers, but when he did it it was music. Yes, it was. That's the sad part about it that there aren't any records around to prove it.

When I was the age of some of you, or a little older, the name bands used to come through this region, playing the parks in the summer and the ballrooms in the winter. I notice you don't get many big bands any more. In fact, I'm told there aren't any, to speak of. But when I was a young fellow there wasn't a name band in the country that didn't play here and all around here. And over and over again. It won't mean anything to you, but I can remember one night when Paul Whiteman, with a thirty-five-piece band, was playing a one-nighter and only two miles away was Vincent Lopez, with *his* big band. How to compare it nowadays, it would be like—I don't know the names of the bands any more. Ray Conniff and Neal Hefti, I guess. But I can tell you this much, one of the singers with Whiteman was a young practically unknown singer with a trio, named Bing Crosby. And if memory serves, the famous Bix Beiderbecke was also with Whiteman around that time. Those of you that collect records will recognize the name Bix Beiderbecke. First name, Leon. Played cornet. Also piano. You have a musician today, Bushkin, he plays piano and horn, but Bushkin was never idolized the way Bix was. They even wrote a novel about him, and if I'm not mistaken, it was turned into a New York play.

Well, what I don't understand is your interest in Red Watson, because Red died around the time I've been speaking of. He was popular *before* Whiteman and Lopez started playing the parks and the ballrooms in this section. The big band then was the Sirens. The Scranton Sirens. Of course you've heard about the Sirens. Both Dorseys played with the Sirens. We had that in our paper when Tommy and Jimmy passed on there a little while ago, and I got a lot of letters from some of your mothers and fathers and I guess your grandparents, that still loved the Scranton Sirens. But with all due credit to the Dorsey boys, the real attraction was Red Watson. Mind you, it was a fine band. None better in the whole United States, because I heard them all. All the big ones of that day. Fletcher Henderson. Earl Fuller. The Barbary Coast. Art Hickman. Oh, my, just saying the names takes me back. Ted Weems. The Original Dixieland. Goldkette. Paul Biese. The Coon-Sanders Kansas City Nighthawks. Jack Chapman. I can remember more than once driving all the way to Atlantic City in a friend of mine's flivver, just to hear a band at the Steel Pier, and then *driving back the same night* so I'd be at work in the morning. That was a long trip then. It's still a long trip, but when we made it—I guess there isn't one of you here that would know how to vulcanize an inner tube. I can see you don't even know what I'm talking about. In those days you could go in any five-and-ten and buy an ignition key for your Ford, and it had a square hole cut in the key to turn on the tank for your headlights. No, you don't register. I might as well be talking about whip-sockets.

You must bear in mind, when I graduated from this school, in other words the same age as some of you within sound of my voice, jazz was such a new thing that they weren't even sure how to spell it. Some spelt it j, a, s, s, and I've seen Victrola records with Jass Band instead of Jazz Band printed on the label. But I'll tell you one thing. If you ever heard Red Watson sing "Jazz Me" you knew it was spelt with two z's. To be quite frank with you, I'm always hesitant about coming here and speaking about Red Watson, because as the I hope respectable editor of a family newspaper, I don't consider Reds a proper subject for a talk before a group of young high school students. If I weren't so convinced that you know as much about some things as I do, I'd have to decline your invitations. Or at least I'd choose another subject. But then I always say to myself, "These young people today, they know a lot more than I did when I was their age, about certain things, and maybe I can sneak over a moral lesson somehow or other."

And I can. You see, boys and girls, or young ladies and gentlemen, Red Watson was an example of great talent wasted. He had a God-given voice, completely untrained, but I was told that he was given many offers to go away and take singing lessons. He came from a little town outside of Scranton and several rich people up there wanted to pay for his vocal training, but he'd have no part of it.

The story was—and those of you that were here two years ago must excuse me for repeating it—but according to the story that I always heard, and I could never summon up the courage to ask Reds to verify it—Reds was a breaker-boy, too. Like that cardinal. But when he was about thirteen years old, working in the breaker, his arm got caught in the conveyor and was so badly mangled that they had to amputate above the elbow. Thirteen, maybe fourteen years old. You can imagine what dreadful torture he must have gone through. The accident itself, and then the amputation which left him with a stump about, well, he used to fold up his left sleeve and pin it with a safety pin just under the shoulder. He was an orphan, living with relatives, and after he got out of the hospital he tried selling papers, but that wasn't as easy as you might think. A paper route was just about impossible to get, and selling papers on street corners was just as hard. You had to fight for the busy corners, and Reds only had one arm. So he used to get a few papers and go around to the saloons and try to sell them there, but somehow or other they found out that he could sing, and he began to make as much money singing for nickels and dimes, and pennies, as he could selling papers. At the age of fourteen he was known in all the saloons, and sometimes the miners used to get him liquored up, even though he was hardly more than a child. They'd give him whiskey and get him singing, and he told me himself that by the time he was sixteen years of age, he could drink beer all night long without getting intoxicated. Whiskey was another matter, but beer he could drink till the cows came home, and it wouldn't affect him. That much of the story is true, because Reds told me himself.

This part I can't vouch for, but you can take it for whatever you think it's worth. I've never been able to make up my mind one way or the other whether it's just imagination on someone's part, or based on the truth, and I never asked Reds. But according to the story that a lot of people believed, when Reds wanted to hit his high note, he'd think back on the time he lost his arm and the pain would come back to him and he'd scream. I don't know. It wasn't the kind of question I could ever ask Reds, although I got to know him pretty well. But I remember hearing a story about Caruso, too. He was supposed to be the greatest tenor that ever lived, and they say he hit his highest note when he was in pain from an abscess in his lung. Who knows? I have a hard time believing it, but I think Caruso died of an abscessed lung, or the effects of it, so there may be some connection between the pain and the high note. I know that Red Watson's stump always bothered him, and he became a heavy drinker to take his mind off the pain. But he wouldn't see a doctor. Oh, no. He said another operation—well, not to be squeamish about it, the stump was so short that there was hardly anything left of the arm, and where would they go after that? He said to me once that he wasn't like most people, because he knew exactly how long he had to live. He said he didn't have to measure it in years, like most people, but in a few inches of bone.

People ask me what Reds was like, because when I was a young fellow, I confess that it wasn't only my duty as a reporter that took me into the various places where alcoholic beverages were for sale. And I guess I was one of the pioneer hep-cats, although they didn't use that expression, and in fact I'm told by the modern generation that you don't even say hep any more. Hip? Or is that passé, too? Well, anyway, I know that the musicians used to call us alligators, because we'd stand in front of a band with our mouths open like alligators, so if you ever heard the expression, "Greetings, 'Gate," that's where it came from. The alligators. And I was one back in the early Twenties, just after the first World War. When we wanted to hear a good jazz band, an orchestra that didn't play waltzes all night, we had to go to the public dances on Saturday nights at the Armory, and whenever I hear you young people being called juvenile delinquents, I have to remind myself that there was plenty of it when I was about your age. Those dances at the Armory, I think the admission was fifty cents for ladies and seventy-five for gents. It may have been less. Fifty for gents and twenty-five for ladies. We had a name for those dances. We called them rock fights. In fact, we didn't even bother to call them by the full name, rock fights. We used to say, "Are you going out to the rocky tonight?" And out of that grew another nickname, the quarry. We used to speak of the rock fights as the quarry. In front of our parents we could say, "I'll see you at the quarry," and our fathers and mothers would think we were talking about going for a swim in the quarry dam. Oh, we were just as wild as you think you are, or almost.

You know, I don't often get to see TV in the daytime, but last year when I was laid up with arthritis I watched you kids, or young people of your generation, dancing on an afternoon program. And one great difference between you and us, *you* don't seem to be having a good time. You hardly even smile at each other. It wasn't that way in my youth. Good Lord, everybody was laughing and jumping around, racing all over the floor when they played a one-step. Now you just glare at your partner and she spins around and you pull her towards you. You don't have any fun. Incidentally, I don't think you dance very well, either, but that's a matter of opinion. I remember a fast tune called "Taxi!" When they played that you moved fast or you got out of the way. That was good exercise, and fun. There'd always be a few fellows pretty well liquored up and they'd take a spill, but that was part of the fun. And there was always at least one fist fight at the rockies. At least one. You see, most of the girls at those dances, they were high school age, but they weren't going to school. They had working permits and a lot of them worked in the silk mill, the box factories, and some of them were servant girls. You hear the expression, going steady, and you think it's new. Well, it isn't. Girls and boys went steady then, and what that meant was that a girl would go to a rock fight and pay her own way in, dance with as many fellows as she wanted to, but she always went home with the boy she was going steady with, and if she tried to go home with somebody else, there'd be a fist fight. That's really where those dances got the name, rock fights. They didn't throw rocks, and they wouldn't have called them rocks anyway. They called them goonies. A gooney was a piece of stone that boys would throw at each other on the way home from school. In some sections of town the boys used to in the winter take a gooney and wrap it up in snow. A snowball with a gooney in it could inflict a lot of damage. See this scar here in back of my ear? That was a gooney wrapped in snow. I never knew who or what hit me at the time, but a bunch of boys from Third Street school were waiting for us boys from Fourteenth Street one afternoon, and I was one of the casualties. My poor mother when they brought me home!

Well, you're very patient with me and I don't know why it is that the mere mention of Red Watson opens up the floodgates of reminiscence, only it's more about me than about Reds. I started to answer the question, what was he like? Well, in spite of his name being Watson, he had a real Irish face, no doubt about it. He wasn't a very big fellow. In fact he was on the short side. But he looked a lot older than his real age. When I first knew him he was only about twenty years of age, but he looked easily thirty. Face was almost purple from drink and he was already starting to get bald. He was usually smiling and he was *always* smiling when he got up to sing. He'd flirt with all the girls around the bandstand that gathered around when he took his place to sing. He was a cake-eater. That was slang for fellows that dressed a certain way. They were also called sharpies. A sharpie, or a cake-eater, wore a suit that was padded at the shoulders and tight at the waist, then flared out. It had exaggerated peaked lapels that went all the way up to the shoulders, hence the name sharpie. The coat was buttoned at the waist with link buttons, sometimes three pairs of link buttons. The cuffs flared out and they were divided. The trousers were very wide at the bottom, and if you were really sharp, they were laced at the sides, like Spanish bullfighters'. The sharpies wore either tiny bow ties, on an elastic, or very narrow four-in-hands. And they wore low-cut vests so that the whole shirt-front was exposed. Tiny little collars. Hair was plastered down with vaseline, and the cake-eaters wore sideburns. And that was the way Reds dressed, with one sleeve pinned up to his shoulder. You boys and girls are even too young to remember the zoot suit of twenty years ago, which was different from the cake-eater's outfit, but if Reds had lived in a later era, he'd have worn a zoot suit. I think.

As to his personality, he had two. One when he was singing, and the other when he wasn't. When he wasn't singing he wasn't a very remarkable young fellow. Good-natured as a rule, although quick-tempered at times. He liked the girls, and they certainly liked him, not because of his looks, you can be sure of that. And not only because of his singing. He had a car, a yellow Marmon roadster it was, and I went on a couple of rides with him after we became friendly, and we'd drive to Reading and Philadelphia, places where they didn't know him at all, and we'd stop some place to get a sandwich. If they had a waitress that was halfway good-looking Reds would start to kid her a little, and always end up with a date. Sometimes he had no intention of keeping the date, but he just had to convince himself that he was irresistible. And he usually was. In fact, too much so. I guess I knew him two or three years before he happened to mention that he was married when he was eighteen and had a baby daughter. He supported his wife and child, but he wasn't a good husband or father by any stretch of the imagination. I could understand his not getting along with his wife, but I've never been able to understand why he didn't seem to take the slightest interest in his daughter. But that was a closed subject, and I decided it was none of my business. In my opinion Reds was one of those people that seem to have a talent for certain things, such as music, writing, art, but they're deficient in the common-ordinary, everyday things that you don't hear so much about, but they're an accomplishment nevertheless. I mean the simple, ordinary things like the sacrifices that some of your mothers and fathers make for you boys and girls, that you may not even know of unless you stop to think about it. Forty boys and girls in this room. How many of you girls had a new dress this year? Don't raise your hands, because my next question is, how many of you girls got a new dress this year because your mother got one for you instead of for herself? And you boys. How many of you have cars—and don't *you* raise your hands, either. Because some of you must know, if you stop to think, that you wouldn't have a car if your fathers didn't decide to spend that money on you instead of on themselves. This isn't a lecture. I'm not at all sure what it is except an informal talk by a newspaper editor to some young people that are interested in the field of journalism. And you don't especially want me to talk about the newspaper business. But in fairness to you, if I'm invited to talk about a colorful character whose example I wouldn't want you to follow, in fairness to you I have to call your attention to the fact that you all have fathers and mothers that do set a good example in love and kindness, and patience and understanding. My conscience won't let me talk about Red Watson, and glamorize him, unless I point out to you that Reds only lived to be twenty-five years of age, and as far as I know—and I knew him pretty well—he never did anything for anybody but himself. With that understanding, I'll continue talking about him. But I had to make that clear. He never did anything for anybody but himself, and he died—well, I'll save that till later, inasmuch as half the members of your Press Club probably are hearing about Reds for the first time. The seniors and juniors were here when I spoke two years ago, but the sophomores and freshmen weren't.

So to continue about his two personalities. The one, he was fun to be with, but I only saw him on his visits to town, maybe four times a year. I don't know how he'd have been as a steady diet. Selfish, and no respect for girls whatsoever, and as I said before, he seemed good-natured, but he had a quick temper, too. I guess if I had to be completely frank about it, I was flattered because he wanted me for a friend. I was just a young fellow starting out in the newspaper business, and I used to enjoy it when some of our local prizefighters and celebrities would call me by my nickname. And in that little world, Red Watson was as big a celebrity as Kid Lefty Williams or Young Packy Corbett, two fighters we had at the time, both since passed on. Made me feel big, even though I had some misgivings about Reds.

But I'll tell you this, you always forgot what he was like when he got up to sing. I mean the things about him that I didn't go along with. It'd come his turn to sing a number and he'd go behind the piano and take a swig out of a pint bottle of whiskey, and a couple of fast drags on his cigarette, and then he'd go to the middle of the bandstand and stand there grinning at the people gathering around while the orchestra played a full chorus. And then he'd close his eyes and put his head back and start singing. It didn't make any difference what the number was. It might be a sort of a risqué song like "Jazz Me" or it might be a ballad. But the dancing would stop and everybody would stand still, as close to the bandstand as they could get, and you'd look at their faces and they were hypnotized. They'd be moving in time to the rhythm, but not dancing, and it was almost as though he were singing for them. Not only to them, but for them. I can remember thinking of him as a misplaced choir boy, and the crowd around him some of the toughest characters in the county. The girls just as tough as the young fellows. They'd all stop chewing gum while he was singing, and even when he happened to be singing a dirty song, they'd smile, but they didn't laugh. And if it was a ballad, he could make them cry. There's a high note in "Poor Butterfly"—"but if he don't come *back*"—that *always* made them cry. Then he'd finish his song and open his eyes and smile at them while they yelled and applauded, and he'd wink at them, and they'd start dancing again. One chorus. No encores, one song every half an hour. That was his agreement. He was paid fifty dollars a night with the band. But then after the dance was over we'd all meet at some saloon and after he had enough to drink you couldn't stop him. He'd get up on the bar and sing whatever you asked him, till the joint closed. The next night it'd be the same thing in some other town, six nights a week.

How he kept it up as long as he did, I don't know. He slept all day, but when he had his breakfast, at seven o'clock in the evening, that was often the only meal he ate all day. By eight o'clock he was hitting the bottle, and usually at half past eight, sometimes nine, he'd be with the band, ready to sing his first number. Naturally he couldn't keep that up, and he began failing to show up with the band. The first few times that happened, he got away with it, but then the crowds were disappointed and the managers of the dance-halls were afraid to advertise that he was coming. Then the band broke up and for about a year I didn't see Reds at all. I heard he was forming his own band, Red Watson's Syncopators. And he was leading the band, himself. But that didn't last long. Two or three months of that was all he could stand. And all the musicians could stand. He'd order special arrangements, but then he wouldn't pay for them, and he got in trouble with the union about paying his musicians, and the first thing he knew he was put on the unfair list. After that he just disappeared, and whenever I'd ask about him from people around Wilkes-Barre and Scranton they had conflicting reports, probably all true. I heard he'd opened a speakeasy in Wilkes-Barre and someone else told me he was in prison for non-support of his wife and child. The last time I saw him I was in Scranton, covering a United Mine Workers meeting, and I asked around and finally tracked him down. I asked him how things were, and not knowing I knew anything about him, he put on a great show. He said he'd got rid of the yellow Marmon and was buying a Wills Sainte-Clare. That was an expensive car. He had offers to go in vaudeville, et cetera, et cetera. And he wouldn't let me pay the check. We were in a speakeasy where his credit must have been good, because he told the bartender to put it on his tab and the bartender made a face, but said okay, Reds. I had a feeling that the bartender would have much preferred my cash. So I said to Reds, approaching the subject in a roundabout way, I said I was glad things were better. And he asked me what I meant by better, and I said I'd heard he'd a little trouble. Well, such vituperation! Such invective! And all directed at me. I was a cheap newspaper reporter that never made more than thirty dollars a week in my life, which was true, but I was also a snooping so-and-so, probably sent there by his wife's lawyer to find out all I could. He took a beer bottle off the bar and smashed the neck off it. That was a weapon known as a Glasgie Slasher, and he held it up to my face and said I deserved to have my eyes gouged out, snooping around and asking questions. I didn't dare move, for fear I'd get that thing in my face. And then I guess because I hadn't made any move he dropped the broken bottle in the gutter in front of the bar, and ran out.

I was given a drink by the bartender, and I needed it after that experience. "He'll murder somebody yet," the bartender said. "He's suspicious of everybody." I asked the bartender how Reds lived, and the man told me. I don't have to go into that here, but Reds was about as low as a man can get to make a living. Any real man would rather dig ditches, but Reds only had one arm and all he ever did was sing. Anyway, he had a place to live and a little cash. And then the bartender, a nice fellow, asked me how well I'd known Reds. Had Reds ever told me that he didn't measure his life by years, but inches of bone? And I said yes, he'd said that to me some years back. And the bartender said, "Well, he's heard the bad news. No more inches, and no more years. Months, and more likely weeks." Then he said he just hoped Reds got through the next couple of months without killing somebody.

Well, he did, boys and girls. The next I heard of Reds was a few weeks later at the office, the city editor handed me a little squib that came in over the U.P. wire. Patrick Watson, known throughout the coal region as Red Watson, the popular tenor, was found dead on the bandstand of the Alhambra dance-hall in Scranton. It was summer, the wrong time of the year for a dance at the Alhambra. So I got Scranton on the phone and checked. Yes, they found Reds at the Alhambra. Nobody else in the place, which was closed for the summer, and the watchman had no idea what Reds had gone there for. There was nothing worth stealing.

But you and I know why he went there, don't we? Yes, I think as I look at you, you know.

Thank you.

The Sharks

Mr. Plastic Rain Cover for His Hat was taking his daily constitutional. "There he goes, Mr. Plastic Rain Cover," said Betty Denning from her position at the window.

"Let him," said her husband.

"But come here and look at him," said Betty Denning.

"I've seen him."

"No, come here. You've only seen him once."

"Oh—" her husband growled, but he got up, took off his reading glasses and went to the window, still holding his newspaper.

"He's looking up here," said Betty Denning.

"Why don't you wave to him?"

"Shall I?" she said. "I wonder what he'd do."

"Well, you can easily find out."

"No, then we'd have him all the time."

"How do you know?"

"He's the type. I wonder which house he has?"

"How do you know he has a house?"

"Because he's on his way back. Yesterday and the day before, he walked toward the west, then fifteen minutes later he walked toward the east and then I didn't see him again. He's going eastward now, which means he's on the way home. That's how I know he has somebody's house. Also, there are no hotels toward the east of us and there are four toward the west."

"Well, you could ask in the village."

"I think I will."

"And then when you have that information safely tucked

away? . . . All you have to do is take the field glasses and see where he leaves the beach. We could easily figure out whose house he has."

"I don't want to stand out in the rain just for that," she said. "And that wouldn't tell me his name."

"Why do you want to know his name? I thought you just wanted to know whose house he has."

"I always like to know people's names when they arouse my curiosity."

"I must say I have damn little curiosity about a man that would wear one of those things. God, they're awful. And the worst of it is, people that wear them never wear good hats."

"You're a sartorial snob," said Betty Denning.

"Indeed I am, and that's hardly news."

"But you don't get anything out of it."

"Of course I do. I get a lot out of it. For instance, a man that wears one of those things isn't likely to be in my circle of friends or any of my friends' circle of friends."

"I know," she said. "I know all that. Therefore you've put your finger on it, why I'm curious about Mr. Plastic Rain Cover."

"How? Or why?"

"Should be obvious," she said. "Who among our circle of friends has rented their house to Mr. Plastic? He's been there now at least three days. Whose house is for rent this summer?"

"Nobody's, up in that direction. All the beach houses are occupied."

"Then who is he visiting?" she said.

"I think you'd better get on the horn and ask around. You could start by calling Fred at the police station."

"Oh, I wouldn't want to do that."

"Fred would know."

"No, I'll ask around more casually when I do the marketing."

"You really don't want to have your mystery spoiled."

"Perhaps," she said.

He began to sing. " 'Perhaps—she's putting on her wraps—

perhaps—she's putting on her wraps perhaps.' Now may I finish Mr. Joseph Alsop?"

"Do," she said.

The three-day nor'easter came to an end in the middle of the afternoon, and they went for a swim. "God, the beach is positively filthy," he said.

"You could pick up some driftwood," she said.

"And put it all in a neat pile, and then some kids would come along for a beach picnic and steal it all. I'm through breaking my back for the little bastards."

"It's good exercise if you remember to bend your knees. Uh-oh. We're going to have company. Mr. Plastic Cover."

"I forgot to ask you. Did you find out anything about him?"

"Tell you later."

Mr. Plastic Cover, now not wearing a hat, came toward them. He had on bathing trunks and a Madras jacket. He was walking eastward, and now there could be no doubt that he would stop. "Good afternoon," he said.

"Good afternoon," they said.

"I was admiring your house earlier. That's your house, isn't it?"

"Yes it is," said Betty Denning.

"I was wondering, is it on the market?"

"No, not really," said Betty Denning.

"Not at *all*," said Denning. "We rented it last summer, but to friends."

"But you don't want to sell. Well, I don't blame you. Nice to see the sun out again."

"Very nice," said Denning.

"Well—pleasure talking to you," said Mr. Plastic Cover.

He moved on and when he was out of earshot Denning said, "What'd you find out?"

"He has the Warings' house for the rest of the season, but he's not renting it."

"Who is he?"

"He's supposed to be some relation of Mona Waring's. He

seems to have plenty of money. He's from out west and he brought a car with a chauffeur and two of his own servants besides, a cook and a maid."

"You wouldn't think to look at him that he had that kind of money. Aren't the Warings coming down?"

"They were, but now they're going abroad instead. A sudden change of plans."

"A sudden deal with Mr. Hat Cover."

"We don't have to call him Mr. Hat Cover any more. His name is Joshua B. Simmons."

"Well, Joshua's going to be in the hospital with second degree burns if he doesn't stay out of the sun. Did you notice his legs, and his nose and forehead? Wow!"

"I don't think that was the sun. I think that's just Mr. Joshua B. Simmons. He put in a big order for liquor. I found that out. And he buys only the most expensive cuts at the meat market. He gets all the New York and Chicago papers and the air mail edition of the London *Times*. He's having five people down this weekend. And he rented one of the large boxes at the post office, the kind that they usually rent to stores."

"You did quite a job on him. Is he married?"

"I had no trouble at all. The natives were more than willing to talk about him. Naturally they all speak well of him. He's spending money. This is his first summer on Long Island. I haven't answered your question about his marital status because I didn't do so well there. Nobody seems to know. The cook does the marketing by telephone. I guess Mona gave her the names of all the clerks."

"Why would he be interested in buying our house?"

"I think that was just to make conversation."

"More than likely. Well, he's exhausted that topic, and now maybe he won't bother us any more."

"Oh, don't be too hopeful. Tomorrow I'm going to the library and look him up in *Who's Who*. I've become fascinated by him."

Betty Denning was not the only one who was fascinated by

Joshua B. Simmons. It soon transpired that he was asking owners
of all the most desirable summer houses if their places were
for sale, invariably getting no for an answer, and always commenting that he did not blame them. "I don't think he wants to
buy," said Betty Denning. "I think it's just a conversational
gambit he thought up."

The Warings apparently had made some arrangement for
Mr. Simmons to be, in Betty Denning's word, whisked into the
golf club and the beach club. It had not been difficult; as soon
as his name came up some of the governors recognized it; he
was on the board of one of the big Chicago banks and of
other imposing corporations. "He was graduated from the University of Chicago," Betty Denning told her husband. "I've
never known anyone that graduated from the University of
Chicago, have you?"

"Walter Eckersall. Eckie. Great football player before my
time, but then he used to officiate. He let me stay in a game
once when he could have put me out. There was a Princeton
guard named Marlow that was holding me on every play, and
I finally smacked him one. Eckie saw me do it and he said to
me, 'All right, he had it coming to him, but don't do that again.'
And I didn't."

"Was that Tubby Marlow?"

"Yes."

"You didn't hit him hard enough. Anyway, Mr. Joshua B.
Simmons is sixty-four years old and not married. Do you want to
know what he belongs to?"

"Sure."

"Well, a whole list of clubs in Chicago, and Phi Beta Kappa,
and something called Sigma Nu. Unfortunately the *Who's Who*
in the village library isn't very up-to-date. In fact, 1940. Nothing about the war, and of course he could have got married
since 1940, but I doubt it."

"So do I."

"Do you think the same thing I do?"

"Yes. I think he's a fag."

"You mean his walk?" said Betty Denning.

"Everything about him, not only his walk. I think he's an old queen."

"Well, you're right. I told you he was having five guests last weekend. He did. All men."

"Well, I hope that's not any criterion. I've had five men here during the duck-shooting."

"Huh. That's not what I worry about when you have five men here. Quite the opposite."

"I've never had any women here when you weren't here, and so stop your innuendoes. What about Mr. Simmons and his house party?"

"I'll get to it. Three of the men were young, two of them were about the same age as Simmons."

"Well, that's handy. They could square-dance."

"They would have been better off if they had. Saturday night they all got very tight and went for a moonlight dip without any clothes on. Old Mrs. Howard was kept awake all night and she reported them to Fred. You can imagine her, looking out and seeing six naked men and looking around for six naked women. Fred and one of the other policemen went up to investigate, but by that time they'd all got in cars and gone some place else. But Mr. Simmons has been given his first warning."

"Fred tell you all this?"

"He didn't tell me but he told Jim Carter and Peg relayed it to me. Jim is boiling mad at the Warings, especially Mona."

"Maybe she didn't know about her uncle, or whatever he is."

"Uncle is right. Her mother's brother. No, I can't go along with that. Mona's never liked it here much, and I think she and Billy just took off for Europe and let Uncle Joshua run riot. You can't tell me *Billy* doesn't know about Uncle Joshua."

"No, I guess not. But Billy will overlook anything if he can make a buck out of it, and I imagine Uncle Joshua sends a few bucks his way. He's probably Simmons's New York broker, and if there's thirty-five cents in it, Billy wouldn't care what the old guy did."

"He's having another houseful this weekend, Mr. Simmons."

"I wonder why we haven't seen him on the beach?" said Denning.

"Oh, I've seen him, when you were taking your nap. He prances by, always looks up, but he doesn't see me. Maybe he has his eye on you, dear."

"Maybe. I've always been popular with both sexes. Next time he walks by, wave to him."

"I will not. I don't find the situation very funny. I love this old place, and when an old pansy and his pansy friends start coming here, things aren't the same."

"Things aren't the same anyway, old girl, as you well know. No, it isn't a funny situation. I'm glad our boys are grown up and married."

"Well, Jim and Peg wish theirs were. The thing is that this nasty old man has been inquiring about properties, and the first thing you know we'll have a colony of them. That'll be the end of this place."

"You thought Simmons was just making conversation."

"I was wrong. He made a firm offer to the Ludlows. Forty-five thousand, and they may take him up."

"They wouldn't! Well, maybe they would. They're not getting any younger and their children don't come here any more. Good God, that would bring Simmons that much closer to our house."

"Why don't you and Jim Carter buy the Ludlows', as an investment?"

"I'm afraid that isn't the solution. We might be able to beat him to it on the Ludlow property, but Jim and I can't go on buying every property Simmons bids on."

"What is the solution?"

"There is none. With the best of good will in the world, people like the Ludlows can't afford to let sentiment, nostalgia, interfere."

"You mean that pansy's going to win? He's going to take over and ruin this lovely old place, where we've had such good times? I can't bear it."

"I've often said to you, the Lord doesn't care much about money. Look who He allows to have it."

"That's no comfort, I must say."

"I didn't offer it as comfort, Betty. We're not young ourselves, so let's try to enjoy this summer and next. After that? Well . . ."

"You wouldn't *sell?*"

"I wouldn't *not* sell if the Simmons types get a toehold."

"Oh, no! Can't we *do* something?"

"Suggest something."

"Let's just kill Mr. Simmons."

"In some ways, the only sensible solution." He squeezed her hand. "You wouldn't even kill a shark."

"What good does it do? Kill the shark, and it only attracts a lot of other sharks."

"Well, we've had a lot of good years here. Between us close to eighty."

"The sixty together were the best. I mean thirty."

On the next Sunday night Mr. Joshua B. Simmons, of Chicago, was murdered. He was stabbed in the chest and neck repeatedly by a young man named Charles W. Randolph. It was all on the radio and in the papers, in time, in fact, for the Monday morning papers.

"Do you know who that is?" said Betty Denning. "That's the boy they call Dipstick Charley, he's always so polite when we get gas. Do you know which one I mean?"

"Sure." Denning was reading the newspaper account of the murder, which differed very little from accounts of similar murders in similar circumstances. The millionaire Chicagoan had taken friends to the station to put them on the Sunday evening train to New York. He had then, according to police, gone to a "cocktail lounge" and there encountered Randolph, whom he invited to his fashionable beach residence for a drink. He made overtures to Randolph, who claimed to have repulsed him, and a scuffle occurred, during which Randolph stabbed him, using a dagger-like letter opener. Randolph then fled in the murdered man's Cadillac sedan and was arrested by state police who suspected him of driving a stolen car. Randolph was brought back to the Simmons beach house, reenacted the crime, and signed a full confession. He was being held without bail in the county prison. There were photographs of Randolph in his army uniform and of Simmons in a business suit, of the dagger-like letter opener and of the beach house and Simmons's Cadillac, and of Randolph in custody between Fred and a state policeman.

Even the tabloids could not keep the story built up for more than the fourth day. "Poor old Mrs. Howard's had a heart attack," said Betty Denning. "She's over at the clinic. Reporters and photographers and you have no idea how many morbid people, mistaking her house for the Warings'."

"They've started to come here."

"What on earth for?"

"The sharks. Do you remember what you said about killing a shark—it only attracts other sharks?"

"Oh, don't remind me."

"It was a very astute remark. While you were doing the marketing I had a caller. He wanted to know if this house was for sale. I said no, and he said he'd been given to understand by a certain friend of his that maybe we might sell. I asked him who the friend was, and he said, 'Well if you must know, it was Josh—Josh Simmons, poor boy.' Poor boy."

"What did you say?"

"I said, 'You get your ass out of here before I kick you out.' He said, 'Oh, you wouldn't do that, would you?' So I showed him I would."

"You kicked him?"

"Of course I kicked him. He won't be back, but others like him will be. You were certainly right about the sharks."

"Oh, dear. Oh, dear," she said.

The Girl from California

The limousine stopped and the driver paid the toll and waited for his change. The attendant in the toll booth looked at the couple in the back of the car and smiled. "Hyuh, Vince. Hello, Barbara," he said.

"Hyuh, fella," said Vincent Merino.

"Hello," said Barbara Wade Merino.

"Going to Trenton, Vince?" said the attendant.

"That's right."

"I knew you was from Trenton. Good luck, Vince. So long, Barbara," said the attendant.

"Thanks, fella," said Vincent Merino. The car moved along. "He knew I was from Trenton."

"Jesus, I'm glad to get out of that tunnel," said his wife. "I get the worst claustrophobia in a tunnel."

"Well, with me it's the opposite. I hate to ride in an airplane."

"I know," said Barbara. "Jack Spratt could eat no fat, his wife could eat no lean."

"We're gonna both of us eat plenty of fat where we're headed for. Today you forget about the calories. *And don't be nervous.* Take it easy. My fathernmother are no more different than your fathernmother. My mother aint even Italian."

"I know. You told me."

He tried to distract her. "You see them broken-down shacks and all? That used to be a pig farm, and you know something? The guy that owned it ran for President of the United States."

"Who cares?"

"Well, your mothernfather are always talking about America, the land of opportunity. Now you can tell them you seen a pig farm on the Jersey meadows, and the owner run for President the United States. I never heard of that in California."

"Thanks for trying to take my mind off it, but I wish today was over. What else will we do besides eat?"

"I don't know. Maybe the old man will make the load. If he's as nervous as you are, he could easily make the load. He could be starting right now. I hope not, though. He starts hitting the grappa, by the time we get there he could be passed out."

"How long does it take for us to get there?"

"About an hour and a half, I guess."

"Maybe I could go to sleep."

"You mean now?"

"Yes. You got any objections?"

"No, no objections if it'll calm you down."

"You sound disappointed."

"Not exactly, but if you go to sleep you're not gonna see New Jersey. I just thought, I know a hell of a lot about California, but you never saw New Jersey except from ten thousand feet up."

"On the train from Washington last year, when I was making those personal appearances."

"Yeah. The only reason why you took the train was because the whole East was fogged in. A hell of a lot you saw that time. All right, go to sleep if it'll relax you."

She put her hand on his cheek. "You can show me New Jersey on the way back."

"Sure. That's when *I'll* want to sleep."

"I wish we were both in bed right now," she said.

"Cut that out, Barbara. You're taking an unfair advantage."

"Oh, go to hell," she said, and turned her back and pulled the robe over her shoulder.

In a little while she fell asleep. She was always able to fall asleep. On the set, when she was making a picture, she could finish a take and go to her portable dressing-room and sack right out. Or if they were home and had had a fight, she would slam the bedroom door and in five minutes' time she would be sound asleep. "With Bobbie it's a form of escape," her sister said. "She's very fortunate in that respect."

"I'm built like a cow, so it's only natural," Barbara would say.

"Don't knock the build," Vincent had said. "It gets you two hundred gees a picture. And me. It got you me. You'd of been one of them boy types I wouldn't of looked at you. I wouldn't of *looked* at you."

The smell of a cigarette or the sound of the radio would wake her up, so he postponed a smoke and sat in silence as the car sped along the Turnpike . . . Then he realized that he had been asleep, too. He looked out on both sides but failed to recognize his surroundings. From his watch he made a quick calculation; they were ten, fifteen—more or less—minutes from the Trenton exit. He put his hand on his wife's hip and shook gently.

"Bobbie. Barbara. Get with it, kid."

"Huh? Huh? What? Where are we? Oh. Hello. Are we there yet?"

"I figured we're not far from it."

"Ask him. The driver," she said.

Vincent pressed the switch that lowered the division. "How much longer we got, driver?"

"We'll be in Trenton in five minutes, Mr. Merino. Then it's up to you."

"Thanks," said Vincent. "How about a little coffee?"

"All right," she said. "I'll do it." She poured coffee from a vacuum bottle. She put a lump of sugar in his cup and drank hers black and unsweetened. He gave her a lighted cigarette.

"Well, we're almost there," he said.

"Is the fellow from *Life* going to be there?"

"I don't know for sure. I doubt it. As soon as I told them it wasn't gonna be every Italian in Mercer County they lost interest."

She looked at herself in her vanity mirror. "Thank God for that, at least. Anyway they make a habit of sending a photographer and bossing everybody around, and that's the last you ever hear of it."

"I know. I don't even know for sure if my brother's coming from Hazleton. Both of my sisters will be there, that's for sure. But I bet their husbands have to work. My other brother Pat, him and another fella from Villanova. You couldn't *keep* them away."

"I hope I get them all straight."

"Pat's the college boy and he looks something like me. My eldest sister is France. Frances. My younger sister is Kitty. She's about the same age as you."

"Frances is the older one and Kitty's the younger one. And Pat's the college boy, and resembles you. What about your brothers-in-law? What are their names?"

"Take my advice and don't find out their names. That way my sisters won't get jealous, if you don't know their husbands' names. Anyway, I bet they won't be there."

"Who else?"

"The priest. Father Burke. And maybe Walter Appolino and his wife. He's a senator. State senator. If he wants us to pose for a picture, why, we better."

"What's the priest gonna be there for?"

"Well, maybe he won't come, being's we got married by a justice of the peace."

"Are they all going to make a stink about that? Because if they do, I'm going to turn right around and go back to New York. I don't have to take anything from them."

"You won't have to. Kitty's husband aint a Catholic and her kids aren't being raised Catholic. I aint worried about that, so don't you be. The only trouble I predict is if my old man makes the load, and Pat starts trying to make a pass at you. I'll give the son of a bitch a punch in the mouth if he does."

"Listen to who's talking."

"Right. Exactly. Listen to who's talking is right. He patterns himself after me because just because he happens to be Vince Merino's brother. Well, hands off Vince Merino's wife, Pasquale Merino, if you don't want to go back to Villanova minus a couple teeth. And don't you encourage him. Don't stand too close to him. He don't need any encouragement in that direction."

"Is there any of your old girl friends going to be there?"

"Not unless my brother Ed comes from Hazleton. I used to date her before Ed did."

"Did you score with her? I don't have to ask, I guess."

"Well, if you don't have to ask, why ask? What's the use of asking a question that you know the answer beforehand? Sure I scored, but not after she started dating Ed. Only Ed don't believe that. I don't think Ed'll be there."

"She probably throws it up to him that she could have married you."

"Hey, you're pretty smart. That's what she does do. And is she ever wrong? I wouldn't of married her even if I'd of kept on living in Trenton."

"Why not?"

"Because she thought she owned me, and she didn't."

"*I* own you, don't I?"

"Well, I guess so, but that was my own free will. I wanted to own you, so I let you own me. But I never wanted to own her. What the hell? I did own her and I never even wanted to. She was all right for then, but I never intended to be stuck in Trenton all my life. I hope they don't come. I hope there's only my two parents, and my sisters without their stupid husbands, and my kid brother if he behaves himself. Oh, Walter Appolino. Walter is more used to meeting celebrities, like he goes to New York all the time and every time he goes to the Stork Club. Walter was the first guy I ever knew that went to the Stork Club, when I was sixteen or seventeen years of age."

"Large deal."

"Come off it, Bobbie. When you were sixteen who did *you* know that went to the Stork Club?"

"When I was sixteen—well, *seven*teen—I was going there myself."

"Yeah, I guess so." Vincent now gave his full attention to the task of directing the driver through the streets of Trenton. In time they stopped at a detached white frame house which had a front porch, a front and back yard, and a one-car garage in the rear. "This is it," he said. "Is it worse or better than you expected?"

"Frankly, better."

He smiled. "My old man's a bricklayer at Roebling's. I bet he makes better than your old man."

"I didn't say he didn't. That's your mother in the doorway?"

"Yeah, that's Mom. Hey, Mom, wuddia say?" He got out of the car and embraced his mother. Barbara followed him. "Three guesses who this is."

"How do you do, Mrs. Merino?" said Barbara.

"I'm pleased to meet you, Barbara." Mrs. Merino shook hands with her daughter-in-law. "Come on in and be introduced to the others."

"Who all's here, Mom?" said Vincent. "Did Pop make his load?"

"What kind of talk is that? No, he didn't make any load. Is that the way you talk about your father?"

"Forget it. Who else is inside?"

"The Appolinos. Walter and Gertrude Appolino. He's the state senator. Senator Appolino, but a great friend of ours. And his wife. And my two daughters. Vince's two sisters, Frances and Catherine. Both married. Barbara, do you want to go upstairs and freshen up first, or will I introduce you to the others?"

There was no need to reply; all the others came out on the porch and Mrs. Merino made the introductions. As soon as all the names were mentioned there was a sudden, blank silence.

"All right, everybody stand here like a bunch of dummies," said Vincent. "Let's go inside or we'll have the whole neighborhood standing around." Two girls and a boy in their early teens came forward with autograph books and held them out to Barbara and Vincent.

"Put 'To my old friend Johnny DiScalso,' " said the boy.

"The hell I will," said Vincent. "Who are you? Pete Di-Scalso's kid?"

"Yeah."

"Your old man arrested me for driving without a license. You're lucky I sign my name for you. Who are you, girl?"

"Mary Murphy."

"Which Murphy? Your old man sell washing machines?"

"He used to but not any more."

"Is this your sister?"

"Yeah, I'm her sister. Monica Murphy. Our father used to sell washing machines but now he don't any more."

"Leo Murphy, Vince," said Senator Appolino. "I got him fixed up as an attendant over in the State House. Very good man, Vince, you know what I mean."

"Oh, sure. Leo's all right. Give my regards to your father, girls."

"Thanks, Vince," said the senator. "All right, girls, run along now. And, Vince?"

"What?"

"Forgive and forget. Put 'To my old friend Johnny DiScalso.' I'd appreciate it, you know?"

"Votes?" said Vincent.

"Sixteen guaranteed, sometimes more," said the senator. "And, Barbara, you, if you don't mind? Just something personal for Johnny? 'To my friend,' or something like that? Appreciate it. Appreciate it very much, Barbara."

"All right," said Barbara.

"Fine. Fine," said the senator. "Vince, I'm sorry Gert and I have to go to a colored funeral, but we'll be back later and your parents said it'd be all right if I brought a few friends back with us. Okay?"

"I don't know how long we'll *be* here, Walt."

"Yeah, but I'd appreciate it very *much,* Vince. I kind of promised these people, you know what I mean?"

"How many, Walt?"

"Under forty or fifty. They just want to say hello and like

shake hands with you and Barbara. Ten minutes of your time, that's all, and a couple pictures for the papers. Ten minutes, fifteen minutes."

"If we're still here, Walt," said Vincent.

"Yeah. Well, I'd appreciate it, Vince. I really would. I more or less promised them, and I sure would hate to disappoint them. It'd look funny, you know, you coming back to the old home town and didn't see anybody. You know what some people would say, and I wouldn't want them saying that about Vince Merino and his lovely bride Barbara. I'm not gonna say goodbye, folks. We'll be back before you know it."

The senator and his wife departed, and the group on the front porch went inside to the parlor. "Pop, wud you tell Walt?" said Vincent after the women went upstairs.

"Huh. I didn't tell him, he told me. Right away he seen it in the paper you and Barbara was in New York, would you be coming to Trenton? Your mother told him yes. Here he is."

"You need him?"

"Well, I don't *need* him. Maybe he needs me as much as I need him, but you got that crazy brother Pat, you never know what he's gonna do, so it's no use antagonizing Walt."

"Yeah. Where is Pat?"

"He'll be here, him and his roommate with his second-hand, third-hand Jag. The roommate keeps the car in Philly. They'll end up with a broken neck, the two of them. Well, it won't be long till the army gets him. He won't be staying at Villanova much longer."

"Why don't you knock a little sense into him?"

"Wait'll you see him and you'll know why. You didn't see him since he filled out. He could take you or me or maybe the two of us."

"Huh. How's Ed?"

"Ed? Oh, him and Karen are like cats and dogs. She was here in Trenton a couple weeks ago but she never came near us. She was here for two weeks last summer and never came around. They're all washed up. Ed was here in March or April, sometime, and he stayed drunk for two days. Your mother and I couldn't get anything out of him, but you can put two and two together."

"Well, give me some *good* news. Are France and Kitty all right?"

"Oh, I guess they're all right. Kitty was fooling around with some married man till your mother and France, and Father Burke got into it. Harry was responsible for that, but that don't give Kitty grounds to fool around with a married man."

"But France is all right?"

"Yeah. Well, you'd never know it now that France was a pretty girl when she was around sixteen."

"No."

"You got a good-looking girl for a wife. She even looks better in real life. You gonna have kids?"

"Well, not for a while."

"Yeah, I see what you mean. She put on weight you might have a hard time getting it off again. I don't blame you. Save your money and then have the kids. What is she? Twenty-three or four?"

"She's twenty-four."

"Well, maybe she could have one the year after next and then wait a while."

"How are *you*, Pop?"

"Oh, hell, I'm all right, I guess. Why? Do I look as if I wasn't?"

"You look all right. How old are you now?"

"I'm a day older than I was this time yesterday. How old do you think I am?"

"I don't know. Around fifty?"

"Well, close. I'm forty-eight. I was bothered with this hernia last year, you remember when I was operated? I was made foreman, so I don't have as much heavy work."

"You still like your booze?"

"Huh. You wouldn't of had the nerve to ask me that five years ago. I don't drink no more. A little beer and a little wine, but no hard stuff. I cut out the hard stuff. Monday mornings I used to start getting dizzy up on the scaffolding, so I quit everything but a little wine and beer. But Ed's making up for it, and so's Pat. They'll scrape him up off the road one of these days. He's a wise guy, you can't tell him anything that he don't know all the answers. Is that your Chrysler outside?"

"Hired."

"What are you driving now?"

"I got an Austin-Healey, but I had it for two years and I'm thinking of getting something else. I only put about fourteen thousand miles on it, being away so much making pictures overseas."

"What happens with Barbara when you go away like that?"

"Well, the only time since we were married, she was in the same picture."

"Yeah, but I see where you're going to Portugal and she won't be there. What do you do then?"

"I don't know. It never happened since we were married."

Vince's father pointed a finger at him. "Start a baby. Take my advice and start a baby right away. Maybe it'll keep you straight. I don't know her, but I know you. The only thing that'll keep you straight is maybe if you have a baby started. Maybe. Forget the money, Vince. Forget it."

"Pop?"

"What?"

"How are you and Mom getting along?"

"What kind of a question is that to ask me? Who the hell do you think you are?"

"Oh-ho-ho. I touched a sore spot. Accidentally I touched a sore spot. Are you fooling around with somebody, Pop?"

"Did she say something to you?"

"When would she have a chance to say something to me?"

"Over the phone she could have."

"No, she didn't say nothing. But you took it so big, as soon as I asked you how you were getting along. I knew if it wasn't the booze it's either a woman or money. And you were never stingy. I'll give you that."

Andrew Merino's blue Tyrolean eyes showed trouble. He put his hand on his son's knee. "You're a man now, Vince, but some things you're still not old enough. I don't want to talk about it."

"Who is she? She older, younger? Married?"

"When I tell you this, it's the God's honest truth. I was never in bed with her."

"Oh, Pop. Come off it. You're a pretty good-looking guy."

"Oh, hell, I was as bad as you or Pat back in my twenties."

"Does Mom know the woman?"

"Don't say it that way, Vince. That sounds as if there was something, and there aint. I have a cup of coffee with her."

"At her house?"

"I never been inside her house."

"Does she feel for you?"

Andrew Merino hesitated, then nodded. "But she won't see me after work. She's in the office."

"Then what's Mom's beef?"

"Huh. Wait till you're married that long. We were twenty years of age when we got married. You'll find out."

"I come here to show my wife a typical Italian family, my folks. My Italian father and my Irish mother by the name of Merino. Mr. and Mrs. Andrew Merino, Trenton, New Jersey. And you wanta know something? The old lady give me a look when I got out of the car, and right away, *right away* I got the whole picture. You hung back and didn't hardly say anything. Then I thought to myself, Pop had this operation a year ago."

"No, it aint the operation, Vince."

"Oh, you don't have to tell me now, but that's what I thought. Five years ago you wouldn't of let Walt Appolino be the take-charge guy, not in your house. You sure you don't have a guilty conscience, Pop?"

"I got a guilty conscience for my thoughts. But what do you want, Vince? Do you want me to tell my own son that I don't love his mother? That's my guilty conscience, but I don't have to tell that in confession."

"You go to confession?"

"No."

"You don't, hey?"

"No, and that's why your mother thinks there's something going on. I been two years without making my Easter duty. She says to me, next Sunday's the last chance to make your Easter duty. I tell her to mind her own business. Then she's positive I'm going to bed with Violet Constantino."

"Oh, Violet Constantino. Johnny's wife. That's who it is? She used to be a good-looking woman."

"She didn't only used to be. But Violet don't have to make her Easter duty. She's a Methodist, so your mother can't keep tabs on her that way."

"Pop, you gotta get this thing straightened out."

"I know. I know, Vince. To tell you the truth, I was hoping I could talk to you about it. I can't talk to nobody else."

"What does Johnny Constantino think of the whole thing?"

"Johnny Constantino," said Andrew Merino. He shook his head. "Him and I go bowling every Wednesday night."

"That don't answer my question, Pop."

"It wasn't suppose to. I was just thinking, him and I go bowling every Wednesday night, plus I give him a ride home from lodge meeting once a month. And I wonder. We been friends all our life, from boyhood, then I reach the age of forty-six and all of a sudden I fall in love with Violet, his wife for twenty years. I don't get anywhere with her, a cup of coffee in the morning, and 'How are you?' "

"Wuddia mean you never been inside her house?"

"I never been inside of their house. The two women don't get along. When do you remember me or your mother being inside the Constantinos'? Never."

"Well, they always lived the other side of town somewhere."

"If they lived over there next door it would be the same."

"Why don't Mom like her?"

"Well, the last couple years you can figure it out why. But before that your mother didn't like any woman that had a job. Violet had a diploma from commercial school and she could always get a job in an office. The best your mother could ever get was waitress or extra saleslady at Christmas. It wasn't her fault. She didn't have the education. But she used to say Violet was high-hatting her. But if it wasn't that she'd of found some other excuse. She don't like Johnny, either. Your mother don't like many people outside of her own family. The Appolinos and Father Burke. But she don't like ordinary people. I'm surprised those Murphy kids and Johnny DiScalso had the nerve to come here today. She chases any kids that run across our lawn."

"Not when I was a kid."

"Oh, not when you was a kid. You know why. She wanted all the kids playing in our yard. That way she'd know where you were. And France. And Kitty. And Ed. But the minute they all grew up, no more kids playing on the front lawn. No more kids in the back yard. It's a wonder France or Kitty ever got a husband. 'Go down and tell them it's time to go home,' she used to say, when one of the girls had a boy friend. Eleven o'clock! Those girls were brought up strict. They might as well of had Father Burke living in the house. You didn't see any of that, but I saw plenty. And what could I do? Give her any opposition and she'd say, all right, if I wanted to be responsible. You remember young Audrey Detmer?"

"On Bergen Street?"

"Got knocked up when she was fifteen and they had five boys that she didn't know which one was the father. 'You want another Audrey Detmer in your own family?' she used to say. Your mother. Well, we almost did, with Kitty. Kitty's first was six months after she got married."

"Listen, Pop, I could of told you a few things about Kitty."

"I wouldn't of been surprised. Well, here they come down. You want a shot of something, or a cocktail? What kind of a cocktail does Barbara drink?"

"She can't handle it. She'll drink a little vino, and that's all I want."

Andrew Merino grinned. "You still got the weak stomach?"

"For liquor."

"Well, you can get drunk on wine, but you don't get Irish-drunk like Ed and Pat."

"Yeah? What about you and your grappa?"

"I never drank it because I liked it, Vince. I only drank it for the effect."

"To forget about Mom, huh?"

"Now, now, you don't have to say that," said Andrew Merino.

"What don't he have to say?" said his wife.

"I was talking to *him*, Kate. I wasn't talking to you," said Andrew Merino.

"All right, have your secrets," said Kate Merino. "I guess we're gonna have to start eating without Pat and his friend. Barbara, you sit anywhere you want to."

"She's suppose to sit next to me," said Andrew Merino.

"Well, she don't have to if she don't want to."

"The place of honor is on my right."

"I was gonna have her sit next to Walt, but he had to go to some funeral," said Kate Merino.

"Yeah. I wish it was his," said Andrew Merino. "Sit here, Barbara. You like Italian food?"

"I love it."

"You got any real Italian restaurants out in Hollywood?"

"Oh, sure. Lots of them."

"Well, my wife is Irish but she knows how to cook Italian food, so dig in. You know what that is, don't you? Thatsa leetla beeta Eyetalian prawn? You like da prawn?"

"Oh, cut the dialect, Pop," said Kitty.

"I no talka the dialect. Me speaka da perfect English, yes-no, Barbara?"

"Sure. Perfect."

"Lay off, Pop," said Vince.

The meal proceeded, and since they were all good eaters, the conversation was incidental to the enjoyment of the food. "I want to help you with the dishes, Mrs. Merino," said Barbara.

"No, we'll leave them till later, but thanks for making the offer," said Kate Merino.

"Would you smoke a cigar, Vince? I got some cigars," said Andrew Merino.

"No thanks, Pop. Maybe Barbara would like one."

"Don't give them that kind of an impression," said Barbara. "But I'll have a cigarette if you'll give me one."

"I ate so much I don't want to get up from the table. I don't want to move," said Vince, lighting his wife's cigarette. He passed his case along to the others, and they lit their own.

"Boy, solid gold," said France. "Can I read what it says inside?"

"From the studio. I know it by heart. 'To Vincent Merino for the Oscar he earned and will some day get. 1958.' That's when everybody said I was gonna get the Oscar."

"It shows what the studio thought of you, and that's what counts," said his mother.

"You're so *right* it's what counts," said Vince.

"We all sat here that night watching the TV," said France. "We were just as nervous as you were, if not more so. They put the TV camera on you, and you sure were nervous."

"Who did you go to that with, sweetie?" said Barbara.

"Renee Remy, who else? Who did you?"

"I don't remember."

"Brad Hicks," said France. "The TV director."

"Figures," said Vince.

"Well, I didn't know you then."

"Was that the front door?" said Kate Merino. "That'll be Pat, just when we're all finished eating."

Kitty Merino got up and went to the hall door. They all watched her, and she held her hand to her mouth and whispered to them: "It's *Karen*."

"Oh, Christ," said Andrew Merino.

"Anybody home?" Karen's voice called out.

"We're all back here, Karen," said Kitty. "Come on back."

"Is that you, Karen?" called Kate Merino. "We're in the dining-room." Then, to the others: "Now don't anybody say anything, then maybe she won't stay. Just be polite."

Karen appeared in the hall doorway. "Hello, everybody. A regular family gathering, eh? Hello, Mrs. Merino. Pop. Kitty. France. Oh, hello, Vince."

"Hello, Karen," said Vince. "Ed with you?"

"No, he had to work but he sends everybody regards."

"Introduce you to my wife. Barbara, this is Karen, my brother Ed's wife."

"Hello, Karen," said Barbara, extending a hand.

"Well, naturally I recognize you, but I'm pleased to meet you personally."

"Did you have your lunch, Karen?" said Kate Merino. "We're keeping stuff warm for Pat and a friend of his, but the way it looks I don't think they're gonna be here."

"Oh, I ate over an hour ago, thanks. At my family's."

"How's your mother?" said Kate Merino.

"She seems better."

"Karen's mother had a serious operation for cancer," said Kate.

"They think they got it all," said Karen.

"We called up when she was in the hospital," said France.

"She told me, yes. She appreciated it."

"How's Ed?" said Vince.

"Oh, just the same."

"I wish he would of come with you. I didn't see Ed since you moved to Hazleton."

"Is it that long? Well, you'd still recognize him."

"Will you have a drink of something, Karen?" said Andrew Merino.

"No thanks. Ed takes care of that department," said Karen.

"Is Ed lushing it up?" said Vince.

"Now, Vincent!" said his mother.

"Yes, speak to him, even if he is the big movie star," said Karen. "Ed's your own brother."

"I just asked a simple question."

"Yeah. Simple," said Karen. "You ever been to Trenton before, Barbara?"

"No, only passed through it on the train."

"Yeah, that's what they say about Trenton," said Karen. "What part of the country did you originate?"

"Well, I was born in Montana, but my parents moved to L. A. when I was two years old."

"I had an uncle worked in Montana. Did you ever hear of Missoula, Montana? It sounds like you ought to use it cooking, but there is such a place."

"I heard of it, but I left there when I was two years old."

"Azusa. You got some funny names in California, too. Is there such a place as Azusa, or did they just make that up for a gag?"

"It's real," said Barbara.

"They got just as funny names around Hazleton, where I live. Did you ever hear of Wilkes-Barre? And they used to have a place called Maw Chunk. M, a, u, c, h, c, h, u, n, k. I don't pronounce it right but then they changed it to Jim Thorpe. From Maw Chunk to Jim Thorpe."

"Let's go sit in the front parlor," said Kate Merino. "It's nicer in there."

"What's wrong with here? I like sitting around the table," said Vince.

"The dirty dishes. Come on, everybody. Andy, bring two chairs for the Appolinos."

"Oh, is Walt coming?" said Karen.

"Walt and Gert. They were here early and then they had to go to a funeral," said Andrew Merino.

"What did you think of Walt, Barbara? Quite the big shot around here, so he thinks."

"He seemed all right."

"Who else was here? Father Burke?" said Karen. "He's usually here, too."

"Is that suppose to be some kind of a crack, Karen?" said Vince.

"You haven't changed."

"No, neither have you," said Vince. "You always came in this house with a chip on your shoulder."

"Take it easy, everybody," said Andrew Merino.

"Goodbye, everybody," said Karen.

"Goodbye? You just got here," said Kate Merino.

"I know where I'm not wanted," said Karen. She looked at everyone in the room, individually, except Vince, then went back in the hall and out the front door.

"Huh," said Vince.

"I wonder when she came down from Hazleton," said Kitty. "I bet she's been here a week or more."

"What possessed her to come over here today, if that's as long as she was going to stay," said Kate Merino. "To see Vince and Barbara, I know, but common politeness she should have stayed longer."

"Well, common politeness or whatever you want to call it, Bobbie and I gotta be going," said Vince.

"So soon?" said Kate Merino.

"Mom, I didn't give any time how long we'd stay. I got an interview at five o'clock at the hotel, and Bobbie has to do a TV tape."

"Well, this wasn't much of a visit, but I guess it's better than none. I don't know what we'll tell Walt," said Kate Merino.

"Vince didn't make Walt any promises," said Andrew Merino.

"I didn't make anybody any promises. I wasn't sure we could get here at all," said Vince.

"I wish I would of thought to bring my camera," said Kitty.

The chauffeur was asleep in the car, and a dozen women and children were standing quietly on the sidewalk when Vincent and Barbara left the house. As though by some tacit agreement the family all stood on the porch to wave farewell.

"Back to New York, Mr. Merino?" said the chauffeur.

"But fast," said Vince. "Go to the end of this street and turn right, then the first left and that'll put us on U.S. 1. After that you look for Turnpike signs." He pressed the button that raised the division.

"If you got anything to say, save it till later," said Vince. "I don't want to talk about them."

"Well, now you know something."

"What?"

"You used to say to me, why didn't we go visit my folks. It was only thirty miles."

"You knew it was gonna be like this?"

"It could have been a lot worse," said Barbara. "You showed good sense leaving. They hate us, they all hate us. Either way, they hate us. If we're nice, they hate us just as much as if we treat them like dirt."

"All but Pop."

"Yeah, I guess he was all right, but he didn't fit in with the rest of them."

"Pop didn't? How didn't he fit in?"

"Don't ask me how. I just felt sorry for him," said Barbara. She took his hand. "What are you smiling at?"

"That Pat. Wait till he gets there and we're halfway to New York."

"Families," she said. "They're just like everybody else. They don't like us. Well, I didn't use to like Ava Gardner before I was in pictures. Or Lana Turner. Who did they think they are?"

"And now they're you, huh?"

"Sure."

"You want to go to sleep?"

"Wait till we get out of the built-up section. They're liable to think I'm drunk."

"I'd like to see the look on Walt's face, with his fifty politicians."

"Erase them from your mind, honey, It's the best way," she said.

A Cold Calculating Thing

For Ada Trimball it was a rush of mail, considering; considering, that is, how seldom she got two personal letters in the same delivery. Sometimes it seemed hardly worth the trouble to memorize the combination of her mailbox, and sometimes it was not worth the trouble to raise that heavy garage door and back the Volkswagen out of the garage and drive it to the post office. But then there were times, too, when nothing seemed worth the trouble; and yet she went on, taking the trouble to make a home for herself and her ungrateful mother, going to the trouble of looking nice, of *being* nice to the people in the post office and the village shops, of watching her money and getting the most out of it, of keeping up with her reading, and voting and attending church and going to the dentist and taking vitamins and getting a permanent and not giving in to that nagging doubt that anything was worth the trouble.

She stopped at the window and laid down the crumpled old card that informed her that there was a parcel too large for her mailbox. "Good morning, Mrs. Dombrowski. You've got something for me?"

"Morning, Miss Trimball. Yes, I think it's a book. Uh-huh. A book." Mrs. Dombrowski pushed the parcel toward Miss Trimball and picked up the crumpled old notice and leaned with her fat forearms on the counter.

"Thank you, and I'd like, let me see—twenty postcards is sixty. Twenty postcards, and ten four-cent stamps, please. A dollar even." Ada Trimball had an adequate supply of postcards and stamps at home, but she wanted to show Mrs. Dombrowski that she was in no hurry to read the two personal letters in this morning's mail, and also to compliment Mrs. Dombrowski by a purchase. She had heard somewhere that the government kept tabs on the sales of stamps in individual post offices, and where sales fell off, the staff was reduced. Mrs. Dombrowski licked her thumb, flipped twenty postcards from a stack, recounted them for Miss Trimball's benefit, and then efficiently tore ten stamps from a page.

"Dollar even," said Mrs. Dombrowski, smiling, again resting her fat forearms on the counter and crushing her comfortable breasts against her arms. "How's your mother?"

"About the same, thank you."

"Well, when they stay the same that's a good sign. I hear Mrs. Diehl took a turn for the worst last night."

"Oh, really?"

"Uh-huh. I was surprised, too, because Monday the report was she'd be home from the clinic by the end of the week. Well, I guess she'll be home, but not the way they expected. But she's more up in years than your mother, Mrs. Diehl. She'd be eighty-five in April. Eighty-five. I never want to be no eighty-five."

Ada Trimball smiled. "Maybe you'll change your mind when you're eighty-four."

"Not me. I'll lose interest as soon as my grandchildren get married. The good Lord willing, I'll stay around to see that, but there isn't much in it for a woman after that. At least that's the way I look at it."

"Oh, I'm not so sure. I'll just bet you'll want to be there to see your first great-grandchild."

"Nup. Not me. What's a lady like Mrs. Diehl had out of the last five-ten years? Crippled with the arthritis and all? And what it costs to be sick nowadays. I guess she has a little put away, but George Diehl told me himself, the week he's had her at the clinic ran him over three hundred dollars. I don't want them spending that kind of money on me at that age."

"Well, it's a long way off, for you." Ada Trimball smiled and departed, knowing that Mrs. Dombrowski would be standing at the counter and smiling at her and thinking what a nice woman she was.

At the drug store and at the dry cleaner's she heard again that old Mrs. Diehl was poorly, and at her last stop, the meat market, she was told that the word was just in: Mrs. Diehl had died shortly after nine o'clock that morning. George Diehl's wife had ordered extra food for the relatives who would be arriving for the funeral.

"What took you so long?" said Ada Trimball's mother.

"I had to hear all about Mrs. Diehl. She passed away this morning."

"Had to hear all about her? What was there you didn't know? I could tell you all about her. She ran around with young men half her age."

"Oh, Mother. She couldn't have. She's been crippled for years."

"I'm talking about when she was in her forties and fifties, before you knew what it was all about. Her husband was no good, either. Karl Diehl. Forty years ago Karl Diehl was a rum-runner. Every night he and his crowd would be off Montauk, bringing in the liquor. And she'd be entertaining some young man, as brazen a performance as you could ever hope to see."

"Well, it doesn't seem to have shortened her life."

"Ada! What a thing to *say*."

"I know. Aren't I just *terrible,* Mother?"

"Sometimes you say terrible things."

"But fortunately I never *do* anything terrible. It's just talk," said Ada Trimball.

"It may be just talk, but you have to think a thing before you say it."

"Well, you *will* let me have my thoughts, won't you?"

"I could never do anything about that, no matter *how* hard I tried," said Mrs. Trimball. "What's the book?"

"I haven't opened it yet."

"I can see *that,*" said Mrs. Trimball.

"Probably the bird book I ordered for you."

"It took long enough to get here," said Mrs. Trimball. "Any interesting mail? Not that you'd tell me."

"Just an invitation to have dinner at the White House, and a cheque for ten thousand dollars. The usual."

"I can't fathom you, you're so flip this morning. A body might think you enjoyed hearing about Mrs. Diehl. If that's what's responsible, let me remind you that human life is sacred. She wasn't a good woman. She was a bad woman. But that doesn't entitle you to gloat over her passing on."

"But I wasn't gloating. I always rather liked Mrs. Diehl."

"I didn't say you had to like her, Ada. All I said was that it isn't right to ignore the fact that human life is sacred. God puts us on this earth for a purpose, and life is a precious heritage. We must do all we can to preserve life, human or otherwise, our own and everybody else's."

"Cora Dombrowski doesn't think so."

"Cora Dombrowski? At the post office? Are you getting your ideas from her nowadays?"

"I'm not getting *my* ideas from her, but I do listen to *hers.*"

"Well, all I can say to that is, don't try to convert *me* to Cora Dombrowski's ideas."

"The two of you see alike in some things."

"Not many. Not very many. It just happens that the Polish Catholics have it in for the Communists, but don't tell me Cora Dombrowski is against the preservation of human life."

"She's done her share, with five children," said Ada Trimball. "No, she isn't against the preservation of human life. But—"

"But what?"

Ada Trimball could not bring herself to tell her mother what Mrs. Dombrowski had said about old age. "Oh, why talk about Cora Dombrowski?" said Ada Trimball.

"You brought her into the conversation, I didn't," said Mrs. Trimball. She put on her glasses and unfolded her newspaper, and Ada retired to her room.

There was something absurdly exciting in the thought that a letter from Walter Hughes and a letter from Alice Wells had been together in her pocket for almost an hour. Ada Trimball took the letters out of her pocket and she saw that they had been crushed together, very much as though in an embrace, wrinkles fitting into wrinkles and the warmth from her own body penetrating through the letters.

She opened first the letter from Walter: he was going to be duck-shooting in the neighborhood, and could he come by for a drink and a chat with her and her mother. He would be at the Mill Pond Inn. The letter from Alice Wells was ridiculous. "Imagine being ten miles away all these months and not knowing it? This was our first summer on Long Island and Gerald is completely won over. We have an option to buy and I am positive we will, we love it so. I have kept the house open through the fall so that we can come down for long weekends. Gerald has a new hobby, painting. Has taken it up with the same thoroughness he does everything. Really quite good too. Do you still play golf? Maybe we could have a game, but I would just as soon just sit and talk. So much to tell you after—oh, dear? Is it fifteen years? Yes. Fifteen. Please do 'phone me. Mill Pond 3-4832 any Thursday, Friday, Saturday, or Sunday. I usually fly down Thursday after lunch and Gerald flies down the next afternoon. By the way, any time you care to fly back to N.Y. with us on Monday morning there is usually room in the Beech for one or two more passengers."

The coincidence could have been nothing more. If Alice and Walter had taken up with each other again, the very last person in the world they would want to know about it would be Ada Trimball. Plainly, Alice was bored in Mill Pond on her long weekends, so bored that she sought relief in the company of a woman to whom she could display her Gerald, with his thoroughness and his option and his painting and his Beechcraft, as well as his unmentioned oil company (or was it companies?) and box at the opera and fairly recent membership in the Links Club.

"Did you take my glasses by mistake?" Mrs. Trimball never bothered to knock on her daughter's door, not even on her bathroom door.

"Mother, you startled me," said Ada.

"I'm sorry, but I have the wrong glasses. Who's your letter from?"

"Do you remember Alice Ryder?"

"I should say I do. Pushy little thing from Englewood, New Jersey. I should say I do remember her. And her mother. They used me to get her in all the dances, then conveniently forgot us when Alice married that Wells man."

"I was a bridesmaid."

"*That* didn't hurt Alice. What's she writing about now, after all these years?"

"She and her husband have a house down here."

"That's no news, surely. They're in the papers every chance they get. That dance they had last summer. Is she apologizing for not inviting you?"

"Why would anybody invite me to a dance for the Jet Set? No, she wants me to telephone her. They come down weekends."

"Of course. Now that there's nothing to do. I remember how hard she tried to get Walter Hughes, right under your nose, and pretending to be your dearest friend. I hope you remember *that* before you jump at her command."

"Walter Hughes. Walter Hughes. Mother, that was all in your imagination. There was never anything between Walter and I."

"That depends on what you mean by anything. He was too much of a gentleman for some things, but what went on between Walter and Alice Ryder is another matter."

"And no concern of ours, is it?"

Her mother looked at her steadily. "No, not now," said Mrs. Trimball. "But there was a time when it should have concerned you."

"Then I was blissfully ignorant, and if you want your other glasses, I think they're on the sideboard, where you usually leave them."

She could not remember when she had won against her

mother, nor could she think of anything her mother had passed down to her, beginning with her looks. At sixty-six and with a bad heart Constance Trimball was a handsome woman, stout but not fat, and vain of her legs and her complexion. Her hair was not as white naturally as for some preceding years it had been when dyed. She wore light blue cashmere pullovers and always a pearl necklace, which was a combination to complement her blue eyes and her teeth. All her life men had been attentive to her and she had had proposals after the death of her husband, but she had been unwilling to better her financial status in exchange for the companionship of the aging men who were her suitors. "We have enough, you'll have enough, and I won't marry a man that wants to be taken care of," she told her daughter. "I took care of your father gladly, but we had thirty-five good years before that." It was a form of defeat for Ada Trimball that her mother was still getting proposals of marriage at the same time that proposals to Ada were for anything and everything but marriage.

A man would study her—sometimes it would be an old friend, sometimes the husband of an old friend—and she had come to know just when he would suggest a week somewhere, a *cinq à sept* in New York, a flight to Paris, a couple of nights on a cruiser. She had a woman's body, she did not get drunk, and as a lady she could be counted on not to make a fuss. And always, when she came home, her mother would refuse to play the game of lies about her absence. The beginnings and endings of her trips were always the same. "I think I'll run over to Philadelphia to see Peggy's new baby," she would say. And her mother would say, "Of course. You're free to go wherever you please." But her mother would not ask her a single question about the Peggys or their babies or Philadelphia. Mrs. Trimball could not more plainly have shown her disbelief and disapproval, and on occasion she had made small effort to hide her disgust. On such occasions Mrs. Trimball would take her text from the newspapers, decrying and denouncing the immorality of the young and the famous for so long as it took her disgust to wear off, by which time she had effectually destroyed Ada's lingering pleasure in the recent rendezvous.

Now her trips were less frequent and of shorter duration, seldom longer than overnight in New York, and the rendezvous would originate with her and her need. She would go to the booth at the village railway station and telephone one of the men—there were three possibilities. "Would you like to see me sometime this week?" she would say. Rarely would all three men have other plans, but it had happened; and when it did she worked a little harder at home, gave herself extra chores so that her mother would not notice her pain. On such occasions she was glad that she had her reading, her volunteer work with the League of Women Voters, her church activities, the things that she called her busy-busy boondoggling. In a peculiar, self-contradictory way she was glad she had her mother. They could come close, but they had never actually lost control during their flare-ups, never said the terrible things, the unforgivable truths and accusations and counter-accusations, and for Ada Trimball the exercise in self-controlled sarcasm was the nearest to triumph that she ever came; for her mother was a rather stupid woman, not really quick, and Ada was sure that she could inflict hurt, even though it might take some time before her mother, retiring to her room, could think back on what had been said and realize that Ada had been cleverly cruel. There was not enough money for them to live apart from each other in the genteel circumstances they required. As year-round residents of the village where once they had passed only the summers, they were able, first of all, to live in a *house*. They were not, as they said, cooped up in a New York apartment. They had three acres of ground behind a tall hedge. They were in residence. They wore their good country clothes and had their economical German car, and they could refer to themselves as having gone native, which pointed up the difference between the true natives and themselves, so that it was hardly necessary to mention that the true natives were never invited to the Trimball house. Likewise, in June, when the summer people began to arrive, Mrs. Trimball and Ada assumed the position of the established, people who had been there all the time, and the more recent summer people were as much strangers to the Trimball house as the natives. Ten miles away was Mill Pond, with its rich and its Jet Set and their children with their T-Birds and Bikinis, and their noise, vulgarity, and publicity. Ada and her mother were unified in their attitude toward natives, summer people, and Mill Pond. Mill Pond was the perfect place for Alice Wells and her husband, and they were perfect for Mill Pond. Walter Hughes would find few of his old friends still there.

Walter Hughes. Alice Ryder.

Ada Trimball wrote him a note. "Do come. Mother and I would love to see you. I am not going to tell her you are coming but will save your visit for a surprise. So please pretend that you have just dropped in." Her complimentary closing was "Cordially."

The note from Alice Wells required no written answer, which suited Ada Trimball's plans. She wanted to have a look at Walter before doing anything else.

On the afternoon of Walter's visit Ada could not resist telling her mother he was coming. It was a small, but complete triumph. "He wrote me and asked if he could come, and I said of course."

"Why didn't you tell me? What was behind *that?*" Mrs. Trimball's anger was barely controlled. "How do you know I want to see him?"

"You can always be upstairs with a headache."

"Ridiculous! I wish when you're having people to my house you'd tell me."

"I am telling you. Now. But why this sudden animosity towards Walter? I've never heard you say a word against him before. Stay upstairs, if you don't want to see him."

"Oh, you miserable fool!" said Mrs. Trimball.

She recovered her composure before Walter's arrival. She wore her blue bouclé dress, her little pearls, and no other jewelry, not even her wedding ring. When he entered the sitting-room she gave him her hand, but he said: "Don't I rate a kiss?" She put up her cheek and he kissed her.

"Would you like tea, or would you really prefer a drink?" said Ada Trimball.

"If there's tea, I'd rather have that. I limit myself to two drinks before dinner," he said. "Well, this is like old times."

"Where is it you live now? Colorado?" said Constance Trimball.

"Denver. Been there ever since the war, and I guess I'm really settled there."

"I'll get the tea things," said Ada Trimball.

"Can I help?" said Walter Hughes.

"Not a bit. You entertain each other for a minute." Ada left them.

"I've always heard that you have to get used to the altitude in Denver. Is that true?"

"It's true. How *are* you?"

"I'm very well, thanks."

"You look well," he said. "Aren't you surprised to see me?"

"Not at all. Alice Ryder's in Mill Pond, so you were bound to turn up there sooner or later."

"Alice Ryder? I didn't know that. I haven't seen her in nearly twenty years."

"Well, you're both in Mill Pond. She and her husband came there this summer, and they're down every weekend."

"Have you been seeing her?"

"Alice Ryder? Hardly."

"You still don't forgive me my one mistake."

"I was the one that made the mistake, Walter. There was nothing to forgive you."

"I never considered what you did a mistake. What we did. I thought it was beautiful, and I still think so. That's why I wanted to see you again. I'm not a boy any more, and as you get older you look back and remember the few beautiful things that happen in a lifetime. Our—whatever you want to call it —romance—love affair—was beautiful."

"No, I'm afraid it wasn't."

"You never told Mr. Trimball about it, did you?"

"I never told anybody. But it wasn't beautiful, Walter. It was a cold, calculating thing on my part."

"That's simply not true."

"Then I must tell you it was. I wanted you to marry Ada, but Alice Ryder had her cap set for you, and I wanted to take you away from her."

"Well, that didn't work very well. I had an affair with Alice anyway."

"Of course you did. And you always thought I didn't forgive you for that. It wasn't a question of forgiving you, Walter."

"Oh. You mean you just gave me up as a bad job."

"A bad job on my part. I failed. What I tried to do didn't work, and there's Ada today, fighting off being an old maid."

"I never *was* in love with Ada."

"I know that, but she'd have been a good wife for you. She was desperately in love with you. There's never been anybody but you."

"Oh, come."

"You know about Ada?"

"No, but she hasn't stayed a virgin all these years."

"No, but as far as love is concerned she has. So be nice to her."

"Hell, I like Ada. I'd even—"

"But don't. She has men friends. She pulls the wool over my eyes, or so she thinks. But it's never been love."

"And you never loved me at all? Did you ever sleep with anyone else?"

"No."

"Just me and your husband?"

"Yes."

"You slept with me to get me away from Alice."

"I thought I could. I was an attractive woman, Alice was nothing but a little chippy."

"You took an awfully big chance."

"Well, when your children are involved, you do. You have children. You must know that. You fight with the weapons at your disposal."

"I suppose so," he said. "What would Mr. Trimball have said?"

She shook her head. "I don't think he would have believed me."

"Would he have believed me?"

"He might have believed you, Walter. And killed you. He would have thought you were, as they used to say, forcing your attentions on me."

"And the cause of it all is over in Mill Pond."

"The cause of it all is in the kitchen," said Mrs. Trimball.

"Yes, if you look at it that way," he said.

"There's no other way to look at it. And not be ashamed."

Walter Hughes stood up and went to her and took her hand. He raised it to his lips.

She touched the top of his head. "Thank you, Walter," she said, and smiled.

You Can Always Tell Newark

Not many people ever see the game and not all those who see it can follow the scoring, and among those who can score it fewer still can play it, and, finally, in the entire world there are probably fewer than fifty men who play it well. It is a beautiful game to watch, requiring a quick eye, a strong wrist, and a dancer's agility of its players; but as is the case with another exciting game, high goal polo, it can become a bore. Too much skill, too much beauty, too much excitement, too much excellence, and the spectator's attention will wander, in polo, at a symphony concert, in court tennis, as in life itself.

The girl had been applauding good shots during the first set, and applauding them in a way that indicated she had some knowledge of the game. She was sitting in the first row of spectators, and from time to time one of the players, when it was his turn to serve, would address some remark to her, apparently not seeing her, but speaking her name. "How'd you like that one, Nance? Who you betting on, Nance?" he would mutter, and she would smile, and the young people sitting near her would turn and smile at her, with what they deliberately intended to be a knowing smile. There was some small joke between her and them, some special knowledge.

There were three rows of benches for the spectators, benches without backs, but the men and women in the third row could rest their backs against the wall. It was cold on the court, and not warm where the spectators sat, and at the end of the second set, when the two players stopped to sip iced soft drinks, all the spectators rose to stretch. It was then that Williams saw that the girl was pregnant, probably in her seventh month.

When play resumed the girl sat down, but now she knew how tired she was, and she sat with her back against the second-row seats, and the young couple behind her, in the second row, made room for her, but it was an uncomfortable position. Williams watched her; she was tired, and once she hunched her shoulders in an involuntary reaction to the cold. Williams, from his seat in the third row, tapped her arm, and she turned and looked up at him, a stranger and an elderly stranger at that.

"Wouldn't you like to sit up here? Support your back? We can make room for you," said Williams.

"Oh, no thanks. I'm all right, thank you." She smiled with her mouth only. Now she sat up straight and lit a cigarette, and there was exasperation in the forceful blowing out of smoke and in her stiff manner of sitting. Plainly she was annoyed that a stranger had noticed her pregnancy and tiredness, and she did not look at Williams again. She wanted no help from anyone. When the match was over and the winner and loser were photographed receiving their silver bowls she did not applaud.

"What's the matter, Nance?" said one of her young companions. "Just because your man lost?"

"Oh, shut up," she said. "And stop *saying* that. Let's get out of here."

"There's free booze," said one of the young men.

"Oh, all right," said the girl. "But let's not stay forever? I'm cold."

"Have a couple of scoops and it'll warm you up," said the young man.

The picture-taking over, the player who had been speaking *sotto voce* to Nancy crossed the court to the place where she had been sitting. "Hey, Joe, where's Nancy?" he said. "Isn't she staying? She go?"

"She's staying. Hard luck, by the way."

"No, he beat me. Listen, tell her to be sure and wait, will you? I have to take a shower, I stink. But I won't be more than ten or fifteen minutes. Will you tell her?"

"Okay, Rex. See you," said Joe.

"Be sure and tell her, Joe. Now don't let her go home without my seeing her. I'll be fifteen minutes at the most," he said, then, in a lower voice: "Is Bud here?"

Joe laughed. "Bud come to see you, especially when you had a chance of winning? Get *with* it, boy."

"Well, I wanted to be sure. I have to go back to New York on the seven o'clock train."

They were all young enough so that what was overheard by someone as old as Williams did not matter. He was fifty, and they were their own world.

"Well, Ned, shall we go have some of that free booze?" said Williams's host and companion.

"Sure," said Williams. The two men smiled.

"Aren't you glad we have all that behind us?" said Smith.

"Sometimes I am," said Williams. "Who is she?"

"I'm all prepared," said Smith. "Her name is Nancy Phillips, married to Bud Phillips. They live in Chestnut Hill. Her name *was* Nancy Standish. That ought to help you."

"*Oh*. That *does* help. The daughter of Bob Standish and Evie Jeffcott."

"Uh-huh."

"No wonder I was drawn to her, so to speak."

"I was terribly amused, you know," said Smith. "I thought God damn it, here is history repeating itself right before my very eyes."

"Is that what you thought?"

"That's what I thought. Don't you think she looks a lot like Evie?"

"Well now I do, but it never occurred to me before," said Williams. "And it isn't actually that she looks so much like Evie."

"No, not terribly much, but at least you're consistent."

"Yes, I guess you could say that. So is the girl, for that matter. Her mother didn't like me the first time she saw me, either."

"She made up for it," said Smith. "We go down this way."

"Why didn't she say hello to you? Where are her manners?"

"What manners? None of them have any manners any more. No manners, no style, no ambition. They're a bunch of self-centered little pigs."

"I wonder what we were?" said Williams.

"Self-centered little pigs, no doubt, but we damn well had our manners drilled into us. These little bastards blame our generation for the state of the world. I think they're taught that in school and college. So they hate us. Really hate us, Ned. I don't think there's a God damn one of them that ever stops to think that we weren't responsible for 1929. We were the victims of it. And World War Two, we get blamed for that. What the hell did we have to do with it? We went, that's all. We had to go, so we went. But these little pricks blame us for the whole damn shooting-match. They don't even know their history. Or Social Studies, as they call it. Jesus Christ! You're lucky you have no children."

"You make me think I am."

"Well, as you know, I have four, and after they're ten years old they start taking pot-shots, and by the time they're fifteen— oh, brother. 'Daddy, you just don't *know.*' That's their stock answer for everything. I just don't know about segregation, or about war. I have one snot-nose about to go in the Army and *he*'s telling *me* how awful war is. And if I *told* him about Guadal he'd accuse me of wallowing in it, so I've never told him. I've learned to keep my mouth shut, the only way to avoid having a scene. 'Daddy, you just don't *know.*' If I'd said that to my father I'd have been clouted over the head. And if one of my sisters had said it to my father, my mother would have taken good care of her. Actually they loved my father, in a way that my daughters have never loved me. They still think he was a great and wonderful man, and all he was was an honest, decent, strict father. The whole purpose of my existence is when I get through paying for their education, to come through with an Austin-Healey for graduation. As a matter of fact I couldn't have paid for their education without help from their various grandparents. Betty and I just get by, and you know how much

I make. This booze is free, so drink it up, boy. Would you like to meet Nancy?"

"Is she like the others?"

"I think so, but you can find out for yourself. She pretended not to see me before, but we'll just go right up to her. Come on. Be brave."

The men pushed through to where Nancy Phillips was leaning against a table. "Hello there, Nancy."

"Oh, hello, Mr. Smith. Have you been here all the time?" She had a drink in her hand and she smiled agreeably enough.

"Sitting right behind you. I want you to meet a friend of your mother's. *And* father's. This is Mr. Williams, Mr. Ned Williams."

"Oh, hello, Mr. Williams. *You* were there, I saw *you*. At least—weren't you the one that . . . ?"

"I'm the one that."

"Did you ever sit on anything as uncomfortable as those benches? Mr. Smith, *can't* this club afford something more *comfortable?*"

"You better take that up with your father. He's on the board. Where was he today, by the way?"

"Oh, hunting, I guess. Saturday, this time of year. Are you over from New York, Mr. Williams?"

"Just for the day."

"Just to see the match?"

"More or less. Partly business with Mr. Smith. How's your mother?"

"Mummy's fine, or I guess she is. I haven't seen her for a couple of weeks. We live in Chestnut Hill, and Mummy and Daddy are still in Ardmore. Do you know Philadelphia, Mr. Williams?"

"I used to."

"Before your mother married your father, he means," said Smith.

"Oh, you were a *beau* of Mummy's? What was she like then?"

"I don't know that she was any different then from now. I

saw her about a year ago. Nowadays I seem to see her and your father at weddings, for the most part."

"I meant as a—what did they call them—flapper? Was she a flapper, my mother?"

"I wouldn't think so, would you?" Williams asked Smith.

"Definitely not. But definitely," said Smith.

"Well, you, Mr. Williams. Were you a—playboy? I guess that would be the opposite of flapper."

"George? Was I?"

"I don't know why you say 'Was I?' As far as I know, you still are."

"Oh, are you, Mr. Williams?"

"You sound incredulous. No, I was never one of the outstanding playboys. As we used to say, I got around."

"Then how did you and Mummy get together, if Mr. Smith is right." She did not wait for an answer but said, largely to herself, "Still—Bud and I."

"Well of course we *didn't* get together or you'd be my daughter instead of Bob Standish's."

"I didn't necessarily mean that close together, Mr. Williams."

"Well, now the conversation is taking a decided turn for the better," said Smith.

"It's taken a turn, all right," said the girl. "So let's turn back."

"Any direction you say," said Williams.

Now, before any more could be said, they were joined by the tennis player, whose hair was wet. "Hello, Nance," he said.

"Hello, Rex. I'd like you to know Mr. Smith, and Mr. Williams. This is Rex Ivers, who played such spec*tac*ular tennis this afternoon. Spec*tac*ular."

"Mr. Smith. Mr. Williams. Oh, hello, Mr. Williams. I've met Mr. Williams."

"I thought you played extremely well," said Williams. "Your only trouble was that you missed the easy ones."

"Four straight. But he beat me. He played better."

"Oh, you're such a good, good sport, Rex," said Nancy.

"Well, what's wrong with that? Anyway, I'm not such a good, good sport. I wish I were."

"Yes you are, that's why you missed the easy ones, as Mr. Williams said. You were playing like a good sport instead of to win, and I consider that insulting to my opponent."

"*He* doesn't feel insulted. He got the hardware, and some of my cash."

"Oh, you actually bet on yourself?" said Nancy. "You had money going on this match?"

"Yes. We bet a hundred dollars apiece. I think you put the whammy on me. Every one of those easy shots I missed, I just happened to be facing in your direction."

"Oh, of course. And I waved my handkerchief to distract you."

"I didn't say that. I meant it as a compliment, what I did say. Where's Bud?"

"He sent his regrets," said the girl.

"I think we'll leave you two," said Smith.

"Say hello to your mother, and your father," said Williams.

"I will, thank you. Nice to've seen you," said the girl.

Smith and Williams rode the elevator in silence and went to the bar, seated themselves, ordered drinks. "Well, that was a happy thought," said Smith.

"Oh, I wanted to meet her."

"I didn't mean that. I was thinking about how she could have been your daughter."

"Oh, I see. Well, is this her first child?"

"It's no excuse. At this moment she's probably raking him over the coals, and he's so much in love with her that it's coming out of his eyes."

"That's very poetic."

"Entirely accidental. Tell me about Ivers. I didn't know you knew him."

"I don't. I just see him at the club and I guess I've met him there a few times. I was surprised he remembered me. Now *he* has good manners."

"Yes, but where does it get him in his own crowd? They not only don't appreciate good manners. Did you happen to notice during the match, he'd say something to her. Nice. And those others with her, they'd all look wise, as if they knew the whole story."

"I did notice that, yes. What's her husband like?"

"He's still in medical school, out at the University. I think he has another year to go."

"Bob Standish has plenty of money."

"Oh, the Phillipses are loaded too. No money problem there. The problem is going to be when she finds out what it's like to be the wife of a doctor. It's tough enough now, of course, while Bud's in medical school, but just wait till she finds out what the first few years are going to be like."

"She seems to be having a very hard time of it."

"For God's sake, why?"

"Oh, well there you've got me."

"Hell of an attractive mother, father's a nice guy, husband working his ass off trying to be something. Plenty of money. A nice young guy in love with her, obviously. And she's having a baby. I don't know what else a young girl could want."

"Is there any chance that this baby belongs to Ivers?"

"Oh, there's always that chance, but she didn't greet him like the father of her child. Is Ivers married, do you happen to know?"

"I happen to know he's not."

"And she's a good-looking little bitch, too. Add that to the rest of her complaints. Quite a shape, when her belly's flat."

"I could see that it would be."

"Ned?"

"What?"

"She *isn't* your daughter, by any chance?"

"Well, you know, George. She could be. Evie never said so, and I was hoping you wouldn't ask, but I was just figuring it out. She could be, mathematically."

"I sort of thought so. At least as a possibility."

"As you said, there was always that chance, but you'd think Evie would have told me."

"I wouldn't think anything of the kind."

"No, I guess not. Evie was a hard one to figure sometimes."

"Why didn't you and Evie get married?"

"Before she married Bob?"

"Yes."

"Because she wasn't in love with me."

"Oh, come."

"She wasn't. She said so."

"She gave you enough proof to the contrary."

"She didn't consider that proof of anything, except of course that she considered me safe to go to bed with. But her family were against it, and God knows I wasn't very reliable in those days, and Bob had been hanging around for years."

"But then after she married Bob?"

"Well—then she discovered she was in love with me. All right, I'll give it to you straight. She wanted to divorce Bob and I was the one that prevented it. Plus the fact that I was leaving for Quantico. It was just before Pearl. Maybe I was running away from marriage, I don't know. But that's why we didn't get married. Mathematically, this girl could be the result of the summer of '41. My daughter. George, I think she is."

"I think so too."

"Something. Even before I knew her name, who she was. I felt protective. You know, when I offered her a seat with us?"

"Sure, sure."

"And it was more than her resemblance to Evie. Maybe not more. Different from. Apart from. She didn't feel anything, though."

"Yes she did."

"Yes, I guess she did."

"Something bothered her. She looked at you, and maybe she saw something without any idea of what it was. Some resemblance to herself, maybe. Not only the color of your eyes, but the shape of them."

"Maybe that's what *I* saw."

"And maybe she did too. That can be very baffling, to see resemblances to yourself in your children. Elusive. And if you didn't know of the relationship, God knows how disturbing it might be. I imagine it must be especially true for girls, who spend a lot more time looking at themselves than we do. You didn't get any feeling that she resented you because you were on the make, did you?"

"No."

"Neither did I. She was annoyed, but that wasn't what annoyed her. Well, we've got it all figured out." Smith raised his glass. "Congratulations, Papa."

"Thank you."

"Now you're one of us. The rejected generation."

"Are we rejected, George? I'd hate to think that."

"Two hours ago you didn't give a damn."

"Two hours ago I certainly didn't. But I'll never be the same as I was two hours ago."

"No, you won't. Are you going to say anything to Evie?"

"I don't know. I don't know whether she'd tell me the truth."

"Do you need to have her tell you?"

"A little bit. Yes."

"Why don't you depend on your instinct, and to hell with what Evie says or doesn't say? Don't even ask her."

"Maybe I won't. I wish I could talk to the girl again."

"That can be arranged. My daughter sees her fairly frequently. That's comparatively easy."

"Before she has her baby?"

"Ned, nobody dies in childbirth any more, if that's worrying you."

"No, but it was cold up there today."

"Nobody dies of pneumonia, either."

"Well then what the hell *do* all these people die of?"

"Worry, so stop it," said Smith. "I don't want to rush you, Ned, but if you're counting on making the seven o'clock train . . ."

The seven o'clock to New York was a train that originated in Washington and it was late, with the result that the train crew wanted no time wasted at the Thirtieth Street station. Passengers were hurried off, passengers were hurried on, and the confusion was worse than usual. An Air Force second lieutenant with a flight kit and a guitar was blocked by passengers trying to board the train, and he in turn refused to budge for them. In the disorder the train was held up for six minutes, and the delay was fortunate for Rex Ivers, who came running down the steps, taking them two or three at a leap. He had a small suitcase and an old pigskin tennis bag of a vintage that had not been manufactured in more than twenty years. He stowed the luggage on the shelf at the end of the car, and considered where to sit. There were vacant seats, but most of them had coats or hats that belonged to passengers who were in the dining-car. "Taken? Taken? Taken?" said Ivers, walking down the aisle. "Hello, Mr. Williams? Is this taken?"

"Probably, but so's the one I'm sitting in," said Williams. "They can eat or they can sit, but they can't do both."

"There'll be a row," said Ivers.

"What if there is? I'm not budging. Have a seat till they come —and I'll bet they stay in the diner till Newark."

"All right. I'm with you," said Ivers. He seemed to be a little bit tight. His hair, now dry, fell down over his forehead. His club tie was crooked, the knot somewhere under the collar. And there was lipstick on his chin.

"I see someone saw you off, affectionately," said Williams.

"Why? Oh, have I got telltale traces?"

"On your chin."

Ivers moistened his handkerchief and rubbed the lipstick off. "All gone?"

"All gone," said Williams.

"Listen, go ahead and read your paper, sir. I don't want to bother you."

"Oh, that's all right. Light's not very good. But I may doze off."

"Yes, I might too."

"I should think you would."

"I had a couple of scoops. If I'd won I'd be high, but I lost, so the only effect is to make me sleepy."

"Have you got your ticket? Give it to me and I'll give it to the conductor."

"Sir, but you want to take a nap."

"After North Philadelphia. Push that gadget and the seat goes back. Get yourself a nap."

"Well—thanks very much. Just a nap's all I want." He handed his ticket to Williams, altered the angle of the seat, stretched out and was asleep in three minutes, heavily, deeply, helplessly, rather sadly asleep.

"Teeks for North Philadelphia. North Philadelphia teeks please," said the trainman.

Williams read his *Evening Bulletin,* saw that the sleeping young man at his right—according to this edition of the newspaper—was one of the finalists in the court tennis tournament. It was strange to come upon this item after the outcome had been decided, like having a look into the future with the certainty that what one saw would take place. Williams read the item again, then turned to the Evening Chat column, which contained society news. At this moment some people he knew in Wynnewood were getting ready to receive guests for dinner: Mr. and Mrs. John Arthur Kersley will entertain at dinner this evening in honor of their daughter Willela Kersley, whose engagement, etc. What if he knew the score of that dinner party, as he now knew the score of Ivers's tennis match? What if he could call up Jack Kersley and tell him for God's sake not to let John Jones sit next to Mary Brown, that before the night was over John Jones would say something to Mary Brown that would wreck their lives? What if he could call Mary Brown and tell her not to listen to anything John Jones said? And what if he had been able to speak to Rex Ivers and persuade him to default, so that he would not have gone to Philadelphia and seen Nancy. "My daughter."

"I beg your pardon?"

"Oh—I must have dozed off," said Williams.

Young Ivers grinned. "Like somebody hit you with a croquet mallet."

"Where are we?" said Williams. He looked out the window but could not identify landmarks.

"We just passed through New Brunswick," said Ivers.

"New Brunswick? How long have you been awake?"

"Oh, I guess I only slept about ten minutes. I woke up just after North Philadelphia. Here's your paper, sir, I borrowed it. Gave me a funny feeling to read about my match before it happened. You know, when this was printed, I was on equal terms with my worthy opponent. Now I'm second banana."

"Do you know Jack Kersley?" said Williams.

"Kersley? No, I don't think so. Should I?"

"No, I just happened to think of him. Lives in Philadelphia."

"I might have met him this week. I met a lot of guys during the tournament. Oh, I did meet an older man named Kersley. Has he got a daughter, Wilhelmina or something like that?"

"Yes he has."

"Then I did meet him. What made you mention him?"

"I don't really know," said Williams. "I guess I'm still in a bit of a fog."

"Why don't you go back to sleep?"

"No, no. A nap was all I wanted."

"You know, when you said Jack Kersley, that didn't register. But the daughter is a friend of a friend of mine. In fact, my girl. My girl is going to a dinner party at the Kersleys' tonight. The girl that saw me off at the station."

"Oh, you have a girl in Philadelphia?"

"Yes. Not the way that sounds, though. A girl in Philadelphia. A girl in Boston. A girl in Chicago."

"This is the real thing? The one and only, we used to say."

"Yes. Married, though."

"Have to watch out for that," said Williams.

"Telling *me*. Do you remember my father? Was killed in World War Two?"

"Sure, I knew him. A fine man."

"That's what everybody says, without fail. But I never knew him. I was three years old when he joined the Navy, and honestly I have no recollection of him except what I hear from my mother and his friends. And I couldn't possibly live up to his reputation. Not possibly. God, at school they had his name on a tablet and every time I got into trouble, sure as hell some master would take me for a walk and steer me in the direction of the memorial. You know. Illustrating the lecture. What I'm getting at is I guess I have some kind of a guilt complex because my father was this idol, and here I am, the original mixed-up kid. It's not something you go to the head-shrinker for, and yet I don't know any minister I'd feel like talking to. That's what it is, too. More of a religious problem."

"Ethical."

"Ethical, right. This girl would marry me. She wants to divorce her husband and marry me."

"Well, if you love her. And you say she's your girl."

"It isn't all that easy. The husband hates me, and he has good reason to. He knows I was there first, she told him. But he's—he's doing something constructive. He's doing something, a line of work, that takes up all his time and energy, and it's worthwhile work. If she left him, it wouldn't only be their marriage. Well, I don't think you know the people, so I'll tell you. The husband is studying to be a doctor and they say he's brilliant. Brilliant. But I know he's dependent on her. Not financially, but for moral support. She's dependent on me—for immoral support. Or was. I hadn't seen her till today, she turned up at the tennis match with her crowd. And she came with me to the station. God, she wants me to get a job in Philadelphia, and she'll get a divorce, and we'll get married, and the hell with her husband. There's a certain reason why she wants me to be in Philadelphia now. Sort of a crisis going on."

"Well, as I see it, Rex, the thing that's holding you back is this ethical problem. Your girl's husband and his career. But where does that leave her and the child?"

"The child? Do you know who it is?"

"I think I sat two rows behind your girl at the match. The crisis is she's having a baby, isn't it?"

"Jesus, yes. Then you know who the girl is."

"Yes, I know who the girl is."

"I know you were talking to her afterward but I didn't figure you'd guess anything. Well, sir, what would you do? As an unprejudiced observer."

"Well, I have an ethical problem, too. My ethical problem is whether to advise you one way or the other. As a matter of fact, Rex, my problem is really more difficult than yours."

"Yes, I suppose it is," said Ivers. "Why should you get into the act, eh? It isn't your responsibility." The young man chewed his lip thoughtfully. "Mr. Williams, I hope you don't think I go around blabbing stuff this way all the time."

"Of course I don't, Rex."

"Well, I *don't*. If you knew me better you'd know that. I don't know whether it was because I had a couple of drinks or what. I wish I could convince you of that."

"Don't let it bother you."

"The thing is, it does bother me. I hope everything I told you is in the strictest confidence."

"It will be."

"Have I got your word on that?"

"You have my word. I promise you I won't repeat any of this conversation to anybody."

"I wish you could forget everything I told you."

"That I can't promise."

The young man was still very uneasy. "You see, Mr. Williams, this girl's had everything she ever wanted."

"Except marriage to you."

"Yes, but it wouldn't work out now. It never will work out. She thinks she wants to be married to me, but it wouldn't last a year before she was discontented. And meanwhile she'd have broken up her marriage and possibly ruined her husband's career, and the kid wouldn't have a father. In other words, this is the time for somebody to make sense, and it's up to me to be the one."

"Probably."

"So—what I'm getting at, the importance of keeping this confidential. Nancy will get over this and stay with her husband, and in two years it'll all be a thing of the past."

"And you don't think you're being tough on her."

"No tougher on her than I am on myself. She's my girl, Mr. Williams. Make no mistake about that."

"Rex, I'm going to ask you a question you may not like."

"You're entitled to ask anything you please."

"What if this baby she's having is yours?"

"If it was, I think she would have told me."

"Would that have made a difference, to you?"

The boy—for now he looked about seventeen—shook his head. "No. It would make things tougher for me, but as long as she didn't tell Bud, her husband, she and the baby are better off."

"Thank you."

"Why do you say that?"

"Oh—thank you for trusting me with your confidences."

"Hell, I ought to be thanking you. And I do. You know, her father and mother, they're your generation, but they don't seem to know what it's all about. I could never talk to them the way I've talked to you. Of course that may be Philadelphia."

"It may be Philadelphia."

"Nancy does a big production of laughing at the whole thing, but you'd never get her out of Philadelphia."

"I guess not. Well, here's Newark. I can always tell Newark, can't you?"

"Yes, you can always tell Newark."

The High Point

One day late in the fifth decade of the century Ruth Styles went to the mailbox, which was in a cluster of mailboxes for the convenience of the rural route man. She extracted the little bundle of mail and took it back with her to her kitchen. Ruth Styles played a daily game of suspense; she always waited until the mail was on the kitchen table, until she had poured herself a cup of coffee and lighted a cigarette, before putting on her reading glasses and examining the items in the post. She would discard the junk—the items addressed to Patron and Boxholder, and the shopping center publications and the more uninteresting catalogs—and she would make little piles of her bills, her husband's letters and bills, the mail for the children, and the mail that was personally for her. In this way she got as much enjoyment out of her letters and out of the daily-except-Sunday ritual as it was possible to get. It was the high point of the morning; sometimes the high point of the day; and on this morning one letter should have been the high point—of years.

The letter was from Ray Kemmerer. The handwriting was instantly recognized; as long as she lived she would always recognize that handwriting, the carefully made letters like precisely enunciated speech; the uniform height of the small letters and of the capitals above the line; the slant; the overlarge part of the small letters and capitals below the line; the flow of ink from the same stub pen—probably the same Parker fountain pen—he had preferred since freshman year in college. She smiled and said aloud: "Now what does Ray Kemmerer, Tonawanda Manufacturing Company, Erie, Pennsylvania, want from Mrs. Edwin

D. Styles, Oak Road, Knollcrest, New Jersey? And how did he get my address?"

The letter was written entirely by hand on a good grade of business paper: "Dear Ruth:—I am sorry to have to tell you that Mother passed away on the 5th of last month. She has been in ill health for over a year & the doctors gave up hope for her several months before the end. Everything was done to make her comfortable, but she must have suffered a great deal in the final months. We welcomed the end to her suffering although she did not complain. She was always very fond of you, as I know you were of her, hence this brief note. I got your address through Sally Moffat when she and Ken stopped by a few weeks ago. Hope all goes well with you and your family. Sincerely, Ray Kemmerer."

She reread the letter twice and put it back in the envelope. Sincerely, Ray Kemmerer. Sincerely, Nobody. Sincerely, Nothing. Sincerely, the man whose presence on the face of the earth had once meant the difference between life with love and life unlived. Sincerely, the object of twenty years of scorn and jest and mockery.

Ted Styles had been thorough, and the arrival of this letter made her realize how completely successful his thoroughness had been. She had smiled in recognition of the handwriting; but the letter itself was the letter of a dullard, a clod, a semi-literate, presumptuous, oversentimental mediocrity. Ray Kemmerer was none of these things, but he might as well have been; it was the way Ted had made her see him. The letter that was supposed to announce the death of a woman who had been nice to her son's friends was in truth a confirmation of the slow murder of Ruth Styles' first love. "Oh, Ted, you really did a job on him," she said. The letter was an embarrassment; she could guess at her husband's every comment, from the handwriting to the vulgar ampersand, to the cautious wording. "Nothing here that couldn't be read in open court," Ted Styles would say. "How do you suppose they welcomed the end of the old lady's suffering? Did they beat on pots and pans? Or with firecrackers, like the Chinese?" She would not show him the letter, but only because she was already certain of his comments, which embarrassed her without being spoken.

She hid the letter in a book that Ted would never take down from the shelf, a collection of pieces by a passé humorist. It was the safest place in the house, and she had used it on other occasions. Ted regarded her continuing enjoyment of the collection as an indication of taste not far above the level of a child's ragbook of animal pictures. The hiding place thus became especially appropriate for Ray Kemmerer's letter. She did not ask herself why she was saving the letter, but in the following weeks she liked knowing that it was there. After a deliberate delay she wrote a reply: "Dear Ray—Thank you for letting me know about your mother. As you say, I was always very fond of her. Since I learned about her too late to send flowers, I have made a small donation to the Presbyterian Missions in her memory. Sincerely, Ruth." Another letter that could be read in open court, and cold enough to discourage further correspondence.

Ruth Styles wanted no correspondence with Ray Kemmerer, and did not wish to see him again. Assuming that his looks had not been damaged or had even been improved upon by the passage of twenty years, he would now be, at best, a handsome man in his late forties, with tight curly hair cut short and parted in the middle, probably deeply tanned in the summer to make darker his dark complexion. Without a doubt he would be a golfer and bridge-player, since he had played golf and bridge as a young man. He had also been a football player at his obscure Ohio college, and golf, bridge, football and the obscure Ohio college had been subjects for Ted's campaign of ridicule. She was not sure what the Tonawanda Manufacturing Company manufactured, but he was vice-president and general manager of it, according to the letterhead. It was easy enough to imagine him, without seeing him, in a white dinner jacket at a country club dance, and if he was not president of the club, he probably had been. Whatever he was now, she was aware that the picture she was creating was strongly influenced by the twenty years' comments by Ted Styles, and the contemporary Ray Kemmerer was not her Ray Kemmerer, real or in fancy. In fancy he was the result of the prejudices introduced by Ted Styles; in the real he was a man whom she had not seen in twenty years, who was married to another woman, and who seemed to have recovered from the disaster to his love affair with Ruth Cooper.

But as months passed after the arrival of Ray Kemmerer's letter she found that now and then she would go to her book-shelf and take down the volume of humorous pieces and hold the letter in her hand. She seldom put on her glasses to read it; there was nothing of interest or warmth or comfort in the words. And yet there was warmth and comfort in the physical letter and in the shape of the blurred words, so little different from the shape of the passionate words he had written in other times. Between the "Ruth" at the beginning of the letter and the "Ray" at the end she could fill in other words of letters she had long since destroyed: "I love you even when I am not thinking about you," he had once written. "I start thinking about you and I realize that I have been loving you all the time." So long as she had the letter in her hand she could substitute, by recollection, the contents of letters she had not saved. And in so doing she would be, for ten minutes, the girl he had written to when he was writing her every night.

She was alone a large part of the day; the children were away at school, and Ted was in New York. It made not much difference to anyone how she passed her time between taking Ted to the train in the morning and meeting him in the late afternoon. It actually made very little difference to anyone how she spent her time *any* time. The children at their expensive schools (paid for by their two grandfathers) spent less and less of their vacations at home, more and more of their holidays visiting friends. Ted had his work, which was more than a job; he designed textiles, and in the firm's interest he frequently lectured at art schools and trade conventions. He was good, he had a reputation, and he had achieved a nice duality in the worlds of art and industry. In either field he partook of the prestigious benefits of the other. "What I am is simply an artistic whore in a Wetzel suit," he would say. "A clean-shaven, solvent beatnik." He was very disarming; his utter frankness was especially effective among new acquaintances, who would immediately credit him with astuteness behind the candor. Most men did not like him, most women did not trust him, but men respected his success and women from time to time had to satisfy their curiosity about him in brief interludes that seldom endured as affairs. His children "adored" him. Ruth said they adored him because he had the gift of treating them as equals, of seeing things their way while subtly making them see things his way. He was bad for her kind of discipline; he gave them sips of wine when they were very young, gave them money when they had exhausted their allowances, taught them naughty limericks, encouraged them to question the authority of their teachers. But he was also quick and sometimes cruel with punishment when they did not instantly obey him, and when she protested that he was being unfair to them his reply was that children did not expect a parent to be fair: "Children are little beasts. They'd knife us in our beds if they could get away with it. Neddy strangled a kitten when he was five years old, don't forget. And I give you Jocelyn Styles and the way she used to beat up on her brother. Fairness? They don't know the meaning of the word."

"But I'm trying to teach them," said Ruth.

"Don't. It's a waste of time, and it's no preparation for life anyway. That baseball fellow, I agree with him. Nice guys don't win."

"Your father is a nice guy," she said. "So is mine."

"My father was afraid of his own shadow, and luckily I found that out when I was three years old. As to your father, Ruth, I don't see any difference between a Philadelphia lawyer and a Pittsburgh lawyer. The whole idea of the practice of law is to learn all the rules so that you can get around them. While we're on the subject of fairness, if there really were any such thing, lawyers would be the worst offenders. Because they're supposed to *know* what's fair. It's all written out for them. And yet they get rich by trickery and distortion of what they've been taught. The only thing that's fair about the law is that there's always another son of a bitch trying to trick *your* son of a bitch. And there's a super-son of a bitch in a black robe to judge the whole disgraceful exhibition. Very amusing."

She had no resources against such arguments. In the very beginning he had seduced her with words before going on to the physical seduction. "You never had an affair with Tarzan?" he had said, in one of his first destructive references to Ray Kemmerer.

"We never went all the way."

"Well, for God's sake, you weren't fascinated by that fine mind. What did you ever talk about?"

They had talked about love and the life they would have together, but she was ashamed to say so to this Ted Styles person. "I don't know, just talk."

"Me Tarzan, you Ruthie?"

"Please don't say any more," she said, and it was as close as she ever came to a defense of Ray Kemmerer or loyalty to their love. She married Ted Styles and allowed Ray Kemmerer to become a tiresome joke. As the wife of Ted Styles she even agreed with his aspersions on Ray's manhood.

"You could always get him to stop?"

"I told you a thousand times," she said.

"But *you* didn't want to stop."

"Yes I did. I didn't with you, but I did with him."

"Something wrong there, somewhere. He looked like a skiing instructor, but he was just too nice."

"Maybe that was it, I don't know. Why talk about him? I never even think about him."

"Maybe you ought to think about him. Think what I rescued you from. He didn't know the first thing about you."

"No, I guess not. I didn't know myself very well, either."

"That's for sure. If you'd married him you'd have been all over the place in six months. Divorced in two years, at the most."

"Probably. I don't know."

"Sure you would. Some son of a bitch like me would have come along and you'd have been the talk of Sewickley."

"We wouldn't have lived in Sewickley. His family came from Erie."

"God, that would have been worse, although I've never been to Erie."

He had compelled her to tell him in detail all there was to tell about her romance with Ray Kemmerer, and since there had been so little to tell, he had allowed his curiosity to subside; but for that very reason it had been easy for him to use Kemmerer as a symbol of the dullness of her life before he entered it. In their marriage, in their conversations, a Kemmerer was a private word as representative in its way as Babbitt to the general public; and until the arrival of Ray's note she had had no sense of loss, no feeling of regret that her first love had been taken away from her, no twinge of conscience for having permitted the denigration of a man who had failed only in ruthlessness. Once there had been a time when his kisses were exciting enough to make her pregnant, if excitement alone had had the secret of potency; there had been a time when death was understandable because it was a form of separation from Ray; the moon and music had once been meaningful because they enjoyed them with each other. And her present habit of saving the best letter for the last had begun in the days when he wrote every night, when she would turn the key in her bedroom door so that no one would interrupt that first reading. One day she had folded a letter and tucked it in the pocket of a tennis dress, and when she had finished playing and at last could read it, it was gone. In terror and in tears she had gone back to the court, searched the clubhouse, questioned the club servants, all without success. It was gone, lost, and gone and lost forever. Nothing could ever replace it, nothing ever did. Ray repeated in another letter as much as he could recall of the original, but it was not the same and there was a hole in her life.

They had two couples for dinner and Ted had a captive audience. "It isn't so much the fear of the bomb," he was saying.

"You hear people spouting forth that the decline of humor is because of the bomb, the times we live in. Hell, we've always lived in *times*. The real reason for the decline of humor is that it's all been said. There were so damn many humorists that they covered everything there was to write about. Ruth has the right idea. *She* still reads Ransford."

"Ransford? God, that dates you," said Emily Choate.

"Not the only thing that dates me," said Ruth.

"Remember *you* said that, not *I*," said Ted.

"All right, I'll remember," said Ruth. "Ransford was terribly funny."

"He probably appealed to a certain kind of background. I mean people with a good, solid, middle-class American background," said Ted.

"That's me," said Ruth.

"It's all of us in this room," said Ted.

"Not you, for heaven's sake, Ted," said Emily Choate.

"Sure me, why not me? You too, and Tom and Alicia and Bud. We all have the same background. I *didn't* say I haven't tried to rise *above* it. I did. And I never was amused by Mr. Ransford." Suddenly he left the room and came back with the Ransford collection. He opened the book, took out Ray Kemmerer's letter, frowned at it and tossed it in Ruth's lap. "I'll read you a sample of Ransford. I think this was in the old *Life*. It's a piece about spending a weekend in the country, and *God*, how many humorists have had a whack at that." He read the piece in a voice pitched slightly higher than his normal speaking voice, and when one of the men chuckled he looked over his reading glasses and stared sternly. "That's funny? I must read it again." He finished the piece, closed the book and tossed it to Ruth. "Ransford got rich on that kind of stuff. He used to get two or three thousand dollars for one of those little adventures, so I was told. And the mothers of the John Mason Brown ladies just doted on him."

At midnight the guests departed, and Ted said: "Who's the letter from?"

"Ray Kemmerer."

"Let me see it," he said.

"No."

"Why not?"

"Because it's my letter," she said.

"Well, we won't have any of that," he said. He snatched the book out of her hands, tossed it back at her and opened the letter.

"I warn you not to read that letter," she said.

" 'Tonawanda Manufacturing Company, Erie, Pennsylvania, September 20th, 1959. Dear Ruth.' " He read the letter aloud, put it back in the envelope and threw it to her. "So poor dear Mummy passed on. What the hell was the objection to my reading that? Is it in some kind of code? Let me see it again."

"No."

"Oh, all right. I don't want to struggle with you." He sat across the coffee table and lit a cigarette. "What interests me is why you'd save a letter like that. And of course it isn't the letter, it's because it came from that All-Time All-American dullard. Do you mean to say that after all these years you've discovered that you're in love with him?"

"I don't mean to say anything."

"Why don't you say something about Emily Choate?" he said. "Isn't that sort of on your mind?"

"Not very much. Not any more."

"Oh."

"Not as much as she was on yours."

"Are you implying that I had an affair with Emily?"

"No, I'm implying that you didn't but wanted to."

"It's there any time I want it," he said.

"I don't think so. A year ago, maybe, but not now."

"You're quite right about that. If she hadn't been so eager."

"And you hadn't been so busy elsewhere. I'm going to bed."

"Sit up and talk a while. I want to find out more about that letter. Why did you keep it?"

"I don't know, but it's really none of your business."

"Take it out of its hiding place from time to time? Sigh over young love? What might have been?"

"Something like that," she said.

"Are you planning to see him? First of all, *have* you seen him?"

"No."

"But naturally you answered the letter."

"Naturally," she said.

"Did you, uh, leave the latchstring out, so to speak?"

"I don't know that I'd say that," she said.

"Well, *would* you say that you raised the drawbridge?"

"No, I wouldn't say that, either."

"You answered him in kind, then, I suppose. In other words, the next move is up to him. Well, you know what that will be, of course. He didn't write you just to tell you about his old lady. So what do you plan to do when he tries to see you, a quiet lunch at the Hotel Astor?"

"If I decide to see him it won't be for a quiet lunch at the Astor."

"Buckity-buckity, eh?"

"Why not?"

" 'Why not'? That's the most cynical remark you've ever made to me."

"Well, why not?"

"You'd better watch out for this kind of thing, Ruth. I'll divorce you, and the Tonawanda Manufacturing Company might not want that."

"Oh, I've thought of that."

"And you wouldn't do it just to get even with me, would you? Maybe a divorce is just what I want."

"I've decided that what you want is of no consequence to me."

"My, we're full of surprises tonight. And if you knew what I thought of this Kemmerer."

"I do know. You've made that clear."

"He's such a dull bastard."

"How do you know?"

"His letter. He hadn't changed."

"I hope not, not too much."

"You sound pretty determined," he said. "I warn you, Ruth. I'm not going to let you get away with anything."

"All right."

"Or him, either. All at once I find myself loathing this slob, much as I hate to admit it. I don't like anyone or anything I don't understand."

"Well, you'd never understand this, Ted. It's too simple for you."

"Explain it."

"You won't get it. It's just that I like having been in love with Ray."

"No, there's a lot more to it than that. He had something else that you never told me. He must have, to make it stick for twenty years. Some dumb, uncomplicated thing that I haven't got. Maybe you don't know what it is. Let me see his letter again."

This time she handed him the letter, and he read it slowly to himself. He shook his head, put the letter back in the envelope, handed it to her. "No. It tells me nothing. It's in him. It's some quality that entirely eludes me. Ruth?"

"What?"

"Have you ever slept with anyone else since we've been married?"

"Yes."

"I thought maybe you had, and I hate it. But that makes this so much worse. It makes Kemmerer so much more formidable." He rose. "Well, I have to go to Atlanta tomorrow. Will you drive me to the airport?"

"Sure. What time?"

"Ten o'clock. I'm only going to be gone for the day—if that makes any difference to you."

"I'll meet you when you come back."

"Oh, I can get a taxi, thanks. Goodnight."

"Goodnight," she said.

"I'll sleep in Neddy's room."

"All right," she said. "You want breakfast at seven-thirty?"

"Yes, that ought to give me plenty of time. Ruth?"

"What?"

"Nothing. Goodnight."

Call Me, Call Me

Her short steps, that had always called attention to her small stature, now served to conceal the fact that her walk was slower. Now, finally, there was nothing left of the youth that had lasted so long, so well into her middle age. Her hat was small and black, a cut-down modified turban that made only the difference between being hatted and hatless but called no attention to the wearer, did not with spirit of defiance or gaiety proclaim the wearer to be Joan Hamford. Her Persian lamb, a good one bought in prosperous days, was now a serviceable, sensible garment that kept her warm and nothing more. She wore shoes that she called—echoing her mother's designation —"ties." They were very comfortable and they gave her good support.

The greeting by the doorman was precisely accorded. No "good morning," but "You'll have a taxi, Miss Hamford?" If she wanted a taxi, he was there to get her a taxi; that was one of the things he was paid for; but he could expect no tip now and she gave him little enough at Christmas. She was one of the permanent guests of the hotel, those whom he classified as salary people because he was paid a salary for providing certain services. Salary people. Bread-and-butter people. Not tip people, not big-gravy, expense-account people. Salary people. Budget people. Instant-coffee-and-half-a-pint-of-cream-from-the-delicatessen people. Five-dollars-in-an-envelope-with-his-name-on-it-at-Christmas people. The hotel was coming down in another year, and the hotel that was going up in its place would have no room for salary people. Only expense-account people.

"Taxi? Yes, please, Roy. Or I'd make just as good time walking, wouldn't I?"

"I don't know, Miss Hamford. I don't know where you're going."

"It is a little far," said Joan Hamford. "Yes, a taxi. *There's one!*"

She always did that. She always spotted a taxi, so that it would seem that she had really found it herself, unaided, and really owed him nothing. He was wise to that one. He was wise to all her little tricks and dodges, her ways of saving quarters, her half pints of cream from the delicatessen. She must be on her way to a manager's office today. Most days she would not take a taxi. "Such a nice day, I think a stroll," she would say, and then stroll exactly one block to the bus stop. But today it was a taxi, because she didn't want to be worn out when she applied for a job. Yes, today was a job day; she was wearing her diamond earrings and her pearls, which were usually kept in the hotel safe.

"Six-thirty Fifth Avenue, will you tell him, please, Roy?"

"Six-thirty Fifth," he said to the taxi driver. She could have given the address herself, but this was a cheap way of queening it. He closed the door behind her and stepped back to the curb.

"Number Six Hundred and Thirty, Avenue Five," said the driver, starting the meter. "Well, you got anything to read, lady, because the traffic on Madison and Fifth, I can't promise you nothing speed-wise. You wanta try Park, we'll make better time going down Park, but I won't guarantee you going west."

"How long will it take us if we go down Fifth?"

"Fifth? You wanta go down Fifth? I give you an honest estimate of between twenty and twenty-five minutes. Them buses, you know. You ever go to the circus and take notice to the elephants, the one holds on to the-one-in-front-of-him's tail with his trunk. That's the way the buses operate. Never no less than four together at the one time, and what they do to congest up the traffic! You see they could straighten that out in two hours if they just handed out a bunch of summonses, but then the union would pull the men off the buses and the merchants would holler to the powers-that-be, City Hall. I'm getting out of this city . . . We'll try Fifth . . . It's Miss Joan Hamford, isn't it?"

"Why, yes. How nice of you."

"Oh, I rode you before. You remember when you used to live over near the River? Four-what-is-it? Four-fifty East Fifty-second?"

"Oh, heavens, that long ago?"

"Yeah, I had one of them big Paramounts, twice the size of this little crate. You don't remember Louis?"

"Louis?"

"Me. Louis Jaffee. I used to ride you four-five times a week regular, your apartment to the Henry Miller on Forty-third, east of Broadway. Fifteen-and-five in those days, but you were good for a buck every night. Well, I'm still hacking, but you been in movies and TV and now I guess you're on your way to make another big deal for TV."

"No, as a matter of fact, a play. On Broadway. I'm afraid I can't tell you just what play, but it isn't television. Still a secret, you know."

"Oh, sure. Then you was out in Hollywood all that time I remember."

"Yes, and I did a few plays in London."

"That I didn't know about. I just remember you rode out the bonnom of the depression in Hollywood. The bonnom of the depression for me, but not for you. You must of made a killing out there. What does it feel like to see some of them pictures now, on TV? You don't get any royalties on them pictures, do you?"

"No."

"Now they all go in for percentages I understand. Be nice to have a percentage of some of them oldies. Is Charles J. Hall still alive?"

"No, poor Charles passed on several years ago."

"You always heard how he was suppose to be a terrific boozer, but I seen him the other night on TV. You were his wife, where you were trying to urge him to give up the Navy and head up this big shipbuilding company."

"*Glory in Blue.*"

"*Glory in Blue,* that's the one. How old was Charles J. Hall when you made that picture, do you remember?"

"How old? I should think Charles was in his early forties then."

"Christ! He'd be in his seventies."

"Yes, he would."

"I'm over the sixty mark myself, but I can't picture Charles J. Hall in his seventies."

"Well, he never quite reached them, poor dear."

"Booze, was it?"

"Oh, I don't like to say that."

"There's a lot worse you could say about some of those jerks they got out there now. Male *and* female. What they need out there is another Fatty Arbuckle case, only the trouble is the public is got so used to scandal."

"Yes, I suppose so."

"You know I was just thinking, I wonder how I missed it when Charles J. Hall passed away. Was it during the summer? I go away in the summer and I don't see a paper for two weeks."

"Yes, I think it was."

"They would have had something in."

"They didn't have very much, not as much as he deserved, considering what a really big star he was."

"But there was a long time when he wasn't in anything. That's when I understood he was hitting the booze so bad. Where was he living during that time?"

"In Hollywood. He stayed right there."

"Wouldn't take anything but big parts, I guess. That's where you were smart, Miss Hamford."

"How do you mean?"

"Well, they forgot all about Charles J. Hall. Like my daughter didn't know who the hell he was last week. But she'd know you. She'd know you right away, because from TV, when you were that lady doctor two years ago, that serial."

"Unfortunately only lasted twenty-six weeks."

"I don't care. Your face is still familiar to the new generation. I don't know what any actress fools around with Broadway for."

"Some of us love the theater."

"Sure, there's that, but I'm speaking as a member of the public. You could be in *My Fair Lady* and there wouldn't be as many people see you as if you went in one big spectacular. When I see my daughter tomorrow night, when she comes for supper, I'm gunna tell her I rode Joan Hamford. And right away she's gunna say 'Doctor McAllister? Doctor Virginia Mc-Allister?' So they took it off after twenty-six weeks, but just think of how many million people saw you *before* they took it off. Up there in the millions. The so-called Broadway theater, that's gettin' to be for amateurs and those that, let's face it, can't get a job in TV."

"Oh, you mustn't say that."

"Well, I'm only telling you what the public thinks, basing it on my own conclusions. Here you are, Six-three-oh. Eighty-five on the clock."

"Here, Louis. I want you to have this."

"The five?"

"For old times' sake."

"Well, thanks. Thanks a lot, Miss Hamford. The best to you, but TV is where you ought to be."

She hoarded her strength during the walk to the elevator, and she smiled brightly at the receptionist in the office of Ralph Sanderson–Otto B. Kolber. "Mr. Sanderson is expecting you, Miss Hamford. Go right in."

"Good morning, Ralph," said Joan Hamford.

Sanderson rose. "Good morning, Joan. Nice of you to come down at this hour, but unfortunately it was the only absolutely only time I had. You know anything about this play?"

"Only what I've read about it."

"Well, then you probably don't know anything about the part."

"No, not really. I read the book, the novel, but I understand that's been changed."

"Oh, hell, the novel. We only kept the boy and his uncle, from the novel."

"The boy's aunt? She's not in the play? Then what is there for me, Ralph? Or would you rather have me read the play instead of you telling me?"

"No, I'd just as soon tell you. Do you remember the school-teacher?"

"The schoolteacher? Let me think. There *was* a school-teacher in one of the early chapters, but I don't think she had a name."

"In the novel she didn't. But she has in the play."

"You really must have changed the novel. How does the part develop?"

"Well, frankly it doesn't. We only keep the teacher for one scene in the first act."

"Oh, well, Ralph, you didn't bring me down here for that. That isn't like you. Good heavens, even if I'd never done any-thing else, I was Dr. Virginia McAllister to God knows how many million people, and I got twenty-two-fifty for that."

"Three years ago, Joan, and you haven't had much to do since. That's why I thought of you for the teacher. I'd rather give it to you than someone I don't know. I'll pay three-fifty."

"What for? You can't bill me over the others, the part isn't big enough to do that."

"I couldn't anyway. The boy gets top billing, and Michael Ware is co-star. Tom Ruffo in *Illinois Sonata with* Michael Ware. But I admit you'd lead the list of featured players."

"You know how these things are, Ralph. Not a manager in town but will know I'm working for three-fifty."

"But working, and I'll take care of you publicity-wise. The theater doesn't pay movie or TV salaries, you know that."

"I understand Jackie Gleason got six thousand."

"He may have got more, but Virginia McAllister wasn't Ralph Kramden. I wish you'd think about this, Joan. It's not physically very demanding. You don't have to stand around or do any acrobatics."

"Or act, either, I suppose. No, I'm afraid not, Ralph, and I really think you were rather naughty to bring me down here."

"Joan, this is a fine play and with this boy Ruffo we're going to run ten months, and maybe a lot longer. For you it would be like a vacation with pay, and you'd be back in the theater. Stop being a stubborn bitch, and think back to times when I paid you sixty dollars a week for more work."

"In that respect you haven't changed, Ralph."

"Four hundred."

"Take-home that's still only a little over three hundred. No, I'm going right on being a stubborn bitch."

"I'll give you four hundred, and I'll release you any time after the first six months that you find a better part."

"Can you write me into the second and third acts?"

"Impossible. The locale changes, and anyway, I know the author wouldn't do it. And frankly I wouldn't ask him to. No more tinkering with this play till we open in Boston."

"Well—still friends, Ralph. You tried."

"Yes, I certainly tried."

She reached out her hand. "Give me five dollars for the taxi."

"Joan, are you that broke?"

"No, I'm not broke, but that's what it cost me to come here."

Sanderson pulled a bill from a money-clip. "If it cost you five to get here it'll cost you another five to get home. Here's a sawbuck."

"I only wanted five, but of course I'll take the ten. In the old days you would have spent more than that on taking me to lunch."

"Considering where we usually ended up after lunch, the price wasn't high."

"I guess that's a compliment."

"You know, you have delusions of Laurette Taylor in *Menagerie*. All you senior girls have that."

"Senior girls. That sounds so Camp Fire-y."

"You're going to be sore as hell when you see who gets this part. I don't know who it'll be, but I'm going to pick somebody you hate."

"Good. Don't pick anybody I like, because I'll hate her if the play runs."

"And yourself."

"Oh—well, I hate myself already. Do you think I like going back to that hotel, feeling sure you have a hit, *hoping* you have a hit, and stuck with my own stubborn pride? But you know I can't take this job, Ralph."

"Yes, I guess I do."

"You wouldn't stretch a point and take me to lunch, would you?"

"No, I can't, Joan."

"Then—will you give me a kiss?"

"Any time." He came around from behind his desk and put his arms around her.

"On the lips," she said.

He bent down, she stood on tiptoe, and his mouth pressed on hers. "Thank you, dear," she said. "Call me, call me."

"I hope so," he said, as she went out.

It's Mental Work

It was nearly half-past four and the last customer had been let out the side door. The barroom was dark except for the weak night light over the cash register. For early risers it was Tuesday morning, but here it was still Monday night. Rich Hickman, the bartender, had his street clothes on, very dapper, and seeming not at all tired as he came in the back room.

"You all through, Rich?" said Wigman, the owner.

"All through *here,*" said Rich, with a smile.

"Yeah, you look as if you had some place to go," said Wigman. "One for the road, as they say?" Wigman pointed to the bottle of bourbon on the table.

"I don't know. Sure," said Rich. He looked at his wristwatch, a hexagonal shape with square hollow links of stainless steel. "You want company a little while?"

"Get yourself a glass and sit down," said Wigman. "I don't know whether I got a date or not. It all depends."

"Yeah, I know," said Rich, speaking while he fetched a shot glass from the bar. "Those all-depends dates. I give that up for a coupla years, but now I'm back playing the field. All depends, all depends. They give you that all-depends chowder, but it's still better than being tied down."

"I don't know," said Wigman. "I don't know which is better, to tell you the truth. I'm forty-four years of age and twice in my life I thought I was settled down. *Settled* down. But it got to be *tied* down, and I was too young for that. I still feel pretty young, but I know what I am. I'm forty-four going on forty-five, and if I'm gonna be ninety years old, I'm halfway there. Halfway to ninety. Cheers, Rich."

"Cheers," said Rich. They raised glasses and drank.

"What did we do tonight?" said Wigman.

"Around three and a quarter."

"Yeah, quiet. Well, a Monday," said Wigman.

"You don't even figure to break even on a Monday," said Rich.

"That reminds me. How is it you never owned a joint of your own?"

"Oh, I don't know. I got offered the chance to, to go partners with a guy in Fort Lauderdale, but I didn't. I didn't like the fellow. And I had a rich dame in Miami Beach used to give me the big talk, but for two years straight as soon as it was April she went back to New York, and I was still on the duckboards. I guess she didn't have the money. The cash, I mean. She had a forty-dollar-a-day room all season, and she had a coupla rings there that shoulda been good for fifteen, twenty thousand apiece. But I know for a fact she was a two-dollar bettor at the track. Her husband wouldn't let her have any cash."

"Were you in?"

"Oh, sure, I was in. I had the use of a big Chrysler and she give me like all my slacks and sport shirts she used to put on the tab at the hotel. They had a woman's shop there that carried men's shirts and slacks and a couple times special orders for an Italian silk suit, sports jackets. And you know, that husband never got wise, because it was a woman's shop. It all went on the tab at the hotel. But cash, no. She was a two-dollar bettor. Didn't cash ten bets all season, all long shots. Every race she had the long shot. That many long shots don't come in."

"That many favorites don't come in either," said Wigman.

"No. Not when I have them at least. So anyway, I stop going steady with her and ever since I been playing the field."

"How old are you, Rich?"

"How old am I? I'm thirty-seven. I'm not so much younger than you."

"You look it, though. I got too much weight on me."

"Well, you think about it and it's very seldom you see a bartender overweight. If he's just a working stiff. An owner that tends bar, he'll put on the weight. But just an ordinary bartender, he's on his feet, moving around. Like a cashier in a bank. A paying teller. How many of them do you see fat? I figured it out why. You're on your feet all day and the lard don't get a chance to grow on you. Furthermore, you don't think of a bartender as using up mental energy, but we do. You carry on these conversations with the customers, you got maybe twenty-thirty customers at one time, and they all say, 'Hey, Rich, will you do this again, please?' and you're supposed to know what every one of them wants. Then the cash register, the prices. And the guys that want the bottle on the bar, you gotta keep an eye on them. It's mental work, and that uses up energy. We're not very different than a paying teller. Except the respectability."

"And the wages, Rich. You get better wages."

"That we do."

"And you're not stuck in the one place all your life."

"No. Oh, I'm not complaining. How long would a teller in a bank last if they found out he was driving some broad's Chrysler and living it up in a forty-dollar-a-day room? I had a room over in Miami, a fleabag over there, but most of the time I was in Miami Beach."

"A good tan goes well with your white hair."

"Oh, I used to pass for ten years younger. This broad thought I was around twenty-six, twenty-seven. Gave her a little priority over the other broads. Priority? You know what I mean. Not priority."

"Superiority."

"That's it."

There was a metallic rap on the window. "I guess I got a date after all," said Wigman.

"I'll get it," said Rich, going to the door. "Howdy do?"

The woman said: "Hello. Is Ernie here?"

"Come on in," called Wigman. "That's Rich Hickman, my bartender. Come on in, June."

"Hello," said June to Rich, acknowledging the introduction.

"Nice to meet you," said Rich. "I'll be going."

"Stick around, don't go," said Wigman.

"I better go," said Rich, looking at his watch.

"Time you meeting your date?" said Wigman.

"Well, I don't know. She was gonna be here or give me a buzz."

"Well, stick around a while," said Wigman. "So she's a little late. They're always late. Hello, Junie."

"*I* wasn't so very late," said the woman. "I told you between four and five, so I'm early."

"What'll you drink?" said Wigman.

"Oh—I don't know," said June. She looked at the bottle on the table. "Not bourbon."

"Well, you can have anything you want, and if you want a mixed drink, this is the guy to do it for you. This guy is only the best. Take my word for it."

"You know what I think I'll have is a Rob Roy. I had a Scotch earlier."

"That's easy," said Rich.

"Live up to your reputation now, Rich. Give her the best Rob Roy she ever hung a lip over."

"What an expression!" said June. She lit a cigarette and Rich went to the barroom. "What happened to the other fellow you used to have?"

"He quit, and I got this fellow. This fellow's twice as good. No spillage. No getting out of hand with the customers. And pretty, too, isn't he?"

"He's almost too pretty. He dyes his hair. Is he queer?"

"If he is, I should be as queer. The women go big for this guy."

"Does he go big for them is the question," said June.

"I got an idea that it's mutual. How was your business tonight?"

"Off. Way off. They're talking about closing Monday nights entirely. I heard they're trying to make a deal with the unions. It may pick up though, towards the end of the week. They moan and groan every Monday, but as soon as it begins to pick up towards the end of the week, you don't hear any more about it."

"I know," said Wigman. "We were way off tonight."

"It starda rain out," said June. "I just got a few drops on me, getting out of the cab."

"I owe you for the cab," said Wigman. He took a bill out of a money clip. She looked at the bill and then at Wigman. She shook her head.

"This five has an *O* behind it," she said.

"I don't need glasses," said Wigman.

"You want to give me fifty dollars?"

"Why are you acting surprised? It isn't the first time I gave you fifty dollars."

"You don't have to give me fifty dollars," she said. "I don't mind when business is good, but you said you were way off tonight."

"We were very good Saturday and Sunday."

"Ernie, you don't *have* to do this," she said.

"But I'd rather," he said. "Here's your Rob Roy. A good way to unload the cheap Scotch."

"I didn't use the cheap Scotch," said Rich. "That's as good as we have in the house."

"Well, that's all right, considering," said Wigman.

Hickman looked at the rain-streaked window. "Hey, you know it's starting to come down."

"You might as well wait here till it stops."

The fifty-dollar bill disappeared into June's purse and she sipped the cocktail, moving her eyes from right to left, left to right as she judged the taste. "Good," she said. "Just right."

"Thanks," said Rich.

"I told you, this guy is only the best," said Wigman. "You better stick around in case she wants another one."

"Well, if it's all right with all concerned," said Rich. "My friend should be along any minute, or phone."

"There's the bottle," said Wigman. "Help yourself. You know the combination."

"Do you mind if I ask you something?" said June.

"Go ahead," said Rich.

"Did you used to be in Miami Beach, driving a big kind of a Cadillac or one of those?"

"A Chrysler, yeah," said Rich.

"Last season. You know you almost knocked me down?"

"Me? I don't remember even coming close. Seriously, are you sure it was me? I don't remember no accident."

"You wouldn't remember me, but I remember you. Corner of Thirty-first and Lincoln. You were so busy talking to your lady friend you never even saw me. Or heard me. I really gave it to you, but it was all wasted. I think you were having a little fight with the lady friend. A blonde with those big sun glasses?"

"That could fit forty-five thousand dames in Miami Beach, but I guess it all adds up. I apologize."

"I knew I seen you some place before. That hair gives you away."

"Next question. Do I dye it? No, I don't. I stard getting gray hair when I was twenty-three years of age."

"I didn't ask you. That's none of my business."

"Well, then you're the exception because they all ask me," said Rich.

"That's funny, because I wasn't," she said. "It's too bad you don't have that big car tonight. You could ride Ernie and I home."

"What is this, the needle? You know damn well it was never my car or I wouldn't be tending bar for a living."

"Ernie, I thought you said this man never got out of hand with the customers."

"You're not a customer, and let's face it, you got the needle in there pretty deep. But enjoy yourself, the both of you," said Wigman.

"Yeah, how much do I have to take when I'm not getting paid for it?" said Rich. "You know what I mean? I got the apron off now, a first-class citizen after four A.M. What do *you* do, June? Are you a hatcheck chick?"

"What if I am?"

"Well, then, relax," said Rich. "You know what I mean? So you take it all night for a lousy buck, so do I. But here it is close on to five o'clock in the morning and we're people now. Not only you, but me. What'd somebody give you the big pitch tonight? Is that what's bugging you?"

"Nothing is bugging me, and nobody gave me any big pitch."

"Maybe that's what's bugging you, nobody give you the pitch. Did I strike oil there, June?"

"Easy does it there, Rich," said Wigman. "Don't get personal."

"You mean I shouldn't call her June? How's the cocktail, ma'am?"

"I must say you're a sarcastic son of a bitch," said Wigman. "I never realized that before."

"Oh, I hold it in when I got my apron on, but this is after hours, Ernie."

"Ernie, huh?" said Wigman.

"All right. *Mr. Wigman,* if that's the way you like it. But I coulda been Mr. Hickman in Fort Lauderdale, and then maybe you'da been one of my customers. Mr. Hickman and Mr. Wigman."

"You coulda been Mr. Hickman in Miami Beach if the broad had the cash, only her husband wouldn't let her get her hooks on any cash," said Wigman.

"Now who's sarcastic?" said Rich.

"I think you're making a fast load," said Wigman. "You only had three sitting here——"

"And one when I was mixing her drink, making four."

"Well, that's a half a pint in about fifteen minutes," said Wigman.

"Do you do everything fast?" said June.

"That depends on how you mean that. Some things I take it slow and easy."

"All right, Rich. Down, boy," said Wigman.

"The lady asked me a question. I thought she wanted to know. Some things I can take it slow and easy, whereas I know some women don't like it if you take it slow and easy. Speaking of shaking up a Dackery, for instance."

"Yeah. Sure. Well, I tell you, Rich," said Wigman. "I think you better take a slow and easy powder out of here while we're all still friends. I see you tomorrow night."

"Okay, Ernie. Okay. Goodnight, Ernie, and good night, June. Watch out for reckless drivers." He got up and went out the side door.

"The idea asking him does he do everything fast?" said Wigman. "You couldn't have but only the one meaning to a question like that."

"So?"

"You mean you go for that guy?"

"I don't go for anybody. I'm so sick of men. I wouldn't care if I never saw another man for the rest of my life, the way I feel now."

"Well, that won't last."

"But you're so *right* it won't last. I didn't say it would last. I was only telling you how I feel now, tonight."

"Well, you want to go home with me or don't you? Either way."

"Put me in a cab and I'll see you tomorrow night. Here," she said, and handed him the fifty-dollar bill.

"Forget it, forget it. It's only human nature. I'm kind of beat too, myself. Let me stash this bottle and I'll get you a cab."

They went out together and he hailed a cruising cab. "That's all I am, Ernie. I'm kind of beat, too. I'll see you tomorrow night, yeah?"

"Sure. Goodnight, kid."

"Kid. Thirty-six years old. Goodnight, Ernie."

Wigman hailed another cab, got in, had the driver stop for the morning papers, and proceeded to his hotel. During the night, his night, he had a heart attack and died. His body was found by the waiter who had a standing order to bring his breakfast at one o'clock in the afternoon. Ernie Wigman's lawyer, Sanford Conn, was out of town and could not be reached, and the place ran itself that night, as it always did when Ernie did not show up. But a policeman had been around, asking questions, and the news of Ernie's death was known to the bartenders and waiters and kitchen help, and to the regular customers. Rich Hickman took charge. "I'll close up," he told the others. They were agreeable; they did not want to have to account for the money in the till.

Rich got the last customer out a few minutes after four in the morning. In the back room was a cop named Edwards, the man on post whom Rich had asked to be there. "I just want you here when I tot up what's in the till," said Rich.

"I'm not suppose to do that," said Edwards.

"Well, do it anyway as a favor."

"Who to?"

"To Ernie. I think he has a kid somewhere, and Ernie was always all right with you guys. That I happen to know. I just want you to witness that I'm not stealing off a dead man."

"I won't sign anything."

"Who asked you to sign, Edwards? I'll count it up in front of you, and lock it up in the register and give you the key. Is there anything in the book against that?"

"Nothing in the book against it, but—well, what the hell? All right. But I don't take any responsibility."

"You don't take any responsibility, but this way no son of a bitch is going to say I robbed a dead man."

"You could of been robbing him all night long, that's the way I gotta look at it, Hickman."

"I couldn't of been robbing him much. All you gotta do is compare tonight with last Tuesday or any Tuesday. If I was robbing him all night long I didn't get rich on it."

"I guess that makes sense," said Edwards. "Go ahead and count it up."

The cop sat bored on a bar stool while Rich made his count. "Cash on hand, five hundred and twenty-eight dollars and eighty-seven cents. Okay?"

"That's what it looks like to me," said Edwards.

"You wouldn't do me a favor and initial this slip before I lock it up?"

"I guess I can do that," said Edwards. "There's somebody at the back door."

"Let him in, will you? No, you keep your eye on the money. I'll let him in. I hope it's his lawyer, a fellow named Conn."

"Conn is a good name for a lawyer," said Edwards.

Rich went to the back door, opened it, and admitted June. "Ernie here?" she said.

"No. Come on in," said Rich.

"What's with the cop?" said June.

"I'll tell you later."

"Trouble? I don't go for cops."

"Then wait here."

"I don't like this. Where's Ernie?"

"Ernie is dead."

"A stick-up?"

"Nothing like that. He had a heart attack. If you'll sit down I'll take care of the cop and then I'll tell you all about it."

Rich returned to Edwards, put the money in the cash register, and gave Edwards the key. "All right, Edwards?"

"I guess so."

"Thanks a lot."

"All right. See you." Edwards left, and Rich mixed a Rob Roy, put it on a tray and took it to the back room. In his other hand he carried a bottle of bourbon with a shot glass inverted and resting on the cap.

"Ernie had a heart attack at the hotel. They found him around one o'clock yesterday."

"That's when he usually had breakfast," she said. "Are they having a service for him?"

"I don't have any idea. He had a kid, didn't he?"

"He had two kids around eighteen and twenty years of age, but I don't know where they are or any of that. I guess they'll show up. He was divorced, that I know."

"I closed up tonight and I had the cop come in to see that I didn't steal anything out of the till. Do you know Ernie's lawyer?"

"Sanford Conn, his name is. He had a piece of the joint. I know him from him going out with Ernie and I a couple times."

"This joint could do a lot better, a *lot* better. Ernie was a nice guy, but I could of told him ways to save a little here and make a little there. You know Conn, eh?"

"That well. Been out with him and his wife, with Ernie. A young fellow about thirty-five. He's the lawyer for four or five joints like this, and I think he's in for a piece of all of them."

"Then he's a guy I could go to with a proposition?"

"If there was a buck in it, he'd listen . . . So Ernie cooled. You know I was almost with him last night."

"How do you mean, almost?"

"Almost is what I said, almost is what I mean. I didn't go home with him. He put me in a cab outside here. I wouldn't of liked that, waking up with a dead man."

"What stopped you from going home with him?"

"Didn't feel like it. I guess I got so burned up with you that I was sick and tired of men. Now I think of it, Ernie said he was tired, too. I wonder if he knew anything beforehand. He *said* he was *tired.*"

"He often said he was tired. I used to say to him, not come right out with it, but he'd sit and put away a quart of bourbon and eat a steak and a whole meal and sometimes he was here for ten-twelve hours, eating and drinking and never get up and walk around. I said to him about a month ago, I said —well, I didn't say anything, if you want the straight of it. But I thought, this guy he never moves out of his chair, and all that booze and rich food. Ten-twelve hours he'd sit here. They get that way, some of them. I worked for guys that did the very same thing. And they kid themselves that they're working, just because they're sitting in their own joint. Work? What work? Why, one of the day men was stealing from him right in front of his very eyes, that's how much work he was doing."

"Stealing how?"

"Oh, there's ways of working with a waiter. There's plenty of ways you can steal. *You* steal a little, don't you? The concession don't get it all."

"Most of it. You know, I'd like to have the concession here."

"Yeah, but would Conn give it to you?"

"Maybe not Conn, but maybe a new owner would. Or a new partner."

"You mean like if I got to be partners with Conn?"

"You must of attended a mind-reading school," said June.

"Graduated," said Rich. "You wouldn't mind working for me? I got the impression last night you wouldn't spit in my eye."

"I wouldn't be working for you, exactly. I'd have the concession, so I'd be working for myself."

Rich thought a moment. "Usually the syndicate owns the concession, and they pay so much for it. You know that."

"I ought to know it after—I been in this business. But here they never had a checkroom. Ernie didn't want one."

"I know. But you were softening him up."

"It's a lot of money going to waste," said June. "I could do a hundred and fifty a week here."

"You could do two hundred, two and a quarter."

"So?"

"Well, that's what I think it's worth, not a hundred and fifty. So if you got it it wouldn't be on a basis of a hundred and fifty. Don't play games with me, June."

"I want to make a little for myself. It's not all clear profit. All right, so you're big-hearted and you give me a concession worth maybe two hundred a week. But first you gotta convince Sanford Conn, and who knows Sanford Conn? I do."

"Yeah, we were coming to that," said Rich.

"One word from me, either way."

"Honey, I'm with you. How much money you got, and how much can you raise?"

"Ha ha ha. Would I tell you? How much do *you* have, and how much can *you* raise?"

"This is serious. If you could get your hands on fi-thousand dollars, I think I could raise twenty-five. With thirty gees I could talk to Conn. Conn don't have to know you got the checkroom till him and I make a deal."

"You want me to put up five thousand dollars for the concession?"

"The way you say that I know you got it."

"Where is your end coming from?"

"What do you care, or what does Conn care, as long as I get it? I don't have that kind of money myself, but I can come pretty close to raising it."

"That dame that you almost killed me with in her car."

"Good for a little, but not much. She don't have any cash, only some jewelry."

"No heist. I don't want any part of a heist. Don't even talk about it. I got no record downtown and I want to keep it that way."

"If I had a record I couldn't work either. And I'm not talking about a heist. But her and a couple others I know, and a couple liquor salesmen. Plus your five, I could go to Conn with a proposition. This is a very good chance for the both of us, June. And me and you could save rent."

"Yeah, that was coming, too. You move in with me or I move in with you. Which?"

"You got an apartment, I'd move in with you. I only got a room way the hell up on West Eighty-fourth Street."

"Where do you think I live? In the Waldorf Towers? I got an apartment but it's only one room."

"By the month?"

"What else?"

"We could save money on a lease. Wuddia say?"

"I don't know. I'd have to think it over. How would I get rid of you if I didn't like you around?"

"How would you get rid of me? Start leaving your stuff on the floor, your hair curlers all over the can."

"I'm tidy."

"I noticed that, or I wouldn't broach the proposition."

"I take a bath twice a day, sometimes more," she said. She snickered.

"What?"

"This way I'd know for sure if you dyed your hair."

"You wanta know something, I touch it. It's near all gray, but I touch it."

"I like it."

"Thanks."

"Well, we didn't talk much about Ernie," she said.

"No, but we didn't say anything against him," said Rich.

"That's true. We didn't say anything against him. I guess he was that kind of a guy, Ernie. He checks out and you start forgetting him right away, but at least you don't say anything against him."

"Well, he done us a favor," said Rich.

"You mean you and I getting together? Yeah, if that's a favor. It's too soon to tell."

"I think we'll work out all right, June."

"Maybe we will. And if we don't—"

"You can start leaving hair curlers around."

She smiled. "Yes," she said. "If they all would of been that easy to get rid of."

"What are you, divorced?"

"Twice. What about you? Are you divorced?"

"No, I never got married. I came close a couple times, but something always happened, so I never had it legal. You know, I go south in the winter, and when the season's over I come north or I been to the coast a couple times, working."

"This'd be the first time you ever settled down? I mean with a place. I don't know, Rich."

"You worried about your five gees?"

"Wouldn't you be?"

"Don't worry about it. I like you. I knew that right away last night. I would of gone after you, Ernie or no Ernie."

"Yeah, and I wouldn't of run away from you. I didn't have anything permanent with Ernie."

There was a banging on the side door and Rich went to the door and peered out at two men. "I don't know these guys," he said. There was a roller shade on the door and similar shades on the windows of the back room. "We're closed," he shouted, and let the shade fall back in place. The banging was resumed.

"Maybe you better see what they want," said June.

"I think I heard one of them say Hickman," said Rich. "Will I take a chance?"

"Talk to them through the door," said June.

Rich opened the door a few inches, and immediately it was pushed against him and he was driven out of the way. "What's the idea?" said Rich.

"What's the idea? What's your idea?" said one of the men. Then he saw June at the table. "Hello, June."

"Hello, Sandy. It's all right, Rich. This is Sandy Conn."

"You're kinda rough, Mr. Conn," said Rich.

"Maybe, and you're kind of stupid. Close the door, Jack," Conn commanded his companion. Jack was obviously a hoodlum, a muscle man.

"I heard you were out of town," said Rich.

"You're Hickman, the bartender?" said Conn.

"Yes. I heard you were out of town and I decided to take care of everything till you got back."

"Yeah, yeah. All right, what's in the till?"

"Five hundred and twenty-eight dollars and some cents," said Rich. "In the register."

"A good thing it isn't in your pocket. Give me the key," said Conn, extending his hand.

"I don't have it. I gave it to Edwards, the cop on the beat."

"You what?"

"I can vouch for that," said June.

"You? I wouldn't ask you to vouch. You're in with this fellow now. Give me the key or do I get Jack here to take it away from you? Whichever one of you has the key, hand it over. I don't care which one Jack has to take it away from. Do you, Jack? You have any objection to wrestling with a woman?"

Jack laughed.

"I guess not," said Conn.

"Call the precinct, if you don't believe me," said Rich. "But if this goon gets any closer to me *or* her, I break this bottle over his head. Then I take care of you, Mr. Conn. You I could handle easily."

"I could almost handle you myself, Sandy," said June. "This man is telling the truth, you silly son of a bitch. He was protecting your interest."

"I aint worried about the bottle, Mr. Conn," said Jack.

"I'm thinking," said Conn. "What'd you say the name of this cop was?"

"Edwards. He's a patrolman."

"You don't have to tell me. If he was a sergeant I'd know him." Conn went to the telephone booth and was gone about five minutes. "I guess I owe you an apology," he said, when he returned. "Edwards has the key." He turned to Jack. "Okay, Jack. Thanks."

"That's all?" said Jack.

"Come around the office tomorrow and I'll give you a check."

"You wouldn't have five or ten on you?" said Jack.

"Here," said Conn, handing him a bill. "Goodnight, Jack."

"Thanks, Mr. Conn. Goodnight all," said Jack, leaving.

Conn sat down, across the table from June. "Too bad about Ernie, but the amount of liquor he consumed. Where you from, Hickman?"

"Why?"

"Well, I liked the way you took charge tonight. I like a take-charge guy. Bill Dickey, you remember used to catch for the Yanks? A real take-charge guy. You ever owned a joint, or managed one?"

"No."

"I know you got no police record, but give me the names of some places where you worked before."

"Why?"

"Well, June here will tell you, I got an interest in five other saloons. I kind of specialize in cafés."

"That's what you specialize in?" said Rich.

"I got other clients, naturally, but I been building up a café-owner practice."

"I thought there for a minute you specialized in something else."

"Like what? Explain."

"Like hiring some goon to beat up a woman," said Rich.

Conn tapped his fingernails on the table and watched Rich in silence. "Don't start anything, Hickman," he said presently.

"Jack ought to be a long way off by this time," said Rich.

"You lay a hand on me and it goes on your record downtown."

"Then I better make it good, huh?" said Rich.

Conn pointed to June. "She don't work, either."

"I'd of been in great shape after Jack got through with me, too," said June.

"What'll we do with him, June?" said Rich.

"If it was me, I'd kill him."

"What'd be the best way?" said Rich.

"Knock him out and dump him in the river. You got a car," said June.

"I told you the car don't belong to me, June."

"Oh, yeah, that's right. You got any other suggestions?"

"They got a walk-in icebox back in the kitchen. We could leave him there."

"I know you're kidding, you two," said Conn. "I tell you—"

"Shut up," said Rich, and slapped him hard on both cheeks. "I got a better idea." He got a hammer lock on Conn's left arm and forced him to his feet. He pushed him forward and kept pushing him through the cellar door, down the steps, and into a closet that was lined on both walls with wine bins and case goods. He closed the door and locked it.

"Will he suffocate?" said June.

"No. But I'll bet he has a headache by the time they find him. He can holler his head off and nobody'll hear him."

"How long'll he be there?"

"Oh, the day man comes on around ten o'clock. That gives him around five hours. In the dark. It's gonna seem longer."

"I hope," said June.

They went upstairs, and in the back room he said: "Well, have a good look at the joint. You won't be seeing it again."

"No," she said.

They went out the side door, and as they headed west she took his arm. "You," she said.

"That's right," he said. "Me."

In the Silence

The two friends were having coffee together after one of their Saturday lunches. As happens in friendships, they could be silent without awkwardness, and during one such silence Charles Ellis casually picked up a small book that was lying on the coffee table. It was a club roster, bound in two colors and with the club insigne stamped on the front cover, and below the symbol a slip of paper was glued on, which in typescript read: "Not to be removed from Lounge." Ellis leafed through the book and was about to put it down when a name caught his eye. "Know anybody named Holderman?"

"No, I don't think so," said James Malloy.

"Joseph W. Holderman 2d, Eagle Summit, P-A. Joined here in 1916. I've seen that name for years and I was always going to ask you about it. If anybody'd know that name, you would."

"I do know it."

"Thought you said you didn't," said Ellis.

"Holderman alone didn't mean anything, but when you gave it the full treatment, I not only know the name. I know the man. Not only know the man, I've been to his house at Eagle Summit. What would you like to know about him?"

"Well, the only reason I'm curious about him is I've seen his name in this book all these years, and I wondered about him. I've never seen him, I've never heard anyone speak of him, and why does a man that lives in a place called Eagle Summit, Pennsylvania, keep up his membership in this club? He's been a member for forty-five years, so he isn't any chicken. Nowadays you hear men like that say they're over-clubbed. Oh, wait a second, he's a life member. Doesn't have to pay dues any more."

"I think Holderman would pay dues anyway."

"What for? So that he can wear the club tie?"

"You may think you're kidding, but that's one of the reasons."

"Sounds pretty stuffy to me," said Ellis.

"He's anything but," said Malloy. "He's no chicken, as you say. He must be in his middle seventies, but I'd like to see him again before he dies. Or *I* do. Have I aroused any more curiosity about Joseph W. Holderman 2d, of Eagle Summit, Pennsylvania?"

"Some. Give."

"I'd love to," said Malloy. . . .

First I must tell you a little about Eagle Summit (said Malloy), where it is and what kind of country it's in. There's almost no such place as Eagle Summit, it's so small. It is, or was, a post office, which was also the general store. A Protestant church, very likely Presbyterian in that part of the country. A garage that was once a blacksmith shop. Mind you, I'm talking about the way it was when I saw it in 1927. There were some private houses, a doctor lived in one and had his office there. There was a little building that was a sort of township hall, with a couple of cells in the back. The village wasn't big enough to have a bank or a movie theater. It wasn't even on the railroad, not even a branch or a spur. It was in the mountains in North Central Pennsylvania, and the nearest town of any considerable size was Williamsport. Eagle Summit was hardly more than a clearing in the woods, and the people that lived there dreaded a forest fire more than anything else in the world. The village could have been completely wiped out without anyone outside's knowing the difference, at least for a week or so. There were only three telephones in the village itself. The town hall's, the general store's, and the doctor's, and one other about two miles away, at the Holdermans' house, but I don't want to get ahead of myself. I want to give you some more geography, et cetera.

The state highway didn't run through Eagle Summit. The

village was on a county road, which was originally, I imagine, scratched out by prison labor, if they could get that many prisoners, or more likely the road was built by the loggers. Timber was the only industry in that part of the State. Thousands and thousands of acres of virgin timber, but so hard to get to it and to move it away that a great deal of it was left unspoiled. It was wild country. Two hundred yards away from Eagle Summit and you were a thousand years in the past, back before Columbus discovered the country. It's doubtful if there were even Indians until the Seventeenth Century, and in two minutes by car you could be transported to a time when there was only bear and elk and deer, panther, eagles, wildcats. And I assure you that if you had to spend the night on the road, if your car broke down, you'd know they were still there. If you stopped to take a leak and turned off your motor the thing that struck you most forcibly was the silence, the enormous silence. If there was no wind—that is, if you were between Eagle Summit and the actual top of the mountain—the silence would be so absolute, such a new experience, that it became spooky, and it would be actually reassuring to hear some animal cry, some bird. And then your reassurance would vanish, because almost immediately you'd get the feeling that you were being watched. And no doubt you were. I'm told that that happens when you're in the jungle. It happened to me during the war, in the Admiralties, but then there was a reason because we'd been told that there were Japs hiding out, sniping at the Seabees. At Eagle Summit it was different. It was a civilized man, me, in a place where I didn't belong. A trespasser. And I knew I was a trespasser and felt guilty about it. This place belonged to the animals and they were sending me thought waves, warnings to get the hell out of there or take the consequences. Boy, the back of my neck was awfully cold. Anyway, I guess that's enough geography. Now for the human element.

As you know, I didn't go to Groton. I went to a school in Niagara Falls that was older than Groton but considerably less fashionable. I probably never would have heard of the school if my father hadn't gone there. It's no longer in existence. But I went there for a year. It was an all-day train ride, or a sleeper jump, and I preferred the day train because I was young and fascinated by any travel. I got a kick out of taking the train to Reading, thirty-five miles away, and any trip longer than that was sheer delight, not to be wasted in sleep. In those days I never took a nap on a train. Too much to see. Well, in 1924, I was on my way back to school after Easter vacation. I was rich, must have had twenty or thirty dollars in my kick, either from bridge or a crap game, and when I changed trains and got on the Buffalo Day Express, as it was called, I bought a Pullman chair. Two of my classmates from Baltimore were on the train, but riding day coach. The hell with them, I said. I'll ride the plush. Splurge. I can see my classmates any time.

So I sat in the Pullman, really luxurious they were then, too. Beautiful woodwork. Mother-of-pearl in the paneling. Big chairs. A brass spitoon. A polite porter who knew his job and had plenty of self-respect, instead of these characters that hate their jobs and hate you. Comfort and ease, and always the *people* that got on and off along the way. Some of them knew each other, some of them didn't.

At a place called Carter City, a station just beyond Williamsport, I looked out the car window to see who was getting on, and I noticed three people. Obviously a man and his wife saying goodbye to a third man. I'll come back to the third man in a minute, but first the man and his wife. This man was about six feet tall. He was in his middle thirties, and wearing a Norfolk suit with knickerbockers, thick-soled shoes with fringed tongues, and a cap made of the same material as the suit. A few years earlier it was collegiate to wear a Norfolk suit, but this wasn't a collegiate-type suit. This was English Country. It had four buttons, like ours, but the top button was left unbuttoned, which we never did. His wife was wearing a tweed suit, too, and a brown felt hat. She was quite short, and she and her husband were laughing very heartily at something their friend was saying. I naturally couldn't hear them through the double

windows of the Pullman. Then the conductor spoke to them—
they obviously knew him and he them—and the third man
kissed the woman and shook hands with the man, picked up
his bag, which was a beautifully banged-up but saddle-soaped
kit bag, and another piece of luggage that I thought contained
fishing tackle. He got on the Pullman-car platform as the train
started to move, and I heard him calling out a final remark in
French. I couldn't understand what he said, but there was no
mistaking it for anything but French. He was holding the door
open, and I heard the woman call out something in French,
and then she and her husband turned and headed for their car.
The car was a grey Pierce-Arrow, a Series 30, or about a 1921
or '22 model. It was a chummy roadster. That is, it seated four,
with divided front seats. Also called a clover-leaf, if you recall.
But it was a hell of an automobile. It had no trouble going
eighty or eighty-five, and this particular job had Westinghouse
shock absorbers. That model was a favorite with people who
wanted a sports car but wanted the weight and size of the
Pierce. There were two of them in my home town, and oddly
enough one of them was painted grey, too.

The whole picture fascinated me, of course. The people, the
car, and the *place*. You wouldn't have given them a second look
on Long Island or the Philadelphia Main Line, but this was in
the woods of North Central Pennsylvania. There were plenty of
rich people in Williamsport, but this wasn't Williamsport. This
was Carter City. Well, as it happened, not entirely by accident,
I had lunch with the third man. He was a really big fellow. Six-
four, two-thirty, and he had a beard. Also he needed a haircut,
and I noticed paint stains on his back hair. I'll tell you about
him some other time, but he turned out to be Rollo Fenner, the
painter. The name struck a vague gong, not that I knew anything about painters, but as we made conversation in the
dining-car he got on the subject of football and then I remembered. He'd been All-American at Harvard. Was with the
Morgan-Harjes Unit during the war, and lived in Paris. I just
didn't have the nerve to ask him what he was doing in Pennsyl-

vania. We got along fine and he gave me his card, told me to look him up in Paris, and he was such delightful company that he really made my trip.

We now perforce skip a year or two. Or three. I got out of school and went to work on a newspaper, working my tail off, loving it, and practically unaware that I was doing grown men's work for twelve dollars a week. The cheap son of a bitch that I worked for—oh, well. Anyway, I had a car, a little four-cylinder Buick roadster, and because of it I got some assignments that you could only cover if you had a car, and on a staff of two women and five men, I was the only one that could drive. So one day the editor called me to his private office, which of course he called a sanctum sanctorum, without knowing a God damn word of Latin, and he said, "James, I have a strange hunch. Read this." He showed me a piece of U. P. copy that had come in over the Morse wire. A flyer had tried to make an emergency landing on a country road near a place called Eagle Summit. Plane caught fire, and the pilot was burned to death, before he'd had a chance to get out of the plane. "Do you know who that might be? It might be Lindbergh! The Lone Eagle!" I thought he was crazy, but he'd convinced himself that Lindbergh, who *was* flying all over the country, getting receptions, was the man that was killed. I think Lindbergh was overdue some place, too. "How long would it take you to drive up there in your car?" Well, four or five hours, I told him. So he gave me some money, swore me to secrecy, and off I went, in quest of the biggest story of the century. Naturally I was to go have a look at the dead pilot, then telephone back if I thought it was Lucky Lindy, and Gibbsville would scoop the world. Or Bob Hooker would have a scoop, not I.

But I was young, so off I went. I knew the roads for the first hundred and fifty miles, and I was convinced that all I had to do was keep the throttle down on the floor-board and I'd have a Pulitzer prize. But after I got off the state highways I began to run into trouble, and the closer I got to Eagle Summit, the more trouble I had. The Buick was developing a tappet knock, or what I hoped was a tappet knock. I much preferred a tappet knock to what I really knew it was—a loose connecting rod. I knew it would be getting dark soon, and I'd seen enough of the territory to know I didn't want to spend the night on the road. Not that road.

But the little Buick made it to Eagle Summit and I went to the town hall and introduced myself to a man there, the township supervisor. I said I was from one of the Williamsport papers and asked him if I could have a look at the pilot. "What's left of him," he said. "I got him back there in a cell." So he took me back and one look convinced me that I wasn't going to win the Pulitzer prize. Whoever he was, the poor guy, he wasn't Slim Lindbergh or Slim Anybody. His face was all burnt away, but the legs and torso belonged to a short stout man. Incidentally, the town supervisor was sore as hell at the dead man. Apparently they all hated airplanes and pilots. "He could of started a fire that would destroy this town," he said. Well, I didn't argue with him. I thanked him and got in my car, but it wouldn't start. I pushed it to the garage and asked the proprietor what he thought. He had a look and confirmed my suspicions. Connecting rod. Could he fix it? He'd have to call up and see where he could get one. It wasn't loose. It was broken. So he called up a Buick dealer in Williamsport and they had a spare, but he couldn't leave right away. I asked him where I could spend the night, and he said I could drive to Williamsport with him and go to a hotel, or I could ask the supervisor to let me sleep in a cell. There were no hotel accommodations in Eagle Summit, obviously, and obviously he didn't give a damn where I slept. While I was thinking it over I heard a Klaxon outside, and I looked and saw a grey Pierce-Arrow, pulled up at the gas tank. At first it was just another grey Pierce, but then the driver got out and it was the man I'd seen at the Carter City station three years earlier. He was even wearing the same Norfolk jacket, but instead of knickers, slacks. He came in and said hello to the garage man, and nodded to me. "Fill it up, will you please, Ed? And fix the puncture in the rear wheel spare." Ed said he wouldn't be able to fix the puncture because he had to drive to Williamsport. And so forth and so on. Leave the spare, he'd fix it the next day. Joe. He called the man Joe.

Well, I was a fresh kid. Twenty-two, and the whole scene at the railroad station came back to me, so I said to Joe, "How is Rollo Fenner?" And of course that baffled him. He tried to pretend that he really recognized me, but all the time racking his brains. Where had he met this kid? Finally it was too much for him and he said so. "I'm sorry," he said, "but I can't remember where I met you." So then I told him the whole story, and he was fascinated that I'd remember. Then I told him why I was in Eagle Summit, and he talked about the newspaper business, about which he knew absolutely nothing, and then about my car. And I told him the truth, by the way. That I was from Gibbsville, not Williamsport. The only reason I'd lied to the supervisor was that I'd learned from experience that if there's anything people dislike more than a newspaper reporter, it's a newspaper reporter from some far-off place. So Mr. Joe Holderman asked me if I knew some friends of his in Gibbsville, and I did, and gave him some details that proved that I knew them pretty well. This conversation took place while Ed was filling Holderman's gas tank, and taking off the spare tire from the carrier in the rear. He didn't have side mounts on that car, unlike most Pierces of that vintage. Anyway, he said it was ridiculous for me to go to a hotel in Williamsport or sleep in the lock-up when he had plenty of room at his house, and after a polite but not very firm protest I accepted his kind invitation. I could tell that Ed, the garage man, thought Holderman was out of his mind. But I could also see that what Ed thought made not the slightest bit of difference to Holderman, and off we went.

He lived about two miles away, in the woods, and the roads were frightful, but when you got there—what a house! It was a sort of super-shooting lodge, is the only way I can describe it. It was in a clearing, but not so much of a clearing that it wasn't protected by the trees when the wind was strong, or in a blizzard. It was a log cabin, luxury style. Two stories and a garage in the cellar, and a porch that went around three sides, and after we put the car away he showed me the view from the porch. From one side of the porch you could see, oh, probably twenty miles that looked like solid timber-land. And from all three sides you saw nothing but acres of forest. It took my breath away, literally, because I just stood and looked without saying a word. It was still daylight, and a wisp of smoke in the distance he said was Williamsport, about twenty miles away as the crow flies, but longer by road. He had a big telescope on the porch, and he gave me a look through it and I could see the fire wardens' towers on the tops of the other mountains. "I'm a sort of honorary fire warden," he said. "Let me show you something." He went to an instrument on a tripod that turned out to be a heliograph. He began working it. "My wife and I have learned the Morse Code. She's faster than I am. I'm signaling to that tower down there to the southeast. He hasn't seen me yet. There! Now he's answering. I'm telling him I just got home. I always tell him when I leave, just so that he can keep an eye on our house. It gives him something to do to break the monotony. He has field glasses but they're not as powerful as my telescope. When I get a new one I'm going to give him this one."

"Have you got a telephone here?"

"Yes, we have, and so has he. But there are times when you can't depend on it. We get some pretty terrific electrical storms in the mountains, and in the winter—you can imagine the snow."

"And at night, I suppose you can communicate with a flashlight?" I said.

"Correct. I have a little flashlight in the shape of a 25-automatic, and that's all I need. Pull the trigger for dots and dashes."

"He can see that that far away?"

"Oh, my yes. When there's no moon I can see him light his pipe. Just the light from his match. He's only about five-and-a-half miles away. Of course I can't always get him right away. He doesn't sit in the dark all night. He'd go out of his mind.

And unfortunately for us, he's only there during the fire season. I mean unfortunately because he varies our routine, too. We like to talk to him."

"Do you know him?"

"Yes, we've had him here for dinner several times. Him and his wife. But frankly he's better company at this distance, and so is she. He talks better by heliograph. In fact, when he's been here he's been very economical with his words, and she's not a very stimulating conversationalist."

"Who, me?"

We turned, and there was Holderman's wife, pretty and short as I remembered her, although not quite so short, with no gigantic Rollo Fenner to make a contrast. Holderman introduced me and explained that I was spending the night and so forth, and she volunteered to show me around the house.

It was what you might imagine. Three rooms and kitchen on the first floor. The middle room was two stories high, with exposed rafters and an open stairway. A magnificent big open fireplace, and on the floor were bear rugs with heads and teeth. All around on the walls were mounted elk and deer and wildcat heads and some stuffed trout and pike. The trophies you'd expect from that part of the world, and a tiger head and a water buffalo and some others from I guess India and Africa. Big tables. Navajo rugs. Big chairs and sofas. In a room on one side of the center room Holderman had a desk and filing case and typewriter and small adding machine, obviously his office. Then on the *other* side of the big room, suddenly you're in an elegant drawing-room. Gilt furniture, light blue carpet. Small paintings, including two by Rollo Fenner. In other words, a completely feminine room. Jade ash trays, for instance. A Chippendale closet filled with bits of china. You couldn't imagine a quicker or more complete escape from the rustic, masculine atmosphere of the center room. But you didn't have to imagine it, because on the second floor, one of the bedrooms was just as feminine, with a canopied bed and a chaise-longue. I almost had to laugh, but I'm glad I didn't. There were three other bedrooms, and they were the rustic type that you'd ex-

pect, heavy furniture, sporting prints, trophies. The feminine
bedroom was next door to a bedroom that you could easily tell
was where they slept most of the time, but there was no connecting door between those two rooms. In her room there was
one bed, not quite a double bed. In the other room, twin beds.
On the other side of the second story, connected by a balcony,
or a gallery, were two guest rooms, and I was given one of
those. Between those two rooms there was a connecting bath,
but the bathroom on the other side of the house was in the rear.
It seemed like an odd arrangement to me. Her personal bedroom had the best view, south and east. It was in the front of
the house, whereas their joint bedroom had only a one-eleva-
tion view. Her room was an escape from an escape, but there
again I'm getting ahead of myself.

All in all, it seemed to me to be the most comfortable house
I'd ever been in. Comfort, informality, and easy luxury. Because the luxury was there, too, don't think it wasn't. The center room downstairs, for instance. Polished hardwood floor.
You wouldn't walk across *it* in hob-nailed boots. And the furniture didn't come from the army-and-navy store. When I said
super-hunting lodge, that's what I meant, and I'm telling you
so much about the house because I spent two nights there and
nearly two days, and all I learned about the Holdermans was
during that time.

They had a couple. I have to invent names for the couple,
because I don't remember their right names. Let's say Jack and
Carolyn. They had their own cabin, back of the main house
and in a different clearing. They were older than the Holdermans. Jack was about fifty. Carolyn, probably in her late forties. Natives, but Joe Holderman and his wife, Violet, had
taught them the little niceties. Jack was a woodsman, but he
functioned as a butler, at least in some things. He wore a lumberjack shirt and no coat, but for instance he unpacked my
small bag and put my things away, and he mixed and served
the cocktails before dinner. But he didn't serve dinner. His
wife did the cooking—or maybe he did. I don't know. But she
waited on table. Not in maid's uniform, but she knew how to

serve. I have to jump around a little bit. For instance, Jack ran my tub before dinner, and while I was taking my bath he pressed my suit, brushed my shoes. And later in the evening, my bed was turned down and one of Holderman's bathrobes was lying on the bed and a pair of bedroom slippers. All done by Jack and Carolyn. Dinner, by the way, was served in the big center room. There was no dining-room as such.

I was pooped. I called up my boss and told him there was no story and that I had engine trouble and wouldn't be back till late the next day. All he said was that I'd have to make it up by working some Sunday. Hell, I worked nearly every Sunday anyway. So after dinner—oh, about nine-thirty or so—Holderman suggested that I go to bed. Had a hard time keeping my eyes open. The long trip, the mountain air, cocktails and a big meal. So I went to bed and slept like an innocent child for about four hours. Then I awoke completely refreshed, turned on the light, and looked around for something to read. I could hear a big grandfather's clock strike the half hours, and I decided to go downstairs and get a magazine. They had everything. *Vanity Fair, The New Yorker, Collier's, Life, Scribner's, Spur, The Field, Country Life, Punch.* And the latest issues, at that. So I put on Holderman's bathrobe and slippers and had no trouble finding my way, because there was a light burning in the big room. Then I noticed that a light was coming from Holderman's office, although the door was closed, and on the way downstairs I heard his typewriter. I felt rather sneaky, so when I'd chosen a magazine I knocked on his door, the office door. He opened it. He was wearing pajamas and a bathrobe, and he had a pipe in his hand. I said I didn't want him to think he was imagining things, and showed him the magazine. "Oh, I heard every sound you made," he said. "Come in and have a chat, if you like." He had a Thermos of coffee and a couple of sandwiches wrapped in waxed paper. He offered me coffee, but I didn't want to get too wide awake, but I sat down and had a cigarette. "This is when I do my writing," he said. "I'm writing a history of the Holderman family, because I'm the last of my line and when I die, we disappear. We weren't very distinguished," he said, "but we did open up a lot of the country around here. I've been at it ever since my wife and I were told we couldn't have children." Naturally he didn't dwell on that, and in fact I was a little surprised that he even mentioned their inability to produce. But he gave me a few more facts, family stuff that I don't remember, but I remember what he told me about himself. He'd gone to school at Andover and that was where he'd met Rollo Fenner, and on a visit to Fenner's house in Maine he'd met Violet Fenner, Rollo's sister. He went to Cornell, but quit college to join the Morgan-Harjes Unit when Fenner did. Then he joined the American army, came home after the war, and married Violet Fenner.

Well, I began to wonder why he was lying to me, and such stupid, insane lying. He was then at least forty years old. And if he'd quit college in 1916, say at the age of twenty, he'd still only be thirty-one. But he was every bit of forty and possibly a year or two older. And yet he was telling me all this with a straight face, to no purpose as far as I could see except that he was off his rocker. And yet he seemed normal, rational, certainly well behaved. He was a polite and considerate host, and at dinner he and his wife had been conventional to the point of dullness. The only out-of-the-ordinary thing I'd noticed at all was her extra-feminine drawing-room and bedroom. And that wasn't too extraordinary. An attractive woman like that, buried in the Northern Pennsylvania woods, it would have been more remarkable if she hadn't wanted some feminine touches, some refuge from this shooting-lodge atmosphere. But I began to wonder what I'd got myself into, and frankly wished that I could get the hell out. But I was stuck, at least till morning, till I could get a ride to Williamsport.

Now this was no wild man. Everything he said was told in the belief that it would be accepted as unquestioned fact. No striving to convince me. And after about a half an hour he very politely suggested that I go back to bed and apologized for boring me with family reminiscence, et cetera. And he never had the least suspicion that I was questioning any of his statements. Nevertheless he had told me some absolutely incredible lies, and to tell you the truth, when I went up to my room, I locked the door.

Naturally I didn't go to sleep for several hours. I put out my light, and then I could look out the window and see that the light was still on in his office, and it stayed on for a couple of hours. I guess I got back to sleep sometime between four and five o'clock, and once I thought I heard people talking, but I couldn't be sure. I slept till about seven-thirty and was awakened by the grey Pierce leaving the property, with Holderman at the wheel. No more sleep for me, so I went downstairs and Carolyn was around, dusting furniture or whatever, and I ordered my breakfast. Then Mrs. Holderman, Violet, showed up. Asked me how I'd slept and so on, and said she was afraid she had bad news for me, although not for her and her husband. She said Ed had called, the garage owner, and he hadn't been able to go pick up the spare part for my car, but would do so that morning. He guessed my car might be ready late that day. So I was stuck with the Holdermans, one of them at least a congenial liar, and the other, Violet, I wasn't sure what. She had a cup of coffee and a cigarette with me, and in the most offhand way she said, "Did you and Joe have a nice chat last night?"

"Yes," I said. "He told me about the family history he's working on."

"Yes, he's been at that a long time," she said. "Sometimes I wish he wouldn't work so hard on it. But he wants to get it all down on paper. When he was in the war he saw so many men die that he developed a fatalistic attitude. The impermanence, you know. Impermanence of life. Don't count on any tomorrow."

"I guess that affected a lot of men's thinking," I said.

"Yes, and especially those that were wounded. My husband was very badly wounded at Belleau Wood," she said.

"In the Marine Corps?" I said.

"Yes. His being alive at all is a miracle, and he's had two operations since the war and is facing another. For two years after the war he was stone deaf," she said. "He hears perfectly well," she said, "but they want to operate again to correct a constant ringing noise. He has a hard time sleeping."

I said, "I hadn't realized he was in the Marines."

"Yes," she said. "He was so pleased to get in. My brother, Rollo, was quite a well-known football player at Harvard, and then he went to live in Paris to study painting, and when the war came Rollo joined the ambulance corps. Came through the war unscathed. Joe had tried out for football at Cornell, but was too light or anyway didn't do very well, and Rollo used to tease him about it. So Joe had something to crow about when he got the Distinguished Service Cross—but at what a price! I don't mean to imply that there's any hostility between them," she said. "If they were real brothers they couldn't be closer than they are." She said her brother visited them whenever he came back to the States, and the two boys, she called them, practically ignored her when Rollo was here. They'd roomed together all through Andover and had gone on a big-game hunting expedition in India the year before she married Joe. She pointed to a tiger head and skin and said that Rollo had shot it. Given it to them as a wedding present, and then gave up hunting. Joe hadn't done any hunting either, since the war. She said I might have noticed something missing in a house like theirs, and I said I couldn't think of a thing that was missing, and she said, "Well, wouldn't you expect to see a gun closet?" And it was true, there were no firearms of any kind visible. "Joe won't have them around," she said. Jack had a rifle and shotguns, but he kept them back in his own cabin.

I relaxed a bit after my conversation with Violet and I got curious about how they spent their days. Also, to be completely honest about it, although she was about forty, which was a very advanced age for me at the time, she looked very inviting in a sweater and skirt and a little pearl necklace. And as the kids say nowadays, she was sending me a message, or so I believed. Let's say the air was heavy with sex, and I wasn't sure whether she knew it or not. I would have been embarrassed to admit to any of my contemporaries that a woman of forty could make me horny, but she did. But the fact that she *was* forty kept me from making a pass at her, although I had several opportunities during the day. I had just enough doubt about what I was feeling, or suspecting, so that I was still a little afraid that if I did make an actual pass, she'd be horrified —or amused. So for the rest of the day I was in a very confused state, hoping for an opportunity to be alone with her, and then when I was alone with her, several times, I couldn't quite carry out my evil intentions. The first move had to come from her.

Well, Holderman came back from Eagle Summit, with the mail and some parcel post, and a report on my car. As to the car, he'd simply *ordered* the garage man to close up and drive to Williamsport. And he could *do* that. He didn't say so, but I inferred that he had money in the garage. But the stuff he brought back from the Eagle Summit post office was interesting. I didn't get to see any of the letters, of course, but he and Violet opened the packages in my presence. For her, some special kind of expensive soap that I forget the name of but I'd heard my aunt speak of it. It was made in France. In his package, two pipes. He'd sent them away to have new bits put in the bowls. I could see that Holderman and his wife got real pleasure out of their parcel post. Like kids. And he explained it. He said, "We live up here in the backwoods, but we don't lose touch with the world. We get all the latest magazines, and we're always sending away for things, little things." And he told me that he kept up his membership in a New York club —this one, without a doubt—although he hadn't been inside the place more than twice since the war, and didn't know when he'd use it again. And every four or five years he'd order a new suit, give an old one to Jack, although the old one hadn't been worn very much, and Jack would give the suit to his son, who was in college somewhere, probably the only boy in the school wearing a hundred-and-fifty-dollar suit. Holderman was getting very close to raising the question why he or they chose to live in the woods, and she was quick enough to anticipate it and she changed the subject. I should mention the fact that nothing he said or did would have aroused the least suspicion as to his being a healthy, normal middle-aged man. Having been alerted to it by her, I could see that he let his hair grow in a strange way around his ear, to cover a bald spot that I assumed was where he'd been operated on. But as far as his conversation and behavior were concerned, he was perfectly all right.

They had two people coming for lunch, a state senator and his wife, who arrived in a big Cunningham phaeton driven by a chauffeur. The wife was related to Holderman, and the senator was just a dull politician who didn't contribute anything and didn't try to hide the fact that he considered the visit a waste of his valuable time. He knew my boss. All those guys knew each other, the subsidized newspaper editors and the politicians that were stooging for big industries in the legislature. They were all grafters in one form or another. They'd all sold out years ago, and they all had big cars and houses in the country or Atlantic City, and I never knew a one of them that didn't overestimate his influence. As long as they voted right they were in, but without the money from the big industries they couldn't have run for dogcatcher. Holderman was rich, but I don't believe he was the big stockholder in any single company of any size. When the senator and his wife left, Holderman was rather apologetic to me. He said his cousin was good company, but she always insisted on bringing her husband. Actually the senator's wife was a rather ordinary woman but at least she'd prattled away during lunch, and she seemed to amuse Violet Holderman. Violet said, "We do our entertaining, such as it is, between Easter and Thanksgiving. After that we can always expect snow, and people are afraid of being marooned up here." So once or twice a week they'd have friends for lunch, but very seldom for dinner.

In the afternoon, after the statesman and wife departed, Holderman and I went for a hike up to the top of the mountain. I was in pretty good shape from tennis and golf, and I lived in a hilly town, but I couldn't keep up with him. On the very top of the mountain he'd put up a sort of shelter. It was open on all four sides, but offered protection from the rain if the rain came straight down. He explained that it was actually a shelter from the rain and the sun. I hadn't thought of the sun. There were no chairs. Only benches, and I sat down to get my breath, and he was quite pleased that a young squirt half his age was winded and he was not. "You see, I'm used to the altitude and you're not," he said. "We're almost three thousand feet above sea level here." Not a great height, but enough to make a difference if you weren't used to it, he said. The view there was of course better than from his house, and he entertained me with a geographical and historical lecture. It was mostly all new to me, and he told it well.

We went back to the house and Violet was waiting for us. That is, she had tea for us and she liked breaking out the best stuff. Holderman commented on it. He said I ought to be complimented, and I was, although I had no way of knowing that she didn't use the silver tea service every afternoon. It would have been in character for her, or them, to use the silver set regardless of guests or no guests. There was a great deal of elegance to the way they lived, notwithstanding the tweeds and lumberjack shirts and the atmosphere of roughing it in the woods. They *weren't* roughing it in the woods. I caught on to the fact that what they were doing was living like the rich on the North Shore, or maybe more like Aiken, although I've never been to Aiken. But with the difference that they didn't belong to any colony, like Aiken people or Westbury people. Then I realized, of course, that the big difference was really the isolation from people. They had people in for meals, but they didn't say anything about going out. No mention was made of going to other people's houses. And then I began to see, with what I'd already found out, that they lived the way they wanted to live because it was the way they *had* to live.

I wasn't finding out much about how they spent their days, what they did with their time, and then within two or three minutes I got some enlightenment on that subject. Holderman finished his tea and said he thought he'd have a nap, and he left us. She said to me, "I'm so glad when he does that. Sleep is *so* important." Then she told me, just as though I'd asked her a direct question, that they never planned anything far ahead, and never had people in more than twice a week. In that way, with such an open schedule, he could go take a nap whenever he felt like it. So that was how they spent their days, waiting for sleep to overtake him. I asked her, "What do you do, Mrs. Holderman?" "What do I do?" she said. "Well, I sew. I do needlepoint." She was teaching Carolyn needlepoint. She'd tried painting, but had given it up because she'd felt that all the talent in that direction had gone to her brother. Very discouraging to look at some of the things her brother had dashed off when he visited them, and she had to work so hard to no avail. She took me to the drawing-room and had me take another look at her brother's paintings, and I dutifully admired them, although actually I was more interested in nature's handiwork —her figure. And ready for the first sign of an invitation from her. But no sign was given. However, the cosmic urge, as we used to call it, was somewhere in her thoughts, in the back of her mind. We went back to the big room and she asked me all about my marital status or engagement status. Did I have a girl? Did I have a lot of girls? Were the girls as wild as older people said they were, or was that exaggerated? Girls had so much more freedom these days, et cetera. The people who'd been there for lunch that day had a daughter that was causing them all sorts of trouble. Sent home from Wellesley, et cetera. Violet said she was glad she didn't have to bring up a daughter in 1927, and that, of course, brought us right back to the house in the woods.

A young newspaper reporter sees so much in the first few years that he begins to think he's seen it all. That makes for a very unattractive wise-guy attitude, what I call unearned cynicism. After you've lived a good many years I don't see how you can be anything but cynical, since all any of us have a right to expect is an even break, and not many get that. But I thought I knew it all, and I didn't. It took me many more years to realize that a reporter covering general news lives an abnormal life, in that he sees people every day at the highest or lowest point of their lives. Day after day after day, people in trouble with the law, having accidents, losing control of themselves—or experiencing great successes. In one month's time a district man would see enough crime and horror and selfishness to last most people the rest of their lives. I can remember a young reporter telling me, when I first went to New York, that when you've seen one electrocution you've seen them all. Well, at that stage of my career I probably would have said the same thing, if I'd thought of it and had seen any electrocutions. God knows I'd seen plenty of nasty things. But I was much too young and comparatively inexperienced to be so omniscient about the Holdermans. At about five-thirty that afternoon, after Violet and I had had our little chat, I was ready to be on my way, quite convinced that I had them ticketed. They'd been interesting enough. Unusual. A war casualty and his reasonably attractive wife, holed up in the woods in an atmosphere of quiet luxury. But they'd become what they call in the newspaper business a one-day story, and I was ready to move on.

From this distance I can be perfectly honest and admit that I was still a little bit hoping she'd make a play for me. I'd never necked or laid a woman quite as old as forty, but there was one in her thirties that used to call me up when her husband was out of town. I don't know why she counted on my keeping my mouth shut. Twenty-two-year-old boys do a lot of boasting. But anyway, Violet was *there,* and *I* was there, and we had a whole evening ahead of us, possibly just the two of us. And she was radiating sex.

Well, she went and had a bath before dinner and so did I, and when I came downstairs she said Holderman was still asleep and we'd eat without him. We did, and after dinner we listened to the radio. They had a special high-powered set, marvelous reception up there in the mountains, and I asked her if she wanted to dance. I'll never forget how she looked at me. She smiled and shook her head, and for the first time I realized that she'd been reading my mind. She didn't say a word. Just smiled and shook her head. She was nice enough not to put it into words. You know—she could have said we didn't dare. Worse yet, she could have danced with me and *then* made a big thing about loyalty to her husband. In any event, I knew right away that she was never going to make a play for me, and that I'd better not make one for her. And with that out of the way, definitely, I relaxed and had a better time. I turned off the radio and we talked. About books and authors. All along the balcony above us the walls were lined with books, and she'd read them. I read a lot then, much more than I do now, and we'd both read a lot of the same things. It wasn't often that I got a chance to pour out what I felt about writing, especially to an attractive woman, and pour it out I did. Then along about nine-thirty Holderman appeared, very apologetic about missing dinner and yet not very refreshed from his long nap. He was in a fog.

She got him something to eat but she wouldn't let him drink any coffee. She wanted him to go back to bed, but he argued with her and as a matter of fact got a little nasty. Nasty for him, that is. "I don't really need you to decide when I should sleep," he said.

"Not deciding anything, just suggesting," she said.

Well, I hung around for a little while, then I said goodnight to them and went to my room. I went to sleep and I don't know how long I slept. Past midnight. And I was awakened by a sound that I thought was some animal. A roaring sound. Not so much noisy as deep, as though the animal were saying the word roar over and over again. Roar, roar, roar, roar. I got fully awake and got up, and by this time I realized that it was not an animal but Holderman, having a nightmare in his office. I was going to go downstairs and actually had my door open, and then I saw her. She was in her nightgown, hurrying across the big room to Holderman's office, and in a minute or so they came out of the office. They had their arms around each other's waists and she was talking to him. I couldn't tell what she was saying because he was talking too. Then they went up the stairs to her room, the fancy bedroom, and she closed the door, and I closed mine.

Try and go back to sleep under those circumstances, but I did, eventually. In the morning I went down to breakfast and

Holderman was there, I remember he was wearing the same old Norfolk jacket and smoking a pipe. "Your car is ready," he said. "I'll take you down to Eagle Summit as soon as you've had breakfast." He was rested and relaxed, and affable. Violet waited on me herself, and she was happy too. I was finishing breakfast and Holderman said he'd go down and get the Pierce started and I could come down when I was ready, no hurry. Soon as I finished my packing.

She lit my cigarette while I was having my second cup of coffee. "Now you understand us a little better," she said.

"A little," I said.

"Oh, you will a lot when you think about us," she said. "I saw your door open last night."

"Oh," I said, which was all I could think of to say.

Then she said, "You're going to be a nice man, you have feelings."

And I said, "Well, you're a nice woman. You have feelings."

"People aren't nice without them. *He* has them." Then she said, "Do you see anything here you'd like to take home with you? As a memento?" I looked around and God knows there were a lot of things, an embarrassment of riches, so to speak, and she obviously wanted me to take something, so I picked up an old-fashioned silver match-safe. "How about this?" I said. "It's yours," she said. "And this," and she kissed me. "Just a token," she said. And she knew what I was thinking—wondering why all the generosity. "Why?" she said. "Because I've watched your young eyes taking in everything, and your curiosity's been very complimentary," she said. "Give me your address, where I can write to you. I think you'll want to know how he comes out of this next operation, and I'd like to be able to tell you. I hardly need tell you that it won't be on his ear," she said.

Well, she never did write to me, never a line. And while I'm on the subject, I haven't the faintest idea what happened to the match box. It was very good-looking. On one side was a picture of a pack of hounds baiting a bear. I think the other side was blank.

First Day in Town

At twenty-five past one Nick Orlando, alone, got out of a taxi, punched the doorman playfully in the ribs, and entered the restaurant. In the foyer there was a crowd, mostly women, who wanted to sit downstairs but who, as matinee time got nearer, were about to decide to go upstairs. Nick Orlando firmly pushed his way forward among these women. At his touch they would turn angrily and say, "I *beg* yaw podden— *oh, Nick Orlando!* It's Nick Orlando!"

The captain of waiters raised his hand high. He had not immediately seen Nick Orlando, whose height only flatteringly could be called average, but the repetition of the Orlando name reached the captain. "I have your table, Mr. Orlando," he said. Then, when Nick Orlando had pushed his way to the rope, the captain whispered, "I don't have a table, but maybe you see somebody." Nick Orlando, who had not said a word since getting out of the taxi, squeezed the captain's arm. He nodded; he saw somebody.

He made his way to a banquette where two women were seated side by side; the one a girl of twenty or so, with a scarf knotted about her neck; the other a woman in her late thirties, who had a ballpoint pen in her right hand and was writing something in a stenographer's dictation tablet. Nick Orlando, heading for this table, picked up a chair without asking permission of a threesome at an island table. He set the chair down so that he faced the two women on the banquette. The girl squinted. "Go away. You're lousing up my interview," she said, laughing.

"Oh, say, this is a treat," said the interviewer. "Nick Orlando. You know where I met you? At Harry Browning's."

"Who is Harry Browning?" said Nick Orlando.

"Get him! Pretending you don't know who Harry Browning is," said the girl. "Five years ago you *didn't* know who Harry Browning is, you'd be telling the truth then, you big faker. When did you get *in,* you dog?"

"What's the interview for?" said Nick Orlando.

"My syndicate. My name is Camilla Strong."

"Your syndicate? I bet it aint the syndicate I got friends in. Syndicate. A syndicate is a man that knows the price of everything and the value of nothing. Who said that, Camilla?"

"Oscar Wilde."

"You *know,* hey? Wud you, go to college, Camilla?"

"I sure did," said Camilla Strong.

"This jerk just stard reading books three years ago, and now the whole field of literature is all his. All his. Nobody ever read anything before him, hey, jerk?"

"Where did you two know each other? Is this a thing with you two?" said Camilla Strong. "Should I have known about this?"

"Her? This tramp?"

"Don't make it too emphatic, jerk, or otherwise she'll think we did have a thing," said the girl. "No, we didn't have a thing, but not for want of him trying."

"That's where everybody makes a mistake with this tramp, is trying. Nobody has to try with this one."

"Oh, I wish I could write this the way it really comes out," said Camilla. "If they'd ever print it."

"Go ahead write it," said Nick Orlando. "You're not gonna destroy any illusions. You seen her that night on the Paar show."

"Aah, shut up with the Paar show," said the girl. "Why'd you have to remind her of that? We been here since one o'clock and not a word about the Paar show till *you* crashed the party."

"Two nominations for Tonys, and one Academy Award, and what are you famous for?" said Nick Orlando.

"You know what really happened, Camilla, was I never

drink. I don't have any tolerance for it. And this jerk made me take two drinks before I was to go on. Two, and one is all I need to get looping. Write that in your article. The inside story of Mary Coolidge getting cut off the air. I think he did it on purpose, too."

"What else? I told you I did it on purpose. You were getting too big for your britches. Your *head* was getting too big for your britches."

"You know, Nick, I really hate you. I hate you with a cold, consuming, venomous hatred."

"I know you do, but I can't get you to admit it."

"You kids, do you talk this way all the time?" said Camilla.

"When we're talking. Sometimes we aren't on conversational terms," said Nick Orlando.

"I wish that was now," said Mary Coolidge. "How did you know I was here?"

"Stop with the kidding. Camilla knows I was with you till an hour ago," said Nick Orlando.

"Oh, now you said too much, Nick," said Camilla. "Unfortunately I've been with Mary since ten o'clock this morning."

"She said you were here since one o'clock," said Nick Orlando.

"Interviewing. But all morning I was with her picking out the dresses for the new play. If you're going to ruin a girl's reputation you've got to do better than that, Nick. What about *you*, by the way? I know you're in town for the opening of *Mad River*."

"You seen it yet?"

"No, I missed two screenings, but I hear you're only great in it. If I call Irving Rudson maybe we could set up an interview. Are you booked pretty solid?"

"Irving don't know I'm in town. I come in a day early."

"To louse up my interview," said Mary Coolidge. "And you succeeded, so go away."

"Oh, he didn't louse it up, Mary. I can have sort of fun with this. It'll read better than just an ordinary interview."

"I don't give ordinary interviews," said Mary Coolidge.

"Ooh, I think this one is burning," said Nick Orlando. "I don't know if it's me or you she's sore at."

"Mary isn't sore at anybody. Where are you staying?"

"Sixteen Twenty-four Pitkin Avenue."

"That's Brooklyn. You're from The Bronx."

"Kidding. I got an uncle living on Pitkin Avenue. I'm at the Sherry. You set it up with Irving."

"And I'll come along and louse it up," said Mary Coolidge.

Camilla Strong pressed the button of her ballpoint, and closed the notebook. "I don't know what your act is, you two. I can't fathom whether you're a thing or not a thing. Come on, level with Camilla before I go."

"I'm mad for him, but religion keeps us apart," said Mary Coolidge.

"Religion? You're both Italian extraction, aren't you?"

"Yeah, but I want to be a nun and he wants to be a priest. So religion keeps us apart," said Mary Coolidge.

"This is a very fast little girl, Nicky," said Camilla.

"Talking, but not running," said Nick Orlando. "She can outtalk anybody but I never heard of her outrunning anybody. Never."

"I kind of think she outran you," said Camilla Strong. "But I'll find that out when I interview you. 'Bye now, kids." She left.

Nick Orlando moved to the vacated seat. "That'll be the day. When that broad interviews me."

"You son of a bitch. I had her in the palm of my hand till you came along. I'm doing the sweetness-and-light bit. The new Mary Coolidge. You know what's in that notebook? All about how I want to do Joan of Arc, for God's sake."

"They all want to do Joan of Arc."

"They all *do* do Joan of Arc, but I'm right for it. I'd hit them with a Joan of Arc that they could smell burning flesh."

"I'd pay to see that. Where did you go last night?"

"None of your God damn business."

"I heard Harry Browning was giving a party. I damn near went," said Nick Orlando.

"Who is Harry Browning?"

"That's *my* line. When did you get my wire?"

"I got your wire Sunday, in plenty of time if I'd of wanted to have a date with you, but I don't. You're a Hollywood hambo."

"Oh, that again. If you were prettier and more photogenic there wouldn't be any knocks on Hollywood."

"You got it mixed up. I said *you* were a Hollywood *hambo*."

"Is that worse than a Broadway hambo?"

"Infinitely. A Hollywood hambo is chicken, sells out for security. At least a Broadway hambo fights for parts, parts he wants. But you Hollywood hamboes take anything the studio says."

"Not me. I don't have to, it's in my contract."

"Mad River. I hear you play a cowboy. You a cowboy?"

"So you're right for Joan of Arc. What the hell are we talking in circles? Why won't you have a date with me? And don't give me that Hollywood hambo answer."

"I could ask you, why do you keep pestering after me? From the first time I ever met you you thought all you had to do was ask, and I'd give you a date. That *paisana* stuff."

"Answer the question. Why didn't you? Why don't you now?"

"Because nobody gets a date with me that I don't want to go out with. You tell me I'm not pretty. All right, then why do you want a date with me? You know why? Because from the first I'd never go out with you and it's no different now with you a star and me a star. You know what the trouble is? You're jealous of me, and if you get me in bed with you you think you don't have to be jealous any more. The kind of a fellow you are, I go to bed with you and it doesn't make any difference if I'm a better actor than you. You can go around and tell everybody you slept with Mary Coolidge. I know bellboys that slept with famous actresses, but does that make them a better actor? You want to get in bed with me, Nick, I'll be proud to —when you're a good enough actor so I can brag about sleeping with you. But not before. So give up. You know who I get phone calls from? From Paris and London and all over? A really big star. Not like you or I, but a *big* star. And you know why I won't have a date with him? Because as an actor he stinks. And you know what his trouble is? He's jealous of me. He's like you. Last season he came to see me every night for a week and two matinees, torturing himself. 'If I could be as good as that little bitch up there, that homely little bitch.' So he wants to take it out in going to bed with me. Like you."

"What the hell is acting?"

"Right! It's a phoney business, but you don't have to be a phoney *in* it. If you're gonna be an actor, don't be a phoney actor. If you're gonna be in a phoney business that's all the more reason why you shouldn't be a phoney in it."

"You're a phoney."

"No. If I was a dishwasher I'd want to be a good one. You know what I'm gonna give this waiter for a tip? Ten dollars. Because he's a good waiter. That waiter over there, I give him ten percent if it comes to forty-eight cents. I count out the three pennies."

"They pool their tips, so what's the difference?"

"Because this waiter I hand him the ten bucks and say thank-you, and the other waiter I just put the money on the dish and say nothing. That's the difference, and they both know the difference. My applause. Don't tell me applause doesn't mean anything to you?"

"You want to know something? I get a hand in *Mad River*. I got two scenes in there where I get a hand."

"How many takes?"

"What?"

"How many takes before you got the scenes right?"

"Ah, nuts," said Nick Orlando. He got up and pushed his way through the matinee-bound crowd. *"Nick! Nick! It's Nick Orlando! Could I have your autograph please? On this menu? On this package?"* He did not stop until he reached the curb.

"Get me a hack, quick," he said to the doorman.

"Right away," said the doorman. He stood in the street, a few feet from the curb, waving for a taxi. "I hear very good reports on *Mad River*," he said.

"Yeah, I'm spreading them all over," said Nick Orlando.

The doorman laughed. "Well, I'll say this for you, Nick. You didn't change. You're just the same. Some of them go out there. . . ." He shook his head.

2

At the next restaurant Nick Orlando was not so well known. He was recognized by the doorman and by the hatcheck boys, but this was not a theatrical crowd, and Nick Orlando could not count on a headwaiter to fake a reservation. "Good afternoon, Mr. Nick Orlando," said one of the proprietors. "You meeting someone?"

"Well, sort of," said Nick Orlando. "I have a sort of a half date."

"Well, if they're here I can tell you. Who is your party?"

The first name that came to Nick Orlando's mind was Harry Browning's. "Sort of looking for Harry Browning."

"Mr. Harry Browning is here, lunching with the eminent playwright Mr. Asa Unger. You know Asa, I'm sure. I'll take you right to them myself. Just follow me, sir."

The proprietor led Nick Orlando to a remote table, in a section usually referred to as left field. Nick Orlando hated every step of the way, which took him farther from the choicest tables, and his only consolation was that Harry Browning, a steady customer, and Asa Unger, a writer of hits, had done no better. Browning and Unger were sitting with their backs to the wall and could see everything that was going on, including Nick Orlando's approach. They both showed some surprise when it became unmistakable that Nick Orlando was joining them.

"Nick-ee, Nicky boy!" said Harry Browning.

"Your party," said the proprietor, leaving them. Nick Orlando did not speak until the proprietor was out of earshot and unable to guess that he had not been expected.

Harry Browning held out both hands and closed them over Nick Orlando's hand. "You know Asa, Asa Unger."

"Sure. Hi, Asa," said Nick Orlando.

"Hello, Nick. Long time."

"Long time is right."

"Cohasset, four years ago," said Asa Unger.

"That's right, you played Spike in *Dangerous Illusion*. Right?" said Harry Browning. "Nicky, why don't you stir up a little enthusiasm for a picture buy? Asa don't need the money, but I'd like to see *Illusion* a picture. I *always* said it was a natural for any studio that had the right man for Spike. Well, you're it, Nicky, and they'll listen to you now. They *gotta* listen to you now. *Mad River*—a blockbuster. I was talking to Irving Rudson before, and he read me the *Time* and *Newsweek* notices over the phone. You see them yet, Nicky?"

"No."

"Irving read them to me over the phone. They echo what the trade reviews said. Nicky, what did they bring *River* in for, do you happen to know?"

"Two million four was the last figure I heard."

"It'll do seven and a half. It'll do eight. You eat yet or you meeting someone?"

"I ate before, but I'll have a cup of coffee with you," said Nick Orlando.

"Listen, fellows, I got a train to catch," said Asa Unger.

"Asa opened in Philly the night before last," said Harry Browning.

"I know," said Nick Orlando, lying. "How'd it go, Asa?"

"Don't read the Philadelphia notices," said Asa Unger. "I'm getting into another line of work."

"They weren't that bad, Asa. Honestly they weren't. You read them over again and the *Bulletin* fellow, he only said what we were saying all along. I'll be over tonight on the six o'clock train. See you, Asa."

"Hang in there, boy," said Nick Orlando.

"Thanks," said Asa Unger. He left.

"Take his seat, Nicky. Sit here," said Harry Browning. "Asa

got a real dog for himself this time. They murdered him in Philly. Sheer murder. He didn't want to show his face in the theater. You know, a sensitive guy like Asa. He wrote a kind of an open letter to the cast, that he wanted to put up on the bulletin board, but I persuaded him. I said id be a mistake. But he's taking it to heart, Asa. Nicky, get the studio to offer him forty thousand for *Illusion*, and I'll let it go for fifty."

"They don't want it for five. They don't want it for free."

"I don't know, Nicky. You may be making a mistake," said Harry Browning. "He may have other properties later on, something you like. This guy's an in-and-outer, and maybe the next one could be very big. Take *Illusion* for fifty now, and I promise you first refusal on his next hit. That's a firm promise."

"I can't do it. *Illusion* stinks."

"All right, well I tried. Now what's with you? Got in when, yesterday? I had a big bash and I looked for you, but I guess you had something lined up."

"Something, yeah," said Nick Orlando.

"There's a lot around. I don't know where it all comes from, but suddenly there's seventy-five new faces. It happens that way every year. Suddenly you look around and while you been busy the new stuff's been catching up on you. At my party there was four or five I never saw before."

"You been busy?"

"As busy as an agent at option-time—and who else should that happen to? Yeah, I been busy. A little thing called Mary Coolidge that I don't doubt for a minute that you know her, but who would ever figure me going for her? Talent and all that, but a mutt. A homely mutt. And egotistical? That's all right if she was doing the intellectual bit with Asa. But I'm not Asa. I like a dumb, pretty broad that looks good without any clothes on and never knew from Ibsen. Nevertheless, I found myself calling her up two-three times a day and couldn't wait, *couldn't wait* till I got her in the kip. And it's nothin' there, believe me. Oh, you know, it's all right, but can you explain to me what I want to bother with her for, when you know yourself, Nicky, like you see that broad just getting up over there? The tan suit? I get a call from her about every two-three months, notwithstanding although she was kept by two millionaires and married one of them." The handsome girl in the tan suit turned and waved to Harry Browning, just a tiny little wave with her fingers to which he responded in kind, an exchange which passed unnoticed by others in the restaurant. "The Ivy League type with her is the husband. I can have that any time I want to, but the last six months I been concentrating on Mary Coolidge."

"Does Coolidge go for you?"

"I gotta be truthful with you there. In three words, I don't know. Here's the situation, Nicky, and you figure it out. This egotistical, homely little mutt, she got two pet names for me. Not dearie or sweetheart. She calls me rascal and scoundrel. Hello, Rascal. Hello, Scoundrel. She says I'm the only pure, unmitigated scoundrel she ever knew. Well, I get called all kinds of names and epithets, but who is she to call me anything? Five years ago she was lucky to get a walk-on in that play of Asa's, *Mainliner*. About the junkies. What was *I* doing five years ago? Well, I had my elder son graduating from Deerfield and I give him a T-Bird for graduation. I had a little piece of property, six acres in Mount Kisco. I had twelve people on my payroll in New York, and I was spending more money in this place alone than Mary Coolidge could earn in two years. Then. She's big now, I grant you. Money-wise and billing-wise, she's big. But I saw bigger ones come and go before she knew if rascal was spelt with a *k*. She's what I call a ten-dollar thinker."

"Yeah? How, Harry?"

"Well, I tell you. She'll give a waiter a ten-dollar tip for a meal that only runs her three or four dollars. Or else she'll give the waiter thirty-five cents, depending on if she likes the waiter."

"I get it, yeah."

"No, I didn't finish. The point is, she has a ten-dollar psychology. Ten dollars is still a lot of money to her. The big gesture. That's the difference between her and some of the dames I used to know. A lousy sawbuck? I used to go out with dames that gave a sawbuck to the woman in the little girls' room. This one, this Mary Coolidge, she'd be good for a quarter, a half a dollar at the most. You know, I wish I'd of known somebody like Anna Held. *There* was no ten-dollar psychology. Or even Bernhardt. Bernhardt was slow with a dollar, but you know what she used to do on tour? She got twenty-five hundred dollars a night, and every night before she'd go on, it had to be all there in gold. In gold. Before she'd go on. Ten dollars for a tip. Big deal. Nicky boy, where can I take you? You want to use my car and shofer for the afternoon?"

"What are you riding in these days?"

"The same. I got the Rolls. You know me, Nicky. I gotta hear that clock ticking. Very soothing. You sure you don't want to help Asa? I gotta go over to Philly tonight, and I wish I had something to tell him on the positive side."

"Well, I know the studio is looking for something."

"You're my boy, Nicky. Offer forty and we'll take fifty, and then you can burn the God damn play. Asa will come up with something one of these days, and he listens to me."

"You're a scoundrel, Harry."

"I know. And a rascal. Thank God I don't have to listen to that tonight. Gettin' weary, Nick. If you want to make a move in that direction, she's all yours."

"Why would I?"

"Well, we did a lot of talking about her. That's what I call buyer-interest. We wouldn't of done that much talking if you didn't show some buyer-interest, Nicky. Hey?"

"A little. I know her, but I never thought of her that way."

"Well, as far as I'm concerned, I've had it. You take it from the top, boy."

"Maybe I'll do that, once around," said Nick Orlando.

3

"Take me over to 414 East Fifty-second. I'm sure you know the way," said Nick Orlando.

"I been there a couple times," said Harry Browning's chauffeur.

"How long did Harry have this rig?"

"This is our fourth year for it."

"You buy it new?"

"Imported it brand new. Mr. Browning has a corporation."

"Oh, yeah. That gag."

"The garage we use, there's eight other Rolls and there's only the one owned private. The government'll slap down one of these days, but we'll still have a good car. We only got less than seventy thousand miles on this."

"Just driving around New York City?"

"Oh, no. I go to Boston for when the boss has a play opening there. Like tomorrow I go to Philly."

"Why doesn't Harry go with you?"

"He gets car-sick on a long ride. Over twenty miles he goes by train or flies. And like some of the clients have the use of the car as a favor. Where you're going now the young lady had me and the car for a week in Boston and a week in Philly, a year ago, during tryouts."

"She a good tipper?"

The chauffeur shrugged his shoulders. "I get a good salary."

"In other words, she's a stiff?"

"I don't want to talk about a client."

"Come on, give. What the hell?"

"Well, you don't have to tell *her* this, but if you're gonna ride around in a Rolls, you don't have to give out with a lot of communist propaganda. I'm not ashamed to wear a uniform. A uniform goes with the job. She wouldn't insult a subway guard, but he has to wear more of a uniform than I do. If it wasn't for the cap you wouldn't know this *was* a uniform.

And the cap ain't so bad. It's just a cap that matches the suit. I wear this suit to Mass on Sunday, with a regular hat."

"What's the most tip she ever gave you?"

"Oh, I don't want to talk about that."

"For a week in Boston? Ten bucks?"

"On the nose."

"And in Philly?"

"In Philly, nothing. I give her an argument in Philly. I told her, I said she had to wear costumes in her line of work, and I wear a uniform in mine, and I didn't see no difference. I don't, either. I'm not a downtrodden servant. I'd just as soon punch you in the nose if I had cause to. Or anybody. But I bet you she wouldn't punch Mr. George Abbott in the nose, or Eli Kazan. Would you punch Spyros Skouras in the nose?"

"I'd think twice about it."

"Well, there you are. Any of those people I'd punch them in the nose if I was driven to it. I'm not show business, see? Oh, where you're going, she don't like me. I seen her for a phoney right away." The back of his neck had begun to redden. *"And you can tell her, go ahead!"*

"What made you so sore all of a sudden?"

"That's the way she affects me. As soon as I begin thinking about her I boil up."

"She's your boss's girl friend."

"Oh, he knows how I feel about her. It's impossible to keep a thing like that from Harry Browning. He's too smart. In some ways. In other ways—but he's learning about this one."

"You think he is, eh?"

"I know he is. Nine years with a man, I can tell when he's getting fed up sometimes before he knows it himself. You're from The Bronx, aren't you? What parish are you in?"

"I used to go to St. Nicholas of Tollentine."

"Yeah? Our Lady of Mercy, not very far away. The same section."

"Our Lady of Mercy, sure. We used to call it Old Lady Murphy."

"This creature you're on your way to, she attended O.L.M., but you wouldn't know it today, to hear the propaganda. Her and the boss have arguments, and there's a man that made a couple million dollars at least. Maybe he don't have it all, but he made it. And *she* tells *him* about the economic system. Why, a day that he don't net a thousand dollars he considers it a waste. He told me that, himself. A funny man. He'll spend forty dollars for lunch any time it'll net him five thousand. That's what he says to me. I could listen to him by the hour. Orlando. Did you've a cousin living on Marion Avenue worked for Con Edison?"

"No, Orlando isn't my real name. I took the name Orlando because my own name was too long. Too many *c*'s in it."

"Pete Orlando. He lived on Marion Avenue near 196th Street. He had a job with the Consolidated Edison, and I used to bowl with him. You know what her name was before she took Coolidge?"

"Cuccinello. Mary Cuccinello. That had a lot of *c*'s in it too."

"Fred Allen would have been just as funny with the name Sullivan."

"Fred Allen? Oh, Fred Allen."

"Don't tell me you're forgetting the great Fred Allen."

"Oh, no, I used to listen to his program when I was a kid. That was on radio."

"Senator Claghorn and Mrs. Nussbaum? Don't you remember them? And the feud with Benny? Jack Benny? That was great entertainment. Who have they got like that today, I ask you? Well, maybe Bob Hope, if he was on oftener. But what do they consider funny nowadays? This young woman you're on your way to, accidentally on purpose saying something dirty."

"You think she did it on purpose?"

"Sure I do. I said to my wife, 'You watch her. Before the night's over she'll say something dirty,' and by God it wasn't two minutes later she come out with the remark and they cut her off the air. They ought to have some way to fine them when they do that, a good big fine, five thousand dollars, and they'd soon put a stop to it. If they knew there was a fine hanging over them, there wouldn't be them slips, so-called."

"How did you know she was going to say something?"

"Because I had enough experience with her, driving her here and Boston and Philly. I know her ways."

"What if I said I was in love with her?"

"Huh. Then I'd say God help you."

"Your boss has been stuck on her for a long time."

"Huh. You don't know the first thing about it. Harry I. Browning knows what he's doing, every minute of the time, whether it's a girl friend or a client or who it is. Well, here we are. I'll be parked along here somewhere."

"You don't have to wait."

"The boss said you could use the car all afternoon and to-night, if you wanted to. I don't mind waiting. I'll be up talking to the other drivers up at River House, in case you don't see me when you come out."

"I don't know when I'll be out."

"Well, you suit yourself about that, Mister. If you don't want me to wait."

"I don't. Here. Thanks." Nick Orlando gave the driver a ten-dollar bill.

4

"What made you so sure I'd let you in? What made you so sure I'd even be here?" said Mary Coolidge.

"I wasn't sure, but I had a hunch you'd be here reading the new play. I know that much about you," said Nick Orlando.

"Smart."

"What is the play? What kind of a part have you got?"

"You don't read the New York papers any more? You got to that stage, hey?"

"I been on location in Idaho. You know where Idaho is?"

"Yeah. Lana Turner comes from Idaho."

"On location, living in a trailer. You weren't in pictures long enough to spend much time on location."

"The name of the play is *A Pride of Lions*," she said, waving a script. "Nobody in Idaho will ever see it because there's no picture in it."

"Maybe that's a good reason for going back to Idaho. Who wrote it?"

"You never heard of him. But you will. He's a young Pakistani, or he was. He hung himself two years ago at Cambridge University, in England."

"Well, that way you're not gonna have any author-trouble at rehearsal. Who's directing?"

"A brilliant, brilliant boy I discovered in an off-Broadway theater last winter. A brilliant, brilliant, brilliant boy."

"Is he grateful, grateful, grateful?"

"Huh?"

"This brilliant, brilliant boy. You know what I like in a director is a director that will take direction, but they're pretty hard to find."

"This boy is creative."

"Oh, then him and you are rewriting the play."

"Wud you come here for, Nick? To rape me or just upset me?"

"I don't know. What do you want me to do?"

"Go back to Hollywood is what I want you to do. You know what I see when I look at you? A dead man. Dead. You started out with something and then you sold out for a Hollywood Cadillac."

"A Maserati. I got a special Maserati. Cadillacs are for Squaresville."

"Then you oughta have one, because you're cubic, man. That's square to the nth degree. Cubic."

"I read you, Maria. Loud and clear. What are you doing tonight?"

"Working, on this. We start rehearsals in two weeks."

"Don't *tell* me you're not up in your part. I thought you were a perfectionist."

"My part? You know how many lines I got in the first act? Four. The second act, ten. The third act, ten or eleven. The fourth act, two."

"What happened to the fifth act? Were you running over? Who has the speaking parts in this play?"

"This play is almost pure pantomime."

"Jevver see a picture, *The Thief,* with Ray Milland?"

"No, but I heard about it. Propaganda."

"No dialog, though."

"Don't mention it in the same breath."

"Then three or four years from now, after you finish your run in this play, you want to do Joan of Arc, you said."

"I don't know if we'll be finished with it in three years."

"We? You mean you and some writer are collaborating on a new one?"

"Not *some writer.* A. R. Lev."

"Who?"

"A. R. Lev, my director in *A Pride of Lions.*"

"Oh, *that* A. R. Lev. I thought you were talking about A. R. Lev that works for J. P. Morgan and Company."

"What's with this dichotomy of yours all of a sudden? Ha' past one you were like a high school teen-ager that I wouldn't give a date. Now you sit here and all you are is destructive. What happened in the meanwhile?"

"I don't know. I guess I finally figured out what a real jerk you are."

"Then why are you sitting here in my apartment?"

"Yeah, but I'm not." He got up. "I just wanted to have the pleasure of telling you. So long, Cuccinello."

"*Nicky!* Don't leave me?"

Exactly Eight Thousand Dollars Exactly

What had once been a pleasant country club, its members consisting largely of young couples on the way up, was now an "industrial park"; and on the old site of the tennis courts was a long, low, windowless building, a laboratory for research in synthetics. The clubhouse was still recognizable beneath the renovations that had converted it into executive offices, but the first and eighteenth fairways were leveled off and covered with blacktop, a parking area for the plant employees. At approximately the location of the second tee there was a roped-off space, with a sign that warned against getting too close to the helicopter which transported plant officials to the municipal airport. One reminder of the former character of the place remained: a golf cart carried officials from the helicopters to the executive offices. A ten-foot-high fence surrounded the entire property and above the fence was strung barbed wire. The fence proper was painted white, but there is no way to make barbed wire look like anything but barbed wire.

The man in the small Renault stopped his car at the gate, and a man in uniform, with a badge that said "Security Officer" and a revolver holster, bent over to speak to the driver of the car. "Good afternoon, sir. May I help you?" The *may* sounded false and sissy, as though it seemed false and sissy to the officer himself.

"Yes, thanks. I'm here to see Mr. D'Avlon."

"Yes sir. Name please?"

"Mr. Charles D'Avlon," said the driver of the car.

"Oh, right. You're expected, Mr. D'Avlon." The guard

could not refrain from a surprised look at the small car. "Will you just pin this badge on your lapel and return it to the officer on duty on your way out?" Charles D'Avlon accepted a plastic square which had a safety pin attached to the reverse side; on the obverse side was printed "VISITOR—D'Avlon Industries—355—This badge must be worn at all times while visitor is on Company property. Please return to Security Officer, Main Gate, on completion of visit."

"Where do I park?"

"A space reserved for you, Number 355, executive parking. That'll be that third row. One, two, three. Please leave your key in the car."

"Oh? Why?"

"That's regulations, sir. All cars."

"My brother's, too?"

"Yes sir. Mr. Henry D'Avlon leaves his key in the car just the same as I do."

"A somewhat different car from mine, though, I imagine."

"Well, you see that black and gray Rolls? That's your brother's. But the key's in it just the same. That's in case we have to move the cars in a hurry."

"In an emergency?"

"Correct."

"Such as an explosion?"

"Any emergency that comes up," said the guard. He did not like the word explosion or the slightly frivolous tone of D'Avlon's remark. "By the time you got your car parked the escort will be there to escort you to Executives' Reception." The guard went back into his glass sentry box and picked up a telephone. D'Avlon drove to the parking space.

The escort was a younger man in a uniform similar to the guard's but without the revolver. "Your first visit, I understand," said the escort.

"My first visit to the plant. I've been here before, but when it was a golf club."

"Oh, yes. That was quite some time ago."

"I would think before you were born."

"I guess *so*," said the young man.

"Are we waiting for someone else?"

"Just waiting for you to pin your badge on."

"Even if I'm with you?"

"Everybody has to wear his badge. You wouldn't get ten feet without it."

"What would happen to me?"

"Be detained. If you didn't have a satisfactory explanation you'd be arrested for trespassing. You saw all those signs on the fence. This is a pretty efficient operation."

"Is that since the explosion?"

"We've always taken security precautions here," said the young man, evasively.

"Why don't *you* carry a gun?"

"What makes you think I don't?" The young man reached in his pocket and brought out a .25 automatic. "It's no .38, but a lot of women have got rid of a lot of husbands with one of these. They aren't bulky, slip into your pants pocket, and some visitors don't feel right walking with a man with a holster. But if you hit a man in the throat with one of these slugs, he wouldn't be much use."

"Can you hit a man in the throat?"

"In the eye, with a little time and the right distance. Some cops call it a jealousy gun. And we practice firing it. The women don't even practice, and look what they do with it. It's a mean little fellow. This way, sir."

The handsome young woman in Executives' Reception bowed and smiled at Charles D'Avlon and apparently pushed a button that released the lock on the door into a corridor. At any rate she did not speak to D'Avlon or to the young security officer. "This way, sir," said the young man. They rode one flight up in an automatic elevator, then proceeded to the end of the second-story corridor, to a door marked President. The young man held that door open for Charles D'Avlon, and a man rose to greet the stranger.

"Okay, Mr. Lester?" said the security officer.

"Okay, Van," said the man addressed. He was about forty-five, wore half-shell glasses and a blue four-in-hand that was embroidered with what appeared to be a long exclamation point. His dark blue suit had narrow lapels and his pocket handkerchief, neatly folded, showed enough to reveal, in the very center, the initials D.W.L. "Have a seat, Mr. D'Avlon. Your brother will be right with you. You have a nice trip out?"

"Out from town, or out from Connecticut?"

"Well—from Connecticut."

"Oh, it was all right. Gave me a chance to see a lot of the country."

"Didn't you use to live here?"

"Oh, sure. We were born here, but it's all changed. I used to play golf here when I was a young man. Do you know where you're sitting?"

"How do you mean?"

"You're sitting in the ladies' can. That's what this was. The ladies' locker-room."

"I wasn't with the company then."

"There wasn't any company then."

"No, I guess not," said Mr. Lester. He sat with his hands folded on his desk.

"Go ahead with your work, if you want to. Don't let me hold you up," said Charles D'Avlon.

"I'm waiting for—there he is," said Mr. Lester. He rose as the door at his right was opened.

"Hello, Chiz," said the man in the doorway. "Come on in."

"Hello, Henry," said Charles D'Avlon. The brothers shook hands and Charles entered the president's office.

It was a corner room with a magnificent view of the rolling countryside and a distant mountain. "I was just telling your man Lester, his office is in the ladies' can."

"Well, that proves one thing," said Henry. "You haven't changed much. You always liked to throw people a little off balance."

"Don't be disagreeable, Henry. It's tough enough to be here under the circumstances. Don't make it tougher."

"Chiz, you're the one that always makes things tougher for yourself."

"I didn't say you made things tougher. I just said they were tough enough. I swore I'd never ask you for a nickel, but here I am."

"Yes," said Henry. "Well, we got right to the point. How much do you want?"

"A lot."

"Oh, I guessed that. If it was a little you wouldn't feel you had to make such a long trip. How much, Chiz?"

"Eight thousand dollars."

"All right. But why eight? Why not five, or why not ten? I'm curious to know how you arrived at the figure eight thousand."

"I thought it would sound businesslike."

"As though you'd figured it out very carefully. Okay, it does," said Henry. He spoke into the inter-com on his desk. "Dale, will you make out a cheque, my personal account, eight thousand dollars, payable to Charles W. D'Avlon, and bring it in for my signature as soon as it's made out? Thank you."

"Aren't you interested in what I want it for?" said Charles.

"Not very much. You have some story, and it comes to eight thousand dollars. You probably need five, but you thought you might as well get three extra."

"That's right," said Charles. "But I hate to waste the story. I had a good one."

"Write it and sell it to a magazine."

"I can't write. If I could write I'd have plenty of material, but first you said you were interested in why I said eight thousand, and in the next breath you don't want to hear my story."

"I wanted to see if you'd admit it was a story. If you hadn't admitted it I'd have had the cheque made out for four thousand. But you were frank, and that's as close as you ever come to being honest. So you get your eight thousand."

"If I'd known it was going to be this easy—"

"No. You might have got ten, but no more."

"Then give me ten."

"Not a chance," said Henry. There were two light taps on the door, Lester came in and laid the cheque on Henry's desk and departed. Henry signed and pushed the cheque toward his brother.

"Cheque protector and everything. Exactly eight thousand exactly," said Charles. "Now I'm interested to know why you gave me any money at all. You didn't have to. Does it give you a sense of power? Does it go with that Rolls-Royce you have down there, and all this high-powered security stuff?"

"To a certain extent I guess it does. But there's more to it than that, Chiz."

"Of course."

"You see, I've always wondered when you'd finally put the touch on me. Not that I lay awake nights, but I knew you would some day. And now you have, for eight thousand dollars. I'm getting off light. Because you must know damn well that this is all you'll ever get from me."

"That occurred to me."

"When we were boys and you used to knock me around I used to feel sort of sorry for you. You'd beat the hell out of me and walk away with something of mine. A fielder's glove, or a necktie. But what you didn't know was that I was dying to *give* you the God damn glove or tie. Anything you asked for of mine, you could have had. But you preferred violence and theft, and naturally I could take only so much and then I began to hate you."

"And still do."

"Does that surprise you? Yes. Because as you grew older that was the way you were with everybody, all through your life. If you look out that window you'll see a research laboratory where the tennis courts used to be. One night after a dance I was getting in that little Oakland I had, that Grandmother gave me for my twenty-first birthday. You ought to remember

it, you smashed it up, you son of a bitch. Anyway, I didn't have
a date and I was by myself and I heard a girl crying. It was
Mary Radley, sitting on the bench between the first and second
courts. She was ashamed to go back to the clubhouse with
her dress all torn. You. You didn't have to be brutal with
Mary Radley. Nobody did, but especially you. But that was
your way, and that was when I first realized that it wasn't
just a question of being a bully to your kid brother. You were
a bully, net."

"Okay," said Charles. "Well, it's your turn to be the bully.
Thanks for the money."

"Wait a minute. I haven't finished. I want you to hear a few
things, and you'll damn well listen or I'll stop payment on that
cheque."

"Captive audience. All right," said Charles.

"You've never changed. Both your wives took all they could
stand, your children don't want to be anywhere near you.
Have you ever wondered why?"

"Not very much. The children were brought up by their
mothers, and their mothers saw to it that I didn't get any of
the best of it. I wrote them off very early."

"Not your daughter. You showed up at her graduation and
made her leave her mother and stepfather to go on some ex-
cursion with you. Whimsical cruelty, that was. Because you
then sent her back to her mother and never did any more about
her. Not a thing, financially or otherwise."

"Her mother has plenty of glue. One thing I did for my children was make sure they had rich mothers."

"Yes. Who also could afford *you* before there were any children, and after."

"The fact of the matter is that both my wives proposed to
me, Henry."

"I have no doubt of it. You were very skillful. I understand
your first wife forced you to accept a wedding present of two
hundred thousand dollars."

"Two-fifty. A quarter of a million. All long since gone, I
regret to say."

"But your second wife——"

"An iron-bound trust. I couldn't get my hooks on any of that. Where did you find out so much about my affairs?"

"When I was around trying to raise the money to get this business started, I encountered a certain amount of resistance because of the name. Even when they found out I wasn't you, people were still very dubious, especially New York and Philadelphia people. Don't ever go back to Philadelphia, Chiz. They really don't like you there."

"I'm desolated."

"You're not, but you ought to be."

"I really am. There are a couple of rich widows in Philadelphia that could make me entirely independent of people like you. But the Girard Trust Company and that other one, they probably take a dim view of me. It's too bad, too, because both of these women, or I should say either one of them could make me comfortable in my old age. I'm crowding sixty, you know."

"Oh, I know."

"The next fifteen years, I don't look forward to them the way things are at present. You may have to take me on as a night watchman."

"Fat chance. And that brings me to another point I was going to make. Or my earlier point about your being a bully. Do you realize that before you came in this room I already knew that you'd been shooting off your mouth about the explosion we had here three years ago? Our Security people couldn't believe their ears. The first man you talked to lost a brother in that explosion. The second man, the young fellow, was very badly burned and had to have skin-grafting operations that took over a year. But your feeble jokes, aside from any question of taste, were your way of bullying people, the way you used to be to caddies and waiters when this was the club. Five men were killed in that explosion, and it's no joke around here. It's no joke anywhere. For your information, both Security officers were convinced that you were an impostor, that you weren't my brother at all. For your additional information, Chiz, I wish they'd been right."

Charles D'Avlon rose. "Well, that sounds pretty final," he said. He went over to the window and looked out at the laboratory. "Mary Radley," he said. "She was certainly a little tramp."

Mary and Norma

There was a pie, a deep-dish apple pie, sitting on top of the light blue bread box, and though a wax-paper sheet covered the pie, Mary Kneely could see that a good-sized wedge had been cut out of it, a slab not quite a quarter of the whole pie. In the sink was a coffee cup and saucer, rinsed out but not washed, and she knew without looking that there would be a dozen cigarette butts in the garbage can. He had waited up for her, smoking, drinking coffee, and finally getting at the pie instead of the whiskey. She wished he had got at the whiskey instead. He had never been able to drink much whiskey; it made him sick or put him to sleep, sometimes both. But now he would be lying awake from the coffee, probably smoking in bed in violation of his own strict rule, and thinking up some sarcastic remark to greet her with.

She covered the pie more securely and put the cup and saucer and knife and fork and spoon on the right side of the sink, where they would be joined in the morning by the breakfast dishes. He had forgotten to clean the percolator, and she dumped out the coffee grounds and cleaned it herself and made it ready for the morning. She ran the cold water over her own cigarette and dropped it in the garbage can with his butts. Then she switched off the kitchen light and made her way to their room.

He was lying in bed, pretending to be reading an old *Field & Stream*, an issue that featured the firearms and fishing tackle that he would never buy. Every year he bought that special issue, if not of *Field & Stream*, of its competitors, and all winter long he would look at the pictures and read the descriptions of the guns and rods and reels and lines; just as in the spring of the year he would pay a dollar for a magazine that contained pictures of boats: big cruisers, yachts for charter, the newest in outboards, and the latest thing in houseboats for the rivers of Florida. Once he had sent away for the plans for building one of those boats, paid around fifteen dollars for the plans; but he did not know the first thing about carpentry, and the boat that had seemed so attractive in the photographs became less so in blueprints. One day he just threw the blueprints away, when she was out of the house.

He looked up at her, then back at his magazine. "You're home early," he said.

"Am I?"

"Yeah, it'll be two-three hours before daylight."

"Oh," she said.

"Who brought you home? I didn't hear any car."

"Came home in a taxi," she said.

"Frank Whalen's?"

"No. The Italian fellow, Joe's."

"Why didn't you call Frank?"

"I did, but he was busy."

"Yeah, and he knows me better than the Italian fellow. He ask you a lot of questions, the Italian fellow?"

"Didn't ask me *any* questions. I didn't have any conversation with him at all. Just told him the address."

"Why did you have to tell him the address? He knows who you are by this time."

"Maybe he does, but I told him the address anyway."

"Did you sit up front with him?"

"I sat in his lap!"

"It wouldn't surprise me."

"Oh, *nothing'd* surprise *you,* Ed. You know all the answers to everything."

She hung up her dress and stood behind the opened closet door to finish her undressing and get into her nightgown and bathrobe. She took a long time in the bathroom, but he was still looking at the magazine when she came out. "Is it all right if I put the light out?" she said.

"Go ahead," he said.

She pressed the button in the base of the lamp. "Goodnight," she said.

"Goodnight, hell," he said, and in the darkness got into her bed. When he returned to his own bed he quickly fell asleep, making the whistling sound that was almost as bad as snoring. She got up and went to the living-room and smoked a cigarette in the dark, unwilling to let the neighbors see a light on. When she began to feel sleepy she went back to bed.

"Where are you going today?" she said, as she gave him his breakfast.

"This morning I gotta go over to Huntington," he said. "Al Proser. I get finished up with Al and then I gotta go see a new fellow in Riverhead. A new fellow just starting out. And if I have time I was thinking while I was over that direction I'd drop in on some of the guys in Southampton."

"And home by way of Center Moriches?"

"Yeah. Why?"

"A few beers with the Kneely family. I won't start dinner till seven o'clock."

"There won't be any beers with the Kneely family. Buddy's in New York for a convention, and Vince and I had an argument."

"Oh, how could anybody ever have an argument with dear sweet Vince? Why he has the disposition of a saint."

"You and your sarcastic remarks."

"That's what your mother says. Vince has the disposition of a saint. She must know some different saints than the ones I ever heard of."

"You can say that again. Any saints *you* know about, my mother wouldn't know them. What are *you* gonna do today?"

"The same thing I did yesterday. Help your sister with the moving."

"Where you were till two o'clock this morning?"

"Why didn't you call her up if you thought I was some place else?"

"Because the two of you are both alike, birds of a feather. I wouldn't believe Norma any more than I'd believe you."

"You're afraid to be right and afraid to be wrong, that's your trouble," she said.

"You're birds of a feather, you and Norma. It's a terrible thing to have to be ashamed of your own sister, but believe me, when the time comes I'm not gonna stand by her."

"When what time comes?"

"The time. When Harry walks in on her some night. Her and one of her boy friends. My own sister. And you stay out of it, too. If Harry starts shooting, and I wouldn't blame him, maybe you'll stop a slug yourself."

"I thought cops were supposed to be able to shoot."

"Harry can shoot all right."

"Well then he won't hit me."

"You just stay out of it."

"All right, I'll stay out of it. If I see Harry coming in with a gun in his hand I'll ask to be excused."

"You know what I mean. You know damn well."

"Maybe it would solve your problems if he did hit me."

"I don't need Harry to solve my problems."

"Well, maybe it would solve *my* problems."

"Aw, go to hell. If I didn't have any more problems than you have I'd consider myself lucky."

"You don't have any problems. The only problems you have are is dinner ready on time, and what's on TV."

"Sure. You never heard of competition in business, I suppose."

"All you do is go to a contractor and ask him how many cubic yards he needs. Or tons. Or truckloads."

"That shows how much you know about sand and gravel. Nine years, and you think all I am is an order-taker. Huh. If that's all I was you'd starve to death."

"I wouldn't mind starving as much as you would."

"Cracks about my appetite don't have the slightest effect, not the slightest. When I lived home, before I was married, the only one of six children that didn't have a good appetite was Norma, your pal."

"Your sister."

"Don't remind me of it. She had to be made to eat her meals, and look at her. A skinny, temperamental, neurotic pushover. My own sister."

"She has two children, and they're healthy. And that stupid cop she's married to, he's not underweight."

"She's a neurotic pushover. I don't know what any guy would see in her. And they wouldn't if she wasn't a pushover. Harry's the one I feel sorry for, but he'll get wise to himself."

"And when he does, bang-bang, huh?"

"It'll be her own fault. Her own damn fault. I won't stand by her. I told her plenty of times."

"Oh, I know you did."

"Well, she can't say I didn't warn her. That much I did, and if she don't wanta take my advice, I did all I could."

"Yeah. You and Buddy and Vince."

"*And Paul.* Even her brother a priest didn't have any effect on her."

"He wouldn't have any effect on me, either."

"Oh, hell, you're a Protestant."

"Whatever I am, Paul Kneely wouldn't have any influence over me, Protestant, Catholic, Jew, Holy Roller."

"You let him marry us."

"As a favor to you, that's all. I didn't pick him."

"You be careful what you say about Paul. He isn't only my brother. He's an ordained priest."

"I'm always careful what I say about him. The only one's not afraid of him is Norma. All the rest of you're afraid of him."

"It isn't fear. It's respect."

"Well don't ask me to respect him."

"Not asking you. I'm *telling* you."

"For the one thousandth time," she said. "If you see any place selling beach plum jelly, stop and get some. It goes good at breakfast."

"I'll see you when I see you," he said, and departed.

She did her morning chores until Norma came to fetch her to Norma's house. "It's as much trouble to move from one end of town to the other as if we were moving to California," said Norma. "More. Nowadays the movers pack everything in barrels, all labeled. The woman I'm moving next door to came all the way from Seattle, Washington, and she says they take care of everything. If you tell them what room to put the stuff in, they'll do that. She and her husband came by car and had a three weeks' vacation driving all over and stopping at places, and the movers got here the day after *they* did."

"That's not my idea of a vacation, three weeks in a car with your husband."

"You'd have different ideas if you saw the husband. He looks like William Holden. They say that about a lot of men, but this one really does."

"Be careful, Norma," said Mary.

"Oh, I only said hello to him a couple of times. But I saw him first, so don't *you* get ideas. Duane Jensen. Nice name."

"Duane Jensen. It's all right."

"He's a major in the Air Force, and he has something to do at Grumman. They have three children. I think she was ready to get snooty when I told her Harry was a cop, but she acted different when I told her Harry was a major fifteen years ago."

"*Was* he?"

"In the Military Police. He sure was. So you could see her doing a little mental arithmetic and figuring if Harry was a major fifteen years ago, he'd be a lot higher than major now. So she stopped acting snooty."

"I know you, Norma, and you better be careful. You get to be friends with the wife first. Then the next thing is it's you and the husband."

"Not always," said Norma.

"Well, pretty often. Don't you ever get afraid of Harry?"

"Harry's a lunkhead or I'd of been dead by now," said Norma. "It isn't Harry I'm afraid of. He's a lunkhead. But those brothers of mine. Especially Ed. He's liable to say something sometime in front of Harry, and that's what I'm afraid of. A lunkhead like Harry, they aren't the ones that make the trouble, but it's when they hear it from a third party. If I ever get in any trouble it'll be Ed that caused it."

"You're so right."

"Oh, sure. I know that. You know what Ed's trouble is— or maybe you don't. No, maybe you don't."

"He eats too much."

"That, and something else."

"He'll eat a whole chocolate cake. I've seen him do it when he gets upset about something, where another man would get drunk."

"Oh, he did that from a kid. Encouraged by my mother. Any time anything happened to one of us, but Ed in particular, Mom would stuff us full of something to eat. But that isn't Ed's basic trouble."

"What is?"

"Well, if you want to know, Ed wanted to be a priest. He was the one that *wanted* to be the priest in the family, but Mom decided that Paul had the true vocation. Therefore, Ed was the one that they always made jokes about girls. Mom used to say 'Our Ed, the girls won't leave him alone,' till he got to believing it himself. But I guess you know plenty about Ed in that department."

"Yeah."

"Vince and Bud, out every night raising hell but Ed was the one Mom called the ladies' man."

"Why didn't she want Ed to be a priest?"

"The only reason I can think of is because Paul was the youngest and that way she could hold on to him longer. She didn't really care what happened to the other brothers, just as long as she could have her Paul. Well, it's a good thing in a way, because God help any girl that would of married Paul after Mom got through with him."

"Did he ever fall for any girl?"

"What chance did he have? She would never of let Ed marry a Protestant if she cared what happened to him. You must of been surprised when she didn't put up more objections. I know Ed was in fear and trembling because you weren't a Catholic, but he didn't have anything to worry about." Norma chuckled. "She almost outsmarted herself, though."

"How?"

"Paul. From the time he was ten years old he got a brainwashing, that the only life for him was the priesthood. And he believed it, absolutely. He was an altar boy and served Mass practically every morning, weekdays and Sundays, and he had holy pictures in his room and all that. Then one day he dropped a bombshell, a real blockbuster. He told Mom he wanted to be a missionary. He wanted to go to China or some place and be a missionary. Oh, was that a catastrophe! I don't know how she talked him out of that, but she did. But believe me, that had her worried. So now he's just a parish priest and doesn't even get to go overseas and travel. His vacation he comes home to Center Moriches and tries to sermonize me. What the hell does he know about me? I think Ed puts him up to it. That's what Vince thinks. Vince had an argument with Ed over me. Did Ed say anything to you?"

"I knew they had some kind of an argument. I didn't know what about," said Mary.

"It was over me. Vince told Ed that what I did was Harry's business, not Ed's business or Paul's business or anybody else's. Vince, you know Vince, he's a holy terror. He'd have an argument with the Pope if he felt like it. You ought to hear him on the subject of Harry. 'That lunkhead,' he calls him. He hates cops, and *I* think he hates *priests*. He'll say anything in front of Paul, just to shock him. He goes too far sometimes. Vince doesn't realize that Paul never had a chance."

"I never thought of it that way, but I guess it's true. To me Paul is just a big fat nothing."

"They all are. And if we lived in Center Moriches, Mom would have Harry, because don't think Vince is all that independent, because he's not. Mom still holds on to the pursestrings, and Vince isn't a very good businessman. He owes Mom over four thousand dollars. And if we lived there she'd figure some way to have Harry obligated to her. And he'd go for it. Sometimes I think Harry's more like one of my own brothers."

They got out of the car and entered Norma's house, their footsteps starting small echoes on the now bare floors. Norma offered her sister-in-law a cigarette, lit it and lit her own. She rested one arm across her waist, giving support to the elbow of the other arm, and holding her cigarette high in the air. She contemplated her next move. "I could do the rest of it myself," she said. "But I'm glad to have your company. I was just thinking, I lived in this house over fifteen years, the only house I ever lived in since I was married. You'd think I'd have some pangs about moving, but I don't. The children don't, either. Harry's the only one that tried to get sentimental about it. God! It's a good thing these walls can't talk."

"I'll say," said Mary.

"I didn't mean you, Mary. I was just thinking about myself."

"Oh, I know."

"The closest I ever came to getting caught, it wasn't Harry. It was my brother Vince. This friend of mine just left by the kitchen door, and two minutes later Vince barged in the front way. He had made quite a load on his way home from the harness races, and suddenly decided to pay a call on his sister."

"Why do you take such chances?"

"Why do you?"

"Yeah, I guess you're right, but I don't have any children, and Ed isn't liable to kill me. Harry would kill you, Norma."

"Maybe, if he caught me. But did you ever stop to think of how many times I thought of killing him? He comes home at five or six o'clock in the morning when he's on night duty. He takes off his uniform and hangs up his gun belt in the closet, and gets into bed with me. The usual thing, then rolls over and goes to sleep, and it's time for me to get up and get the kids' breakfast. How many times, I wonder, have I looked at that gun and thought, 'You lunkhead, what do you think I am? Some kind of a cow?' No consideration, nothing nice about it. Wakes me up out of a sound sleep just so I can be some kind of a cow. If that's all there is to it for him, it isn't enough for me. Oh, I'd never shoot him, but if he knew how many times I thought about it, he wouldn't bring his gun home."

"Ed is always looking at pictures of guns."

"Oh, I know. He always did. He even asked Harry—maybe I shouldn't tell you this. But I will. He asked Harry one time last winter how to go about buying a gun. It's against the law in this State. A revolver. Harry told him it was practically impossible in New York. Possession is illegal without a license, and you had to go through a lot of red tape to get a license."

"I'm not afraid of Ed."

"No, I wouldn't think you would be. But I'll bet there'd be times when you'd be afraid of yourself if you had a gun in the house."

Mary stood in the middle of the emptiness, not thinking of what Norma was saying. "You lived here fifteen years," she said. "I remember when you papered this room. I guess the people that bought the house, the first thing she'll want to do is re-paper it."

"I wouldn't blame her. I was beginning to get sick of it," said Norma.

"And then there won't be anything left of fifteen years you lived here."

"Yes there will. She bought the icebox and the washer and the dryer."

"But nothing personal. Wallpaper I consider personal. Like appliances, I don't."

"Oh, yes. I see. No, I guess there won't be much of that left. It could have been anybody lived here."

"Nine years I've been married to Ed, but we lived in four different places. You lived here fifteen years."

"Mom's in the same house over thirty-five. They put additions on it, but it's the same house. Now it's too big for her, but she won't let go of it. She could save money if she did, but then she couldn't have the whole tribe around at Christmas, queening it over everybody. Making everybody eat too much. You've been there, you've seen her."

"Sure have. I sure have. 'Mary's lucky. She won't have to get up and go to early Mass.' Every Christmas Eve for nine Christmases. 'Mary can sleep late.' "

"I know."

"The funny thing is, I went and got myself mixed up with another Catholic."

"You don't have to tell me unless you feel like it."

"Joe Angelo."

"That has the new taxi business?"

"Yes."

"He's married, Mary. You know that."

"Sure, I know it."

"I guess he's all right. It takes money to get started in the taxi business, and he doesn't have a criminal record. Harry seems to think he's all right, and he'd know if anybody did. But don't let Harry find out about this, or he'll make it tough for Joe."

"That's what Joe's afraid of. He's more afraid of Harry finding out than Ed."

"I was wondering who it was," said Norma. "I knew you had somebody, but I didn't want to say anything till you told me yourself."

"Yes, since last spring."

"Well, all I can say is good luck and be careful."

"If it isn't me telling you to be careful, it's you telling me."

"Yes, but I had more experiences in that line, Mary. I'm married to a real lunkhead, but Ed Kneely's no lunkhead. He's shrewd, mean and shrewd. And one of these days he's going to be a rich man."

"Ed?"

"He's like my father. My father didn't start making any money till he was well up in his thirties, and Ed's branching out. He's getting known over in Suffolk. You know, five years ago Ed wouldn't have had an argument with Vince. Vince was always kind of the big shot, the one that made the most noise.

But like now Vince owes Mom over four thousand dollars, and she doesn't figure to get that back. It'll be taken out of Vince's share when she dies. Ed'll get his full share, and if she hangs on another five years he'll come into it just about when he needs it in the business. Ed Kneely's going to be a rich man, so don't spoil it for yourself. You're entitled to reap the benefit."

"The benefit of what?"

"Sticking with the son of a bitch all these years. The only thing that'll stop Ed is if he eats himself to death. Which he'll do if you worry him too much. Keep him off the pies and cakes till he makes his fortune."

Mary smiled. "Then what?"

"Then let him enjoy himself. Give him waffles for breakfast and pie à la mode every night. He'll eat it, and you'll be a rich widow when you're still in your forties. I wish it was as easy as that with Harry, but Harry didn't gain ten pounds since he got out of the Army."

"I wonder if they hate us as much," said Mary.

"If they didn't, we wouldn't be talking this way."

"I guess not."

"I got the look from Duane Jensen. He knows. But I'm 'way ahead of him. I'm thinking of when he begins to wish he never saw me, when he wishes he was back in Seattle."

"Yes. Joe said last night I ought to use Frank Whalen once in a while, just to throw people off."

"That's one of the first signs," said Norma. "He wouldn't have told you that last spring. *I* hate *them*. It isn't only them hating us. But what are you gonna do?"

The Cellar Domain

Not just anyone and everyone got their hair cut and their faces shaved at Peter Durant's shop. Peter had a system to discourage new customers who in his opinion had not earned the right to join his clientele. Peter had, of course, the first chair, but he kept his eye on the other six chairs in his shop and on the order in which his customers arrived and should be attended to. A barber would finish with a customer, and Peter, almost without missing a snip at his own customer's hair, would call out: "You're next, Judge. Bobby, take Judge Buckhouse." Customers and barbers alike accepted Peter's decisions without argument, and an unwelcome newcomer would sometimes find that he had been passed over in favor of five or six men who had not been in the shop when he arrived. Once in a while there would be one who would say: "I think I was next."

"Can't help that," Peter would say, and that settled it. If the customer didn't like it, he was free to go elsewhere, which was exactly what Peter Durant intended. A young businessman, a young lawyer or doctor making a first appearance at Durant's, would know better than to risk a scene in the presence of Peter's established customers, who were the county's most prominent professional and financial men and some others who had received Peter's approval. In those long-gone days it was an important occasion when Peter Durant would say to a customer: "I'm ordering you a mug. Do you want your name on it or just your initials?" No one had ever declined the honor of a mug at Peter Durant's or hesitated to pay the two dollars for the mug and its gilt lettering. It was a diploma, the acceptance of a man's racing colors, membership in a club like the Philadelphia Union League, a rating in Bradstreet's, a commission on the Governor's military staff. It was all these things, because there were men in the county who had achieved one or another of these things but had not been invited to pay two dollars for a mug at Peter Durant's.

Although the shop was in the cellar of the hotel, it was not a convenience for hotel guests. Traveling salesmen were accommodated at Durant's only in the less busy hours of midafternoon, and even though some of his barbers might be shaving themselves, or sitting on the customers' bench and reading the Philadelphia *North American* or the London *Illustrated News,* Peter sometimes would take a quick look at a stranger and say: "Be an hour's wait."

"What about those men?" the stranger would say, nodding toward the idle barbers.

"That's my business. Better go down the street. You got a good barber down towards the railroad station."

The stranger would glare at Peter, but depart, and Peter would say: "That's the kind of a son of a bitch would ask for a manicure." Peter's barbers would laugh. They liked Peter; he paid them well, he did their thinking for them, and he backed them up in any dispute with a customer. There were only two rules they had to obey: a barber was not supposed to work if he had liquor on his breath; if he wanted to go on a drunk he could take the day off; and the other rule was that no barber, no customer for that matter, was permitted to address him as Pete. He was not deceived by the obsequious newcomer who called him Mr. Durant; but no judge, no doctor, no clergyman, no bank cashier, no retired millionaire got an answer when he said Pete instead of Peter. But then they never made that mistake; they knew better. Casual use of the diminutive had kept some men from getting a mug.

The shop sold nothing but shaves, haircuts, and facial and scalp massages. No tonics, no combs or brushes, no cigars or cigarettes, and only one special service: some men who shaved themselves would bring their razors to Peter for honing. A great deal of betting went on among the customers, especially during political campaigns, but Peter Durant participated only to the extent that bets made in his shop were recorded in a notebook he kept in his cash register. Both parties to a bet would see what he wrote in the notebook, sign their initials, and Peter would say: "Now nobody has to ask me do I remember who bet what." But Peter thus became the repository of valuable information that he kept confidential, and inevitably his customers' trust in his discretion got him in on some good things. He went on shaving men whom he could buy and sell, even though they might not know it.

Generally Peter Durant discouraged the favorite-barber custom, and among the newer customers it was not permitted. "One's as good as another in this shop," he would say. "Harry's as good a barber as me, and Elmer's as good as Harry." But Peter had his own favorite customers, and he would linger over a haircut, or speed it up, so that one of his favorites would get in his chair. Peter's chair, the first, was nearest the street windows, and certain customers would stand on the sidewalk and look down into the shop until they had attracted his attention. If he nodded, they knew he would fit them into the order so that he would cut their hair; if he shook his head and made a face, they knew it to mean that they would have to take another barber. The other barbers, who were not fools, made every cooperative effort to see that Peter's favorites got to his chair, but it was a different matter altogether for them to understand why Peter Durant preferred some customers to others. They could understand why Edwin E. Patterson was entitled to the first chair, but most of the barbers could not understand why Andy Keever got in the shop at all.

Ned Patterson was in town a lot because he had business at the court house; not a large amount of business, and obviously not highly profitable, what there was. He usually got off the trolley-car from Swedish Haven at the corner across the street from the barber shop on mornings when he was to be in court. On court days he liked to be shaved by Peter Durant, and it did not escape the notice of the barbers that Peter often trimmed

Ned's hair—"neatened it up," he called it—without charging him for a regular cut. "Now I guess you look all right," Peter would say.

"Thank you, Peter. Thank you very much," Ned would say, and lay down the same quarter and nickel—twenty cents for the shave, and ten-cent tip—and be off to the court house. At this time, shortly after the First World War, Ned Patterson was in his sixties, a good ten years older than Peter Durant, but nearly everyone still called him Ned. On court days he wore a black suit, black necktie and shoes, and starched collar and cuffs and shirt-bosom. Walter, the bootblack-porter at Durant's shop, could not have improved on the shine Ned had already given his shoes. Ned Patterson seldom encountered other lawyers in the shop; he was there too early in the day. But Judge Buckhouse sometimes arrived for a shave as Ned was leaving, and Ned would say: "Good morning to you, sir."

"Good morning, Ned. If you're not in too much of a hurry I can give you a lift."

"Very kind of you, Judge, but I've got a man waiting." He was fifteen years older than Judge Buckhouse, and the last two blocks to the court house were a steep climb, but he never accepted the judge's offer. Always, when the offers were made, Ned would explain that he had a man waiting, presumably a client, but Buckhouse knew that Ned Patterson sometimes came to the court house, wandered up and down the corridors, listened to trials, mingled with colleagues in the lawyers' room, and represented no client. Just by being there at every session of every term, Ned sometimes would be appointed by the court to defend a case and receive a fee that he would not get by staying in Swedish Haven. Sometimes a colleague would put something his way—a dreary job of searching in the prothonotary's records—that would be worth twenty-five dollars. Ned Patterson rarely went home empty-handed at the end of a term of court, but the juicy receiverships went to other lawyers, more aggressive or younger or more learned in the law. "In a jury trial," a lawyer once said, "it ought to be worth a few dollars to have Ned sitting with you at counsel table. That white hair and smooth skin, and that undertaker outfit he wears. He's the next thing to having a bishop on your side. But I don't know how often it would work. The jury might start wondering why God didn't examine the witnesses, or why He didn't make the closing address. Some juries would begin to think that maybe Ned didn't—quite—go along with you, and they'd smell a rat. And as for letting him examine a witness, you'd be taking a chance of ruining your case then and there. I like old Ned, but to tell you the truth he doesn't even copy things right. He knows his law, and loves it, and in some respects he'd have made a good judge. But not for the County. He'd never send anybody to prison." And so, in his late-middle sixties, Edwin E. Patterson, Esq., attorney-at-law, sole surviving member of the firm of Patterson & Patterson, was still waiting for the success that had seemed to come so easily to his father many years ago, the success without which Ned could not have continued his own unprofitable practice of law. For the truth was that Ned and his wife subsisted on the small income from his father's estate, and his professional fees provided him with the luxury of being a lawyer. He was a gentleman-at-law, an amateur of the law, who went to the court house as some men, old friends in Philadelphia, went to the opera. Some of *them* could not sing a note, but they loved Verdi. In much the same way, on court days, Ned Patterson would come to town, humming, as it were, the Rule in Shelley's Case.

In a sense, then, Ned Patterson's visits to Peter Durant's barber shop were time spent in the dressing-room, before the performances at the court house in which he might or might not take active part. The quiet dignity he maintained while covered with lather was genuine enough, lifelong and natural, but Peter Durant had no way of knowing that Ned at such times was especially content because he was already enjoying the promise of the day's later developments. "Never seen that man when he wasn't at peace with the world," Peter Durant would say. "Shaving him's a good way to start the day." The more remarkable, then, that Peter Durant's other favorite customer should be Andy Keever.

Andy Keever's membership in the Durant clientele was offensive to more than one of the regulars. He knew everyone by name, and as he made an entrance in the shop he would walk past the waiting customers on the bench, speaking to each—"Mr. Hofman . . . Dr. English . . . Mr. Chapin . . ."—and shedding his outer clothing, removing collar and tie, and apparently not noticing that there would be a closing of ranks so that the men of substance would not have to make a place for him. He would stand at the far end of the shop, hanging his clothing on the rack, and call to the owner: "Hey, Peter, you coming to the hose company picnic?"

"Oh, sure," Peter Durant would say, smiling because everyone knew that he never went to hose company picnics. "I'll be there with bells on."

"Never mind the bells, we'll bring them." Andy would stand at the clothes rack, surveying the room and waiting for the exactly right moment, and then he would move quietly forward until he reached Elmer Bitzer's chair, without being seen by Elmer. He would goose Bitzer and simultaneously whistle through his teeth, a loud, piercing whistle, and Bitzer would jump. Everybody would laugh, but the hardest laugher was Peter Durant, who would drop his hands to his sides and bend over, weak with giggles. "That fellow, he kills me," he would say to the customer in the chair. "I can't help it, he makes me laugh." Even Bitzer, the perennial victim, would grin.

Andy Keever would find a place on the bench, look about him, stand up and say: "Any reverends here?"

"No," one of the barbers would say.

"Who's that under the hot towel? Not a reverend, sure?"

"Mr. Miller."

"Then I got a good one for you. Hey, Peter, I got a good one for you. There was this railroader come home and found his wife in bed with a Chinaman. You know, a Chinaman . . ."

Andy Keever never laughed at his own stories. When he finished one he would look around at all the men, and if one of the men had not been listening, was reading a newspaper,

Andy would make a face at him and raise his voice and tell a dirtier story. Sometimes he would have French postcards and phallic toys that he would hold out to a barber, and then as the barber reached out his hand, Andy would quickly pull away. "Naughtee, naugh-tee. You're too eager," he would say. "I'm saving this for Walter. Hey, Walter, I bought you something in Philly."

Andy Keever was new in town, had come there after being mustered out of the Army early in 1919. One of the breweries, resigned to what was about to happen, was making the change from beer to ice cream, and Andy Keever was put in charge of a crew that canvassed candy stores and poolrooms and the like, signing up customers for the new product. Andy Keever was a live wire, a hard worker, and in a few short months it was understood that the brewery family were so pleased with him that it was only a question of time before he would be made general manager of the ice cream plant. He was a charter member of the Legion post, a sports fan, a founder of the Lions Club, a forward on one of the businessmen's basketball teams at the Y.M.C.A., and, within a year, one of the leaders of the small group who got things done. They were virtually a standing committee of Rotarians, Merchants Association members and Masons who ran the drives and campaigns that represented community activity, and Andy Keever was the first new face in that group in five years. Some of these men were patrons of Peter Durant's shop, which was the only place where they would frequently encounter those other men, men who were known as the Lantenengo Street crowd, the Gibbsville Club crowd, the plutocrats and "our would-be aristocrats." As individuals, in man-to-man relations, the members of the two leading groups got along nicely; but as group members they kept to themselves, recognizably different in clothes and manners. At Peter Durant's shop, there never was any doubt as to the proprietor's preference, and after waiting in vain to be sold a mug, some of the Rotarians would take their business elsewhere, invariably complaining of the service at Peter Durant's and omitting mention of the fact that a Ned Patterson got more cordial treatment than a director of the Building & Loan Society.

"I think Mr. Keever goes a bit too far," said one of Peter Durant's favorites one day.

"Fresh as paint, but he puts me in stitches," said Peter. "I don't know what there is about that fellow."

"Well, if *you* can put up with him," said the customer. "But I wouldn't like to be in Elmer Bitzer's chair, with Elmer holding a razor at my throat."

"Oh, you take notice sometime. Keever don't do that to Elmer when Elmer's shaving. Keever has more sense than that."

"Good. Glad to hear that, anyway."

"Oh, sure. That's something I never *would* put up with. In this business you learn to have an awful lot of respect for a razor."

"I should think so," said the customer.

"When I was learning the barber trade, if I nicked a customer my old man would fine me a week's pay, even if it wasn't my fault."

The customer closed his eyes, the signal to end conversation that was always respected by Peter Durant. There were other men who in other conversations revealed a distaste for the presence of Andy Keever, and Peter thought about the matter; but Keever's jokes and little pranks went on, and Keever remained a customer. Peter began to feel that criticism of Keever was by way of being criticism of himself, and he had had little experience of that. He ran his shop to suit himself, a first-class shop with first-class barbers, where the best men in the county sat with their collars and ties off, and one man—Peter Durant—was the only boss.

"You don't know a fellow named Andy Keever, do you, Ned?"

"Andy Keever. Keever? That's a new name to me," said Ned Patterson. "What does he do?"

"He's up there at the new ice cream plant. They got him in charge of the salesmen," said Peter Durant. "He's a customer, but never this early in the morning. Ha' past ten or eleven he usually comes in."

"Don't know him, but why do you ask?"

"Well, he rubs some people the wrong way. Other customers, and I kind of wondered did you ever hear them say anything."

"No, but you've always been able to get rid of men like him. True, you have to serve him, legally, but you have your methods."

"I don't want to get rid of him."

"Then by all means, don't. I've seen men in this shop that despise each other, but they behave themselves here. You have a gentlemen's institution here, Peter, and you've made it that and kept it that."

"Keever isn't what you'd call a gentleman."

"Well, I didn't mean that they're all the cream of the crop, but they behave like gentlemen."

"Not Keever."

"*Not* Keever? Then I don't see what your problem is, Peter. Very few places that men gather together and conduct themselves as well as they do here, but this is one of them. If this Keever man—-what sort of thing does he do that annoys the other patrons?"

"Oh, jokes, and stuff like that."

"Well, if you mean dirty jokes, I've never heard you tell one, or enjoy one. I don't mind them myself, if they're really funny and well told. Abraham Lincoln. Mark Twain. John Kendrick Bangs. Arthur Twining Hadley. An off-color story didn't bother them, and I certainly wouldn't condemn your man Keever on *that* evidence. Unless, of course, you're referring to the reverend clergy. I know you have two ministers and I believe Monsignor What's His Name comes in here."

"He don't tell them in front of them."

"Then what's troubling you, Peter?"

"I don't know whose side I'm on, that's my trouble. Andy

Keever makes me laugh till I'm weak, but a lot of my best customers—you can tell by the way they look at him. But on the other hand, is it my shop or does it belong to the customers?"

"I begin to see your problem, yes," said Ned Patterson.

"*You* see my problem."

"I do. One: does the proprietor claim the right to select his customers? Two: having selected his customers, have they in turn any inherent rights? Three: do those inherent rights include that of rejecting a new customer?"

"I follow you."

"I'm trying to see it as a lawyer might when he prepares a case for a judge's opinion. But now I have to follow a different procedure. The question really comes down to a matter that isn't governed by set rules. In other words, it becomes a matter of personal preference, Peter. Taste, on the one hand, and business expediency. Do you want this man around, and do you want him around enough to jeopardize your business? From what you've told me, and from what I know of your clientele, you may be running a real risk."

"That's what I've been thinking about."

"And now that you've told me as much as you have, you've suddenly shed some light on something else."

"What's that, Ned?"

"Well, you and I've been friends for a long time."

"Close on to thirty years," said Peter Durant.

"When court's in session I make it a habit to have my lunch at the club."

"The Gibbsville Club."

"Yes. Otherwise I never go near the place, and I hardly ever know what's going on up there, although I've been a member since my twenty-fifth birthday. But I *have* heard some talk, let me see, during the present term and during the May term— of putting in a barber chair. Putting in a chair and hiring a barber. I paid very little attention, but it's just possible, Peter, that some of your customers may be deciding to act."

"Oh, they are, eh?"

"It's a possibility. It's a probability. Most of the men at the club are customers of yours, and it may be more than a coincidence that there's been this talk of hiring a barber."

"You didn't hear who they were thinking of hiring, did you?"

"No, but there I'd draw the line at confiding in you. You understand that, of course."

"You wouldn't tell me if it was one of my men they were hiring?"

"No, I wouldn't. I don't mind passing this information on to you, since it may help you to decide your problem. But it would be quite another matter, Peter, to reveal any names. Either names of customers or the name of the barber, if I knew it. So, this conversation may only have added to your dilemma, but you've been warned."

"Well, I wouldn't expect you to name names, Ned. Just to tell me if it was one of my men."

"No, I wouldn't tell you that, either. Out of six men that you've had with you for a long time, you wouldn't have much trouble narrowing it down."

"You bet I wouldn't," said Peter Durant. "And I got a pretty good idea already."

"A word of caution. Better think about Mr. Keever and how much you like to have him as a customer. Don't spend your time wondering if one of your men has been offered another job. I don't think *I'd* like Mr. Keever, but I'm just throwing that in, free gratis."

Two days later Peter Durant fired Bobby Little, the second-chair barber who had been in the shop for more than twenty years. Bobby denied having had business conversations with Gibbsville Club men, but Peter Durant called him a liar. The firing took place in the evening, after the last customer had gone and the shades were drawn. "You think I'm stupid, you think I don't know what's going on behind my back?" said Peter to Bobby and to the other five barbers.

"You're gonna find out you were wrong, Peter," said Bobby Little. "But don't ask me to come back. I don't work for no man calls me a liar." He went to his post, wrapped his razors and scissors in the black leather case that he used on visits to sick customers, and held out his hand. "Give me me time."

"I'm giving you two weeks' pay."

"Give me me time, up till tonight. I don't want no favors from you. Two weeks' pay after twenty-one years. Calling me a liar. Pay me up till tonight and that's all. But believe me, Peter Durant, you got some things to learn."

Peter Durant handed Bobby three five-dollar bills and Bobby turned to the others. "Goodnight, fellows." The others said goodnight to him and stared at the curtained door after he left.

"I hope you're sure, Peter," said Harry Slazenger. "As far as I'm concerned, Bobby never said nothin' to me about no Gibbsville Club offer."

"That's a bright one," said Peter Durant. "Why the hell would he want to tell you? He'd be afraid you'd tell me."

"Well then he'd of been wrong, because I wouldn't of told you," said Harry Slazenger.

"No? Maybe you're in it, too. Maybe they're gonna have *two* chairs up there."

"I don't know. This is the first I heard about it that they were gonna have *one,* but if you don't believe me, Peter, why don't you come out and say it?"

"All right, I will say it," said Peter Durant. "I think you knew about this. Bobby's your brother-in-law."

"Are you calling me a liar?"

"Yes, I'm calling you a liar," said Peter Durant.

"Give me me time."

"With pleasure," said Peter Durant. "You want to be proud, like your brother-in-law, or will you take the full two weeks?"

"I'll take the two weeks. I'll take all I can get. If you want to give me two months I'll take it." Slazenger turned to the other barbers. "How many you fellows gonna show up for work tomorrow?"

"Leave me out of it, Harry," said Elmer Bitzer. "You and

Bobby have your fight, but that don't say we gotta go without work."

"You trying to call a strike?" said Peter Durant. "This aint a union shop."

"Too bad it isn't," said Slazenger.

"You'll get three days and not another nickel," said Peter Durant. He opened the cash register, took out the money and slapped it on the shelf in front of Harry Slazenger's chair. Slazenger packed his equipment in a case similar to Bobby Little's.

"Something got into you, Peter. We all been noticing it. *They* won't admit it, but you got something festering inside of you."

"Take your God damn stuff and get out of here," said Peter Durant.

"You want me to tell you something?" said Slazenger. "Pretty soon you won't need six barbers. You'll be able to do it all yourself. Ned Patterson and that fellow Keever, that's who you'll have for customers."

"You worried about if I'm gonna have enough to eat?" said Peter.

"Oh, you got money, Peter. We know that. But you lose Bobby and now me, and even so you didn't find out who's going to the Gibbsville Club. One of those four, maybe. But which one, eh, Peter? Which one?"

"I got the right ones," said Peter Durant.

"No. But it's one of these four," said Slazenger. He laughed and departed.

Peter Durant looked at the remaining four barbers, but decided against making a speech. "Whose turn is it to open up tomorrow?"

"Bobby's," said one of the barbers.

"Well, I'll take his turn tomorrow," said Peter Durant. He locked the cash register and went about pulling the cords of the ceiling lamps, and the men said goodnight and departed.

The news that Peter Durant had fired two of his oldest employees got about very quickly, but during the first few days most of the regular customers were too tactful to inquire for details. On the Friday morning, however, Judge Buckhouse, who was president of the Gibbsville Club, asked Peter to join him in a corner of the hotel lobby upstairs.

"You made a mistake, Peter. You shouldn't have discharged those men. There *was* some talk about putting in a chair at the club, but I don't think it's going to come to anything."

"You'd say that now."

"I beg your pardon?"

"Maybe you decided you wouldn't put a chair in, but how do I know you didn't dicker with Bobby Little?"

"You don't know, but you can take my word for it," said the judge. "We never got to that stage."

"You didn't talk to any of my men?"

"The whole idea never got beyond the discussion stage."

"I don't know," said Peter Durant. "He acted very suspicious. And that Harry Slazenger! That son of a bitch."

"*What* don't you know? I said that the idea never got beyond the discussion stage, and you said 'I don't know.' Are you doubting my word?"

"I doubt everybody's word."

"Then there's nothing more to be said. That's all, Peter. Good day."

"Good day? What do you mean by that?"

"Goodbye, is what I mean."

"You're not coming in any more?"

"Certainly not. I wouldn't think of it."

"Well, I guess I'll have to get along without you, then. Where do you want me to send your mug? You paid two dollars for it, so it belongs to you."

"Oh, I don't care what you do with it, Peter."

"Your mug?"

"Throw it in the wastebasket. Now I have to be getting along." The judge crossed the lobby to the revolving door and entered his waiting limousine. Peter Durant slowly walked through the door marked Barber Shop—Gentlemen and down the steps to his shop. He removed his suit coat and put on his white jacket and took his place at his chair.

"All right. Who's next?" he called.

"Hey, Peter, you didn't say hello to me. Am I fired, too?" Andy Keever, from his place on the bench, was pleased with the big laugh he got.

"Oh, go to hell," said Peter Durant.

The Properties of Love

Mrs. Henry D'Avlon thanked the pilot and copilot of the airplane. They were employees of her husband's company, but they were not his servants, and they required a special courtesy due their professional expertness. At the same time they were not executives; they wore a uniform that went with their job. It was a dual purpose uniform: a grey double-breasted suit when the pilots were off duty. It became a uniform when they pinned on their pilots' badges, silver wings with the company's trademark tastefully cut into the shield. The badge, in a miniature version, also appeared as a cap device for the Air Force type caps that matched the grey cloth of the suit. Mrs. Henry D'Avlon had chosen that material and had designed the badge.

Joe Barton, assistant to the vice-president in charge of public relations, was waiting on the landing strip, smiling up at Mrs. D'Avlon as she descended from the airplane. "Good morning, Joe," she said.

"Good morning, Mrs. D'Avlon," he said. "Good flight?"

"Very good. A few bumps over western Pennsylvania, but otherwise serene. As a matter of fact, Pete and Ernie got me here ten minutes ahead of our E.T.A."

"I know," said Joe Barton. "I just got here."

The company Cadillac was standing in the reserved parking section, and Matthews, the company chauffeur, seemed genuinely glad to see Mrs. D'Avlon again. "Hello, Bert," she said. "My, you make this car glisten."

"Thank you. Nice to have you notice it," said Matthews.

She thought she detected an implication directed at Joe Barton, who probably never complimented Matthews on the appearance of the car, but it was not her wish or her place to take sides. Matthews put her luggage in the rear deck and they left La Guardia and headed for the hotel.

"Sorry the boss couldn't make the trip with you," said Joe Barton.

"Yes, it's too bad, but he hates to fly when he has a cold."

"I don't blame him. So do I," said Joe Barton. He was a very Christian young man, a thought that she had had on first meeting him five years earlier and which she did not quite understand until one day she realized that with his blue eyes, clean-cut features, perfect teeth, blond hair and gold-rimmed spectacles he had instantly made her think of Y.M.C.A. And there it was. Association. Young Man. Christian. Y.M.C.A. He was thoroughly male, and completely sexless. At thirty-seven he was as far as he would ever go in the company. He would be paid more money, and he would get a better title, but he would never achieve the policy level. He had a wife and two children and he commuted from Rye, and there was no reason to suppose that he was not saving his money. Fredericka D'Avlon had never met Barton's wife and was not likely to, but she knew that Mrs. Barton would not be a bit jealous during the next two days, when Barton would be her escort at dinner and the theater in place of Henry D'Avlon. Mrs. Barton—any woman who would be the wife of Joe Barton—would know that that was part of his job, and that Fredericka D'Avlon was fifty-two years old. Mrs. Barton, in Rye, would probably make little jokes about Joe's being out with the boss's wife; but they would be prideful little jokes, too. "Joe's at the theater with the big boss's wife," she would say. "How about coming over, you two, and watching TV?" And when Joe got home after the theater, Susie, or whatever her name was, would make *safe* little jokes, as though there were no need to be jealous of a woman in her fifties. And Joe Barton, being a Joe Barton, would *expect* his wife to make the safe little jokes. Well, it was only fair; Henry D'Avlon would make safe little jokes about Joe Barton when *she* got home.

They were on the approach to the Triboro Bridge, and as

always in clear weather, the view of the skyline gave her a single, brief thump in the stomach. It always happened, and it always took her by surprise in spite of her knowing the cause of the dull, quick pain. That first look at New York from the ground had the same impact as the time in a restaurant when she heard a man at the next table saying, "George Reed is downstairs." It was all she heard, but it was enough, as the first look at the skyline was always enough. George Reed was downstairs all over New York for those two seconds in which she had a new glimpse of the tall buildings that were not Chicago or Detroit or Cleveland.

"I'm very lucky," she said. "I almost never get colds."

"I wish I could say that. I'm good for one cold every winter, usually when I'm taking my two weeks in Florida. And another one in August, around Labor Day weekend."

"You ought to be able to guard against that. Whenever I feel a suspicion of a cold I take some ascorbic acid tablets. You ought to try them. I forget who recommended them. I think I read about them somewhere. Dr. George Reed."

"Oh, *well,* if *George Reed* recommended them they must be the best. I'll get some."

She was mystified by her lie. George Reed had never recommended anything in any publication that she was likely to read. George Reed was a surgeon, who avoided personal publicity as though it were that staph-something infection that terrified hospitals. Nevertheless she had deliberately and wrongfully attributed to him a cure-all for the common cold, and that was not justifiable or excusable by her simple impulse to say his name. Yes, she admitted to herself, she took pleasure in saying his name.

"Do you *know* Dr. Reed?" she said.

"I don't, but he operated on my wife's uncle. A seven-hour operation for cancer of the lung. I don't understand the technicalities, but they say he's an absolute genius. No question about it."

"Yes, you hear a lot about George Reed. I don't think he

was the one that recommended ascorbic acid tablets. It was somebody else."

"Well, frankly, it didn't sound much like him."

"No, it *didn't* sound much like Dr. Reed. I realized that as soon as I said it. Have you ever met him?"

"Yes, once, in the hospital. And I must say he *looks* like a great surgeon."

"Oh, why do you say that?"

"Well, he gives you the impression of strength. Confidence. He's quite tall. Over six feet. And he has this iron-grey hair cut very short. Actually, when I think of it, he could also be taken for a general. A four-star general. I guess that's responsibility and being accustomed to giving orders. Giving orders and expecting them to be obeyed. A lot of people can *give* orders. I almost studied medicine. I sort of wanted to when I was in high school, but my family couldn't afford that long expensive education. God, they're in school for at least seven years and they're two more years before they start making any money at all. I guess it must cost close to thirty-five thousand dollars minimum to get an M.D., and my family didn't have that kind of money. I imagine it was a lot different when George Reed was starting out."

"It was, but—well, I don't know why I say that. I just take for granted that it was," said Fredericka D'Avlon.

"But if my son wants to study medicine, I'll find the money somehow. He hasn't said anything yet, but he likes biology and gets very good marks. English, he can't write a two-page letter. But I'll be interested to see if he's any good in chemistry, and if he is, I'm going to encourage him to study medicine."

"Heaven knows we need doctors," she said.

"And where are they going to come from? How many men can swing thirty- thirty-five thousand dollars for a son's education? You know much more about the company than most executives' wives do, so you must know approximately what I make. And I'll be able to put Buddy through. By the skin of my teeth, but I could make it. But how about—well, Bert Matthews up there. What if he had a son that wanted to study medicine? This darn income tax hurts him every bit as much as it hurts people like me, in higher brackets. I'm sure Bert's the kind that saved his money, but a man in his job probably never earned more than six thousand dollars a year top. Top. And if he was able to save a thousand a year, every year for thirty years, he was darn lucky. In fact, I don't believe he could save that much. I'm a little better off because the company gives us those stock options and the bonus plan. Oh, I'm all right as long as D'Avlon Industries is all right, and you might as well say as long as the country is all right."

Fredericka D'Avlon let him prattle on, with his mixture of frankness and loyalty to the company. For a moment he had been a person, an individual, but he was competing for her attention with her thoughts of George Reed, now made more delicious by her having spoken his name for the first time in so many, many years.

So now he was giving the impression of strength and confidence. A four-star general. She knew that he had operated on a king, that he had saved the life of an opera singer, that among his patients had been a first-rate movie star and a prime minister and at least two men who were the opposite numbers in their corporations of Henry D'Avlon in D'Avlon Industries. She had read his brief bulletins on the condition of his famous patients, and the newspaper articles in which it was reported that Dr. Reed declined further comment. The Queen had given him the O.B.E., and Harvard, an honorary degree; but Fredericka D'Avlon had seen no photographs of him, had not heard his voice, did not know, for instance, where he spent his summers or what kind of cigarettes he smoked or whom he was having dinner with that night in 21. This little man, Joe Barton, had seen him and talked with him and had described him as he was today. What chaos there would be in the back of the limousine if she were to say: "George Reed is the love of my life." But she was not strongly tempted to confuse and embarrass Joe Barton. His astonishment and incredulity and fears were so predictable. He was such a *Christian* young man. But if she would not shock him, she still could use him, and before she had had time to plan with her customary thoroughness she was uttering the words: "Joe, I wonder if you could keep a great secret? It's something you can't even tell your wife."

"Why, yes, of course, Mrs. D'Avlon."

"Could you arrange to get me an appointment with Dr. Reed?"

"I'm almost sure I could," he said. "Are you—worried about something, Mrs. D'Avlon?"

"I haven't told my husband, or anybody. But I think I'd like to have more than just a routine check-up."

"You are worried, aren't you? Listen, Mrs. D'Avlon, I'll get to work on it right away. You're going to find out that D'Avlon Industries carries a lot of weight in unexpected places. I will have to mention your name, but it will be top-secret."

"How will you go about it?"

"There are several ways, but first we want to guard against any rumors that would affect D'Avlon Industries itself, don't we?"

"Oh, good heavens yes."

"That rules out a friend of mine at the bank who's on the hospital board. Ordinarily that would be the obvious way. But I can call Dr. Reed's secretary because she knows who I am on account of my having paid the bill for my wife's uncle. You see? Then I ask to speak to Dr. Reed, and he won't be there, but I'll say it's Mr. Barton of D'Avlon Industries, and he'll call me back. Not because of my uncle, but because of D'Avlon. And D'Avlon is the magic word not because Dr. Reed needs money, but because we distribute about two million a year on research projects, and I'm sure he'd like to get some of that for the hospital. I'll explain that you don't want any publicity, and believe me that's something he'll respect. You want an office appointment first, don't you?"

"I hope it's all I'll need," said Fredericka D'Avlon.

"So do I, and it probably will be. But you're wise to play it safe. I'll be back to you on the phone within an hour."

She had a bath and changed her clothes, and the telephone

rang. "You have an appointment at his office, two o'clock this afternoon. I spoke to him myself on my first call, and I didn't have to do any skulduggery. He remembered meeting me, and when I told him who the appointment was for he said he'd change his other appointments to accommodate you. Now don't you worry, Mrs. D'Avlon. You're in good hands, the best in the world."

The receptionist at George Reed's office said: "Go right in, madam. The doctor is expecting you." It was ten minutes of two, and Fredericka D'Avlon noticed that there were no other patients in the waiting-room.

She knocked twice on his door and heard him say "Come in, please."

He rose and stood behind his desk with his hand outstretched. "Hello, Fritzie," he said.

"Hello, George."

"I've just been having a sandwich. Have you had your lunch?"

"What did you have? Chicken with mayonnaise, and no lettuce?"

"Exactly," he said. "Do you want half?"

"No, you finish it."

"Would you like some coffee? I'd feel better about eating my sandwich if you'd have some coffee with me," he said.

"All right, yes. I'd like some coffee, if it's made."

"This place is like the Navy. There's always some coffee," he said. He spoke into the inter-com. "Some more coffee, please, Miss Ryan. And another cup and saucer."

"Is that all you have for lunch? After twenty-five years haven't you learned to eat more sensibly?"

"That's the kind of question I'm supposed to ask," he said. "I vary it sometimes with a hamburger. Tuna fish. But chicken is my favorite."

"Well, you've kept your waistline. But what have you done with your hair?"

"It's more comfortable this way when I'm operating. Ah,

here we are. Thank you, Miss Ryan." The receptionist served the coffee and went out.

"May I smoke?" she said.

"Sure."

"How about you? Will you have one?"

"All right, I'll have one thanks."

"You say that as if you didn't usually."

"I don't carry them, and I don't keep any in the office. That's my way of cutting down. I haven't given it up entirely." He lit his cigarette.

"Finish your sandwich, George."

"Well—all right."

"There's nothing wrong with me. I'm here under false pretenses."

"I see. You want to ask me about your husband?"

"No. I don't want to ask you about anybody. I just came to see you."

"What prompted your curiosity?"

"I don't know exactly, but this morning I had occasion to speak your name, the first time in all these years, and I had to see you. Our friends are beginning to die, and I'm going to, sometime, and so will you. And I wanted to see you. Do I have to say any more than that?"

"No. But if you do, I won't hold it against you. Shall I say it first? I love you, and I've never stopped."

"And I've never stopped."

"No, we could never stop, could we?"

"Well, of course we did stop," she said.

"Seeing each other. But we had to do that," he said.

"*I* had to. Or I thought I had to."

"You did have to, Fritzie. You did the right thing. I couldn't have gotten married for another five years, and I didn't. For another seven or eight, I guess it was."

"Has your marriage worked out well?"

"Very well, at least for me. I've never been sure that Polly's as happy as she deserves to be. She knows about you, of course."

"That was a mistake. Henry D'Avlon *doesn't* know about you."

"How did you manage that? You weren't supposed to be a virgin, were you?"

"No, but I didn't have to tell him about you. There was somebody else after you."

"Who?"

"What difference does it make?"

He laughed. "You're quite right. But I'm jealous, all the same."

"You have a nerve," she said, smiling.

"I know," he said. "Isn't it odd, we two sitting here like this, studying each other, more or less like strangers, when we should be just about getting ready to have our twenty-fifth anniversary? You've had two children, I've had three. But little by little we're going back to what we used to be."

"Yes. I love you as if none of it had happened."

"It's nice, isn't it?"

"I guess it is. As long as we *don't* think about five children and a husband and wife."

"We don't have to think about them, not for the present. I'm glad you came to see me, and I wonder why you did. I mean, why just now?"

"I don't know. It could have been any time. Well—no, not the first five or ten years I was married. I was still very busy getting you out of my life, and I couldn't possibly have seen you. But then my life began to be regulated by my husband, my children, home, taking an interest in my husband's business. And I was safe. Then I could admit to myself that I was in love with one man. You. But that took about ten years."

"Very much the same thing happened to me, too. I remember reading an article about your husband. I guess it was in *Fortune*. It said that you were one of the modern corporation wives, very active. Very helpful to your husband. Have you got a keen business sense, Fritzie?"

"It didn't say that."

"No, but something like it. Oh, I don't know. I'm more in-

terested in finding out what brought you here today. I'm glad
you came."

"Are you, George?"

"Yes, I'm glad you didn't put it off much longer."

"Why? Is there something the matter with you?"

He nodded. "Yep."

"You mean you're going to die?"

"Yes, I think so. I'm going to have what's called exploratory
surgery, but I'm fairly sure I know what they'll find."

"Why didn't you have the operation before?"

"Oh, hell, I was so busy, and a few months wouldn't have
made much difference. The interesting thing is, Fritzie, you
knew I was going to die, didn't you?"

"I guess I did."

"*I* think you did. I think our loving each other is the explanation. We never stopped. And we never will, will we?"

"No."

"You see, in my business, you never know it all. Things
I was taught twenty-five years ago are now no longer true.
Some young guy in Pasadena, California, may be holding up
a test tube at this very minute and shaking his head and saying
he doesn't understand it. But he will understand it, maybe two
years from now, and out goes everything we believe today. And
good luck to him. But no guy in Pasadena or Paris or Moscow
or anywhere else is going to be able to tell why you came to
see me today. They thought they had it when Freud began publishing, and lately they've been doing things in the extra-sensory
line. But I think they're a long way off. The poets are closer.
They do a lot of research and make their reports, but they're
very careful not to commit themselves to a definition. They go
right on describing the properties of love, but by avoiding a
definition they keep an open, scientific mind. But if anyone
wants the proof of it, here we are. You and I."

"Oh, my dear, I'm too much of a materialist."

"You always were, but what of it? It didn't stop me from
loving you, or you from loving me. You have everything a
woman is supposed to want, and you're a successful materialist.

Just as I'm a successful alleviator of suffering and a non-materialist. But this morning you discovered that the man you love is going to die, and the only person in the world that also knows it is me. And how did you know? The only way you could know. The poet's way. The scientific way. And not the dull, unimaginative way of some near-sighted son of a bitch in Pasadena."

She smiled. "This is like our talks on the top of the Fifth Avenue bus. Do you remember when I used to ride up to the hospital on the bus, and have to come home alone? Goodness, we used to talk."

"Remember? Do I remember?"

"I wonder what ever happened to Mr. Cletus Connaughton."

"Who?"

"Mr. Cletus Connaughton. Our favorite bus conductor."

"You're making that up," he said.

"I am not. He had a badge that said Mr. Cletus Connaughton. He was a red-faced Irishman that used to hold the bus for me while we said goodnight. Mr. Cletus Connaughton."

"The one with the advanced case of acne rosacea. Was that his name?"

"Mr. Cletus Connaughton. He was sweet," she said.

Reassurance

Henry and Olive Rainsford stood on their porch, observing that moment of silence between the saying of goodbyes and the starting of their departing guests' car. Olive Rainsford, in sweater and skirt, had her arms folded close against her bosom; the air was chilly. Henry Rainsford, in tweed jacket and mole-skin slacks, had his pipe in one hand and a kitchen match in the other, and he was smiling. Mary Roberts lowered the window on her side of the car, and said in a quiet voice: "It was such fun." Her remark was a kind of afterthought; it did not belong with the already spoken farewells.

"It was, wasn't it?" said Olive Rainsford. Her remark was immediately lost in the roar of the engine turning over.

"Okay, Keith?" said Henry Rainsford. Keith Roberts did not hear him; he put the car in gear and turned it toward the gate. By the time the Robertses' car was halfway down the driveway, Henry and Olive Rainsford were inside the house. "You're shivering. Let's have a cup of coffee?"

"All right," said Olive Rainsford. Elsie, the maid, was coming down the front stairs. "Elsie, would you bring us some coffee, in Mr. Rainsford's den?"

"Yes ma'am," said Elsie. "Mrs. Roberts forgot this."

"What is it?" said Olive Rainsford.

Elsie handed her a small blue leather case. "Cosmetics," said Elsie. "Facial tonic, and cold cream and stuff."

"Well, we'll have to mail them to her."

"Maybe she'll be back for them," said Henry Rainsford.

"No, she won't miss them till tonight, and by then they

ought to be in Savannah. They're planning to spend the night in Savannah. All right, thank you, Elsie. And the coffee."

Henry Rainsford lit his pipe and seated himself in the tufted leather chair. "I love them dearly, but one night is about as much as I can take," he said.

"I don't see why you don't go right ahead and smoke your pipe while she's here. It's your house."

"Mary knows that I know she can't stand my pipes. So if I lit up, she'd know I was doing it deliberately," he said. "Once a year. It's all we ever see them."

"Why do they insist on *driving* to Florida? That must take it out of Keith, and he's no young boy."

"He's sixty. Just my age."

"Well, I wouldn't let *you* drive those long distances. I can think of nothing more exhausting. It must take them a week to recover, even her, just sitting there. She's fifty-five."

"She's fifty-six. Well, they want to have the car while they're there. And I think driving gives them an excuse to visit us."

"To have an annual look. To see if we're still speaking to each other."

"I suppose so. It isn't as if Keith didn't have all the money in the world. He could ship the car, or rent one while he's there."

"And it isn't exactly a car for a man sixty years old."

"Oh, I don't mind that. As long as he lives Keith will be driving the latest thing, and I wouldn't take that away from him."

"No, I guess I wouldn't either, if he has to go on living with her."

Elsie brought the coffee and departed.

"I don't think that's the way it is, exactly," said Henry Rainsford.

"The way what is?" said Olive Rainsford.

"It isn't that Keith has to go on living with her, unquote. She has a lot to put up with, too."

"Your great love," said Olive Rainsford.

"Yes. Till I was twenty-two. You say that every year, and I guess I always have the same answer."

"You have."

"But the woman who stops here every year on her way to Florida isn't eighteen-year-old Mary Vondermuhl. And I'm not twenty-two-year-old Henry Rainsford."

"How very true, but while she's in this house you're both back at Princeton."

"Yes, we are, in a sense."

"Innocent?"

"No, I said, in a *sense*. Oh, innocent, sure. Good Lord. Innocent to the point of stupidity. Then."

"When she lost her innocence it's too bad she didn't lose her stupidity."

"Well, she had sense enough to latch on to Keith, and God knows he wasn't a very bright prospect when she married him. She gave up a pretty good thing when she divorced Miles Larkin. Financially, at least."

"I wonder what they're saying about us, right this minute," said Olive Rainsford. " 'I never thought it would last this long.' "

"Oh, hell, Mary'd be saying a lot worse than that. She doesn't spare anybody else while she's here, so I'm sure she doesn't spare us when she leaves."

"All right. What *would* she say?"

"Well, considering that she doesn't really like you—"

"Putting it mildly."

"And on a basis of her remarks about other people, she probably does a lot of speculating about our sex life."

"Which wouldn't interest Keith."

"Which would interest Keith more than almost anyone I know."

"Really? Keith?"

"Clinically, yes. You see, he's only known you for ten years, and that's about as many times as he's seen you, ten, so he wouldn't open up in conversation with you. But he'd be interested, don't think he wouldn't. All his life."

"So that when I thought he was falling off to sleep, he was actually studying you and me."

"Sure. All the time."

"Horrid thought."

"Oh, well."

"Horrid thought, because it's like being told later that some-one watched you taking a bath. Being told by the person that watched you."

"Except that Keith would never admit to you that he'd been studying you."

"Then after he's been studying you all evening, I suppose he tells her what he's found out, or thinks he's found out."

"More than likely."

Olive Rainsford nodded. "That's what she meant by that remark. 'It's been such fun.' "

"No, I don't think she meant anything by it. I don't think she's all that subtle, Mary. But I'm sure she listens to all of Keith's analyses of people. He does it scientifically, clinically, and she listens because underneath it all, Mary's a twenty-four-karat bitch."

"That's surprising, coming from you."

"Well, you never really inquired as to what I really thought of Mary."

"I can almost feel them listening to this conversation, can't you?"

"They're probably talking about us." He looked at his wrist-watch. "At five minutes of ten, fifteenth of January, 1961, we were talking about them and they were talking about us. It would be amusing if we could check up on that, but of course we never can. What are you going to do this morning?"

"I'm going over to Betty's to pick up some things she bought for me in Washington. She'll want me to stay for lunch, but I won't, unless you're going to be out for lunch. What are your plans?"

"I'll be right here, working on my speech."

"What speech?"

"Oh, my speech. You know, next month. The dinner for Tom Whalen. New York."

"Why do you have to make a speech for Tom Whalen?

Aren't you doing enough, just by going to New York? Three days shot."

"Not really. I'll get some things done in New York. It's a good idea to show your face at the Trust Company every once in a while. I go see Snyder and he tells me what he thinks I ought to get rid of and what to hold on to—things he can do by letter or telephone. But then at lunch he tells me about his son at Columbia Law School, and his new grandchild, if he has one. He always has. And he always ends up by telling me how smart I was to get out of the rat-race."

"Do you have to be told?"

"Well, it helps. Fifty was pretty young to retire."

"You didn't retire. You changed from being a banker to a farmer. You had the money, so you did what you always wanted to do. Do you need reassurance, Henry?"

"Sometimes. Not often, but sometimes."

"When? For instance?"

"Oh, when Gene Black asked me to go to India with him that time. And when Eisenhower used to have those small dinner parties, most of the fellows were friends of mine. I'd have enjoyed having dinner with the President of the United States in the White House. My daughters would have been proud of me. So would you."

"I'm just as proud—well, not proud, but pleased, when I compare your blood pressure now with ten years ago. If you want to give this up—"

"Don't even think of it! This *is* the way I want to live. The only thing that ever causes me doubt is once in a while I wonder about you. Are *you* happy, stashed away in Virginia, away from your friends and New York?"

"I wouldn't go back to that life no matter what happened."

"Not even if I died?"

"I'd stay right here. I'd get a job teaching school, or something."

"It's settled, then."

"It was settled when we came here. I knew what I wanted,

too, Henry. And it wasn't a question of geography. It was *you*."

"Thank you," he said. "It wasn't a question of geography with me, either. Or switching occupations. I never would have made the move with anyone else."

"Some more coffee?" she said.

He smiled. "Why of course some more coffee. *Please.*"

She was back a few minutes before one o'clock, and he was sitting at his desk in his shirtsleeves, his tweed jacket lying on the seat of the tufted chair. "How's Betty?" The room was full of smoke.

"Limping. A horse stomped on her toe."

"Painful, especially at our age. Broken?"

"No. The skin's broken, but not the bones. She had X-rays. She's probably going to lose the toenail. Did you finish your speech?"

"No. I wasn't satisfied with the way it was going, so I started all over again. I think I have it this time. The first draft I tried to be funny, and I'm not a humorist."

"And they'll all try to be funny."

"Exactly. So I began all over again, starting with the question, why are we giving Tom Whalen a dinner?"

"Thirty-five years with the bank, isn't that why?"

"That's the official, public reason."

"Oh? What's the real reason?"

"Tom's been given the bad news. He has about a year to live, if that. Cancer."

"Is he going to know that you all know it?"

"No, and only three of us do. Me, Brownie Johnson, and Jack Stegall. Mollie told Brownie and he told Jack and me, swore us to secrecy. Then *Tom* told Brownie, because he thought somebody ought to know at the bank. So Tom will know that Brownie knows, but he won't know that anyone else knows."

"Does Tom want a party?"

"Yes. Very much. The day after the party they're going to announce his retirement from the board, and he wants to see the whole crowd before the announcement. He's not going back. I mean, he's not going to go to his office again. He wants to see the whole crowd, but he doesn't want a lot of individual farewells. So most of the fellows are going to the party in a jovial mood, for a festive occasion, and that's what Tom wants."

"This makes me like Tom, and I never have. That big, gruff Princeton football player having such sensitivity. I think of how he used to bore me when Princeton would lose."

"He bored everybody, but that happened to be one of the things he cared about. Princeton football got Tom Whalen a lot of things he never would have got without it. He made good on his own at the bank, but first he had to make the original connection, and football did it for him."

"How serious are you going to be in your speech?"

"I'm going to make the point that a man has to care about something besides his work, and that in Tom's case it was Princeton football. It isn't very profound, but Tom will like it. In recent years he's had to take a lot of kidding on that score, and some of it wasn't very nice kidding. Some of it wasn't kidding at all, although it was put in an ostensibly kidding way. And Tom knew it. He didn't talk quite so much about Princeton football in recent years, and I know why. He told me that he shut up about football because he was afraid his enthusiasm was beginning to hurt the bank. Well, he was right, there. To quite a lot of people he symbolized the bank, the only name they knew on the board. And there was a certain amount of criticism on that score, having a perennial undergraduate as the bank's representative. I don't know why it was any worse to have a football nut on our board than some other banks that wanted nothing but Skull & Bones types, but football is supposed to be juvenile, and Skull & Bones is supposed to be mature. I *guess*. I always failed to see the difference, but then I'm a Princeton man."

"I never appreciated Skull & Bones *or* Princeton football," said Olive Rainsford. "Is it true that they wrestle in the nude at Skull & Bones?"

"Search me. I always heard they had a swimming pool down in the cellar. Or maybe that was the other one, Keys."

"Lunch, ma'am," said Elsie.

"Thank you." They said no more until they had had their tomato juice. "I meant to ask you, what reason are you giving for this dinner for Tom, in your speech?"

Henry Rainsford touched the napkin to his lips and cleared his throat. "I'm trying to more than say something nice about Tom. I'd like a lot of the fellows there to realize that they're not wasting their lives. More and more they confide in me that they wish they'd done what I did. But what if they all had quit? Consider the fantastic notion that all the fellows from our bank and all the other fellows that will be at Tom's dinner—that they had all followed my example ten years ago. There'll be seventy-five men at that dinner, practically all of them between the ages of fifty and seventy-five. I don't imagine that a single one of them hasn't at some time or other thought of chucking the whole thing. So let's consider the mathematically unlikely possibility that they all had quit, ten years ago, when I did."

"All right, let's consider it."

"In my honest opinion, if that had happened the effect on the country would have been as bad as the loss of a major battle. I've been tempted to compare it with the dropping of an atomic bomb on one of our big cities. But we don't know anything about that, so I say the loss of a major battle. The men that will be at that dinner carry around in their brains the financial-economic, long-range and day-to-day plans of the nation. There'll be fifteen or twenty men at that dinner who have the experience and information that enable them to make decisions that affect every man, woman and child in this country for at least the next twenty-five years. Not one of those men is indispensable, of course. But any five of them are, and fifteen or twenty of them disappearing all at once—it's frightening to contemplate."

"Well, it didn't happen, and it won't happen."

"No, it didn't happen and it never will. That would be carrying coincidence too far. But the fact—and this *is* a fact, even if it's conjectural—that if you concede the fantastic possibility, you have automatic chaos, and I say it's frightening to contemplate. And I'm going to say all this in my speech, because in a way I represent an outsider's opinion, and these guys get an awful lot of abuse from outsiders. It's time someone said something that will make them feel good. Important. Responsible. They aren't all in it for the money. All of them could quit. I did, and they all have more money than I have. I'm not going to say it's patriotism that makes them stay on the job, because that wouldn't be true. And yet it is a kind of peacetime patriotism. Take Tom Whalen, for instance. The bank has eighteen hundred employees, and he's thinking of them when he quits. That's what the bank is to Tom. But then take Charlie Bennington, who'll be at the dinner. His company employs over two hundred thousand, and I know that Charlie never makes a decision without considering them as a factor. The effect on them, and the secondary effect on the entire public. Charlie's grandfather was a master mechanic in Quincy, Illinois."

"Charlie Bennington?"

Henry Rainsford nodded. "A master mechanic, in the railroad roundhouse."

"I thought Charlie Bennington was from a long line of Harvard Benningtons."

"A long line of two. Charlie, and his father. I guess with a name like Bennington if Charlie wanted to go back far enough he'd find some Harvard men in his background, two hundred years ago, but the family fortune as he knows it dates from the master mechanic in Quincy, Illinois. And he's never forgotten it. Nor should he. A master mechanic puts in as many years learning his trade as a Harvard A.B. In fact, more."

"Are you going to say all *this* in your speech?"

"No. But it's going to be in my mind as I prepare the speech. I'm going to get up there and tell those fellows how good they are. Something I never would have thought of doing while I was still in their midst, so to speak. I would have been embarrassed. But this way I say my say, and the next morning I'm on the train for home."

"Your good deed done."

"My good deed done. I won't have to slobber over Tom, but what I say about all of them will apply to Tom, and he'll sense it. Even if he doesn't get it right away, he'll get the underlying meaning when he has time to think it over."

"Very good. I approve of that. I was afraid this was going to be—"

"Sloppy sentimental, induced by too many Martinis. I know."

"Yes, and 'Rah, Tiger, Sis-boom-bah.' "

"There'll be some of that, but we'll keep it to a minimum."

Elsie entered. "Ma'am, you're wanted on the phone. It's Mrs. Roberts."

"Did you tell her you found her case?"

"Yes ma'am, but she wanted to talk about something else. I'll take your plate and keep it warm."

"Thank you," said Olive Rainsford. She made a face and her husband laughed. "Well, she must *know* we're in the middle of *lunch*." She took the call in Henry's den. "Hello, dear. We found your case. At least Elsie did. I'll mail it to you this afternoon."

"That isn't why I called," said Mary Roberts.

There was silence. "Mary? Mary? Are you still connected? Hello."

"I'm here. Olive, I'm calling from the hospital in Blake Falls, North Carolina. It's Keith."

"Oh, dear. What, Mary?"

"It's all over."

"You mean he's dead?"

"He collapsed at the wheel and we ran off the road."

"Are you all right? I mean were you hurt?"

"I'm all right. We weren't going very fast. We'd just stopped for a traffic light and were starting up again. And it happened. He just fell forward, slumped over the wheel. He didn't say a word, Olive. Just slumped over the wheel."

"How awful for you, dear. Do you want us to come and get you, or anything?"

"I'm all alone, Olive. They're all so nice. The doctors and

the police, but I don't *know* anybody. I don't know what to do. I didn't know which way to turn."

"Well now you just take a room at the hospital, and Henry and I'll be on our way in ten minutes. How far is it?"

"I don't know."

"Never mind. I can look it up on the map. If you can't get a room at the hospital, go to the hotel, if there is one. But anyway be sure and leave word where you'll be. We'll go straight to the hospital. And you tell the doctor that Henry and I will be there as soon as we can. Two hours, would you think?"

"Yes, I think it's about two hours from your house."

"You get some rest, dear, and don't worry. Henry and I will take care of everything."

She hung up and then saw that her husband was standing in the doorway. "Keith die?" he said.

"I gather he had a heart attack. They're in Blake Falls, North Carolina. He died immediately, at the wheel. Car went off the road, but she's not hurt."

"Well, at least it was quick."

"I was just thinking. I'll have to pack a bag for New York. She's all alone, and I'll have to go back with her."

"She could call her sister, lives in Englewood."

"She could, but she didn't. She called us. She *really* called *you*."

"No she didn't, Olive."

"She doesn't know it, but she did. Oh, I don't mind. She talked to me, but she was appealing to you."

"Well, maybe, poor thing. Keith's brother's in New York. And as far as that goes, Mary has children of her own."

"I know all that, Henry. But she didn't call them, she called us. Her own age, and an old love, you. That was instinct, and we have to respect that."

"Okay. We'll both pack for New York, but I hope we don't have to go."

The car was heated; the citizens of the Virginia and North Carolina villages were staying inside, and the nearly deserted streets seemed a continuance of the bleak countryside, with its patches of hardening snow and the brittle branches of the pine trees. "Could we have the radio on?" said Olive Rainsford, a half hour away from home.

"Sure. Take your pick," said Henry. "Rock and roll, hillbilly, commercials, and news. Mostly commercials." They heard two mentions of the death of Keith Roberts, New York millionaire sportsman, in Blake Falls, North Carolina, while en route to Hobe Sound, Florida.

"Roberts was at one time intercollegiate doubles champion and captain of the Princeton University tennis team, later turning to golf and served as a governor of the United States Golf Association. He was also a collector of modern art and donated numerous paintings to museums," said the announcer.

"How did they know that in Blake Falls, North Carolina?" said Olive Rainsford.

"That came from the Associated Press," said her husband. "Probably Washington or New York."

"Nothing about Mary except that she was with him, so I guess she wasn't hurt," said Olive.

"She said she wasn't, didn't she?"

"I thought she was possibly being brave."

"Not that brave. If she'd been hurt she'd have told you."

"You *don't* like her, do you?"

"No."

"Why not?"

"You were right this morning when you guessed why they always stopped to spend the night with us. She was making an annual check on our marriage. And she didn't wish us well."

"Then why on earth are we going to all this trouble?"

"You answer that, Olive."

"In a situation like this we had no choice."

"You had no choice, or gave yourself no choice. You acted on a decent instinct. If it'd been me, I don't know. I think I'd have tried to get out of it."

"No, you'd have done the same thing."

"Well, maybe."

"We neither of us like Mary, but when we're needed we do

what we can. We've got to that age, where we don't have to like our friends. They just have to be our age."

He smiled. "I couldn't have said it better," he said. "'We don't have to like our friends. They just have to be our age.'"

"Well, you know what I meant."

"Sure. I most certainly do. The thinning ranks, and baby, it's cold outside."

The name Blake Falls was beginning to appear more frequently on billboards and direction signs. "Don't leave me alone with her," said Henry Rainsford. "Stick with me every minute."

"All right," said Olive Rainsford.

At the hospital the head nurse took them to her room. "We didn't have a room for Mrs. Roberts, so I was only too glad to let her rest in mine," she said.

"Very nice of you," said Henry Rainsford. "The death certificate and the undertaker?"

"All being taken care of, Mr. Rainsford. Ah b'lieve Mrs. Roberts' brother in New York City did the talkin' with Dr. Mercer, he's our chief of staff. Dr. Julian K. Mercer? Ah'm sure you must of heard tell of heeum."

"The name is familiar, yes," said Henry Rainsford. "So the local undertaker will put the body on the train, and so forth?"

"Yandell Brothers, they're the best in town."

"How is Mrs. Roberts?"

"Taking it very well. Didn't want a sedative, and I took her in a cup of chicken broth and a lamb chop at ha' past two. She's been on the telephone a great deal of the time, naturally, and Ah b'lieve her brother is taking a four o'clock plane from New York. Then he has about an hour's drive from Charlotte. About an hour."

"She sounds much better than when we talked to her," said Olive, half to her husband, half to herself. "Nurse, you've been really wonderful with her."

"My name is Miss Coleman. Ah'm the head nurse. C, o, l, e, m, a, n. Well, that's what we're here for, to do the best we can, and Mrs. Roberts *was* in a state. Didn't *know* a soul, and everything happened so suddenly as those things do sometimes. Uh-oh, that's my light blinkin'. Is there anything else I can tell you before you go in?"

"I don't think so, thank you," said Olive Rainsford.

"Then if you'll excuse me, that light means I'm wanted on the phone. I'll come by when I can."

Mary Roberts rose from the white iron chair and silently embraced her visitors. "You were so good to come. And it was such an imposition, but I was panic-stricken. As if I'd got in trouble in a foreign country. Are you exhausted, Henry?"

"No."

"I reserved a room for you at the hotel. You don't want to drive back tonight, do you?"

"We just got here, so we don't know," said Olive Rainsford. "We want to be sure everything's all right with you."

"Ralph is flying down, Keith's brother, and he said something about chartering a plane."

"And going back to New York tonight?" said Henry Rainsford.

"Yes, I don't see any point in staying here. Actually Ralph has a friend in Charlotte and this friend's company has a plane that they'd let us use, if it's here when we're ready to leave. Otherwise we'll charter one. I don't think I could bear to spend the night here."

"Well, you seem to have things pretty well under control," said Henry Rainsford.

"Thank you, Henry. I didn't want to let myself go to pieces, and when I knew you and Olive were on the way I began to make some sense. This Coleman woman has been very efficient, and Dr. Mercer, the head doctor, he couldn't be more charming. One of those real Southern charmers. *Knows Bob Hawthorne.* Went to P. and S. with Bob, and as soon as I told him I knew Bob, why the sky was the limit. Have either of you got any cigarettes? They have a machine out in the hall, but this would be the day it broke down."

"Here's an extra pack," said Henry Rainsford. "Well, what

would you like us to do, Mary? Do you need any cash, for instance?"

"Luckily I have about a thousand dollars in traveler's cheques, and they turned over the cash Keith had in his pockets, so no, I'm all right for money, thanks. I would like to go for a walk. The hospital smell. I've been here all the time. Henry, would you take me for five or ten minutes in the fresh air?"

"We'd love to," said Olive Rainsford.

Mary Roberts looked at her. "Uh-huh. I was thinking if there were any phone calls for me—oh, I'll just open the window. I guess I don't really want to go for a walk. Oh, do you know who called and was so nice you couldn't believe it, Henry?"

"No, who?"

"Miles."

"Miles Larkin?"

"Heard it on the radio, and then saw it in the afternoon papers. Miles Larkin was my first husband, Olive. I don't think you ever knew him. *He* knows somebody that has a company plane. One of the cigarette companies. And within five minutes after Miles hung up this perfectly charming gentleman called up from Winston-Salem—that's somewhere around here—and said everything was at my disposal. Car and chauffeur. Plane. Lawyer if I needed one. Imagine Miles, after all these years. I guess you'd better put down the window, Henry. It's gotten colder. I never knew that Miles had any connection with the cigarette business, did you, Henry?"

"He hasn't, as far as I know, but Miles is a pretty well-known man, in financial circles."

"And yet with *all* his money, what's it got him?"

"Oh, I brought your little case," said Olive. "It's in my bag, in the back of the car, Henry. It's a blue leather case about so big."

"I'll get it," said Henry Rainsford.

"Don't make him go," said Mary Roberts.

"Oh, yes," said Henry Rainsford, leaving.

"Go on about Larkin, Mary. You were saying that with all his money?"

"First I want to tell you how much I appreciate your coming all this way, Olive. The nicest thing about it is that Henry and I were never anything. You know? I'm sure you know who he's had affairs with and who not. So it isn't as if I had that claim on him. It was boy and girl and nothing more with Henry and I."

"Yes, I knew that, Mary."

"Then you see why it's nicer that he came all this way, and you, of course. Both of you. Just as nice of you, because you and I've never been very close. Henry's a very lucky man, and I'm so pleased for both of you."

"I'm a very lucky woman, and Henry's a fine, wonderful, decent man."

"Yes, I was very lucky, too. To have Henry for my first love, and then Miles as my first husband. Even if it didn't work out as a marriage, it was a good relationship. Well, the proof of it today. After all these years Miles came through, and he didn't have to. He could have just sent flowers. Or nothing. After all, he had good reason to dislike Keith." She smiled. "Henry had good reason to dislike Miles, too. Did Henry take you away from your husband?"

"No, I guess I took him away from his wife. His wife, and New York, and Wall Street, and all that life. Didn't you know that, Mary?"

"Well, I must say you're frank about it. Yes, there was naturally some talk at the time, but nobody can criticize the results after ten years. It is ten years, isn't it, didn't you say last night?"

"Ten years, that we've been married. Twelve years we've been together."

"You did the right thing, the intelligent thing, whisking him off to Virginia. I've always thought that, and I remember having a lot of respect for you when I heard it. It was the one sure way to keep him interested. A whole new life, away from those same people in those same surroundings. It wouldn't have worked with Keith, of course. Keith was determined to make a lot of money, and the place to do that was New York, and for the first years of our marriage that was uppermost in his mind, the prime consideration. I'd left Miles, a very rich man, and Keith was determined to make it up to me. Finally the day came when I said, in effect, 'All right, Keith, you have enough. Now let's enjoy life and stop thinking about making money.' And that's what we did. For twenty-five years he'd had a certain goal, a certain sum, and when he reached it I made him call it quits and do the things he wanted to do. His paintings, his golf, and his books. He was a great reader, you know. Terribly interested in things like psychiatry and psycho-analysis. Loved to study people, and in his will I happen to know he's left a very substantial sum to a thing they have at Princeton, a mental research thing."

"Oh, really?"

"Isn't this a depressing little room? Do you suppose Miss Coleman *lives* here? She's Southern. I imagine her family live somewhere near. Do you suppose this is her father and mother? And this. Her brother, I would imagine. A resemblance there. But you'd think they'd have nicer furniture for a head nurse instead of this hospital stuff. Heavens. She graduated in 1938. I wouldn't have *my* diploma hanging where everybody could tell my age. I wonder what's keeping Henry?"

"Oh, opening the rear deck, and unlocking and locking my bag," said Olive Rainsford. "Maybe taking time out to smoke his pipe."

"Henry and his pipes," said Mary Roberts. She put her hand on the telephone. "I have a feeling that I ought to be calling somebody, but I don't know who. I've called everybody that I had to call, family and so on, but then there are so many almost-family, you know. People like Charlie Bennington and Tom Whalen. That bore, but he adored Keith and every year they went to the National together for a week of golf."

"They'll have heard by this time."

"Yes, Miles did."

"So did we, on the car radio, several times."

"Oh, what did they say on the radio?"

Henry Rainsford entered and placed the blue leather case on Miss Coleman's iron desk.

"Thank you, dear," said Mary Roberts.

"You're welcome. I was thinking, Mary, you seem to have everything under control."

"I hope you're not thinking of leaving."

"Well, that's what I *was* thinking. Not if you need us, but you are going back to New York tonight, and everything's being taken care of. And I'd much prefer my own bed to a room in the hotel. Ralph should be here around six o'clock."

"Oh, how do you know?" said Mary Roberts.

"I've been talking to Dr. Mercer. He spoke to Ralph just before he left Idlewild. Or maybe it was La Guardia. Or maybe it was Newark. Anyway, one of the New York airports. Ralph got hold of Charlie Bennington's plane, and that's what you're going back in."

"See, Olive? I should have called Charlie."

"So, I think we'll plan to go back to the farm when Ralph gets here."

"Oh, don't wait. If Dr. Mercer's in the hospital I'll feel all right. I have confidence in him. You two go. I insist. You've done enough for me, and I'll always, always appreciate it. Just knowing you were coming made all the difference."

Henry and Olive Rainsford bade her farewell for the second time that day, and now their car was headed for home. "Do you want the radio on?" he said.

"No, do you?" said Olive Rainsford.

"No."

"When you get tired I'll drive," she said.

"All right. That'll be pretty soon."

"Let me drive now and you have a nap," she said.

"No, I'm good for the first hour."

"Well, the minute you begin to get tired, say so," she said.

"And you doze off if you feel like it."

"I'm not tired, and I want to keep you company."

"Why?"

"Oh, you know why," she said. "It's been a very unrewarding day."

"Yes," he said. "But it's over now."

"And we're going home."

"And we'll have a fire," he said.

"Yes, and you won't have to work on your speech."

"And we won't have to like our friends."

"No matter what age," she said.

"These bastards never dim their lights," he said.

The Free

Art Schwartz was finishing up the raisin pie, and his wife Rhoda was running her hand through her back hair, reading the newspaper spread in front of her, smoothing the ash from the end of her cigarette on the saucer, now and then taking a little sip of her coffee.

"Somebody at the kitchen door," said Art Schwartz.

Rhoda shrugged a shoulder, took off her glasses and put them on the table, and went to the kitchen.

"Hello," she said. "Oh, hello, Red."

"Is Art in?" The man was Red Moyer, town police officer, and behind him was George Pease, another policeman.

"Yes, he's in. Just finishing supper. Come on in," said Rhoda. "It's Red Moyer and George Pease," she called.

"Come on in," said Art Schwartz. "We got enough coffee, Rhoda?"

The dining-room seemed instantly smaller as Moyer, with Pease lagging behind, came in. They were in uniform and with all their equipment—extra-wide belts, pistols and holsters, handcuff and chain-twister holsters, blackjacks, double rows of cartridges, extra-large belt buckles, black leather jackets and silver-plated shields—they seemed to take up a lot of room.

"No coffee, Art. We're here to make an arrest," said Red Moyer.

"Did Rhoda do something, or me?"

"You," said Red Moyer.

"What did I do? You got a *warrant!* What's the charge?"

"Murder. Suspicion of homicide, in the warrant," said Red Moyer.

"You're crazy. Who was I suppose to kill?"

"Miriam Denby. Come on, Art. Get your hat and coat," said Red Moyer.

"When was I suppose to kill her? And what with?"

"You'll find out. Come on, get going."

"Wait a minute, for Christ's sake," said Art Schwartz. "I got a right to see what it says in the warrant."

"You shot her in the head with a .38, between one o'clock and ha' past five this afternoon," said Red Moyer.

"I did no such thing," said Art Schwartz.

"I guess you weren't with her this afternoon," said Red Moyer.

Art Schwartz looked at his wife.

"Were you with her?" said Rhoda. "That's all I want to know."

"She's gonna find it out," said Red Moyer. "Yes, he was with her, Rhoda. We lined up four people that seen him with her."

"You don't care if I killed her or didn't kill her. Is that it, Rhoda? All you care is if I was with her."

"You promised. You swore an oath," she said.

"She wanted a hundred dollars," said Art Schwartz. "But I didn't kill her."

"Come on, Art," said Red Moyer.

"Quit hurryin' me," said Art Schwartz. "I gotta talk to my wife."

"Your wife," said Rhoda.

"Is that final?" said Art Schwartz.

"I told you how it would end up. I gave you one chance after another," said Rhoda.

"And you think I killed her?"

"I don't know whether you killed her or didn't kill her."

"And if I did kill her, you wouldn't stick with me. Okay, Red."

"You better take your coat. You'll need it," said Red Moyer.

"Why? Don't you want me to catch cold? So long, Rhoda. I would of stuck with you. *J.R.* You remember that, or don't you? Just remember *J.R.*"

"I kept *my* promise," she said.

"Yeah, sure. Sure. Come on, Red. *Look at George,* with his hand on his gun. Christ, you're bloodthirsty, George. I think George wants me to make a run for it."

"Try it," said George Pease.

"George was a very good friend of Miriam," said Art. "Where were *you* all day, George?"

"Lay off, Art," said Red Moyer.

Within a week Art Schwartz was a free man. A frightened, but conscience-troubled woman came forth and testified that she had seen Miriam Denby place the revolver to her head and fire; three witnesses testified that at that moment they were shooting pool with Art Schwartz; a girl friend of Miriam Denby's reluctantly testified that Miriam was going to threaten suicide if Art did not give her the hundred dollars. The district attorney had no case, and knew it.

The people of the town were glad; only a few of the pious had been able to convince themselves that Art Schwartz would commit a murder. He was bad in some ways, very bad about money things, lacking in respect for some authority; but two of his grade school teachers had wanted to take the stand in his favor if the case had come to trial.

"You can go home now," said the warden.

"As far as you're concerned, yeah."

"Stay out of trouble, Art," said the warden. "You're not a kid any more. You ought to get a regular job."

"I make more shooting pool. That's what I'm best at."

"Shooting pool is no way to earn a living. With a good eye and steady nerves, you ought to be able to learn some trade."

"What?"

"Well—something that takes good eyesight and steady nerves."

"Right. Shooting pool," said Art. "It's what I'm doing. Thanks, warden. I appreciate what you done."

"Your father and mother were good people, Art."

"Yeah, but not my uncle, and he raised me."

"I know, I know. Well, good luck, and keep out of trouble."

"Or I'll be seeing you, huh? So long, warden. Now where?"

"Go home. Straighten that out first," said the warden.

"The warden is right, Arthur," said Wallace Webster, Art's lawyer. They were walking down the stone steps in front of the prison. "Straighten that out first."

"Mr. Webster, the warden wants me to learn a trade, and you both want me to straighten it out with my wife. I'll learn a trade about as quick as I'll straighten it out with Rhoda."

"This could be the turning-point in your life, Arthur. You could make a whole new start in every way."

"Wait a minute, Mr. Webster. I was just found innocent, wasn't I?"

"It amounts to that. The charge was dropped. You weren't found innocent or guilty, since there was no trial."

"I know, I know. But don't that make me just as good as you are, or the warden, or anybody else? I was arrested, but for something I was found innocent. So I'm just the same as if I wasn't arrested."

"Well—yes."

"So then why should I be the one to change my ways? I'm even better off than some people. I was charged with something and then they *prove*d I wasn't guilty."

"Have a cigarette, Arthur," said Webster. They were sitting in the front seat of Webster's parked car.

"Thanks," said Art Schwartz.

"You're out of this thing a free man, and that's as far as my duty goes, as lawyer to client. But your old ways got you into this position, Arthur. Your wife didn't stand by you as I think she should have, but it must have been a shock to her. It all came at once. The police come to your house and arrest you, and in the course of the conversation it develops that you'd been seeing a woman you'd promised to give up."

"Yeah, that's all she thought of, Rhoda. Not if I was on my way to the chair, guilty or innocent. She didn't even ask me that."

"No. You were guilty, in her eyes, of breaking your promise."

"And she cared more about that than if I fried."

"Momentarily, maybe she did. Momentarily. She's a woman."

"Yeah, there's plenty of proof of that, Mr. Webster. Some I didn't tell you. I'm all the one that has to change, I'm the one that the whole town knows I was with that crazy Miriam before she shot herself. I know what you were gonna say a minute ago."

"What was I going to say a minute ago?"

"Simple. If I get in some other kind of trouble, this goes against me, innocent or guilty."

"That's taken into consideration, rightly or wrongly. And my point is that although you didn't commit a homicide, your old ways got you into a situation where you could be charged with suspicion. Logically, you ought to be able to convince yourself that the best protection for your future is to change your ways. Your domestic life is your first problem, and as to your second, I'll help find you a steady job. You have brains, and you have other aptitudes, so even if you start at low pay, you ought to get ahead fast."

"That's what we used to say in Fourth Street Grammar. 'You'll get ahead—you need one.' "

"They even said that in my day," said Webster. "Well, shall I take you home?"

"Oh, hell, sure. The rent's paid, and I paid it."

"Be careful, Arthur."

"Why? In case I lose my temper? Mr. Webster, you never saw me shoot pool. If I scratch, I don't let it get me down. I make my living off guys that want to smash their cuesticks. They scratch, or miss a cock-up, and they want to smash their cuesticks, and it takes them a whole frame to get their stroke back."

"I used to play a little in college. I had a high run of eighteen."

"Not bad. You went into the second frame."

"I had a good break shot in the second frame, I remember, but then I guess I got overanxious. The record for high run in our fraternity was somewhere in the thirties. Thirty-two, something like that."

"Uh-huh. My high run is twice that. Sixty-four, but a college boy that can run thirty-two, he could of been a good pool-player if he stuck to it."

"He didn't. He's a surgeon in Allentown. Maybe you could have been a surgeon."

"Yeah. Rhoda gave me a book last year. The cover for a book. Do It Yourself Brain Surgery, or Brain Surgery Made Easy. I forget exactly. We didn't have no books to fit the cover *on*. When they had me in the clink was the first time I ever wanted to read a book. Then I did have the desire to read a book."

Webster smiled. "Maybe you should have stayed in a little while longer."

"And get to be a reader, yeah. And strain my eyesight. My wife can't read print this high. If she don't have her glasses on she can't read the big headlines. No thanks, Mr. Webster. I got two things I don't want to fool with. My eyesight, and my coordination. You never saw me shoot with a gun, either. I can break those bluerocks all day, if I got somebody there to pull them. Or unless the guns get too hot. I'd like to go up against some of those rich guys at the golf club. I hear they shoot for three-four hundred dollars a match."

"You're looking for easy money again," said Webster.

"Why is it easy money? What's wrong with that, if I'm good at it? Shooting pool I have to give everybody fifty to thirty-five, fifty to twenty-five, fifty to twenty. I'd have to give those men at the golf club a ten or twenty handicap, a hundred to ninety, a hundred to eighty. Or I might even lose to some of them even up, but I'm willing to take the chance. Very little easy money around when you got a reputation like I have."

"Well, maybe it isn't easy money, but it's still no way to make a living."

"Mr. Webster, I don't think you ought to tell me how I should make a living if I don't cheat. And where I play pool they got their eye on me every minute. It's skill, and a little figuring the percentages. And *you* used to play pool, so you know if you play pill pool you often lose before you even get a shot. And maybe I have a good night playing pool and then blow it all in a crap game."

"Maybe, but not often, from what I've heard, Arthur."

"No, not often."

"Here's your house. If you change your mind, I'll see if I can help you get some other work."

"Thanks. Thanks very much, Mr. Webster."

"You're welcome. Shall I send my bill here, or to the poolroom?"

Art Schwartz grinned. "My office, the first table at the Pastime Billiard Parlor. Office hours seven to closing."

"You're incorrigible, Arthur," said Webster, and drove away.

Art Schwartz entered by the kitchen door and quickly ascertained that the house was unoccupied at the moment. "Good," he said to himself. "I won't have to talk to her." But he was only half finished packing his suitcase when Rhoda appeared.

"I was over next door and I saw you come in," she said.

"How come you're off today?" he said. "You didn't quit your job?"

"I traded my day off with another girl."

"Well, you want to have a look at what's in the suitcase? You won't find anything belongs to you."

"No."

"You can keep the stuff I paid for, I don't want it. The TV and the radio. That kitchen stuff. All I want is my clothes and my guns."

"Where are you going?"

"I'll get a room some place."

"The battery's dead in the car."

"The battery's dead?"

"I didn't use it while you were away, so it ran down, I guess."

"How do you know it's dead if you didn't use it?"

"I tried to start it this afternoon. I was going up to meet you when you got out, but it wouldn't start. The horn didn't blow, so I guess it's the battery."

"You were going to meet me when I came out of the clink? Why?"

"I decided to."

"Why did you decide?"

"I talked to Mr. Webster."

"Oh, he decided. Not you. I *thought* he was kind of stalling up there."

"You don't have to spend that extra on a room. The rent's paid up till the end of the month. I'll go to my parents'."

"That's where I thought you'd be now."

"No, I been here all the time."

"Yeah. With J.R., probably."

"With nobody but my sisters and one night my brother. I got afraid to be here alone."

"Don't tell me Joe Rieger wasn't here at all?"

"He called up, but that's all. He knows that's finished."

"Then what'd he call up for?"

"Oh, he wanted to take me out. He wanted to start up again, but now he knows it's finished."

"Don't brush him off on my account. I'm a free man, you're a free woman."

"That's what my parents said, and my sisters and brothers."

"For once I agree with them."

"For once they agree with you. They said I did the wrong thing, I should have stood by you, no matter what."

"Don't say 'no matter what.' I'm just as good as anybody, you know. I was judged innocent, legally. No case against me."

"You kept on seeing her after you gave me your promise. I kept *my* promise."

"I wasn't talking about that. I was talking about the murder charge."

"I was talking about your promise. My parents were against me, but my friends weren't. Everybody in town knows you had her pregnant."

"Everybody but me. That's why I wouldn't give her the hundred dollars. I wasn't the only guy she was going out with, so why should I be the chump? George Pease, the cop. Stan Wilson at the Pastime. I got her to admit it that she didn't know *who* got her pregnant. That's why she shot herself. I told her to go to hell and get somebody else to be the chump, not me. And I got out of that car and I wasn't sure if she was gonna shoot me in the back. First she wanted me to marry her, and then she wanted me to give her a hundred dollars. But I didn't even know for sure if she was pregnant. She didn't look it, and maybe she was gonna take George and Stan for a couple hundred, too. Well, I would of given her the hundred dollars if I thought she was that desperate, but I didn't *know* that. When I got back to the Pastime I asked Stan if she put the bee on *him*, and he said no, not yet, but that same morning she called him up and said she wanted to see him. You know, she didn't threaten to kill herself. She threatened to kill me, and I don't threaten as easy as that. She said if I didn't promise to marry her she'd kill me, and pulled out this .38. I said go ahead and shoot and see where that got her. Then she said she had to have a hundred dollars and threatened me again, but I told her to go to hell and got out of the car. You should of heard the names she called me. Screaming and yelling and crying. And I walked down to the main road and took the bus."

"What did she do? Just sit there, I guess, and work herself into a state. Three men she was sleeping with and didn't know which one was the father. And all three married."

"There was four men," he said.

"I know."

"How do you know?"

"He told me."

"Oh," said Art Schwartz. "Well, it could of been him or it could of been me, or it could have been Stan or George Pease. Why would he tell you he was mixed up in it too?"

"Joe Rieger?"

"Yeah, now we got his name out in the open. Why would he tell you?"

"He was scared. That's why he called me up."

"Oh, come on, Rhoda."

"That's half why he called me up. First I told him I wouldn't go out with him, and then he wanted to know if you were going to mention his name in court, in the trial. There was a rumor around that Mr. Webster was going to subpeeny all Miriam's boy friends. So Joe was trying to find out if he was going to get a subpeeny so he could leave town. I told him I didn't know anything and he didn't believe me, so I understand he left town."

"Well, he'll be back now."

"Who cares?"

"He'll be back."

"She must of been desperate." Rhoda suddenly picked up an odd-shaped book, the only volume in a glass-fronted case that was half filled with china figurines of animals and brass and wooden knickknacks. She put her tongue on her thumb and rapidly turned the pages. "There. There she was when she was a cheerleader. I was a soph and she was a senior. She certainly was pretty. This is our Annual, my sophomore year. Here she is in High Jinks, the musical comedy show. Too much makeup on, but you can see how pretty she was. Here's all about her, the four years she was in High. 'She walks in beauty, like the night.' Miriam Denby, 204 South Fifth Street. Basketball. Field hockey. Gamma Gamma Gamma. Assistant cheerleader. High Jinks. Honor Roll, sophomore and freshman years. Not when I was there. She was bright, but she didn't study. Junior Prom Committee. Senior Ball Committee. Plans to enter college, probably State or Drexel. She didn't, though." Rhoda closed the book. "From High she went to work for Davison's. I guess she was one of the first models they ever had. If not *the* first. Part of the time she was a saleslady and part of the time she modeled."

Art Schwartz closed the lid on his suitcase. "When you get done talking about Miriam, how about you and me having a talk?"

"I'm ready whenever you want to. I was just talking while you did your packing up."

"Yeah. Well, you understand, Rhoda, I paid the last rent I'm gonna pay."

"I know."

"And other expenses. I don't pay any more of them."

"I don't expect you to. If we're not living together, I don't want you paying my bills."

"Well—that's all right then. You're not gonna have me hauled up for non-support?"

"No."

"Understand, you could make it tough for me if you got a lawyer. I might as well tell you that, because you'll find it out sooner or later."

"I knew it already. I heard about non-support. My sister had her husband up for non-support one time."

"Stella?"

"Yes. Ted had to put up some kind of a bond or he'd of been sent to prison. Mr. Webster wasn't the one that made me decide to meet you when you got out. It was Stella."

"Stella?"

"Well, look at Ted and her now. Three kids, and Ted's as good a husband as any woman has. They had their troubles, and they got over them. Ted drinks a little, once or twice a year he don't come home on payday. But that's better than some have it. And Stella said, 'You go and be there when Art gets out,' but then the car wouldn't start. I guess that's an omen. I wouldn't of known what to say anyway, and I'd of *died* if you walked away from me in front of Mr. Webster. So the car not starting was an omen. Where were you thinking of getting a room?"

"I don't know. Some place. I could probably rent a room from Stan Wilson."

"You'll be in the same kind of trouble again if you do. Phoebe Wilson's as bad as Miriam, if not worse."

"Everybody knows that."

"Then what do you go there for? Why don't you just stay here till the end of the month, and I'll go to my parents'. You can find a better place than Phoebe Wilson's."

"What are you being so big-hearted for?"

"For God's sake, Art! I got nothing but my whole family telling me how wrong I was, not standing by you. My father, my mother, my sister, my brother, and I even got it from Ted."

"But not your friends."

"Well, somebody had to be on my side."

"You go stay with your parents, they'll give you hell all the time?"

"Well, a person takes so much and then you get used to it. Oh, I don't intend to stay there, either. I'll get an apartment with one of the girls at the store."

"What one?"

"I don't know, but they're always talking about it. The single ones, and the ones that are separated, you hear them talking about getting an apartment. And if I have the TV and some of those other things I could probably fix it so I wouldn't have to pay the first month or two rent."

"And you could have guys to the apartment."

"Well, if I was divorced, or separated, and that's what we're gonna be. You're not gonna wait very long, Art. I doubt if you'll wait till tonight, if I know you. Phoebe Wilson, probably. She's on your mind."

"Well, that's none of your business any more."

"No, I admit it. You got a perfect right. Phoebe. Some other tramp. Go where you please. You're free."

"Well, so are you."

"*I* know, Art. *I* know."

"Yeah. What other phone calls did you get while I was up the hill?"

"What makes you think I got any?"

He laughed. "That was a wild guess, but now I *know* you did. Who?"

"You mean fellows?"

"You know God damn well what I mean."

"I'm not gonna get anybody into trouble. I didn't date anybody, so why should I tell you who called me up? No. You got your suitcase all packed, Art. If you want to stay here, I'll go to my parents. If you don't, why do you prolong the agony? You want to stay here?"

"With you."

She shook her head. "Oh, no, Art. Hunh-uh. What's through is through. What's over is over."

"All right, we're back to you being Rhoda Bevan and I'm Art Schwartz. I never saw you before."

"No. It has to be more than that with me. That's all right for Phoebe, and Miriam, but not me."

"It was more than that with Joe Rieger?"

"Yes, for a while. I told you. We don't have to go over all that again. I thought I was in love with him and he thought he was in love with me, only we weren't. It was you and that damn Miriam."

"Joe was with Miriam."

"I didn't know that then. I was just getting even with *you.*"

"You did."

"Well, are you staying?"

"No." He picked up his suitcase, and started down the stairs, with her following. In the kitchen they halted.

"I could offer you a piece of raisin pie. Cup of coffee," she said.

"You eat it."

"I don't like raisin. You know that. You want to take it with you?"

She opened the cakebox and brought out an uncut pie.

"You want me to go along the street carrying a raisin pie in my hand?"

"Well, then eat it, and I'll save the rest for my brother."

He looked at the pie. "All right." He put his hat on one of the kitchen chairs, but kept his overcoat on. She poured him a cup of coffee and sliced him a wedge of pie. He began to eat, and the telephone rang. The telephone was in the living-room, adjoining the kitchen.

"Hello," she said. "Oh . . . Yes . . . All right." She hung up and returned to the kitchen.

"Who was it?"

"It was for me."

"I know that much. One of your boy friends, judging from the conversation. This time you said yes, huh?"

"What if I did?"

"You did, didn't you?"

"Yes," she said.

"And you said 'All right.' That means he's coming here? When?"

"I'll tell you who it was, for your own good. It was George Pease, and he's gonna be here at six o'clock."

"George was one of those that phoned you when I was up on the hill?"

"Yes, and I said no, but now I said yes. So eat your pie and go, Art."

Art ate the rest of his pie. "I never liked that George Pease, from the time we were kids. I'm out of cigarettes."

"Here." She handed him a pack, and he lit one.

"I remember the night we were sitting here and they came to arrest me. I thought a lot about that, up on the hill. Red Moyer, kind of embarrassed. Red never thought I did it. But there was George, hoping I did it, and hoping I'd make a run for it. And as soon as I was put away, he calls up my wife." He stood up.

"Where you going? Where you going, Art?"

"Getting something I forgot." He went to the living-room, closing the door behind him, and she sat at the kitchen table, afraid to admit to her mounting terror. The door opened quickly and she looked at him.

He was grinning. "The pump gun," he said. "My old Ithaca, 37-S. Five shots."

"Don't, Art. Please?" she said.

"We just wait. Just sit calm and wait."

The Compliment

George Remsen saluted his wife with a home-from-the-office kiss and placed the refolded newspaper on the sofa beside her work-basket. She rather liked the custom, one of the few old ones remaining since the children were married and the Remsens had taken a hotel apartment. All through their married life George Remsen had brought the afternoon paper home to Jan. The custom had originated as an economy, but now George Remsen's economies consisted only of large ones: giving up a house in town that had too many servants and too many stairs; hiring limousines for weddings and funerals instead of maintaining a car and chauffeur (both car and chauffeur had seemed to spend most of the time in the garage on East Seventy-eighth Street, with other chauffeurs and similarly useless cars); giving up, not reluctantly, those annual trips to Europe; and in general ruthlessly abandoning the habits and possessions that George Remsen had worked so hard to achieve. The hotel apartment cost seven hundred and fifty dollars a month, but in floor space it was almost identical with the walkup in which the Remsens had begun married life for a tenth the price.

Jan Remsen watched her husband as he picked up his half-dozen letters and culled the impersonal items and put them to one side. He held up one large, square blue envelope. "This looks as though it ought to be interesting, but I'll bet you it's a benefit. A hundred dollars a ticket to see some damn play I wouldn't go to on a pass. And inside there'll be a card saying 'Do come. This is really a worthy cause. Signed, Mary McA.'

Then we have to go through the whole list of patronesses to figure out who Mary McA is. Well, let's see." He slit the envelope with Jan's plain silver opener, and her attention was rewarded by his instant interest. He quickly turned to the signature, frowned, and commenced to read. "It's from a girl I used to know, years ago," he said.

"*Not* from Mary McAndrews. I rather guessed that."

"No, before I ever knew Mary McAndrews. In fact, before I knew you. Hazel Dobson, from Batavia, New York. She's visiting someone in New York. Can't quite make out the name. Congratulations on my success. Very nice. Friendly. Buzz-buzz-buzz. Ah! Has a letter I wrote her in 1916, when I was eighteen years old, before I joined the Army. Wants to keep it, but would like to bring it and show it to me. Will lend it to me if I want to have a photostat made. But it's such a remarkable letter that she wants to hold on to it. No strings. Doesn't want to be a nuisance. Well, she wouldn't be a nuisance anyway. She was a terribly nice girl. Thinks you would be as interested as I'd be. Let's call her up and ask her to come over tomorrow?"

"All right," said Jan Remsen. "Is there a phone number? Do you want me to invite her?"

"Here, see if you can make out the name. I can read the number, and it's a Butterfield 8 exchange. Yes, you call her. She'd feel better about it, knowing Hazel. Hazel Dobson Chandler. Mrs. Dwight Chandler. Go ahead, give her a call."

Jan Remsen dialed the number and said, "May I speak to Mrs. Chandler, please? This is Mrs. George Remsen . . . Mrs. Chandler? Janet Remsen, yes. George and I would love it if you could stop in for a drink tomorrow afternoon, say about six? And please bring the letter . . . Oh, is that so? I don't think George ever knew that, or at least he didn't tell me. Well, I'll be expecting you, *we'll* be expecting you. Thank you." Jan Remsen hung up. "She sounded very nice."

"What was it that I never knew or never told you?"

"That she used to know Tom."

"Your brother Tom? I didn't know that. I guess she's just trying to tell you that she's all right. Reassure you. Nothing between *her* and me."

"Wasn't there?"

"I would have married her in a minute when I was twenty-one or -two, but she had other fish to fry. Other irons in the fire. In other words, it was all one-sided, on my side. But she was one hell of a girl."

"How old would she be now?"

"Sixty-two. Exactly my age."

"I'm reassured," said Jan Remsen.

"There was never anything. Nothing but a nice friendship between a very attractive girl and an awkward boy that needed someone to talk to," said George Remsen.

Jan Remsen looked at her husband, and the quick reassurance was gone, but she said nothing.

Hazel Dobson Chandler was announced at ten minutes past six, and Jan Remsen stood at the open door of the apartment to greet her guest as she got out of the elevator. "How do you do? Sometimes we don't hear our doorbell. It's only one of those buzzers," said Jan Remsen. "George will be here any minute."

"I'm *very* glad to meet you after so many years. I always felt as if I knew you," said Hazel Chandler.

"Where did you know Tom? At Cornell, I imagine."

"Yes. My brother Frank was in Kappa Alpha, a class ahead of Tom. Frank was killed in the war, in 1918, and I remember I had a very sweet letter from Tom after the war. Speaking of letters, Mrs. Remsen, I hope you don't think I'm some sort of crackpot, but I saved this letter of George's because I always felt that he was going to be a great success. I always felt that. You know how you do, with some people?"

"Yes. Will you have a cocktail, or shall we wait for George?"

"I'd just as soon wait, if you would."

"We could have tea, but George never takes tea."

"I'd rather talk. You see, I'm not sure, on thinking it over, I'm not at all sure I want to show George the letter. I'd rather show it to you first."

"He'll be here any minute. He's never later than six-thirty."

"It isn't terribly long. You can read it in five minutes, and then you decide whether to show it to him or not."

"I can't wait to read it," said Jan Remsen.

"Well, here it is," said Hazel Chandler. "You'll see why I hesitate."

Jan Remsen read the letter, the first few lines to herself, then, at Hazel Chandler's urging, aloud:

Ithaca, N. Y.,
Oct. 15, 1916

Dear Hazel:

Just a few lines to tell you I received the copy of *The Genius* by Theodore Dreiser and wish to express my thanks altho' I do not see how you managed to get hold of a copy. They are at a premium here & perhaps I should accept the book with thanks and "no questions asked." It is pretty raw in some places, at least as much as I have read so far but very true to life. I have never read anything by Dreiser before this but have great respect for your judgment, therefore will read the book and when I complete it will let you know what I think of it. Am not very good at book reports but I like a book that is true to life in preference to the average novel or many of the classics. Do not have very much time for reading these days as it is hard enough to keep up with my studies but they say it gets easier after freshman year. However, if it does not begin to get easier I may give up college and enlist. Saw your brother Frank last week, getting ready to go up to Canada and enlist in the Canadian Army. He said your parents are very upset. Can't say I blame them in a way as Frank is very bright and should stay here until he graduates, then enlist if he still wants to. I do not know what came over me because I suddenly said to Frank "Why are you planning to enlist in the Canadian army and get yourself killed over in France?" He became very angry with me for which I do not blame him as it is not my place to make such remarks but it was out before I realized what I was saying. If looks could kill I would be lying dead in Ithaca, N. Y., not Frank in France. I hope he gets over being angry as I always admired Frank & he is entitled to enlist if that is his wish. It would be different if I enlisted as I am not very optimistic as to midyears, therefore I could better myself in the army. However, am planning to stay here as long as I can until we "get in it." That will be sooner than most here think. I fail to see how we can avoid getting in it much longer. The Germans know who's side we are on or they would have to be very ignorant. If you look at it the way a German would they ought to declare war on us before we have any more opportunity to get ready for it. If I were a German I would take heed from all this talk about "preparedness" and declare war.

Hope you do not think I am a cheap skate afraid to waste a 2-cent stamp but I did not finish this letter altho' that was over a week ago. Saw Frank before he left and apologized. "That is alright, George," said Frank. However, I wish I had not said it in the first place as I should learn self-control instead of speaking without thinking, not that I think Frank is going to be injured. I am sure he will return safe & sound. Glad we parted on friendly terms as I may be over with him sooner than you expect, judging by the way things are going both scholastically and diplomatically (bet. U. S. A. and Germany). I am getting into the right frame of mind to enlist. I do not like mud or cooties but I will be ready when the time comes. The war will not last very long because there are so many modern inventions that as soon as we get in the tide will turn. When it is over I have decided that I will not try to get back in my class here but will try to get a job in one of the banks at home to learn the business, then go to N. Y. City. Would like to take the business course at Harvard but the next best thing is to get a job in one of the banks, then N. Y. City. The only time I was ever in N. Y. City I said to myself that I would be back some day and here that day is not far away! I am willing to put in two yrs in the army and two yrs in a small bank, then N. Y. City, here I come! That's the place for me. I appreciate your efforts to encourage me to take an interest in literature, etc., but that is not my bent. Please do not be disappointed in me, but you know the old saying about a silk purse and a sow's ear. I have a knack for figures, could always add 2 columns of figures when the other kids were learning to add 1. Also discovered that it was fun for me to do the problems in pounds Sterling and francs, etc. altho' others in my class found it impossible or were much slower at it. Therefore do not see the good of wasting time & money studying a lot of stuff I will never have any use for. I will be better off in a bank after we have licked the Kaiser, then I can start making my "first" million. I have never told this to anyone else, even you, but I am convinced of it that some day I am not going to stop at my "first" million. I cannot explain why, but it is a premonition. Do not think me conceited as that is the last thing I want you to think. I value your good opinion more than that of anyone I know. Hope to see you at Christmas if your "date" calendar is not monopolized by a certain Deke from Hamilton.

> Yours sincerely,
> Your friend,
> George K. Remsen

Jan Remsen smiled and handed the letter to her visitor. "I don't see why he shouldn't read it," she said. "What would be the harm?"

"Probably none, if you think it's all right. After all, I haven't seen George in almost forty years and I don't know what he's like now."

"Well—he's as nice as the boy that wrote that letter, but of course not as naïve."

"Oh—well, I wouldn't have said naïve. It isn't often a boy of eighteen is so sure of what he wants to do, and then goes ahead and does it, as George did. And his premonition about my brother Frank. Notice he said in the second part of the letter that Frank was going to return 'safe and sound,' but George didn't believe that, did he? Do you think?"

"No, I think that's fairly transparent. Didn't want you to worry."

"And his predictions about the way the war would go."

"Yes, he certainly gave that some thought. And I see what you mean about his not being naïve. Naïve was the wrong word. But I don't see why the letter should upset him now. I still don't see that."

"It's just that my reaction to the letter, when I first reread it, was amazement that a boy of eighteen could predict so accurately. Then, as I thought it over, if *I'd* ever predicted things so accurately, I'd wonder what had happened to me that I'd lost the power."

"Oh, I see," said Jan Remsen. "But he didn't make any other predictions, did he? Or did he?"

"Yes, he did. The Deke from Hamilton that he mentions in the letter?"

"Yes?"

"That was my husband, Dwight. George made a prediction about him. That Christmas. He said, and I can hear him this minute, 'Don't get serious over Dwight Chandler. He's a natural-born crook.' Well, I was very cross, naturally, and put it down to jealousy, but George said it wasn't jealousy. Did George happen to tell you that he was a little bit in love with me years ago?"

"Yes."

"But I thought he was too young. You know how boys your own age seem terribly young?"

"Oh, yes."

"So I wasn't in love with George, although I considered him a really dear friend. Well, anyway, I was very cross and I stopped seeing him. I got so serious about Dwight that I married him, and three years later he was sent to prison. For embezzling. He embezzled twenty thousand dollars from his grandfather's lumber business, which was a partnership, and the partner saw to it that Dwight went to jail. My husband died in prison. A ruptured appendix."

"Oh, dear. And what happened to you?"

"Oh, I did various things. I taught school, and I ran a little bookshop and then I got a job as librarian. People were very nice to me, and I managed to educate my son and daughter."

"I'm just adding up years. You were married three years and then you had these other jobs. George could have helped you by then. Why didn't you ask him? Not that he could have done very much, but you know George."

"Yes, but you don't know me, Mrs. Remsen. George was the last person I'd have gone to."

Jan Remsen looked at her visitor. "I can understand that, Mrs. Chandler. Maybe we'd better *not* show him the letter. Not because he lost the gift of prophecy."

Hazel Chandler returned Jan's look steadily. "No, not because he lost it or ever really had it. He was just very good about people."

"Very good about people. And you don't want him to know you had such a bad time."

"He must know some of it, but he doesn't know how bad it was, some of the time."

"You're all right now, though, I hope?"

"Yes, I'm all right now. I have a job in the hospital and a little money from a legacy, and I don't need much."

"What *do* you need?"

"What do I need? Nothing, really."

Jan Remsen leaned forward and put her hand over the back of her visitor's hand. "You just want to see George, is that it?"

Hazel Chandler nodded. "Just to see how he is. How he looks."

Jan Remsen smiled. "That's the least I can do, Hazel."

"Why?"

"Think what I owe you for staying away all these years."

"That's the dearest compliment any woman ever gave me," said Hazel Chandler. "Thank you."

Sterling Silver

The woman with the white, white skin two cabañas away called out: "Norman, come here a minute, please. Nor-man?" From her tone we expected that a small boy would respond to the call, but the man who separated himself from the group on the sand was well in his forties, furry as to chest and belly and shoulder blades, all but bald above the forehead, and deeply browned by the sun. He wore a gold identification bracelet, Hawaiian print bathing trunks, web-strapped clogs, and carried a raffia hat shaped like an oldtime planter's Panama. He looked at his half-smoked cigar, then on his way to the cabaña he dinched it in the concrete flower-pot.

"What is it, Irma?" we heard him say.

"I wanted a Collins," she said.

"I know, but when the waiter comes around," said the man.

"He was just here, but I wasn't ready for one."

"I know, but by the time he gets here you could have ordered one and you'd have finished this one. Wuddia want? Another rum Collins?"

"Well naturally I don't want a Tom. Gin on top of rum."

"No. You want a rum Collins—"

"Exactly like this one. This was just right."

"Well, now how was that so I can tell them?"

"I don't know, but it had just enough sugar."

"In other words, not too sweet."

"Not *too* sweet, but you could taste the sugar."

"Two spoonfuls, about?"

"I honestly don't know, but *they'll* know."

"Which waiter brought you this one? Joe?"

"No, I didn't like the one Joe brought me. It was *too* sweet."

"Then it was Mark?"

"Is that his name? The thin one."

"That's Mark. All right, I'll go find Mark and he'll take care of it for you."

"Oh, I don't know," she said.

"What?"

"Well, it's close to ha' past one. There won't be any lobster if we don't get there before two. They were all out yesterday. You take another dip and then we can go up and have lunch."

"You mean cancel the drink? You don't want it?"

"I'd rather have the lobster. I was so disappointed yesterday. I just felt like lobster."

"We could have lunch served here, or I guess it's too late today, but it's only a buck apiece extra to have it served in the cabaña."

She shook her head. "I'd rather go buffet. I hate to see those dirty dishes sitting around after I eat. You have a dip."

"No, I'll put on my bathrobe."

"Don't do that, Norman. Change into your slacks and your Filipino shirt. Don't let's go up there in your bathrobe."

"All right."

He entered the cabaña and came out a few minutes later wearing a white ruffled shirt and orange-red slacks. "Y'all set?" he said.

"Yes, but let's wait till those two go up. I don't care to stand in line next to them," she said.

"Who are they?"

"They're in 24. Their name is Mr. and Mrs. Copeland."

"How do you know?"

"It says so on the cabaña list. Here." She handed him a card, which listed the numbers and names of cabaña occupants.

"What have you got against them?"

"If she's his wife, I'm Lady Mountbatten."

"Lady Mountbatten is dead."

"Well, so am I, if that's Mrs. Copeland or Mrs. Anything Else."

"You could say that about quite a few here," he said. "Live and let live."

"I'm surprised they allow Bikinis in a place like this," she said.

"Oh, it isn't a regular Bikini," he said.

"If you can see a woman's belly-button, that's a Bikini for my money."

"Well, you can't see anything now. She's all covered up, right up to the neck. Come on, Irma, or we won't get any lobster. Or *you* won't. I don't want any. The roast beef was good yesterday, and it satisfies my appetite."

"You haven't lost any since we've been here."

"No, but I haven't gained. I just don't want to go over one-ninety. That's what I gotta watch out for. One-ninety. God, you're lucky. You take in the calories. One of those rum Collinses is more calories than I take in in a whole breakfast. And how many did you have?"

"What are you, counting my drinks again?"

"Oh, Irma. Lay off. Let's go eat."

They were Mr. and Mrs. Norman Borse, Cabaña 18, and they had arrived from Los Angeles in a black-and-grey Rolls-Royce. There were some Borse brothers who had lately got their names in the newspapers in connection with several fairly spectacular real estate deals, and we assumed that he belonged to that family. At the hotel he was on familiar terms with four or five men, but his wife kept to herself. In the late mornings she sat in the cabaña, and after lunch, while he was playing golf, she presumably retired to their room. They dined late, together, and for about four hours in the evenings she displayed her Paris originals and jewelry in the bar, then he would go with her to their room, returning to take his place in a bridge game with the same three men every night.

"Irma, Irma, Irma," said my wife. "And where have I seen that face before? You're no help at all."

"Yes I am," I said. "I told you she was never in the movies

and never on the stage. That saves you a hell of a lot of trouble."

"Are you sure she was never in the movies?"

"She was never even a Wampas baby star. Not even a Meglin Kiddie. I'm sure of it. Think back on some ax-murderers."

"No, and she wasn't the Pig Woman, in Debussy's Lane."

"De Russey's Lane. I could easily find out who she was."

"How?"

"By asking him. But that would take the fun out of it."

"Have you spoken to him?"

"Yes, today. We were held up on the first tee and we made conversation. He asked me where I got my putter, and I'm playing in a foursome with him tomorrow."

"If I don't figure it out tonight, ask him tomorrow who she was."

"If I can. It may be an embarrassing question."

It was not. Norman Borse and I were partners in the golf match, and he immediately became a fraternity brother, with the right to overpraise a good shot, to suggest changes in my stance, to recommend a tailor, to convert me to a vitamin preparation, to inquire into my financial investments, to give me a guided tour of the development he and his brothers had created near Santa Ana. "You're a married man, I take it," he said.

"Yes," I said.

"Some evening you and your wife might like to have dinner with my wife and I. You staying a while?"

"Another week," I said.

"Yes, now I know which one is your wife. She was the charming lady you got out of the station-wagon that she was at the wheel. I been married to the same woman for twenty-two years. Three to go before I have to go for that big silver number. I have it all planned out. Do you remember the girl with the beret?"

"I didn't notice her."

"Oh, I don't mean today. I mean the one that first they ran a picture of her on the cover of *Life* magazine. The girl with the beret, she got to be called. Black beret and trench coat, and then her picture was in all the ads every time you picked up a magazine. That was my wife, Irma Hopwood."

"Oh, of course," I said. "Billboards, all over the country."

"That's it. Bradford Petroleum put her under exclusive contract. She was practically their trademark there for a while."

"Yes, I remember her very well. She was like Betty Furness and Westinghouse, on TV."

"Well, she's my wife, and what I'm going to do, I'm going to get one of those sculptors and get him to make a statue of her in the beret and trench coat and present it to her on our twenty-fifth. Solid silver, of course. I don't care if it costs me a fortune, it's something I been wanting to do for over twenty years. I'll bet she's the only woman in the United States that has a contract that precludes her from wearing a beret."

"Really?"

He nodded. "If she wears a beret and has her picture taken and it gets into like the society page, she's in violation of contract. Oh, hell, they wouldn't go to court now, but they could. And twenty years ago don't think they wouldn't. I guess at one time her face was as well known as the President of the United States. There's no doubt about it."

"I'm sure you're right."

"The Bradford Petroleum Girl. The Girl in the Beret. We used to count how many billboards we saw her picture on. On a five-hundred-mile trip it used to average around fifty, depending on what part of the country."

"I remember. She'd be standing there with her hands in her pockets and her feet spread apart. Very dashing. Beret and trench coat."

"And you know what they did, don't you?"

"No."

"They used to give her a bonus of Bradford stock. That's what they thought of her. Oh, she needs me like a hole in the head. I didn't start making mine till after the war, and what I got in the Seabees you can imagine, but I made her hold on to that Bradford and I don't know how many times they split it."

"Irma Hopwood, eh?"

"That's it. Hardly anybody knew her name. To this day they don't. The Bradford people didn't want her name known."

"Then what happened?"

"Oh, what you might call a combination of circumstances. I never knew exactly. But somebody in the Bradford organization conceived the idea that the public was sick of trench coats after the war, and then they began publicizing that big B, you know. You know, the black-and-yellow B you see on all their pumps and all. And I guess an oil company couldn't go on forever with the same girl advertising their product. Irma wasn't sore. She got bored with it, to tell you the truth. You know, a woman likes to dress up, but every time she had to pose for a new painting or some photographs, always the beret, always the trench coat. And she gets paid, you know. She gets a couple thousand dollars a year today to enforce the contract. And she has that beautiful Bradford stock, and it's oil stock, don't forget. Tax-wise, very nice."

"Yes," I said.

We were standing together on the fairway, waiting for the foursome ahead to hole out. "It's an advantage when the wife has money of her own," he said. "I got one of my brothers that everybody knows the only reason why his wife is sticking to him is the money. We weren't always millionaires, the Borse brothers. Al married very young and she'd of been all right for like if he'd of stayed where he was, making a nice living but never very big. He had a used-car lot on Cahuenga, and a nice home in the Brentwood section. But he came in with my other brother and I and inside of three years if you wanted to find her she'd be in Bullock's-Wilshire or I. Magnin's, spending. There, or trying to get the fat off her in some reducing salon. Which was all right, understand. A man makes a lot of money, his wife is entitled. But she got so she hated him. The more he made, the more he gave her, the more she hated him. Al's no

Gregory Peck, this I got to admit. He's undersized and he has a high-pitched voice that he sounds like everything he said was an argument. So all right, that's what he was when she married him. It shouldn't be any news to her. Go ahead hit, you're away."

I made my shot and got on the green.

"You'll get your four," he said. "You got a chance for a birdie, but I'll be satisfied with a four." He hit his own shot, and it went in the trap. "Short," he said. "That may cost us, partner. It's when I get thinking about my brother." We walked in silence to the green, and when it was his turn he blasted the ball out of the sand and laid it an easy two-foot putt from the cup. He winked at me. "This is a game of concentration," he said. But on the next hole he returned to the subject of his brother. "Al used to play this game better than I do, but he never gets time for it any more. We used to play in Griffith Park. That's where they invented the saying, 'A ball is not lost till it has stopped rolling.' I was telling you about Al and his wife. So anyway, how do you think he feels, knowing that she'd walk out on him today if it wasn't for the money. Whereas, I always have the consolation that Irma could walk out on me any time. It's an advantage when the wife has her own. It gives a man the feeling that he has more to offer. Whereas, Al, the harder he works, he's only getting in that much deeper. He makes it and she spends it, and every dollar he gives her she gives him back five dollars' worth of hatred. This is living? I don't see it. He don't even get any consolation out of their children. She took away all the pleasure he got out of the children. We came from a very strict family and it nearly kills Al, the way they don't show him any respect whatsoever. Like I was over at his house a couple weeks ago and he went around looking for the evening paper, and Daphne was reading it. The older daughter. 'Never mind,' he said. 'The hell with that,' I said. 'Give your father the evening paper.' Oh, they hate me. They really hate me, but I get more respect out of them than their own father. When I see what's happening with his kids, I don't regret it not having any of my own. I wouldn't hold still for the way they treat their parents nowa-days."

"It's a problem, all right," I said.

I liked him, he sensed it, and when our match was ended he took me back to the hotel in his Rolls and invited me to play again the next day. We arranged to meet at two-thirty, and he declined my invitation to have a drink in our cabaña.

My wife was sunning herself at the pool. "How'd it go?" she said.

"We won. He's damn good," I said.

"Did you find out?" she said.

"Oh, yes," I said, and told her about Irma Hopwood, the Girl in the Beret. She did not receive my report with as much interest as I had anticipated. Instead, when I had finished, she resumed reading her novel.

"What's the matter? Lost interest?"

"Not exactly," she said.

"Here I come home with a good story and forty dollars I didn't have when I left, and all I get is Cloud 90."

"Relax," she said, and from her smile I knew she had some-thing on her mind.

Norman Borse and I won again the next day, and as he was leaving me near the pool area he suggested dinner for four. I said I would speak to my wife and call him in his room.

"No thanks," said my wife, when I relayed the invitation. "Let's not get involved with Mr. and Mrs. Borse."

"Why not? He's not a bad guy, and she might be amusing for one evening."

"I don't like women that sleep with waiters."

"Who? Borse's wife?"

"She and the waiter called Mark. Yesterday I saw him going in their room. Today I saw him leaving."

"You're sure?"

"Yes, I'm sure. Are you playing golf with Borse tomorrow?"

"No, he's going to be in Los Angeles all day, but we have a date to play the day after tomorrow. He's flying back tomorrow night."

"He'd better not get back too early," said my wife. "Who are you playing with tomorrow?"

"It's ladies' day, so I'm skipping a day."

"Then let's drive around. You can show me that house you used to have."

There was a house in the foothills I had rented many years ago, a comfortable, isolated, overgrown cabin, with its own tennis court and a view of the desert—and rattlesnakes. We found the house, now no longer isolated but in the midst of a colony of modern ranch-type units. "That's it," I said.

"I imagine it had charm then, but not now," said my wife. "Why do they have to build so close together when they have the whole desert?"

"Probably the water supply," I said. "Expensive pipe lines."

"Yes, I suppose so," she said. "And yet it isn't a low-cost housing development. There's one family that have a Rolls."

"The people that own that particular Rolls don't live there," I said. "Let's turn around and go back."

"Why? Whose car is it?"

"Belongs to Norman Borse."

"Oh," said my wife. "Well, you're not surprised, I hope."

"No, you were right. But he isn't a bad guy, you know."

"Do you really know that?" said my wife.

"No, I guess I don't. But this is so disrespectful, flaunting the Rolls, and he was so outraged by the disrespect his brother's children show."

"I'm not on her side, but after twenty-two years he must be awfully obtuse."

"You think he knows about these things?" I said.

"That's the only way I could forgive him."

"Forgive him?"

"Well, excuse him," she said. "If he doesn't know she sleeps with waiters, he's too stupid to live. If he does know it, and still loves her enough to ignore it, he may be kidding himself, but as you say he's not really a bad guy."

"But you don't like him," I said.

"I don't have to like him," she said. "Neither does she.

She's just a sterling silver bitch that he has to live up to. A girl he stole from a billboard. Don't play any more golf with him."

"I was just thinking, I didn't want to," I said. "Why?"

"Because you don't really like him, and you'll come home depressed. He's not a bad guy, but that's all he is. Just not a bad guy, and that isn't enough when you're our age."

"And this place is too damn expensive anyway, for what you get."

"For what you get," said my wife.

The Trip

Harrison Deering was apprehensive of his coming trip to London, his first in many, many years. On his last visit he had seen royalty, in black satin butterfly tie and white waistcoat, playing the drums at the Kit Kat; in recent years he had seen the same royalty briskly walking in Park Avenue and several times having lunch at his, and Harrison Deering's, club. "I suppose I look as old as him," Deering would say. "Or maybe I should say he looks as old as me. But by God he had style, and he still has it. I don't know what London's going to be like without him." Harrison Deering did not mean to imply that he had been chummy with royalty. No such thing. His approach to London and Londoners was and always had been American-English: American, in that he had no wish to be taken for anything else; English, in that he was not a man to scrape up acquaintance with strangers on trains and on shipboard. He liked most of the English ways, since they were very much his own ways. But in London during his forthcoming trip he would be seeing other Americans like himself and *their* English friends, just as he had done on previous visits. He had no English friends of his own, and his best reason, or excuse, for going to London at this time was to confirm his hope that a great deal of the London he was fond of was still there. Royalty would not be playing drums at the Kit Kat—if there was still a Kit Kat. No one wore butterfly bows or white evening waistcoats any more. The firm that had always made Harrison Deering's shoes had moved from Oxford Street to some place else. Gertie Lawrence was dead, and Noel Coward was over sixty. Harrison Deering did not expect to be invited to parties by Fruity This or Porchy That or Jack What's His Name. Harrison Deering had never done anything for the Englishmen who came to New York, and he did not expect any Englishman to do anything for him. He was not going to London for parties; he no longer went to parties in New York. "I'm going to London because I have four thousand dollars to blow-in," he told one friend. "How long that would last me in Florida, I don't know. I could probably sponge off a few people and make it last a couple of months. But it's too damn cold in Florida and they won't admit it. I was there two years ago and I wore a sweater every day I was there. No heat in the houses. Rain. Cold. Cold that gets into your bones and stays there. And who do I see? The same damn people that are just as sick and tired of my face as I am of theirs. So I'm going to London. At least it'll be different."

"Yes, but different in what way, Harry?" said his friend.

"Well—they drive on the left-hand side of the road," he said. "Intentionally."

He gave other explanations and excuses for choosing London, but his private one was that hope of finding a scene of his youth that had not undergone alterations or, indeed, total obliteration, as was the case with so many neighborhoods in New York, Philadelphia, Boston, Palm Beach, and Long Island and the Main Line. "You should *see* what they've done to Princeton," he said. "I went there to a wedding last week, and they have a new station at the Junction."

"That's not new, Harry," said his friend. "It's been there ten years. The old one burned down."

"I didn't know that. Burned down? I didn't see anything in the papers about it."

"Oh, yes. It was in the papers, but that was ten years ago. I think it happened during the Christmas holidays."

"Hmm. Then they couldn't blame the undergraduates?"

"Much as you'd like to, you can't blame the undergraduates," said his friend.

"I have nothing against the undergraduates. At least they're not responsible for the rest of what's been going on there. *You* are, you alumni. That new library."

"New?"

"New to me. It looks like one of those department stores in Manhasset. The Sunshine Biscuit Company."

"Then I advise you to stay away from Oxford on your trip abroad. I understand they've put up some buildings you won't like at all."

"I had no intention of going to Oxford. I don't know a soul there. Not even at All Souls. Joke. My father once had some notion of sending me to Oxford, but considering the fact that I never got a degree at Harvard, he was probably very wise to give up the whole idea. And I never would have fitted in there. I was there for two days once, and they all seemed so much younger than I'd expected. I'm sure they knew a hell of a lot more than I did, but they were so damn young. There's nothing younger than a young Englishman, is there? Or as old as an old Englishman. God, when an Englishman gets old, he looks as if he'd been around since 1066. Wouldn't surprise me if some of them had been."

Harrison Deering was a widower among widows. He knew that his widows liked to think that they were taking care of him; protecting him from loneliness; seeing to it that he was invited out at least one night a week; remembering his birthday and his widowerhood at Christmas with rather expensive presents of fine handkerchiefs, good cognac, re-orders of his favorite pipe tobacco (he had a good-sized credit at Dunhill's on that account), and other consumable gifts that would not clutter up his small apartment. "A useless stallion with a brood of old mares," he would say to describe the situation. "Quid pro quo. I give them something to do, somebody to fuss over." He had only to say the word and any of two or three of his widows would marry him, but he did not at sixty-eight feel up to breaking in a new woman to his habits, and his habits contained the secret of his comfort and to be comfortable was as much as he could reasonably expect out of life. Six days a week he would get his own breakfast of orange juice, toast and coffee; rinse out the glass, cup and saucer, and occupy the morning with his moderate calisthenics, his newspaper, his shave and bath, his mail, a telephone call or two. So would go the morning until it was time to go to one of his two clubs. As a much younger man he had invested in life memberships in the clubs, so that he now had no dues to pay, and lunch at either club was cheaper and in more congenial surroundings than anywhere else that he knew of. After lunch he always took a fifteen-minute nap before the bridge or backgammon games. At the club where the game was backgammon he would be one of the same five chouetting, and at the other club he was one of a foursome who had been playing bridge together for fifteen years, with one substitution caused by death. There was some criticism of Charley Borden, who collapsed and died while playing a hand. The criticism was mild enough, but it was voiced, one player to another: it was simply that Charley had been told by his doctor not to play bridge, but he had insisted on playing, with the inevitable, extremely disturbing result. Harrison Deering defended Charley. "I admit it's a hell of a thing to do to your friends, especially when you know it's going to happen. But we all loved Charley, and I wouldn't like to think that *I'd* deprived him of a little fun those last few years. Damned sight better to have him keel over here, among friends, than out on the public street. Policemen going through his pockets to find some identification. Taxi drivers pointing to him. 'Look, a dead man.' No, God damn it, we owed that much to Charley." The man who joined the foursome in Charley Borden's place was about ten years younger than the average of the others, and a son of the oldest living member of the club.

Harrison Deering did not stay around for the late-afternoon drinking at his clubs. The distance to his little apartment was just long enough for him to stretch his legs and get a breath of fresh air, work up an appetite for dinner. Miriam Washington came in five afternoons a week at four o'clock and cleaned the apartment and cooked his dinner, which he ate at seven; and if he was spending the evening at home, he had the television set which two of his widows had given him, the interesting short-wave radio that another widow had bought for his bedroom, and always two mystery novels from the lending library in Lexington Avenue. The evenings passed quickly, and as he moved about in his apartment Harrison Deering, who had a nice bass, would sing, "Last night I was dreeeeeming, of you, dear, was dreeeeeming." He had never learned the entire lyric, but he always came in strong at the end with "Once more to —my heart." It was a song his father had liked, sung on a record by John McCormack, who was certainly not a bass, but Harrison Deering loved it, and often sang it when he was alone.

A trip to London was such a radical deviation from Harrison Deering's established routines that nearly a full year elapsed between the first spoken announcement of his decision and the date for sailing. At his widows' little dinner-bridges his friends would ask him how his plans were coming, and he usually had some small item of progress to report. In the beginning he would say: "Well, I stopped in at the Cunard Line yesterday and got all their literature. Did *you* know that the Cunard Line has an office at Fifty-sixth and Park? I s'pose you did, but I didn't." A similar surprise awaited him with the discovery that he did not have to go all the way downtown to get a passport. He collected information on the ship of the line, and the kind of accommodations to book, the advantages to be gained by out-of-season travel, and so on. His widows and some of his men friends—among whom were a few who went abroad every year—jotted down notes to give Harry Deering, and item after item showed him how very different things were these days. On one subject there was unanimous agreement: flying was out of the question. Flying had no style, and even among those friends who went abroad every year and were quite casual about their own arrangements, the trip that Harrison Deering was planning had to be done with as much style as modern circumstances would allow. Months ahead of time his widows planned a series of small farewell dinner parties, and Harrison Deering himself was going to splurge with a farewell luncheon for all those who had been so kind.

After all his friends returned from the summer hiatus and the sailing date was weeks away the imminence of the trip was on all their minds. Harry was now at the packing stage; that is, the logistics of packing. He worked out the number of evening shirts he would have to have on shipboard (no laundry on the *Queen Mary*, which he was taking on the eastward passage). He would wear his grey flannel to the ship and take a tweed jacket, using the grey flannel trousers as slacks. He was slightly disappointed to be advised that he would not need his tails, although this gave him extra room in his luggage. He looked well in tails and knew it, and while he was forced to agree that his friends knew present-day London better than he, he was going to put in one wing collar, one stiff shirt, one white evening tie and the appropriate jewelry in case a white-tie occasion arose, and without telling any of his friends he also made a note of his miniature medals: his 1916 Mexican Border, his Victory Medal, and his Croix de Guerre with bronze star. They would not take up much room, and he was ready if the right invitation came along. He might have to hire a tailcoat, but be damned if the lapel would be bare.

It went without saying that he would be stopping at Jordan's Private Hotel, and he was delighted to be told that they could give him the same room he had occupied in 1922. In his correspondence with Jordan's, which was carried on over a period of two months because neither Harrison Deering nor Jordan's used the air mail, he was assured, or reassured, that the room would be just the same except for the wallpaper, which he did not remember anyway. The room rates were considerably higher, but he expected that. He was completely reconciled to the expense all around; he did not actually speak of this trip as the last one he would make, but he planned everything with that thought in mind. He would have precious little left of his four thousand dollars when he got back to New York. Tommy Long and Erskine Rockwell, his American friends in

London, were going to keep him busy every minute, or nearly every minute, and he was already planning a big bash, as the young fellows said, for Tommy and Skinny and their wives in the Savoy Grill the night before he sailed for home. That would leave him enough for tips on the westward passage, and that was exactly the way he wanted it to be.

And then one day when the sailing date was less than a fortnight away, he went to the club, had his lunch and his nap, and to the card-room. Bobby McGowan was there at the usual table. Bobby, by two years the oldest of the foursome, was always first at the table, always a bit impatient to get the game started. "Well, Sir Harry," said Bobby. "Only a few more chances to take your money."

"Looking forward to taking yours and converting it into sterling," said Harrison Deering.

"The luck I've been having lately, you won't have any trouble," said Bobby. "You know, I rather envy you your trip."

"Come along. Do you good," said Harrison Deering. "You can get a passport in two or three days, and surely you'd have no trouble booking passage."

"Oh, my passport's good for another year, and I guess I could wangle a stateroom, but Marjorie wouldn't hear of it. Where the hell are the other two? Oh, here you are." He thus greeted John Banks, who seated himself and filled his pipe.

"No Williams?" said Banks.

"Not so far," said Bobby. "And I know he wasn't here for lunch."

"No, I didn't see him," said Harrison Deering.

"Well, we'll just have to wait," said Bobby.

"Getting all ready to shove off, Harry?" said Banks.

"Just about. Four more chances to take your money, and then off I go."

"Harry, call downstairs and see if Williams is in the club, will you please?"

"Oh, he'll be here," said Harrison Deering.

At that moment Jimmy Walsh, the club servant in charge of

the card-room, came to the table. "Gentlemen, I'm afraid I've bad news for you," said Walsh.

"What's that, Jimmy?" said Bobby.

"Mr. Williams. He fell over dead in a taxicab."

"Old Mr. Williams?"

"No sir, *your* Mr. Williams. Mr. J. L. The taxi brung 'im here because this is the address he gave. But he was dead. Too bad. A *nice* man. I'm very sorry, gentlemen."

"Oh. I see. Thank you, Jimmy," said Bobby.

"Yes sir. Can I get anything for anybody?"

"Yes. Yes. Three brandies, I guess," said Bobby. The others nodded their approval of the order.

"Three brandies, sir," said Walsh, and left.

"First Charley Borden, and now Jerry Williams," said Bobby McGowan.

"Exactly what I was thinking," said John Banks.

"Yes," said Harrison Deering. "Alone in a taxi. Heart, I suppose."

"Must have been," said Banks. "But his father's over ninety."

"Ninety-one, but I don't see what difference that makes," said McGowan.

"Well, I was thinking of longevity running in families," said Banks.

"Alone in a taxi," said Harrison Deering. "I can just see that driver, if he's a typical New York taxi driver. Sore as hell because he probably has to make out some police report. Lose fares. The last man poor Jerry ever spoke to. At least Charley had us with him."

"Yes, that's one way to look at it," said McGowan.

Walsh served the drinks and McGowan raised his pony. "To Jerry."

"To Jerry," said Banks.

"To Jerry," said Harrison Deering.

They drank their brandies and Banks rose. "I think I'll go downstairs and find out what happened. You fellows staying here?"

"For a minute or two," said McGowan.

"You'll excuse me," said Banks. "I don't think I'll be back."

"All right, John," said McGowan. "Goodbye."

"Goodbye, John," said Harrison Deering.

"Jerry was sort of a cousin of his, wasn't he?" said McGowan, after Banks had gone.

"I believe so, yes. There was some connection," said Harrison Deering.

"Yes, I think Jerry was about a third cousin, something like that."

"I believe you're right. Jerry's mother was a Thatcher, and I think old Mrs. Banks was a Thatcher, too," said Harrison Deering.

"Yes, she was. John's mother and Jerry's mother were I think second cousins. Not very close, but there was some connection. John took it rather hard."

"Well, remember it was John that got Jerry in this game. They were in a couple of things together."

"Oh, were they? Business things?"

"Yes. They both had money in a small electronics plant in New Jersey. I never knew much about it."

"No," said McGowan. "Well, Harry, I don't suppose I'll see you now before you sail."

"Jerry's funeral."

"Of course, of course. Then I will be seeing you."

"Yes," said Harrison Deering. "I'm not so sure about sailing. I may change my mind."

"Oh, don't give up your trip. You've looked forward to it for so long."

"I'm not afraid of dying, Bobby. It isn't that. But I'd be such a damn nuisance if I checked out in a London taxicab."

"Oh, that won't happen, Harry."

"No, maybe not. But after today . . ."

"I know," said McGowan. "It *is* something to think about."

In a Grove

In this obscure little California town, far away from Hollywood and not even very close to the Saroyan-Steinbeck country, William Grant once again encountered Richard Warner, as he had always known he would.

Johnstown—to give it a name—was one of those towns that vaudevillians used to describe as "a wide place in the road" and that had owed its earliest existence to the gold strikes of more than a century ago. But in the intervening years it had been all but abandoned until irrigation began to help agriculture, and Johnstown got a second life; unspectacular, unromantic, unexciting, and obviously unprofitable—the last place Grant would expect to find Warner, and yet, since his disappearance had been so complete, the kind of place that was just made for a man who wanted to leave the world in which he had once been widely known.

Grant stopped his car at a filling station. "Fill it up, will you please? The oil is okay, but will you check the water and tires?"

"Right. What do you carry, twenty-six pounds, the tires?" said the attendant.

"Twenty-six, right."

"You been driving a distance, they'll all be a little high, you know. You want me to deflate to twenty-six?"

"Yes."

"Some don't, you know."

"Well, I'm one of those that do," said Grant. "What's the name of this town?"

"Johnstown. Johnstown, California."

"Is that a cigarette machine in there?"

"It's a cigarette machine that's out of order. The nearest place is the supermarket. You can see it there on the edge of town. They call it a supermarket, but nothing very super about it. It's only what used to be the Buick agency, that's all it is."

"But they have cigarettes there."

"Oh, they have cigarettes. They have most everything you find in a supermarket, but I don't know who they think they're kidding, calling it a supermarket. It's no bigger than when it was the Buick agency."

"What happened to the Buick agency?"

"What happened to it? This was never a town for Buicks. You wait here a few minutes and you'll see a couple Model-A Fords, still chugging away. Maybe some International trucks, been through various hands, one rancher to the other. Way back, when I was a kid, one family had a Locomobile. You ever hear of the Locomobile?"

"Yes."

"Another rancher had a big old Pierce-Arrow. Those big ritzy cars, but I'll tell you something. You look on the running-board of those cars and every one of them carried canteens. Ed Hughes, that owned the Locomobile, I remember he had like a saddle holster he had strapped to the right-hand door, to carry a 30-30 rifle in. They didn't buy those cars for show. They bought them because they stood up. That was before they thought up this planned obsolence."

"Planned obsolence. Uh-huh."

"You know, 'Here's this year's piece of junk, come back and see what I allow you on it two years from now.' That's where all the trouble lies. Now what you got here is a foreign car, and it aint even broke in at forty-five thousand miles. This is an automobile. You don't mind if I take a look under the hood? I know, you said you don't need oil, but—"

"That, that just went by. That was no Model-A," said Grant.

The attendant had missed the passing Jaguar, but now waved to it. He smiled. "No, that was Dick Warner. He's a fellow lives here. You ever hear of the expression, as queer as Dick's hatband? I think that's who it originated with, Dick Warner."

"Dick Warner? How long has he lived here?"

"Oh—I guess fifteen, maybe twenty years by now. Why, do you know him?"

"Possibly. Where did this fellow come from?"

"Oh, well I'm not even sure about that."

"Is he a tall thin fellow? Brown hair? About my age?"

"Well, I guess he'd answer that description. What are you, the F.B.I. or something like that?"

"Hell, no. If I were the F.B.I. I'd go looking for the deputy sheriff, wouldn't I?"

"You found him. *I'm* the deputy sheriff, and I never had any bad reports on Dick, bad or good for that matter. He pays his bills, don't owe nobody, and his fingerprint's on his driver's license. Well, now he's making a U-turn. Maybe he recognized you."

"I doubt it."

"Heading back this way. Yeah. Moving slowly. Wants to get a good look at you. Mister, are you armed? You got a gun on you?"

"No."

"Well, Dick has, so get behind something. I am."

"There's not going to be anything like that."

"All the same I'm getting out of the way till I make sure. I'm going in and put my badge on. And my gun."

"Go ahead. I'll stand right here."

The Jaguar drove past slowly, the driver staring at William Grant. After the Jaguar had gone past the filling station it stopped, then backed up into the parking area. Dick Warner got out.

He was tall and thin and wore a planter's Panama with a band of feathers, a safari jacket with the sleeves rolled up, sun-tan slacks and leather sandals. "Is it you, Grant?"

"Yes it's me. Hello, Dick."

"Christ Almighty," said Warner. He put out his hand, and Grant shook it.

"No, just me," said Grant.

"What the hell are you doing here?"

"I was looking for a good place to hide out from the law."

"Then get going. There isn't room for two of us. Well, God damn it, Bill. Hey, Smitty, come on out and meet a friend of mine. This is Mr. Grant, Mr. Smith. See that you give him four quarts to the gallon."

"Now, Dick. Now, now."

"Mr. Smith thought you might be going to shoot me," said Grant.

"Now why'd you have to tell him that? I didn't know but you were somebody snooping around and Dick didn't want to see you."

"I hear you carry a gun, Dick," said Grant.

"Smitty, whose side are you on? You talk too much."

"This fellow stard asking me questions. He's the one with the big mouth. That'll be four-eighty, Mister, and the next time you come here there's another filling station the other end of town."

"You decided not to check the air for me?"

"I decided if you wanted to check the air you can do it yourself, and there's the hose if you need water."

"All right, Sheriff. You owe me twenty cents," said Grant, handing Smitty a five-dollar bill.

"Mr. Grant's a nice fellow, Smitty. You shouldn't take that attitude."

"I know what attitude to take without any advice from you, Dick."

"I know. Your gums are bothering you again," said Warner. "Smitty has a new upper plate, and he won't give his gums a chance to get used to it."

"I don't think it's his gums. I think he's just a disagreeable guy."

"Move on, Mister, or I'll give you a ticket."

"What for?" said Grant.

"Obstructing traffic. Failure to pay for parking on my lot. I'll think of a few things."

"He will, too, and his brother-in-law's the mayor," said Warner. "Smitty, this is no way to treat a visitor to our fair city."

"We don't encourage tourists. If this fellow's a friend of yours, Dick, you get him off my property pronto."

"All right. Follow me, Bill. And don't go through any stop-signs."

"I'll get out of here as quickly as I can."

"Thirty-mile zone," said Smitty.

"I think that dentist gave you the wrong plate, Smitty," said Warner. "Come on, Bill."

The built-up section was four blocks of one-story white stucco business buildings, which changed abruptly to a stretch of one-story frame dwellings, all badly in need of paint, and then there was country, bare in the rolling hills where the irrigation was not effective. Grant followed Warner for about a mile, until Warner blew his horn, slowed down, and made a right turn into a dirt road. A few hundred yards along that road Warner again slowed down and entered a dirt driveway that ended in a grove of various trees, in the center of which was a ranchhouse. Two horses in a small corral looked up as the cars approached, and a collie ignored Warner's car to run along beside Grant's, barking ferociously. Warner signaled to Grant to drive up alongside him.

"Stay in your car till I put Sonny away. He's liable to take a piece out of your leg," said Warner. He got out and the dog came to him, and he grasped the dog's collar and snapped a leash to it and attached the leash to a length of wire that ran between two trees. The dog could run only between the trees. "You're safe now."

"What do you feed this dog? People?"

"I don't have to. He helps himself. Particularly fond of Mexicans. Itinerant workers. Salesmen. Hollywood writers, he hasn't had any but I can tell he's willing to have a taste of you."

"I can tell that myself."

"Well, just stay out of reach."

"All right, Lassie," said Grant. "Maybe if I gave him a good swift kick."

"You'd never leave here alive if you did. Even if I let you get away with it my wife wouldn't."

"Oh, you're married."

"Good God, do you think I could live here if I wasn't?"

"Well, what the hell. Itinerant workers, Mexicans."

"Lay off the Mexican angle. My wife is half Mexican."

"What else do I have to look out for?"

"Well, at certain times of the day, down there near the ditch, rattlesnakes, but they don't come up here much. I've done a pretty good job of exterminating them around the house. Anyway, you won't be here that long. You're on your way somewhere, obviously. Come on in and meet my bride and have a cooling drink."

"And I forgot to get some cigarettes."

"We have plenty. The señora's a heavy smoker. There she is."

A girl, not readily identifiable as Mexican but wearing a multi-colored peasant blouse and skirt and huaraches, opened the door of a screened porch. "Hi," she said.

"I brought somebody out of my past. This is Bill Grant, used to be with me at Paramount. Bill, this is the present Mrs. Warner, Rita by name."

"Hi," she said. "And what's with that present Mrs. Warner bit?"

"We can only wait and see."

"You wait and see. Come on in, Bill. What would you like to drink? I got some cold beer."

"Thank you, that's just perfect."

"Where did the great Warner run across you? Or you across him? He never has any company. From Hollywood, anyway. Dick, you get the beer."

"All right," said Warner, and went to the kitchen.

"I'm working for TV now, and I came up this way scouting locations. Have you been in pictures?"

"No, but I know what scouting locations means. I went to high school in L. A. Fairfax."

"How did you stay out of pictures?"

"You think I'm pretty enough? I guess I'm prettier than some of those dogs, but I was never discovered. Except by his majesty."

"Where did he discover you?"

"You better ask him, he has a different story for everybody. He told a couple people in Johnstown I was his daughter. The son of a bitch. I *am* married to him though. You married?"

"Sure. I have a daughter around your age."

"Well, so has Dick, although I never saw her."

"I know. She lives back East."

"And he has a son. You don't have to be cagey about that side of him. Three ex-wives, a daughter and a son. A brother, a sister, a mother—all that I know. Did you know him a long time?"

"A long time ago I knew him pretty well. Then we had a falling-out. I can't remember what about."

"Well I remember," said Warner, bringing in a tray of bottles and glasses. "I fired you because you went on a three-day bender and never let me know where you were."

"I guess that was it."

"You made me look bad on my second picture as a producer."

"Yeah. You behaved like a jerk producer, that's right."

"Why do you say jerk producer? What other kind is there? You're one now, only in a worse medium. I've seen your name in the paper once in a while. The hell with that. What are you up here for?"

"What are you?"

"I asked you."

"I'm scouting locations."

"Stay away, will you? Go on up to Marin County. I don't want a bunch of those bastards coming to Johnstown. I went to a lot of trouble to get away from them, so don't spoil it for me, will you?"

"I won't promise. Anyway, I might make you a few dollars. I could rent this place for a couple of weeks."

"I don't need the money."

"Hey! Who don't need the money?" said Rita. "I could use a few bucks."

"On what? We have enough."

"I was wondering about that," said Grant. "You do have enough? This is a nice place and all that, but I remember when you were playing polo."

"I could still play polo if I wanted to, but who plays polo these days? For that matter, who makes pictures these days?"

"His majesty thinks the movies stink," said Rita. "That's why he never goes to them, and that's why he knows all about them."

"You don't smell with your eyes. The beautiful odor is wafted all the way from Culver City," said Warner.

"Culver City is where I work. I shoot a lot of stuff on the Metro lot," said Grant.

"Speaking of shooting, what was that conversation with Smitty?"

"He told me you carried a gun. Apparently he doesn't know anything about you, your background, where you came from."

"I've seen to that."

"But this is the strange part. He was willing to believe that you were ready to shoot it out with the first stranger that asked about you. That's an odd impression to leave after living here fifteen years."

"I've told Smitty what you might call conflicting stories. It's nobody's business what I did before I came here, or what I do now, if I stay within the law."

"What *do* you do now?"

Warner pointed to a wall that was completely covered with bookshelves containing paperback books and old magazines; western stories, detective stories, science fiction, popular delvings into the human mind.

"You write them?" said Grant.

"I steal from them and then write my own. I have five by-lines, and I make anywhere from five to fifteen thousand a year, turning out stories. I'm what we used to call a pulp writer."

"It must keep you busy, but do you need the money? I thought you left Hollywood with plenty of glue."

"Don't give this greedy little Mexican the wrong idea," said Warner. "We live on what I earn."

"Except when you want to buy a Jaguar, or send away to New York for some clothes," said Rita.

"My extravagances, my spirit-raising expenditures, they come out of my capital, the money I took out of Hollywood," said Warner.

"You let him get away with this, Rita?"

"She's devoted to me, you can see that. Sit on his lap," said Warner. "He's wondering if he can make you, so let him have a try at it."

"You want me to sit on your lap, Grant?"

"Of course. He's right."

She put down her glass and sat on Grant's lap. Grant took her in his arms and kissed her and felt her breasts.

"Cut!" said Warner. "Now go back to your chair."

The girl returned to her chair and picked up her glass.

"How do you feel, Chiquita? Would you have gone on?"

"What do you think, king? Of course I'd have gone on."

"Then why didn't you?"

"Because I knew you were going to say 'Cut.' "

"That isn't the answer you're supposed to give."

"That's the answer I gave, though. I told you I have a lot to learn."

"She has spirit, this girl," said Warner.

"Plenty."

"Oh, not only what you mean. She still has a mind of her own."

"I always will have. His majesty thinks he rules me, but he doesn't tell me to do anything I don't want to do. You can't hypnotize somebody against their will."

"Yes you can," said Grant. "But there's some theory that while they're under hypnosis they won't do anything they don't want to."

"I guess that's what I meant."

"Let me remind both of you that this has nothing to do with hypnosis. I am not a hypnotist."

"Maybe not, but you like to think you have hypnotic powers," said Grant.

"There you're perfectly correct."

"I'd like to know why you said 'Cut'? It wasn't just to show your power. It was because you were afraid."

"Nonsense," said Warner. "Afraid of what?"

"Ho! Afraid that Rita and I would get in the hay. She was willing to stop because she was getting embarrassed."

Warner gave a short laugh. "Embarrassed? Rita? Tell the man what you used to do for a living."

"I was a hooker," said the girl.

"A fifty-dollar girl that got tired of the grind," said Warner.

"And several other things," said Rita. "You don't only get tired of the grind."

"My wife doesn't embarrass easily, Grant."

"I guess not," he said.

"The complexities and deviations are all old stuff to her. What did you think of Grant when you first laid eyes on him?"

"Well, I knew by the car that he was probably some Hollywood friend of yours."

"Yes, but what else?"

"Well, he'd make a pass at me if he had a chance."

"So far nothing very complex," said Grant.

"Well, I knew he didn't like you."

"Now we're getting somewhere. Do you know why you thought that?" said Warner.

"That I couldn't tell you."

"All right, never mind. Tell us some other first impressions and reactions."

"I thought I wouldn't mind getting in bed with him."

"She doesn't see many men here," said Warner.

"Let her tell it," said Grant.

"But he wouldn't be much fun after a while. You're still the most fun, king."

"Why is he so much fun, Rita? Not just sex," said Grant.

"Don't knock sex. And it is sex. With this character everything is sex. Want to ask you a question, Grant. Did he lay all those picture stars?"

"He had his share, but not many of the big ones. He was afraid to go after the big ones. He was afraid he'd get a turndown and it would get around that he'd made a pitch and was unsuccessful. In Hollywood, honey, that's losing face. No, your husband didn't score with the big ones."

"I knew you were lying about that," said Rita to Warner.

"Grant is only telling what he knows. There's a hell of a lot he doesn't know."

"What Academy Award winner did you ever lay? Now don't give me any best-supporting actress. I mean the Number One. Or what star that got top billing, her name over the main title? Or a hundred percent of the main title."

"What's that?"

"Your name in letters as big as the title of the picture," said Grant. "The only one was Ernesta Travers, and she was giving it out to projectionists. She actually laid a projectionist while he was running a picture for her."

"You've got the story wrong, but no matter. I even forgot about Ernesta."

"I didn't know she was ever a big star," said Rita. "Have some more beer, Grant."

"All right, fine," said Grant.

"You, king? You want another?"

"If you get it, yes," said Warner.

She left them.

"Yes, what you're wondering is true. She was a hooker."

"Well she was a damn pretty one. Is. I have to be careful of my tenses. Is damn pretty, whatever she was."

"Would you give her a hundred dollars now?"

"Sure."

In a loud voice Warner called out: "I've got you lined up for a fast hundred dollars."

"With Grant?" she responded from the kitchen.

"Yeah."

"All right," she said. She brought in three bottles of beer, clutching them by the neck. She put a bottle in front of Warner, then sat herself beside Grant and poured beer into his glass. "Do I get to keep the whole C-note?"

"Certainly," said Warner.

"Do I get shot in the back?" said Grant.

"That's the chance you take."

"Just so you don't shoot him while he's in the kip with me."

"That's the chance *you* take, señora."

She looked at her husband. "Listen, how much of this is kidding and how much is kidding on the square?"

"I'm not kidding at all. If you'd like to make yourself a quick hundred dollars, Grant and I made a deal. Ask Grant if I'm kidding."

"Just like old times, back in the Thirties," said Grant.

"I don't know," said the girl.

"What don't you know?" said Warner.

"Well, what the hell?" she said.

"It's how you used to earn your living," said her husband.

"I don't deny that. But the first friend of yours ever came to the house and you promote him into a party with me," she said.

"Don't you want the hundred dollars?" said Warner.

"I always want a hundred dollars."

"Well, you necked him, you let him give you a little feel."

"Yeah, but I thought that was—I was just playing along with the gag."

"Grant wasn't playing along with any gag, were you, Grant?"

"To tell you the truth I guess I wasn't."

"And it was no gag when you said you'd give her a hundred bucks."

"No, I'd give her a hundred bucks."

"Well, you son of a bitch, if you meant it, I'll level, too," said the girl to her husband. She reached out her hand. "Come on, Grant."

Grant stood up. "You'll excuse us, I'm sure," said Grant.

The girl looked at her husband. "You can't be on the level," she said.

"Why not?" said Warner.

"God damn you. God damn you!" She ripped off the peasant blouse and, naked to the waist, put her arms around Grant and kissed him. "Come on," she said, and led him by the hand.

She lay on the oversize bed, and Grant shed his clothes and got down beside her. She looked at him. "Don't worry, I won't welsh on it now," she said. She put her arms around him and began running her little hands up and down his spine, slowly, caressingly.

"Perfect." Warner's voice was cold and calm.

The girl saw her husband in the doorway, then she screamed. "No! No!" The first shots struck Grant in the spine, he shuddered and died. The girl tried to hide behind his body, but Warner grasped his hand and pulled him aside and took his time firing the remaining four shots. Then he went to the telephone and dialed.

"Smitty, come on out here. I've got something for you," he said.

The Old Folks

The house stood a mile to the north of the main road, on land that was flat and covered with snow. It was a large, white house, with the pillars that made it describable as American Colonial, and set in among a dozen now leafless walnuts and elms. It happened that there were no buildings whatever between the main road and the house, so that the side road that eventually reached the farm and cut through it seemed like a long, private driveway. So it had been, in the previous century.

"That's home?" said the man.

"That's home," said the woman, who was driving the car.

"Looks good," said the man.

"Yes, it always looks good from here," said the woman. "After I've been there a while I want to go away, but it always looks good when I come back."

"Is all this yours? This land?"

"Heavens, no. Not any more. It was when my grandfather was alive, but now we only have two hundred and forty acres."

"As compared with what, when your grandfather was living?"

"I have no idea. Maybe a thousand acres. Maybe more. Beginning with the road we just left, and then quite a sizable piece of land on the other side of the house, where you see the barns and the silos. And to the east and west."

"That would be a lot more than a thousand acres, if I'm any judge."

"Probably. Grandpa was one of those people that liked to

be able to say that it's all theirs as far as the eye can see. Although I don't think I ever actually heard him say it. In fairness."

"What was he? An oldtime landowner?"

"No. Not if you mean did he make his money that way. He bought it all after he'd made his money elsewhere. Grandpa made his money in the steel business. This was where he lived after he retired."

"To become a country gentleman?"

"Exactly. He bought this from the widow of a friend of his. Grandpa knew the property from visiting here, but he had nothing to do with the development of it. Mr. Frick and Mr. Carnegie built big houses on Fifth Avenue, and Grandpa, not being that rich, bought a farm in Ohio. Now you get a better look at the house."

"Looks fine. Comfortable."

"I keep it up. I'm glad now that I did. There was a long time when I never saw it, and I was often tempted to sell, but now I'll never sell unless I really have to. I had good times here, and I was very fond of my grandfather. I'm very lucky to have this place to go to. By the way, my daughter and her husband won't be here till tomorrow. She telephoned as I was leaving to meet you."

"Are we terribly distressed about that?"

"Not unless you wanted to play bridge. It certainly won't interfere with any other arrangements. Nancy has no illusions about me. In fact she may be thinking she's giving her mother a break."

"By leaving the old folks to themselves?"

"Precisely."

"Well, she is. I'd rather be alone with you tonight than have to play bridge, or make conversation with Nancy and her husband."

"I'd rather be alone with you, too. I'm glad Nancy's going to be here part of the time. I'll concede that much to Ohio morality. But your first time here should be just the two of us."

"You're dead right. I can see how much competition I have from the house, and you can make up your mind whether I'd fit in."

"That's a very disarming trait you have. Suddenly you'll state the whole case when I least expect it. You *have* got competition from this house, and I *do* want to see if you'd fit in. But I wouldn't have had the honesty to put it all into words. You're a nice man, Arthur."

"Oh, hell. Why should you and I practice small deceptions? You and I? We know everything except whether we want to spend the rest of our lives together."

"At this moment I have no doubt at all, but I'm very different here from what I am other places you've seen me. I never feel I have to *try* here. You could see me for ten years in New York and never know that I have this side."

"What side?"

"This side. You'll see. The side that loves this house. You'll notice things."

"So will you."

She stopped the car at the front door. "Take your bag in and I'll put the car away. We won't need it again tonight. If you want to wash—under the stairway. I'll be right back."

"Why can't I wait, or go with you?"

"Because it's cold and it's almost four hours since you left your office. Go on, don't be polite."

"Is this one of the things I'm supposed to notice?"

"I hadn't thought of that, but I guess it is. If you'd like to fix me a bourbon and water, you'll find everything in the little room on your right."

He handed her the drink when she returned from the garage. "It's weak, I hope," she said. "I go for days here without anything to drink."

"What do you do on an average day?"

"On an average day I have a cup of coffee in bed at half past eight. I take my time about dressing and breakfast, so that I'm seldom really up and about before ten in the morning. Drive to the village, which is six miles away, and do whatever market-ing there is to be done. Come home, and by that time the mail and the New York papers have arrived. Read both, and if there's any mail to be answered, I answer it, and the morning's just about gone. After lunch I go for a walk, then I come home and do my needlework, with the radio going, till it's time to have my bath. At seven I have my supper, and then I read and watch television——we get very good reception, but a lot of it's wasted on me. After the news I go around with a flashlight and see if everything's secure for the night. Glass of milk and so to bed. And that's an average day, at this time of year."

"Don't you see anybody?"

"Well, literally, yes. The people in the village, the postman sometimes, the cook and the maid, and my farmer and his family. I don't lose the power of speech. In the spring and early fall I may play golf at the little country club that we passed on the way out, but I don't enter into the social life. There are three or four women that I play golf with, but they never come here. My grandfather and grandmother discouraged that. When I was a girl I could have anyone I wanted to come here and play tennis, before there was a country club, and swim in the pool. But the fathers and mothers weren't invited. Grandpa and Grandma's guests were from Pittsburgh and New York."

"Where were your father and mother?"

"Traveling, or at a place we had on Murray Bay. But I was here more than any place else, every summer till the year I came out, and even then. I actually looked forward to my visits here, until boys began to enter my life. Then my mother bought a house in Southampton to launch me socially, and I promptly disrupted everything by eloping. Well, you know that. Number One on my hit parade."

"Why did you elope?"

"The real reason? The real reason was because I was so terrified of Southampton. I didn't think I was very pretty and I was afraid of being unpopular. Boys liked me, but the girls were horrid, and this boy got tight and when he suggested that we run away and get married, I did. Anything to get out of Southampton. Instead of which I got into it more deeply than before. All three of my husbands were Southampton types."

"Roy I know, but did the other two have any dough?"

"Oh, yes."

"But you never got any of it. Didn't you ask for alimony?"

"No. I should be embarrassed to tell it, but my first husband could have named my second husband as corespondent, and my second could have named my third."

"And Roy? Who could he have named?"

She shook her head. "He's married and living with his wife again. I won't tell you. At least I won't tell you now, and maybe I never will. Roy doesn't know, and that's why he's so bitter about me. But why should he know? Why should I tell him? I told him I was in love with another man, having an affair, and wanted a divorce."

"Why didn't you marry the other guy?"

"He didn't want to marry me. That was quite a blow. I told him that I'd asked Roy for a divorce and he said, 'Now wait a minute. I didn't ask you to get a divorce.' Which was perfectly true. He hadn't. I'll certainly never forget that little scene. We were on the train together on a Monday morning, coming in from Southampton, and I made my announcement. I thought it was going to be greeted with love and enthusiasm, instead of which my brave lover was terror-stricken. When I saw that I got up and went to another car, and I've never spoken to him since."

"But you went ahead with the divorce anyway."

"Of course. I'd told Roy everything but the man's name. I couldn't ask Roy to overlook my indiscretion, not after telling him I was in love with another man."

"Roy isn't the soul of forgiveness."

"No man would be, under the circumstances. Roy might have excused me for having an affair. The reason I say that is because I always felt that he was *waiting* for me to have an affair. But a silly affair is one thing, and telling your husband that you love another man is very different."

"Roy wouldn't have forgiven you for an affair. I know Roy. He thinks I'm kind of a traitor now, even if you are divorced."

"Do you mind?"

"Being on Roy's jerk list? Not a bit. Roy demands absolute loyalty from all his friends, you know that. If he sees you having lunch with another stockbroker he immediately suspects you of getting ready to transfer your business. If you go out with a woman he slept with twenty years ago he thinks you spent all your time talking about *him*. So I knew I'd be on his jerk list, the moment he heard you and I were seeing each other."

"Especially since he automatically assumes that every man I ever danced with was a former lover or about to be one."

"In fact, how did you put up with him for ten years?"

"I put up with him for five. The first five were pleasant, the second five—that's when I started coming back here again."

"Alone? I hope that doesn't sound too much like Roy."

"I was about to say, it did sound a little like Roy. Yes, I always came here alone—at least, not with a man."

"So this became your refuge. Your Shangri-la."

"I guess so. I always think of Shangri-la as that place that Roosevelt used to go to. This has a different connotation. This is a place where I was a princess, and knew it, the way children do know. And my grandfather and grandmother were sweet and kind. And *I* was nice. That's the important thing, Arthur. *I* was nice. I never had to be punished here. At home, which was Pittsburgh, with my father and mother, I got away with everything I could, and that was damn little. But as soon as I came here I was in a different atmosphere. I went to bed when I was told to, and I was on time for meals. I always wanted to get married from here."

"Why didn't you?"

"I spoiled that by eloping, and my other two marriages were civil ceremonies."

"What about the one in between, your second husband?"

"Mike? Well, he's Nancy's father, and I find that increasingly hard to believe. When I have to see him about Nancy—

money, legal things—it's usually in a lawyer's office. 'Good morning, Dorothy,' he'll say. Kisses me on the cheek, and Mr. Charlton, my lawyer, is so relieved that there's not going to be any fireworks. We sit there, Mike and I, and Mr. Charlton drones on about tax advantages and all that, and I find myself staring at Mike and his bow tie. He always wears bow ties. And his father's watch-chain. And I *know* the intimacies we shared. I know them, but I can't believe them. Six years together, which included the war years, some of them. Me pregnant part of the time, and other times following him from one place to another when he was in the Navy. Where's it all gone? Does it mean as little to him as it does to me? And yet I used to move heaven and earth to be with him. Black market railroad tickets. Black market gasoline. Bribing hotel clerks."

"And then the roof fell in. How did that happen?"

"The war did it. He came back from the Pacific and was in Washington and I went down there to be with him. But he didn't want to do any of the things I thought he'd want to do. I'd have people in for cocktails, *his* friends, not mine particularly, and then he'd give me hell because he said I didn't realize that he wasn't going back to that life. Well, I *didn't* realize it, because he hadn't *told* me. I was supposed to guess that. He was very disagreeable, and all I was doing was try to please him. Well, you can take just so much of that, and then you let ding. We had several bad fights, in which I was accused of failing to realize that there was a war on, and trying to make a Southampton out of Washington, and neglecting the baby. That really got me. Neglecting the baby. He'd come in and look at Nancy in her crib, sometimes play with her for as much as five minutes, and that was being a good father. No thought whatever about the 365 days a year I was taking care of her, without any help at all. Oh, well, Mike took it big, the war, and I was the convenient one to blame for the cocktail parties in Washington, and my grandfather was a merchant of death, having made his money in steel. And what did I know about the wave of the future. Well, nothing, but I didn't see why I should take the blame for Pearl Harbor or the sinking of the

Hornet. Or for that matter, Mike's friends. Under those circumstances I was a pushover for somebody like Roy. Yes, literally. He built me up, flattered me, was sympathetic. Got a nice colored woman from Tennessee to help with Nancy, and that was it."

"And now where is Mike?"

"Living in Providence, where he belongs. Married and has two children by his horse-face of a wife, who I'm sure regards me as a nitwit that he had to get over the way you do measles. He's active in politics, goes around making speeches in Italian. And writes me letters about Nancy, how she ought to take things more seriously and would I please cooperate. I don't know what I'm supposed to do. Nancy has a husband, a very serious-minded young man studying law at the University of Pittsburgh. I wrote and told Mike that it seemed more important for Nancy to be a good wife than to nip over and help Dr. Schweitzer. But Mike isn't one for the light touch. He wrote back and said that Dr. Schweitzer was doing a noble work and wouldn't take Nancy unless she had the right qualifications, such as a degree in nursing. Oh, a long diatribe, ending with the suggestion that since she was living in Pittsburgh, perhaps she could take some courses and volunteer to work with Dr. Salk. So I wrote him just a note and asked him who was Dr. Salk. You should see the answer I got. I wish I'd saved it. There probably isn't a mother or grandmother in the whole United States that hasn't heard of Dr. Salk, but Mike didn't stop to think of that. First he told me all about Salk, and polio shots, and polio. Then ever so gently he used it all as an excuse to—as a text for a sermon. My ignorance of Dr. Salk was typical of me and the kind of life I lived. They say that religious converts are the most bigoted, but for pomposity, for sheer pomposity, that sermon on Dr. Salk was the end. The reformed aristocrat turned progressive, liberal, whatever you want to call it. And his horse-face wife looking over his shoulder at every word he wrote. Well, why not? I'm sure Mike and his wife are descended from a long line of witch-burners, so it's perfectly natural."

"What did you see in him in the first place?"

"The exact opposite of my first husband. Mike was a quiet, conservative young man. Almost painfully shy, but not really. It wasn't shyness. It was just that he wasn't flamboyant, and that made him seem shy after my first husband."

"But you had an affair with this Mike while you were still married to the first one."

"Don't kid yourself about people like Mike. They have affairs, too. Just like you and me."

"How old are you, Dorothy?"

"I'm forty-three, and I know what you're thinking. It's quite a crowded record for someone forty-three, but I was nineteen when I married for the first time. I should be older, and most people think I am, but forty-three's the correct age."

"You may be a bit young for me. I'm coming up fifty my next birthday."

"Roy's fifty-two, although I don't know why that matters, except that he's that much older than you, or you're that much younger than he. If we reach the point where we really seriously discuss getting married, our ages will be important, but there are other things much more so."

"Such as?"

"Such as where we'll live."

"I have to make my living in New York."

"How much money would you have if you didn't work in New York?"

"Not much. I couldn't live on it."

"Do you mean your present style of living?"

"Oh, hell, no. No, I mean—well, I have an income of about seven thousand a year, apart from what I earn. We wouldn't get very far on that."

"What do you make all told?"

"Around fifty thousand a year."

"And you'd never be content to live here, with just your seven thousand and my income."

"I couldn't. Fifty isn't young, but it's too young to quit, to retire and live on an Ohio farm that isn't really a farm. What would *I* do, Dorothy? You don't think I could live the kind of day you described as your average day. I've been a go-getter all my life. I worked my way through college in the bottom of the Depression, and I was just getting on my feet when the war came and I joined the Army. Four years less a month in the Army, and I had to hustle when I got out. And I have responsibilities. I have my mother and two sisters. My sisters work, but I'm probably going to have to take care of them sometime."

"If you don't work yourself to death in the meantime. It's a grim thought, but you have to think it."

"Oh, I've thought it. But the grimmest thought is that the way things are constituted, you and I can't afford to get married. Not on your terms. Not if it means we'd live here. I'm making fifty thousand a year, and I'm just getting by. If I stopped working, it would make a difference to my mother and my sisters. Fifty thousand a year, but I couldn't really afford this visit on my own. I had to make it a business trip to Columbus. I'd never go anywhere, I'd never leave New York if I had to pay my own way. I've been to London twice this year, Seattle, Mexico City, Montreal, Phoenix, Arizona. But on company business. If a trip to anywhere costs more than twenty dollars, and isn't company business, I don't take it. So you see, Dorothy, I don't fit in, and this house *is* competition. Jumping way ahead, if we were married and you insisted on living here, I wouldn't be able to see you more than once a month."

"I see what you mean."

"I got out of the Army in '45 and as I say, started hustling. I was thirty-five years old, and I met a girl I wanted to marry, but she married someone else. I didn't have any money. What I'd saved I spent during the war, on myself and my family. I came out a major, but majors were a dime a dozen in civilian life. I even had a Silver Star and a Purple Heart, in case anybody was looking for an ex-major with a Silver Star and a Purple Heart. But they weren't. So I lost out on the girl and began to hustle. Then suddenly I'm almost fifty, with a mother and two sisters who aren't very well off, but I'm making fifty thousand a year and riding in jets and staying at the best hotels. And you're trying to make some sense out of your life. We both are. You have this place, and you love it, and you'll meet some guy that you'll want to marry and that can afford to live here with you. But I'm not the guy."

"Oh, you're the guy. I fully believe that, Arthur. But I could never live in New York again. I wouldn't be nice. That sounds insipid, but you know what I mean."

"I know exactly what you mean, just from seeing you here this short time. It's a good thing we're not in love."

"No, it's a pity we're not in love and twenty years younger."

"I stand corrected."

In the silence she got up and closed the draperies.

"What are you thinking?" he said.

"I was thinking that nobody would feel sorry for us."

He smiled. "No, they wouldn't," he said.

"We have everything. We have money, we're free to marry."

"That's the way they'd describe it. I'm a fifty-thousand-dollar-a-year man, and you're an attractive divorcee. What's keeping them apart? Why don't they get married and settle down, instead of this silly middle-aged affair of theirs?"

"And they're not getting any younger," she said.

"They're not getting any younger, and—"

"And it's very unbecoming for people their age, when there's nothing in the way. It isn't as if she hadn't been around long enough to find out what she wants."

"And when is *he* going to stop ratting around?"

"She'll be a grandmother any day now. Out of consideration for her daughter—*let's not play this any more*. It isn't very funny after a certain point. What is your mother like, Arthur?"

"Oh, I don't know. She was a schoolteacher and so was my father and so are my two sisters. What were your parents like?"

"Not were. Are. They're still alive, living in Santa Barbara. Mother keeps hoping that Nancy doesn't turn out the way I have, marrying so young. But that's hardly an original thought. I hope so, too."

"Still alive? How did you happen to get this house?"

"Grandpa left it to me because Mother didn't want it, and he knew I did. Or knew I would, when I got older. And he was right, I do want it and I am older. But I wish I didn't."

"Don't say that. Anything that you've loved as much as you do this house, and as long, must be good. You *are* nicer here, Dorothy."

"But I'm a little afraid that from now on I won't be. I may come to hate this house."

"No, as long as you can live here you'll have a nice memory of yourself. In fact, you'll always feel that you have at least one more chance in life. And believe me, that's worth holding on to." He rose and stretched his arms. "I think I'll have a quick bath before dinner."

"Your bag's in your room. Have a nap if you're tired. I'll wake you at seven-thirty. It's just you and I for dinner."

"I know," he said. He put his hand on her cheek. "Nice Dorothy."

"Nice Arthur," she said, and covered his hand with her own.

A Case History

For ten months at the outset of his professional career Dr. Drummond had served as ship's surgeon in various liners that called at South American, Australian, and Asiatic ports. In his front office hung framed photographs taken on some of his voyages, pictures of himself in tropical whites posed with men whom he would identify as presidents of banana republics, opera and concert performers on tour, forgotten financiers, the inevitable Englishmen of title, and Orientals in native costume or western dress. At home, his den was furnished with drums and spears, shrunken skulls, lovely brassbound boxes, Chinese gongs, and more photographs. The brass was now tarnished, the wooden objects now brittle dry, the drumheads crinkly and the photographs fading after nearly forty years of sunlight, but almost nothing had been moved from its original resting place. Dr. Drummond had always been delighted when a new patient commented on the photographs in the office or a visitor to his house showed curiosity about the primitive weapons. "Yes, that's me, if you can believe it," he would say. "On my right is Sir John Humberland. He wasn't Sir John then. That's when he was Leftenant Humberland, of the Yorkshire, uh, Yorkshire some regiment, but of course you probably read about him at Tobruk. On my left, that's a friend of mine named On Ling, he was a financial adviser to one of the famous war lords. An Oxford graduate, spoke beautiful English, of course. That was on a voyage from Auckland, New Zealand, to Hong Kong, and an interesting thing about that picture, it was the only time those two got that close together. Jack Humberland was thought to be a British intelligence agent, but if he was he never got anything out of On Ling. On Ling would bow to him very politely, but he'd never sit down with him, never engage in conversation. I finally got the two of them together long enough to pose for a photograph, but On Ling didn't like it very much. You can tell by his expression.

"Now this is a young lady that we had with us on a trip from Havana to Santiago, Chile. Through the Panama Canal. Very attractive. Her husband was a chemist, worked for one of the big chemical companies . . . The man on her left. An American. I don't know what he did, if he did anything. He was three sheets to the wind all the time he was aboard. Glad to see him go, I can tell you . . . These, of course, you can guess where this was taken. Bali. That was before the Dutch made them cover up. I always manage to stand in front of this picture when the Reverend Hostetter's here for dinner, but I guess he must have seen it by this time . . . I bought this in Sidney. It's an authentic boomerang. Needs a bit of waxing, but I keep putting it off. My housekeeper before I had Mrs. Brophy took it upon herself to do a job on my collection, and she put her thumb through one of my drumheads, so I don't let anybody touch any of my souvenirs . . . That, that's a blowgun. You've heard of them. They use them to blow poison-tipped darts. Some of the tribes use curare, others have their own particular poison that you won't find listed in the U.S.P. United States Pharmacopoeia . . . I shot that tiger from the back of an elephant, but I didn't have enough money to bring the skin home with me so all I have is this snapshot. Oh, it's all a long, long way from Gibbsville, P A, in miles and in years . . . These teacups, aren't they delicate little things? The last ones I have left out of a set. Lucky to have these two, after forty years and the clumsy women I've had working for me."

The doctor was a widower, childless, whose wife had died of liver trouble during the Second World War. The late Mrs. Drummond had money, some of it her own, most of it the income from a trust fund established by her first husband. When she died everyone agreed that Buz Drummond had fully earned the money he inherited; he had been nice to Sadie, done all he could to make her stop drinking though knowing it to be a hopeless task, and for a time he had practically given up his practice to take care of her so that she could have her wish, which was that she not be sent to a hospital. Sadie loathed hospitals; her father and mother and first husband had all died in the same hospital, on the same floor, in the same year, and she was bounden determined that the only way they would get her into a hospital was if they put her in a straitjacket. That, as a matter of fact, was done, but Buz honored her wish and did not take her to a hospital. As soon as she died he again became more active in his practice, and he kept busy until the younger men returned from the war; then he announced that he was taking no new patients, and during the late Forties and the Fifties he more or less retired to play golf and bridge and to devote his time to writing. He had missed out on two great wars, but he had seen a great deal of the world and he had a lot of good stories to tell.

The news that Buz Drummond was writing a book immediately caused some alarm, since the town had not fully recovered from the notoriety that followed the publication of several novels by a former resident. But on second thought Buz Drummond's friends were able to reassure themselves with the knowledge that first of all Buz was a gentleman, and in the second place, he intended to live out his life in Gibbsville. He was, moreover, an M.D., and there certainly were some written or unwritten rules to govern the degree and kind of revelations a doctor could make, even in the guise of fiction. After the early alarm Buz Drummond's friends, with few exceptions, began to take a friendly interest in his new writing career. Most of his friends would ask him how his book was coming, and he would reply that there was a lot more work to it than he had anticipated but it was *fascinating* work. Those acquaintances who were inclined to be apprehensive or suspicious—other doctors and former patients—were in accord on one thing: they knew a thing or two about Buz. But most people relied on his good sense, his good taste, his professional ethics, his decision to remain a resident of the town, and the now comforting knowledge that he had never really completed anything he had set out to accomplish.

His contemporaries recalled that after serving his internship in a Philadelphia hospital, Buz had come home for a round of farewell parties. According to his announced intention he was about to take off for South America on the first leg of a journey to last five years, during which he hoped to make a special study of tropical diseases and their cure. The high point of the bon voyage festivities was a dinner dance at the brand-new country club, for which two hundred were invited and Markel's orchestra played. The dance went off without unpleasant incident, other than the too-frequent repetition of a song called "Tell Me Little Gipsy," which had to do with fortune telling and an obvious connection with the adventurous young doctor's future. Buz got moderately tight, and the next day departed for Baltimore and his first berth in a fruit boat bound for Honduras. His closer friends had chipped in for a farewell gift—a doctor's emergency kit in an alligator-hide satchel— but he accidentally left it on the train.

When he returned to Gibbsville in less than a year his friends supposed that he was merely on a holiday between voyages, and they said so, thus supplying him with an explanation of his return. "Waiting to hear from the Dollar Line," he would say. Then, as the weeks passed: "Oh, that Dollar Line proposition fell through." Meanwhile his friends were getting postcards and little gifts he had sent them before his return, and several boxes of stuff arrived at his mother's house on Frederick Street. Then, in the autumn of '21 he opened an office on lower Lantenengo Street, in a neighborhood nicknamed Pill Row. He bought a Dodge coupe—one of the standard doctors' cars—and became a regular attendant at the meetings of the County Medical Society until he noticed that the only men who seemed to find time for the meetings were the young fellows just starting out, the arthritic old men, and the mediocrities of the profession. His own practice at first surprised him. His office hours were from one to three in the afternoon and six to eight in the evening, and he always had one or two patients, at least, in the waiting-room. Some of them were deadbeats, but they were patients; quite a few of them were the servants of his well-to-do friends; high school boys with their first gonorrhea; consumptives from the Negro section; old men and old women with real or imaginary illnesses to talk about; schoolteachers who, in the vernacular, doctored with him because he did not charge too much.

He lived at home with his mother, who was financially secure but not rich, and he watched his expenses, but at the end of two years he owed money at the bank. Like every other doctor in Pill Row he was offered a substantial sum by one of the local bootleggers in return for his liquor prescriptions, but professional gossip had immediately identified those physicians who dealt with the bootleggers, and Buz declined their offer even though it would have got him out of debt and with money to spare. The solution to that problem, the respectable solution, was to marry a girl with money. There were of course other solutions less respectable, and still others that were respectable enough but, for a young man, a too-early admission of failure. He could sign up with one of the coal or iron operators, he could be the official examiner and physician for the middle-class lodges that provided insurance benefits. But one of the older men advised against either arrangement. "You'll find out that for their God damn fifty-cent fees they think they own you, and as far as the big companies—the surgeons are the only ones make any money out of them. The lodges and the coal companies will crowd the other patients out of your office." A nice girl with money would also complete the picture of the up-and-coming young physician that Buz Drummond wanted very much to impress on the public mind; he was anxious to have the townsfolk think of him as a well-traveled man, but he wanted them to believe that the curtailment of his five-year trip had been a decision of his own, a desire to settle down to something constructive.

He found that his mother had been proceeding along the same line of thought, was just as far along as he. "You'll be thirty any day now," she said. "That's not old for a man, but it's not young either. And there are two or three nice Gibbs-ville girls that aren't getting any younger either. Well situated financially. Mary Bowen, but unfortunately she's a Catholic. But there's Minnie Stokes, you've always liked Minnie. And you'd go a long way before you'd find a nicer girl than Josie Entwhistle. All the right age to get married, and just waiting to be asked."

"You can rule out Mary and Josie."

"Well, then, Minnie."

"Minnie's the only one of those three. I've already had too many arguments with Mary, about her religion. And Josie has you fooled, Mother."

"Well, I'm not insisting on either one of them, but find *some*body. Doesn't have to be a Gibbsville girl necessarily, but people would be that much more pleased if you married a town girl. And she doesn't have to be one of our friends. This town has a lot of money and it isn't all on Lantenengo Street."

"Oh, I know that."

"Look at some of the names of the directors of the banks."

"I have."

"Well, don't let the grass grow under your feet," said Mrs. Drummond.

Henrietta Moore chose this inopportune moment to inform Buz Drummond that she was pregnant and was taking her name off the nurses' registry. "I can go to Philly and have it taken care of, but, honey, I'm going to lose a couple months' work and I don't have much saved up."

"How the hell—"

"Oh, what's the use of complaining about it? I should of known better and you should of known better, but we took our chances, so I'm not taking any calls till maybe January or February. That's thirty-five dollars a week I'm out, times twelve weeks. Twelve fives sixty, twelve threes thirty-six and six to carry is four hundred twenty dollars."

"You're better at arithmetic than you are at some other things."

"You be careful I'm not too good at multiplication. Or addition. Catch wise?"

"Very witty, I'm sure. Well, you want me to raise five hundred dollars."

"I didn't say that. Five hundred is only what I'm out. Don't you expect to pay for the abortion and while I'm in the hospital? I need a thousand, Buz."

"A thousand dollars?"

"Do you want to do it yourself? You'll still have expenses. I want to be in a hospital. I don't want to start hemorrhaging in a boarding house. Listen, Buz, I'm not holding you up for anything, but I want to go to Philly and be in a hospital. I'd have a hard time getting it done here, in the hospital. I had my appendix out five years ago, so I can't use that old excuse."

"When do you have to have the money?"

"I have to let them know I'm coming at the hospital, two or three days' notice. A girl I trained with is the head nurse there."

"What hospital is it?"

"As if you didn't know. Every intern in Philly knows, and most nurses. And those society bimboes."

"All right, I'll get the money."

"You certainly are good-natured about it, I must say. *God!*"

Mrs. Drummond handed over a bond. "I'm not giving you this," she said. "This is a loan, and you must pay me back. I don't object to helping you when I know what the money's for, but you've told me two versions of why you need a thousand dollars and frankly I don't believe either one of them. I want the money back and forty-five dollars interest. I mean it, this time I do."

"You'll get it back, and I'm no child, Mother. I don't see why I have to account for every nickel I spend."

"There are a lot of nickels in a thousand dollars. And I'm no child, either, by the way. I think you're ashamed to tell me what you want the money for."

"Have it your own way," he said.

Henrietta Moore did not go back to work as soon as she had

said she would, but when she did go back, Drummond's first knowledge of it was through the nurses' registry. He telephoned to find out what nurses were taking calls and Miss Moore's name was mentioned. "Tell her to call Dr. Drummond," he said.

She telephoned him. "Good evening, Dr. Drummond. This is Miss Moore."

He was alone in his office. "So you're back at work?"

"Yes, I'm going on a case for Dr. English, starting night duty tomorrow. Why?"

"Are you calling from some place where you can't talk?"

"No, I'm in a booth at the drug store. I stopped in after the movies and I saw you phoned. I can talk all right—if I want to. Only I don't want to. The least you could do was send me some flowers, all the time I was in Philly. I could of had a septicemia for all you cared."

"But you didn't have. And I take it you're all right again."

"You asking for a date?"

"No, I'm not, Henrietta."

"That's good, because you wouldn't of got one. Goodnight, Dr. Drummond."

She was a good nurse, was asked for by the leading physicians of the county, and if they guessed among themselves which of their number had gone to bed with her, they got no confirmation from her. She was equally discreet in the matter of passing professional opinions of the doctors. She had never been known to commit the unforgivable sin of expressing any but the most impersonal, complimentary comment on a member of the medical profession. Nevertheless she managed to convey favorable and unfavorable impressions of doctors without uttering a word, without making a face, and men like Malloy, English, and the Woodman brothers easily guessed that Henrietta Moore's opinion of young Buz Drummond was not very high. Oddly enough it was her non-professional opinion of Dr. Drummond that had the greater influence on the leading men. They could make up their own minds about Drummond as a physician, but if he could not stay out of trouble with Moore, if he antagonized such a good-natured old war horse—she was thirty-two—he could not be much of a fellow. They had been through too many vigils with her, been awakened by her from too many naps in too many Morris chairs, had drunk too many cups of her coffee and glasses of her iced tea, not to feel something that was part comradeship, part affection, part gratitude. She had helped them put chains on tires and taken the reins when they fell asleep in zero weather, and all of them knew that when she got them out of bed at four o'clock in the morning the patient had taken a turn for the worse. In her career as a nurse she had even seen one or two doctors cry.

She took herself out of Buz Drummond's life and was soon enjoying the company of a jovial cigar salesman from Reading, but Drummond's coldness during her brief pregnancy and the let-down after the abortion had done something to her spirits. The cigar salesman was new and therefore did not know that it was unusual for Henrietta to need a shot of rye to pep her up. But then one day, on a confinement case, Dr. Malloy said to her: "Did I smell whiskey on you?"

"Yes, Doctor. For cramps."

"Pack your bag and go home."

"Are you going to report me?"

"Not this time, but believe me if you'd lied to me I would have. What's the matter with you, Moore?"

"I don't know."

"Come and see me at my office tonight."

"I'm not sick."

"Then whatever's the matter, drinking on a case won't do you any good. You know how I feel about whiskey. You've been taking Sen-Sens, but I could smell that booze the minute I went in the room. God damn it, Moore, I'm giving you fair warning. Do you need money?"

"No thank you, Doctor."

"Maybe you'd better get married. I'm going to tell this patient I need you on another case. But this is the last time. God damn it to hell. Whiskey!"

On Malloy's word alone her name could have been stricken from the nurses' registry (nurses who detected whiskey on doctors' breath kept silent), and the threat to her livelihood and to the work she loved was effective for a few weeks, but the cigar salesman complained of her lack of pep and she had a few shots of rye with him. When she turned up on her case to relieve the night nurse she was so badly hung over that the night nurse had to stay with the patient. "Any doctor could tell what you've been doing, Moore," said the night nurse. "I'll do a double trick, but you're gonna get caught."

"Oh, don't sermonize to me."

"Listen, if that's the thanks I get for protecting you, I'm supposed to report you anyway. You're drunk."

"Mind your own business and leave me alone," said Henrietta Moore.

The nurses had been raising their voices during the altercation and the patient's household later in the day reported to the attending physician, who quickly discovered that the night nurse was shielding Henrietta Moore. He telephoned her at her boarding house and there could be no doubt as to what had kept her off duty that day. She was incoherent, coddling, insulting. "Lay off me, Dr. Fabrikant. You lay off me and I'll lay off you," she said. Within the hour he had reported her to the Medical Society, and her nursing career was ended. In a couple of weeks she had vanished and no one in Gibbsville ever saw her or heard from her again.

Buz Drummond made an effort in the direction of Minnie Stokes. He took her to two programs of the cultural series— the Philadelphia Orchestra and the Denishawn Dancers—and to the Lions Club Ball. If it had been the summer season he could have played tennis or golf with her, and the conversational gaps would not have been so painfully noticeable; but Minnie Stokes was not deceived, no one was deceived. It was apparent that Buz Drummond had decided that Minnie Stokes would make him a suitable wife, and he was going through the perfunctory motions of courtship. Everybody was all for it: home town young doctor, home town rich girl. The only one who was not all for it was Minnie Stokes, whose self-respect and sense of humor caused her to vacillate from annoyance to laughter, and when he proposed to her she said, "No, Buz."

"I admit I haven't been very romantic, Minnie, but we've known each other all our lives. To suddenly act like Romeo . . ."

"Oh, it isn't that."

"Well then think it over. Don't say no right away."

"It'll always be no, Buz. At least *my* answer will always be no. I'm looking for a husband, but if we can't have love at least we ought to have some fun."

"What kind of fun?"

"Any kind. But you seemed to think the whole thing was cut and dried. Take Minnie to the concerts and a few dances, and then propose and get married. I know doctors are always thinking about their cases, but is that what you were so preoccupied with?"

"I suppose I was. It's my life work."

"Well, it's not going to be mine. That's what you can tell people if you want to. Tell them I wouldn't have made a good doctor's wife. As a matter of fact I probably wouldn't. Why don't you transfer your attentions to Mary Bowen? She's very serious, and she's free. And—well, why don't you?"

"What was the third thing about Mary?"

"She's well off. I somehow don't see you marrying a poor girl, Buz."

"That has nothing—well, why should I?"

"That's better. We couldn't even be frank until now, when it's too late. Shall I say something awful? This is the first time I've liked you since our first date. Buz, we're such old friends —why don't you marry Mrs. Loffler?"

"Mrs. *Loffler?*"

"She's only about thirty-five, and she has all that money from Mr. Loffler. Go on, marry Mrs. Loffler, and make her spend some of that money on someone besides herself. She's dying to, you know. She'd love to give parties and travel, and you like to travel, don't you?"

"How do you know she's only thirty-five?"

"Her class in high school."

"Seems older than that to me."

"That's because she's been wearing black since Mr. Loffler died, and you think of her as older because Mr. Loffler was older."

"Do you know her?"

"Worked with her at the Red Cross during the war. She's gained a little weight since then, but not too much. Love to hear her laugh. Daddy says she's worth over four hundred thousand dollars."

"From that musty old store?"

"And buildings. He owns most of the 300-block, or did. She's not afraid to spend money but she doesn't know how. She did over the Norton house when they bought it and she has very good taste. Well, *quite* good."

"I don't even know who she was."

"Sadie Gardner. Her father was Squire Gardner, where they used to take people when they were arrested."

"Of course, I remember her now. I had trouble placing her. Didn't she work in the telegraph office?"

"I don't know. I didn't get to know her till the Red Cross, during the war."

"She doesn't play golf or tennis, I imagine."

"No, she isn't in the club, and I doubt if she'd play if she were. But if you want me to I can have her here some afternoon and you can drop in, accidentally on purpose." Minnie put her hand on his arm. "Aren't you pleased, the way this is working out?"

"The way you're working it out. You're the one that should be pleased, Minnie."

"I am. I know you have to marry someone with money, but as long as it isn't me I'm in favor of it."

He put his arm around her. "I want to kiss you."

"All right," she said. She gave him a full kiss, then stopped. "That's the way we should have started, Buz. You should have taken me out in your coupe and parked."

"I didn't know that that's what you wanted."

"Oh, yes," she said.

"Do you now?"

She nodded. "If you'll take precautions."

"I haven't got any with me, but I could go downtown."

"No, then just let's be like this."

They were not long in advancing from lazy kisses to ardent demands on each other, and she amazed him with how much, how desperately she seemed to center her very will to live in the motions of her hips. She was going to be hard to give up now, with what he knew about her. It was not going to be easy to let her go.

Minnie's plan to effect a proper meeting between Drummond and Mrs. Loffler was dropped. He was evasive because he did not want Minnie in on his conquest of the widow, for no other reason than a kind of squeamishness; it would embarrass him to have Minnie see him polite and attentive—and crafty. Instead he made a habit of driving past the old Norton house, now the Loffler house, when he was out on calls, and as he intended, his opportunity came. On some days he passed her house a dozen times, and finally he saw her hurrying home during a shower. He stopped his car at the curb, opened the door, tipped his hat, and said, "Jump in, I'll take you home."

"Oh, it's Buz Drummond? I mean Doctor. How nice."

She got in. "You sure you know who I am? You don't think I'm someone else? I'm Mrs. Loffler."

"Oh, come on, Sadie. Gibbsville isn't that big. We've both lived here all our lives."

"You never spoke to me before."

"The other way around. I've spoken to you, but you've never spoken to me."

They were only a couple of blocks from her house, and they reached it in a minute.

"Have a cigarette till the rain stops," he said.

"Shouldn't you be taking care of your sick people?"

"They'll wait till this clears up." He gave her a cigarette and lit it for her.

"I was never allowed to smoke while Mister was alive. He said a cigarette was the sign of a fast woman. Maybe he was right."

"Then there are a lot of fast women."

"Yes, and I'll bet *you* know a lot of them."

"Me? I'm a hard-working country doctor."

"Oh, yeah? That's what they *all* say."

"Too busy for that sort of thing, I'm afraid."

"Oh, sure. Oh, of course. Mr. Innocent talking. How come you're still single?"

"I just told you. Too busy."

"Oh, yeah? Too busy with what? I'll bet all those lady patients, not to mention those pretty young nurses."

"Neither men nor women are at their best when they're sick, and nurses only lead to trouble, so I'm told."

"That's not what I heard. A young doctor with S.A. Sex Appeal. How many of those lady patients really have something the matter?"

"Well, take yourself, for instance. You're an attractive young widow, but you never sent for me."

"I doctor with English when I have to have a doctor, which is very seldom."

"There's none better."

"But you wouldn't call him loaded with S.A. . . . Rain's stopped. Come on in and have a cup of tea, or something stronger if you wish. Or do you have to go?"

"I'll have a cup of tea, just to prove you're wrong about the medical profession."

"I wasn't talking about the medical profession. I was talking about Buz Drummond."

"And you're not afraid of me?"

"What's there to be afraid of?"

She went upstairs to take off her wet shoes, but she came down in a complete change of attire, a flowery print dress with a short skirt that revealed her pretty legs.

"I like your dress, or do you call it a frock?"

"You could call it a frock. It's old. I didn't have it on since

Mister passed away. Just been hanging there waiting for me to wear it. You want tea, or liquor?"

"What are you having?"

"Tea. Liquor's supposed to be fattening, and I'm trying to reduce. Do you know anything I can take to reduce?"

"Yes."

"What?"

"Take in your belt a few notches, and when it fits you, that's how much you ought to eat every day."

"I don't wear a belt. You should see what I wear. I'm too stout. I'd give anything to take off ten pounds. Do you know what I weigh? I weigh a hundred and thirty-four in my birthday suit. That's too much for five foot three, don't you think so? A hundred and thirty-four with nothing on?"

"You wouldn't have any trouble losing ten pounds if you put your mind to it."

"The trouble is, the extra weight always goes to the wrong places, if you know what I mean. Well, I guess you do know, being a doctor. If I ask you a question—maybe I better not."

"Go ahead."

"Well I always wanted to ask it but Dr. English isn't—well, are you sure you don't mind? It's a personal kind of a question."

"I ask a thousand of them a day."

"Well, how do you feel when you have a lady patient, and you have to examine her, and she's somebody you know socially?"

"When you say examine her I presume you mean her Eustachian tube?"

"Like that."

He stood up. "Well, if I were going to examine your Eustachian tube—"

She held up her hands. "Go away, go away! I didn't ask you to examine me."

"Hold still!" he said, in the voice of command. She obeyed, though she was apprehensive.

"Now if I wanted to examine your Eustachian tube, Mrs. Loffler, what is the first thing I would say to you?"

"Well—I don't know, but something like 'Take off your dress,' or something like that."

"Why should I?"

"Well, because it's customary."

"Not in my office."

"It was when Dr. English examined me."

"Made you take your clothes off to examine your Eustachian tube? That old rascal, Billy English."

"He was a perfect gentleman. I wasn't a bit embarrassed."

"Mrs. Loffler, I might as well stop kidding you. The Eustachian tube is here, in your ear." He tapped his ear.

"Oh, *you!* And all the time I thought—I really thought there for a minute you were going to—well I wasn't sure exactly what I thought. You have a sense of humor. I must say I like a person with a sense of humor. You wouldn't think it, but Mister said a lot of funny things. He had that *dry* humor, you know. If some of the people in this town ever heard what he used to say about them."

"Do you miss him?"

"Well, I do. Not as much as I did, but I would have if we'd kept on living in the other house. This house he never lived long enough to get used to. But I miss him. After all I was married to him for eight years and you get used to a person. A lot of people criticized me for marrying a man so much older, but when two people get along, you forget about the age. And no woman could ask for a better husband. He lavished presents on me, really lavished them. I could go to Philadelphia and go hog wild in Wanamaker's, Strawbridge's, but it seemed to give him as much pleasure as me. Of course I didn't take advantage, too much, and in a business deal I guess Mister was one of the smartest men in town, if not *the* smartest. Starting out clerking in Boyle's dry goods store for four dollars a week. That's all he got. Four dollars. He had to open up in the morning and lock up at night. Twelve hours a day, six days a week, and no vacation the first two years. Old Terence Boyle liked him so much he wanted him to marry one of his daughters, but Mister wouldn't turn Catholic, and that was how he happened to go in business for himself. You know, it isn't generally known around town, but Mister was never very fond of the dry goods end. People thought he was, but he wasn't. He was more interested in buying and selling properties, real estate. But he kept store because—to show you how clever he was, he didn't want people to think he was a real estate man. A dry goods and notions man, people wouldn't think he was as smart as a real estate man when it came to buying or selling a property. Oh, he was very good to me. I never would of ended up in a house like this if it wasn't for Mister."

"Well, obviously you made him happy, too."

"If we'd of had children. But he ruptured himself when he was younger and he blamed that on why we never had children. It's a big house for just one person. I miss the war."

"The war?"

"Well, I don't mean the bloodshed and all those boys going away, but the Red Cross. During the war I used to go to the Red Cross four-five days a week and I made a lot of friends, but after the Armistice they didn't have the Red Cross any more and I didn't see as much of them. I'm thinking of learning to drive a car. A lot of women do now. Mister didn't like a woman to drive a car, but he never said I *shouldn't*. They're trying to sell me a Pierce-Arrow, but I want to start out with something smaller. The Fierce-Sparrow. Imagine me driving a Fierce-Sparrow? What make is that little car you brought me home in?"

"That's a Dodge."

"Are they hard to drive? Mary Bowen has that Paige, but that's more of a big car. Minnie Stokes gave me a ride in her car and I watched her manipulating all the things. She says it's much easier than it looks. You get so it becomes second nature, she says."

"Minnie has a Templar."

"Oh, I wouldn't want anything as sporty as that, but I like that size car. The Dodge sedan is a nice car. I noticed a lot of them around with women driving. Everybody says don't buy a Ford, because it has no gear shift."

"It has a gear shift, but you operate it with your feet."

"Well, you see how much I know about it. I'm pretty sure I won't buy a Fierce-Sparrow, because then I'd have to hire a man to drive it, and a woman my age driving around with a man all the time. It's all right for Minnie's mother and ladies that age, but I wouldn't feel right about it."

"Why don't you let me teach you to drive?"

"Oh—but how long would it take for that to get around? Can't you just hear them?"

"It would probably get around in two days, but do you care? I'm sure I don't."

"Well, will you give me a couple days to think about it? I'm not worried what they say about me, but—"

"Don't worry what they say about me."

"I was thinking of Mister. It's all his money. Or it was."

"You smoked a cigarette."

"I guess you're right. I'll ring you up, if you really mean it."

The estimate for the circulation of the news that Buz Drummond was giving Sadie Loffler driving lessons was fairly accurate. "Well, I just heard the latest," said his mother. "You and Sadie Gardner."

"Did you?"

"I did, and I guess everybody else has too if it's got to me."

"Have you any objections?"

"Depends on which way you look at it, I guess. But I guess you're looking at it financially."

"Your idea wasn't so good. Minnie turned me down."

"I know, but Sadie Gardner won't. She's older than you are, a good five years. She hasn't long to go before she's forty, and you're not going to get any children out of her."

"There's no proof of that, but anyway I've never longed to have children."

"Every man wants children, sooner or later."

"No, not every man. Not every man wants a wife, either. What's the matter with Sadie? Because her father was Squire Gardner?"

"If I have any objections to Sadie they're the same ones you'd make. Don't try to make me feel like a snob, when you're one yourself. A Frederick Street snob is worse than a Lantenengo. You and Joe Chapin, very much alike."

"I wish I had his money."

"Well, you won't have as much marrying Sadie Gardner, but it's a nice nest egg. You gave up very easily with Minnie, and she has more than Sadie Gardner Loffler, or will have."

"Minnie and I will always be very good friends, but I'd never propose twice to the same woman."

"You'd be making a lot more money if you'd become a surgeon. Why didn't you?"

"Can't stand the sight of blood."

"Don't be impertinent, Buz. A man that's rude to his own mother."

"All the rudeness has to be on the one side, eh, Mother? Is there anything else you want to say before I retire?"

"No. Yes. But you're so thin-skinned you might just as well go to bed."

"You pique my curiosity. What is it?"

"Did you ever have anything to do with a nurse named Henrietta Moore?"

"I had her on a lot of cases. Why?"

"If you're planning to marry Sadie Gardner, Sadie Gardner Loffler, make it quick. A story reached me that you paid this nurse a thousand dollars to leave town. And thinking back, you borrowed a thousand dollars from me just about that time."

"Jesus."

"There's something to it, isn't there?"

"What do you do when people come to you with stories like that about me?"

"I brazen it out, deny everything or else say I know nothing about your affairs, personal or professional. But alone, I think a good deal."

"Have you any more juicy tidbits?"

"Well, two in one evening. That seems to me a lot."

"Yes. Well, I guess I'd better get married before I get into more trouble. Isn't that what you'd suggest?"

"I suggested it a long while ago. Now I suggest you get married before it's too late. Squire Gardner's daughter probably has very old-fashioned, conventional ideas. They're great ones for respectability, people like Sadie. They're the ones that don't tolerate certain things that you and I might overlook."

"*You* might overlook, Mother?"

"Only because I have to, sometimes. My ancestors were among the people that made those rules, those ideas. Pity we didn't all live up to them."

"Didn't Father?"

"Well, he tried. Goodnight, son. I'm going to read a while."

"What are you reading, that has you in this mood?"

She held up her book, the spine toward him. "It's a library book, Miss Williams recommended it. Called *Winesburg, Ohio,* by a Sherwin Anderson. Sher*wood* Anderson. It's not for young people like you. It's for the old, like me. Full of plain, unpleasant truths. Very gloomy little stories that could have happened right here in Gibbsville. And did, some of them. Don't read it."

"I won't. I was just wondering what you were reading."

The book was in her lap when he came down in the morning and saw her sitting there, one side of her face contorted, but her appearance otherwise that of an aging lady who had stopped rocking her chair to let herself be overcome by a deep sleep.

2

Dr. Drummond's reappearances at the meetings of the County Medical Society were welcomed, since what he may have lacked in purely professional standing he possessed in civic prominence. He had money now, was not dependent on his practice to meet his bills. He was a doctor, he treated sick people, but as he said, he had time for other things. The more skillful members of the profession were perfectly willing to have Dr. Wallace P. Drummond represent the medical art at luncheons and banquets, and they conceded that he represented them well. Some of the ugliest men in town were among the most successful healers, but Buz Drummond's appearance on a dais was a great asset to the profession, to the enterprise of the moment, to the community, and to Buz Drummond. His light brown hair had grown darker, then patches of grey had appeared. He was clean shaven at a time when most doctors still grew moustaches. He was nearly six feet tall and flat-bellied. And since his marriage he had been going to a Philadelphia tailor. In this new phase of his life he discovered that he could talk on his feet, but no matter what he said or did not say, people liked to look at him while he told his introductory funny story, waxed persuasive in the inevitable appeal for funds, and ended with a winning smile and a modest disclaimer in advance of the applause that would follow. If most of this was directly or indirectly the result of marrying Sadie Loffler for her money, then it was worth it. There was no doubt that it was worth it to Sadie, to whom he was courteous in public to a degree that was a lesson to other husbands. She took pride in his new popularity and in being half of Dr. and Mrs. Wallace P. Drummond of Lantenengo Street. When he invaded the meetings of the County Medical Society he did so with a purpose. He wanted to be elected president of the Society, he was so elected, and he handed the honor to Sadie like a present. Thenceforth in print he was not merely Dr. Wallace P. Drummond, but Dr. Wallace P. Drummond, president of the Medical Society of Lantenengo County, his full style and title. He took care to remind the editors of the newspapers that the correct usage was Medical Society of Lantenengo County, and not the more abrupt Lantenengo County Medical Society.

No layman, of course, could successfully challenge Buz Drummond's authenticity as a doctor. There were those citizens who were inclined to be cynical about the well-barbered, well-tailored personality, but Buz Drummond could smell their hostility and in their presence he made a point of using medical language they could not possibly understand, a protective device employed by doctors everywhere to defeat lay criticism. Buz Drummond had few occasions to use it. In two or three years of the new prosperity he had made a remarkable advance from his earlier mediocrity, and some of the admiration for him that counted most came from other doctors. "Put Buz Drummond on it, he gets things done," they would say. He could telephone the mayor, the chief of police, the county judges, and even the governor and get an audience. He did not deal with lieutenants of local industry but captains only, and possibly because he looked like the canon of a cathedral, he was influential with the clergy of all denominations. No one paused to consider what the consequences might be for opposing Buz Drummond. In the beginning of his civic career no one said, "What if I don't?" The original power was all persuasion, when Buz Drummond had no latent power of reprisal against those who could have refused him. Then in a few years it was too late; too many men had yielded too many favors gracefully or unquestioningly, and now the power was real. He had prestige. Now he could quickly summon the support of the men who had inadvertently given him his power, and since it was true that he seemed to want nothing for himself, he usually got what he asked for.

Politicians so thoroughly convinced themselves that he was an ideal candidate for public office that they could not understand his refusal to run. The smartest politician in the county, Mike Slattery, said to his wife Peg Slattery, "I keep asking myself, what does this fellow want? I have a hard time understanding a man like that. Everybody wants something, and he was about ready to tip his mitt a year ago, but it's nothing in my line."

"Ready to tip his mitt, how?" said Peg Slattery.

"I mean he was ripe. All these good works and civic activity. Usually I can tell when they're ready to announce. With him it was about a year or so ago. But I asked him did he have his eye on anything, and he said yes. He had his eye on a big new wing for the county hospital. That was in the machinery, I told him. What about for him, what did he want? To stay out of politics, he said. To stay out of politics! That fellow's in politics up to

his ears, every day of his life. I'm not afraid of him, but I sure as
Satan want him working for me. The one thought did occur to
me."

"What's that?"

"The man may just be stupid."

She shook her head. "No. That you can't say about him."

"Yes I can, and I do. The only man I came across in my
reading that doesn't seem to want anything for himself is that
little fellow in India. Mahatma Gandhi. And we can forget
about him. He's not coming to this country, and if he did they'd
lock him up."

"The little man with the goats, wears a shroud?"

"That's the man. I'd put Buz Drummond up against him
and Buz would win every precinct. Here. Not in India, mind
you. Oh, no. But those Hindus, they're a hundred and fifty
years behind us, woman. We got free of England a hundred
and fifty years ago, and that's all the farther they are now.
When they get their independence that's when they start being
like us, the way we started to be back in 1776. They won't need
their little man then. They can start fighting amongst themselves, as we did. And do. You need a little fellow like Mahatma
to lead the fight for independence, or a great fellow like George
Washington with Jefferson's brains behind him. Men that don't
want anything for themselves. But this is 1925, and we have
our independence for a hundred and fifty years, and everybody's out for themselves. Those that don't are stupid, because
this country is a nation of competition. Either Buz Drummond
wants to be Mahatma, or he's stupid. Politically, I'm speaking
now. And financially. Politically and financially he's stupid not
to strike while the iron's hot. What else does a man like him
want? Well, we have a dirty file on Buz. I started collecting
items for it about two years ago."

"There was some story, but I don't remember it."

"Yes. There was one story got out. He knocked up a nurse,
back a few years ago, and he gave her money to leave town. He
sold a bond he got from his mother. A thousand-dollar bond.

The nurse disappeared from the face of the earth. If she's alive or dead we don't know. The tip on that story came from Billy English. It isn't much of a story till we find out more what happened to the nurse, and that seems hopeless. Then I began delving into a trip he took, working as a ship's doctor. He was supposed to be gone five years, but he was home in less than one. Why? Well, he met some young woman that fell for him and they had a romance on the boat. She was supposed to get off some place in South America, but when the boat sailed she was on it. Left her husband because she was stuck on Drummond. Some place in Australia the American consul came and took her off the boat and they shipped her back to South America with a nurse. She went out of her head."

"Over him? Over Buz Drummond? She must have been *crazy*."

"She was. That's what I said. That's what I just got finished telling you."

"I meant it differently."

"Then as I understand it he was on two other boats over in that part of the world, and on the second one an Englishman with a name like Cumberland took a shot at him."

"At Buz?"

"Yes, woman. Who're we talking about? Shot him in the arm. The official report says that Buz accidentally shot himself, but I don't always go by official reports. Buz had to stay in China or some place till the arm got better, and then he was quietly given the sack and shipped back home. How's that for Mr. Dr. Buz Drummond?"

"He doesn't know you have any of this?"

"Oh, good heavens, no. We spent a lot of money collecting this data. Most of the dirty files the data doesn't cost you a cent. But I had to know a few things about Buz when he began getting strong a year ago. What I told you cost us about eighteen hundred dollars. But wait. I'm not finished. The prize data didn't cost us anything at all, and it isn't a lot of stuff that happened when he was a young fellow, way out on the other side of the world. The prize is what's going on now, here in town."

"Wuddia want me to do? Say please? You're going to tell me, so go ahead. The prize data."

"*Who*—is Buz Drummond's girl friend?"

"Don't know, and didn't know he had one."

"None other than Miss, Minerva, Stokes, alias Minnie Stokes."

"That's old. She jilted him, oh, four-five years ago."

"Did she now? Peg, sometimes you're not as smart as I give you credit for. Dr. Wallace P. Drummond, alias Buz, and Miss Minnie Stokes have been carrying on together since before he got married, and right under Sadie's nose. Whenever Minnie jilted him, she turned right around and began having a passionate love affair with him that if this town ever finds out about it, I wouldn't be surprised if they stoned her. And what they'd do to him I can't in my wildest dreams imagine. Pillars of society, eminent practitioner of the medical profession. And underneath it all they're like a couple of alley cats. He puts his car in the garage at night, and there she is, waiting for him. The carriage-house, the old Norton place? Going on now for I guess five years. Just in the past year they stayed together as man and wife twice in New York and three times in Philadelphia. Dr. and Mrs. W. P. Drum, they go as. Oh, the sinning that goes on, Peg."

"You don't have to make a joke of it. I suppose it's useless to ask how you found out, and if you're sure."

"The meetings in the carriage-house, how that was discovered—well, not to make a joke of it but it was funny. Sadie Loffler had a maid, and *she* was using the room in the carriage-house to meet *her* boy friend. And one night she went up there and heard voices. Sneaked up the stairs in her bare feet and guess who she saw, using her hideout."

"Is that the Chapman woman, that works for Sadie?"

"Correct. She puzzled over whether to blackmail him or not but she asked the priest in confession, as if it was happening to a friend of hers, and the priest said he couldn't give absolution to a blackmailer. So she never said anything to Buz. But when I began making some inquiries she said she'd talk to me but no one else. I offered her some money, but she said she was afraid she wouldn't get absolution if she took money."

"Huh."

"Now don't start complaining about the dirty files. You couldn't run politics without them."

"I didn't say anything."

"You grunted. But I notice you always listen to every story I tell you."

"Well, I agree with you he is stupid."

"Sure he is. I could *make* him run for office if I had to. Usually the dirty files are used for the opposite effect, but if I ever need Buz Drummond, I've got him. And console yourself, Peg. I never used the dirty files to make a nickel in my insurance business. Not a nickel."

"Huh."

"There you go again," he said. "Can I get you a bottle of beer?"

"I'll have a bottle of beer."

"All right. But it's illegal. Ten years ago it wasn't illegal. Ten years from now it won't be. But now it is. That's law for you. And the Church changes its laws, too, Peg. What's your penance when you go to confession? Five Our Fathers and five Hail Marys. But you used to have to do sackcloth and ashes, in front of everybody. Think I'll have a Coke."

"You're a rascal. An old-time rascal."

"No, I'm not. I'm a man living in a world full of people, Peg. And I must be fond of them or I wouldn't study them so much. I'll bet you Lincoln and I would have a great time swapping stories together."

"Oh, tonight it's Lincoln. Who was it the other night, the Italian fellow?"

"Niccolò Machiavelli. Him, too. This is the most fascinating work there is, Peg. I wish I knew all those ones in the past, and the ones to come."

"Get the beer, will you, please? We can talk then."

3

Happy Sadie Drummond, fetching and carrying for people, giving of her money and her time, had wanted to go back to the days of the Red Cross, but the early years of her marriage to Buz Drummond made the Red Cross days (and marriage to Mister Loffler) seem like some sort of rehearsal. Every day she had something to do, somewhere to go, or new plans to engage her attention. Buz, she said, kept her busy. She had automatically become a member of the country club on her marriage to Buz, and she dutifully took some golf lessons, but she gave them up and did not even try to play tennis.

In the third year of her marriage her feelings were hurt, and she sulked and brooded until Buz had to give her a good talking-to. Minnie Stokes had invited Sadie to attend the meetings of the Wednesday Afternoon Bridge Club, not, at first, as a player but as one of the learners, along with a few younger girls who were just starting the game. In the second year Sadie had picked up enough of the rules and basic mechanics of the game to become a playing member, and one of her happiest times was in making preparations for the day when it was her turn to entertain the ladies. Her chicken à la king was all white meat; her dessert was not just ice cream but ice cream in molds, George and Martha Washington, cherry trees, hatchets, drums, stacked muskets, all appropriate to the third Wednesday in February; and she had not only a first prize and a booby prize, but favors for everyone. She completely ignored the custom of a five-dollar limit for first prize and two dollars for the booby. Her first prize was a silk-and-hand-embroidered-lace camisole from Bonwit's, Philadelphia; her booby prize, a pair of hand-painted salt and pepper shakers; and each lady received a cute little sterling silver bridge pencil with her initials engraved on it. "Oh, Sadie, you *shouldn't* have," said Minnie Stokes, the first-prize winner.

"Oh, I know, but after all why not? When a person has as

much fun as I did selecting the things. And everybody *came*. I didn't have to ask anyone to substitute." She had dreaded the prospect of having to ask a non-member to fill in, since any acceptable substitute was probably more truly eligible than she.

In the third year, as October came and went and November was half over, and Sadie had not been notified of the resumption of the meetings, she said to Minnie Stokes: "When are you going to start the Wednesdays again, Minnie?"

"Well, we still have the Wednesdays but with a different bunch of girls. More serious bridge players, you know. They all play for blood."

"Oh."

"Not as much fun, of course, but some of the girls thought we had too much conversation and not enough bridge. After Christmas we may decide to have another club, more like the old one."

"I see," said Sadie. She saw plainly when she saw a group of cars parked at Josie Entwhistle's house. Josie Entwhistle was one of the girls whose bridge game was of a caliber to give Sadie confidence in herself.

"Mean, nasty stuck-up things," said Sadie to Buz. "And I don't trust that Minnie Stokes. I think she kept me out. She always looks at me funny."

"Now you listen to me, Sadie," said Buz. "You told me over and over again you were never going to learn the game. And there's nothing worse than playing bridge with somebody that doesn't *care* about the game. Spoils it for everybody. Minnie's a very good player. She plays with men."

"Maybe that's her trouble. If she played with them in other ways maybe she'd find herself a husband, before it's too late. Her and her golf and her tennis and playing cards."

"Well, perhaps so. But you like Minnie and she's never been stuck up with you, you *have* to admit that."

"She didn't used to," said Sadie. "But now she looks at me funny."

"Something you imagine."

Happy Sadie Drummond could not long sulk over a snub by other women when her intimate life with Buz was so exciting, full of things that were so exciting that she could not tell them to any of her friends. Sometimes he would stay away from her for weeks at a stretch, but she knew, because he told her so, that abstinence so deliberate stored up desire. He introduced her to methods of pleasure that he himself had not heard of until his voyages to the Orient, and he assured her that periods of abstinence were essential to the creation of a desire strong enough to conquer her feeling of wickedness. "I guess I ought to feel more wicked than I do," she once told him. But instead she only felt a superior pity over the girl she had been as Mrs. Sadie Loffler. Most of the time she could hardly remember that side of her life with Mister Loffler, and she was glad that Buz had no jealousy of her first husband. It would have embarrassed her to reveal now the unrefined pleasures of her first marriage. Sometimes at a banquet, when Buz was making a speech, she would steal a look at the faces of the women in the audience and think of them with their Lofflers and of herself with this man who was her husband, and her sense of possession would become almost unbearable. It was especially lovely torture when she had reason to guess that a period of abstinence might end that night.

4

"One of these days," said Buz Drummond, "I'm going to have to do away with her."

"Why do you say that?" said Minnie Stokes.

"You'll see why," said Drummond.

"No I won't, so tell me," said Minnie. "You'll never do away with anybody, darling, but why do you think you have to say it? About once a year you say something like that."

"Some day, some year I won't say it, but just do it."

She shook her head. "Never," she said.

"Don't be so know-it-all. It's very exasperating," he said. They were lying on a bed in a hotel in Newark, New Jersey, a city in which neither of them knew a single human being.

"You're more apt to do away with *me,* as a matter of fact."

"Why?"

"Well, I can make you very cross. You lose your temper with me, but she only bores you. You might push me out of a window, but in anger. Or want to kill me when I can't go away with you, but then I wouldn't be there, when you lost your temper. But the only way you'd ever do away with her would be like giving her small doses of arsenic or something like that."

"I've thought of that."

"I'm sure you have."

"But that isn't the way. There are doctors in this town—I don't mean here, I mean Gibbsville—that are going to want to be damn sure there's nothing suspicious about the way she checks out, when she does check out."

"Yes."

"If she fell from the court house tower, in full view of everybody, there'd be doctors ready to do a post-mortem. If she ever gets sick I'm not even going to give her an aspirin tablet. I'll call in Billy English or somebody equally respectable, let him be responsible from the word go. Of course I wouldn't have these murderous thoughts if you'd marry me."

"Well, I don't intend to."

"She'd give me a divorce. I know she would."

"Yes, she probably would. If you told her that you were in love with me, she would."

"What kind of a life is this for you, Minnie?"

"Hmm." She smiled faintly.

"No, really?"

"Oh—it's all right I guess." She knelt on the bed and kissed his mouth.

"Well, it isn't," he said.

"No, of course it isn't. But you love me, and I love you. You love me as much as you can love anybody, and I love you the same way, which is more. You haven't got much love to offer, have you, Buz?"

"Well, that's what you keep telling me."

"But what there is is for me, isn't it?"

"Yes. All of it. A nasty little eyecupful of love, according to you."

"You're sweet," she said.

"But let me tell you something. An eyecup full of arsenic is a fatal dose, and the same amount of love has just as big an effect on me."

"How do you mean?"

"I mean, well, don't you get it? Whatever love I have to offer is yours, whether it's enough to fill a bathtub or an eyecup."

"Oh, yes. I see. I guess I see."

"Why don't you marry me? I'll make you happy."

"Maybe you could. You make *her* happy."

"Oh, Christ."

"But maybe the trouble is—I don't know—I love you, and never, never anyone else. But I've always shied away from you."

"I wouldn't say that, exactly."

"Oh, heavens. This? If you asked me to I'd do this in the middle of the floor at a club dance. Not really, of course, but I've often wanted to."

"Yes, I can think of times."

"There were other times that you didn't know about, too. Other boys I've danced with have got the benefit of what I was thinking about you."

"Who?"

"Oh, I don't know. Ever since I stopped thinking like a nice girl I had some such thoughts about you. But then you were so *dull* when you came a-courting. Fate protected me."

"Oh, shit."

"Don't say that. I don't like that word. You can say anything else."

"Well, to go on. You've told me this before, that if I hadn't been so considerate of your virginity we'd be married today."

"Yes. I expected to be swept off my feet, and was ready and willing. The second time I went out with you I even wore underclothes that wouldn't interfere. But you brought me home from the concert and didn't even try to kiss me."

"I know, I know. But why was that a mistake? You've never been able to tell me why. Do you know why?"

"Oh, I do now."

"Money-proud?"

"Not exactly. It was just that—as if I'd been looking forward to an affair with Don Juan and he spent the evening discussing iambic pentameter."

"I didn't discuss iambic pentameter."

"Or anything else. You just put in the time with Minnie Stokes, making a cold-blooded, calculating effort. And that made me realize that you could be cold-blooded and calculating. Gave me time to get my breath. I wasn't in awe of you any more."

"I see. Should have taken it right out and given you a jab with it."

"Well, something like that. Anything would have been better than yawning through Mendelssohn's Scotch Symphony. That's what they played."

"How do you remember that, or do you?"

"Oh, I do, Buz. I remember everything about us, things you've forgotten or never knew."

"The question is, when are you going to be a mature woman and marry me? You're over thirty, and people aren't going to say nasty little Minnie broke up Dr. Drummond's marriage. Everybody's grown up—except you. There are no young kids in this triangle."

"Do you know what people can do?"

"What?"

"Well, I won't say it, but you know what they can do."

"You mean they can go fuck themselves?"

"Yes. Thank you for saying it for me."

"It's a word that occasionally passes your lips. Minnie, do you *want* to stay single all your life?"

"I'm not single now, to my way of thinking. I couldn't be more double than I am with you."

"But I'll be forty before very long, Sadie's past it now. The longer you delay, the worse it's going to be for her, if that's what you're thinking about."

"Partly."

"The question of children. You've been very careful, but you've never said you didn't want to have children."

"I'm resigned to not having them. And you *don't* want them."

"Is that why you're resigned?"

"Partly. Principally."

"What is life going to be for you when you're, say, fifty? Do you think now that you and I will still want to go on like this? You won't be able to stand it. Love won't last that long, Minnie."

"Maybe not."

"Well, what will you have then?"

"When I'm fifty? Oh—I'll have you. By that time this won't be so important."

"You don't know much about biology if you believe that. Are you aware of the fact that after the climacteric, the menopause, many women get more pleasure out of sex than they ever did?"

"I don't believe it. I've heard it, but I doubt it very much."

"Take my word for it, free. No charge. See, I'm not just after your money."

"Ah, Buz, don't say that. Sweetheart."

"Well, Christ, what else is there for me to think? The fact of the matter is that I don't need Sadie's money any more. Or yours. If I wanted to I could make fifty thousand a year, in perfectly legitimate business. If I wanted to go into politics I could make a lot more. A *lot* more. But I won't do it as long as I'm married to Sadie. Why should I? I'm respectable and respected now. I carry a lot of influence, and incidentally I've given Sadie a good run for her money."

"Yes, you have. Nobody can take that away from you."

"The squire's daughter has gone as far as she'll ever go, and much farther than she had any right to expect. She's not on my conscience, even if she is on yours. She is, isn't she?"

"On my conscience? Yes, I guess so."

"You know so. That's the whole damn trouble."

"No it isn't. The truth is she bores me, too, intensely. I have to put up with her friendship, which I don't want. You have no idea how many times I've been tempted to describe a night with you, in vivid detail."

"Why don't you sometime?"

"That would do away with her, more quickly than arsenic. But why don't *you?*"

"Describe a night with you?"

"Yes."

"I don't know, I never thought of it. I guess I couldn't do that."

"You couldn't do it to her, or couldn't do it to me?"

"I don't think I could do it to her, because I know how she'd look. And I couldn't do it to you, because I couldn't tell anybody about you. I used to talk about girls and everything about them, everything. Naming names. But I wouldn't even admit that you have nipples on your breasts. You and I are—us."

She put her hand on his cheekbone. "The eyecup turns into a bathtub," she said.

"Yes, and I still don't get my answer."

"My darling, whatever answer I gave you would be a thinking answer, and false. The real answer is a feeling one, and I don't know what it is."

"All right," he said. "What would you like to do? I have another pint of Four Roses, bottled in bond. Shall I send down for some ginger ale? Or do you want to take the next train back to Philadelphia? Or do you want to just lie here and see what happens?"

"I certainly don't want to take the next train back to Philadelphia."

"One of these days you will," he said.

5

It was the day after Thanksgiving and the year was 1939, in which there were two Thanksgiving Days: the officially pro-claimed, or FDR holiday, and the second a week later on the traditional fourth Thursday. Sadie and Buz were in a Chestnut Street jeweler's, doing their Christmas shopping.

The clerk stood patiently while Sadie contemplated a silver dish. "I tell you what you do," she said. "You take it over and ask my husband what he thinks of it. That's him over at the leather-goods counter. And while you're gone I'll have a look at these other things."

The clerk said, "Thank you, Mrs. Drummond," and de-parted. He always waited on her for silver articles. She busied herself for a moment, then turned to look at Buz and the clerk. But the clerk was talking to another customer, paying no atten-tion to Buz, and the other man was shaking his head. The man was at least sixty-five years old and did not have the look of a regular customer of the shop. The clerk shrugged his shoulders and returned to his post. "I guess your husband must have moved to another counter," he said.

"He did not. He's still there. The tall man wearing the brown overcoat."

"Oh, I beg your pardon. Oh, *that's* Mr. Drummond?"

"Dr. Drummond."

"My mistake," said the clerk.

It was only one of several incidents that did not seem to an-noy Buz as much as they annoyed her. In this instance Buz had been unaware of the incident, but she was unable to keep it to herself. "Are you ever sorry you married me?" she said, back at the hotel.

"When you make a mountain out of a molehill. You could have pointed me out and prevented that mistake."

"Then you'd have seen me point and thought I didn't have **any** manners."

"Oh, what balls, Sadie. You're forty-nine years old, and I'm forty-four. We're neither of us young people."

"But you should of seen what he picked out to be my husband. And not only the age. Practically an old tramp, in off the streets."

"Well, what do you want me to do? Try to look older? Let my appearance go to hell? Well, I refuse to. And I also refuse to pamper you. Every woman has to go through change of life and you're just being selfish. I won't put up with it. You overtire yourself with this damned Christmas shopping and you take offense at the least little thing. I'll give you something now to put you to sleep and I'll go over and have dinner at the Union League."

"Anything to get away from me, that's what it is."

"Right. I don't care for your company, and I'm sure you don't care for mine."

"One of these days I'll kill myself. You mind. I will."

"Will you indeed? Here, take this and go to sleep."

"What is it?"

"It's something to put you to sleep, and I hope you'll wake up not feeling so sorry for yourself."

"Why shouldn't I feel sorry for myself? Nobody else does."

"Now listen to me, Sadie—"

"I don't want to listen."

"If you don't listen I'm going to pack my bag and leave you, this minute."

"If you do I'll jump out that window."

"No you won't, so just listen to what I have to tell you. Are you going to listen?"

"All right."

"You promised me a month ago that you weren't going to drink except before meals. Did you have something at the hairdresser's this afternoon?"

"No."

"Yes you did, or if not at the hairdresser's, somewhere. Now don't lie to me."

"I had a cocktail downstairs."

"You had three cocktails downstairs, or four."

"I had three, not four. And they were small ones, not doubles. They only give you a half a cocktail here anyhow. This place is a gyp."

"When we get home you're going to go see English."

"I am not, and anyway he's too old."

"Then somebody else, but you're going to make an appointment to see a doctor next week. So you decide which one you want to see."

"There's nothing the matter with me. You said so yourself, every woman goes through the change."

"Sadie, you *know* what else is wrong with you. I'm a doctor, remember. And even if I weren't, you couldn't keep it from me forever. You never used to take a drink unless I was there."

"Yes, but you're never there when I want one."

"I'd have to be there pretty much of the time, it seems to me."

"Are you calling me a drunkard?"

"I'm telling you that you're on the verge of becoming an alcoholic, and I'm telling you that your liver isn't going to be able to stand what you've been doing to it."

"It's the only pleasure I get out of life any more."

"Do you call it pleasure, sitting with Josie Entwhistle and getting drunk every afternoon?"

"I didn't see Josie all week, and what's the matter with Josie? She's one of *your* friends, the only one that's nice to me. The only one that ever shows any appreciation."

"You can't buy people's friendship." As soon as he said it he realized it was a mistake. Josie Entwhistle was the last of the Wednesday bridge players who continued to be companionable with Sadie.

"That was a nasty mean thing to say, and you said it to hurt me. You took all the pleasure out of my Christmas shopping. I wish I never would of married you. If I hadn't of been rich you never would of looked at me."

"That's insulting."

"Minnie Stokes wouldn't have you, that's why you married me."

The harm was done, and so he continued. "Well, I married you and I didn't marry Josie Entwhistle, if she's the one that gave you that idea. And she is." He had now spoiled her only companionship.

"I notice you don't deny it about Minnie Stokes."

"Josie Entwhistle has been jealous of Minnie all her life, long before you ever knew Josie or Minnie, and I'm not here to discuss Minnie."

"What are you here for?"

"To watch you go to sleep, and then have a few minutes' peace by myself."

At the word sleep she tried to fight it, but almost immediately her eyes closed. He watched her for five minutes and then went out. He walked over to South Broad Street and at the club he telephoned Minnie.

"I just wanted to hear your voice," he said.

"Is something wrong?"

"Yes. You're ninety-five miles away, and you always are."

"Yes, most of the time. I'm sorry, darling, but you caught me at a bad time. I'm going to dinner."

"Who's taking you out to dinner?"

"Mr. McHenry."

"Haven't you started to call him Arthur yet?"

"Well, yes I have, but it doesn't come naturally."

"It will."

"I don't know. Darling, I have to hang up. Shall I see you next week?"

"Come to the office, tomorrow evening?"

"No, I don't like that. You know I don't."

"All right. Next week. Monday night?"

"Tuesday night."

"Not Sunday night?"

"No, it'll have to be Tuesday at the earliest. Goodbye, darling. Sorry I couldn't be more help."

After Pearl Harbor he tried to get a commission, but he was not wanted. He was younger than some of the new majors and lieutenant commanders, lieutenant colonels and commanders, colonels and captains, but he was neither young enough nor good enough to overcome the Army's and Navy's indifference. There was a vague irony too to the fact that Sadie, with her fond recollections of the Red Cross of the First War, was asked to contribute money but not her services. The only people who knew her now were also tolerantly aware of her addiction to the bottle. "No, Buz," said Minnie Stokes McHenry. "We simply couldn't have her disrupting things."

"It might help her. It really might," he said.

"It might for a while, but what if she turned up drunk? Or had to be taken home? Then everybody in town would know, instead of just a few. No. I'm sorry."

"You've done a pretty thorough job of getting the Drummonds out of your life. Drummonds. It almost sounds like gremlins."

"She was never in my life, and you'll always be in it."

"What do you tell Arthur?"

"He has never asked."

"Can any man be that incurious?"

"He isn't incurious, but I told him I'd only marry him on condition that he not ask. I told him I'd had love affairs, but I wouldn't tell him how many or with whom."

"Some day you *will* tell him."

"Yes, some day I probably will, when I want to get some comfort out of my past, when I have to think back on how attractive I used to be. But I don't need that quite yet. A few years from now, probably."

"I hate Arthur McHenry."

"Well, I guess I hated Sadie but wouldn't admit it. If I'd given in to it I'd have been miserable, all those years."

"And might have married me. Do you remember one time I wanted to kill her?"

"I do. We were in Newark, New Jersey. You talked about it other times, too, but I remember that because there was something in your voice that day that—it was the one time I was afraid. You weren't angry. You were bored and weary, and I had a feeling it was getting you. You used to have a habit, you know, or you don't know but you did have a habit, when something bothered you."

"I'd lower my voice, speak more softly."

"No. This was completely unconscious. You'd start rubbing your scar, where the Englishman shot you. You were completely oblivious of it, but I noticed it."

"I'm sure Arthur McHenry has no such scars."

"He has no scars of any kind, that I've been able to find."

"Have you discovered any of your own?"

"Oh, a deep one, yes." She laughed. "But I can't rub it, and I can't blame anybody for it but myself."

"Tell your physician."

"I'll tell you. It's what hurts when I think of how much I loved you and how happy we could have been. But every time I have my palm read they always say my head rules my heart. You've never read much. Did you ever read anything by Joseph Conrad?"

"No, I don't think I did."

"He said a very strange thing for an author to say. He said that thinking is the great enemy of perfection."

"That's why I don't read novels. Statements like that. But he has a point, at least in love affairs."

"Well, he included love affairs, as I remember it."

"And so you have a scar, too, Minnie?"

"Uh-huh. But it doesn't show. It doesn't show."

"When it does what's McHenry going to do?"

"Oh, he knows what love is. He loved his other wife, too. You never really loved anyone but me, did you? Or I anyone but you. What did that prizefighter say? We were robbed."

"We wuz robbed. Don't be so prissy."

"And don't you be so bossy. I'm a married woman now."

"Yes. That's what you are, Minnie. A married woman. And you have the scar to prove it."

"Don't make it hurt, please. That's not what a doctor's supposed to do."

"Well, you tell me a good anaesthetic to use on myself."

"If I knew of one I would."

"I guess the best is what I tell some patients. Those that haven't got very long. 'Keep busy. Don't overdo, but keep yourself occupied.' It never made a one of them live a day longer than he should have, but at least some of them felt useful for a few months."

"You're useful."

"At the moment, I am."

"That isn't what I meant, Buz, but there are lots of ways, aren't there?"

"Oh, sure. As a matter of fact, what *did* you mean?"

"You thought I meant your practice, but I meant Sadie and myself. I don't know what either of us would do without you."

"You seem to be doing very well without me. Sadie is another story, one that we'll see the end of fairly soon. Two years, three years."

"Two or three years? I could almost laugh, couldn't you?"

"Sure. Often. But only almost. And in a way I'm glad you didn't wait."

"Why?"

"Well, my ethical problem is bad enough as it is, and if you were still single it would be much worse. Sadie is drinking herself to death, literally, and I know as her husband that she's doing it deliberately. Not in any mean or vindictive way, but because she has nothing to live for. Nothing. Sex is no pleasure for her any more. Dressing up. Giving parties. None of the things she enjoyed for a while. She doesn't want to look at herself in the mirror, and she doesn't, or when she does she cries. So she drinks. She gets what she calls sozzled. For about two hours a day, in the middle of the afternoon, she makes a little sense and I try to go home and see her then. But the rest of the time she's intoxicated, or sozzled. I could probably have her committed, but she's not going to respond to any treatment that I know of, including psychiatry. I could compel her to go to a hospital, but she has a genuine terror of hospitals, and in these times I have no right to put her in a hospital, with the shortage of nurses, and sick people sleeping in corridors. Can you imagine Sadie in a corridor? And would you put her in a private room when the demand is what it is today? Have you been to either of the hospitals lately?"

"Yes."

"Then you know. So I have Mrs. Brophy in the house. She's not a nurse and she's not young, but she's pretty strong and conscientious, and at least I know that Sadie isn't going to set fire to the house with a cigarette she left burning, or fall asleep in the bathtub. And if she has a bad fall, Mrs. Brophy always knows where she can reach me."

"What about Sadie herself?"

"Most of the time she doesn't know what's going on."

"Have you had any other doctors in to see her?"

"No, not yet. I know what they'll say. The younger men will say psychiatry, and pass the buck that way. One or two might recommend surgery, but why subject her to that ordeal when I know damn well that as soon as she comes home from the hospital she's going to start drinking again? I'm not giving her little doses of arsenic. My wife is a hopeless case. She's going to die from the things that are wrong with her organically, and even if they could be cured, she'd still die. There's a thing I've noticed about Sadie and others as well. There are some people that don't seem to be interested in themselves, seem to be more interested in other people. And we tend to think of them as unselfish and so on. But I wonder. Sadie, for instance, has always been outwardly generous and so forth, but I don't believe that she ever spent much time thinking about herself, about her own mind, her motives, her limitations. And if she did, possibly she didn't like what she learned, and therefore stopped. She was safe, comfortable, as long as she didn't do any thinking about herself."

"Escapism."

"Of course. But a case of escapism like Sadie's is a form of death. Not suicide, but death. Sadie probably died of shock years ago, when she got a good look at herself and didn't like what she saw."

"I never thought of it that way."

"Well, I never would have if I hadn't been married to a case of it. I think Sadie murdered Loffler."

"Oh, come on, Buz. He died in the hospital. That's why she hates hospitals."

"He not only died in the hospital. I also went to the trouble of looking up his death certificate. He died of normal causes. A heart condition. Billy English signed the death certificate. No post-mortem. No suspicious element in the whole business. But I think she hoped so much for his death that she got her wish."

"Oh, well that's a different matter."

"Is it? I think that's what she saw that she didn't like. I think that after Loffler died she took the one and only look inside herself and was horrified by what she saw. Horrified. Admitted to herself that she had wanted him dead."

"Is she a witch? Is that what you're implying?"

"A kind of one, yes. Fat, and not very bright, not skinny and clever, the way witches are supposed to be. You said something a few minutes ago about fortune-tellers. Were they skinny?"

"No, as a matter of fact the fortune-tellers I went to were both stout women. I only went to two. One in New York and one in Collieryville, but they were both heavy-set."

"Well, I saw them in China, the Hawaiian Islands and several other places when I was out there years ago, and they were all fat women. Rather jolly fat women, except when they were fat men."

"Are you making this up?"

"No. If it sounds that way it's because I've never put it into words before. Even now I'm not going to tell you everything."

"What is there to keep back?"

"Things I don't like to tell, and that you wouldn't like to listen to."

"Oh, in the sexual line?"

"Yes."

"Well, without going into detail, what kind of thing? Be objective."

"Well, medically objective, which is to say things she didn't know herself, she was a sadist. But not in the obvious ways. With a man like Loffler, a man that couldn't have known there was such a word and was probably frustrated anyhow, she could have been very dangerous."

"How?"

"Well, I don't think he'd had much sex life before he married Sadie, and he was fifteen years older than she when they got married. He was always fifteen years older, of course. When I married Sadie I discovered that I was expected to function every night of the week."

"But you didn't."

"No, I didn't, but apparently she had Loffler trying every night. When it got dark, you went to bed, and when you went to bed you had sex. That must have been quite a strain on Loffler, who wasn't accustomed to any at all during the first forty years of his life. I can see how this conversation could become embarrassing to you, Mrs. McHenry."

"Well, yes, it could. But I'm fascinated by the witch theory. Since it's come up, I admit I always thought Sadie was—strange. I remember one time at a dinner at the hotel. You were making a speech for the Community Chest, I think it was, and I happened to notice Sadie. She wasn't looking at you at all. She was studying all the women, one after another. Pride, I thought it was at first, but that wasn't it. I decided it was more like jealousy, trying to guess which of the women wanted to go to bed with you. Why wasn't she more jealous of me? Why didn't her instinct tell her about us?"

"Who knows? She wasn't jealous of women patients, either. She once asked me what a doctor thought when a woman patient also happened to be a friend of his. I told her that sick women were completely devoid of any attraction for a doctor. She accepted that. She also accepted my statement that doctors never fool around with nurses. Those were the days when she accepted everything I told her. These past few years she doesn't believe anything, but that's not only directed against me. She doesn't believe anybody. Mrs. Brophy, me, anybody. Oh, if I were just out of medical school I wouldn't say this, but Sadie is crazy. Take away all the language of anatomy and diagnosis and therapy and prognosis—and I'm married to a crazy woman."

"Then she's not a witch, Buz," said Minnie, smiling.

"No? In the tropics the chief conversational topic after sex and money is witchcraft, whether you're in Port-au-Prince or Honolulu. I never knew a ship's officer that didn't have some favorite witchcraft story. But you have a word like poltergeist, which comes from the German, meaning a noisy ghost. Those things aren't confined to the dark-skinned people. The banshees. *Macbeth.* And I know this much about my wife. When Mrs. Brophy has to sit with her at night, she won't do it without her rosary beads. Don't ask me why, but I guess Mrs. Brophy has heard her say things in her sleep."

"What are you grinning at?" said Minnie.

"Something that might amuse you. Should, if you haven't lost your sense of humor."

"What?"

"Mrs. Brophy told me that Sadie thinks there's a ghost in the garage."

"*Us?* You mean to say she knew about us?"

"No, positively not. This ghost has only been there in the past year or so. It's over three years since you and I've been up there. This is completely imaginary."

"Unless one of your maids is going in for hanky-panky."

"Which one? Agnes, the cook? Or Mary Chapman? Agnes couldn't walk that far, and Mary could walk that far but who'd want her to?"

"I guess Sadie has nightmares."

"Of course she has. Delirium tremens nightmares. But I thought it would amuse you, ghosts in the garage."

"What if that had ever got out about us? Think what a sensation we'd have caused."

"I often think of the sensations we caused, Minnie."

"Never mind, never mind," she said. "Well, this is the first good talk we've had in three years."

"Yes, and think how many years since we had such a good talk fully dressed."

"I won't think about that, Buz, and don't you." She got up and left him as the crowd began to gather for the meeting of the Lantenengo County Red Cross Executive Committee, Dr. Wallace P. Drummond, chairman.

6

A new doctor, wholly new to the town, created a place for himself that was made up in part of Buz Drummond's former position and in part his own. "I've only been practicing a little over thirty years," Buz said one evening at the Gibbsville Club. "Well, not quite forty. But already I'm obsolete, thanks to three things. Psychiatry. The wonder drugs. And the New Deal. If I were just getting out of medical school, knowing all I was supposed to know in 1921, I couldn't get a license to practice today. Not in this State. Most of us my age won't admit that, but it's true. You take thoracic surgery. I watched a man do an operation the other day that in my early days, if he'd have attempted it he'd have been expelled from the Gibbsville Hospital, kicked out of the Medical Society. It was a heart operation. Oh, our men operated on the heart, true, but this man went in and took care of the obstruction and then put a sleeve over the aorta—too complicated to explain to a layman—but the patient will live ten more years. In my day we'd have let him die, without any surgery. I started out with a Dodge coupe, but in reality I was one of the last of the horse-and-buggy doctors. Nowadays if a patient is too sick for an office call they send him to the hospital. Doctors are just too damn busy to make house calls, not to mention the fact that there aren't enough nurses to take care of private patients at home. Not to mention the bloody awful expense, and the fact that the hospitals have the facilities that aren't available at home. When I was starting out, though, if I sent a patient to the hospital the family would begin to wonder whether Pop had made a will."

"You mentioned the New Deal. Where does that come in?"

"Socialized medicine."

"But you're holding the line against that, you and the County Medical Society."

"Every two years we elect a new president—the same old new president. Me. But this year I'm not running again. I'd get licked, and I want to retire undefeated, bow out gracefully, if not graciously. You see, Arthur, the Society is still made up of men like me, who can outvote the new men, but every two years the new fellows are a little stronger. Officially the Society is opposed to socialized medicine, but the new young men are just waiting for a form of it that will be acceptable to them. And it won't be acceptable to me. The monthly meetings aren't what they used to be, a few nonentities getting together to talk shop, swap a few dirty stories and adjourn to the Elks for beer. We get a bigger attendance these days and some of the best men. And they're so damned serious. Oh, hell, Arthur, I'm on the shelf. Do you know that two doctors in this town have telephones in their cars?"

"No, but I'm not surprised."

"It doesn't surprise me either, except that I came across a discussion in the minutes of a meeting back around 1902, 1903. Old Dr. Wainwright, long since dead, led the discussion. The question was should doctors charge a fifty-cent fee for talking to patients over the phone. The vote was thirty-five to one against charging them. Today we charge two dollars, to those who can afford it. Wainwright brought up the point because he hadn't decided whether to put in a phone or not, and he wanted to be sure it would pay for itself. He was outvoted on the fifty-cent fee, so he didn't put in a phone. Now nearly every doctor in town has an office phone, a residence phone, an unlisted residence phone, and the answering service. And two of them, phones in their cars. How things have changed!"

"Yes."

"I was never very fond of Malloy. Too brusque, too domineer-

ing. But he was nice to me when I first started out, and I remember him trying to get me to stop smoking. A doctor must
rely on all his senses, he said, and one of the most important is
the sense of smell. Smoking ruins your sense of smell, he said.
The reason I bring him up is how can you smell a patient over
the phone, sitting in your car? I'm older now than Malloy was
when he died, but he practically belongs in the Dark Ages, and
where does that leave me? Sitting here in this club, waiting for
our bridge partners. Standing on the first tee, waiting for the
other members of a foursome. I have an M.D. on my automobile license plate, and sometimes I think I get it under false pretenses. However, last Sunday coming up from the club a state
policeman pulled me out of a traffic tie-up. He saw my license
plate and escorted me to an auto accident. I was too late for one
poor son of a bitch, but I stopped another from bleeding to
death. Not that a chiropractor couldn't have done the same. Or
a first-class Boy Scout."

"How are you coming along with your book?"

"Oh, you've heard about my book? Well, I've been making a
lot of notes. I have a dozen school tablets filled with them, and
I could go on filling them with the things I remember. The
trouble is I'm not sure what kind of a book I want to write."

"At least you know what kind you don't want to write."

"What kind is that?" said Buz Drummond.

"Like that piece of tripe Dr. Malloy's son wrote a few years
ago," said McHenry.

"Oh, but that was a novel. Fiction. He made all that up."

"But he certainly gave this town a black eye."

"That's what I don't understand, Arthur. If it was all made
up, what were people so sore about?"

"He gave the town a black eye, that's why. And not one
damn thing he wrote about actually happened."

"That's what I said. But you as a lawyer, and I as a physician, we know that things *like* them happened."

"Oh, hell, as far as that goes, I know some things that if
young Malloy ever heard about them . . ."

"So do I, Arthur," said Dr. Drummond.

THE CAPE COD

LIGHTER

APPEARANCES

Howard Ambrie stopped the car at the porte-cochere to let his wife out, then proceeded to the garage. The M-G was already there, the left-hand door was open, and the overhead lamp was burning, indicating that their daughter was home. Ambrie put the sedan in its customary place, snapped out the light, rang down the door, and walked slowly toward the house. He stopped midway and looked at the sky. The moon was high and plain, the stars were abundant.

In the kitchen his wife had poured him a glass of milk, which rested on the table with a piece of sponge cake. "I'll be able to play tomorrow after all," said Howard Ambrie. "There's hardly a cloud in the sky."

"Oh, then you've thought it over," said Lois Ambrie.

"Thought what over?"

"Jack Hill's funeral. You're not going."

"Was I thinking it over?"

"You said at dinner that you hadn't decided whether to go or not," said Lois Ambrie.

"That was only because I knew the McIvers planned to go."

"I don't understand your reasoning," she said.

"Well, then I'll explain it to you. Peter and Cathy *want* to go to the funeral. I don't. No reason why I should. But

I didn't want to inflict my *not* wanting to go on their *wanting* to go. Impose, I guess, would be a better word. Influence them. Or for that matter, take away their pleasure in going to the service. I said I hadn't made up my mind, and so there was no discussion about it. If I'd said I definitely wasn't going, or if I'd definitely said I wasn't going, they would have wanted to know why."

"What would you have told them?"

"What would I have told them? I'd have told them that I'd much rather play golf tomorrow."

"Well, that would have started a discussion, all right," she said.

"I know it would," he said. "And I know what the discussion would have been. Wasn't Jack Hill one of my best friends? Couldn't I play golf after the service? And so forth. But I disposed of all that by simply saying I hadn't made up my mind."

"You disposed of it as far as the McIvers were concerned, but will you tell *me* why you're not going?"

"I don't mind telling you. In the first place, I've never considered Jack Hill one of my best friends. He wasn't. He was a lifelong acquaintance, a contemporary, our families were always friends, or friendly. And if you wanted to stretch a point, we were related. All of which you know. But in a town this size, at least until just before the War, damn near everybody is related in some way or other."

"Yes, and damn near everybody will be at that funeral tomorrow," she said. "Therefore your absence will be noticed."

"Maybe it will. I thought of that. But the fact is, I never liked Jack and he never liked me. If the circumstances were reversed, I'm sure he'd be playing golf tomorrow. There won't be many more days we can play this year. I noticed driving by this afternoon, they've taken the pins out of the cups, and I wouldn't be surprised if they filled in the holes. The golf shop is boarded up for the winter. In fact, Charley closed up a week ago and went to Florida. I hope there's enough hot water for a shower. I hate to come in after playing golf in this weather and find no hot water."

"You're playing in the morning," she said.

"Playing in the morning. We're meeting at ten o'clock, playing eighteen holes. Having something to eat. Probably the usual club sandwiches. And then playing bridge. I'll be home around five, I should think."

"Who are you playing with?"

"Same three I play with every Saturday, and they won't be missed at Jack's funeral."

"No, they certainly won't be. None of Jack's old friends, and none of your old friends, either, not in that foursome."

"Lois, you talk as though the whole of Suffolk County were going to be at the church tomorrow, checking to see who stayed away. Are *you* going to the funeral?"

"Yes, I'm going. Or I was. I don't know whether I want to go without you."

"Oh, hell, call up somebody and go with *them*."

"No, if you're not going, I won't. That would make your not going so much more noticeable. 'Where's Howard?' 'Playing golf.' "

"Listen, I'm not going, so don't try to persuade me."

"I think you ought to go," she said.

"No."

"I'll make one more try. I'm *asking* you to go," she said.

"And my answer is I think you're being God damn unreasonable about this. Jack Hill and I have known each other over fifty years, we were thrown together by age and financial circumstances. His family and my family had about the same amount of dough. But when we got older and could choose our friends, he never chose me and I never chose him. We were never enemies, but maybe if we had been we'd have found out why we didn't like each other. Then maybe we could have been friends. But we never had any serious quarrel. We never had a God damn thing."

"He was an usher at our wedding."

"I *knew* you'd bring that up. That was twenty-five years ago, and I had to have him and he had to have me because our parents were friends. It was one of those automatic things in a small town. I couldn't ask one of the clammers, and he couldn't ask one of the potato farmers, but that's *all* it was. And since you bring that up, about being ushers, Celia didn't ask me to be a pallbearer or whatever the hell she's having. Celia has more sense about this than you have."

"There aren't going to be any pallbearers, and you know it."

"All right, I do know it. And she's very sensible, Celia."

"I'm asking you again, Howard, please. Put off your golf till after lunch, and go to this funeral with me. It isn't much to ask."

"Why do you care so much whether I go or not?"

"Because I don't want Celia knowing that you stayed away."

"Oh, Christ. All right. Although why you care what Celia knows or doesn't know—you and Celia were never that good friends."

"But you will go?"

"Yes, I said I would, and I will. But you certainly screwed up my weekend."

"You can play in the afternoon and Sunday."

"Father O'Sullivan can't play Saturday afternoon, he has to hear confessions, and he can't play Sunday at all. And Joe Bushmill is going skeet-shooting this Sunday. It's not only my schedule you loused up."

"I'm sorry about that, Howard, but I do appreciate it."

"Oh, sure. You have no idea how you complicate things. We had to get a fourth for bridge, because O'Sullivan has to be in church at three o'clock. And now they'll have to get someone to take my place at golf *and* bridge."

"I'll do something for you sometime."

"Why didn't you make your big pitch before tonight?"

"Because I took for granted that you'd be going to the funeral. I just took it for granted."

"I suppose the same way that people took for granted that Jack Hill was a friend of mine. Well, he wasn't. I'm going to bed. Oh, Amy's home. The M-G's in the garage."

"I know. Goodnight, dear."

"Goodnight," he said. He bent down and kissed her cheek.

Light showed on the floor beneath Amy's bedroom door, and he knocked gently. "Amy? You awake?" he said softly.

"Father? Come in."

She was sitting up in bed, and when he entered she took off her reading glasses. "Hi," she said.

"What are you reading?" he said.

"Detective story. Who won?"

"Oh, your mother and I took them. We always do, at their house, and they usually win when they come here." He sat on the chaise-longue. "As Mr. McCaffery says, what kind of a day's it been today?"

"Fridays are always easier than other days. The children seem to behave better on Friday. That is, their behavior is better, probably because they're in a better mood. Their schoolwork isn't as good, but you can't have everything."

"Do you like teaching?"

"Not very much, but I like the children."

"Well, it's nice having you home for a year."

"Thank you, Father. It's nice being home."

"Is it?" he said.

"Have a cigarette?" She held up a package.

"No thanks. You didn't answer my question."

"I know I didn't. Yes, it's nice being home."

"But that's as far as you'll commit yourself?" he said.

"That's as far as I want to commit myself."

"You mean you don't want to think more deeply than that?"

"Yes, I guess that's what I mean. I'm comfortable here, I have my job, my car to run around in, and I had no idea we had so many detective stories. This one was copyrighted 1924."

"There are some older than that, early Mary Roberts Rinehart," he said. "Believe I will have one of your cigarettes." He caught the pack she tossed him and lit a cigarette. "Are you making any plans for next year?"

"Not exactly. I may get married again. I may not."

"This time you ought to have children right away."

"It wouldn't be so good if I had a child now, would it?"

"It might have kept you together, Amy, a child. We had you the first year, your mother and I."

"Father, you're practically implying that if you hadn't had me—"

"I know what I'm implying," he said. "And I know you're no fool. You know it's often been touch and go with your mother and I. You've seen that."

(8)

"I guess it is with everybody. But a child wouldn't have kept Dave and me together. Nothing would."

"Well, what really separated you?"

"Well, it wasn't his fault. I fell in love with someone else."

"The man you're thinking of marrying?"

"No."

"The man you're thinking of marrying is that doctor in Greenport?"

"Yes."

"But the man you left Dave for was someone else?"

"Yes."

"And what's happened to him? He's gone out of your life?"

She looked at him sharply. "Yes."

"Why? Was he married?"

"Yes."

"Where did you know him? At Cornell?"

"No, Father. And don't ask me any more questions, please. You voluntarily said you wouldn't ask me any questions, you promised that when I came home after my divorce."

"I did, but with the understanding that when you were ready to tell us, you would. It isn't just idle curiosity, Amy. Your mother and I have a right to know those things, if only to keep you from making the same mistakes all over again."

"I won't make that mistake over again. And I'm not ready to tell you what happened to me with Dave."

"As far as I know, Dave was a hell of a nice boy."

"He was, and is, but I wasn't a hell of a nice girl. No father likes to face that fact about his daughter, but there it is."

"You're not a tart, you're not a chippy."

"No. But that's not all there is besides virgins, Father."

(9)

"Oh, I know that."

"Well, when does a girl get to be a tart in your estimation? Is it a question of how many men she sleeps with?"

"It most certainly is, yes."

"How many?"

"Yes, I walked into that one, didn't I? Well, a girl who sleeps with more than two men before she gets married, she's on her way. I can see a girl having an affair the first time she thinks she's in love. And then the second time, when she's more apt to be really in love. But the next time she'd better be damned sure, or she's going to be a pushover for everybody."

"Well—that's more or less my record. The second time was also the man I left Dave for."

"Oh, you had an affair and married Dave and continued to have this other affair?"

"Yes."

"What's going to prevent your having an affair with this same guy after you marry your doctor? . . . You had an affair with a married man before you married Dave. He sounds like a real son of a bitch."

"I guess maybe he was, although I didn't think so. I guess he was, though."

"You're not still seeing him?"

"No. I did after I divorced Dave, but not after I began dating the doctor."

"You're—to use an old-fashioned word—faithful to the doctor?"

"Oh, you're so smart, Father. You've tricked me into admitting I'm having an affair with the doctor. The answer is yes."

"Hell, I knew you were probably having an affair with the doctor. I'm no fool, either, you know. Well, it's been a very interesting conversation between father and daughter.

It's a good thing I'm not *my* father, or you'd be—well, you wouldn't be here."

"No, but we wouldn't have had this conversation, either."

"You have a point. Goodnight, dear." He kissed her cheek and she squeezed his hand. "There *is* that," he said. "We wouldn't have had this conversation. Goodnight again."

"Goodnight, Father," she said.

The girl sat in her bed, holding her glasses loosely with her right hand, her book with her left, both hands lying on the pink comforter. Her mother came in. "What was that all about?" said Lois Ambrie.

"Our conversation? Oh, mostly about Dave and me."

"He didn't say anything about Jack Hill?"

"No."

"I'll be glad when Jack is buried and out of the way."

"I know," said Amy.

"Your father is getting closer to the truth, Amy."

"I guess he is."

"I had a very difficult time persuading him to go to the funeral tomorrow."

"Why did you bother?"

"Appearances. 'Why didn't Howard Ambrie go to Jack Hill's funeral?' They'd be talking about that for a month, and somebody'd be sure to say something to Celia. And then Celia'd start asking herself questions."

"I wonder. I think Mrs. Hill stopped asking questions a long time ago. She should have. I wasn't the only one he played around with."

"You can be so casual about it. 'Played around with.' And you haven't shown the slightest feeling about him, his dying."

"I didn't show any because I haven't got any. Other

than relief. I'm not grief-stricken that he died, Mother. As long as he was alive I was afraid to marry Joe. Now I think I can marry Joe and settle down in Greenport and be what I always wanted to be. But not while Jack was alive. That's the effect he had on me."

"He was no good," said Lois Ambrie. "Strange how your father knew that without knowing why."

"I know why," said Amy. "Jack was the kind of man that husbands are naturally suspicious of. Father was afraid Jack would make a play for you. Instead he made a play for me, but Father never gave that a thought."

"I suppose so. And in your father's eyes it would be just as bad for me to cover up for you as it would have been for me to have had an affair with Jack. I'll be glad when he's out of the way. Really glad when you can marry Joe."

"Did you go over and call on Mrs. Hill?"

"I went over this afternoon, but she wasn't seeing anyone. Fortunately."

"She *is* grief-stricken?"

"I don't think it's that. No, I don't think it's that. As you said a moment ago, Celia probably stopped asking questions a long time ago. I'd put it another way. That she's known for years about Jack. Now she doesn't want to see anybody because whatever she's feeling, she doesn't want anybody to see *her*. Grief, or relief. Maybe she doesn't even know yet what she feels. Fear, maybe. Whatever he was, she stuck with him all those years, and suddenly he's gone and she's fifty-two or -three. I don't know what's in Celia's mind, but I'm glad I'm not her. Did you see Joe tonight?"

"Yes, I had dinner with him. We had dinner at his sister's house in Southold. Spaghetti. She's a very good cook."

(*12*)

"That will be quite something, an Ambrie marrying an Italian boy. Will you have to turn Catholic?"

"I will if he wants me to. If it means that much to him. I'm not sure it does, but it would probably make a difference to his family."

"Can he marry a divorced woman? I have no idea what the Catholic church says on that."

"We haven't discussed it, so I don't know either."

"Your father's great friends with the new Catholic priest, O'Sullivan. They play golf and bridge together every Saturday."

"So I gather. When the time comes, whatever they say I'll do."

"It would be quite a feather in their cap, an Ambrie turning Catholic."

"They may not see it that way. I understand they can be very tough about some things."

"Well, I suppose it's their turn. Goodness knows I still can't get used to the idea of having one in the White House. Can I get you a glass of milk or anything?"

"No thanks, Mother."

"Then I guess I'll be off to bed."

"Mother?"

"What?"

"I'm sorry I caused you and Father so much trouble. You especially. All those lies you had to tell."

"Oh, that's all right. It's over now. And it was really harder on your father. He never knew why he didn't like that man."

"And *you* couldn't tell him, *could* you, Mother?"

"What?"

"Oh, Mother."

Lois Ambrie looked at her daughter. "Is that another

(13)

detective story you're reading? You mustn't get carried away, Amy." She smiled. "Goodnight, dear," she said, and closed the door.

THE BUCKET
OF BLOOD

The place had several nicknames before Jay bought it and it more or less permanently became Jay's. Once it had been known as the Bucket of Blood, a name that did not stick because it was not really all that tough, and because there already was another Bucket of Blood in another part of town that deserved that name. The original, genuine Bucket of Blood was in one of the Italian sections of town, a neighborhood known as the Gravel Hole, that was entirely populated by the families of day laborers who worked on the navvy gangs for the railroads. They were miserably poor, scorned by the Italian grocers and fruiterers and barbers and cobblers, and so feared by the town police that they ignored everything that went on in the Gravel Hole. "Let them settle it among themselves," was the attitude. When there was a Black Hand War, which would break out every two or three years, and word of a homicide would leak out of the Gravel Hole, the town police would notify the State Constabulary, who were good cops and among whom were men who spoke Italian, some of whom were themselves Italian. The staties would put on civilian clothes and drive to the Bucket of Blood, which was the first building at the north end of the Gravel Hole and considered to be the deadline for outsiders. In a couple of hours the staties would usually come out with a prisoner, and he was usually the murderer. If they did not get the right man it was because the guilty party had had time to hop a coal train and get out of town. The only outsiders who were tolerated in the Gravel Hole were Father Guglielmo, the pastor, and Dr. Malloy, who spoke Italian, but even Dr. Malloy carried a gun. Other outsiders who had business in the Gravel Hole would have to wait on the steps of the Bucket of Blood, and sometimes that was as far as they got.

That was the original Bucket of Blood, and to give the name to Jay's place was rather unfair, although not entirely so. Jay's offered whiskey, beer, and, in the winter, a place to come in out of the cold. You could not get a sandwich at Jay's; the only edibles were bowls of salted peanuts on the bar and on the tables in the two back rooms. Jay had an alarm clock on the back bar and on the wall a large Pennsylvania Railroad calendar, showing a passenger train coming out of the Horseshoe Curve. Otherwise the saloon was devoid of decoration; there was no name on the windows, not even a ladies' entrance sign on the side door.

The neighborhood was as rough as any in town except the Gravel Hole. Within two blocks were four whorehouses, all owned by the same unmarried couple but differing in price and clientele and in the youth and beauty and cleanliness of the staff. The tracks of the Reading Railway ran parallel with the street, behind a fence which was broken by gates opening for spurs of track that led into warehouses and lumber yards. There were two blacksmith shops and half a dozen garages in the neighborhood, an old factory that was used as a drop by the beer mob, and such small businesses as a welder's shop, the shop of a man who repaired band instruments, a tinsmith's, a plumber's, and the headquarters of other artisans who had to make a lot of noise by day and went home quietly at night. No one had any legitimate business in Jay's neighborhood after seven in the evening, and the municipality spent very little money in lighting up the area. When darkness came the visitors to the neighborhood were there to drink or hire a woman, or both, and if they could have paid for better whiskey or better women, they would have been some place else. Nevertheless Jay managed to keep out of serious trouble.

He began by letting it be quickly known that he gave good value. He would explain how he cut his booze to anyone who asked, and he made a point of calling it booze in the aggregate and an individual drink he called a steam. Alcohol, caramel, and water were the principal ingredients of his booze, and he charged twenty-five cents for a shot in a two-ounce glass that he filled to the brim. He drank it himself out of the same bottle he poured for the customers, and he drank moderately but steadily all night long. "The party I get my white from, my alcohol, he knows I drink it myself," he often said. "If he wants me to stay in business, he gotta give me good stuff." The house bought generously; if two men were drinking together, the house bought every third round; if there were six at a table in the back room, the house bought the seventh drink. Nearly everyone could establish credit after a third or fourth visit to Jay's, and he would carry a heavy drinker even though he knew the customer had exhausted his credit elsewhere. But he made no effort to hide his preference for booze drinkers over the customers who drank beer. "I can't help it if the beer comes to me with ether in it. That's the way it comes. I'd have to charge a man a half a check for a good glass of beer, supposing I could get it in the first place. I bet you if you went to every joint in town right now, this minute, you wouldn't be able to find a barrel of real beer. Maybe the Elks. I understand they get delivery, but you have to be an Elk or with an Elk. I'm talking about where an ordinary fellow can go in and order a glass of beer, pay ten, fifteen cents for it. What they do at the breweries, they make good beer, then they take the alcohol out of it to stay out of trouble with the law. Then they get word that it's okay to make a shipment, and they quick needle it with ether. So a man comes in my place and drinks ten or fifteen beers and he's putting away a lot of ether. Bad for the disposition. I get more trouble out of my beer drinkers than I do out of my booze drinkers. They get sleepy and they try to stay awake and all they get is disagreeable. I'll tell you something else. Nine times out of ten a man don't know the difference between near beer and good beer. Nine times out of ten. If they want the taste of beer, they ought to drink Bevo. If they want a belt out of it, they ought to drink a boilermaker. I don't make a nickel out of my beer drinkers, but I have to accommodate them. Most of them don't have no place else to go, and I can't be so choosy."

Jay was *formal* with his beer trade. He gave them no cause for complaint; he was polite to them, and he would listen, hear them out, when they tried to hold him with conversation; but when he bought them a beer he would not drink with them, and when they tried to buy him a beer he would say, "That's all right," or "No thanks, it bloats me." But he would drink steam after steam with his booze customers, and he was such a little man to have that capacity. He was in his middle thirties, but already the upper half of his thin little face was shaded blue and his eyes were teary. He would lift a shot glass, take a breath, knock back the liquor, stare straight ahead as it went down, take another breath, and plunge the glass in the rinsing tank. He never said so, but he wanted and needed every drink. He seemed

(18)

grateful for the company of booze drinkers, and he was; he had a personal superstition against taking a drink by himself. He respected solitary drinking in others; that was how some men preferred to drink. But he knew that he was in control of his own drinking only so long as he could make a rule about it and stick to it. The booze was there, gallons of it, and one little nip more or less would not do him any harm, but if it meant breaking his rule it could be, would be, the sign that he had lost control, and no one had ever seen him in that condition. Well, no one in this town.

Jay's last name, Detweiler, was fairly common in the town. There was a Detweiler a butcher in the west end of town; Detweiler Brothers had a furniture store and undertaking parlor on the main drag, out of the high-rent district; Clara Detweiler taught French in the public high school; Billy Detweiler had had half a season at third base with Reading, in the International League, before breaking his leg; Isaac Detweiler was janitor and night watchman of the Citizens Bank, a former fifer with the Spanish-American War Veterans Fife & Drum Corps. There had been Detweilers in the town for seventy-five years, and they had paid their bills and minded their own business, attended the Lutheran or the Reformed church, and they were respected. Jay had no idea of their existence when he arrived in town, nor had he had any intention of getting off the train. He was on his way to a county fair sixty miles away to join a carnival show in the fall of 1919, when he was stricken with acute appendicitis. The conductor put him off the train at the first town that had a hospital, having wired ahead to have an ambulance meet the train. The appendix ruptured while Jay was riding to the hospital and he nearly died of peritonitis. It was inferred from papers in his pockets that he was some connection of the local Detweiler family, and he became temporarily the beneficiary of all those years of respectability. He was in the surgical ward for three weeks, a free patient, and by the time he was able to convince the hospital people that he was not a Detweiler of Gibbsville and that the eighteen dollars in his pocket was all the money he had in the world, he had also made a good impression with his courage and appreciation for everything that was done for him.

"What are you going to do when you get out of here? You're going to have to wear a belt for six months, maybe a year," said the doctor.

"A belt? What kind of a belt?"

"A surgical belt. You won't be able to do any heavy work. Not that you have been, judging by your muscles."

"No, I always stayed away from that, if I could."

"But you spent a lot of time outdoors."

"I sure did, Doc. I sure did."

"What *do* you do?"

Jay smiled. "Well, I didn't exactly lie to you, but I didn't exactly tell you the truth either. I told you I was a salesman. Well, I sell, but I don't sell carpet sweepers or kitchen cabinets. I'm a pitchman."

"A pitchman. Oh, yes, I've heard of that. With a side show, a carnival."

"That's correct, sir."

"Three-card monte and that sort of thing?"

"Well—if necessary."

"Hasn't been very profitable for you. You didn't have very much money on you when you were admitted."

"I was on my way to Bloomsburg, to the Fair. I had a job waiting for me with a friend of mine, but he don't know where I am. But I'll get in touch with him. He has an address in New York City."

(20)

"How old are you, Detweiler?"

"I'm just turned thirty."

"Just turned thirty. Why don't you turn honest? You seem like an intelligent fellow, and I guess you have to be sharp-witted to make a living in your profession, if I can call it that."

"And quick on your feet."

"I'll bet. You're quick with the booze, too, aren't you?"

"It's a weakness of mine."

"Yes, and I know what the other one is, too."

"How could you tell that? I'm clean as a whistle."

"The tattooing."

"Oh, Norma. Christ, that was in Muncie, Indiana, a long time ago. I'll bet she weighs a ton by now. Undying love. Well, she got J. D. tattooed on her rump. Not very big, about a half an inch high. She wanted it, I didn't ask her. But she couldn't have it too big. She done the dance of the seven veils and she had to cover up my brand with makeup, working. Norma. I was twenty years of age and I guess if she leveled with me she was thirty. The first real woman I ever had. Gave me up for a knife thrower, Captain Jack Montague. Johnny Muntz was the real handle, but I let him be Jack Montague, he was awful handy with them shivs."

"You're going to need some money. What do you plan to do?"

"I'm going to pay back this hospital. And you."

"You don't owe me anything. I'm on surgical duty. But you're expected to pay the hospital for medicines. Your belt."

"That I intend to. I'll work here, an orderly, till I'm off the nut. Of course what I could do, you give me a deck of cards and let me go upstairs where the rich patients are."

"Wouldn't *that* be nice?"

"No, I wouldn't do that here. You people here saved my life. Just give me a cot to sleep on and my scoff, my three meals a day, and I'll work as long as they say till I'm in the clear. Meantime I can get in touch with my buddy through *Billboard* and maybe he has something lined up. I can put the arm on him for a little walking-around money, *if* he answers my letter."

"You can't be an orderly. Too much lifting, and a lot of things you'd have to learn. But maybe you could run an elevator, something of that sort."

"It's a funny thing. I want to get out of here, but all the same I got a feeling for this place. I was ready to cash in, wasn't I?"

"Yes, you were."

"I come to in the ambulance, heard that bell ringing and I got it through my head, that nurse, never seen me before, nobody ever seen me before, but they're doing all they can for me. Then I guess the thing popped, huh? And the next I remember I was in a bed with clean sheets. Thirsty! God, I was thirsty. For water, not booze. Water. And I hurt good . . . That conductor, *he* was a nice fellow. *He* went to a lot of trouble. You know, Doc, I had him pegged for a mark. I only had eighteen bucks in my kick, and we don't generally take a risk with railroad conductors, but this guy I was gonna make a pitch. And then what'd he do? He saved my life."

"Well, young fellow, think about it."

"I do."

"Because it's something to think about. These were all people that you call marks. Easy marks, I guess that means. But one after another they helped save your life. You should have seen the pus in your belly. So do think about it, Detweiler, and stop being a wisenheimer."

Jay, seated in a white enameled iron chair, ran the elevator, worked off his debt to the hospital and made himself agreeable to the staff and patients. They were sorry to see him leave, but he had located the crap game that is to be found in every town the size of Gibbsville. In his cake-eater clothes, now not fitting him too well, he was obviously neither a cop nor a muscle man, and he was admitted to the game. He quickly identified the professionals in the game, and he bet their way; right when they bet right, wrong when they bet wrong. He was not interested in handling the dice himself and he passed up his turn; but he nursed his $10 case money until he had won $100, and then quietly departed. He was followed into the alley, and he knew it. He suddenly stopped and turned. "Get any closer and I'll rip your gut," he said.

"I ain't after your dough. I want to talk with you."

"You can talk standing in front of the restrunt, around the corner."

"All right, I'll meet you there."

The stranger, whom Jay recognized from the crap table, led the way to the Greek's all-night restaurant, which lighted up the sidewalk. He offered Jay a cigarette, which Jay declined.

"I oughtn't to smoke either. I just got out of the hospital, too."

"I don't remember you," said Jay.

"I be surprised if you did. You want to make a couple dollars?"

"Always do, but first who *are* you?"

"My name is Bartlett. Red Bartlett. I live here in town."

"Doing what?"

"Well, this and that."

(23)

"Like time? You done a little time, I know that much."

"Yeah, I been in the cooler. Nothing big. Breaking and entering. Assault and battery. I guess you done a couple of bits yourself."

"Uh-huh. I was hung for murder, and I did twenty years for holding up a stagecoach. What do you want, fellow?"

"I seen the way you were playing them dice. You look to me like a fellow was trying to get enough to leave town."

"And you got a proposition that me and you go in it together, we cut it up, and I leave town."

"You're pretty cute," said Bartlett.

"I'm cuter than that. They don't pin it on you, but they pin it on me because I blow town. Mister, I just as soon they didn't see me talking to you, anybody as dumb as you are."

"Six or seven hundred dollars, your end. Five, anyway."

"Listen, God damn you, I wanted to blow this town tomorrow, and now I can't. A thick-headed son of a bitch like you, you're gonna go ahead with this, whatever it is, and now I gotta stay. I gotta stay, and I gotta be able to account for every minute. You son of a bitch, I wish I never saw you. Goodnight, mister." Jay entered the restaurant and sat at the counter, drinking coffee and eating the bland filler of custard pie, until daylight. He went to his rooming house, carefully reminding the landlady of the time in case questions should be asked later. The precaution was unnecessary: at four o'clock in the morning Bartlett had already been shot and killed while resisting arrest during the burglary of Detweiler Brothers furniture store—undertaking parlor. It was a Saturday night, the beginning of the month, when instalment payments were due, and there was more than $4,000 in the strongbox to be banked on Monday

(24)

morning. Bartlett had once worked as a helper on Detweilers' delivery van, and even then had been fired for clumsiness.

Jay went back to the crap game that afternoon and watched it for a while without playing. It was a different game. The night before it had been professionals and working men with the gambling itch; today it was high school kids, the easiest kind of marks but the worst kind of trouble makers, who rightly suspected each other of using the tees, the miss-outs and plain ordinary loaded dice. Bad news. The house collected a nickel a pass, and the professionals stayed out of the game, waiting while one or two of the kids became big winners and cleaned out the small bankrolls, Mom's money from the sugar bowl. The professionals sat against the wall, staring at the caps of their shoes until they heard a kid say, "I'm shooting five dollars. Five dollars open here." The professionals jumped down from their high wire chairs; the men had been separated from the boys.

Soon the game resembled that of the night before, with the appearance of the winners from the night before and the losers who had promoted new bankrolls.

"Two to one no six," said a man.

"He sixes," said Jay, and he was back in the game. It was a long evening, less profitable than the previous one, but when at last he was $50 ahead on the night, he quit. Once again he was followed into the alley, this time by two men who immediately took him by the arms. They were two of the men he had identified as professionals. "Where we going?" said Jay.

"Up the street."

"Where up the street?"

One man laughed. "They call it the Bucket of Blood."

"And what happens there?" said Jay.

"We have a couple of shots," said the man.

"Out of a gun, or a bottle?" said Jay.

"Oh, a bottle. Why did you say a gun?"

"My little joke," said Jay.

"Maybe we'll throw you in front of a train, but we don't carry a gun."

Immediately Jay broke loose. "Well, I carry this," he said. He backed away, and they could see his knife, which he held as though he were shaking hands with it. "One of you gets it for sure, right up the gut," he said.

"Cut it out, Detweiler. We got business to talk."

"Like throwing me in front of a train. Lousy bastards."

"That was kidding. We both got guns, if we'd of wanted to knock you off."

"And I'm a cop," said the less talkative of the men.

"A cop?"

"You should of known that."

"A town cop?"

"A town cop. Put away that sticker and we go have a drink. Go on back to the dice game and ask anybody if I'm not a cop. Chapman, my name is."

"What kind of cops do they have in this town?" said Jay. "You *are* a cop. I can tell it now, but I didn't before."

"You're a sick man, Detweiler," said Chapman. "The two of us could make a run for it and I could shoot you as quick as I gave it to Bartlett."

"You gave it to Bartlett?" said Jay.

"Yeah."

"Who's this other fellow?" said Jay.

"Me? You heard them say my name. Dave Bangs."

"I know both your names, but what do *you* do, Bangs?"

"I hustle a buck," said Bangs.

"This town is wider open than I thought," said Jay.

"This town ain't wide open, only a couple streets," said Chapman. "You satisfied now, or do we run and shoot?"

"I'll say one thing about this town. It got the coldest-blooded cop I ever run up against. All right, buy me a drink."

The whiskey was so bad that Jay was almost afraid to finish his drink even after he had diluted it with water. "My first since I got out of the hospital," he said.

"The beer's even worse," said Chapman. "I'll send you around a couple of pints of drug-store rye tomorrow."

"Make it the first thing in the morning," said Jay. "Tomorrow's get-away day for me."

"Well, maybe. Listen to us first," said Chapman.

"Listening," said Jay.

"I owe you a favor, Detweiler. When I seen you talking to Bartlett I figured he was ready for something. What, I didn't know, but it was pretty near time he needed money."

"Where were you when I was talking to Bartlett?"

"Across the street. I follied you out in the alley. I seen you pull the toe-jabber on him, too. You know how to use that thing, don't you?"

"Now that I'm talking to a cop I gotta watch what I say."

"All right," said Chapman.

"This here guy's the smartest detective on the force," said Bangs.

"Out of how many?" said Jay.

"Two," said Chapman. "But last night didn't take much brains. You gave Bartlett a no, and all I had to do was hang on to him. I no sooner saw which way he was headed than I knew where he was going to."

"Tell me some more about how smart you are, Chapman. How did you know I wouldn't go in with Bartlett?"

"Well, I heard you call him a son of a bitch. Your voice carries, for a little fellow. Secondly, why should a smart little guy like you go in with a dumbhead like Bartlett? What was the percentage for you?"

"Yeah. He said my take would be five or six hundred. I understand there was close to five thousand dollars at the furniture store. He was a muttonhead, all right."

"He sure was. I went to school with him till fifth grade, he never got no further. They had him in Glen Mills for a couple years—"

"What's Glen Mills?"

"Reformatory. He come out of there worse than he went in. Strong as an ox, but used to beat up his old lady, a scrubwoman over at the Pennsy station. Kids with paper routes. A hooker down the street, she had him arrested for a. and b. He broke into a couple stores and we sent him up on one. He was what you call a habitual criminal, and if he ever had a hundred dollars in his pocket, I doubt it. Maybe a hundred, but I'll bet he never had two."

"Never two," said Bangs.

"No, I don't think he did either," said Chapman. "He said to me, the time I put the collar on him, he said, 'I'm gonna excape outa here. Excape. And I'm gonna come down and kick your brains out.' You know what? The warden told me Bartlett was a model prisoner, so model that he *liked* it up on the hill, and I wanta tell you something. Our county jail ain't one of your model prisons. They got rats up there the size of a fox terrier. I was up there one day and I seen a rat this big right on top of the warden's desk. I shot it. The warden was sore as hell, but I don't want to be in the room with a rat that big."

"And Bartlett was even bigger," said Jay.

"Yeah, Red was bigger. But not as smart. How smart are you, Detweiler?"

"Ah, now comes the pitch," said Jay. "Well, I been known to have two hundred dollars in my pocket. Maybe three. Maybe four. But there's a lot of guys smarter than me. Maybe if I was a little smarter I would have been a detective."

"Uh-huh. It's gonna take a week or ten days, but we'll find out how smart you were."

"What's the capital of Michigan?" said Jay.

"Michigan? Detroit, I guess. Why?"

"Illinois?"

"Well, I know it ain't Chicago," said Chapman. "Springfield? Why?"

"The capital of Michigan is Lansing, and you're right about Springfield. That's where the records are kept, and that's what you want to do, isn't it? Find out if they have a sheet on me? They have. But why should I save you the trouble? That's what they pay them clerks for."

"Illinois we know about. You did a year and a day in Joliet, assault with deadly weapon or something like that. We got an answer from Illinois. That was where your sharpie suit came from, Illinois. Some little town. The hospital reported you to us. New York State you're in the clear. Pennsylvania you're in the clear. You had eighteen bucks on you when you went in the hospital, and you were headed for the Bloomsburg Fair. I could run you in now and fingerprint you if I wanted to."

"But you won't, because you want something."

"Yep. You know who owns that crap game, and the joint we were playing in?"

"Well, I thought it was Jerry, the house man. But you ask me the question like that, who does own it? You? You and Bangs?"

"I and Bangs, we both got our fifty percent," said Chapman.

"Nice," said Jay.

"Yeah, but it's all I get. I don't take another nickel. I don't get to collect from the hookers. The saloons. The ordinance violations. Carnivals. Circuses. Taxi companies. Fortune tellers. All the other poolrooms in town. If you started another dice room in town, I'd close you up inside of fifteen minutes. But if you wanted to open up a saloon you'd have to see someone else."

"Well, that's the way it should be. Nobody gets too greedy. And the mayor and them, I guess they cut themselves in on your take," said Jay.

"That's none of your business, Detweiler."

"Right, it isn't," said Jay. "Well, wuddia got in mind for me?"

"We're looking for a man to take Jerry's job, and we gotta have one right away. Jerry got consumption and they're sending him to the sanitarium. The way I see it, winter's coming. That's your worst time of the year, but it's our best. When it's cold weather we got fellows waiting for tables to shoot pool, eleven o'clock in the morning to midnight. We make good money off the pool tables. But the big money, naturally that's the dice room. Payday at the mines. Payday out at the steel mill. And you know who's good for a bundle every week?"

"No."

"These traveling orchestras. Every week beginning October to April they get a famous jazz orchestra, famous ones that make Victrola records, one right after the other. They all like to shoot dice."

"And what you don't get, the hookshops do. I know them traveling orchestras," said Jay. "Do you handle muggles?"

"Them marijuana cigarettes? No, that's handled by a

(30)

fortune teller and one of the hack drivers. Or there's a doctor on Lantenengo Street, if you got the right send-in. Nose candy. The needle. That's pretty quiet around here. Not much call for it except the hookers."

"And Jerry."

"Yeah, Jerry. Cocaine."

"And Dave, here," said Jay.

"Not me," said Dave.

"Have it your own way," said Jay.

"How about you?" said Chapman.

"Not so far, but there's no telling. Is that why you're giving Jerry the boot?"

"Partly. But he has consumption, too," said Chapman.

"He looks it. In other words, he was stealing too much."

"A little too much, yeah. You don't mind a little, but Jerry all of a sudden began stealing ten-fifteen dollars a day."

"A broad," said Jay. "Most likely some broad he was paying for her dope."

"What makes you think I took it?" said Dave.

"Yeah, we're back to that," said Jay. "Well, I guess I knew over a hundred men and women that took it."

"Were you ever wrong?" said Chapman.

"I been wrong."

"And you could be lying, too. I mean about you not taking it," said Chapman.

"I could be lying, but I'm not. It'll come to that, maybe, but my weakness is the booze. That I admit. Even this lousy rat-gut, now I started, I want another. What's the job, and what does it pay?"

"Fifty a week. You're house man. The pool tables, we got a kid racking up and shooting for the house. The dice game, you don't handle the dice. That is, you don't play. You collect on every pass, and a guy craps out, you say who gets the dice. And you keep the game honest."

"How honest?"

"Well, the dice have to hit the board on every roll or it's no dice."

"That's not what I meant."

"I know what you meant. There's two guys you never take the dice away from."

"Dave is one," said Jay. "And a fellow named Sol Green."

"That's correct. Anybody else you get suspicious, you change the dice. But not Dave, and not Sol."

"What if there's trouble? A chump starts a fight?"

"Usually it's an out-of-town guy that starts a fight. If I ain't there, Dave and a couple our friends can handle it. I don't want you pulling that toe-jabber unless the guy goes for you. But the way we handle a squawker, the first thing we do is get him out in the alley. Stop the game, and get that guy out in the alley."

"What about them kids?"

"There's a kid named Lefty Permento, they're all scared of him. We give him ten bucks a week and he shoots pool for free. An ugly bastard, but he sure likes to fight."

"Fifty dollars a week," said Jay. "Should I have a talk with Jerry and see how much I can steal?"

"Don't steal too much. Remember, this is all I got except my hundred and twenty a month from the police department. And it's *all* Dave got."

"And I'm there all day and all night," said Dave.

"Yeah, what are *my* hours?" said Jay.

"You come on at six o'clock. Very seldom you're there after ha' past one, two o'clock in the morning. Saturday and

Sunday afternoon, you come on around one. You get Mondays off."

"Who does the bookkeeping?"

"We do, in our head. The Greek owns the building, we pay the rent in cash. Everything is cash. Electricity. Everything. Dave pays that stuff."

"Well, we'll give it a try," said Jay. "Say, I want to ask you—why do they call this place the Bucket of Blood?"

"Search me," said Chapman. "They got a place the other end of town, down in Little Italy. They call it the Bucket of Blood, too, but there they got reason to. This joint, I don't see how he keeps going."

"Who's the owner?"

"The fellow tending bar, Matt Hostetter. He's on his last legs, too. And yet when I was a kid this place did business. My old man and all the guys from the car shops and the freight yards used to come in here. Why? You want to buy it?"

"You never can tell."

"Just don't buy it with our money," said Chapman.

"*Some* of your money," said Jay.

He ran an orderly game for Chapman and Bangs. The dice players made him prove that he knew what he was doing and what they were doing. He could be witheringly sarcastic, but generally he was good-natured and he talked continually. "The man's shooting twelve dollahs, five covered, seven dollahs open, now two dollahs open. Fi' dollahs he's right coming out, fi' dollahs he's wrong. Shoot the dice, and his point is eight. Eight's the point and it's two to one he eights for fi' dollahs and five to two no eight the hard way. And—crap it is. The dice go to Mulligan. Mulligan, your dice. The man shoots two dollahs and he's covered, and you watch Mulligan run that deuce up to sixteen thousand dol lahs. Well, not this time, Mulligan, a pair of beady little eyes. But Mulligan's a dead game sport and it's two dollahs open. Two dollahs. He's wrong for five dollahs, five dollahs he's wrong coming out and—*no dice!* The money *got* to be on the table, not in the air. No ghost bets here, gentlemen. The money *got* to be on the table. That's better. All right, Mulligan, roll them."

Beginning with his first night, he held out five dollars that was due the house and on big nights he got away with ten. He ran a faster, more efficient game than Jerry had run, and he stole a great deal less. All winter he made between eighty and a hundred dollars a week; he paid his room rent punctually, subsisted largely on eggs, and kept a pint of fair whiskey always within reach. And he saved his money. When warm weather came and with it a slackening off of business, he persuaded Chapman and Bangs to close the dice game for a month except for the big paydays, and he and Chapman would make tours of the amusement parks. During intermission and after the dance was over they would get a crap game going among the touring musicians and the concessionaires, and Chapman was delighted to discover that he had not lost a nickel by closing down the indoor game. On this deal Jay and Chapman went halves, and Bangs was not in it at all. Jay encountered some old carnival acquaintances among the concessionaires, and he could always get a carnie friend to act as a shillaber. The shill would win a little money and make a noise about it, and the musicians and concessionaires and the roustabouts would be ready to be taken. It was seldom necessary to sneak in the educated dice more than two or three times during a game, but it had to be done at precisely the right moment and under the suspicious eyes of the concessionaires. The smarter men among the concessionaires could tell when Jay and Chapman *ought* to throw in the educated dice, and they would drop out of the game temporarily, but even with this knowledge the concessionaires were never sure enough of their suspicions to risk a challenge. And most of them knew that Chapman was a cop, carrying a gun, and that Jay had done time out West for cutting up a fellow with a knife. At the end of the summer layoff, Jay had saved up nearly six thousand dollars.

"The parks all close Labor Day," said Chapman, one night when they were driving back to town.

"Yeah, nothing lasts forever," said Jay.

"You must have a pretty good little bundle."

"Pretty."

"Dave wants to get a new man," said Chapman.

"I'd be sore too, if I was Dave, but we didn't need him. He would have been a li'bility. Clumsy. If he'd of been with us I'd of spent all summer waiting for him to throw out three dice."

"He wouldn't throw out three dice. He's too good for that. But you're right, he's getting clumsy."

"Chappie?"

"What?"

"Have you got a new man?"

"Well, we talked to a fellow down at the shore. Bangs knew him before. I just as soon get rid of Bangs and go partners with you, but Bangs has the money and you don't. I don't either, you know. I ain't finished paying for my house and my wife's old lady has to have an operation."

"That's all right. A year ago this time I was almost dead. Now I'm alive and a little ahead. If I bought Matt Hostetter's would I get any help from you?"

"As long as you don't open up a dice game. And as long as you don't mean you want any money from me."

"Just a good word with the right people. Hostetter wants five thousand dollars. He's crazy, but if I offer him thirty-five hundred I think he'll sell."

"I could make him sell. Not me, but Schmidt. All I do is I say to Schmidt, put Hostetter out of business and put a real go-getter in there. You'd be better for Schmidt than old Matt is. Matt's on his last legs."

"I wouldn't want to muscle him out. That wouldn't be good for business."

"You'd be doing him a favor. You understand, though, you have to get your goods where Schmidt says."

"I'd have to talk to Schmidt about that. Hostetter's been taking anything they send him. It's a wonder they don't go blind, drinking the stuff he sells."

"Well, you work that out with Schmidt. I wish you and me could go in together, but right now Bangs has the bankroll. Why do you want to run a broken-down joint like Hostetter's?"

"I tell you why, Chappie. From Hostetter's the only way you can go is up. I'm in business for about as little money as it's possible. And the main reason, I got a place of my own. No partners, my own boss."

"Yeah, I wish I didn't have so many partners. I got Dave, I got the mayor, I got the chief of police, I got my wife, my wife's old lady, my two kids, a couple broads always asking for stocking money. Maybe you think I got it good, but if you want to know the truth of the matter, I'm in hock to Dave for over four thousand. I owe on this car, and it's two years old. My house ain't paid for. Where does it all go? I don't live high, but if I had to live on my hundred-and-twenty cop's pay, I couldn't do it. My wife says to me, quit. Quit running the dice game, she says. Where would she be if I quit? And her old lady with a private room in the hospital? Don't be surprised if one of these days I come around and put the arm on you."

"Wait till I get on my own two feet, though."

"You'll be all right. I got a feeling. I just got a feeling. Jay, I'm gonna let you off at the Greek's. I got a date with a broad. You don't have that trouble, do you? I never seen you with a broad. What do you do when you want to get your ashes hauled? Not that it's any my business."

"Sophie."

"Sophie? The waitress Sophie? At the Greek's?"

"Uh-huh."

"She's kind of big for you, ain't she?"

"You mean I'm kind of small for her? I always liked big broads, and *I* don't have to *feed* her."

"Sophie, huh? Well, wuddia know. You know who else is there, don't you?"

"Sure. Dave."

"Just so you know. He could get her fired from the Greek's, and he would in a minute. He don't like you, Jay."

"That's a pleasure. *I* don't like *him,* and I got a word of advice for you, Chappie. That's a fellow that carries his own deck. We all carry our own deck—you do, I do, we all do. But Dave is the kind of a guy, he lets you think he's Big Hearted Joe. Like you owe him that four thousand dollars. Yeah, but whose four thousand dollars? I guarantee you, that was never money he had his hands on. I'm willing to lay the odds it was money you held out on him and told him. Am I right?"

"Yeah, but I don't think you're guessing."

"That's all I am, is guessing. Nobody had to tell me that about Dave. If you ask Dave for the *loan* of a thousand dollars, watch him try to wriggle out of it. He wouldn't like to part with money once he has it."

"You're a hundred percent right. I held out on him, once for fifteen hundred, the other time for three thousand. I told him I had the money and I was ready to give it to him but would it be all right if I held on to it. So you're right, he never had the money in his hands."

"Yeah, I met all kinds, including a lot of Daves. If you ever get the chance to get rid of him, do it. Not that you'd do a favor for me, but a favor to yourself. Well, goodnight, Chappie."

"I'll talk to Schmidt. Goodnight, Jay."

During the first week of his ownership Jay had Matt Hostetter back of the bar with him. "The new owner," Matt would say, serving a customer. At the end of the week Jay handed Matt five ten-dollar bills. "That's for the good will, Matt. Now so long, and don't ever come in here again. It's my joint, and I don't even want you for a customer."

"No hard feelings, young fellow. You treated me all right," said Hostetter. Matt went home, sat in a rocking chair, and in three months died of an embolism. Jay was among the mourners at the service in the Lutheran church and among the contributors when the hat was passed by the undertaker. Jay held a folded five-dollar bill between thumb and forefinger, suspended over the hat, and before he dropped it he said: "Three months ago he had enough to bury him."

"I guess he did, yeah. Don't know where it all went to," said the undertaker.

"Wild women, probably," said Jay.

"Oh, no. He was too old for that." The man was deeply shocked, but he took the money.

Schmidt, the cop who exercised authority over the lower-grade speakeasies, was surprisingly tractable when Jay announced he wanted to change alcohol dealers. "I'm for it," he said. "They were palming off some terrible stuff on old Matt. If somebody went blind, it'd sooner or later come back to me and it'd be my rap. You go ahead and get your alcohol where you want to. But beer, beer you have to stick with the same people. That's over my head, *I* take *my* orders on who supplies beer. And you take your orders from me. If I see you putting in some other beer, I'll come down here and close your place. That's my orders, Detweiler, so no trouble, you understand?"

"Sure," said Jay.

There was a noticeable improvement in the class of people coming in. The old customers stayed, but now the place began to attract the low-salaried white collar men who could not do without their booze; the artisans who had to have cheap whiskey; the pensioners who had nothing much left in life but the conversations and long silences they could share with other pensioners. The word had got around that Jay Detweiler served the cheapest decent drink in town. Among the new customers were a few men who were fearful of patronizing Matt Hostetter's old place, which they had always heard to be a dive for cutthroats in a neighborhood that was occupied by the most lawless element in town. But when they went to Jay's on a trial visit they found it to be not nearly so bad as they expected. The badly dressed, unshaven derelicts were there, but the place itself, though bare of beautifying features, was scrubbed clean and smelt clean; in among the beer and whiskey smells was the smell of strong soap, and the smell of disinfectant in the toilet was almost overpowering, but reassuring. The new owner, Detweiler, appeared to be rather young to be the proprietor of such a place, and he was certainly not equipped by nature to handle a fracas. He was frail and polite, and though he had a blackjack hanging on the back bar in plain sight, he seemed too agreeable as well as too fragile to be effective if trouble broke out. He wore a collar and tie and a waistcoat in which he kept fountain pen, pencils, pocket comb and a notebook. His customers were not aware that Jay had changed his style of dressing; he no longer wore his cake-eater suit, with its low-cut vest, or a string tie or striped silken shirt with a tiny, too-tight collar. He could easily be taken for a ticket seller in a railway station, standing behind his bar and dispensing his goods. After a while the timid ones enjoyed the cheap thrill of patronizing a place that was nicknamed the Bucket of Blood but that was hardly more disorderly than any hose company on a Saturday night.

The new proprietor was there every day but Sunday, from nine o'clock in the morning till one or two the next morning. On Sundays he would not open up until dark, and his customers had to do the best they could to get through the day without booze. The rest of the time Jay was at his place of business from opening to closing. At lunch time and at supper time he would have his food brought in from the Greek's by a waiter known as Loving Cup because of the size of his ears. Jay would put the tray on one end of the bar and eat the food standing up. He never licked the platter clean; he ate only because he knew how important it was for a drinking man to get some food in him.

At the end of his first year his pocket notebook showed him that he had recovered nearly half his investment. His bookkeeping was simplicity itself: it had cost him just under five thousand dollars to get going; twelve months later, after paying all his bills, including the payments to Schmidt, he had about two thousand dollars in cash, and he owned the business to boot. He refused to complicate the bookkeeping; the first year had been a gamble. He had put five thousand dollars into a game, and he came out of that game with two thousand cash, a business, and his living expenses for a year all taken care of. He had never worked so steadily and so hard in all his life, and he had never enjoyed himself so much. He was strongly tempted to give a party on the first anniversary, but decided against it; instead, he waited until midnight and then announced that thereafter until closing, all drinks would be on the house. He gave no reason except, "I just happen to feel big-hearted tonight." His custom of buying free drinks was so well established that his explanation was accepted without curiosity.

It amused him to think back over his first year and to realize that in all that time he had lived in an area that was roughly four blocks by three—squares, the town people called them. He had never so much as taken a stroll two blocks to the north, two blocks to the south of the Greek's, one block to the east of his rooming house, or one block to the west of his doctor's office. He read the town papers thoroughly and he knew what was going on, but he had not had time to look around. The area in which he had confined himself was not much larger than the area to which he had once been confined by the State of Illinois—with the great difference that when he was in the pen he had not been free to wander. Twice in his lifetime—once by a judge's sentence and the other by his own preference—he had stayed put for a year.

He had run away from his uncle's farm at fourteen, and since that time he had wandered up and down and across every state east of the Dakotas, north of Tennessee, west of Massachusetts, and south of the Canadian border. He had stayed out of the South, where the small town cops and sheriffs were said to be mean; and he had stayed out of the West because of the distances between towns. Up and down, back and forth, with circuses, carnivals, medicine shows, Chautauquas, Tom shows, and working the county fairs alone or with a companion. He had put cardboard in his shoes and newspapers under his shirt to keep warm; ridden in the caboose with a too friendly brakeman and had two teeth knocked out by a special cop on the Nickel Plate; slept in a van with a dog and pony act, and driven his own Cole Eight after a highly successful week at the Columbus State Fair. He had seen all the awful things that can occur in a circus train wreck; and he had felt the dull, sickening hatred of a "committee" in a town in southern Indiana, where a man from a previous carnival had raped a little girl. He had comforted a tent-show girl whose six-hundred-dollar boa constrictor was shot by a drunken miner in Kentucky. He had been taken for his only aeroplane ride by an Army lieutenant in Rantoul, Illinois, whom he had taught the O'Leary belt trick. He had got crabs at a fraternity house in southern Illinois and gonorrhea from a corset demonstrator in Fort Wayne. He had run twenty dollars up to sixteen thousand in a crap game in Louisville on the eve of Derby Day and was about to drag his winnings when a friend almost imperceptibly shook his head, and Jay took the motion as a signal to make one more throw. But the friend was only being bothered by an insect on the back of his neck, and the dice came up a deuce and an ace. And now, after about twenty years of knocking around, he owned his own business in a town he had never heard of two years ago.

Jay had often pondered the mysterious ways of fate. Throughout his life accident and coincidence and luck had governed his actions with the unpredictability of a pair of honest dice. To some extent you could figure the percentages; they were known. It was easier to make an eight than a nine, harder to make a five than a six. You could shake the dice noisily in your fist—a pair of honest dice—and if you were very good you could improve your percentage by little tricks, like holding one die in the grip of your little finger. But in his study of the behavior of dice he had often given them an honest shake and an honest roll, and still come up with some strange sequences. Once he had rolled fourteen (or fifteen?) four-three sevens in a row, without manipulating the dice during the shake or the roll. And he had seen experts, using his dice, roll out numerical sequences in arithmetical order from two to twelve and downward from twelve to two. You could improve your chances legitimately or semi-legitimately. But you could not always explain accident and coincidence and luck; you just had to believe in it because it was there.

If he had not been put off that train, he would have died. But he *had* been put off the train, in a strange town that was full of people who had the same last name as his own. In all his wanderings he had never met another Detweiler, and in this town there were thirty or forty of them. He still had not met any of his namesakes; he was sure they would not like to claim kinship with him. And he knew so little about his parents that he would not be able to establish—or deny—any connection with the local Detweilers. He had no recollection whatever of his father and almost none of his mother. He had been raised by her brother, always with the reminder that he was another mouth to feed, with no credit for doing a man's work from the time he was able to lift a pitchfork, and to take a man's beating before that. His uncle was named Ben Russell, and he had always called him Mr. Russell, not Uncle Ben. He had never called Ben's wife aunt. She was, if possible, harder to get along with than Ben. Even now Jay hated to see a counterman cut into a fresh pie; it reminded him of the hundreds of times Mrs. Russell had sliced a pie into six wedges for the six Russells and nothing for Jay.

Now he could cut the pie the way he wanted it—all six wedges for Jay Detweiler. Unlike Chapman, the detective, he did not consider himself in reluctant partnership with people who were essential to his business, and, also unlike Chapman, he did not regard as partners the people who were essential to his pleasures or who were dependent on him for a living. He paid a scrubwoman to keep his place clean, he paid room rent to Sadie Tupper, graft to Sergeant Schmidt, so much to the beer mob, so much to the alcohol mob. He took what he needed out of his own till, and he gave Sophie George ten dollars every Sunday.

The first sign of discontentment in his new way of living was the discovery, on awakening one Sunday morning, that he had no desire to go to Sophie's room and spend the day with her. He had desire, but not for Sophie, and in a little while he was knocking on the door of the second best of the whorehouses. It was eleven o'clock in the morning, and the door was opened by the bouncer, a booze customer of Jay's, a man known as Sport. "The girls are all asleep," said Sport. "If that's what you came for." He was in a pair of pants pulled over a union suit and his hair was uncombed. "Come in, have a cup of coffee."

"Thanks," said Jay. "When do they start getting up?"

"Well, those with their regulars, they'll be getting up any time now. A couple the girls got Sunday regulars. You ever been here?"

"No."

"I thought you weren't. I didn't remember seeing you. I wasn't sure. You want cream and sugar? I make good coffee and I like it good and sweet. They say it spoils the taste, but I say it gives a different taste. My coffee you can drink black, and it's good that way, or you can put cream and sugar in it and it's just as good, only different. All the girls here say my coffee spoils it for them when they go to a restrunt."

"It has a nice aroma," said Jay.

"That's the tip-off. If it don't have a nice aroma, it ain't gonna have a good taste. You might as well start a new batch."

"I don't want to wake up any of the girls. Ain't any of them up yet? They all asleep?"

"I'll call upstairs," said Sport. He went to the hall. "Hey, anybody up?"

"Who is it?" a woman's voice replied.

"A friend of mine," said Sport.

"I'll be down," said the woman.

"That's a girl named Jenny," said Sport. "She come here from Fort Penn a month or so ago. Good-lookin' broad. She'd pass for respectable—if you didn't look too close. She don't dress like a hooker, is what I mean. Age, maybe thirty, maybe a little younger, a little older."

The woman, wrapped in a kimono, appeared. "I smelt that coffee and it woke me up. Hello, mister."

"Hello, Jenny," said Jay.

"You want me to take him on? Can I have a cup of coffee first?"

"Well, what do you think, Jay?" said Sport.

"Fine, fine," said Jay.

"A friend of yours?" said Jenny.

"Great pal of mine," said Sport.

"As soon as I have a cup of coffee, all right?" said Jenny.

"Sure, sure," said Jay. "There's no rush."

"Sport, you're gonna have to get the doctor for Beulah. She got a pain in her stomach and the sweats."

"That sounds to me like appendicitis. I had that," said Jay.

"Can she die from it?" said Sport.

"She sure as hell can," said Jay.

"I'll say she can. I had it too. I was operated four years ago," said Jenny. "I nearly died from it."

"So did I," said Jay. "Did yours rupture?"

"I thought only men got ruptures," said Jenny.

"That kind, but appendicitis can rupture," said Jay.

"They didn't tell me anything about that," said Jenny. "I just remember I had the gripes so bad, and the sweats. Did you have to wear a belt after? I had to wear a belt and I was out of work for over two months. Went back to work too soon anyway, the doctor told me. I got a thing they call adhesions, and had to be operated again. So you better get the doctor for Beulah, Sport."

"I will. I'll call him up on the phone," said Sport.

"And don't take all day about it, or you'll wheel her out of here to the undertaker's," said Jenny.

"Keep your shirt on," said Sport.

"If she keeps her shirt on I get a reduction," said Jay.

"You're a kidder, mister," said Jenny. "Anyway, I don't have a shirt. Well, any time you're ready, I am."

Jay became a Sunday regular of Jenny's, and she became a customer of his, as much, she told him, for the conversation as for the booze. He had never encouraged Sophie George to visit his saloon, and strictly speaking he had not extended a more than casual invitation to Jenny; but he was pleased with Jenny's visits. The other women among his customers were not much different from the men; drinkers in skirts, nothing to look at, and only too well aware that they had to stay out of trouble or be barred. Jenny was welcome—so long as she too behaved herself, and didn't come in too often. That she liked Jay personally was obvious to him.

Once in a while she would drop in of an afternoon, alone or with another girl, and take only a soft drink—a "temperance," she called it. She had been shopping for a bottle of perfume, a hat, a new kimono, and she felt like chatting before going to work. "It does a person good to get a breath of fresh air," she would say. Some of the girls in her house never left the place except to go to Dr. Traff's for their weekly examinations. "Which is a laugh, the inspection he gives you," said Jenny. "But if you don't go once a week, Sport won't let you work. He's under orders, just the same as the rest of us. Oh, I guess it's some protection, for a while. Sooner or later you're going to run into hard luck, but it's the same in your business. Sooner or later you're liable to get a bad shipment and they'll all go falling out of here with the blind staggers."

"It ain't the same thing, Jenny," said Jay. "I get a report on every shipment before I mix a batch of booze. Don't forget, I drink more of this than anybody."

"Yeah, and I don't see how you do it and stay on your feet."

"I don't let it get control over me."

"It will, though," she said.

"Yeah, the odds are it will, some day," said Jay.

He liked her friendly interest in him, and it was only old-time caution and not anything she said that put him on his guard with her. It was a long time coming, half a year or more, but he was ready when she made her pitch. "I want to get out of working in a house," she said, one afternoon.

"How do you mean? You'd have a hard time working

independent. You couldn't rent a room, the cops'd make it tough for you. This is a small town, Jenny."

"I know. I was thinking if you and me, the two of us lived together."

"Married, you mean?"

"Well, either way. But I could make seventy-five to a hundred a week here."

"Hustling?"

"How else? And the two of us could stash away a nice buck."

"Not a chance, Jenny."

"You got that little room back there and I notice it has a sofa."

"That's for if a man and woman don't have no place else to go," said Jay. "And they gotta be people I know. Another thing, I don't charge them. If I charged them the cops'd raise their take. You got pipe dreams, Jenny. You wouldn't make any seventy-five, a hundred a week here. Not my customers."

"Let me go to work and I'd show you."

"No," said Jay. "Oh, I ain't saying you couldn't pick up a few dollars. Any place that sells booze, it don't take a very smart hustler to make coffee and cakes. Even the old men I got coming in here, you could hustle them, but they don't have the ten dollars to spare, and you're a ten-dollar girl. Some of my old guys make a sawbuck stretch out for a whole week, and you'd take it away from them in ten minutes. No."

"I could make twenty dollars a day, six days a week."

"No dice, Jenny. The whole place'd change."

"It's nothing much now," she said.

"Not to you, maybe."

"Well what the hell are you so stuck up about it? They

call it the Bucket of Blood, for God's sake."

"Not any more. They used to, but not as much."

"Why don't you give *me* a break?" she said.

"A break, yeah, but I don't want to ruin a business I built up."

"I'll give you half, Jay. I tell you what I'll do. I'll bet you five dollars I can hustle the next guy comes in, I don't care who he is or how old or anything."

"Sure you can. You can hustle me, but that ain't saying you're gonna work here."

"You're a mean little bastard. Next Sunday go some place else."

"You don't have to take it personal."

"Well, I do, see? And next Sunday, stay away. We don't have to work Sunday if we don't want to. Sunday we can have anybody we want to, and I—don't—want—you, see?"

"That's your privilege. Have a steam?"

"The hell I will, now or any other time," she said.

He was sorry to break off with Jenny, and amidst his regret was deep appreciation of the compliment to himself and to his business in her willingness to marry him. It was easy to find a woman who would marry a man with a successful business, but Jenny had been willing to be a partner, to bring to the partnership her earning ability. It was a high compliment indeed, and it made little difference whether it flattered his business or himself, since one was the same as the other. He wondered how many other Detweilers in the town had had this satisfaction.

There was no one else in the saloon, and he was pleased that that was so. He poured himself a steam and raised his glass and faced the door. "Good luck, Jenny," he said.

(*49*)

THE BUTTERFLY

Mrs. Benner opened the newspaper wide and raised it in front of her. "I don't want to discuss the matter—*no—more*," she said. "I have no wish to discuss the matter and that's final."

"Mom, that's no way to be," said Hilda Benner Vogel. "Discuss it? We didn't discuss anything. You just said your say and then hide behind your paper."

"Hide? I don't have anything to hide. If it's hiding, you ought to be the one to hide." She lowered the paper. "As long as you're living in this house, just as long as I pay the electricity and the taxes and I'm the one forks over at the supermarket, you'll listen to me."

"All right, I'll listen. I'm willing to listen, Mom. But don't just say something and my God, I'm willing to listen but you don't *say* anything."

Mrs. Benner moved from side to side, shifting her weight in the chair as she lit a cigarette. It was a filter-tip cigarette but from long habit she spit an imaginary fragment of tobacco from her lower lip. "Willing to listen? When are you willing to listen? Hilda, you gotta get work and that's all there is to it. It isn't I mind the drain on my finances. You don't eat that much, and the heating for one room isn't that much extra. But as long as you got nothing to do you're going to get into some kind of trouble. Idle hands are the plaything of the devil. I never seen that to fail. There's not a family I know that whether it's a man or a woman, boy or girl, if they don't have work, they're the ones that get into trouble."

"I *agree* with you—"

"I didn't ask you to agree with me, Hilda. I'm stating a fact, only you don't seem to know it. Thirty-three years of age but some ways you never learned any more responsibility than a kid sixteen. Last night you come home at ten of three. Ten of three this morning. Ten of three on a Monday night? A Tuesday morning? In this neighborhood that's late for a Saturday night, let alone a Monday or Tuesday."

"If they're all asleep they wouldn't know *what* time I came home," said Hilda.

"See? You don't want to listen. You just want to give me an argument."

"I don't want to give you any argument. You asked me who it was and I told you."

"You told me some man named Tom Reese, but who's that? I don't know any Tom Reese. I never heard of him. What does he do for a living? I suppose he's married."

"Yes, I told you that."

"And how old is he? Did you tell me that, too? If you did, I don't remember, I was that upset you coming home at three o'clock in the morning with a married man."

"He's around thirty-eight or -nine."

"You still didn't answer my question, what he does for a living. Does he have a job?"

"He's getting a job."

"Oh, another one. Birds of a feather flock together. Maybe while he's looking for a job he can look for one for you, too."

"I couldn't do his kind of work. If I could I would. He makes plenty when he's working. He's a steeplejack."

"A what? A steeplejack? That paints church steeples?"

"And other jobs like that on tall buildings. But he has to lay off on account of the weather."

"Why don't he get work in Florida, then?"

"He just came back from there. As soon as the weather gets good he has a job down at the shore, Atlantic City."

"What company does he work for?"

"No company. He works independent."

"Oh, inde*pen*dent."

"Pop was independent till he sold the store. There's nothing wrong with working independent if you can. I'd rather be my own boss any day."

"Yes, but Pop built up a business from nothing or the chain wouldn't have bought him out. Don't compare your father with some fly-by-night steeplejack. How many children does this Reese have?"

"Two."

"Well, just you be careful he don't make it three. I'm not that hard up for a grandchild, believe me."

"That won't happen."

"Where did you meet this Reese?"

"He was at that party I went to at Stella Cosgrove's."

"His wife was there?"

"Yeah, she was there."

"But he liked you in preference to her?"

"Well, he asked me for a date."

"What kind of a looking person is she, the wife?"

"Well, I don't hold a candle to her for looks, but she has a lousy disposition."

"Oh, he liked you because you were more the retiring kind."

"Maybe. I don't know. Yes, I guess so."

"But he doesn't sound like any retiring kind himself, asking you for a date the first time he ever laid eyes on you."

"He isn't. He's not the retiring kind."

"A boozer?"

"No. He can't, on account of his job."

"Oh, but he likes women. Was he married before?"

"Yes."

"Did you tell him about Roy?"

"I told him I was married but separated. He said he could tell that by looking at me."

"Yes, I guess he could, a man like that. Some of them can take one look at a woman and tell you all about them, whether they're married or separated, or a widow. *I* can usually tell. Do you have another date with Reese?"

"Tonight."

"Oh," said Mrs. Benner. "Tonight, huh?" She scraped the end off her cigarette and picked up her newspaper. "Then you won't be home for dinner?"

"No," said Hilda.

"Some men can get away with it," said her mother.

Shortly after seven-thirty the doorbell rang and Mrs. Benner went to answer it. "Good evening," she said. "Will you come-in-sit-down?"

"Yes ma'am, thanks," said Tom Reese.

"I'm Hilda's mother. She's near ready but take off your coat."

"Thanks," said Reese. He was wearing an overcoat, very short, hardly came to his knees, the type that was advertised as suburban or sports-car. The upper part of the garment was dark blue, the rest of it grey. The material was something like a tweed, and it was very new. As he walked he seemed to be bow-legged and he was a shorter man than

(53)

he had given the impression of being. He was very thin, still somewhat sunburned, and had blue eyes and cheekbones that stood out. He offered Mrs. Benner a cigarette, which she accepted, and when he held up a lighter she noticed the back of his hand was tattooed in a design that was interrupted by the cuff of his white shirt.

"I notice you have a tattoo," she said.

"Which one?" he said. He raised the sleeves over his right arm and displayed a dragon that went up to his elbow, and he showed her the tattoo on his left arm, a fouled anchor with a line that wrapped around his arm to the wrist. He kept his cigarette in his mouth while showing her the decorations, and breathed out smoke as he described them. "I got some others, too," he said. "But I guess I won't show you *them*."

"Did it hurt when they did it?"

"Sure, but not bad. I had these since I was seventeen years old. The first couple days they fester and itch, that's worse than the needle. They do it with an electric needle. But the worst part is the itching. Oh, and it don't look very appetizing the first few days."

"I'll bet it doesn't," she said. "Can I offer you a drink of something?"

"Don't touch it. I get high enough in my work, you know what I mean? Did Hilda tell you, I'm a steeplejack."

"High enough in your work, so you don't get high on the ground?"

"That's it. You got a beautiful house here, Mrs. Vogel."

"Benner. Mrs. Benner. Hilda's married name was Vogel."

"Sure. You don't look old enough to have a daughter her age."

"I am, though. Not saying how old she is."

"She told me. That's why I can't believe it."

"Well, appearances are sometimes deceitful."

"Yeah, and it's how old a person feels. My grandfather got married for the third time when he was seventy-four years of age. He married a woman forty-five and he outlasted her. People don't get enough fresh air, that's what it is. I'm the first one in my family didn't go to sea, and stay at it, that is. I went to sea when I was sixteen but I got better money as a rigger so I give it up. But my father, my grandfather, and a whole bunch of uncles all went to sea, some in the Navy, some not. Tattooing runs in the family. That's how I happened to have these. I understand my grandmother had a tattoo on her leg where it wouldn't show. Except to him, if you know what I mean."

"I wouldn't have it done for any man."

"You don't know. Maybe you would. A lot of women are tattooed."

"The ones in the circus you mean."

"Not only them. Regular women. Women like you."

"Not like *me,* I can tell you," said Mrs. Benner. "I wouldn't be tattooed no matter how much you paid me."

"The best work is a fellow in London. London, England. He's famous. One of these days I'm thinking of flying over there and letting him do a job on me, if he's still alive. I don't know whether he's still alive."

"Well, don't ask me to accompany you, because I wouldn't have it done no matter how much you paid me."

"You be surprised how many women got tattoos on them. I had a friend, a girl friend in Frisco, and she made me take her to a tattoo artist."

"She must have been high."

"Well, she was. She had a few in her, but it was on her

mind when she was sober, too. She kept asking me when was I, so I finally took her to a tattoo artist in San Francisco. A Chinaman."

"Where did she have it done?"

"In San Francisco . . . Oh, you mean where on her?"

"Yes."

He grinned. "Well, you'd have to be pretty well acquainted before you could get a look at it."

"Even if she had one of them Bikinis?"

"With a Bikini you could see it."

"Imagine taking off your clothes and letting some Chinaman. Were you there?"

"Was I there? She wouldn't of done it if I wasn't there."

"What was it? What kind of a design?"

He chuckled. "You know what it was? It was a butterfly."

"Well, go ahead and tell me. *Where* was it?"

"Where was it? Well, I tell you. If she was a steer, it was like she was branded."

"Branded, she sure was. Branded for life. Every time a man asked her—I guess we better change the subject. High up?"

"About halfway. It'd show in a Bikini but not a regular bathing suit."

"Did you pay for it?"

"Forty-fi dollars."

"Forty-five dollars for a thing like that. You don't care how you get rid of your money."

"I'm a spender."

"I don't mind a spender if you get value received. You're a nice dresser, and I thought maybe you'd be coming here in blue jeans. But forty-five dollars just because some foolish woman wants a butterfly on her rear end."

"Many a time I spent forty-fi dollars more foolish than that."

"Oh. You mean value received," said Mrs. Benner. "And she wanted it done? You didn't put her up to it?"

"That's not my motto, Mrs. Benner. My motto is always make the woman ask for it. Always make the woman ask for it, then she don't blame you later."

"Sensible if it works. Don't you ever ask for anything yourself?"

"Never."

"That's a funny way to go through life," said Mrs. Benner.

"Well, the way I look at it, we pretty near all want the same things, only I figured out if you make the other person ask first, they can't blame you if it don't work out."

"Is that business, too, or just personal relations?"

"Oh, business is altogether different. I mean personal."

Hilda appeared, and they left immediately, so quickly that Tom Reese carried his overcoat on his arm. Mrs. Benner followed them to the porch and saw them drive away in a large station wagon with a Florida license plate. She had somehow expected a Cadillac, but maybe he used the station wagon in his business. It had different kinds of racks on the roof, and steel angle-irons along the sides where he could probably hang ladders and things. But it was a well taken care of car.

It was not like Hilda to come rushing in like that. You could almost say she was bossy, rushing in like that and interrupting a conversation. Mrs. Benner enjoyed talking to Tom Reese, even if she didn't agree with him on some things; and it occurred to her that Hilda could have been eavesdropping. If so, the thought must have run through her mind, as it had through her mother's, that Tom Reese had as much as said that Hilda had asked him for a date, not Tom her. Hilda was not a liar; she was an unusually truthful girl, for a woman, but Mrs. Benner would almost bet that if she had a tape recording of the original conversation it would show that Hilda had asked Tom to take her out, maybe without even realizing it. Some little thing, like saying, "I don't have anything to do Monday night," and then Tom saying, "All right, do it with me." Tom Reese *was* a liar, Mrs. Benner believed. A liar in that he would not feel bound to tell the truth. A man so clever about women would have no trouble outsmarting a girl like Hilda.

Hilda came home shortly after eleven. As the front door opened Mrs. Benner could hear the station wagon zooming away. He probably had not even got out of the car.

"You're home early," said Mrs. Benner.

"That's what you wanted," said Hilda.

"Where'd you go?"

"We went to a motel," said Hilda.

"You look here, young lady—"

"You asked me where we went and I told you. If you asked me last night I would of told you the same thing."

"I could of guessed that much. Tomorrow night the same."

"*That's* where you're *wrong*. Tomorrow night he's going to ask *you*."

"It's a good thing you're out of my reach or I'd give you a good slap in the face."

Hilda, still wearing her coat and with her handbag looped over her wrist, stalked out of the room and ran up the stairs. Mrs. Benner lit a cigarette and stared at the TV. The man was drawing curvy lines across a map of the North American continent and accompanying his drawing with references to Bismarck, Denver, and Galveston, but

Mrs. Benner did not take in what he was saying. The lines he was drawing were all so female, so buxom and female, and now as he drew another line his hand moved as though in a quick caress, as though he were creating sections of a woman's torso that she could only anticipate until the line was drawn.

She got to her feet and snapped off the TV. She went around turning out lights because she knew that once she got to the second story she would not want to come down again. In a few minutes the first floor was dark and Mrs. Benner climbed the stairs and she could see that the light was on in Hilda's room.

Hilda had not taken off her coat. Her aluminum suitcase lay open on the bed and was partly filled with clothes.

"What are you, going somewhere?" said Mrs. Benner.

"Looks that way."

"You going for the night, or what?"

"For the night and all the rest of the nights," said Hilda. "My things in the wash, you can send them to me."

"Where to?"

"I'll send you a postcard."

"You don't have any money. How are you going to live?" said Mrs. Benner.

"I'll get something."

"But what?"

"Oh, stop asking me questions. Something."

"You got a better chance of getting something here, where you know people, than if you went away some place."

Hilda said nothing.

"That's the whole problem, Hilda. What I been trying to drum into you, only you won't listen. If you don't have work, something to do, you get miserable."

Hilda stopped packing and stood erect. "What were

you talking about before I came down tonight, you and Tom Reese?"

"What were we talking about? He was telling me about his tattoo."

"I thought as much. And the woman with the butterfly on her behind?"

"Yes, he told me that."

"Huh."

"What do you mean, huh?"

"What do I mean? I mean you're gonna be like that woman in Boston."

"What woman in Boston?"

"That got herself tattooed."

"You mean San Francisco."

"Boston. Boston, Massachusetts."

"He told me San Francisco. Maybe there was two of them."

"Maybe there was two hundred of them. Maybe there wasn't any. But I know this much, I'm not gonna stay around here and watch my own mother make a fool of herself. You ought to hear what he said about you."

"What did he say about me?"

"I'll tell you what he said. He said he bet me inside of two weeks you'd have a butterfly tattooed on you."

"Huh."

"So go on have a date with him tomorrow night. You won't have to go to any motel. I won't be here. And don't forget to tell me when you get the butterfly tattooed on you."

"Up and down these stairs all day, I think I'll sell this place," said Mrs. Benner.

"Didn't you hear what I said?"

"I heard what you said, Hilda, and it's in one ear and out the other."

"Are you sick or something?"

"I don't have to be sick to be disgusted, the kind of men you go out with. You go to a motel the first night you go out with him, no wonder he can talk dirty about your own mother. Do you want some money?"

"I have thirty dollars."

"You'll need more than thirty dollars, that won't last you three days if you want to live decent. You want to live decent, or don't you?"

Hilda was silent.

"You can't go any place this hour of the night, alone. You can go to the bank with me in the morning and I'll draw out some money for you. A woman can't stay decent in this world if she don't have some money to fall back on." Mrs. Benner went to the bed and picked up the aluminum suitcase and turned it upside down. "Your stuff'll be back from the laundry tomorrow. Put these things away for the night, anyway. And for God's sake take off your coat."

Hilda opened the closet door and hung up her coat.

"Straighten it out," said Mrs. Benner. "You gotta learn to take care of your things, or you won't have anything."

CLAUDE EMERSON, REPORTER

For thirty years Claude Emerson got up every morning at six o'clock, put the coffee on, shaved himself with one of his two straight razors, took a cup of coffee in to his wife, and then went back to the kitchen and sat at the table and drank two cups by himself. He would sit there, staring straight ahead, slowly stirring the coffee between sips, and when he had finished the second cup he would put on his glasses. There was a small mirror on the kitchen wall, and he would stand in front of it while putting on his collar, in which his necktie was already inserted. He would knot the tie and pull it a little to one side, a little to the other, until he was satisfied that it was in the right place, then he would smooth it down with the palm of his hand, throw back his shoulders until the tie bulged the right amount, and *then* he would insert his stickpin at the right place, slide the safety catch over the pin, and draw away to inspect his work. His next move would be to put on his toupee, which took less time but no less care than the tying of his tie. In thirty years and more Claude Emerson's toupee had deceived no one. It had never quite matched the color of his own hair, which went gradually from an orangey red to a reddish grey. Claude Emerson was always a little behind the natural color changes. He bought a new toupee every five or six years, but he could not afford to keep up with nature. Indeed, he had never been able to afford even one first-class matching job. His friends, his wife, and Peter Durant, his barber, urged him to abandon his toupees, but Claude Emerson refused because, he said, he always caught cold when he went without one.

And so, every morning, there was that part of his personal ritual; putting the toupee in place, smoothing it down gently with the palms of both hands, the final adjusting pull over one ear. After that, his coat and waistcoat, which he put on together, and the business of his watch and chain, which he could do while on his way to the clothes-tree in the front hall. He would put on his seasonal hat and the outer wear appropriate to the weather—rubber coat, gumshoes, umbrella—and he was ready for the street.

On very few mornings he failed to find someone to walk with, and he tried not to walk with the same man on successive mornings. His companions were the bookkeepers and store clerks and men who worked in the offices of the railroads and the coal companies, white-collar men like himself, but whose jobs were nowhere near as exciting as Claude Emerson's. "I'd like to have gone in the writing game," they would often say. "But I was never much of a speller."

Claude Emerson would reply consolingly: "Well, with me it was always arithmetic. When I was in High they tried to teach me bookkeeping, but I could never strike a trial balance."

Most of his morning companions were men who *had* learned bookkeeping, but their work did not furnish much of a topic for conversation. Claude's work, on the other hand, was of the stuff that conversations are made on: last night's meeting of the Borough Council; yesterday's burglary; the untimely passing of a Civil War veteran; a two-alarm fire in the Sixth Ward; tax millages; church picnics; a new movie theater; the Burton Holmes lecture; the gilding of a church steeple; the birth of twins; the price of strawberries; the new uniforms for the band. To the man who spent his days perched on a bookkeeper's high stool, the life of Claude Emerson seemed full of variety and stimulation; and Claude Emerson thought so too, for he loved his work.

He was a big man: six foot two, never less than two hundred twenty pounds. In High he had not liked football, but because of his size he had had no choice but to play. He lacked aggressiveness, but he stood head and shoulders over most high school players, and in helmet and noseguard, shoulder harness and kidney pads, he was valuable to the team even before the game began. For four years he heard opposing players say, "Get a look at that big son of a bee. I'll bet he's a ringer." Claude's own coach would say to him: "Just watch the center, Emerson, and as soon as the ball's snapped back, fall forward, *fall forward!*" In Claude Emerson's football days there was no forward passing and not much running around the ends; the principal play was the center rush, and Claude's bulk made him worth two line players, leaving, as it did, one extra guard free to engage the opposing line players on every scrimmage. In spite of the hard-rubber noseguard-mouthpiece, Claude lost four front teeth during his playing career, but he gained a reputation as a stalwart son of Old High which lasted all his life, and, better yet, football introduced him to his lifework; he was paid $1.50 for his reporting of the out-of-town games in which he played.

The paper had no sports section or regular sports writer in those days. Claude Emerson's account of the previous Saturday's game seldom appeared before Tuesday, and often did not appear until Wednesday. Nevertheless his stories usually ran a full column in length, and when he was ready to graduate from High he was taken on as a general news reporter at $1.50 a week. At the end of two years, when his salary had reached $3.50 a week, he asked to be raised to $10; he was keeping company with Clara Stahlnecker, a high school classmate, and her father would not give his consent to Clara's engagement until Claude was earning $60 a month and had at least $200 in the bank. The editor of the paper, though heartily approving of marriage, could not see his way clear to a salary jump from $3.50 to $10, and took the opportunity to caution Claude against such an impulsive step as matrimony at the age of twenty or twenty-one. "Think these things over, Emerson," said Bob Hooker, the editor.

"I did think it over, Mr. Hooker," said Claude Emerson. "And I guess I have to tell you, I can get ten dollars at the *Telegraph*."

"I don't believe you," said Hooker. "When did they tell you that?"

"Four or five months ago."

"Bosh! If that was true you would have said something then."

"I almost did, but I was hoping I'd get a bigger raise this time."

"Even if you're telling the truth, which I doubt, you realize that the *Telegraph* is on its last legs? So go on over to them, but don't come back looking for work here when the *Telegraph* shuts down," said Hooker. "I'll give you six dollars a week and a dollar-a-week raise every six months."

"Two years before I get ten? No sir, I can't wait that long."

"You haven't got the Stahlnecker girl in some kind of trouble?"

"I don't have to stand for that kind of talk," said Claude. "Now I quit!"

From time to time during the next dozen years Bob Hooker would try to re-hire Claude Emerson. To more and more citizens of the town Claude Emerson was becoming a symbol, the only symbol, of newspaper reporting. They saved their news items for him and would give them to no one else. They would stop him in the midst of his morning rounds and shyly hand him articles they had written. "You fix it up so it reads right, Claude," they would say, and he would do so. They were fascinated and not antagonized by the changes he would make, and when they saw their items in print, written in Claude Emerson's ornate style—"the festive board groaned under the weight of delicious viands" —they became members of Claude's small army of volunteer reporters. Nor was it only the humble who relied on Claude Emerson for the proper presentation of news items; doctors and bankers trusted him; lawyers and clergymen had confidence in him; rich old ladies, who had heard of him through their medical and spiritual and financial advisers, would make their rare announcements only to Emerson, that nice young man at the *Telegraph*. He was summoned to the homes of certain citizens who had never spoken to Bob Hooker, homes to which Mrs. Hooker had never been invited. In such surroundings Claude Emerson was awkward and perhaps over-polite, but he also had the big man's dignity, and he confined his questions to the matter in hand. He seemed to know instinctively that these ladies felt it their duty to make public the information they gave, while wishing to keep out of the papers themselves. "I don't want this to look as if it came from me," they would say, and so Claude Emerson would begin his story: "Word has been received here of the untimely passing of John W. Blank, former town resident, who for the past forty years has made his home in St. Paul, Minnesota," or, "Through the generosity of a donor who wishes to remain anonymous, a handsome, new, mahogany Chickering piano has been installed in the Parish House of Trinity Church." Claude Emerson's stories appeared without a byline, but Bob Hooker recognized the Claude Emerson touches. In an Emerson story an oyster was always a succulent bivalve and every funeral had a cortege, but all the names and the middle initials were always there and invariably correct.

"Claude, I'd like you to come in and see me one of these days," said Bob Hooker, in his first attempt to re-hire him.

"I don't know if that would look right, Mr. Hooker," said Claude.

"Then I'll say it now, here. I'll pay you twenty a week," said Hooker.

"I'm getting better than that at the *Telegraph*."

"I don't believe you, but if you are, you won't be getting it for long. That rag is on its last legs."

Several times in the next seven years Claude Emerson had reason to know that the *Telegraph* was having financial difficulties. His pay envelope contained $12.50 and not the full $25. "That's as much as I could scrape together, Claude," said George Lauder, the editor and publisher. "I'll give you my note, but right now things are slow. They should pick up after Labor Day. I'll give you my note, or I'll give you some stock, but I advise you to take my note. Gives you a better claim in case things don't get better around here." Things never got much better at the *Telegraph*, and they would have been much worse without Claude Emerson, who, as in his football days, did the work of two men. The difference now was that he liked what he was doing, and George Lauder was not a coach who failed to appreciate him. It was a sad day for Claude Emerson when George Lauder, unable to face another slow summer, drank a pint of cheap whiskey and put a bullet through his heart. He owed Claude Emerson $412.50 in back wages. The money was uncollectible, since Claude Emerson had never taken one of George's notes and for more than a year George had failed to keep any books. The bank realized as much as it could on the sale of the equipment, and Claude Emerson, literally with hat in hand, went to call on Bob Hooker.

"Well, you see, Claude," said Hooker. "I've got this young lady, a college graduate, that does all the social-and-personals. I don't pay her anything. She's doing it for the experience, and she works like a mule. When she leaves I'll get another like her."

"I didn't want to apply for social-and-personals," said Claude Emerson.

"All you have to do is look at the paper to realize I have no other place for you. The other jobs are filled by fellows you know."

"Well, if you hear of anything elsewhere in the county—"

"Why don't you put an ad in Fernald's Exchange, Springfield, Mass.?"

"No, that'd be a waste of money for me. I'll have to look for something else, maybe up at the court house."

"You mean give up reporting?"

"I guess I'm going to have to," said Claude Emerson.

The threat of this waste of a good reporter was too much even for Bob Hooker. "I wouldn't want to see you do that, Claude," he said. "I'll tell you. I can pay you twenty dollars a week and a commission on any new advertising you bring in."

"Couldn't you make it twenty-five? I have the two children starting school. I tried to sell ads for George Lauder, but I was never any good at it."

"Well, you're a family man, and you're not a drinker," said Bob Hooker.

"No, Mr. Hooker! That's not it. I'm good at my job! I get more news than any two reporters in town. You know that. I could go uptown this minute and get five or six items that won't be in your paper tonight."

"Say, you're pretty sure of yourself."

"About that I am. I didn't use to be, but think how many times I had items in the *Telegraph* that you never had. Or maybe had them a day late."

"I never expected you to get conceited," said Hooker.

"Let me say this, will you, please? The *Telegraph* stopped printing three weeks ago tomorrow, but I made my rounds every day, just the same as usual, just as if the paper was coming out that afternoon. And every day I got at least one story that you would have run on Page One. Let me show you some, here in my pocket. I'm not conceited, but when it comes to getting the news, I don't have to take a back seat for anybody. No, Mr. Hooker, I have to start at twenty-five, and no selling ads." He rose, and the sweat ran down from beneath his toupee. He wiped his forehead with a bandana handkerchief and blew his nose loudly. His speech to Hooker had left him momentarily without a sense of direction, and he made for the wrong door.

"That's the toilet," said Hooker.

"Oh, excuse me," said Claude Emerson. "Well, good day."

"All right, Emerson. I'll start you Monday. Twenty-five a week."

"Is it all right if I start today? I have a story."

"What is it?"

"The Second National bought the Eisenhauer property at Main and Scandinavian. They're going to move there and put up a five-story office building over the bank."

"That's just a rumor."

"The papers were signed last night. I got that from J. Edward Stokes himself."

"I saw him this morning. He didn't say anything to me about it."

"I saw him this morning, too, and he gave me the whole story. I asked him if he'd keep it quiet for a few days, and he kept his promise . . . Do you want a few lines on Dr. and Mrs. English getting back from their trip to Egypt?"

"When they get back."

"They're back. I was with him earlier this afternoon. He has some very clear pictures of him and the missus in front of the Pyramids. Both riding camels. I talked to Father McCloskey. He has his silver jubilee on the twenty-fourth day of next June, and plans are under way—"

"All right, Emerson. Go on upstairs and go to work," said Hooker. "The other door."

That was in 1908, a year that could be said to mark the beginning of the golden era in the career of Claude Emerson. He was thirty-three years old, an age at which he had grown up to his size. His face had lost the last of the baby-fat look that remained with him through the mid-twenties. He had become, in more than one sense of the word, a prominent figure, instantly recognizable at council meetings, fires, parades, and his volunteers could easily find him. For the same reason it was easier for those who wished to avoid him to keep out of his sight; but few citizens had anything to fear from Claude Emerson. What he knew, he knew, and his inside information was considerable, but the paper he worked for was not a scandal sheet. Even in the heat of the primary election campaigns, when the rules of fair play and reticence were suspended, the paper refrained from publishing the dirtier truths about the opposition candidates. A candidate for the Republican nomination could expect to be called a grafter and an incompetent, and the paper would ask, in large type, what this faithless public servant had done with his share of the looting of the public treasury; but it was never hinted that the man had spent any of the money on women or booze. That sort of accusation was harder to take back when and if the man under attack happened to win the nomination. If there had ever been a threatening Democrat the paper would have used—invented, if necessary—anything it had on the man. Democrats, however, were so few in number that they could not present a formidable candidate. Some Democrats registered as Republicans in order to vote Republican in the primaries, in the fantastic hope that the weaker Republican would be nominated and thus give the Democratic candidate a tiny chance in the November elections. There were some spiritual Democrats who had never voted for a Democrat in the primaries. There were, to be sure, a few Democrats who had never voted for a Republican at any time.

Within two weeks of Claude Emerson's return to the *Standard,* Bob Hooker's paper, there was a noticeable increase in the paper's circulation. It was the custom to place a pile of papers just inside the front door, where workmen could pay their pennies and pick up a copy on the way home.

"We're getting new readers," said Bob Hooker to Claude Emerson, late one afternoon. "We're selling fifty to sixty more papers off the pile, every evening."

Claude Emerson smiled. "Oh, yes. Yes indeed."

"A lot of them I don't recognize," said Hooker. "Who are they? Friends of yours that followed you from the *Telegraph?*"

"I'll tell you who most of them are. They're Democrats. They used to read the *Telegraph*. Now they read the *Standard.*"

"Then they *did* follow you? I knew George Lauder was a Democrat, but don't tell me you're one."

"No sir, but I know most of them. Most of those men, you can tell by looking at them, they work in the car shops. I cultivated them. They didn't read the *Standard* when I worked here before, but these past years when I worked for the *Telegraph* I made a practice of chatting with them during lunch hour. It wouldn't surprise me if you got another fifty or seventy-five taking the paper on home delivery."

"Maybe we could get them to vote the right way, in time."

"I don't know about that. Not these fellows," said Claude Emerson.

It was a poorly kept, impossible to keep, secret that the *Standard* was subsidized by the Coal & Iron Company. It was known as a scab rag, a company sheet, anti-labor, anti-union. It had no circulation in the mining patches, and even in the town its circulation was smaller than the opposition paper's. But the Coal & Iron Company subsidy was one of the two factors that made the *Standard* a superior paper. In losing years the deficits were covered, and in profitable years improvements were made. The other factor in the *Standard*'s favor was Bob Hooker himself, who was actuated by greed and inspired by his love for the newspaper business. The greedy man had begun life as a poor boy, whose formal education ended with grammar school. He was of Yankee and Pennsylvania Dutch stock, a common enough combination in the anthracite region. Among his ancestors was an early president of Yale, and on his mother's side there were numerous Lutheran clergymen. His father, however, was a drunkard who died young, and Hooker's mother supported herself and her son with work as a seamstress until her eyesight gave out and she had to take in washing and ironing. She died of consumption in the year that her son finished grammar school. He was a frail boy with an outsize head, and the only job he could find seemed cruelly unsuitable inasmuch as he suffered from defective vision. The job was printer's devil, paid him a dollar a week and a cot to sleep on in the back of the shop. In spite of his bad eyesight he learned his trade quickly and well, and he read his mother's Bible from habit every day, learned three new words out of the dictionary every day, and on Sundays he read every line of all the out-of-town newspapers that he was able to store up during the week. At sixteen he got a job as printer on the *Standard,* and at nineteen he owned it.

As the new owner of the paper he wrote his own editorials in a day when small-town newspapers ran no editorials or meekly reprinted the political opinions of the metropolitan dailies. The small-town public was usually startled to find a local reference in an editorial, and the *Standard,* and its youthful publisher, attracted the attention of the educated citizens. Under the influence of Henry Wadsworth Longfellow and William Cullen Bryant the young editor wrote a weekly poem in which he introduced the local place-names of Indian origin—Lantenengo, Nesquehela, Taqua, Swatara, Mauch Chunk—and on other days he wrote short paragraphs with the standing head, This & That, which failed as humor but were of local, topical interest.

Bob Hooker was only five years older than Claude Emerson, and had had four years' less schooling, and yet there never was any question as to who was in command. The power rested in something other than the authority to hire and fire, although both men were continually conscious of that authority. The two men had remarkably similar backgrounds. Claude Emerson was a Mayflower descendant, a genealogical fact that was passed down to him by his father and mother and almost never mentioned outside the family. (Once in a great while someone would ask Claude: "Is that a baby ring?" and he would touch the smooth-worn gold ring on his little finger: "No, it belonged to my father," he would say.) Alexander Emerson, though not a drunkard, had died at a fairly early age, leaving a wife and fourteen-year-old son Claude. Alexander's widow had a mortgage-free house on Scandinavia Street and her husband's life savings from his job as cashier-bookkeeper with a dry-goods concern. She did not touch her inheritance. She returned to her old job of teaching seventh and eighth grades in the public school, and continued to teach until Claude married the Stahlnecker girl. The then newlyweds lived with her in the Scandinavia Street house for the first eighteen months of their marriage, at which time the senior Mrs. Emerson suffered her third stroke and passed on. She was very tall for a woman—slightly taller than her husband— and everyone said she tried to do too much; coming home tired after the long hours in the classroom, and pitching in to do a lot more than her share of the housework. She had never got used to letting Clara Stahlnecker sweep and scrub and cook, and possibly Clara should have taken a firmer stand, but Clara was so tiny compared to Mrs. Emerson, and Mrs. Emerson all her life was accustomed to giving orders, not taking them. No one could possibly blame Clara, and, after a time, no one did. Some of the neighbors thought Claude could have been firmer with his mother.

The obvious differences in the respective backgrounds of Bob Hooker and Claude Emerson were inherent in the similarities, the principal difference, of course, being the considerable fact that Bob Hooker was practically a homeless waif while Claude Emerson, at the same period in his life, enjoyed the love and protection of his mother. And yet Claude, compelled by the accident of his size to play a brutal game in which he took no pleasure, may have been no better off than Bob Hooker, who at least was no more uncomfortable than the child Mozart. One thing was certain: that Claude Emerson, protected and loved throughout his boyhood, inspired affection in later life, even or perhaps especially among men who treated him with something less than complete respect. No one, on the other hand, was ever known to speak with affection of Bob Hooker, even those men who treated him with respect. Claude was not particularly conscious of inspiring affection, but Bob Hooker was aware of it and mystified by it. Why was that overgrown clod so popular? He was almost a clown, with his ridiculous unmatching toupee, his squarish derby from September to May and his planter's Panama from May to September; his big, pigeon-toed feet and his dainty short steps: his black undertaker's suit with its pockets bulging with wads of copypaper. Claude Emerson's popularity was particularly galling after such incidents as the visit of old Mrs. W. S. Hofman. Her barouche and sorrel pair stopped one morning in front of the *Standard* office, and Bob Hooker rushed out to greet her.

"Good morning, Mr. Hooker," she said. "I have something for Mr. Emerson. A little item that I think might be of some interest."

"Emerson's uptown on his morning rounds, but I'll be pleased to take it," said Hooker.

"Oh, he is? Do you expect him back soon?"

"No, not for another hour or so," said Hooker. "But I'll be glad to see that it's taken care of. Would you care to come in my office?"

"Thank you very much, but it'll keep. Mr. Emerson knows how I—he usually comes to my house, but since I was in the neighborhood. If it's convenient I'd like him to stop in this afternoon. Half past five, we usually meet. But thank you, Mr. Hooker. All right, Clancy. We'll go to the bank, now, please."

It was no consolation to Bob Hooker that Claude Emerson not only would be treated almost as a servant but that he would conduct himself almost as a servant. It was no comfort, either, that Mrs. W. S. Hofman saved her news for the *Standard*. The irritating fact was that Claude Emerson had a place in Mrs. W. S. Hofman's scheme of things while Bob Hooker had not. The old lady had not even been rude; she had treated him with automatic, impersonal, infuriating politeness, and closed the door of her barouche in his face.

The power, the strength, that Bob Hooker exerted over Claude Emerson was the strength of envy, and it endured because Bob Hooker refused to acknowledge its existence. Instead he kept Claude Emerson on his payroll year after year, raising his salary when necessary, working him hard, diluting his compliments on Emerson's industry with humorously tolerant remarks about his cliché-ridden literary style. Claude Emerson had never pretended to be a writer. He learned early that there was a set journalese phrase for nearly every detail of every event that made a news item, and when he had acquired them all he saw no reason to originate another batch. The people read what he wrote, they understood what he was saying, and they were subtly complimented by his frequent use of elegant expressions. It was nicer to have your daughter united in the bonds of holy matrimony than merely married; the last sad rites were so much more appropriate than a funeral; and Jupiter Pluvius, with his torrential downpours, was more exciting than a two-inch rainfall. It was supposed to be a private, mild, office joke when Bob Hooker would say, in the presence of the other reporters, "Well, I noticed in yesterday's paper that that robber brandished a wicked-looking blue steel automatic." He would not mention Claude Emerson; he did not have to. "Anybody here ever see a holy-looking black automatic?" The city editor and the other reporters would laugh, and so would Claude Emerson. No one, not even Claude, thought Bob Hooker was being cruel. "Emerson's an excellent reporter," Hooker would say privately to the city editor, "but I have to jack him up once in a while. Inclined to get a swelled head."

In spite of Bob Hooker's criticisms in the office Claude Emerson retained his self-confidence "on the street." Again and again he was paid the ultimate compliment by a civic organization to a reporter: they would hold up the start of a meeting until he made his appearance. It was almost as high a compliment as its corollary: "Don't let Claude Emerson find out we're having this meeting." It was finally through a compliment, the second-grade kind, that Claude Emerson became vulnerable to an act of revenge by Bob Hooker.

It was now 1926. Claude Emerson's silver anniversary as a member of the Fourth Estate had passed unnoticed. His son and daughter were married, his wife was content with a daily box of Lowney's, Samoset, Page & Shaw's or Whitman's to assuage her craving for candy, and at $40 a week Claude Emerson was the best-paid reporter in town. He was fifty-one years old and without realizing it he had written the history of the town for all there was of the Twentieth Century and a few years beyond. He had recorded marriages of a hundred young persons whose births he had written up for one paper or another. He had covered all the details of the rebirth of the town from a borough to a third-class city, and he had written the story of the passing of the last horse-drawn fire-fighting equipment. He had seen the vanishing of news value in items concerning local reception of radio programs from Kansas City, Missouri. An Old High teammate had a Princeton son who was on Walter Camp's Second All-America team, and the *Standard* not only had a regular sports department but carried accounts of golf tournaments at the country club. The new hotel was no longer a novelty, and three Philadelphia brokerages had branch offices, complete with stock quotation boards, competing for local investors' business. Two county judges posed for photographs in white linen knickerbockers, and four state troopers went to prison for accepting bribes from bootleggers. The largest and oldest brewery was now an ice cream plant. Bob Hooker was one of the newest members of the Union League in Philadelphia. War was so much a thing of the past that there were only two officers left in the National Guard companies who had seen service on the Mexican Border and in France. A sound Yankee was President of the United States and a sound Pennsylvanian was Secretary of the Treasury . . . The town had no archivist, but it did have Claude Emerson, and his word was accepted as final in the settling of bets. ("I say it was 1911, you say it was 1910. We'll ask Claude Emerson.") In a peculiar, intangible sense he owned the town, the town was his, because he possessed so many of the facts of its life.

Then one morning in 1926, having given Clara her

eye-opener cup of coffee, and adjusted his toupee, and taken his bumbershoot out of the hall stand, he fell in step with Marvin F-for-Frederick Nerdlinger, a friend who lived two squares west on Scandinavia Street. Marvin worked in the laboratory of the Coal & Iron Company. He and Claude Emerson had been classmates at Old High, and the Coal & Iron gave Marvin a job as soon as he graduated. There was even some talk of sending Marvin to Lehigh for college chemistry and physics, but Marvin did not want to waste a lot of time on English and history and the other stuff they made you take in college. Now, at fifty-one, he had college graduates working under him at the lab, although they did not as a rule stay with the company after two years.

"Morning, Marvin," said Claude.

"Claude," said Marvin Nerdlinger, without breaking stride.

"A light precipitation," said Claude, holding his umbrella over his shorter friend.

"Thanks, I don't mind a little rain," said Marvin. "You weren't around yesterday."

"Should I have been?"

"Might have been worth your while, I expected you," said Marvin.

"You had a story for me?"

"No, I didn't, but I thought you'd be around trying to get one."

"Come on, now, Marvin. Don't tantalize me. Something happened. What was it?"

"Fourth of July came early this year."

"Fourth of July? You had an explosion? Anybody hurt?"

"Not hurting any more. Never have another moment of pain."

"Who? You mean someone was killed?"

"All I said was the Fourth came early this year. The rest you'll have to find out for yourself."

"That's what I'm trying to do."

"Oh, no. Not me. I said as much as I'm going to."

They parted company at the corner of Main and Scandinavia, and Claude Emerson hurried to his office and the telephone. After calls to the hospitals, the Coal & Iron doctor, the coroner's office, and the fire chief, Claude Emerson said to Frank Carter, the new city editor: "I'm up against a stone wall."

"I wasn't listening," said Carter. "What stone wall?"

"I understand there was an explosion yesterday over at the C. & I. lab. That's over on Coal Street. They keep it separate from the main building."

"What do they do there?"

"Well, a lot of things. Chemical things. I don't understand much of it, but one thing I know they do do, they analyze dynamite and caps. The lab is a little stone building near the car shops. Built of stone and brick. Walls two feet thick. Looks like a guardhouse. They're not allowed to have it in a residential or business area."

"Then why don't you go there and have a look?"

"I will, but the way I always work, on a story like this I don't go and ask them if the thing happened. We know it happened."

"You're sure of that?" said Carter.

"I'm sure. And I'm sure a man was killed. I'd like to have the man's name and some of the details before I go there. The more I have, the less they can deny."

"They can't deny it if a man was killed."

"Oh, can't they?" Claude chuckled. "Wait till you're here a few months. You'll find out they can deny anything. Do me a favor, don't tell the boss I'm working on this."

"If he asks me, I'll have to tell him."

"I understand that, sure. But wait till he asks you. He won't be in for another hour or so, but when he comes in just don't say anything. By that time I may have some facts."

"Are you going to get me into trouble?" said Carter.

"Just stay out of it and you won't get in any trouble."

"Why do they want to be so secretive? Accidents happen all the time. Miners get killed every day, it seems to me."

"This is a different matter. They never had a man killed at the lab, to my recollection, and when this gets out it's going to make people nervous. You're not supposed to keep any dynamite in the city limits. That's an old ordinance from the borough days. Gibbsville Supply Company had an explosion back around 1892, two men killed and a conflagration that gutted three buildings. There was hell to pay, and they passed an ordinance. No more dynamite in borough limits. It's right down there in black and white."

"Well, get after it."

"I'll do that little thing," said Claude Emerson.

Police Sergeant Biddle said there was nothing on the blotter, but he avoided looking at his old friend. "Anyway, it's not a police matter, Claude."

"I know. The fire chief. But Billy McGrew is making himself scarce. I've been after him all morning."

"Go have a look in his book. If there was an alarm turned in, he has to keep a record of it. What time was this supposed to happen?"

"You know darn well when it happened."

"Not a police matter, I told you. You start calling me a liar and I'll kick your big ass out of here."

"I don't have a big ass, and you didn't use to, before you were promoted to sergeant."

At the word sergeant, Biddle looked up. As much as to any politician he owed his chevrons to the daily favorable mentions he had got from Claude Emerson. "Is there anybody out there?"

"No," said Claude Emerson, peeking out in the hallway.

"This didn't come from me, mind you?"

"Hell, you know me better than that," said Claude.

"Somewhere between four P.M. and a quarter after, we got a still alarm. Fire reported at 220 South Coal. Billy McGrew answered it in the chief's car, and the combination truck from Perseverance and some other apparatus in the First and Second Ward. The usual still alarm equipment. When they got there the fire was out, or under control. But there was some scraps of a human body, what was left of it, scattered all over the lab. Name of the man, Kenneth W. Cameron. Age twenty-seven. Married. No children. Employed as chemist by the C. & I. Home address, 22 North Frederick. Moved here from Wilkes-Barre about six months ago. Cause of death, accidental explosion of unknown chemicals. The rest you're gonna have to find out for yourself. Now don't say I never gave you anything."

"I won't say anything, not about you, anyway. What did you say your name was? John J. Jones?"

"Huh? . . . Oh, I catch on. Well, you better not," said Sergeant Biddle.

The deputy coroner was an undertaker, Miles T. Wassell, and Claude Emerson found him in his office in back of the funeral parlor. "Morning, Miles. I hear you won't have much to work with, that young fellow yesterday."

"What young fellow was that, Claude?"

"Oh, I thought the deputy coroner was supposed to know all these things. Well, that'll have to go in my story.

'Deputy Coroner Miles T. Wassell was not informed of the fatal accident to Mr. Cameron.' "

"You better not print that or I'll sue you."

"Then you better tell me what you know—that I didn't find out already, and without any help from you, Miles. I don't have to tell you, the coroner's records are public property. How much dynamite did they have at the lab?"

"I didn't say they had any."

"Then what caused the explosion? Maybe he was making tea and put too much sugar in it."

"I don't know anything about any dynamite."

"Or anything else, so it appears. But remember, if you want to try to make a fool out of me, it'll be tit for tat."

"The man was killed by some unknown chemicals exploding."

"You don't have enough of him for an autopsy. When is the inquest?"

"I'm waiting to hear from the Coroner."

"Yes, I'm waiting to hear from him, too. You can tell him that when you talk to him. Is he taking personal charge?"

"Yes."

"I see. You're under orders to him, then. Well, you just tell him I tried to reach him this morning, and I'm not going to try again. I can be reached at the *Standard* after twelve noon."

The windows of the laboratory were boarded over and a Company policeman stood in the doorway. He was a stranger. "You can't go in there," he said.

"Why not? I'm going to see Mr. Nerdlinger."

"You work for the Company?" said the policeman.

"No, I didn't say I did."

"Then you're not allowed in. I got orders to keep

everybody out. Does Nerdlinger know you're coming?"

"He was expecting me yesterday."

"Well, that was yesterday. I wasn't here yesterday, all I got is my orders for today. What are you, a salesman?"

"Tell Mr. Nerdlinger that Mr. Emerson is here. And tell him I don't enjoy standing out here in the rain."

"Well, I guess you can stand here in the doorway. Wait here a minute, but don't go inside. You're not allowed inside till Nerdlinger says it's okay. Emerson?"

"Claude Emerson."

"Claude. Huh. Claude. All right, Claude, stand here, but don't go any farther, or as big as you are I'll throw you out in the gutter."

"Don't talk that way. Captain Wingfield wouldn't like it."

"You know Captain Wingfield? Are you a friend of Captain Wingfield?"

"I'm a friend of everybody's, unless they try to throw me in the gutter. Yes, I know Cap Wingfield, very well indeed. I knew him before he worked for the Company."

"Are you a lawyer?"

"Listen, go on in and tell Mr. Nerdlinger I'm here, and stop asking me questions, will you?"

Still in doubt, the policeman went inside, and as he opened the door Claude got a strong whiff of the odor of chemicals and stale smoke, but the policeman closed the door too quickly for a good look at the laboratory. Claude tried the door; it was locked.

The policeman returned. "He can't see you. He's busy," he said.

"Well, I'm willing to wait, but not long," said Claude. He made a sniffing noise. "Sure is some smell."

"It's a hell of a lot worse in there," said the policeman.

"Would you mind going back in and ask Marvin—that's Nerdlinger—ask him when he can see me?"

"He didn't sound like he was going to see you. He just said to tell you he was busy."

"Nonsense. What is there to do in there today? Clean up, but he can do that any time."

"No, they have to do it today. They found a piece of the fellow's jaw this morning."

"I didn't think there was that much of him left."

"Oh, that was just talk," said the policeman.

"I thought he was blown into a thousand pieces."

"Nah. From his waist down you wouldn't know he was hurt. The trunk and the head were all blown apart."

"Did you have to look at him?"

"Hell, I seen worse in the army. I dug a grave for worse. Yeah, I saw him. The undertaker put him in a canvas bag last night, the bottom half of him and the big hunks. The piece from his jaw, they found that up on the top shelf where they keep them glass jars, look like Mason jars."

"Oh, I understood all the glass was broken."

"Nah. Dynamite acts funny. You take now for instance a Mills grenade. That goes off and all those little squares, they go in all directions, every which way. But there's a lot of stuff in that labbatory, it wasn't even touched. Smoky, from the fire, but all in one piece."

"There was one report that it was nitro-glycerin."

"Dynamite. This poor son of a bitch was making some kind of a test, and—hyuh, Captain. Friend of yours here."

Captain Thomas L. Wingfield, chief of the Coal & Iron Police Division, stood in the rain and stared at Claude Emerson. "What are you doing here, Emerson?"

"Trying to get in to see Marvin Nerdlinger," said Claude.

(85)

"Have you been gabbing to this man?" said Wingfield to the policeman.

"No, I just got here," said Claude.

"You shut up, Emerson. You, Chapman. What was that about some son of a bitch making a test? What have you been telling this fellow?"

"Now wait a minute, Cap," said Claude.

"You didn't let this fellow get inside, did you?" said Wingfield, ignoring Claude.

"Who is he, this fellow?" said Chapman.

"He's a God damn reporter."

"You God damn son of a bitch!" said Chapman. He went at Claude Emerson with both fists driving into Claude's belly. One punch was enough; Claude Emerson had not been physically attacked since high school days, and he was fifty-one years old.

"Cut that out," said Wingfield, and the beating stopped. "Emerson, you're sticking your nose in where you ought to know better. Go on, get out of here."

"I have to sit down a minute," said Claude. "Can't get my breath." He lowered himself to the stone stoop.

"Let him sit there," said Wingfield.

"Solar plexus," said Claude Emerson.

"You ought to know better," said Wingfield. "Get up and walk around. It'll do you good."

"I don't know if I can."

"Go on in and bring him a drink of water," said Wingfield.

"Yes sir," said Chapman, and went inside.

"What the hell is the matter with you, Claude? Bob Hooker isn't going to print anything about the accident. He's on the Company payroll the same as me."

"I know."

(86)

"This Chapman is a bully-boy, as tough as they come. The next thing would have been the boot for you. One of the toughest men I have."

"Could you send around and get me a taxi?"

"Where do you want to go? Home? I'll drive you there."

"The office."

"I advise you to go home and go to bed, and stay there. You took a couple of mean punches. He goes in there like a pile-driver, with both hands. Come on, I'll drive you home."

"No, I have to go to the office, Cap. I'm getting my breath back."

"I wish this wouldn't have happened," said Wingfield. "Fellows our age, that's real punishment." He helped Claude to his feet and they got in Wingfield's car. It was only about seven blocks to the *Standard* office, and the cold rainy air helped to revive Claude, but he and Wingfield maintained silence until the car stopped at the office. "I wouldn't have had this happen for the world, Claude. You know that. But you should have known better."

"Both doing our jobs, Cap. Thanks for the ride."

"I wish I could fire Chapman, but the trouble is I need him."

"Doing his job, too. So long, Cap," said Claude.

He had to stop and rest a couple of times on his way up the stairs, and when he reached the newsroom it was immediately apparent to Frank Carter and the others that he was not well. "Are you all right?" said Carter.

"Had a kind of an accident, you might call it. I'll be all right after I had a little rest." He hung his hat and raincoat and umbrella on the clothes-tree, and made his way to his desk. "I got a lot on the explosion, but I need more. Did you get anything on it?"

Carter reached in the wire basket and took out two

pieces of paper, one typewritten, one in pencil. "I got this," he said, handing it to Claude. "The Boss wrote the story *and* the head."

"A Number 30 head? For this story?" said Claude.

"Read the story. A 30-head is all it's worth," said Carter.

Claude read aloud:

"Kenneth W. Cameron, age 27, of 22 North Frederick Street, was fatally injured yesterday while conducting an experiment in the laboratory at 220 South Coal Street. The accident occurred, according to eyewitnesses, when Cameron apparently misjudged the proportions of chemicals in a test he was conducting as part of a safety program.

"Cameron, who recently came here from Wilkes-Barre, was the son of Mr. and Mrs. James D. Cameron, of that city. He was a graduate of the Rensselaer Polytechnic Institute, at Troy, N. Y. He was a member of Sigma Chi and Sigma Xi, the latter an honorary fraternity. In addition to his parents, his wife, formerly Miss Nancy Benz, of Nanticoke, survives. Funeral arrangements have not yet been completed. Burial is expected to be in Wilkes-Barre."

"And that's all? That's it?" said Claude Emerson.

"And the head. 'Chemist Dies in Safety Test,'" said Carter.

"And the Boss wrote it all himself," said Claude. "Where are you going to run it?"

"Page three."

Claude Emerson handed the story and headline back to Carter. "I had a little more than that," he said.

"I'll bet you did," said Carter.

"I even had the name of the company Cameron was working for. I see the Boss doesn't mention that."

"I noticed that, too, Claude," said Carter.

"I hope the Boss didn't have as much trouble getting his story as I did mine," said Claude.

"What happened?"

"Ran up against a stone wall. Not the same one I mentioned earlier. Although it was, in a way," said Claude. "Frank, I don't want to leave you short-handed, but I'm going to have to take the rest of the day off. Would you do me a favor and call the cab company? I don't feel much like walking. Or anything else."

"Listen, I'll get one of the boys to drive you home. The circulation department has a car."

"Any other time, but today I'd rather take a taxi. This is the first time in thirty-two years I wished I'd been a book-keeper."

"Not you, Claude," said the city editor.

THE ENGINEER

Work on the big dam had been suspended in 1917 and '18, but after the War the engineers began to arrive in considerable numbers. They were all sorts, running in age between the middle twenties and the early fifties; college men and practical men; married and single; brilliant and barely competent; construction men, electrical men, supervisory men, financial men; men who had worked together in far corners of the world, men who were meeting for the first time; the ambitious, the washed-up, the healthy, the drunkards, the womanizers, the cheats, the gipsies, the dedicated, the dullards, the mysterious, the dependable. Some came and did their jobs and were off and gone in a month or two; others, on jobs that took longer, brought their families; and a few stayed on and became residents of the town, usually because they had had some mining experience and found work in one of the independent coal operations. But whether they left in a month or stayed forever, as a class they were a positive addition to the life of the town. They were educated, well-traveled men; scoundrels or worthy citizens, they were The New Engineers in Town, and no other group of men ever enjoyed quite the same welcome. If some of them abused the welcome, they were usually punished by their confreres' ostracism or efficiently banished by the Company.

They all came to a town already respectful of engineers as a class—the successful and the mediocrities among the native-born mining engineers prepared the way for the new men. And except for the gipsies, the chronically footloose, they could look around and see that for an engineer it was not a bad place to be. Indeed, several of them partnered up to form small engineering firms of their own, with the town as home base, and a couple of those firms are now in the hands of the second generation, not getting rich but getting by.

But in the early Twenties the New Engineers were all strangers in the town, fresh or not so fresh from Cornell and Case and M.I.T., from Wyoming and Montana and Alabama universities, and from Sweden and Scotland and Turkey and France. They took rooms in the Gibbsville Club and the Y.M.C.A., in the hotels and boarding houses, whatever they could get that was appropriate to their position and pay. A man who had had five servants in China was lucky when his bed got made in his boardinghouse on North Frederick Street; and another man who as a colonel had rated his own batman now had to polish his own shoes. But as a group they were adaptable.

Chester L. Weeks arrived in town in 1921, after most of the first wave had gone on to other jobs, and the big generators were in. He checked in at the American House, the oldest and largest hotel, but not the best and by no means the worst. "You understand," he told the desk clerk, "as soon as there's a room with a private bath, I want it. I'm going to be here for some time."

"We understand that, Mr. Weeks," said the clerk. "As soon as Judge Boxmiller checks out."

"How soon do you think that'll be?"

"Well, that's hard to say. Another two-three weeks. He's an out-of-town judge, from over Nesquehela County.

There's some special case he's hearing, I don't exactly know what."

"But when he leaves, I can have the room with bath— and hold on to it? I don't want to give up my private bath every time a judge hears some special case."

"No, this don't happen but once every two-three years."

"Good. Now I have a lot of pressing, and laundry."

"You can give all that to Jimmy, he'll take care of it for you. You can have your laundry back the day after tomorrow."

"Not before then?"

"Well, if Jimmy wants to take it home, his wife can do it special if you're in a hurry."

Chester L. Weeks turned to the colored man beside him. "Are you Jimmy?"

"Yes sir, that's me. Jimmy."

"Is your wife a good laundress?"

"Don't like to brag, but she does the best work I know. All hand work, fifteen cents a shirt."

"And how late is the barber shop open?"

"Oh, ha' past eight, nine o'clock, depending," said Jimmy.

"What time do they open in the morning?"

"In the morning?" said Jimmy.

"They're open around eight o'clock in the morning," said the clerk.

"Fifteen cents for a shirt, eh?" said Weeks.

"Maybe she do it for—twelve?"

"Or maybe she'll never do it again, if she doesn't do good work this time," said Chester Weeks.

"She do good work, that I guarantee you," said Jimmy.

"Do you know what I've been accustomed to paying for a shirt?"

"No sir."

"One cent."

"One cent! A penny! You couldn't even get that low a price from the Chinaman."

"This *was* a Chinaman. In China."

"Oh, in China. That's different. Everything cheaper over there, so I'm told. Them Chinamen, they eat rats and rice. I wouldn't like that. Who'd ever want to eat rats and rice?"

"I have. It can be quite a delicacy."

"Not me. Rice I don't mind. I eat lots of rice, but don't give me no rats with it."

"You probably wouldn't like sheep's eyes."

"Sheep's eyes. You mean eyes out of a regular sheep? Ha ha ha ha. Listen to you talk. Sheep's eyes. Mister, now I *know* you joking me. Mister?"

"What?"

"What else you eat?"

"Oh—fried grasshoppers."

"Fried grasshoppers. Ha ha ha ha ha. What else?"

"Bamboo shoots."

"Bamboo shoots. Ha ha ha. You ever eat any—any— I don't know."

"Thigh meat. I got sick from it."

"What that, thigh meat?"

"Thigh meat, from a man's thigh. They said it was pork, but it wasn't pork."

"Huh? You ate a man?"

"I ate part of a man."

Jimmy was disturbed, and very near to anger.

"Some of the places I've been, and the things I've eaten, it was better not to ask what they were. What are we waiting for? Oh, the rest of my luggage."

"It's coming by Penn Transfer, Mr. Weeks. You don't have to wait. I'll send it up as soon as it gets here. One trunk and one large suitcase?"

"All right, send it up."

In the silent ride up the elevator and the walk to Chester Weeks's room Jimmy decided that no disparagement of his color had been intended by the newcomer, and his anger subsided.

"I'll unpack these bags," said Weeks. "You can take the dirty linen with you, then come back and get the rest when my trunk arrives. Do you send my suits out or are they done here in the hotel?"

"We got a tailor in the basement, he does them."

"No creases in the sleeves, will you tell him?"

"Yes sir. No creases in the sleeves."

"Does your wife know how to wash a linen suit?"

"Yes sir. Sir?"

"Yes?"

"What that sign there, say Raffles?"

"That's the name of a hotel. Singapore. Asia."

"You was in Asia?"

"China's in Asia."

"Oh, yeah. Yeah. Raffles. Some name for a *hot*el, hey?"

"Some hotel, too."

"Man!"

"What?"

"Look at them guns. Mister, how many guns you got?"

"Three. Just these. This one's a Webley. English. This one is French, and this one's American."

"All countries."

"Well, three. That's so it would be easier for me to get ammunition. Couldn't always get American cartridges everywhere I went. And some places I couldn't get British, and so on. But I could usually get one of the three."

(94)

"Was you in the War?"

"Yes. At least I was in the army. Were you in the army?"

"Yes sir, I was a lance corporal. Orderly in the Quartermaster Corps. Served ten months at Frankford Arsenal. Honorable *dis*charge."

"Frankford Arsenal? Where's that?"

"Philadelphia, P A, sir."

"Oh, yes. Here, will you hang these up, please?"

"Hmm. Silk. I never saw a suit made out of silk."

"They won't do me much good when winter comes. How cold does it get here?"

"Oho. Cold. Hot in summer, cold in winter. In the mountains, here. Trolleys don't run. Snow plows get stuck. River gets froze. Poor people don't get enough heat. Children take sick and die. Men got no work. Get drunk and fight, every night, not only Saturday. Folks stay home, ain't got shoes, can't even *look* for work. Men like me, got a steady job in a *ho*tel, they let us take home stale bread for our neighbors. But winter's no good for us, no good at all."

"Why do you come North?"

"Sir, I didn't come North, I was born North. My pappy was born North, *his* pappy born North. We's always here in town, since *I* can remember."

"Then why don't you go South?"

"Huh. South. You can freeze there, too. Wintertime ain't no good anywhere if you don't have wood in the stove and bread in the box. It don't get cold in China?"

"You bet it does. And hot."

"Huh. Guess I'll stay here."

"You might as well. Who polishes the shoes?"

"Me. They got another boy in the barber shop, but the people in the rooms, I shine them."

"Do you take the laces out?"

"When they ask. I run them under the tap and rinse 'em out to look nice and fresh. I do it right. But some don't ask."

"Well, I ask."

"Yes sir, I seen that."

"I like to have my things just so. If I gave you a fixed sum every week would you see to it that my shoes are always polished, and my clothes in order? My hats brushed and so on?"

"Like a valley?"

"Yes."

"A fixed sum? How much is that, a fixed sum?"

"Two dollars a week?"

"Two dollars—I don't know. I got a lot of work to do."

"Five dollars."

"Five? Yes sir, I can do it for five. I come in early or stay late for five. I tend to your shoes, take your suits down when you need a press. Brush your hat. Brush it with a brush, no whisk broom."

"All right, five dollars a week. Here."

"Six dollars?"

"Five dollars for your first week, the other dollar is for today. And don't think I always tip a dollar, because I don't."

"No sir. Thank *you* sir."

The hotel staff and, very soon, the friends of the hotel staff were fascinated by the latest member of the corps of engineers. There had been other strange ones, nutty ones, but this Weeks man was the first they ever heard of who had eaten human flesh; a white cannibal. Chester L. Weeks in a week's time attained a celebrity among the hotel and domestic servants and their friends in advance of his first invitations from the resident engineers and non-engineers of the town. But that is not to say he went unnoticed. It was summer, and the business and professional men of the town wore their Palm Beaches and mohairs, and a few of the rich wore linen suits; but Chester L. Weeks had a tropical wardrobe that was just different enough to attract attention every day, everywhere he went. He changed his suit every day, from spruce, crisp linen to luxurious silk; from Panama to Leghorn to Bangkok to sailor, with puggree bands and the colors of remote clubs to add brightness to his headgear. The stuff was not new, but the style and the variety were new to the town, and in those first days the men with whom Chester L. Weeks had to do business were so bedazzled by his wardrobe that they were slow in realizing that he was no mere dude. He was quick, sharp, and knew his business. The other engineers had dressed very conservatively, casually, or even shabbily; but then Chester L. Weeks was not, strictly speaking, an engineer. He had an engineering degree, and he worked for an engineering firm, but he was essentially a financial man. He was not exactly an accountant, although he discussed accounts; he was not a purchasing agent, although he was keenly interested in prices; he was certainly not a lawyer, but he knew the language of contracts. Nor did he come under the head of the fairly new and somewhat suspect designation of efficiency engineer. One thing was certain: he was not the kind of engineer who put on hobnailed boots and carried a transit on his shoulder.

Whatever the precise nature of his job, he seemed to rate on equal terms with the supervising engineer of the entire hydroelectric project, J. B. Wilcey, who had been in charge of the dam building and the plant construction since the earliest blueprint stage, and who was now something of a fixture in the town, with a good-sized house, a wife who played bridge and tennis, and two children in private schools. Jess Wilcey took Chester L. Weeks around and introduced him to the top men of the business and financial community, who did not fail to notice that Wilcey's manner indicated a willingness to please Weeks. "Thank you, Jess," Weeks would say, politely but unmistakably telling him to go and leave him with the new contact. It did not take long for the business men to get it through their heads that this new fellow, with his blue shirts and linen neckties and highly polished oxfords, was very well thought of in the home office back in New York. The concurrent stories that had somehow got around, to the effect that Weeks had once escaped from Chinese bandits and had seen a companion slaughtered to provide food, probably had enough basis in fact, the business men believed, to prove that dude or not, his manhood could not be questioned. It was hard not to question the manhood of an American who carried his handkerchief in his sleeve.

He was a rather small man, with no extra fat on him anywhere, the skin drawn tight over his cheekbones and a mouthful of large, even teeth. He was nearly bald, and on his face and pate and hands, in a fading suntan, were numerous large freckles or liver spots. He had a sharp nose and thin lips that he had a habit of moistening while he studied a business paper. His concentration was intense and he was liable to be impatient when it was interrupted, but his memory, especially for figures, was remarkable. "Thirty-two cents a foot, I think you said," he would say to a business man, referring to a minor detail of a large sheet of figures.

"I can easily look it up," the business man would say.

"Never mind. It was thirty-two," Weeks would say. "But couldn't you have saved us money on those shipping costs? Why the Lehigh Valley instead of the Pennsylvania?

We had our own trucks, and the Pennsylvania railhead is only four miles farther than the Lehigh Valley. But you took this roundabout way because the Lehigh Valley was four miles closer to the dam. Just at a guess I'd say that made a difference of between eight and ten thousand dollars, without having a table of freight rates at hand."

"You're right except for one thing."

"Where am I wrong?"

"You weren't here, so you don't happen to know that the Pennsy was having a strike. A rump strike."

"Then I apologize. It must be very annoying to have me come here, a total stranger, and start right in by questioning your judgment. I'll be more careful in the future. Next time I won't go off half-cocked. But that doesn't say there won't *be* a next time."

He was as unconcerned over the obvious fact that he antagonized some reputable business men as he was by the admiration of others. ("Show the son of a bitch whatever he's entitled to see, but keep him away from me.") The respect that was shown him automatically by virtue of his position in Wadsworth & Valentine was followed by respect he quickly earned on his own, in his relentless preoccupation with facts and figures and his apparent passion for work. "Don't you ever take time off to relax?" said Jess Wilcey, after two weeks of Chester L. Weeks and his zeal.

"Am I going too fast for you, Wilcey?" said Weeks.

"No, but there's no use killing yourself. You don't have to do it all in a month. In fact, you can't. And my wife's waiting for you to say the word, when we can entertain for you."

"That's very nice of her. Tell her any time from now on. The usual Company dinner?"

"Yes, I guess that's what it'll have to be, the first one.

You haven't met any of the wives, have you?"

"No. How many are there?"

"Six," said Wilcey. "Seven couples and you."

"All right, tell Mrs. Wilcey she can get that over with any time next week or the week after."

"Do you want to join the clubs? You almost have to join the Gibbsville Club, but what about the country club?"

"I'll join it. Company pays for it."

"I don't imagine you want to rent a house, but any time you want to move out of the American House you can probably live at the Gibbsville Club, or my secretary will find you an apartment."

"I like the American House. It's a bit broken down, but I like the atmosphere. How many Company dinners do I have to go to?"

"Just ours. The other wives will ask you to Sunday afternoon tea, but you know which ones you have to go to. Then whenever you're ready, Maria—"

"I know. The dinner to meet the natives. You seem to like it here."

"Yes, I do. We both do."

"Have you had any good offers to stay?"

"Yes, although you have a hell of a nerve to ask that question."

"Well, I *have* a hell of a nerve. That's no news to you, Wilcey. Don't tell me you haven't had a half a dozen letters telling all about me. I've had to play Company politics, too, don't forget. I found out all I could about *you* before I came here. That's part of the fun of working for a big company."

"I don't consider it fun. I stay out of Company politics as much as I can."

"Then you'd better seriously consider that local offer, because when you get to where you are and I am, that's when the Company politics is playing for high stakes."

"I'm a construction man."

"Then I don't have to worry about *you*, since you're planning to settle down here."

"I didn't say that."

"You didn't have to, and I could almost tell you what your next job'll be. But that's fine with me, Wilcey. You and I make about the same money, and the next step up is for you, or me, or McDonald, in Manila. You've eliminated yourself, so it's between McDonald and I. That ought to make for harmonious relations between you and I. Fine. Excellent."

Wilcey smiled. "Where did you learn your politics? In China? I was only out there for one year. Maybe I should have stayed longer."

"You're a construction man, Wilcey. And a good one. You stick to that. Ten years from now we may be able to do business."

"When you're president of Wadsworth & Valentine?"

"Chairman of the board. You're the type of man they make president. I don't want it. I want to settle down in New York. Well, now we understand each other perfectly. I thought we'd be six months getting around to this conversation. I hope you're as relieved as I am."

"I wouldn't say we understand each other perfectly, Weeks. But we made progress."

"I stand corrected. Let's say we understand each other as well as we ever have to. And you're a little keener than I gave you credit for."

"Thanks."

Maria Wilcey's Company dinner for Chester L. Weeks went according to protocol except that the guest of honor was the last to leave.

"Where do you get Scotch around here?" said Weeks.

"I got this through the Gibbsville Club."

"Pretty good. It actually tastes like Scotch. Mrs. Wilcey, may I congratulate you on a very nice dinner party? I hope it wasn't too dull for you."

"No, it went off pretty well, I thought. I'm sorry we couldn't have a young lady for you, but next time there'll be all local people and the town is full of attractive girls. Withering on the vine, I may say."

"I look forward to that."

"So are they," said Maria Wilcey. "They've all been wondering who you were, and by the way they've heard the most awful stories about you."

"I have a spotless reputation."

"No you haven't. Morally, yes, but did you know that you're supposed to be a cannibal?"

"A cannibal, did you say?"

"It isn't a subject I cared to bring up at a dinner party, especially a Company dinner party. But I've been asked whether it was true."

Weeks smiled. "Well—I once partook of human flesh. It was fed to me as pork, but I knew damn well it wasn't. That was in Borneo, when a party of us were sent looking for oil. But how did that get all the way back here? Oh, of course. I know. The bellboy at my hotel. What other damage to my reputation?"

"Do you carry a revolver?"

"No, but I know where that started, too. Same source."

"And you never were a spy," said Maria Wilcey.

"I was a military intelligence officer."

"But not a spy, running from one country to another."

"I've run from one country to another, but always for the greater honor and glory of Wadsworth & Valentine, Incorporated."

"Isn't that a military ribbon you wear?"

"It's the Croix de Guerre, but I got that in France three years ago. I think I'll stop wearing it, now that I'm back in the States."

"You didn't get it for spying?"

"No. My company happened to be next-door neighbors to a French outfit, and they gave all the American officers the Croix de Guerre. Our colonel got the Legion of Honor, and their colonel got the D. S. M. The French outdid us in courtesy, but of course they always do."

"He's lying to you, Maria. He got the Distinguished Service Cross," said Jess Wilcey.

"But not for spying, and that's what Mrs. Wilcey wanted to know about. I wouldn't have made a good spy. Too obvious. Too secretive."

"You had a very good war record. One of the best," said Wilcey.

"Well, all right, I did, but I'm not trading on it," said Chester L. Weeks. "Although of course I always wore my medals whenever the British wore theirs, in China. I have the Military Cross, and that did me no harm—or the Company."

"You're all for the Company, aren't you?" said Wilcey.

"I'm all for Chester L. Weeks, just as you're all for J. B. Wilcey."

"If the truth be told," said Wilcey.

"How long have you been with the Company?" said Maria Wilcey.

"Twelve years, with time out for the army. Do you want to know my age, Mrs. Wilcey? Thirty-seven. Your husband could have told you that."

"He didn't tell me anything about you, except that you were coming, and that you were here." Maria Wilcey was annoyed. "I heard much more about you from outside sources."

"A full description of me—or pretty full—was sent to your husband at least a month before I got here. It always is. You know how the Company works."

"Yes, but you obviously don't know how Jess works."

"Mrs. Wilcey, my job here is going to take about two years, then I'll be sent somewhere else. Maybe back to China. Mexico. We're going to have to see a lot of each other these next two years, and suddenly I seem to have gotten off on the wrong foot with you. Was it that remark about my age?"

"Yes."

"Well, I apologize. You see, I'm accustomed to wherever I go, the Company wives take it upon themselves to play Company politics with me, as happened several times this evening. Then they want to marry me off to their sisters. Well, I don't want to play Company politics with the wives. And I'll be damned if I want to marry their sisters. So I'm on my guard at all times, and if I was rude to you, I'm sorry."

"Well, let's have another Scotch-and-soda and forget about it," said Wilcey.

"First I want to know where I stand with Mrs. Wilcey. Do you accept my apology?"

"Of course," said Maria Wilcey.

"Thank you. Now I'll tell you something. I think you are the most charming, and probably the most intelligent Company wife I've met in many years. I would have thought so anyway, but I might not have told you so if we weren't going to be friends. Wilcey, think twice about taking that other job. I hate to see this charming lady wasted on this town."

"She likes it here," said Wilcey.

"You will too, when you've been here a while, Mr. Weeks."

"Not if I can help it. Your husband knows which way I'm headed."

He refused a lift home, and when the Wilceys had turned off the porch light they could hear the precise tapping of his heels on the sidewalk as he marched homeward. "Listen," said Maria Wilcey. "He even walks like a pouter pigeon."

"A pouter pigeon—"

"I know. Hasn't got leather heels. But isn't he a strutting little man?"

"Oh, I guess he's all right."

"I'll turn Mary Beth Huber on him. She's the last thing he'd expect to encounter here."

"Why do you want to do that?"

"Because he's so darn patronizing about this town."

"So were you, at first."

"So I was."

Mary Beth Huber, the most widely traveled young woman in the town, and soon to be off on another trip, sat next to Chester L. Weeks at Maria Wilcey's second dinner party. At the meat course she announced: "I refuse to apologize for monopolizing this man, but he has news of friends of mine I haven't seen in aeons. Now, Mr. Weeks, tell me about Jack and Lydia Banning-Douglass. Did they ever patch it up?"

"No. She went home, and he stayed in Hong Kong."

"And married the Russian? I can't believe *that*."

"No, she was around Shanghai for a while, then she disappeared."

"I didn't think that would come to anything," said

Mary Beth. "Did you ever know Hans van Blankers?"

"Van Blankers? Was he with Shell?"

"I don't think so."

"Where would I have known him?"

"In Bangkok."

"Oh, well you see I haven't been there since before the War."

"No, he was there after the War."

"My particular friends in Bangkok were the Van Egmonds."

"Still there. I had a Christmas card from them last year."

"So did I. Picture of a Dutch boy and Dutch girl skating on the canal."

"And the windmills in the background. Homesick, and afraid to go home after so many years. Just like so many of our friends out there. Did you find that to be the case?"

"Almost invariably, if they stayed in one place. The people that shifted around, or got home every two or three years, they didn't want to stay put. But some of the others you couldn't budge."

"And no wonder. I don't imagine they could live on the same scale back in England, or Holland."

"Although it was the women that usually wanted to go home."

"Well, that's understandable, too. Nobody ages very well in the tropics, but it tells more on the women. Physically, I mean. Are you going back?"

"I just got here, don't send me back so soon. I've just unpacked. Truthfully, I don't know. I'll be here about two years, then I don't know what comes next. We never do, especially we bachelors."

"If you had your way what would you do?"

"Oh, I have my way, Miss Huber. I'm not doing anything I don't want to do. But I suppose you mean if I had the money to do everything I want to do?"

"Yes."

"I'd go on working. I'd be doing more important things than I'm doing now, but working just as hard, using the same brains."

"The tropics haven't affected your ambition."

"I haven't spent all my time in the tropics, and in any case I wouldn't use that as an excuse for laziness. My offices in Hong Kong and Shanghai were no more uncomfortable than my office here. The electric fan was a great invention. The electric fan, used in conjunction with the paperweight."

"I'm going abroad next week. I'll be very much interested to see how you like Gibbsville when I get back."

"Where are you off to?"

"I'm taking my mother to the French Riviera. We'll take trips to North Africa, but I don't expect to see any of our mutual friends. I might go out that way again next year. It would be fun to. Did you play polo in China?"

"Yes, some."

"Then you must have known a man called Pat Dinsmore."

"I was wondering how you happened to miss Pat."

"Oh, I know, Mr. Weeks. But you must admit he has charm."

"Carloads of it."

"I fell for it, just like all the others, before and since. Was he a friend of yours? Do you hear from him?"

"Hear from him? He can barely read and write. No. I don't expect to hear from him. As for his being a friend of mine, he doesn't need friends. He has charm. But I suppose if I wrote to him I'd get an answer, some time in the next year."

"Don't on my account. But how is he?"

"Well, I saw him in June. He came to a stag farewell party for me, and that was one night he left his charm at home."

"And I guess that wasn't the first time. But you forgave him. Why *do* we, people like that? We're so intolerant of little faults in nice people, and yet we're prone to overlook big faults in people like Pat Dinsmore."

"Since you honor me with your confidence, I'll tell you that I never did forgive Pat Dinsmore. And if you ever do see him again, please don't mention my name, when I'm not there to defend myself. Will you promise me that?"

"Of course. Not that I ever expect to see him."

In her remaining days at home Mary Beth Huber did more than dispel some early suspicions that Chester L. Weeks was somehow phony. Especially among the younger men of the town, and particularly among those who had gone to good prep schools and colleges, the social judgment on him was severe. They conceded that his engineering degree from a Western Conference university was probably authentic; Wadsworth & Valentine would have checked on that. They accepted the Wadsworth & Valentine opinion of his professional ability. But his manners and his taste in clothes were a little wrong—and therefore all wrong. The word of Mary Beth Huber, world traveler, was indisputable in fixing Chester L. Weeks's previous social position in the Far Eastern polo and gin sling world. And yet he was not right. He made no claims that were probably false; he made few claims at all, and in two spheres of admirable activity—his work, and his war record—he did not take the credit he was entitled to. The same kind, and a lesser degree, of offense had been given when the leading bootlegger's younger brother had blossomed forth in a five-hundred-dollar raccoon coat. The fact that Chess-turr (they dragged out his name derisively) did not lie and that his credentials were valid was frustratingly infuriating, and it was not particularly pacifying to call him a wet smack and let it go at that.

He was at his most offensive at the bridge table. He was exceptionally good in a community where the standard of bridge was high. He would sometimes, after the fourth or fifth trick, lay down his hand and say, "I'll give you the king of clubs and a diamond trick. The rest are mine," and pick up a pencil to mark the score.

"Let's play it out," someone would say.

"Why? If you insist, all right, but I assume you're going to follow suit. All right, *let's* play it out." He was, of course, always right in such cases, and he was annoyingly over-patient with slow players.

"Is that your lead, Mrs. Walker?" he would say.

"Yes. The ten of hearts."

"I see the ten of hearts, but I want to make sure it's your final decision. Mrs. Walker has led the ten of hearts. From dummy, Mr. Weeks plays the queen. The queen of hearts, Mr. Forbes. Your king, Mr. Forbes? My ace. And now I lead my jack in the same suit. The jack of hearts, led. Mrs. Walker. The knave."

"Oh, dear."

"Why don't you play your four of hearts, Mrs. Walker? *Or* your five. I'm almost sure you have one or the other, because I see that little deuce and that little trey sitting over there in dummy. Ah, the four! Thank you, Mrs. Walker. From dummy I shall play the little deuce. And Mr. Forbes, I count on you to have the six-spot. Yes, the six. Nice distribution, isn't it? But I don't think we'll try that again. What's that they say about the children of London?"

"The children of London are starving because their fathers wouldn't lead trumps."

"I *thought* you'd know that, Mrs. Walker."

At least once a week he would play at a dinner-and-bridge or a bridge-and-supper, and if in the course of the evening there was always someone to feel the sting of his sarcasm for a wrong bid or an unreturned lead, no one could deny that Chester L. Weeks had the game to back it up. He played regularly in another foursome of two other men and a woman who were generally conceded to be the bridge sharks of the town, and he was equally tyrannical with them, although in this foursome the others fought back. The game was never played for high stakes; a quarter of a cent a point, in stag games at the Gibbsville Club, was the limit. But social prestige and the entree to certain formidable houses were reward enough for a man in his first winter in the town. And as he improved his position it seemed foolish and futile to maintain a hostility toward him that was based on little more than a hunch that he was somehow a faker. At the end of his first year in the town he had demonstrated his superiority in bridge, which could not have been faked; he was respected by the men of business and, obviously, by the Company that employed him; he really had played some polo in China; he had some first-class military decorations for bravery under fire. It was ridiculous to say that no one knew anything about him; no one knew very much about any of the new engineers' pre-Gibbsville history, and because of the special animosity toward him, more questions had been asked about his background than about any other man's in the Company. In a year's time the active animosity toward him practically vanished because it had become a bore, and it disappeared without having done anything to mollify or appease the young men who contemned him. They could have beaten him at golf and tennis, but he not only declined their invitations to play; he wondered aloud why presumably grown men wasted their energies on such silly pastimes. Then, to prove that he was not merely anti-sports, he won a mile race against a recent captain of the Penn swimming team.

All this was observed and duly noted by the mothers of nubile young women, most keenly by those mothers whose husbands had accurate information on Chester L. Weeks's personal finances. He was a long way from wealthy, but he was making fifteen thousand a year and his capital was somewhere around a hundred thousand. He was, moreover, thirty-eight years old, and according to Maria Wilcey, next in line for an important position in the home office in New York. He had distributed his attentions evenly among the young women of good family, and he had been classified as elusive; but no conscientious mother believed that an elusive bachelor was a confirmed one, and Blanchette Moseley was the conscientious mother of Ida Moseley, age twenty-five, graduate of Miss Harper's School for Girls, near Ardmore, and of Wellesley College. Blanchette Moseley was convinced that her Ida was just the kind of girl who ought to appeal to a man like Chester L. Weeks. *"You've* got to do something about it, Adam," she admonished her husband.

"All right, but what?" said Adam Moseley. "We've had him here for dinner a couple of times."

"Oh, *that*. So has everybody else. Get him interested in the bank."

"Oh, positively. I can just see the expression on certain faces when I say we ought to put this new fellow on the board. Apart from the fact that Weeks doesn't own a single share of bank stock."

"Wedding present."

"Well, if you want to give him your stock, that's all right with me."

"You don't have to give it to *him,* do you? We can give it to Ida."

"Bee, we don't want to get in any money competition to buy a husband for Ida. She'd hate that, and anyhow, we wouldn't necessarily win that kind of a competition."

"Have a talk with Ida and see how much she'd hate it. She thinks Chester's the most interesting man that ever came to town."

"In some ways he is, but how does he feel about Ida?"

"He has to be prodded, that's all. They have a lot in common. Don't forget Mary Ku."

"Mary Ku? Oh, that Chinese girl."

"Ida's best friend at Wellesley. Through her Ida knows a lot about China. And Ida loves to travel."

"I know that, all right. But so does Mary Beth. I'll do anything and everything I can, but first Weeks has to show some interest."

"He does not! That's exactly where you're wrong. He's so set in his ways that he'll never marry anybody if somebody doesn't prod him."

"You keep saying prod him. I don't quite know what you mean."

"Let's invite him on a trip, away from here."

"Just the four of us? You can't just up and invite him to go along on a trip with us and Ida."

"You don't have to do it that way. Take him up to the camp and Ida and I'll come along later."

"Well, that might work out. If he'll go."

"Ask him. He's not going to hear it by Ouija board."

"It won't look right if it's just he and I. I don't know him that well. I ought to ask a couple other men."

"Ask as many as you please, but not their wives and daughters."

An invitation to spend three or four days at Adam Moseley's camp with two or three men of equal substance would not be taken as a black mark on Chester L. Weeks's record at the home office. Jess Wilcey, for example, had not been given such an invitation until he had lived in Gibbsville three years. "I can guarantee you a buck if you know which way to point a rifle, and there's some trout fishing. In the evening we usually get up a game of bridge or poker. What size shoe do you wear?"

"Eight-B," said Chester L. Weeks.

"Then I guess I can fix you up with all the clothes you'll need. Not very dressy up there, you know. But plenty of hot water. You'll want a hot bath, especially after that first day in the woods. I notice you're a Scotch drinker, and we also have plenty of Canadian ale. We can leave here the afternoon of the fourteenth, about three hours' drive. Have a good dinner and turn in early so we can be up first thing in the morning. You familiar with the Thirty-O-Six? That's the rifle most of us use."

"Know the rifle very well."

"Good. I have four of them, and you can take your pick. Or you can use a different one every day till you get the limit. Our limit, that is. Our limit's one buck to a man. That's over the legal limit, but it's fair. The game wardens use common sense."

"I haven't brought down a deer since I left Michigan."

Here, at this precise point, by naïvely accepting an invitation he considered a simple compliment, Chester L. Weeks had made a decision he would regret throughout the rest of his life. On Wednesday afternoon Adam Moseley picked him up in his Dodge coupe. They arrived at the camp approximately three hours later, to be greeted by the other hunters, Samuel D. Lafflin, a Wilkes-Barre coal operator, and Malcolm Macleod, division superintendent of the Pennsylvania Railroad, both good shots and good bridge players. They had a steak dinner, cooked by Moseley's guide and caretaker; three rubbers of bridge after dinner, and a good night's sleep. They left the cabin at five-thirty in the morning, and were back at eleven, Lafflin having got his buck in the first hour. Toward dusk MacLeod, Moseley, Weeks, and the guide went out again, and Weeks shot his buck while there was still enough light for a good photograph of the animal and the overjoyed hunter. "Another fifteen minutes and you wouldn't have gotten him," said Moseley. "I'm going to make you a present of his head, mounted. I know a good taxidermist in Allentown."

"Why wouldn't I have gotten him fifteen minutes later? Too dark?"

"Yes. You could have still seen him, all right, but I wouldn't have let you shoot. If you'd missed, you know. Buck fever. A spent bullet from a Thirty-O-Six could kill a man a mile away and you'd never know it."

"But I didn't miss, and anyway I don't get buck fever."

"No, you certainly don't," said Moseley.

"We have two more days," said Weeks. "If you and MacLeod don't get your deer by Saturday afternoon, is it permissible for me to take another shot?"

"Well, yes. But you have to let MacLeod have first shot. That's the usual understanding."

"And what about you?"

"You can have my shot."

"Thank you."

In spite of Moseley's guarantee, no more deer were shot, but Weeks remained keyed up until late Saturday afternoon. His disappointment at not getting a second kill was offset by his being, with Lafflin, one of the two lucky hunters, and the arrival of Mrs. Moseley and her daughter in the middle of the afternoon furnished him with a new audience. "Do you shoot, Mrs. Moseley?" he said, at dinner.

"Only with my camera. Ida has. Ida got her first deer when she was fourteen."

"Fifteen, Mother," said Ida Moseley.

"Your first? And how many have you shot since then?"

"Six, here. Two years ago, in Maine, I shot a moose." She pointed to a head over the fireplace. "That one. Everybody thinks that was Daddy's, but it wasn't. It was mine. Daddy *wishes* it was his, but it isn't."

"I don't wish it was mine," said Moseley. "I just wish it had been T.R., instead of a poor inoffensive moose."

Blanchette Moseley's apprehension that Weeks might resent the feminine invasion of the stag party was unfounded. Rather, he seemed to be stimulated by the presence of women, and he was gracious and entertaining until after lunch on Sunday, when they were all ready to leave for home. "I wish I could spend a month up here," he said.

"It's all yours, if you can persuade Wadsworth & Valentine to give you a vacation," said Moseley. "But it'd probably get pretty lonely up here with only Joe Mossbacher to talk to. He doesn't have much to say."

"The less he said the better. Maybe I might even send him away."

"I don't know," said Moseley. "It'd be quite a change for you, you keep pretty busy."

"Isn't that what I want? A change?"

Blanchette Moseley easily maneuvered Weeks into Ida's car for the homeward journey, and herself into Adam Moseley's Dodge. "It went off very well," she said.

"Nothing forced, nobody got self-conscious."

"No, but don't count on me for any more cooperation. I don't like this fellow."

"Oh, now what? I knew you had something plaguing you."

"I don't want him for a son-in-law. No, it's not that. I don't want Ida to be his wife, that's what I don't want."

"I hope you'll respect Ida's wishes in the matter. You'll get a very different story from her. What terrible thing did you find out about him?"

"It's nothing you'd understand."

"Irritating. What is there that you'd understand that I wouldn't, pray tell?"

"The effect it had on him when he killed his buck. Right away he wanted to go on a killing rampage. He wanted to kill Mac's buck and mine."

"You didn't get one, neither did Mac."

"No, you wouldn't understand it at all. He's the kind of a fellow that comes up here and kills three or four deer, as many as he can kill, and leaves them to rot. Doesn't even bother to skin them out."

"You were willing to let him stay here a month."

"That was a safe invitation. There's something about this man's character, I don't pretend to know what it is, but I don't want to see him married to Ida."

"Well, I hope for Ida's sake that she can overlook these mysterious flaws in his character. And don't you help her go looking for them."

"We're going to have snow," said Moseley. "They're having a blizzard in Montana, I read."

"Oh, pish and tush, Adam Moseley."

Ida Moseley had her friends, and throughout that

fall and winter Chester L. Weeks was so frequently asked to call for Ida—he would walk to her house, and they would proceed to parties in her car—that it began to be taken for granted that he would be her escort at the social functions of the younger set. She was not so beautiful that habitual propinquity to her was likely to turn a man's head; there was no compelling urgency in a friendship with Ida Moseley, and no unbearable suspense was created for her friends. With Ida it was said you could have a good time without getting serious, and plainly Chester Weeks had a good time with Ida, a jolly good time. But Ida was unable to confide in even her closest friends that Chester had misbehaved, made passes, got fresh, or stayed late at her house. He was of course an older man, a man of the world who had himself under control at all times and one who was more likely to protect a girl's reputation than some of the young bachelors and young husbands in Ida's set. It was somehow understood that he *probably* had secret affairs with some of the women in the town who were understood to have secret affairs with men like Chester L. Weeks; those well-dressed dressmakers and nurses and manicurists who went out with traveling salesmen but rarely were seen in public with town men. It would have been so easy for him to have just that kind of extremely private life while living at the American House. He had refused to take advantage of the vacancies at the Gibbsville Club when they occurred, and the American House was known to be lax about women visitors in men's rooms. And Chester himself, so secretive and so independent and self-sufficient, was just the kind of man who would be too discreet to patronize one of the whorehouses but would make elaborate, secret arrangements for his pleasure. Without a doubt he had had concubines in China, and on the word of Mary Beth Huber he had moved in a fast set on the other side of the world.

Among the older men and women, contemporaries of Adam and Blanchette Moseley, the belief in Chester Weeks's clandestine affairs was so fixed that they expressed some cautious concern for Ida's future: if, as seemed reasonable to suppose, he were eventually to marry Ida, would he give up his other women? Ida pretended to be a sophisticated girl, but did she know what she might be getting into? A man like that could ruin a nice girl's life, and for all her sophistication—reading books by Schnitzler, shooting crap with the young men, driving her Hudson Speedster at eighty miles an hour, and the black silk one-piece bathing suit that had got her a strongly worded note from the club—Ida was a nice girl. Friends of Adam and Blanchette Moseley hoped Ida would not make a fool of herself over this man, and they would be glad when his two years were up and he went away.

Not much was left of his two years at the end of that second winter, and Ida Moseley faced the spring in a mood that sickened her because she would not treat it as desperation. Every day was lost time, and the first of August less than four months away. Chester thought he knew where he was going next: the Company had already asked him how he would feel about being "loaned" to the Irish government.

"Would you like that?" said Ida.

"Hard to say," said Chester. "It could be a big step forward, or it could turn out to be a waste of time. One thing that would interest me."

"What?"

"Well, the language. In China we used to hear that Gaelic and one of the Chinese dialects—I forget which—

had words in common. I'd know as soon as I heard them. And of course living in Ireland is much cheaper than living here. I'd save a lot of money there."

"You never worry about money."

"I don't worry about it, but I think about it."

"When would you go, if you went?"

"I get a month off in August, then I report to the home office. Probably the middle of September, late September."

"Won't you be at all sorry to leave Gibbsville?"

"No. I'm not like Jess Wilcey. He's staying here, you know."

"Yes, I know. Maria told me."

"And that's why he's staying. Because Maria likes it. And I guess he does too, although it's Maria that makes the decisions."

"You don't like Maria."

"No. A man as good as Jess shouldn't stop here. He should have made at least one more step upward."

"You've made a lot of friends here."

"Name two. You, but who else?"

"Oh—dozens. You've been one of the most popular men we've ever had. You could be going somewhere every evening if you wanted to."

"Only to escape another kind of boredom. If I had to, I could finish up my job here in four or five weeks. I'm 'way ahead of my schedule. As a matter of fact, I've thought about doing just that, finishing up and taking a leave of absence before the Irish job."

"What other kind of boredom did you mean?"

"Sitting in my room with no work to do."

"Before you go I want to see your room."

"Why? There's nothing to see. Half a dozen prints, and

a mantelpiece full of photographs. But my own furniture's in storage in New York."

"I'd still like to see it, where you've lived for nearly two years."

"No. Can you imagine the buzzing if you were seen leaving the American House?"

"Well, naturally."

"If I had my own things it might be worth it. I have some really lovely pieces I picked up in China. Some jade, naturally. And some tapestries that date back to the twelfth century."

"Haven't you any of the jade here?"

"Four pieces, minor items in my collection because I know what hotel chambermaids can do. But the good stuff is stored in New York till I have a house there. Has to be a house. No apartment for me."

"I still want to see your room at the American House."

"It can't be done. Your mother would not approve."

"What if I went there with her?"

He smiled. "Sure, if your mother's interested in brass beds and Grand Rapids rockers."

"Tomorrow, after dinner?"

"Day after tomorrow. I'd offer you dinner, but they don't set a very good table at the American House. You and your mother come in any time after half past eight."

At nine o'clock on the second evening Ida Moseley appeared in the hotel lobby, went to the house telephone, and was connected with Chester's room. "We're downstairs," she said.

"Come right up," he said.

He stood in the hall outside his room, and said nothing when she walked past him through the doorway. He closed the door.

"This could get you in all sorts of trouble, Ida," he said.

"Well, I'm here, so it's too late to do anything about it now," she said. "Don't be cross, Chester. Give me a drink."

"I'll have to send downstairs for some ice. That means the bellboy, getting a good look."

"Jimmy Scott? I've seen him already. Jimmy used to work for us, in our garden. Just give me whiskey or gin and some water from the tap. And a match, please."

He lit her cigarette and made two Scotch-and-waters. She took off her hat and tossed it in a chair.

"What exactly did you have in mind, Ida?"

"I wanted to put you in a compromising position."

"Compromising positions are passé, but endangering your own reputation is just damn foolishness. And that's all you're doing."

"Well, let's have a drink on it."

"It won't be your first, either."

"No, I sneaked a few at home. Is it noticeable? I only had two. No, three. I had a brandy with Daddy, and two by myself."

"Where's your car?"

"Parked down the street in front of the bank. Why?"

"Finish your drink, and we'll go for a ride."

"No hurry."

"That's just the point, there is. If we go now, right this minute, you might be able to get away with it. Not even that evil-minded night clerk could accuse you of much in five minutes."

"Oh, you have a portable. Have you got any new records?"

"Ida, let's cut out the nonsense."

"Now, you've made your honorable gesture, honorable Chester. Honorable Chester with the honorable gesture. But having done so, your conscience is clear and I, for one, would like another Scotch. How about you?"

"No more, for me or you,"

"Don't be an Airedale. I'm not some sixteen-year-old virgin, unacquainted with the facts of life. Surely you don't think I'm so hopeless that I could reach the age of twenty-five without being seduced. I wouldn't call that a compliment, not a bit. Chester?"

"What?"

"Don't make me talk this way. I don't want to get tight. But I have to have something to get up my nerve. If you knew the times I wanted you to kiss me. And if you had, you could have gone the limit. Did you know that? Is that why you didn't kiss me? You could tell that, couldn't you?"

"I suppose so."

"You know so. I don't know whether I love you or not. I think I do. But whether I do or not, I'm sort of hypnotized by you. And that's just as good or just as bad as being in love. I don't care a *thing* about that other boy. He was just a—well, he was a *darling* boy. I won't say anything against him. And I admit it, I was crazy about him. But with you it was sex without being sex, if you know what I mean, and you probably don't. Or maybe you do. Do you?"

"Yes."

"Oh, you do? Then you knew about me, and you didn't want to start something. See, that's where Neddie was inexperienced. Neddie was the boy. He never would have understood that, but you do. That's where you're experienced. All those women, probably Chinese girls and

heaven knows what all. You know we're a lot alike, you
and I. You were probably seducing me all that time
without even holding my hand, and I felt it. I knew what
you were doing. You learned that in China, didn't you?
I read it somewhere, something to that effect. Or India.
It takes immense concentration. But I have a lot to learn,
haven't I?"

"Yes, you have."

"I'll be with you in a minute," she said. She went to
his bathroom, and came out in a few minutes, wearing her
slip and shoes. "I'm still a bit shy," she said.

"So I see."

"You hurry, though, please? And while you're in there
I hope you don't mind if I turn out the light."

"I'm not going in there, Ida."

"All right. Come here and kiss me, darling."

He sat on the edge of the bed, took her in his arms,
and kissed her. "There," he said.

"No, I think the light's too strong," she said. "It's the
light, it's much too strong. And take off your coat. Your
coat and vest, take them off."

"No, Ida, I'm sorry."

"I'll take off this slip."

"No, don't."

"I have a nice shape, I really have."

"I know you have. It's quite lovely."

"One of the best in my class."

"I'm sure."

She smiled. "But you don't have to take my word for
it."

"I'd rather," he said. "I'd really rather, Ida."

"Don't you want to *see* me?"

"I don't really want to see you."

"You want to wait a while?"

"It isn't that. Seeing you won't make the slightest difference. Nothing will."

She was silent. She gazed thoughtfully at the brass posts at the foot of the bed, and she frowned. Then she remembered that her hand was on his shoulder, and she took it away.

"You mean you can't?" she said.

"I can't because I don't want to."

"Oh."

"It isn't you, Ida. You're very sweet. Very sweet. And I'm sorry."

"Wouldn't you just like to lie here with me, gently?"

"It wouldn't be any use, and I wouldn't like it. No, I don't want to."

"Is it men?"

"When it's anything, yes."

"But that's terrible, Chester. I feel so sorry for you."

He smiled. "That's because you're nice. You are nice, you know."

"I never guessed. You know—I'm supposed to be pretty blasé."

"Well, now I guess you will be. When you've had time to think it over."

"I don't need time. And I don't like being blasé."

"No, it isn't much."

"It's nothing. Really nothing."

"And now I'm nothing, am I?"

"I don't know. Kiss me again."

He kissed her cheek. She shook her head. "It's much too much for me to understand. I'll have a drink, please."

He went to the table, and while his back was turned she slipped past him to the bathroom. She came out fully dressed, and accepted the glass he held out for her. She sat down and gave him a quick smile, but looked away from him.

"Is this one of the jades you brought from China?"

"Yes, not a very good one."

She put it down without examining it very carefully. "I don't know anything about jade. I have one in my room at home that's supposed to be pretty good. Given to me by a Chinese friend of mine."

"Mary Ku," he said.

"Yes, you've heard me speak of her. She's been here. Everybody adored her."

"Go on home, Ida. Don't make talk-talk."

She finished her drink quickly. "I think I will. Are you coming for dinner Friday?"

"No, I don't think so."

"You can if you want to."

"No."

"I guess you're right, really."

"If I sent you one of my good jades would you keep it?"

"Oh, you know I'd like to, but——"

"Say no more."

"I need a little time to straighten things out in my mind. Oh, heavens, Chester. *You* know."

"Of course."

"Goodnight," she said.

Her car went off the road at a turn about five miles north of Reading, some time around half past ten. It was quite possible that she was blinded by the headlights of a bootlegger's truck, but no one knew why she was so far from home, and alone, at that hour of the night. But they found a considerable amount of alcohol in her stomach, and that was when the questions led back to the American House. Dr. Mary Ku came all the way from Massachusetts General to attend the funeral.

THE FATHER

Miles J. Berry, forty-two, assistant foreman and head mechanic at the Clinton Motor Company, Trenton, New Jersey, entered the kitchen of his home on the outskirts of Trenton, took a can of beer out of the refrigerator, put the can and a glass on the kitchen table, pushed his cap to the back of his head, and let go with a long sigh. From the second story came his wife's voice. "Is that you, Miles?"

"Yes, that's me, Miles. Who the hell'd she expect?"

"Wha'?"

"I said yes it was me."

"There's a letter for you, I put it on top of the TV. It looks like it was from one of your sisters."

"Which one?"

"Wha'?"

"Which one?"

"I do' know. I didn't open it."

"But you're sure it's from one of my sisters."

"Wha'?"

"How'd you know it was from one of my sisters?"

"I seen the postmark on the envelope. Nyack, New York, and it isn't your mother's handwriting."

Miles Berry sipped his beer and lit a cigarette. Slowly he reached down and untied his right shoelace, then untied his left shoelace. He had another sip of the beer, then pulled the laces out of the top eight eyelets of both shoes, took the shoes off and pulled his socks away where they were stuck to his feet. He sighed again. "Ah, Christ," he said.

"What are you beefing about now?"

He had not heard his wife, in her canvas wedgies, coming downstairs, and now she stood at the dining-alcove door, with a bundle of dirty laundry in her arms. "I wasn't beefing," he said. "Where's Ava?"

"She's out, I guess."

"She's out you guess? We don't have all that big a house. She's out or she's in."

"She's out," said Vilma Berry.

"Where, out?"

"Where? At a friend's, maybe. Or down at Al's. The kid's young, she has to have some relaxation."

"You ought to keep her out of that Al's. I know that Al. I knew him ever since I was a kid and any joint he runs I don't want my kid hanging around."

"Then you tell her. What's the harm in having a Coke and maybe smoking a couple cigarettes?"

"You look inside of one of those cigarettes and maybe you won't find any tobacco."

"What are you, inferring they get reefers at Al's?"

"Not inferring anything."

"Well, if you want to give her an order to stay out of Al's you do it. But Ben Lightner the cop's daughter goes there, and if there was reefers for sale Ben ought to know about it."

"Ben is a traffic cop. What does he know where they sell reefers?"

"All right, all right, all right. If you got information you ought to report it."

"I didn't say I have any information. I just said I know Al. I went through school with him and I was in the army with him."

"Whenever your feet hurt you start getting strict with Ava. Why don't you buy a new pair of shoes instead of torturing your feet with those clodhoppers? Then we'd have a little more peace around here."

"Wuddia want me to do? Wear loafers to work? I gotta wear shoes that keep my feet dry. It might inarrest you to know we *wash cars* at the garage, not to mention oil and grease on the floor. I can't wear any other kind of shoes and keep my feet dry."

"Well, I just wish you'd find some solution. You got your bad feet from the army. Make them give you the right shoes."

"It's too much red tape."

"You got anything you want to put in the laundry?"

"No."

"You want to wear what you got on to work tomorrow?"

"Yes."

"It wouldn't hurt you to wear a clean shirt and pants."

"What's wrong with what I got on?"

"Because this is the day I put them in the laundry, otherwise you'll be short next week. You'll want clean next Monday, and I won't have them for you. You got two clean pants in your drawer and two clean shirts, but you'll need clean next Monday to start the week in. Wednesday you'll want clean, Friday you'll want clean, Monday you'll want clean, but you'll only have dirty. How'd you get those so dirty today?"

"I thought you were suppose to wash on Monday? My mother always did her washing on Monday."

"Listen, I got a system worked out, so don't start screwing it up after all these years. The least you can do is go to work with a clean shirt and pants, and nobody can say I'm not a good housewife. This washer isn't big enough for all the laundry I have to do."

"Three people and this house? Wuddia want, the Stacy-Trent washing machine? We only got three people and the sheets and towels. What's so big about that?"

"Because I send my daughter to school clean and my husband to work clean and I do the marketing clean, and anybody comes into this house don't see a lot of dirty towels—you know how many towels you use up in a week? And since you took to wearing that long underwear."

"You rather I got pneumonia?"

"Oh, you're just beefing about anything and everything. Why don't you go read your letter from your sister?"

"Curiosity killed the cat."

"Well, what's *she* writing you a letter for? If she has anything to say why doesn't she say it over the phone, those Friday night calls from Nyack. Collect. God Almighty, you'd think you were living in South Dakota somewhere, and they never saw their brother Miles."

"Well, they don't hardly."

"There's nothing stopping you from taking the car and driving up to Nyack any Sunday you want to."

"Nothing but fifty thousand cars on the Turnpike. I don't get any pleasure out of driving that way."

"Go read your letter."

"When I finish my beer," he said, finishing it.

The letter was leaning against a light blue, temporarily empty flower pot on top of the television apparatus. The handwriting was that of Dot Berry, Miles Berry's older sister. The envelope almost matched the color of the flower pot, and Berry held it up to the light because he could tell it contained two items, one besides the notepaper. Good old Dot.

He tore open the end of the envelope and took out the contents, the notepaper and an old newspaper clipping. Whenever Dot wrote him she always enclosed a newspaper clipping or something like that. The clipping seemed to be from the *Daily News,* although he was not sure. It was a photograph taken in 1943, and it showed four-and-a-half teen-age girls, some grinning, some in the midst of rolling their eyes, huddled together behind a sign that said: "Frankie Boy Is the Most— The Sinatra Swooners Trenton N. J." The caption gave the names of four of the girls, and the second girl from the left was Vilma Schrock, 17, Trenton.

"For God's sake," said Miles Berry. He read the caption again. The girls, it read, had been waiting outside the Paramount Theatre in New York City since seven o'clock in the morning, and at the time the picture was taken they had been waiting four hours and probably would have to wait four more, because the kids who were already in the theater were refusing to leave when the show was over. Vilma Schrock, 17. And he knew the others, too. Mary D'Isernia, 16; Carmen Quisenberry, 17; Rosemary McEntegart, 17, and Betty Dougherty, 16. They were all married, all living in or near Trenton, with their husbands and a total of about fifteen or sixteen children. He read Dot's note:

Dear Milo:
I came across this old paper underneath a pile of stuff in the attic. I guess it was when Mom used to save up Dick Tracy to send you before

you went over seas. She does not remember why she saved it altho we looked all thru the paper to see if there was some article in it. You were over seas when this picture was taken & did not know Vilma then. Therefore we did not save the paper on acc't of Vilma being in it. Just a coincidents. I bet she gets a big laugh out of it today.
Mom is better. Will phone Fri.

Sincerely,
Dot

There she was, the way she was at seventeen, looking as though she were about to charge the photographer and bite him. She had better teeth than the other girls in the picture, but did she have to look like a charging tigress? The photographer probably had said something disparaging about Frankie Boy, to get her reaction.

The kitchen door swung open and Ava came through. "Hi," she said.

"Hi," he said.

"What are you reading?"

"I got a letter from your Aunt Dot."

"Aunt Dot? What does *she* want?"

"She doesn't want anything. She isn't like some people, the only time you—"

"I know, I know, I know. The only time you hear from them is if they want something. I know. What's the matter with the TV?"

"Who said anything's the matter with it?"

"Well, turn it on, then. Gee, Pop. Wuddia, just sitting here?"

"What channel do you want?"

"Six."

"What's on Six?"

"Clutch Cargo."

"Clutch Cargo? What's that?"

"Oh, here we go again. You say it in that tone of voice and I know what's next. Why don't I watch Hunkley Hinkley Brinkley. Pop, I got all the homework I need, without watching Hinkley Hunkley Brinkley."

"This is the time when you ought to be learning something, instead of hanging around Al's all afternoon. I don't like you hanging around Al's."

"Where else do you *want* me to go? I suppose Jimmy's."

"What's Jimmy's?"

"See, you don't even know which places are all right."

"What's Jimmy's?"

"It's another candy store two squares up past Al's. It's where the Emperors hang out. Johnny D'Isernia and Chip Quisenberry. Them."

"I know all about them all right. You stay away from them."

"Then how do you know so much about them if you never heard of Jimmy's?"

"I know enough."

She appeared about to say something, but she kept silent and proceeded to the front hall and up to her room. He could tell when she reached her room: her record-player began to broadcast the melancholy, despairing music that her generation loved, and soon her thin little voice, thin but true, joined in the tune. She could not be thinking of the words she was singing along with the boy vocalist; something about his little sweetheart, his little dove, lying dead on the highway. But her voice went along with the music, and Berry found that there were tears in his eyes, for Ava and for Vilma Schrock, 17, but mostly for Ava. And for every father, too, but mostly for Ava and the years ahead.

THE FIRST DAY

On Monday morning at ten minutes of eight Ray Whitehill entered the Ledger-Star Building, walked quickly through the business office and on to the news room, and came to a halt at Lester Bull's desk. "Hello, Les, here I am," said Ray Whitehill.

"Good for you, Ray. Welcome back. Let's see, I'll take you over and introduce you to the only other member of the staff that's in so far. Or do you know her? Mary McGannon."

"No, I've never met her."

At the last desk in a row of five a young woman was at a typewriter, copying from a notebook, which she peered at through heavy glasses.

"Mary, this is Ray Whitehill. Ray, Mary McGannon."

The young woman quickly removed her glasses and stood up. "Oh. Well, goodness. How do you do? Welcome back, Mr Whitehill."

"Thank you."

"Needless to say, I've heard a lot about you, and we're all so glad you're going to be on the paper again."

"That's very nice of you. What have you got there? A P.T.A. meeting?"

"Well, just about. The League of Women Voters, but the names are almost the same."

"Get them right," said Whitehill. "And always remember that Mrs. J. Stanton Keene spells her name with three e's and the other Keens get along on two."

"Oh, Mrs. J. Stanton isn't with us any more," said the young woman. "She's been out of circulation over two years."

"You mean *more than* two years," said Whitehill. "I didn't know the old girl had cooled."

"Mary writes it *more than,* but in conversation she always says *over,*" said Bull.

"Yes, she brought down her last gavel two years ago."

"Well, don't let me interrupt you," said Whitehill.

"Will you excuse me?" said the young woman. "I've got forty names to copy before I go on my rounds. Very glad you're back, Mr. Whitehill."

"Very glad to be back, thanks."

The girl put on her glasses and sat down.

"I thought it would be nice to get you your old desk, but it's nowhere around," said Bull. "We got all these new ones in a couple of years ago. All new desks and typewriters."

"My old one would have looked out of place here."

"Yeah, I guess it would, but I asked anyway. So I've put you here, temporarily. If you want to change later I'll get one of the other boys to trade places with you, but you don't want to be over on the sports side, do you?"

"Makes no difference where I sit, Les. Although that's where I started. The sports side. When I first came on the paper I *was* the sports side. I did the whole thing myself."

"Well, we have four men doing it now. You know,

every township has a high school now, with a stadium and a swimming pool, and a band. Scholastic sports really sells papers, we found. More so than the junior college."

"What junior college? You mean to say the town has a junior college?"

"Oh, since 1947. Twelve hundred students, but sports-wise they don't cut as much cheese as the high school leagues."

"I've been away a long time."

"Yes, when you left I wasn't even in kindergarten."

"That was 1927."

"I'm thirty-seven. I've been here fifteen years this June. I've never worked anywhere else."

"God knows I have."

"I should say you have. I wish I had your experiences to look back on, but when you're married and three kids you think twice about making a drastic move. And I can't complain. They've treated me very well. When the two papers merged I got this promotion, and I'm in on participation. It would have been fun to get around more, but it looks like I'm here the rest of my life unless there's something drastic."

"Well, this is where I began, and this is where I end up, if that's any consolation."

"Yeah, but I never interviewed Winston Churchill, and I never palled around with Heywood Broun and Damon Runyon. Was it true that Runyon couldn't speak, that he had to write on a pad of paper?"

"Yes, the last years."

"I saw a picture of Heywood Broun, he was wearing a raccoon coat and a high silk hat. Did he really dress like that? The unmade bed, somebody called him."

"He didn't care how he looked."

"But he could write. We used to have to read old columns of his. By the way, I've arranged to have the New York papers on your desk every day. The boss said you wanted the *Trib* and the *Times*. They come in around ten o'clock, by mail. Okay?"

"Fine, fine. Thanks, Les."

"You make yourself comfortable, then. I've got to start getting out a paper. Oh, Ray, this is Bud Freedman, our assistant sports editor."

"Hello, Ray," said a young man.

"Hello, Bud." They shook hands.

"Les, I have a story you might like to run on Page One and jump to the sports page."

"What's the story?"

"Marty Moreno's been offered the job coaching the St. Joseph's varsity."

"Why don't you stop? You come in with that story every year."

"This time he's going to take it."

"When he does we'll run it, but never on Page One. Go to work and stop trying to win the Pulitzer prize."

"Where is Marty Moreno coaching now?" said Whitehill.

"Queen of Angels. You know Marty?" said Freedman.

"Look in the files, around 1925, and under my byline you'll find a story that says Marty Moreno has been offered the job of coaching at Villanova. I went for that in 1925, the first year Marty was coaching."

"You're kidding," said Freedman.

"Find out for yourself."

"Thirty-six years ago? Yeah, I guess he could of been coaching then."

"He was coaching, all right. Queen of Angels.

Marty will be coaching with the Queen of Angels when he meets the real one."

"What was that? Let me have that again."

"It isn't all that good," said Whitehill.

"He'll be coaching the Queen of Angels when he finally meets the real one. Wait'll I see him. Will I give him that for a needle? Thanks, Ray." The young man went to his desk.

"Eager," said Les Bull.

"Young," said Whitehill. He went to the assigned desk and inspected the contents: a drawerful of *Ledger-Star* stationery in assorted sizes; typing paper and flimsies and carbons; a neatly folded clean hand towel; an area telephone directory; a box of pencils; a stapler and a package of paper clips. The neat efficiency brought back memories of a room he had once occupied in an *Essex* class carrier, even to the matching pencil and ballpoint pen set. He pulled the typewriter out of its hiding place in the desk, and the typewriter was almost new. He rolled a couple of pieces of paper into the typewriter and tapped out his byline. He saw Les Bull looking up from his work and smiling.

"Attaboy, Ray," said Bull. "That's good to hear."

"My byline," said Ray Whitehill. "That may be as far as I'll get, today."

"Hang in there," said Bull.

One by one the other members of the staff reported for work, all strangers to Ray Whitehill except John J. Wigmore, the county editor. The others wasted little time in the amenities, and Whitehill made no attempt to hold them in conversation, but John Wigmore was a contemporary, had started on the paper a year ahead of Whitehill. He kept his hat on and he was smoking a cigar. "Ray, it's like old times to see you back," said Wigmore. He sat on Whitehill's desk. "Do you recall the big fire of '26?"

"I sure do," said Whitehill. "That was the first time you ever let me cover a news story."

"Yes, and I guess you might say that gave you your start. Hadn't been for that you'd still be covering basketball. Not really, though. You'd have been discovered sooner or later. They couldn't keep you down, Ray. You had the old zing, the old razzmatazz, and you could write. If I'd been able to write worth a damn they wouldn't have put me on the desk."

"The boy editor," said Whitehill.

"I was the youngest city editor in this part of the State. Now I'm damn near the oldest. Where you living?"

"I took a room at the 'Y' temporarily."

Wigmore looked from right to left, lowered his voice and said, "If you're looking for a nice apartment, I can fix you up."

"What's the angle, John?" With Wigmore there was always an angle; that much had not changed.

"Oh, no angle, exactly. Strictly legitimate. You pay rent. But this new apartment building just went up at Fourth and Market."

"I noticed it."

"A little trouble with the building inspector that I happened to be instrumental in fixing up for the Roach brothers. They're the ones put up the building. So naturally I know Jerry Darby, the building inspector, and I got him together with the Roach boys. Now it's all straightened out."

"I imagine the builders are very grateful."

"Well, their apartment house could have sat there empty for six months or a year if somebody didn't take some action. Where they made their mistake was antagonizing Jerry right at the beginning."

"Were you the bag man, John?"

Wigmore smiled. "You know, the funny thing is, no money changed hands. Not a nickel." He studied the end of his cigar. "Now just between you and I, Ray. Jerry has a daughter just got married and it wouldn't surprise me if her new house was built with surplus materials from the apartment building. It's a brick house, and so's the apartment, and I understand she got the same make of refrigerator and dishwasher you'll find in the apartments. Surplus, of course. Hard to trace. But that way everybody's happy."

"And what's your end?"

"Don't worry about me, Ray. My old motto, ask me no questions and I'll tell you no lies. But anyway, there's only two vacancies left and I can get you one for a hundred and a quarter that somebody else'd have to pay two-fifty. Do you have your own furniture?"

"In storage," said Whitehill. "New York."

"We'll send a truck for it," said Wigmore. "Like to have you meet the Roach boys. They're going to be doing a lot for this town, Ray."

"Why not? I'll be glad to meet them."

"Then I'll tell them to hold one of those apartments for you? They're both the same identical size and layout, so whichever one they hold won't make any difference. And you're more or less a prestige tenant, so don't have any hesitation."

"Just a mild payola?"

"Just a mild. Well, I gotta get to work. Where you having lunch?"

"Having lunch with the boss, at the University Club."

"Lousy food, but it's the University Club. I usually eat at the hotel. Are you going to join the University Club, Ray?"

"I don't have to. I was made an honorary member in 1943."

"Oh, that time you came back and lectured. They made you an honorary member. Does that still hold good?"

"As far as I know."

"Don't have to pay any dues, then, hey?"

"Nope."

"That makes you and the boss the only members in this shop. And you're in for free. Pretty nice, pretty nice."

"At those prices," said Whitehill.

The New York papers were delivered punctually, but in the time before their arrival he had written nothing more than his signature. The other staff members were busy at their typewriters and telephones, and when they spoke it was only to each other. They were a little in awe of him, he knew, and they could not know that that was not what he wanted now. He wanted to be made to feel at home in what had been his professional birthplace, but most of them had not been born when he was already too big for the paper and the town. He had felt more at home in bureaus in Hong Kong and Helsingfors, in tents and Quonset huts in the western hemisphere; he had been more at ease with Nehru and Ben-Gurion than with the assistant sports editor of the *Ledger-Star*. He could not concentrate on the available newspapers, the exchanges from the nearby cities in the State, and when the New York papers arrived he read them eagerly, like letters from friends, which indeed they were in at least a manner of speaking. He knew Lippmann as Walter, Alsop as Joe, Reston as Scotty, and to them he was Ray or Whitey. He read the papers and some of his confidence came back to him, and he thought of a piece he might write for the morrow's *Ledger-Star*. But now it was time to keep his date at the University Club, with the boss.

It was a three-story, red brick and white trim building, just off one of the main streets, and he could remember when it was being built, then later when he would go there to cover banquets, then—in 1943—when he went there as guest of honor. The biggest men in town had been there that night, listening respectfully to his report of the fighting against the Germans in Italy. He spared them nothing, that night. They needed to be told some hard, ugly truths after the let-down that followed Mussolini's surrender. When he sat down they were momentarily silent, but then spontaneously they rose and burst into applause and he knew he had done some good. They made him an honorary member and gave him a Revere silver bowl, and the president of the club said how appropriate the bowl was, although accidentally so. "None of us knew beforehand that Ray was going to be a modern Paul Revere," said the president. "But he sure is riding and spreading the alarm, and we'll always be grateful to him."

Ray Whitehill entered the club and started to give his name to the sixtyish attendant. "Don't you remember me, Ray? Al Redmond."

"Aloysius Patrick Xavier Redmond, for God's sake," said Whitehill. They shook hands and Redmond took his hat and coat. "Do they let you play pool here?"

"Tell you the truth I could beat most of them, even with my eyesight the way it is. You're here to stay now, Ray?"

"I think so. I hope so. Maybe we can get in a game sometime."

"Bring your money, I could always give you fifty to forty," said Redmond. "Mr. D. B. Otis would like for Mr. Whitehill to meet him in the bar. I guess that's one place you could always find your way to, Ray. Anyhow, it's to the end of the hall and down them stairs."

"Thanks, Al. See you soon," said Whitehill.

Dexter Otis was standing with his back to the bar, and as soon as he saw Whitehill he waved and pointed to a table for two against the wall. "Got wedged with a bore, and I don't even know his name," said Otis. "Will you have a drink, Ray?"

"No thanks."

"You don't drink anything at all any more?"

"Two years."

"That long, eh? Well, I seldom do during the daytime. Let's order, shall we? I'm going to have the sausage cakes and mashed potatoes. If you stick to the plain things the food here's all right, but otherwise, no. I noticed you're an honorary member, so you'll probably come here a lot, but don't expect fancy dishes."

"I'll have the sausage cakes. Yes, they made me a member in '43."

"I was in the Navy then. I guess that was when I first began to read your stuff. You were doing a lot of magazine stuff."

"Quite a lot. That, and the radio."

"And you sold one book to the movies."

"Two."

"Do you mind if I ask you a personal question?"

"No, go right ahead," said Whitehill, sensing what the question would be.

"Where did it all go, the money I mean, the dough you made?"

"Well, I sometimes wonder myself. I was married twice and divorced both times, and I had a daughter by my first wife. Her education took quite a bit, although I don't regret a nickel of that. I guess I don't regret any of it."

"But weren't you living on an expense account a lot of the time, when you were overseas?"

"Very few guys got rich that way. All that seemed to do was help us acquire expensive tastes."

"Have you any idea how much money you made?"

"All told? You mean since I left the old *Star?*"

"Yes."

"Well, I never stopped to figure it out, but thirty-four years. Over all I probably averaged twenty-five thousand a year in salary. How much would that be?"

"Uh, that would be eight hundred and fifty thousand."

"Books. Lectures. Radio. And two movie sales. And I had that television show a few years ago. I don't know, Dexter. I'd have to put it down on paper. Maybe a million. Taxes always gave me a lot of trouble."

"But you made around two million dollars."

"Yes, I guess I did."

"You make us look like chiselers at the *Ledger-Star.* I wish we could pay you more."

"I'm satisfied. I may not be worth what you are paying me. I may not work out at all."

"Well, we both agreed to try it for a year."

"A year should be plenty long enough," said Whitehill. "I just don't want you to keep me longer than a year if you're not satisfied."

"Well, frankly, we couldn't afford to, but we're hoping that by the end of a year's time you'll be syndicated. With your name, your reputation, once you get back into the swing of things—we discussed all that."

"And I'm glad to say you're more optimistic than I am."

"The way we see the picture, Ray, the paper's making money, no doubt about that. We have a monopoly, and some people will tell you that's not a good thing. But one paper that makes money is better than two that are losing money, and that's just about the way it was when my Dad bought the *Star*. The *Star* was on its last legs, and the *Ledger* hadn't shown a profit since the end of the war. So Dad merged the two papers and four years ago we began to see daylight. But what we've got we want to hold on to. It isn't only circulation-wise. It's readership-wise. We could throw the paper into every mailbox in the county and still go out of business, that's what circulation counts for. It's readership, the competition from TV. Do we pull, or don't we? It comes down to this fact, namely, do Sam Jones and his wife Minnie want to read the *Ledger-Star* six days a week? As long as they do, we stay in business. Now we have a lot of good features, syndicated stuff, but it lacks the local identification. That's why when you wrote me for a job we decided to gamble on you, to give us local identification and a well-known name. Confidentially, Ray, you're getting more than anyone else on the paper, and it's a gamble, even if it doesn't seem like much compared to what you've been accustomed to. Les Bull, our managing editor, doesn't know what you're getting. You're not on the regular editorial budget. You come out of the executive budget."

At this point the sausage cakes were served.

"Well, as you say, Dexter, it's a gamble. Maybe Minnie Jones isn't going to like me."

"That we'll have to wait and see, but just go at it relaxed, as if you had all the time in the world, and I think you'll get a good response. We'll be able to tell in a month or six weeks, but you mustn't be discouraged if some of them don't know you, your reputation. Some of the younger ones don't, you know."

"A lot of them don't."

"I probably shouldn't say this, considering that you used to hobnob with F.D.R. and Hitler and Stalin, but you realize, Ray, those names are ancient history to a young housewife that wasn't born when the Japs hit Pearl."

"Yes, I realize that. My daughter isn't much older than they are. She's a young housewife."

"Then you know that. They don't even remember Korea very well."

"I didn't go to Korea. I was having booze trouble then. Booze trouble, wife trouble, income tax trouble. And I panicked whenever I looked at a typewriter."

"But you straightened yourself out. You made a lot of money after that."

"Yes, I went back to work. That was when I covered the Berlin airlift."

"When was that, Ray?"

"What I just said. When the Korean trouble started I was having trouble with my wife and I took to the bottle, but I got straightened out, and then I went over and covered the Berlin airlift."

"No. I think the Berlin airlift was before the Korean trouble. I'm pretty sure of that, Ray."

"Was it? Wait a minute. Yes, I guess it was. You're right."

"I wouldn't correct you on a thing like that, only I happen to remember wondering whether I'd have to go back in the Navy."

"It was before the Korean business, you're right."

Throughout the rest of the meal the conversation was awkward and forced. Young Dexter Otis had embarrassed himself, but it was his own fault. How could he expect a man to remember everything that had happened in those crowded years? Dexter Otis, probably a j.g., if that, at the very moments when Mitscher and Nimitz and Halsey were welcoming their friend Ray Whitehill to the Pacific Ocean Area. Would Eisenhower give a grin of recognition upon seeing Dexter Otis? Bradley? Patton? Clark? De Gaulle? Montgomery? Was he ever even sneered at by Goering, barked at by Mussolini? Of course not.

"I beg your pardon, Dexter."

"I was just asking you, in your lapel. Is that the Legion of Honor?"

"Legion of Honor, that's right. I don't often wear it, or any of them."

"How many have you got?"

"I guess about six. Purple Heart. Air Medal. Oh, I guess I have maybe six or seven." He chuckled. "Sometimes I put one on when I want to spruce up a bit, like today, my first day in the new job. Then maybe I go for two or three months without taking them out of the box. The only time I never go without this is in France. The French like you to wear it. They figure it's a courtesy to them when an American wears their decoration."

"Well, it is."

"But not many people around here know what it is, so I think I'll put them all back in the box. All that's in the past anyway. and I'm more interested in the future. As you say, Minnie Jones doesn't care what I did ten, twenty years ago."

"That's a good, healthy way to look at it, Ray."

Plainly the man was pleased to be relieved of his embarrassment. "It just occurred to me, Dexter. I have all the medals, in storage in New York. What would you think if I donated them all to Franklin High? That's where I went. Might be good promotion later on. I have the medals and in addition I have, oh, plaques and scrolls and diplomas, not to mention autographed pictures. It might have some promotional value, and I had four walls from floor to ceiling filled with the stuff. That way the stuff would have some historical value, instead of just gathering dust. And underneath, of course, a discreet little plate to remind everybody that yours truly is a staff member of the *Ledger-Star*. Oh, we'd get that in."

"Yes. Yes, I think it might be good."

"I have a very wonderful picture of me with the old man. Churchill. Completely informal, relaxed. We wouldn't want any Hollywood stuff, would we? I have any number of pictures of me with movie people. And a lot of other celebrities. Writers. Ballplayers. But I was thinking I could give the other stuff to Franklin High, and we might make use of the Hollywood and sports people somewhere in the Ledger-Star Building. You know, it does no harm to remind the old home town that a character named Ray Whitehill was on a first-name basis with the most famous people in the world, and has the pictures to prove it."

"Right. Well, we have plenty of time to talk about that, Ray. I have to go to a meeting, if you'll excuse me."

"Of course. I think I'll stay and have another cup of coffee," said Whitehill.

The younger man departed, and Ray Whitehill sat alone, he knew not how long. The waitress came to him and said, "That coffee must be cold, Mr. Whitehill. Let me give you some fresh."

"All right, thanks," he said. But it would take more than coffee, more than anything he could name, to put warmth where he felt a chill.

JURGE DULRUMPLE

On long trips—to see the cherry blossoms in Washington, to hear the music in the Berkshires, to visit relatives at distant points—Miss Ivy Heinz and her friend Miss Muriel Hamilton sang two-part harmony, not only because they loved to sing but as a safety measure. Muriel Hamilton had never learned to drive, and their singing kept Ivy Heinz from getting too drowsy. They sang well together, especially considering that both were natural altos. Muriel Hamilton carried the melody, since it was a little easier for her to get out of the lower register and also because she was more likely to know the words. Ivy Heinz could go awfully low, and sometimes for a joke she would drop down in imitation of a man's bass, and whenever she did that, just about *every* time she had done it, Muriel Hamilton would say, quickly, without a pause in the singing, "George Dalrymple."

"No, *no!*" Ivy would say, and they would laugh.

Any mention of George Dalrymple was good for a laugh when Ivy Heinz and Muriel Hamilton got together. It was an extremely private source of amusement, sure-fire or not. Shared with a third party it would have been an act of cruelty to George because an explanation of the laughter would have involved revealing a secret that concerned only

George and the two women. It went back to a time when all three were in their middle twenties, the summer in which George Dalrymple proposed first to Muriel Hamilton and then, a month later, proposed to Ivy Heinz. Neither girl had been enormously complimented by a proposal from George Dalrymple, but they knew that from George's point of view it was a compliment, a terribly serious one that was no less serious or sincere because he had gone so soon from Muriel to Ivy. George Dalrymple was a serious man, a fact that made it fun to have a private joke about him, but in public you had to treat such seriousness seriously.

Other people, in discussing George Dalrymple or even in merely mentioning his name, would often lower the pitch as far down as they could get. They would pull their chins back against their necks, and the name would come out, "Jurge Dulrumple." His speaking voice was so deep, his enunciation so economical, that his vocal delivery was his outstanding characteristic, more distinctively his than those details of appearance and carriage and manners that he might share with other men. There were, for example, other men just as tall and thin; others who swayed their heads from side to side independently of their bodies when they walked; and others who were as quickly, instantly polite in such things as standing up when a lady entered the room, lighting a girl's cigarette, opening doors. George did all these things, but what set him apart was his way of talking, his words coming from down deep in his mouth and expelled with a minimal motion of his lips. His friends, such as Ivy Heinz and Muriel Hamilton, knew that he was not self-conscious about his teeth, which were nothing special but all right; and it was not in George Dalrymple's character to go around talking like a jailbird or a ventriloquist. George Dalrymple talked that way because he was serious and wanted people to realize that everything he said was serious.

When George came back from his army duties in the winter of 1919 he was twenty-three years old. His military service had largely consisted of guarding railroad bridges along the Atlantic Seaboard, a task he performed conscientiously with the result that he was discharged a corporal. If the woor—the war—had lasted six months longer he would have been a second lieutenant and probably sent to Brest, France, or some such point of debarkation; his congressman had been practically promised the commission by the War Department. But once the Armistice was signed George was anxious to get out of the Urmy and resume work at the bank. He had already lost practically two years, and in the banking business it was wise to start early and stick to it. The time he had put in at the bank before he was drafted was now just about matched by the fifteen months he had spent protecting the railway systems from German spies. The bank took him back at a slight raise in pay and with full credit in seniority for the time he had been in the service of his country. It was a pleasant surprise to find that one of the newer bookkeepers at the bank was none other than his high school classmate, Muriel Hamilton.

Two of the women who had been hired during the hostilities were let go, as they had been warned they would be, but Muriel Hamilton was kept on. The recently inaugurated school savings plan, for children in the public and parochial schools, owed at least some of its success to Muriel Hamilton and her ability to get along with children. She was painstaking and patient, and the bank officials put her in complete charge. Once a year she went around and gave a talk to all the classes from seventh grade to senior high, and the bank could see the results immediately. No one was more surprised than Muriel herself,

In her four years at High she had been so near to failing in Public Speaking—which almost no one ever failed—that it had pulled down her general average and kept her out of the first third of her class. George Dalrymple's marks in Public Speaking were as bad as Muriel's, but his other subjects kept him in the first ten in a class of eighty-five boys and girls, the largest class in the history of G.H.S. It surprised no one that George Dalrymple, on graduation, had a job waiting for him at the Citizens Bank & Trust. His high school record merited the distinction, a fact that delighted his father, the assistant cashier. John K. Dalrymple was not a man who would have forced his son on the bank.

In his pre-army days as a runner at the bank George Dalrymple and his father always walked home together for noonday dinner. Each day John K. Dalrymple would take the opportunity to review George's morning activities in detail. The father had George repeat all the conversations he had had with the tellers at the other banks, and he would suggest ways of improving the impression he created in the banking community. "It's all very well to have the light touch," John Dalrymple would say. "But it can be carried too far. It's better to be all business at your age. Time enough for ordinary conversation later on." There was no actual danger that George might get a reputation for frivolity, but he was young and did not know all the ropes, and his father did not want George's natural gravity to be affected by nervous unfamiliarity with the work.

John Dalrymple, as assistant cashier, did not have to stay as late as his son, and they did not walk home together at the close of business. But as soon as George got home he would get into his overalls and join his father in the flower garden, or, during the cold months, in the odd jobs about the house that John Dalrymple claimed kept him from getting stale. Father and son had very little time together in the evenings; John Dalrymple liked to stay home and read, while George had choir practice one night, calisthenics and basketball at the "Y" two nights, stamp club another, Sunday evening services at the Second Presbyterian Church, and the remaining evenings he spent with his friend Carl Yoder. Sometimes the boys would be at the Yoders' house, sometimes at the Dalrymples', and once in a while they would take in a picture show if it was Douglas Fairbanks or a good comedy.

It was a terrible thing when Carl passed on during the influenza epidemic. George could not even get leave to come home for the funeral. In fact, there was no real funeral; the churches and theaters and all such public gatherings were prohibited during the epidemic; the schools were closed, and you could not even buy a soda at a soda fountain. The death rate was shockingly high in the mining villages, but death by the wholesale did not affect George Dalrymple nearly so much as the passing of funny little Carl, the Jeff of the Mutt-and-Jeff team of Dalrymple and Yoder in the Annual Entertainment at G.H.S., senior year. George Dalrymple knew that things would not be the same at home without Carl trotting along after him everywhere they went.

One of the first conversations he had with Muriel Hamilton at the bank was about Carl Yoder, their classmate, and George was quite surprised to discover how fond she had been of Carl. "I always thought it was mean to call him The Shrimp," she said. "He didn't like it, did he?"

"No, he certainly did not," said George. "But he wouldn't let on to anybody but me."

"I didn't like it either, because remember in the Annual Entertainment when he wore girl's clothes? I loaned

him that dress. And if Carlie was a shrimp, then that
made me one too."

"Oh, yes. I remember that dress. That's right, it was
yours. But that wouldn't make you a shrimp, Mure. Girls
aren't as tall. I never think of you as a short girl."

"Five feet two inches."

"That makes me ten inches taller than you and ten
inches taller than Carl."

"Oh, I thought you were taller."

"No, it's because I'm skinny, and so much taller than
Carl. Just six feet and maybe an eighth of an inch."

"I never saw you in your uniform."

"Well, you have that treat in store for you. I'm going to be marching in the parade, Decoration Day."

She was a girl, not a short girl, and soon after that first
conversation he formed the habit of walking part way
home with her after the bank closed for the day. He would
say goodnight to her at Eighth and Market, slowing down
but not stopping when she entered her house. His new duties at the bank included opening up in the morning, a full
half hour before Muriel reported for work, and he did not
see her in the evening after supper except by accident. His
schedule also had been rearranged so that his and his father's lunch hours did not coincide, and George was not entirely displeased. His father's questions about army life indicated a belief that it had been far more exciting and sinful
than was actually the case. Some aspects of army life had
disgusted George and he hoped never again to see some of
the men in his company; the bullies, the drunkards, the
dirty talkers, the physically unclean. George Dalrymple had
come out of the army a somewhat coarsened but still innocent young man; he had lived closely with men who really
did so many of the things that George and Carl Yoder had

only heard about. He had heard men tell stories that they could not possibly have made up, and some of the stories were told by men about their own wives. Nevertheless George Dalrymple had no inclination to discuss that sort of thing with his father. It would have been almost as bad as discussing them with his mother. The war was over, he was through with the army, he had not liked being a soldier, but the whole experience was his own, a part of him, and to speak of it to his father would be an act of disloyalty to himself and the army that he could not explain to himself but that he felt deeply. It was private.

The time would come, he knew, when it would be no more than the right thing to invite Muriel Hamilton to a picture show and a soda afterward. If, in those circumstances, she showed another side of her, he would start keeping company with her and, eventually, ask her to marry him. She was exactly his own age, but he did not know any younger girls. She was what some people called mousy, but she was very well thought of at the bank, and he liked her femininity and her neatness. As soon as there was a tiny daub of ink on her finger she would scrub it off; she never had a hair out of place; and he was sure she used perfume, although that may have been perfumed soap. He had watched carefully the tightening of her shirtwaists over her bosom, and concluded unmistakably that marriage to her would be a pleasure. She had not been one of the prettier girls at G.H.S., and yet she was not by any means homely, and it was remarkable that she was still single while other girls, less attractive, were already married. She belonged to a group that called themselves the H.T.P.'s, who went to the pictures and had sodas together and had been doing so since senior year. One of the group dropped out to get married, and shortly thereafter it became common knowledge that H.T.P. stood for Hard To Please. Now the only ones left of the original H.T.P.'s were Muriel Hamilton and Ivy Heinz.

Muriel so readily accepted George Dalrymple's first invitation to take in a show that he felt sorry for her. She was not really an H.T.P.; she was merely waiting to be asked. They went to the movies, they had a soda. "There'll be a trolley in about seven minutes," said George.

"A trolley, to go eight squares?"

"I forgot to ask you before," he said.

"The only time I ever take the trolley is if it's pouring rain and I'm going to be late to work," she said. "I like walking. It's good exercise."

"So do I, now. I got pretty tired of it in the army, but that was different."

Watching the movie, they had not had any conversation, and now, walking her home, he began a story, about his army duties, that he had not finished when they reached her house. She stood on the bottom of their front steps while he hurried the story to an ending. "Well, thank you for taking me to the movies, George. I enjoyed it very much," she said.

"The pleasure was all mine," he said.

"See you tomorrow," she said.

"Bright and early," he said. "Goodnight."

He said no more than good morning to her the next day. He was determined not to let their outside relationship alter their conduct at the bank. Nevertheless he waited for her when the bank closed, and he soon discovered that their relationship had been altered. "George, I, uh, maybe I ought to wait until you ask me again, but if you have any *intention* of asking me—to go to the movies, that is—then maybe we oughtn't to walk home together every day. Walking home from work, that's one thing. But having a date, that's another. And I don't think we ought to do both. Maybe that's rather forward of me, but if you had any intention of asking me for a date?"

"Yes. Yes, I see."

"Half the people at the bank knew we had a date last night."

"Oh, they did?"

"You can't do anything here without everybody finding out about it."

"Well, personally I don't mind if they find out about that."

"But I do, George. Walking home from work, that's just politeness, but when a fellow and a girl have dates at night in addition, then that's giving them something to talk about."

"I'd be willing to give them something to talk about, but that's up to you, Mure."

"It is and it isn't, if you know what I mean. It all depends on whether you were going to ask me to go out with you in the evening. But if you were, I'd have to say no. And I don't want to say no."

"On the other hand, I don't want to give up walking home with you."

"Then we haven't solved anything, have we?"

"Not exactly," he said. "But maybe I can solve it. How would it be if we kept on walking home every day, but didn't have *regular* dates? Most fellows and girls have date-night on Wednesday, and when they start going real steady, he goes to her house on Sunday."

"We're a long way from that," she said. "All right. We'll walk home after work, as usual, and if you want to take me to a picture, you say so and sometimes I'll say yes and sometimes I'll say no. Is that all right with you?"

"Anything's all right that you agree to."

They violated the agreement immediately. He saw her every Wednesday night, and on Sunday evenings he walked home with her and Ivy Heinz. He and Ivy would say goodnight to Muriel, and he would then walk home with Ivy. But though Muriel had never invited him inside her house, Ivy simply opened the door and expected him to follow her, which he did, on the very first night he walked home with her. She called upstairs: "It's me, Momma. I have company."

"All right, but if you're going to play the Vic don't play it too loud. It's Sunday. And don't forget, tomorrow's Monday morning."

Ivy wound up the Victrola and put on Zez Confrey's "Kitten on the Keys."

"Do you still dance, George?"

"Oh, I'm terrible."

"Well, we can try," said Ivy.

He knew as soon as he put his arm around her waist that the dancing was only an excuse. She stood absolutely still and waited for him to kiss her. They kissed through three records, one of them a non-dance record of Vernon Dalhart's, and at the end of the third she stopped the machine and led George to the sofa, stretched out and let him lie beside her. She seemed to be able to tell exactly when he would be about to get fresh, and her hand would anticipate his, but she kissed him freely until the court house clock struck eleven.

"I-vee-ee? Eleven o'clock," her mother called.

"You have to go now," said Ivy.

Sunday after Sunday he got from Ivy the kisses he wanted from Muriel, and after several months it was more

(159)

than kisses. "Next Sunday you come prepared, huh?" said Ivy, when their necking reached that stage.

"I am prepared, now," he said.

"No. But next Sunday Momma's going to be away and I'll be all alone. We won't have to stay down here."

He had grown fond of Ivy. From the very beginning she had understood that he was in love with Muriel and had never brought her into their conversations in any way that would touch upon her disloyalty to her friend or his weakness of character. Nor was she jealous of his feeling for Muriel. Nor was Muriel so much as curious about what might go on after they said goodnight to her on Sunday evenings. But fond as he was of Ivy, it was her taking him to bed with her—his first time with any woman—that compelled him to propose marriage to Muriel. He had no doubts about himself now, and among the doubts that vanished was the one that concerned his marital relations with Muriel. As husband he would be expected to know what to do, but before the night in Ivy's bed he had not been sure himself.

He took Muriel to the picture show on the Wednesday following the Sunday in Ivy's room, and when they got to Muriel's house he said, "Can we go inside a minute?"

"It's after eleven, George."

"I know, but I didn't have much chance to talk to you. I wish you would, Mure."

"Well, I guess they won't object, a few minutes. But you can't stay after half past eleven."

His manner did not show it, but he had never been so sure of himself or wanted Muriel so fiercely. He stood behind her as she was hanging up her things on the clothesstand, and when she turned and faced him he did not get out of the way. "I want to kiss you, Muriel."

"Oh, George, no. I noticed all evening—is that what you were thinking about?"

"Much more, Muriel. I want you to marry me."

"Oh—goodness. You're standing in my way. Let's go in the parlor."

She switched on the parlor chandelier and took a seat on the sofa, where he could sit beside her. She let him take her hand. "Did you just think of this?"

"Of course not. I've been thinking about it for over a year," he said. "Maybe longer than that, to tell you the truth. You're an intelligent girl, and you know I've never dated anyone else."

"As far as I know, you didn't. But I never asked you and you never told me. You could have been having dates with other girls."

"Maybe I could have, but I never did. Ever since I got out of the army the only girl I wanted to be with was you. And that's the way I want it to be the rest of my life. I love you, Muriel."

"Oh, George. Love. I'm afraid of that word."

"You? Afraid of the word love? Why, you, you're so feminine and all, love ought to be—I don't know."

"Well, marriage, I guess. I guess it's marriage I'm afraid of."

"I guess a lot of girls are, but they get over it. Your mother did, my mother did, and look at them."

"You have so many wonderful qualities, George, but I don't think I could ever love you the way Mama loves Father. And your parents. It's nothing against you, personally, it's just me. And any fellow."

"My goodness, you love children."

"You mean when they come in the bank? But that's what they are. Children. You're a man, George."

"Don't tell me you're a man-hater."

"No, not a man-hater. Heavens. But I could never—I never want to get married! Why don't you help me? You know what I'm trying to say. I wouldn't like a man to—I was afraid you were going to kiss me, in the hallway. *That.* That's what I'm trying to tell you. I could never have children. When we were in High didn't you use to feel the same way about girls? I used to think you did. You never went out with girls, George. You and Carlie had more fun than anybody."

"But I always liked girls."

"Well, I liked boys, too, but I never wanted to be alone with a boy. You know how old I am, and I've never kissed a boy in my whole life. And I never will."

"You're wrong, Muriel. You'll fall in love with one some day. I wish it was going to be me."

"How wrong *you* are. I wouldn't let you sit here if I thought you were like the others." In the conversation she had taken away her hand, and now she put it back on his. "I want a man for a friend, George, but that's all. When I was little I read a story about a princess. She was forced to marry this king or else he'd declare war on her father. I couldn't do that. I'd sooner kill myself."

"Why?"

"Don't ask me why. I think all girls feel that way, underneath. I don't think they ever get used to some things, but they pretend to because they love their husbands for other reasons. I could love you that way, George, but you wouldn't love me. You wouldn't be satisfied with just being nice. You'd have to be a man and do those things that are so ugly to my way of thinking."

"But girls have desires, Mure."

She shook her head. "No. They only pretend. Most

girls have to have a man to support them, but if they had a job they'd never get married. I have a job and Ivy has a job, so we didn't have to have a man to support us."

"The rich girls on Lantenengo Street, they don't need a man to support them."

"Not to support them, but that's the way they stay rich. The rich girls marry the rich boys and the money all stays together."

"I hear some pretty funny stories about some of those girls."

"Yes, but most of them drink, and the men take advantage of them. The girls are nice, but when they take too much to drink they're not responsible. That's why the men up there encourage them to drink."

"Well, I know very little about what goes on up there, but at the rate they're spending it, some of them won't have it very long."

"I feel sorry for the women. I don't really care what happens to the men, especially one of them."

"Did something to you?"

"Not to me, but to a girl I know. One of the H.T.P.'s. One night at the picture show, he did something. Don't ask me any more about it because I won't tell you. But they're all alike, up there."

"You'd better not say that at the bank."

"Oh, I should say not. But whenever that man comes in I think of what his wife has to put up with. And they're supposed to be the people everybody looks up to. Rich, and educated, the privileged class."

"I wouldn't be like that, Muriel."

"I know you wouldn't, George. But maybe men can't help themselves."

"It's a good thing we talked about this."

"Oh, I wouldn't have married you, George. Or anybody else."

"I was thinking of something else. You make me wonder about women, how they really feel. You're a woman, and I guess you ought to know."

"We just don't have the same feelings men do."

"Then if women all had jobs the whole race would die out."

"Yes, except that don't forget women love children and they'd still go through it all to have them."

"Would you?"

"No, I don't love children that much."

"What do you love, Mure?"

"What do I love? Oh, lots of things. And people. My parents. Some of my friends. The music in church. Singing with our old bunch. Nature. I love nature. I love scenery, a good view. Flowers. Nearly all flowers I love, and trees on the mountains. The touch of velvet, like this cushion. And I love to swim, not at the shore, but in a dam if the water's not too cold. And my one bad habit. Smoking cigarettes."

"Now I never knew you smoked."

"I don't get much chance to, except when I go to Ivy's. Mrs. Heinz has something the matter with her nose, some condition, and we can smoke one right after the other and she never catches on. If my parents knew I smoked they'd disown me."

He looked at her hand. "Muriel, some day the right fellow will come along, and all these things you said tonight, you won't even remember thinking them."

"Don't say things like that, George. You don't know me at all, what I really feel. Nobody does, not even Ivy."

"Your trouble is, you're just too good, too innocent."

"Oh, I don't like that, either. You meant it as a compliment, but it shows a great lack of understanding. Of me, that is. You think that some fellow with wavy hair—"

"Maurice Costello."

"Or Thomas Meighan. I'll meet somebody like that and forget the things I believe. But you're wrong. I'd love to have Thomas Meighan for a friend, but honestly, George, I'd just as soon have you. At least I know you better, and I don't know what I'd ever find to talk about with Thomas Meighan." She looked at him intently. "George, I don't want to put you off proposing to someone else. You'll make some girl a good husband. But when you do find the right girl, if you want to make her happy, don't be disappointed if she doesn't like the kissing part of married life. You know what I mean, and it isn't just kissing."

"I know."

"A friend of mine, a girl you know too, she got married, and now she comes to me and cries her heart out. 'You were right, Muriel,' she says. 'I hate the kissing.' I used to try to tell her that she wasn't going to like it, but she wouldn't believe me. She said if you love a person, you don't mind. Well, she loved the fellow she married but now he hates her. Isn't that awful? And I feel just as sorry for the fellow, George. He can't help it that he has those animal instincts. All men have them, I suppose. I guess even you, because I admit it, I had that feeling earlier that you were going to want to kiss me, and that's the first step. I've always known that about boys, and that's why I've never let one kiss me."

"Well, I guess we'd better not have any more dates."

"Oh, we couldn't now. And maybe you'd better not wait for me after work tomorrow. I've told you so much about myself, I don't know how I'm going to look at you in the morning."

"Do you feel naked?"

"George! Oh, why did you say that? Go home, go home. Please go, this minute." She was in angry tears, and he left her sitting on the sofa.

At the bank in the morning she seemed cool and serene, but he was not deceived. At moments when once she would have given him a bright, quick smile, she would not look at him. In the afternoon he stayed behind longer than usual, to give her a chance to leave well ahead of him. On Sunday night she was not at church, and he walked home with Ivy.

"You can't come in," said Ivy. "My mother's still downstairs."

"Then she must be sitting in the dark," he said.

"All right, you can come in, but it won't be any use," she said.

He put a record on the Victrola, but she braked the turntable. He put his arms around her, but she turned her face away and sat in a chair where there was not room for him. She lit a cigarette before he could get out his matches. "Muriel told you, huh?" he said.

"Sure. She tells me everything. I don't tell her everything, but she tells me. Now you'd better leave her alone."

"Oh, I will. She's a man-hater."

"Just finding that out? And what if she is?"

"At least you're not."

"Maybe I should be."

"Oh, she handed you some of her propaganda," said George.

"Think back to one week ago tonight, George Dalrymple. Then Monday, Tuesday, and Wednesday you proposed to Muriel."

"Ivy, you knew all along that some day I was going to ask Muriel to marry me."

"No I didn't. I thought you'd find out that she was never going to marry anybody. You had a lot of talks with her."

"Not about that subject. What's the matter with her?"

"Does there have to be something the matter with her?"

"Well, there's nothing the matter with you. You want to get married some day."

"Maybe I do and maybe I don't."

"Yes you do. What if I asked you to marry me?"

"You didn't ask me."

"Then I do ask you. Will you marry me?"

"No."

"Well, maybe that's because you're sore at *me*. But you're going to marry somebody."

"There you're wrong."

"You'll have to have somebody."

"I have somebody—now."

"Who?"

"Wouldn't you like to know?"

"That's why I'm asking you. Harry Brenner?"

"No, not Harry Brenner."

"Chick Charles?"

"Not him, either."

"Oh, that new fellow in the jewelry store."

"Wrong again."

"I can't think of anybody else you had a date with. Is it a married man?"

"Give up, stop trying."

"All right, I give up. Who is it?"

"That's for me to know and you to find out."

"Don't be sore at me, Ivy."

"I'm not really sore at you, George."

"Yes you are, but when you get over it, let's take in a movie next week?"

"No. Thanks for asking me, but I'm not going to see you any more."

"You're sore about Muriel. Well, I couldn't help it."

"Honestly, George, I'm not sore about Muriel. Not one bit."

"Well, I'm going to keep my eye on you. I want to find out about this mystery man."

"It's a free country, George."

On the next Wednesday night he happened to be at the movies with Harry Brenner's brother Paul, and sitting two rows in front of them were Ivy Heinz and Muriel Hamilton. Later, at the soda fountain, George walked over and reached down and picked up the girls' check. "Allow me, ladies?" he said.

"Oh, no, George, you mustn't," said Muriel.

"My treat," he said. "I guess thirty-two cents won't break me." He paid the cashier on the way out, and stood on the sidewalk. The girls stopped to thank him again, and Muriel, somewhat ill at ease, made some polite conversation with Paul Brenner. George, in his muttering way, spoke to Ivy. "Using Muriel as a disguise, eh?"

"Curiosity killed the cat," said Ivy.

It was a long time, many Wednesdays, before George Dalrymple allowed himself to believe that Ivy was not using Muriel as a disguise. But they were just as nice about his secrets, too.

JUSTICE

There was nothing in or about the house that had been in being more than four years, nothing that gave promise of lasting more than five. The land itself, I knew, had been bulldozed and shoveled into its present contours to provide the setting for the house, which was split level on several levels. For the most part the house was made of glass, stained woods, and aluminum. I had heard that the house alone cost ninety-five thousand dollars, but driving up to it for the first time, seeing it from a distance, I could not help thinking that it looked like an advertisement for a trailer. Trailer advertisements have a way of looking like ads for children's playhouses, and I suppose that what made me think of trailers was that general air of impermanence. Or maybe it was the other way around. The roof supports on the front terrace of the house were thin poles of aluminum, as though they were meant to be folded and tucked away when the trailer, or the house, moved on in the morning. The whole house, or so it seemed on my first look, could be folded according to a trailer designer's plan, and driven off to Maryland or Arizona or Florida or Oak Ridge, Tennessee.

I knew that at one time a man could have stood on the site of the house and seen General George Washington and his Continentals. The view from the house was superb: rolling country, still largely held by dairy farmers whose family names were repeated in the names of the townships and "corners" and villages of the countryside. I was sure that Harry Rupp and his wife and children had never looked out from their terrace and tried to imagine Washington and his men in the snow. But it didn't matter. Barbara Rupp, with her contact lenses, could not see that far, and from what I came to know of their children, they hated history, which they called "social studies." As for Harry, his imagination was active enough but he had trouble recalling any date prior to Pearl Harbor . . .

I parked my car, that first day, and climbed the steps to the terrace level, where Mrs. Rupp was sunning herself and Harry was standing, in Hawaiian print shirt, plaid shorts, blue ankle-length socks, and huaraches. He had a cigar in his left hand, which he held rather daintily high. "Hi, Mr. Daniels," he said. "You didn't have to come all the way out here."

I was a little out of breath.

"Steps are pretty steep," said Harry Rupp. "But they keep my legs in condition. Sit down a minute. Like you to meet my wife. Barbara, this is Mr. Daniels. He's the chairman of the hospital drive."

"No, only the special-gifts committee," I said.

"Make yourself comfortable, Mr. Daniels," said Barbara Rupp. She was wearing wrap-around sun glasses and I don't think she saw me very well. She barely raised her head from the deck chair.

"You have quite a place here, Mrs. Rupp," I said.

"Well, it's what *we* wanted," she said, closing her eyes.

"She did most of the work. I gotta be away a good deal of the time. What would you say to a little libation? Smoke a cigar?"

"Well, a Coke or something like that," I said. "I don't often drink in the daytime. And I'll have a cigarette in a minute or so."

Rupp poured a Coke and handed it to me.

"You live in the town, Mr. Daniels?" said Barbara Rupp, without opening her eyes.

"On the edge of town," I said. "Lakeside Road. It used to be called Kouwenhoven Road."

"I know where it is. How many acres do you have?"

"We have four and a half acres."

"Four and a half acres? Oh, you must live in that big old fieldstone. That's a nice property."

"Thank you."

"Is that your family home?"

"Yes, I was born there. It's been in my family a long while, though not in its present form. My grandfather added on to it. He had a large family."

"They're coming back, according to some people, but I wouldn't have more than two," she said. "If you get one of each, what else do you have to prove?"

"Yeah," said her husband. "Well, Mr. Daniels, what did you have me down for?"

I smiled. "Well, I don't know that we had you down for any set sum. My job is to tell you what we're trying to do at the hospital, and then rely on your generosity."

"I know about that pitch, Mr. Daniels. But what did you have beside my name, in pencil? What was Harry Rupp supposed to be good for?"

"You must have had some experience in this sort of thing," I said. "Very well. We had two figures for you. One was a thousand, the other was fifteen hundred."

"You gave yourself plenty of leeway," said Rupp.

"Not really," I said. "We had you down for a thousand, but the fifteen-hundred figure was for you and Mrs. Rupp."

"Count me out," said Barbara Rupp.

"Well, I'll go for a thousand."

"That'll be fine," I said. "But what about you, Mrs. Rupp? I'd like to put you down for something. Say two-fifty?"

"I'll bet you would. No, when I said count me out, I meant count me out altogether."

"I see," I said. I stood up. "Well, Mr. Rupp. Thank you very much. You've been more than generous, and I won't take up any more of your time. I'll leave this folder with you, in case you'd care to learn about what we're doing at the hospital. And on the back page, the address and so forth. Where to send your cheque."

"Don't leave any folders, will you please?" said Barbara Rupp. "Harry can make out the cheque to the hospital and send it to you direct, can't he?"

"Of course," I said. "Well, thanks again. And nice to have seen you both."

"Well, one of us, anyway," said Barbara Rupp.

I had, of course, acted under instructions: never have an argument with a potential donor. Barbara Rupp was not exactly a potential donor, but her husband had given freely and generously, and would go down on our list as a favorable prospect in years to come. "Oh, and thanks for the Coke," I said, on my way down the steps.

Our community is not a large one, but I literally did not see Barbara Rupp again until the hospital had its drive a year later. Occasionally I would encounter Harry Rupp at our little golf club, but my friends and I had a table of our own in the smoking-room and our golf matches were made up of men from that group, all considerably older than Harry Rupp and his friends. I was sometimes in the club when Harry Rupp was there, but we did not always speak.

When I was again given Harry's name for my special-gifts list I said to him, at the club: "Harry, may I come out and see you, possibly this weekend?"

"Going to cost me a thousand dollars, Norman?" he said.

"At least that, I hope."

"Tell you what I'll do. I'll send you a cheque and spare you the trip," he said.

"Well, of course if you'd prefer. But I was also hoping I could get Mrs. Rupp to change her mind."

"What the hell, you can try. I'll tell her you're coming out Sunday afternoon. Make it late, around five. I won't be there, because our kids got some other kids for Sunday lunch, and then they slop around the pool. But by five she'll be by herself."

"Oh, why don't I do it some other time?"

"Listen, either way it's gonna be a waste of time, whether you go this Sunday or a week from Thursday."

She was wearing a playsuit, and her face and body were dark brown from the sun. "Harry said you were coming," she said. "But the answer's gonna be just the same."

"Yes, he warned me. But I can't think of a better way to spend at least part of Sunday afternoon than trying to collect money for the hospital."

"Don't you go to church?"

"Yes, I do as a rule."

"Church is another one of those things like hospitals."

"How so?" I said.

"Neither one of them will ever get a nickel out of me. Harry does it because it's deductible tax-wise, but also because it looks better if you're in business."

"Is that the way you feel about all charities?"

"In other words, don't I give to charity? No."

"I should think Harry would encourage you to, if only for tax purposes."

"That's a phony. I don't want them to get my money, even if I do get a little deduction for it. If you're not related to me, or you're not some close friend of mine, I wouldn't give you five cents if you were starving. That's not personal. I mean anybody. I don't know you, so I got nothing against you. But I wouldn't give you any money whether it was for you or the hospital or your Aunt Tillie."

"Well, it's an interesting point of view."

"And you're dying to know why. Shall I tell you why you'd like to know, Mr. Daniels? Because everybody wishes they had some excuse to stop giving away money. Take away that tax deduction and the charities would starve to death inside of six months."

"There again, an interesting point of view. I don't happen to agree with you, though."

"How do you know you don't? You didn't take time to think about it. You got it ingrained in you from your parents and *their* parents, give to charity. So you give. That's all."

"Haven't you ever given to any charity?" I said.

"Are you asking for the hospital or for your own information?"

"My own information, I guess. The hospital is a losing cause, it seems to me."

"Then I'll give you the information. You want to fix me a scoop? I'll have a bourbon on the rocks and you help yourself." She lit a cigarette and seated herself in one of those things that pass for chairs and that look like a salad bowl on a tripod. "Yes, I used to give to charity. Just like everybody. The Salvation Army. The Red Cross.

Somebody got married in the store—I was working in a department store—I chipped in. Or if I saw some blind man on the street, even if I was sure he was a phony. A dime. A quarter. Then I got in an automobile accident and they kept me waiting in the hall. They didn't pay a God damn bit of attention to me till I almost died on the stretcher. Then they had the nerve to charge me for blood transfusions, irregardless of my two brothers and friends of mine from the store were donating blood. I was in that hospital six weeks and when I came out I was minus the sight of one eye. I had a concussion. What they call a concussion of the brain. Nothing wrong with my brain, but my eyesight. It finally cleared up so I could see out of that eye, but the hospital ate up all my insurance and what I had saved up. So that's when I stopped giving money to charity."

"Hospital facilities——" I began.

"Sure, sure, sure. And it was right after the war. Sure, sure. Don't *you* give me that. I can recite it backwards and forwards."

"I thought you might have some philosophical reason, some principle based on objective reasons. But it isn't that, is it? It's just a very unfortunate experience. If you'd been bitten by a dog, you probably would have a prejudice against dogs. You don't deny that the hospitals do some good, Mrs. Rupp?"

"I don't deny anything, friend. Harry's got it made now, and if I have to go to a hospital, my bills get paid. But that's all they get out of me. Or any other charity. They can all go to hell."

"Well, fortunately most people don't feel that way," I said.

"You mind if I say something? You're a stuffed shirt," she said. "You're a real stuffed shirt, Daniels."

"Quite possibly," I said. "And not very good company, so I think I'll take my leave, if I may tear myself away."

"Sit down, for Christ's sake," she said. "I don't insult a person unless I like them. You know what I do? I ignore them. I'm not saying I like you as much as some people. I only saw you these two times. But there's two kinds of a stuffed shirt. Those that are stuffed shirts because that's all they are, and those that act like stuffed shirts but aren't. You're the latter."

"I see. But you'll concede, won't you, that when you tell a man's he's a stuffed shirt, he's not likely to wait around long enough to discover that there are *two* categories of stuffed shirt. Tell me why you like me. I may not like your reason for liking me, and then I *will* be a stuffed shirt."

"I think you're regular. You're all manners and politeness and all that, but get you with a load on and you'd be just like anyone else."

"Well, I can't help but feel you have a point. However, I don't often get a load on."

"Let's get stiff," she said.

"No thanks," I said. "As a matter of fact, Mrs. Rupp, I have to take my wife to a cocktail party and should leave this minute."

"What's she like, your wife? How old is she? How old are you?"

"I'm fifty-five. My wife is younger than that."

"A lot younger? Ten years younger?"

"Not ten years, but let's not get too precise."

"Do you have any children?"

"Two daughters. Both married. One in Philadelphia, one in New York." I stood up.

"You know something?" she said, getting out of her salad bowl.

"What?"

"Fifty-five's not so old."

"It's not so young, either," I said.

She moved toward me until her body was actually resting against mine. "I could get you to stay here," she said.

"Yes, if I didn't leave right this minute, you could."

"And you'd be glad you stayed," she said.

"No, there I think you're wrong. I'd be sorry, and so would you."

"You mean on account of Harry."

"Harry, in your case. My wife, in mine."

"You never cheated?"

"If I say no, you won't believe me."

"You're damn right I wouldn't," she said. "Well, go ahead go. I won't detain you, Mr. Daniels. I'll let you chicken out this time."

"You're right. That's exactly what I am doing," I said. "One question. Why me?"

"Ah, you want a little flattery, don't you?"

I laughed. "I guess so."

"Well, I tell you, honey. It's your grey hair. Will that satisfy you?"

"You know, you're quite a naughty woman," I said, smiling.

"Ho-ho. You can say that again. Why do you think Harry has me stashed away up here?"

I left her, and for a few days I seemed to have come to life again. They were disturbing days, full of disturbing thoughts, and when I attempted to treat the thing lightly, to laugh off the episode and its immediate effect on me and on the even tenor of my ways, I was only partially successful. The only thing to do *was* to laugh it off, I told myself, but in honesty I knew that I was not so invulnerable that my sense of humor could banish the thoughts that disturbed me. I felt her in her playsuit resting against my body, and that was all too real. So real that, as I have said, I came to life again. But in a week or so the routine of my life took hold once more. The disturbing thoughts became less disturbing and intruded less frequently. My business affairs, my home life, my social life, the afternoons of golf and the comradeship of my old friends, what I had done for so many years, what I had *been,* came to my rescue. Now I could look upon the episode with amused tolerance. When I was safe again I encountered Harry Rupp at the club. He apparently had been away on business. "Hi, Norman," he said. "I understand you got nowhere."

"I got absolutely nowhere at all," I said.

"She's tough," he said. He was standing naked with a towel wrapped around his middle, and his hairy chest and shoulders and arms and back and belly made me think of him as not a man alone but as a partner to her. I had never before been so close to a naked man whose wife had offered herself to me. I cannot explain what I felt; it was almost but not quite as if I were he but he was not I. His hairy body had done what I had refused to do but had been tempted to do, and my body had felt the very beginnings of what his body had felt completely and often. I was glad the towel covered his middle. I think I would have stared at him and he would think I was something I am not.

I was safely away from her, and I could calmly ask myself why I had even for a moment been so affected by her that for nearly a week she had been disturbingly in my thoughts. I had no reason to like her. Beyond a slight curiosity as to her reasons for being opposed to charities, she had not interested me. She was a woman I could have seen at the supermarket; one of many women I could have seen on the half-fare special Wednesday trains; overdressed, over-talkative, undistinguished; spending their husbands' new money in a competition among themselves. In her play-suit, with its white ruffled edges and gingham material, she was making a foolish effort to be girlish in spite of having produced two children who were in their early teens. Her figure was of the kind that I describe negatively as not bad rather than positively as good. During the war, when I was stationed in London with the Air Force, I had had two brief, meaningless affairs with women who had the same sort of figure: they looked much better in clothes than out of them, and would not take off their brassieres while the light was on.

Those women in London had faded in my memory (and in my conscience) as completely as the details of the paperwork I was then doing for the Air Force. With a strong effort I suppose I could recall an evaluation of some of our daylight bombings over Germany, and with the same effort I could recall the name of one, but not both, of the women. I knew, as a private statistic, that I had been unfaithful to my wife, but if my wife guessed it she never let on, and after the war she had no grounds for suspicion. I came home and got busy and did rather well in my real estate business, and we settled once again into the kind of life we had lived before the war. When the materials were available we repaired and improved our house, we saw our friends, I took part in the less demanding community activities, we watched our daughters through adolescence and young womanhood, and we acquired three grandchildren. We even interceded when two friends of ours talked wildly of getting a divorce, and they have been kind enough to say that Millicent and I kept them together.

With Harry Rupp at the golf club Saturday after Saturday, I cannot say that I forgot about her. Whenever I saw him, I would instantly think of her, but my mind would be occupied with the brief conversations he and I had, and that happened often enough so that I can truthfully say that the encounters with Harry had the curious effect of reminding me of her existence but reducing her to unreality. Harry seldom spoke of her, unless it was to mention her in connection with a trip he had taken with her, or some such joint activity. He rarely mentioned her by name, and I had become so sure of myself that I was able to do so. He said, one afternoon: "I see your wife's in the ladies' semifinals."

"Yes," I said. "Never got that far before. Barbara never plays, does she?"

"Golf? The most exercise she gets is bending over to paint her toenails. Oh, maybe swim the length of the pool. But no sports. Nothing competitive, you know what I mean. She just likes to sit."

"Well, the way I played today I'd have been better off just sitting," I said.

"Yeah, but that don't happen very often. I can belt them off the tee, but Jesus I wish I had your short game."

"I didn't have it with me today," I said. "See you, Harry."

"Right, Norm. Right."

For a while after that conversation whenever I heard their names or had other reason to think of them I would get an instant mental picture of Barbara Rupp in her playsuit, sitting in the sun and bent over to paint her toenails. The picture somehow offended me: the land that had been intact for a million years, now capriciously bulldozed and gouged out to make a site for a silly house for a silly woman, who had nothing better to do than decorate herself with paint and let the sun darken her skin to falsify her age. I had not set foot inside her house, but town talk was that she had all sorts of trick lighting, and built-in loudspeakers for a high-fidelity phonograph, and the very latest electrical appliances and deep-freeze units. They of course had television antennae as complicated as the radar installations on an aircraft carrier, and I gathered that her interior furniture was of a piece with the salad-bowl chairs on the terrace. It had cost ninety-five thousand dollars to build the house; that figure was a matter of public record. How much more was spent on furniture and gadgetry was anyone's guess. Knowing Harry, and after my two interviews with her, I was sure they filled the house with items from catalogs; funny toilet paper and tricky highball glasses and that sort of thing. They had been living in our neighborhood about four years, and the wives of my close friends had yet to meet Barbara Rupp. Some of them had not even seen her, and their initial curiosity about the Rupps' house had subsided.

The men, of course, were acquainted with Harry Rupp. He was already a rich man when he came to inspect building sites; from absolutely nothing he had built up a business that fascinated me, as any simple, fabulously successful enterprise fascinated me. During the war, while working in a defense plant, he sold black market cigarettes and candy to his fellow workers, then wangled a concession to serve coffee and doughnuts in the plant, legitimately. Thereafter he never again had to lie about his source of income; he became a sort of concessionaire in small, then larger, industrial plants, supplying and managing and taking a good profit from cafeterias and executive dining-rooms. He came to our town with a top credit rating and an impressive amount of loose cash. He was a big man, direct and even blunt, according to those of my friends who had dealings with him in his early days in town. But as one of them said to me, "He's a fellow that's definitely on his way to much bigger things. You sense that after talking to him for five minutes." He was away a good deal of the time, usually arriving home on Friday afternoon. In his blunt fashion he told the right men that he and his wife had no social ambitions, but that he wanted to get his kids in the private schools and he himself wanted to play golf. "After that," he said, "you can forget about us." He almost immediately fitted into a group of men at our golf club that consisted of several retail merchants, two young doctors and a dentist, the Catholic priest, the district manager of the telephone company, and one of my younger competitors in real estate. Among them were the best golfers in the club and the hardest drinkers, and they shook dice not only for drinks but for sums of money that caused some alarm among the older members of the house committee. "Somebody's going to get hurt," the committee chairman said.

"True," I said. "But we already have rules against gambling on club property. We either enforce the rules and stop gambling entirely, or we just look the other way. Then when someone does get hurt, they may come to their senses."

As it happened, Harry Rupp, who everyone knew had plenty of money, rescued the house committee from the embarrassing predicament. "This game's getting too damn big for fun," he announced one afternoon. "I don't mind thirty or forty bucks, but when we get up around two hundred dollars on the table, I begin to take it seriously. Furthermore, we got Father Mulcahy sitting here like a bump on a log. One of these days he's gonna get in the game, and

that's the day the bishop better count the Sunday collec-
tions. So wuddia say, fellows? Wuddia say we don't play for
any paper money?" Rupp was the only man who could
have done it, and I found out later that my friend the committee chairman had spoken to the priest, who then spoke
to Rupp, and that Rupp's immediate reaction had been
favorable. "Woodburn," he said, referring to the telephone
company manager, "is too nice a guy to get in trouble over
a lousy dice game. But I seen him turn pale last week when
he dropped seventy-fi' dollars. He don't have that kind of
money. I'll break it up."

That was the kind of man Harry Rupp was among
men, and then as chairman of the hospital's special-gifts
committee I learned a little more about him, but what I
learned was really only more of the same: his quick generosity to the hospital drive was to be expected of the kind
of man I had seen in the golf club smoking room. Moreover, his sort of heartily virile man's man would not necessarily be guilty of basic disrespect in calling his wife "tough"
or even in speaking scornfully of her laziness. His attitude
toward his wife, and toward women, had only been hinted
at in Barbara's remark: "Why do you think Harry has me
stashed away up here?" The remark could have more than
one meaning. It might be flirtatiousness on her part; it
might have been the plain truth; it might have been indica-
tive of resentment or loneliness or boredom. But it told me
almost nothing about *Harry's* attitude, and toward the end
of that summer it became important for me to know just
what his attitude was.

As always, there was that one day in late July or early
August that Nature sends us creatures as a reminder that
autumn will come. August and September can be warm, but

we have been given that brief warning, although we highly intelligent human animals seldom act upon it. I took no deliberate action on it, to be sure, but I found that inexplicably I was having a recurrence of my disturbing thoughts of Barbara Rupp. I think it was because autumn could be sensed, and in the autumn I would not see her. When I had seen her it was spring or early summer, and for me she did not exist in cold weather. How can I explain to myself what happened to me? I came to life again, as I had before, but this time it was the thin chill of a distant autumn and not the recollected pressure of a real woman against me that brought me to life so desperately. I hardly even thought of *her;* I thought of myself. And then I began thinking that this new life would remain incomplete if I did not go back again to that hideous house. This new life I was feeling was hideous, too, but I had lost any sense of beauty that I had ever had. Yes, I thought, killed by an early frost, and to hell with it. One thing killed, another thing come to life; and what was gone was truly gone and better gone and useless. Only this hideous new life was not dead.

I have never been a devious man. In our business, waiting is half the game, and since Millicent and I both have small private incomes, I could always wait till I got my price before selling a piece of property. In my personal life I was equally secure: Millicent and I were completely compatible, understood each other perfectly, lived in an atmosphere of mutual respect, and were, of course, very much in love. My London episodes can be properly attributed to physical necessity and wartime strain; and since they occurred at a distance of three thousand miles and during a universal moral blackout, I did not get involved in deviousness. But now I seemed to have developed a talent for intrigue. Through the most casual questions I determined that Harry

Rupp would be absent from home from Monday through Friday of the second week in August and that his two children would not yet be home from summer camp. I drove out to the Rupps' house.

To my momentary dismay Barbara Rupp was not alone. She introduced me to a young woman who was the wife of a young farmer nearby. With my new talent encouraging me I recovered quickly from my first disappointment. "I don't want to make a nuisance of myself, Mrs. Rupp," I said. "But I have a client's interested in building a house like yours. Would you mind if I just paced off a few measurements to give me some idea?"

"Help yourself," said Barbara Rupp. "You want a tape measure?"

"No thanks," I said. "I'm used to making rough estimates. You ladies forget all about me."

"I was just leaving," said the farmer's wife.

"You're not gonna leave me all alone with Mr. Daniels," said Barbara Rupp.

The farmer's wife tittered out of embarrassment for me and my decrepitude.

"I hope I'm not *quite* that harmless," I said, as stuffed-shirtedly as I could sound.

The farmer's wife went down the steps, accompanied by Barbara Rupp, while I, with pencil and paper in hand, paced off the dimensions of the terrace. Barbara Rupp returned to the terrace. "You could have got that information by phoning Harry," she said.

"I happen to know he's away."

"What is it? Just an excuse to see me?"

"Yes," I said.

"Yeah, I thought so. I saw the look on your face when you spotted Dora. You know I have two kids."

"I know they're not home from camp," I said.

"Oh, this is for real, huh?" she said. "Wuddia you, been brooding over the pass I made at you?"

"I'm here," I said.

"Well, yeah," she said. She looked at me. "Yeah."

"Can't we go inside?"

"Sure. Why not?" she said. "You want a Coke? I think you better have a *real* drink."

"So do I," I said. I fixed a bourbon on the rocks. She already had a long drink in her hand. She sat in a bright green chair and stretched her legs on the matching hassock.

"What brought this on? A little domestic quarrel with your wife?"

"Not a bit. I just wanted to see you. Had to see you."

"Yeah, that's better, because if it was only a fight with your wife it isn't worth it. A wife getting suspicious, and that's what she'd be. I don't care what you fight about, right away the wife starts getting suspicious. I got myself to think about, too."

"Does Harry trust you?"

"No, and I don't trust him either, but you picked the only time of the year when I don't have two bodyguards age fifteen and thirteen. Hell, I know Harry never passes up anything, but I have to behave myself. I used to wrap hamburgers when Harry and I were just getting started, and I'm not taking any chances of losing out on a deal where he has over eight hundred people working for him."

"You don't seem to be getting much out of the deal now."

"Who says I'm not?"

"I didn't mean financially," I said.

"Neither did I," she said.

"Oh."

"You don't think I was waiting seventeen years till you came along. I said I had to behave myself, but that's for Harry's benefit. I wouldn't give a hoot in hell for a woman that just waited around while Daddy-O was out cutting up . . . Now I got you thinking about your wife."

"It's quite true, you have."

"You want to think about her some more?"

"No."

She put down her drink. "Then why don't you try one on for size? A nice kiss."

She stood up and I took her in my arms and kissed her.

"Say, you're hungry," she said.

"Yes," I said, and we went to her room.

The strangest thing was that I was new to myself, as new as she was new to me. The self-reproach and the disgusted weariness I had expected did not occur. I did not want to leave her, and because I did not want to leave her I knew that I never would leave her entirely. She put on a pale blue kimono and walked with me to the terrace door. "Maybe in a week or so," she said. "I have ways of getting rid of my little bodyguards. And listen, don't worry about Dora. She owes *me* a few favors."

"Are you planning to tell Dora?"

"I don't have to tell her. All we ever talk about is men anyway."

"I know her father-in-law."

"So do I. A damned sight better than you ever will. So there's nothing to worry about there, either, Daniels."

"Don't call me Daniels," I said.

"I'll call you whatever comes into my head," she said.

But she was not destructive. She was me, and if she

had continued only to be me the affair might have had a self-destructive effect on me. But it soon became a shared experience, and one day she said, "Harry says I'm getting quieter."

"Well, are you?"

"With him I am."

"Does that mean he's getting suspicious?"

"Just about. He has an old trick he tries. Like out of the blue he'll suddenly mention some fellow's name, and watch for my reaction."

"Has he mentioned my name?"

"Not so far. But all the names of his golf friends. He had it kind of narrowed down to Woodburn there for a while. But don't you start getting careless."

"Never fear."

"Don't say never fear. Always fear. Because I'm apt to get careless. I'm smarter than Harry Rupp, but him noticing that I'm getting quieter. That was careless. But you know what the trouble is, Norman. You know why I'm getting careless."

"Why?"

"I'm the next thing to falling in love with you."

"You are, Barbara?"

"Just about. It's all I can do to fake it with that ox any more. I didn't use to mind. Enjoyed it, in fact. What's two men when the one don't mean any more than the other? Dora's father-in-law Wednesday night, Harry Saturday night. I don't hate Harry Rupp. I think the world of him, in some ways. But I never told him I loved him since we got the Schwarzberg contract, that was our first big contract. Some nights he didn't get three hours' sleep. Architect plans. Bank loans. Unions. Wholesalers. And me big as a house with Harriet. We had a semi-detached in Kew Gar-

dens. You would of thought he had the entire responsibility
for the atom bomb. Huh. Two years later he wouldn't re-
new with Schwarzberg. They weren't *big* enough any more.
He said he was doing it for me and the kids, but not Harry.
Harry's a born big shot. The only trouble is, I don't like it
when he big-shots me. Him or anyone else."

I smiled. "I'll try to remember that."

"You better more than try, Norman. I could turn on
you," she said.

She was now contentedly in my thoughts, where before she had been a source of disturbance. We saw each
other on an average of once a week, usually at her house,
but when Harry did not go away we would meet at Dora's.
My real estate business is a modest operation, not requiring
the services of a full-time secretary, and my office is in the
second-floor rear of a two-story building on a side street.
In the morning there is no one but me to answer the telephone, and it is normal for me to be seen in all parts of
town and the nearby countryside, afoot or in my little car.
My recently discovered talent for intrigue was being given
few tests.

I say she was contentedly in my thoughts and that is
true, and I am mindful of a certain ambiguity in the statement. Her confession of love for me did not come as a surprise. A man knows those things. I was able to recognize,
for instance, the difference between her somewhat crude
tenderness and Millicent's habitual gentleness. Millicent's
behavior, her gentleness, was universal, not limited to her relations with me. Barbara, on the other hand, was learning
tenderness for the first time. She loved her children, in her
special way, but she sometimes would compare their childhood with her own. She had had to drop out of high school

to go to work at sixteen, and the contrast between her children's private schools and summer camps and luxuries, and her struggles to earn a living, was a source of resentment. "I don't begrudge it to them," she said. "Harry has the money. But if I don't slap them down once in a while, they start correcting my grammar and all." And slap them down she did, with the result that their father's weekly homecomings were fun for him and the children, but not for their mother. For that and other reasons it was not so remarkable that she should turn to other men and finally to me.

I could not tell her that I loved her. I had never said that to anyone but Millicent, and it was the one thing of the old me that the new me withheld from Barbara. No, there was one other: she was fascinated by my affairs in London and coaxed me for all the details, and I saw no reason not to tell her as much as I remembered. She was correspondingly revealing concerning the men she had known before and since her marriage to Harry Rupp. But I refused to discuss Millicent on such terms, and my refusal infuriated Barbara. As a matter of fact my apparent loyalty to Millicent was not solely based on a question of taste; Millicent and I, as I have said, "understood" each other, but when I said that, I was speaking of the mutuality of a successful marriage. Actually there had been times in my marriage when I did *not* understand Millicent, when it seemed to me that she was taking advantage of her femininity to behave capriciously. Millicent was the last woman in the world I would call neurotic, but on several occasions she pretended that I had been neglecting her and then, with beautiful inconsistency, locked me out of our room! As for the kind of detail Barbara Rupp sought, there was nothing much to tell.

And I could not bring myself to pay Barbara the compliment that I could have done in all sincerity: that she, and not Millicent, was the woman in my life. I had every intention of staying married to Millicent as long as I lived. I would maintain the same courtesy toward her and protect her from gossip and scandal. But she would have to find her own reasons for the change that had taken place in our relationship, and I was sure she would do that. My hair was grey, my golf handicap had been raised, I needed new glasses every year, a fourth grandchild was on the way, and it was not unusual for me to go to two funerals in the same week. It was my own secret, not even shared by Barbara, that in a few days I would build up such a fierce desire for her as nothing in my old life—the early days with Millicent, the wartime days in London—had prepared me for. I had laughed, with my friends, over jokes about "the last call to the diner," and *l'age dangereux*. The jokes, though I laughed, had always seemed to be in questionable taste, possibly because I have always felt that a man's dignity is more important than his demonstrated virility, and the jokes demonstrated just the opposite at the cost of his dignity. Such jokes, however, usually concerned an aging man and a young girl, and Barbara Rupp was not a young girl. She was a woman who did not have too far to look for a dangerous age of her own. And, as she had said, fifty-five was not so old. There was this, too: that since she had fallen in love with me, we were in this thing together.

I now come to the part of this story that is the most difficult to tell. It is told by the old me, about the man whom I have called the new me; and while they are essentially separate and distinct persons, who will believe that they are not one and the same? The old me and the new me had the same name; I signed my cheques the same way, and the bank never questioned them. The new and the old occupied the same pew in church, and no one noticed when the old became the new. And the old me, now writing, can reveal the innermost thoughts of the new me without taking any so-called literary license. My insistent plea that the old me and the new be considered separately is not the whimpering of a coward: what happens to me happens to the outer me, the only me that the world can see. Nevertheless, I have the same right as anyone else to be judged fairly. I intend to write this all down and destroy it immediately, but I have come to believe that there are many things we do not fully comprehend. I believe that a man can be two men, can even have two souls, for I was two men and have had two souls. And I believe that if I put this all down, somehow the truth will get into the air, even though I destroy these pages immediately and without showing them to anyone. If I tell the truth, sparing neither myself nor anyone else, it will show in my face and in my actions, and people will at least be less positive that my punishment is completely and unquestionably just. If I can create some doubt, this painful confession will have served its purpose.

Barbara abandoned her attempts to extract information of an intimate nature on the subject of my relations with Millicent, and I was glad that we had buried that bone of contention. But without at first seeing any connection, I next had to resist her wish to *meet* Millicent. She had no desire to advance herself socially; but she was increasingly curious, to the point of obsession, about Millicent, about the woman who had been my wife for nearly thirty years. Once again I took a firm stand. "You warned *me* against getting careless," I said. "But this is simply asking for trouble. Your paths haven't crossed, so why should they now, after five years?"

"I want to meet her, and I'm going to."

"I forbid you to do any such thing," I said.

"Forbid me? Who the hell do you think you are? You sound like a God damn schoolteacher."

She wasted no time. The very next afternoon, when I got home from work, Millicent said: "You should have been here earlier. I had a caller. Mrs. Harry Rupp."

"What the devil did she want?"

"I don't know. I thought maybe you'd know. She said she wanted to talk to me about the hospital, serve on one of the committees. But she didn't impress me as the kind of woman that wanted to do any work. She had some other reason."

"Wanted to have a look inside our house," I said.

"Not from what I've heard of hers," said Millicent.

"No, and not from what I've seen of it."

"She mentioned that you'd been there twice."

"I went there to collect money, remember?"

"Oh, I remember."

"Well, are you going to try her out?"

"No," said Millicent. "She wouldn't fit in."

"I don't think she would, either." I said. "What did you tell her?"

"Well, I hope you don't mind, but I said I'd got the impression from you that she wasn't really interested in charities."

"You shouldn't have said *that,* Millicent."

"I wouldn't have, ordinarily. But I wanted to get rid of her, so I wasn't exactly polite. If she wanted a look at this house, she got it, but I don't imagine she'll pay me a second visit."

I was incensed at Barbara for her defiant disobedience, and she was furious at me for the snub Millicent had given her. She appeared in my office on the morning after her visit to Millicent, and said things that could be heard down the hall, things that, overheard, could leave no doubt about the character of our relationship. I fought back with complete silence, until she had run out of vituperation for Millicent and for me. Then I got up and opened the door and looked down the hall. No one was in the hall, and I said, "Now go, and never come here again." What I wanted most was for her to leave the building unrecognized. It was about a quarter to eleven in the morning, a busy time in the building, but there was no one in the hall or on the stairway, and she left.

My reputation, of course, was endangered. I held out no foolish hope that she had not been overheard. All I could hope was that people in the neighboring offices would not identify the woman who had been in my office. That hope was not an entirely foolish one, since it was possible for her to go downstairs and out the rear door to the parking lot, and that is what she did.

But the damage to my reputation had been done. Next door to my office was a tailor's establishment, conducted by a man who had often been behind in his rent. I had had to warn him so many times that there was no cordiality left in our daily greetings. But at noon that day he grinned and smirked. The other two rooms on my floor were rented to a milliner who was not renewing her lease but was moving to a larger store on the main street. The tailor's daughter worked for her as a saleslady, and there was no chance that the three of them would miss this opportunity to wag their tongues.

As a rule I lunched with friends of mine in the coffee shop of the hotel, and I could now tell, from day to day, the progress of the gossip about me. It was two weeks before anyone actually said anything, but if I happened to miss a day at our table, the next day I could detect uneasiness and small silences that revealed they had been discussing me in my absence. The first man to come out with it was Millicent's brother, Harvey Crimmons, who was a lifelong friend. He walked back to my office with me after lunch. "Norm, are you in any trouble?"

"You wouldn't ask me that if you didn't know I was," I said.

"It's going to get to Millicent," he said. "It's spreading like wildfire. Norm, I'm no saint, and if I can help you, say so. Is there anything *to* this talk?"

"I don't know what the talk is, by this time, but you're referring to a visitor I had in my office a couple of weeks ago?"

"Raised hell because you cut off her money or something," said Harvey. "Nobody can figure out who it is you're keeping."

"That's the story, is it?"

"I'd go to Millicent if I were you. I think I know my sister pretty well."

"Harvey, I couldn't bring myself to tell her. And yet the minute she hears anything at all, she's going to guess who the woman is."

"Then you're only postponing it. It's like the dentist. You're going to have to go sometime."

"It isn't really like the dentist, Harvey."

"No, not really, but——"

"It isn't just one tooth. It's several sets of teeth, if you want to think of it that way," I said. "And nobody's going to look very pretty when this dentist gets through."

"I still say tell Millicent before someone else does."

"I'll think about it some more, but thanks anyway," I said.

I stopped in at the tailor shop. "Why, hello there, Mr. Daniels. What can I do for you?"

"Schneider, you're going to have to find another room," I said. "I want you out of here by the first of the month."

"Where can I find a place in that short time? I gotta look, and find some place is in my price range. Why are you kicking me out, Mr. Daniels?"

"You're not a good tenant, and you haven't lived up to the agreement. Three times in the last eleven months you've been behind, and I could have kicked you out the first time."

"You talk about good tenants, Mr. Daniels. I could talk about bad landlords. Noisy ladies cursing and swearing in the landlord's office, that's no good for business."

"That's what I wanted to make sure of, Schneider," I said. "Be out of here by the first of the month. You'll get a registered letter tomorrow."

"It wasn't only me that heard her," said Schneider.

"The first of the month, Schneider," I said. I was satisfied that he had not identified my visitor and that the milliner and her saleslady were likewise in the dark. Why was that important?

Because I wanted to be with Barbara again. For whatever time we had left, I wanted to be with her. Before Millicent learned the truth, before Harry Rupp learned the truth. I was convinced that no one knew it was Barbara who had made the stormy scene in my office. If I could see her only one more time, then it had to be that, but that it had to be. And I was not sure that it would be only one more time. Harry Rupp, for instance, might hear gossip about me, but he would not place me under suspicion. As for Millicent, if she guessed the identity of my mistress, I would lie to her, not lies of denial but lies that promised never to see Barbara again. I had no intention of giving up Barbara Rupp. Once again she was me, in my blood, and once again I was thinking of myself rather than of her. It was just like before, when I had come to life again, except that now I knew it was for the last time, whether that meant one afternoon or meetings over a period of months.

The shady character I had become dropped in at the golf club, not to play golf but to learn a few things about Harry Rupp. I must say he behaved astonishingly well. He made no mention, direct or indirect, of my new status. No one, as yet, had treated the gossip as a subject for humor in my presence, but Harry Rupp was always unpredictable, to say the least. I did not for a second doubt that he had heard the gossip; his group were as fond of gossip as a woman's sewing circle. But however much he may have joined in the gossip and jokes when he was with his cronies, he gave absolutely no indication that he had heard anything that reflected on my character. As for his suspecting that Barbara was involved, the notion was preposterous: Harry Rupp was not a man who could so convincingly hide his feelings. At all events, I ascertained that he would be absent on one of his usual Monday-to-Friday trips, and on the following Tuesday I telephoned Barbara from my office. I came right to the point. "I'll be at your house at half past one," I said.

"Are you crazy?" she said. "You know what I heard about you? You're supposed to be mixed up with a married woman!" She chose the wrong time to be funny.

"One-thirty," I said.

The autumn, that by a hint of its coming had started this thing, was now here, with colors so gorgeous that it was hard to believe there had ever been a summer or ever would be a winter. As I drove out along the country roads to that trailer-camp house I actually forgot that an unpleasant scene would occur at the end of my drive. But I was shaken back to reality by the sight of Dora's car in the driveway.

Barbara and Dora were drinking coffee in the "family room," a room so designated for no other reason that I could make out than to distinguish it from the livingroom. Both women simultaneously raised their eyelids as I entered, both expressing the same disapproval and hostility. They waited for me to speak.

"I see we're going to be chaperoned," I said. "Or were you just ready to go, Dora?"

"I'm staying," said Dora.

"Would you care to join in the fun?" I said, hoping to shock her.

"I'm here to protect Barbara," said Dora.

"What from? She hasn't needed your protection thus far."

"She sure does now," said Dora.

"Harry didn't go away," said Barbara. "He only went to Newark. He'll be back this afternoon."

"And I'm staying right here till he gets back," said Dora.

"What made him change his mind at the last minute?" I asked Barbara.

"How should I know? But that's the way it is," said Barbara.

"Was it your idea to have Dora here?"

"Partly mine, partly Dora's."

"Well, I certainly haven't got much to talk about with Dora here," I said. "I'll be in my office every morning except Thursday. Will you phone me?"

"No, she won't," said Dora.

"Dora, you're rapidly becoming a bit of a nuisance," I

said. "Barbara and I have a lot of things to talk about—"

"You son of a bitch, don't you see she's scared stiff?"

"Are you scared stiff, Barbara?"

"Harry was never this way before," said Barbara. "Maybe he didn't even go to Newark. And he was suppose to go to Newport News. He was suppose to be there just about now. But he called up and cancelled his appointment, in front of me. He won't hardly talk to me."

"Well, let's see what he does tomorrow," I said.

They took that as my parting remark. They looked at me in silence, and said nothing when I left.

I never saw Barbara again, and I have no better information as to the later events of that day than has any other reader of the newspapers. No one else ever knew what happened that afternoon after Harry Rupp came home and Dora left. The driver of the school bus saw Harry Rupp, alone at the foot of the driveway. Rupp told the busman to take the Rupp daughter to Dora's house (the boy was at boarding school). That was at approximately fourten. At five o'clock Harry telephoned the state police and told them to come and get him. Barbara, beaten and choked, was stretched out on the sofa in the family room.

I, of course, was never charged with any crime, and even when I was made to testify as a material witness the State objected so often to the defense questions that a transcript of the trial contains only a few pages of my testimony. But if ever a man was on trial, it was I. The jury found Harry Rupp not guilty, but I was convicted of an unnamed crime by my friends and fellow townsmen. I was convicted and sentenced before I ever took the stand, and the district attorney was a fool to go against the weight of public opinion. I do not know what kind of reasoning it is that blames me for the murder of Barbara Rupp, the breaking up of

Harry Rupp's home and business, the disgrace to my children and grandchildren. The only person who could legitimately claim to have suffered by my infidelity was Millicent, but she and my children no longer bear my embarrassing name. For Millicent the scandal was a release, the divorce proceedings were humorously perfunctory, and she married a man who, I am told, is another Harry Rupp with fifteen years added. They live in a place called Petoskey, Michigan.

Perhaps it is too late for any real good to come of this confession. I did not expect to be judged fairly during the near-hysteria of a murder trial, with one of the New York papers referring to me as "Barbara's aging aristocratic lover." I, an aristocrat? My ancestors fought and died two centuries ago to free this land from the aristocrats, and down through the years my family have stood for justice and fair play. For that very reason I hoped, throughout my ordeal, that when the trial was ended and my fellow townsmen came to their senses, they would see this thing in its true light. I naturally released my clients from our business commitments, with the expectation that they would return to me voluntarily. Indeed, I counted on their return as the first indication of a general return of sanity after the orgy of gossip and persecution. But I have been disillusioned on that score. Younger firms, and newer firms, seized the opportunity of my temporary retirement, and timidity has overcome my former clients. My last dealings in real estate have been the sale of my house, that had been in my family for five generations, and the business property in which I had my office. I am barely able to afford my small room in the hotel, which is situated two stories above the bus terminal. I gave my golf clubs to the pro in part payment of my account with him when I resigned from the club. And Millicent extracted her pound of flesh, down to the last ounce.

I walk the streets of this old town as a convicted criminal, waiting for a word or a sign that justice is being tempered with mercy. Friends of a lifetime speak to me when they cannot avoid doing so, but they never stop to chat, although I have given them openings. It is not so much that I need their companionship; it is rather that I want to be helpful. I know that one of my lifelong friends is going to need the kind of help that I could give him; every morning and afternoon he drops in for a chat with the comely young woman who sells tickets at the bus station. If I could tell him that people have no time for compassion—but perhaps he too feels that he is coming to life again. The young woman is certainly prettier than Barbara and has a much better disposition. I go to the bus station about once a week to weigh myself. Every man over forty-five should watch his weight.

THE LESSON

To the young half of the people in the little church the name Godfrey Gaines meant almost nothing. He was Mr. Gaines, father of two of their number, and a sufficiently close friend of the deceased to be selected as an usher at the service. But it had been a long time—the lifetime of the young people in the church—since Godfrey Gaines had done or been anything to attract the attention or stimulate the curiosity of anyone born after 1930. The young people were there to pay their last respects to Mr. Barton, father of the Barton twins and a man whom it was easy to call Rex. People of all ages called him Rex, and in the church that day were twenty or thirty young people who throughout their lives had called him Uncle Rex. As for Mr. Gaines, Godfrey Gaines, it so happened that none of his nieces or nephews had made the trip East to attend Rex Barton's funeral, and therefore no one present had ever called him Uncle Godfrey.

It was a little strange, or so it seemed to the young people, to see how many of the older half of the congregation greeted Mr. Gaines with warmth. The fathers, the actual uncles, all shook his hand and whispered something; the women, the mothers, the actual aunts quite obviously expected to be kissed, and were kissed. All this was strange because he was a stranger to the young people, but it was also strange because there was nothing about him now that called for any demonstration of affection or pleasurable greeting. Mr. Gaines, Godfrey Gaines, was not what you would call a distinguished-looking man, and in his blue serge suit and black four-in-hand he could easily have been mistaken for a paid pallbearer or one of Walter J. Mc-Ilhenny's assistants. The young people knew Johnny Gaines and Miriam Gaines Loomis because Johnny and Mimi had been brought up by their mother and stepfather, who lived in the neighborhood. It was known that Johnny's and Miriam's father was to be an usher at Rex Barton's funeral, and he thus escaped being identified as a paid pallbearer or an undertaker's assistant. But it was all pretty strange, to see Johnny's and Mimi's father, whom most of them had never seen before; to see him so warmly greeted by the older people; and for him to be an usher and thereby presumably to have been an intimate friend of Rex Barton. And perhaps the strangest thing of all was that Godfrey Gaines was such an ordinary-looking man.

The young people watched him with his contemporaries, recognizing them, failing to recognize them, being recognized by them. When recognition occurred it was with a quick smile, a smile as close to elation as the circumstances would permit, and the young people, seeing the smile, had a clue to the warmth of their parents' greeting. When Godfrey Gaines smiled the fathers and mothers and uncles and aunts seemed to be remembering good times, memories that needed the appearance of Godfrey Gaines for the reawakening. A father would whisper something to Mr. Gaines and Mr. Gaines would grin and nod; the mother would kiss Godfrey Gaines, sometimes putting both hands on his shoulders as she did so. Then they would all remember where they were, the solemnity of the occasion, and the mother, the woman, would take Godfrey Gaines's arm and be led to her pew. Mr. Gaines would leave them then and come down the aisle, an ordinary-looking man who could have been mistaken for one of McIlhenny's lugubrious helpers.

The little church was known to them all. Three generations were represented on this day: Rex Barton's generation, and the preceding and succeeding generations. No one had ever seen a speck of dust on the woodwork or a smudge on the brass, and only the most faithful of the faithful noticed the difference when the floor matting was changed. Everything else was the same, year in, year out, and by some mystery of time and human association, even Godfrey Gaines began to fit into the hour. In the midst of the prayers and hymns, the friends and relations, the banks of flowers and the sacred furniture, Godfrey Gaines was one minute a stranger and the next minute a member. Everyone was extraordinarily conscious of time and the passage of it outside the church and down to the moment of entering a pew and becoming part of the congregation; but then time was suspended, minutes and fractions of hours ceased to be the measure of time. Outside, and in the past, there were years and more years or fewer, and when the service ended there would be other years, many or few, but during the ceremony a man in the pew ahead had never been anywhere else, a woman across the aisle had been there throughout eternity. And the young people had known Godfrey Gaines all their lives.

McIlhenny's six men marched beside the casket as Brendan McIlhenny, at one end, pushed it down the aisle. Mrs. Barton and the twins and their husbands darted across the transept and out a side door, and after a moment of hesitation the first pews' occupants commenced to leave. They gathered on the steps of the church and on the sidewalk. ("Are you going back to the house?" "No, nobody is. Mrs. Barton and the others are leaving right away for Manchester, Vermont. That's where he's being buried.")

Godfrey Gaines got his coat and hat out of a limousine and put them on, then went back to the gathering on the church steps. He looked for and found a group of five: his former wife, her husband; his son, his daughter and her husband.

"You're staying with Tom and Edie?" said his former wife. She was standing very close to her husband and holding the collar of her coat close to her throat.

"Staying with Tom and Edie," said Godfrey Gaines. "How are you, Bill?"

"Pretty well, thanks," said Bill Whitehill, calmly.

"Our friend here looks very well," said Godfrey Gaines.

"I wish you wouldn't refer to me as our friend," said Miriam Whitehill.

"All right," said Godfrey Gaines. "I was being polite, that's all. I thought you were going to invite me for lunch or something."

"Far from it," said Miriam Whitehill. "I only wanted to be sure where you were staying."

"So you wouldn't go there?" said Godfrey Gaines.

"Something like that," said Miriam Whitehill.

"But would it be all right if Johnny and Mimi went to Edie's for lunch?"

"I'm sorry, but I can't, Father. I have to be in New York this afternoon," said Johnny Gaines.

"Where do *you* have to be, Mimi?" said Godfrey Gaines.

"I'll go with you," said his daughter. "George is driving back to town with Johnny, but I can go to the Taylors', if that's what you want."

"That's what I do want. Very much. In fact, it's all I

want. Let's go." Without another word to the others he
turned and led his daughter to the limousine. "Mr. Taylor's
house, please," he said to the chauffeur. "Cigarette, Mimi?"

"No thanks. I've given them up."

"Permanently?"

"I guess so. Haven't had one in four months . . . I'm
having a child."

"Well, that's good news. Congratulations. What do
you want?"

"I don't care. A boy, I suppose. I'm sure George would
like to have a boy, and call it George the Third."

"Not if he knows his American history. When is it
due?"

"Probably the second week in June."

"How does your mother feel about being a grandma?"

"She's looking forward to it. All her friends already
are."

"Yes. That would be her reason."

"Oh, Father. Must you? You two, still so bitter after
twenty-five years. Why don't you grow up?"

"Would you speak that way to her?"

"I have."

"In her hearing?"

"I'm not afraid of Mother, or I wouldn't be here now.
I didn't ask her permission to come with you."

"No, you didn't. And she didn't like it a damn bit."

"Well, I'm not going to like it either if all you're going
to do is make cracks about her."

"All right. I'll stop. But I want to point out that she's
had all these years to make cracks about me. And don't tell
me she didn't take advantage of that opportunity."

"I wouldn't think of trying. She's made you sound like
such an awful son of a bitch that you couldn't possibly live

up to it. She made you seem like Errol Flynn."

"Errol Flynn? That's reaching for one."

"No. What made me think of him was when he died, Ma said he couldn't have been any worse than you."

"A charming thing to say to a man's daughter, you have to admit that."

"She didn't exactly say it to me. To George."

"Well then it was nice of George to pass the information along to you."

"He thought it was funny. Don't criticize George."

"Did you think it was funny?"

"In a way. I only remembered Errol Flynn dressed in a pirate's costume, I think it was. And I can't picture you as a pirate."

"I have to weigh that remark. How do you picture me?"

"As you are. And every once in a while I come across a picture of you in a football suit. Did you see yourself in *Sports Illustrated* last fall?"

"Every time that picture's reprinted people send it to me. Sure, I saw it. But you never knew me when I looked like that. My Errol Flynn days, you might say."

"I can't imagine Ma falling for a football type."

"She didn't. By the time she knew me I was a golf type. Although my football reputation had preceded me."

"Lefty Gaines."

"Only because I learned to pass with my left hand. I was never lefthanded in anything else, but I spent a whole summer practicing forward passes with my left hand, and that was really how we beat Yale my sophomore year. When we played Harvard they were ready for me, in spite of the no-scouting agreement. I always used to rib Rex Barton about that. At first he maintained that Harvard hadn't broken the agreement, but I finally got him to admit that some kind alumnus had managed to convey the essential information. Well, what the hell, it was a ridiculous idea anyway. All you had to do was read the Sunday papers, the play-by-play. The New York *World* had charts of the big games."

"Were you an All-American?"

"Second. I lost out to a fellow at the University of Michigan. I'm sure Walter Camp had never seen him play, but I guess it was a fair choice."

"Only you don't really think so."

"Of course I don't, but I'm so used to saying it, I can say it in my sleep. You don't really care anything about football, do you?"

"Not very much. Sometimes people used to ask me if you were my father."

"Not very often, I'll bet. At least not people your age."

"Nobody my age, but a few years older, and of course the father of boys I went out with."

"Then why do you encourage me to talk about it? Not that I needed much encouragement. You were being nice to the old man."

"Why not?"

"Well—yes. Why not? Do you think I've had a rough time, Mimi?"

"Yes, I do."

He took his daughter's hand and looked at it, and then he put it back on her lap. "I have," he said. "But God damn few people know how rough. How did you?"

"I don't know, exactly. Stories. Not exactly stories, either. All the people around here liked you, but they talked about you as if you were dead. Uncle Rex didn't, but a lot of the others did. I knew you didn't have any money, and I heard about your divorce."

"That was in the papers."

"Yes. You married that woman to annoy Ma, didn't you?"

"Well—that may have been part of the reason. I didn't have to marry her, God knows. Nobody did. And she wasn't a bad dame. The only trouble was, she saw me with men, men that knew me as Lefty Gaines. She thought if she married me, my men friends would give her a background. Do you know what I mean? These Yale guys and Harvard guys and Princeton friends of mine, they were the big money and the social leaders of the town. But when I married Jenny my friends' wives never had us to their houses, and she began to think I was some kind of a phony. She wanted like hell to be respectable, and that's where I failed her. She took me for plenty, too, but I had no right to expect anything else. She was, let's face it, a whore."

"That was easy to guess."

"And that's what she is now. A madam. She runs a whorehouse in Kentucky. She's married again, so I don't have to pay her any more alimony. But she took me for everything I had when I walked out on her. It wasn't much by Bill Whitehill's standards, but it was all I had, and I had a hard time getting on my feet again. Your Uncle Rex helped me there. Not with money. With a job."

"I never knew Uncle Rex to be tight-fisted."

"Don't get the wrong impression. He never was tight-fisted. He'd have let me have any amount of money, within reason. But I didn't ask him for money. Him or anyone else. You know, when you get in a jam your friends will often let you have five hundred or a thousand in the hope of getting rid of you. I know. I've done it myself. But a job is a different story. So I called Uncle Rex on the phone and I put it to him straight. All he had to do was pick up the phone and I'd have a job. Rex was a director of a lot of big corporations. 'What kind of job, Lefty? What do you want to do?' And I told him, not just some stopgap kind of job. I wanted something where I could get a whole new start, and I thought the place where I'd fit in best was in some kind of personnel work. Well, to make a long story short, that's how I happened to get with Midlands Incorporated. I knew less than nothing about food processing, but all my life I had a knack of dealing with people. It's mighty interesting work, too. I make twenty thousand dollars a year. Maybe your husband makes that much, a little over half my age. But that twenty thousand represents four big raises in ten years. I started at ten. So they like me. I get results."

"That's wonderful, Father."

"I come back here and see the old crowd I used to know before you were born. Some of them probably expected to see me with my tail between my legs. Beaten. Abject. But I don't think I gave that impression, do you?"

"Not a bit."

"Were you—you weren't embarrassed or anything, were you? I can't tell about Johnny. A son takes his mother's side instinctively, and I don't know whether he had to go back to New York or not."

"He really did. I happen to know he did. He said so before the service."

"Well, I'm glad he wasn't just ducking me. I'd hate to think he didn't have any more character than that. I'm sure Bill Whitehill's been a good father to him and all that, but I know Bill, and if Johnny was only making up some excuse, Bill Whitehill wouldn't have much respect for him. You get along with Bill all right, don't you?"

"Very well."

"Bill's all right. I won't say anything against Bill. Not everybody that inherited as much money as Bill came through as well as he has. He always did everything by the book. He was in love with your mother long before I entered the picture, and when she married me instead, he took it with good grace. You *could* say he was biding his time till the roof fell in, but I never held that against him. Your mother was very lucky she had Bill to turn to. So were you, for that matter. And Johnny."

"Father?"

"What?"

"I probably shouldn't ask you this."

"If it's what I think it is, don't ask it," said Godfrey Gaines.

"How will I know we're thinking of the same thing?"

"Because there's only one question you could ask me that you'd have to soften me up first. When you say, 'I probably shouldn't ask you,' there aren't that many things that you're curious about."

"You *are* good about people," said Mimi. "Up to a point."

"Up to a point? What do you mean by that?"

"Well, you guessed the nature of what I was going to ask you, and you refused to hear the question. But where you're not good is that you don't know me."

"Not as well as I'd like to," said Godfrey Gaines.

"Thanks, but I'm not going to be diverted by compliments. Up to a point you know people, Father, but you don't know that you can't stop me from asking the question. Was it Mrs. Barton?"

"Was what Mrs. Barton?"

"Was Mrs. Barton the one that made Mother so bitter? Was Mrs. Barton your girl?"

Godfrey Gaines smiled faintly. "You have it all figured out, haven't you?"

"Yes, I think I have."

"All the wisdom of your years, all the sophistication of Long Island. You just have to know, don't you? Is that why you came along with me?"

"Not entirely, Father. But for years I've suspected that Mrs. Barton was the one that came between Mother and you. She always seemed the logical one."

"You looked over the field, and Mrs. Barton seemed the logical one."

"Yes. She must have been beautiful when she was young."

"She was indeed, and in my view she still is."

"Then I'm right. It was she?"

"No," said Godfrey Gaines.

"Is this a gentlemanly denial? Are you going by the book, too?"

"No. But I kissed Mrs. Barton once."

"Is that all?"

"That's all," said Godfrey Gaines. "I kissed her once, and then I went away."

"It doesn't sound like you at all, Father."

"No. It doesn't sound like Errol Flynn, either, I imagine." He leaned forward. "Driver, don't go to Mr. Taylor's right away. We want to drive around a while. Just take us anywhere till I tell you." Godfrey Gaines pressed the button that raised the glass division in the front seat, and looked at his daughter. "I haven't been a very good father, Mimi. I've been a lousy father. In fact, practically not a father at all. Bill Whitehill's been your father, not I, and he's a man that goes by the book. Always goes by the book. Which is all right, most of the time. But there comes a time when you have to throw the book away. I have a lesson for you, and it isn't in the book. Okay?"

"Of course."

"The first rule in the book, of course, is that a gentleman doesn't talk. Right?"

"And the rule that's broken most often."

"Right. And now your father is about to break that rule, because it's much more important for a father to teach his daughter something about life than it is for him to observe the rules."

"I'm waiting with bated breath, Father."

"All right," said Godfrey Gaines. "After you were born, and it seemed like the time had come for your mother and I to resume normal relations, she decided to go away for a while. The doctor had told me it was all right for us to sleep together, but your mother begged off. I had another talk with the doctor, and he said that while your mother was physically able to have relations with me, still it wasn't unusual for a woman after her first child to—to be reluctant. Unwilling. Indifferent. And in some cases he said the whole idea was repulsive to a wife, especially if she'd had a bad time in her pregnancy. That wasn't the case with you, at least physically. Your mother didn't have a particularly bad time having you, but then as Jerry Murphy, Doctor Murphy, said, we couldn't overlook the psychological factor. So your mother went South for four months. She was to be gone two weeks, originally, but that became a month, then two months. Then four. She'd never say she was staying another month, and several times when I said I wanted to join her, she said she'd be home the next week and there was no point in my going South. Then she'd stay another month.

"Well, I didn't suspect anything wrong, but I was young and vigorous and a couple of times I more or less picked up where I'd left off with a girl I'd known before I was married. In plain language, I slept with this girl several times while your mother was in the South, and in some way or other your mother found out about it. I don't know to this day how she found out, and it really doesn't matter. The point is, when your mother came home she accused me of being unfaithful, told me the girl's name and where she lived, and had me dead to rights. No use denying it. Her facts were too good. I asked her if she wanted a divorce, and she said she'd have to think it over. She thought it over for quite a while. She took so long, in fact, that I began seeing the girl again, and one day I realized that it had been a whole year since I'd last slept with your mother. I was never the most sensitive man in the world, but it dawned on me that this was getting to be a hell of a marriage. I was crazy about you, but you weren't the most brilliant conversationalist at that age. Goo and gah were about the extent of your conversation when you weren't yelling your head off. And it was just about that time that I realized that I wasn't in love with your mother any more. We were living in the same house and we went everywhere together and entertained a lot. But don't forget I was still kind of on trial. She was still thinking it over, whether to get a divorce or not, and finally one day I asked her what she'd decided, and she said it didn't really make all that difference unless I wanted one. That was the first inkling I had that she knew I'd been seeing the other girl again. Then, just a shot in the dark, I asked her if she was seeing anyone, and she said yes, she was. I couldn't believe it. I wasn't in love with her any more, but no man wants to feel like a chump, and believe me I did. I regret to say that I threatened to kill her and the guy. I hit her, and she ran to her room and locked the door and telephoned the Bartons. It was about eleven o'clock at night, but the Bartons came over and Rex more or less took me in hand and Mrs. Barton went in and pacified your mother. It was decided that the best thing would be if Rex and I went in town and spent the night at the club, which we did.

"Oddly enough, the quarrel seemed to be just what we both needed. I returned home next afternoon, full of remorse and apologies, and your mother said it wasn't all my fault, that I'd had provocation, and I don't remember who first suggested it, but we decided to take a trip together and see if we couldn't make a fresh start. That lasted about three weeks, or just long enough for me to bring up the subject of the other guy. She said it was part of the bargain that we weren't to talk about what had happened before, but if that was part of the bargain, I certainly didn't remember it. In fact, I didn't remember any bargain. We returned to Long Island, and shortly after that your mother announced that she was having a baby. Johnny. It should have occurred to me that she'd gone into the second-honeymoon very enthusiastically, considering that we'd been on the verge of very serious trouble. But I didn't say anything. The reason I kept quiet was because I was secretly ashamed of myself. I'd got her pregnant, but I really didn't love her. The only love in my life was you, saying goo and gah."

"Hadn't I progressed beyond goo and gah by that time?"

"Conversationally, you were in a rut."

"I was practicing up to be a good listener," she said.

"Maybe."

"All right. So you'd got Mother pregnant," she said. "Or someone had."

"Really, Mimi."

"Well, isn't that why she went away on this second honeymoon?"

"Listen, kid, I don't mind not going by the book, but you *want* me to throw the book away."

"Father, all this talk about the book, going by the book, that came from you."

"Then I guess I don't know how to talk to you," said Godfrey Gaines.

"Yes you do. I'm enjoying the conversation, but when you talk about Bill Whitehill and yourself and this non-existent book, I wonder where you've been the last twenty-five years. You were married to a woman that runs a whore-house. I should have thought—well, go on with your story, Father."

"I don't know how to. In my job I have to give a lot of talks, but there I know my audience. This time I don't."

"Well, try. Assume that I take it for granted that you weren't responsible for Mother's pregnancy. Who was?"

"Rex Barton," said Godfrey Gaines. He looked at her again.

"That doesn't surprise me."

"God, in your way you're as smug as I thought I was."

"But Father, I've known for *years* that Uncle Rex and Mother were a thing. Who around here doesn't know it?"

"Bill Whitehill?"

"Maybe he does and maybe he doesn't."

"Has he got somebody?"

"Well, if he hasn't it's only because he doesn't want anybody."

"What about *you*, Mimi?"

"What about me?"

"You and George?"

"Have I got somebody? No. But I happen to like George."

"Gee, that's a positive declaration," said Godfrey Gaines. "That's the old-time religion."

"Don't be sarcastic, Father. You had the old-time religion, you and Mother, and where has it got you? Twenty-five years of hating each other, not to mention a home broken up, and you marrying a whorehouse madam. That's the book you keep talking about. Well, you can have it."

"What would George do if he found out this child wasn't his?"

"What do you mean, found out? He wouldn't have to *find out*. I'd tell him."

"If you knew," said Godfrey Gaines.

"Father, ask the driver to take us to the Taylors'."

Godfrey Gaines did so, and the car wound along the roads that long ago and now once again had names that seemed so odd—Muttontown, Matinecock, Skunks Misery. Godfrey Gaines could not have found his way now, where the chopped-up estates had lost all identity.

"Father. When did you kiss Mrs. Barton?"

"Oh, you want to go back to that? Well, when I went to say goodbye to her. Your mother and Rex Barton were off somewhere together, and I decided I wouldn't be there when they got back."

"Did you know they were together, or just guess?"

He smiled. "I was like you. He seemed the logical one."

"Why?"

"Well, she'd turned down Bill Whitehill, the other logical one, and that left Rex Barton. And who did she rush to the phone to when I threatened to kill her? Oh, hell, it had to be Rex. He was all over the place anyway."

"Where was I?"

"In the nursery, where you belonged. I had no intention of taking you away, then or later. Personally I considered your mother a slut, but what did I know about raising a one-year-old daughter?"

"So you went to see Mrs. Barton."

"I told her I was leaving Miriam, and she said I was making a great mistake. I'll never forget it. 'Rex will get over it, and so will she.' That was the first I ever knew that Mrs. Barton was hep to the jive."

"Oh, Father. Not slang. Not *that* kind of slang."

"All right," said Godfrey Gaines. "She knew where they were, and she offered to make Rex come home, but I said no. Then she suddenly became very attractive to me, Mrs. Barton, and I suggested that she and I go away together. She laughed. She said she'd do a lot of traveling if she went away every time she got that kind of an offer. But she said no. 'I like you, Lefty,' she said. 'And maybe this is a good idea, your going away. But if you do go, don't ever come back. Don't *ever* come back,' she said. 'Cut them all out of your life, all of us,' she said. So that's what I did."

"And you kissed her."

"Actually it was more like she kissed me. It wasn't a pass on either side. It was affection. So I stayed away—till she sent for me, the day before yesterday. I guess most people around here wouldn't have thought of me to help give Rex Barton a send-off, but she did. And I guess she must have had her reasons. I didn't even ask. There's nothing I wouldn't do for Cyn Barton," said Godfrey Gaines.

"If you ask me, you've done quite a lot," said his daughter.

MONEY

The money was divided three ways: Ellen Brosnan got her
widow's share, and as soon as possible she left town and
went back to Buffalo, New York, where she had originally come from; the remaining two-thirds was split between
Nan Brosnan and her sister Marietta Brosnan Kelly. The
whole thing amounted to about two hundred thousand
dollars, quite a sum in those days, but the distribution did
not cause much talk in the town. A few said Ellen Brosnan
was lucky to get anything, but they were quickly reminded
by the knowledgeable that under the law it was almost
impossible to cut Ellen off. It could be done, they said, but
she would have had to agree and it would have had to be
so stated in Clete Brosnan's will. He would have had to say
that Ellen had been provided for during his lifetime (and
God knows that would have been the truth) and consequently consented to accept the nominal sum of one dollar in
exchange for waiving her dower rights. All were unanimous
that the way Clete disposed of his estate was the best
way: give Ellen her third and let her go back to her Buffalo,
New York, without any excuse for making a fuss, and let
the Brosnan girls enjoy life in peace and quiet, gratefully
remembering their brother with Month's Mind and Anniversary Masses said for him and a simple urn of Indiana

limestone to mark his grave. He had not had much peace and quiet during the latter portion of his life, but at least he could rest in peace now—that was what *"requiescat in pace"* meant, wasn't it, after all?—with Ellen back in Buffalo and Nan and Marietta home and keeping the name up. All were unanimous that Clete had managed to bring about in death the kind of order and dignity that he had so longed for in life.

They got a good price for the house in Oak Road. The house was only five years old, well built of the best materials and with all the latest modern conveniences. Electricity everywhere, and two full-sized bathrooms. A high antenna for the Stromberg-Carlson so that Ellen could get Kansas City and Chicago as clearly as other people could get Pittsburgh and Schenectady. The garage door lifted easily with one hand instead of being a swinging door that had to be swung outward into the driveway. The Vic was an Orthophonic, and Ellen was the only housewife on Oak Road who had a telephone extension in her kitchen—although for the time she spent in her kitchen it seemed like a waste of money. Ellen even had an electric contraption for polishing the hardwood floors, although no one thought for a minute that Ellen was the one who pushed the contraption around. That was a job for her maid. A maid—for a house containing eight rooms and no children, where there were seldom any visitors to take care of but always fresh candy in the cut-glass jars, where there was a baby grand piano with no one who could play a note. Completely furnished, rugs and all, the house brought twenty-eight thousand dollars, which had to be divided up three ways under the terms of Clete's will. "I'd as soon let her have the whole thing," said Nan Brosnan.

"Well, not me. I wouldn't. I'd as soon she got none

of it," said Marietta Kelly. "She already got more than she's ever entitled to."

"Yes, but she's going to get all's coming to her or we'll have some shyster lawyer hauling us into court."

"I didn't mean we should try any funny business. What Clete wanted we have to conform with. But if she got what she was entitled to, a roll of toilet paper'd be sufficient."

"It doesn't come by the roll in that house," said Nan Brosnan.

"Just a figure of speech," said Marietta.

"I know. And don't think I was having generous thoughts, lamb. If I let her have the whole thing, it'd only be to get rid of her, to have nothing more to do with her whatsover . . . I'll say this for her. You'll hardly find a mark on any of the furniture, not a scratch, and in some ways the stuff is better than new."

"Why shouldn't it? At our place it's just the opposite, but I brought up my three children in our place. Why shouldn't her stuff look new? A hired girl with nothing to do but clean and dust—and run that electric floor polisher. You'd think she was getting ready to give a ball."

"And it's what killed Clete, too. Those slippery floors," said Nan Brosnan. "That spill he took the summer before last, Clete was an old man after that. Never the same."

"Oh, we can't blame her for that, Nan. Clete was delicate from as far back as I can remember. True, he got a bad shaking up, but when was Cletus Brosnan ever a Gene Tunney? You or I could always put him down, as children."

"He wasn't a muscular man, but he made up for it in brains," said Nan.

"With only the one blind spot, but men are easily

swayed. I ought to know, with a husband and three sons."

"You don't have to be married to know that," said Nan. "I didn't enter the convent at some tender age."

"I wasn't inferring anything, Nan. Don't always have a kind of a chip on your shoulder when the subject comes up about men."

"I didn't think you were inferring, lamb. But it's you with your husband and three sons that sometimes you act a *little* superior. I see all kinds of men at the office, away from their women, and many's the time I'm glad I never married. A woman in an office sees an entirely different side of things. I know I wouldn't want to be talked about the way some men talk about their wives, or have my husband say the things I've had married men say to me."

"Well, the more credit to you, Nan."

"Thanks. Just don't feel sorry for me."

"I don't. There've been times I envied you, and you know that."

"Well, we're not dependent on anyone now, you or I," said Nan Brosnan. "We can do as we please now, if we want to."

"Yes, and I hope you stick to it, your decision."

"To quit my job? Nothing'll shake me now, lamb."

"Oh, that I'm sure you'll do. I was thinking of your other decision."

"To give up my room? Well, if you still want me."

"Still *want* you?"

"You didn't say anything these last couple of weeks. I thought maybe you talked it over with Luke and he was against it."

"Good heavens, no. We got all that extra room, what's the use of paying room rent when we have all that extra room?"

"Well, I was thinking it over."

"Oh, Nan, there you go again with that chip on your shoulder. In other words, why didn't we ask you to stay with us before? Well, the only answer I could give to that question is the truthful one. We never thought of it before. You seemed content boarding at Bess Stauffer's, a few minutes' walk to your office. Me asking you to come live with us has nothing to do with your legacy, Nan, if that's what worried you."

"I'm not saying it did."

"No, but it stands to reason that's what you were thinking, your remark about thinking it over. After all, Nan, I have as much as you have from Clete, so don't start conjuring up some ulterior motive. It never would have occurred to me to ask you to live with us, only you said you were giving up your job, and then I thought why does Nan go on living at Bess Stauffer's, downtown? It was too far a walk from our place as long as you had your job, but if you're not going to an office every day, why not keep me company? I get lonesome for someone to talk to. I sound like another Ellen but it's true. You devote your whole life to making a home for a husband and three boys and then the boys all go off and get married and all those years you didn't make any friends of your own."

"You? You have a lot of friends, friends by the dozen."

"No. I have neighbors and acquaintances but not a single close friend. Don't confuse me with Luke, Nan. Luke has the Knights and the Legion he goes to and always some kind of a political thing, but I never could join the Daughters or the Auxiliary when they wanted me to, and now I don't want to."

"They want you now, surely."

"Since the news of Clete's will, indeed they do. But

(*223*)

I was always careful who I made friends with, and this is the time to be more careful than ever. That's a good thing for you to keep in mind, too, Nan."

"Oh-ho! Don't think I won't."

"Especially look out for men, Nan."

"The fortune-hunter type of man I can see through a mile away."

"I'm glad to hear that, Nan. Very glad to hear it. There's no more pitiful a figure than a woman suddenly come into money and no one to ward off the leeches and sponges."

"I can spot one of them a mile off. Don't forget, I've been a bookkeeper since I was seventeen years of age."

"I know, but with we Brosnans the heart often rules the head. Look at Clete and Ellen. Suddenly at almost forty-five years of age one of the cleverest businessmen in the county, Cletus Brosnan, J. Cletus Brosnan, what does he do but become infatuated with a pretty face in a nurse's uniform. If he could have seen her the first time dressed in something else there might be a different story to tell. But I had to sit there one day and listen while he told me about this angel of purity."

"Angel of purity is what he said to me, too. Did you ever think she was that?"

"Her? You're not seriously asking me that question, Nan. That kind of a bust development, I was sure she had one or two children."

"Oh, you can't tell anything by that. Remember Sister Mary Alexander?"

"I do. But in a black habit she still looked more like an angel of purity than Ellen in her white nurse's uniform. Could you ever picture Ellen in a nun's habit?"

Nan laughed. "No, that I couldn't."

"We have fun together, Nan. You come and stay with

us. You'll get used to Luke, if that's worrying you. Once in a month of Sundays he comes home stewed to the gills, but he always has enough sense to sleep in the cellar those nights. 'If you come home in that condition,' I tell him, 'you don't deserve better than the dog. Sleep it off in the cellar,' I tell him. But that's only maybe once or twice a year."

"I've never seen Luke with one too many."

"That's the Legion. The brewery sends them good beer, a couple halves at a time, and they don't stop drinking till the barrels are empty. At that I'd rather have him get drunk on good beer than take a chance on going blind from bootleg hootch."

"Oh, any day. And if not blind, I heard of some that died of convulsions."

"Luke won't often take a drink of whiskey. He likes his beer, but the hard liquor he leaves for the younger fellows. He has that much sense, and that's something to be thankful for."

"You got the best of the Kelly boys. Clete always had only the nicest things to say about Luke. And I remember during the war people saying Luke didn't have to go, but he went."

"Well, there'd always been a Kelly in the Civil War and the Spanish-American, and our boys weren't old enough, so he went. He couldn't have gone if we didn't have Clete to help out, but Clete was glad to. You remember."

"I do. Clete was mortified when they wouldn't take him, but at least he could make some contribution."

"Mind you, it wasn't much. Two thousand, and Luke paid it all back. It took him five years, but he paid back every cent. Oh, yes. Every red cent. Luke was bounden determined he wouldn't go through life owing money to his brother-in-law."

"I never knew that. I never knew that at all."

"See? Here we are, sisters, living in the same town all our lives, and there's so many things we don't know about one another." Marietta Kelly was abruptly silent.

"What, lamb?" said Nan Brosnan.

"*Please* come and live with us, Nan."

"What's the matter? Is there something wrong? Tell me "

Marietta nodded. "I'd tell you, but I took my oath. You'll find out soon enough, God help us."

Nan Brosnan, in the weeks of accustoming herself to her new surroundings and leisure and to the constant close company of her sister, respected the mysterious oath Marietta had given. There were times when she had the guilty suspicion that Marietta had invented a crisis in order to persuade her to become a member of the Kelly household. But against that was the genuineness of Marietta's entreaty; it was not like Marietta to show any sign of weakness. In years gone by Marietta had taken things from her older sister, taken them without permission, stolen them on occasion; and when she asked favors she had always managed not to say please. Nan Brosnan could not remember ever hearing Marietta say please, and if she had actually uttered the word, the implication that the word carried was never in her tone. The word "please," and its significance as a sign of weakness, convinced Nan that Marietta had taken an oath and that the oath was necessary to hide a real, a desperate secret. Marietta was cheerful and chatty, sarcastic and revealing, but in those early weeks she did not again refer to the oath. It took weeks, but Nan Brosnan discovered that among all the persons and things that Marietta was so eager to talk about, one topic was omitted: not once, not ever, did Marietta tell a story that had Luke Kelly for the principal character. She told wonderfully funny stories about school days and the eccentricities of some of the nuns; stories about departed curates that she would never have told in front of a third person; anecdotes about her three sons growing up, and hearsay gossip about the inside maneuverings and machinations in the Legion Post and the Knights of Columbus Council. But Luke Kelly was never made the principal character of these reminiscences, and once Nan Brosnan discovered this omission she realized that the thing that troubled Marietta surely concerned Luke. Her mind leaped to a suspicion that it concerned Luke and Ellen, but as she listened further to Marietta's criticisms of Ellen, Nan Brosnan dismissed the suspicion: Marietta despised Ellen, but she was not jealous of her for any reason that had to do with Luke.

Nan grew fonder of Luke. Living in the same house with him she surprised herself with her quick acceptance of Luke as a sort of living substitute for Clete. He would never be Clete; he was too jolly and careless about every thing; his manners, his appearance, his outlook on life made him totally unlike Clete. Clete was hardly out of bed in the morning before he was shaved and wearing collar and tie, and if you ever saw Clete in his shirtsleeves it was only because he was doing some handyman chore about the house. His coat went back on the minute he finished the chore. But Luke would come down in the morning needing a shave, carrying his coat and vest and collar and tie, rubbing his whiskers, scratching himself wherever he felt the need and without regard for Nan's presence. "Hello, girls. You got the old man's breakfast ready?" he would say. "Nan, what are you doing up at this hour? You're supposed to be a lady of leisure. Go on back to bed." He would put an elbow on the table and rest his head on his hand as he spooned up big globs of Cream of Wheat, and while waiting for his eggs and bacon he would sit and smile sadly at Nan. "No rest for the weary, Nan," he would say. Sometimes in the interval between cereal and eggs he would stand up and put on his collar and tie. He would finish his breakfast and say, "Goodbye, girls. Anybody phones, I'll be at the barbershop." He was a collector for a furniture company, which allowed him to bring a Dodge coupé home at night, and he would be out of the house by half past eight, although he seemed to be dawdling and delaying. It was just that his way of doing things, unlike Clete's way, made him seem to be wasting time when he really wasn't. One morning the sisters were in the kitchen, and at eight-fifteen he had not made his appearance. "Will you go up and see if he went back to bed? He wasn't up when I came down."

"I thought I heard him moving around," said Nan. "I'll call him. I don't feel right about going up."

"If he went back to bed, calling won't waken him."

"Then you go up. I'll fry the eggs," said Nan.

Marietta was gone about five minutes. She returned to the kitchen and looked at her sister. "I can't move him. He's lying on the floor in the bathroom."

"Who do you doctor with?" said Nan.

"Young Michaels. The number's one-three-five-oh. But I think it's too late."

"They'll know where he is."

"Too late for Luke, I mean. I think he's gone."

"*No*, lamb. I'll phone Michaels and maybe he'll bring a pulmotor. You go on up with Luke."

Nan admired Marietta's calm without understanding it, but she understood it better when Marietta said, "It's what I've been expecting. What we both been dreading."

"The oath you took?"

"He had the one stroke, but he made me swear to keep it secret. He wanted to be Post commander and he was afraid they wouldn't vote for a man'd had a stroke."

"Go on up with him, lamb."

Marietta shook her head. "I can't, Nan. It isn't him," she said. "You can put the eggs back in the icebox, unless *you* want them."

"Oughtn't somebody to be up there with him? You phone Michaels and I'll go upstairs."

"Will you, then? You can wait out in the hall. But I just can't go up there, Nan."

Everyone said what a brave woman Marietta was throughout her ordeal of the next few days. When they compared notes they found that no one had seen her break, although some noticed that at the requiem Mass, while Joe Denny was singing "Beautiful Isle of Somewhere," she put her handkerchief to her eyes under her heavy veil. But that was the closest to a display of emotion that anyone saw during those days. "A brother and a husband in less than a year's time," they said. "It's lucky she's got her three boys."

"And Nan. It isn't as if she was all alone in the house."

"And at least they won't have any money worries."

Luke's insurance and the house and his savings came to nowhere near the size of Clete's legacy, but Marietta for the first time in her life could be considered comfortably well off. The boys were all self-supporting in more or less distant cities, and before they returned to their homes Marietta spoke to them about money. "Thanks to your Uncle Clete and your father, you won't have me to worry about. Aunt Nan and I'll be living here and sharing expenses. So you don't have to support me. Use your money to raise your own families."

The two older boys nodded silently, but the youngest,

Bob, spoke up. "I was counting on a thousand dollars from Dad," he said. "I was *counting* on it, Mom. He as much as promised it to me."

"He didn't say anything in his will," said Marietta.

"I know, but when I married Polly, Dad said he was sorry he could only give me a hundred bucks for a wedding present. He told me he was paying off Uncle Clete and a hundred was all he could spare. He said he'd make up for it some day."

"I don't hear the others claiming a thousand dollars," said Marietta. "And as far as that goes, I don't hear *anybody* offering to chip in for the funeral expenses."

"Oh, wait a minute, Mom," said Gerald, the oldest brother. "The funeral expenses come out of his benefits from the Knights."

"Partially only," said Marietta. "If you want to see the bills, I'll show them to you when they come in. Are you going to say Dad promised you a thousand, too?"

"Well, he told me the same as he told Bob," said Gerald.

"And me," said Ray, the middle son.

"It's funny I never heard about any of these big promises, although Dad and I never had any secrets from one another. Especially about financial matters. And you, Robert, you're a strange one to bring it up, considering how we scraped and pinched to send you to pharmacy school."

"If I had a thousand dollars I could use it for downer money to open my own drugstore," said Bob.

"A thousand dollars to open a drugstore?" said Marietta.

"And Polly's father willing to go on my note, and the little I managed to save."

"If it wasn't for your Uncle Clete I'd have to sell this

house and you'd all have to chip in to support me. Or I hope you would. It certainly would look nice if I had a son owner of a drugstore and another son a telegraph operator for the United Press and another son making carpenter's wages, and not enough from the three of them to keep me out of the poorhouse."

"Poorhouse? Bushwah!" said Bob. He stood up. "Dad made me a promise, and Jerry and Ray, too, and Dad always kept his promises. But I promise *you* something, Mom. This is the last time you'll see me in *this* house."

"Sit down, Bob," said Gerald

"Don't have a fight over money with Dad hardly——" said Ray.

"Oh, go to hell," said Bob. "Stick around, maybe she'll give you my share."

"That calls for a——" Gerald began, but Bob went out.

"Sit down, Gerald," said Marietta. "I won't have any rough stuff in the house of the dead. Let him go, and I hope he keeps his promise, because I don't want any son of mine in my house that talks that way to his mother."

"He was telling the truth, though, Mom," said Ray. "Dad said the same thing to me he said to Bob."

"I don't doubt it for a minute, that Dad would say those things. But where the money was going to come from, that was another matter entirely. All the years we were married he used to say he was going to take me on a trip to Ireland. Five years from now, ten years from now, he used to say we'll go back and pay a visit to Roscommon and Waterford and look up the Kellys and the Brosnans and the Dooleys. But the only trips anybody ever made was when Dad was delegate to the Legion conventions. I never held him to any of those promises, although dear knows I'd of welcomed a trip anywhere. You'd a wonderful father, you boys, but he had a forgetful habit of saying we were going to do this and going to do that and then the whole thing would completely pass from his mind. He'd mean it at the time, but I soon found out it was like playing some kind of a game. 'Sure,' I'd say, 'we'll visit Ireland five years from now,' but when the five years were up I had more sense than to remind him. I'm surprised he didn't promise you *five* thousand, but it shows how little you understood your father if you took those things seriously. Paying back your uncle, getting rid of the mortgage on this property—it cut him to the quick that the only money I ever had of my own had to come from my brother, not from him."

"Oh, let's drop the subject of money," said Gerald.

"Well, if you two honestly believe I'm holding on to money that rightfully belongs to you—if you honestly believe that? I'll give each of you five hundred as soon as Lawyer Phillips finishes with the legal end, and five hundred apiece next year or the year after. But not Robert. Robert's behavior in this house today puts him beyond the pale. Let him and his Polly and her father start their drugstore, and luck to them. Is that agreeable to you?"

"Whatever suits you, Mom," said Gerald.

"You, Ray?" said Marietta.

"The same for me," said Ray.

"I'll do the best I can for the two of you," said Marietta. "And don't forget, I'm not going to live forever, either. Just remember, no man knows the day or the hour."

Nan Brosnan joined her sister in double mourning. "As long as you wear black I'll wear it too," said Nan.

"Not you," said Marietta. "I'll always wear black, but a year's plenty long enough for you. You won't be criticized."

"I wasn't afraid of that. It's the way I felt about Luke. The next thing to a brother."

"Well, when the year's up for Luke I'll wear a little white in my hats, and you can start wearing colors."

"Well, we'll see," said Nan.

"I'm sure if you took a trip to Buffalo, New York, you wouldn't find a certain Mrs. J. Cletus Brosnan in widow's weeds. Oh, did I tell you? She sent Monsignor fifteen dollars for Masses for Luke. Imagine the gall! Never a word to me, never as much as a bunch of forget-me-nots for the funeral. But fifteen dollars for Masses."

"Well, it's one way of showing spite, if you want to look at it that way. Or maybe something's come over her since Clete passed on. Maybe she's finally learning to appreciate him, now that it's too late."

"Yes, and maybe she's having a high old time with poor Clete's money and what's fifteen dollars?"

"For me it's a lot of money when I think of how much you have to have in capital to get fifteen dollars' income."

"How much?" said Marietta.

"Well, fifteen dollars is three hundred dollars at five per cent."

"Yes, I guess it is," said Marietta. "It doesn't seem like much, does it, to only get fifteen dollars from three hundred."

"You don't get anywhere near that much from the bank."

"You hear about so many that are making money hand over fist in the stock market. Oughtn't we to go in the stock market, Nan?"

"I've been thinking about it. I was always afraid to when I only had my salary and my building-and-loan."

"Well, find out more about it. You're better at business than I am. Who do you go to for advice on such matters? Who did Clete go to?"

"A fellow named Ralph Fexler."

"Who's he? I never heard of him."

"He manages the local office for Westmore & Company. That's a New York stockbroker firm. Fexler goes around with the country-club outfit. He's a young fellow in his early thirties, I'd say."

"Oh, you know him?"

"I know him to say hello to, from coming in the office. He knew me as Clete's sister. Don't worry, you'll be hearing from him."

"Clete trusted him?"

"Oh, he's honest. Westmore & Company's a big firm, and a lot of the country-club outfit buy their stocks through Fexler. He'll be around to see us one of these days."

"Maybe we're losing money by not going to see him," said Marietta.

"Well, I had the same thought, but I didn't want to say anything till things got more settled. But now don't get the idea that everything you put money in guarantees a hundred-per-cent profit. You don't hear as much about the ones that lose money in the stock market."

"Oh, I know that much."

"Well, as long as you do. It's taking a chance when you buy a stock, lamb. If I lost all my money I'm pretty sure I could get a job, but I was a head bookkeeper. I wouldn't go in too deep if I were you. A little at a time. Risk five hundred or a thousand, and if you make a profit reinvest it. If you lose it, well, you learn by experience."

"That sounds like a very sensible idea, Nan. But don't you think maybe we ought to get started? Couldn't you go to see this Fexler man?"

"Not go to see him. He has a big office all full of men smoking cigars and watching the stock market."

"Watching the stock market?"

"A blackboard with the names of the stocks, and young Jimmy Shevlin—"

"Jule Shevlin's boy?"

"Uh-huh. Young Jimmy up there marking down the latest prices with a piece of chalk. I was never inside the place, but I often had to pass it and I could see in."

"Jule Shevlin'd never let her Jimmy work in a place if it wasn't reliable."

"Oh, I said it was reliable, and Clete did business with them for years, years. But I wouldn't just walk in and ask for Fexler. I'll write him a little note and tell him we were interested. If I put up five hundred and you put up five hundred it'd only be a thousand, small potatoes to Fexler, but he knows there's more. And remember this, lamb. He's a broker, and makes a little every time whether we buy or sell. He knows that between us there's over a hundred thousand dollars, and he'd love to have us for customers. You watch. When I tell him we're interested he'll come running, even if it's only a thousand to start with."

Marietta Kelly was quite taken with Ralph Fexler. "Did you notice his complexion?" she said to Nan. "Skin like a baby's. And isn't it nice to see a young fellow wear a stiff collar these days? I noticed his hands, too. He'd hands like Monsignor's. Clete had hands like that."

"And Ray, and Bob. Maybe Jerry would have, too, but a carpenter gets his hands banged up with a hammer, I guess," said Nan. "Anyway, we're in the stock market, lamb. Is it a thrill for you? It is for me."

"I feel as if it was the first day of school and Mom bought me a new dress," said Marietta.

(235)

They made money: their thousand-dollar investment grew to fifteen hundred in a year's time—"Makes bank interest look sick," said Nan—and along the way they learned about margin trading. They also overcame their shyness about sitting in the big room surrounded by men smoking cigars watching Jimmy Shevlin. One day Marietta was offered a cigarette by a man sitting in the next chair. "I believe I will," she said and grinned at Nan.

"So will I," said Nan Brosnan.

They added another fifteen hundred to their fund. Although their accounts were kept separate, they bought and sold the same shares in the same amounts, and calculated their winnings and losses in terms of a joint account. They were at the office of Westmore & Company nearly every day, all day, and when the market was being particularly active they had sandwiches and coffee sent in, just like the big traders among the men. They were at the Westmore office one day and heard the town fire whistle blow five times. "Five times," said Marietta. "That's the Fourth Ward, our Ward."

"Oh, good Lord," said Nan.

"What?"

"I'll be back in a minute," said Nan. She went to a telephone booth, and when she came back she was holding her hand over her breast and shaking her head. "It's our house, lamb. It's my fault. I'll pay you back, every cent."

"The fire? My house?"

"Maybe Mr. Fexler'd drive us there in his car," said Nan.

On the way to the house in Fexler's car she explained. As soon as she heard the alarm she remembered that on the way down to the office she was almost sure she'd left a cigarette burning in the kitchen. "I couldn't be altogether sure," she said. Marietta was very angry, but she did not want to say anything in front of Mr. Fexler.

"Fire must be out," said Fexler. "Here come two of the engines. The hook and ladder and the chemical."

The chief's car and another engine were standing at the curb. The house showed no damage, looked the same as usual except that the front door was open and a hose line ran from the fire plug, through the doorway, to somewhere inside the house. "Thank God," said Nan.

"Wait'll we have a look inside before thanking God," said Marietta.

"I'd be glad to wait for you ladies," said Mr. Fexler.

"No, no, that's all right. Thank you very much for being so accommodating," said Marietta.

"Well, let me know if I can be of any assistance," said Mr. Fexler.

Ed Sharp, the fire chief, was in the hall when the sisters entered. He shook his head. "Don't you know better than to leave a curling iron attached? For God's sake, if you're going to curl your hair, at least disconnect the thing when you're done with it. You got off easy this time, but—"

"How do you know it was the curling iron started it?" said Marietta.

"It's my job to know, that's how," said Ed Sharp. "Your God damn fire started in the bathroom and your God damn curling iron was the only thing hooked up. That was a dumb thing to do. Who do you insure with?"

"Joe Denny," said Marietta.

"Well, lucky he's a friend of yours."

"Do we get the insurance?"

"If it was up to me you wouldn't, anybody that would do a dumb thing like that. You got all that money, why don't you spend some of it on a permanent wave? Yeah, you'll get your insurance, this time. But I hope they make you pay double after this."

"Who discovered the fire, Ed?" said Nan Brosnan.

"The woman next door. Schrope. She noticed the smoke coming out the bathroom window, and she knew there was nobody home. Nobody home, I'll say. Nobody home." He made a revolving-wheel gesture with his finger over his ear. "Ten more minutes and this house would have been a vacant lot."

In her total humiliation Marietta could extract some consolation from the fact that even if the insurance company refused to pay, she had made enough money in the stock market to cover the damage. It was not as easy as that to take the blame away from Nan and assume it herself. "Well, why don't you say it? Say it was my fault," said Marietta.

"It could have been mine," said Nan. "I feel just as guilty."

"Like hell you do. You're standing there telling yourself I blamed you and all along it was my fault. Well, what if it was my fault? What's to stop me from putting a match to my own house if that's what I wanted to do?" Aloud, but to herself she added: "We ought to had the whole house rewired years ago. Luke was right." Then, to Nan she said: "Would you be willing to chip in to have the whole house rewired?"

"Well, being's you don't charge me any rent, sure. But why do we put money in this house? Why don't you sell it instead of putting good money in it?"

"And live where?"

Nan shrugged her shoulders. "Depends. An apartment is big enough for just the two of us. Or, if you want to splurge, we could buy a house on Oak Road."

"Oak Road," said Marietta. "Oh, if we could get back Clete's house, wouldn't that be delicious, Nan? Nan, we're rich. The two of us worked hard all our lives. Aren't we entitled to enjoy ourselves with the time we got left?"

"Clete's house has gone up since we sold it. But we might be able to get it back, if we offered that young couple a quick two or three thousand profit. How high would you want to go? They paid twenty-eight thousand. We could offer them thirty."

"I'll go to thirty-five! It's an investment, isn't it?"

"Well—nobody's going to refuse a seven-thousand-dollar profit on a twenty-eight-thousand investment. That comes to a twenty-five-per-cent profit in less than two years. If you want it that much, it's all right with me. But there we get into a legal problem. Who takes title to it? You, or me?"

"I will. I have more money than you have."

"Oh. You want to buy the whole thing yourself?"

"As I think it over, yes. I'm not crowding you out, Nan, but I think I ought to be the one to own the house, and maybe you wouldn't object to paying me a little rent."

"Like for instance, how much?"

"What did you pay at Bess Stauffer's?"

"I paid Bess fifteen a week for my room and breakfast and supper. That's sixty a month, seven-twenty a year. You wouldn't have any trouble getting a mortgage."

"Well, what do you think of the idea?"

"Well, it isn't what I started out thinking about, but maybe it's better for all concerned," said Nan.

"You'll always have a home with me, Nan. You know that," said Marietta.

Lawyer Phillips strongly advised against it, but within two months the purchase had been made and the sisters took up residence in the house their brother had built.

"They must be crazy," their friends said. But even Lawyer Phillips was forced to admit that luck was on their side. A woman paid ten thousand dollars for Luke Kelly's old house and immediately converted it into six apartments. "Maybe that's what you should of done," said Nan. "She's going to have between two and three hundred a month from Luke's house."

"I'm satisfied," said Marietta. "I'm not out of pocket, and I own Clete's house. That's the real satisfaction, us living in Clete's house. Wait till Ellen hears that. Us sitting in her chairs. Can you still play the piano, Nan?"

"I guess I could pick it up again if I practiced."

"Have a few lessons. I'll make you a present of them," said Marietta.

"No, I wouldn't take lessons at my age, but I'll practice and see if it comes back to me. I'll buy some music at the five-and-ten."

"You practice your piano, and do you know what I'm going to do? I'm going to practice how to drive a car."

"Are you going to buy a car?"

"I am. An Essex coop. I told Jim Denny if I could learn to drive inside of a month, I'd buy one. I start tomorrow. Living out here one of us has to learn to drive a car, and I know you wouldn't care to."

"I might. I'm not as afraid of them as I used to be."

"Then so much the better. When Jim takes me for my lesson, you come along."

"No, you learn and I'll watch you."

"Yes, I can practically drive now, from watching Luke. He wouldn't let me drive, because the Dodge belonged to the store, but he showed me how everything worked. I understand the gearshift is different in an Essex, but the general idea is the same."

"You'll learn in no time," said Nan.

She began to feel deserted already. She would never learn to drive a car, and her eyesight was so bad that if anything happened to her glasses she would not be able to see the radiator cap. No matter what Marietta said to re-assure her, Nan Brosnan felt far less at home in Clete's house than she had in Luke's. It was not only the mere act of paying rent in Clete's house—which she had not done while living at Luke's. Nan enjoyed spending money when she had it to spend. But her first mention of a house on Oak Road was a chance remark, not intended to interest Marietta specifically in Clete's house. She had not gone to the house very often while Clete was alive, not nearly as often as Marietta and Luke had been. The married couples had made a pretense of conviviality in the early years of Clete's marriage, partly because it was the right thing to do, and partly because Ellen had bought some, but not all, of her furniture through Luke, which meant a small commission for Luke even at reduced prices. In a sense every article of furniture in the house meant some-thing to Marietta, either as a chair that had been bought through Luke, or a rug that Ellen had bought at Wana-maker's, and thus an item that contributed to Marietta's hatred of Clete's wife. There was little in the house that Marietta did not, as it were, know personally. In the final two years of Clete's life, when Ellen was supposed to be carrying on with the manager of the hotel, nothing new was added to the house furnishings. But Nan was accus-tomed to living in surroundings that had been chosen by other women: her mother, Bess Stauffer, Marietta, and now Ellen Brosnan. In what would soon be fifty years she had never bought so much as a footstool for herself, and now that she could afford to furnish a whole house she had neither the inclination nor an established taste to express in purchases of sofas and tables and draperies. For more than thirty years she had been making her neat little figures in ledgers, under lighting conditions that were not of the best, and now if she took off her glasses a picture on the wall was only a blurred square outline.

"Jim Denny says I'll be driving in a week," said Marietta, returning from her first lesson.

"Then we can start going to Westmore's again," said Nan.

"Well, I don't know about that, Nan," said Marietta. "Do you want to?"

"Don't you?"

"Well, we don't have to, you know. And I don't think it looks right, two women going there every day."

"We've been doing it, and we weren't the only women there."

"No, we weren't, but I don't have to tell you who one of the women was."

"But we never had to sit near her, and she never tried to get friendly or anything."

"No, and a good thing she didn't. But she was there every day and for a long time we didn't even know who she was. But believe you me, all the men knew. The worst madam in the county."

"Well, there was old Mrs. Lucas, she went every day."

"As queer as Dick's hatband," said Marietta.

"And Sylvia Levy."

"Yes, but always with her husband. Levy was there most of the time, but she only came up a little while in the morning and just before the market closed. I don't want to start going every day."

"Why? Since we're living on Oak Road?"

"All right, yes. Since we're living on Oak Road. We're not on a party line here, Nan. If Ralph has anything to tell us, like for instance a margin call, he can get us here almost as quick as if we were there in the board room."

"We can't be watching the board from here."

"Well, if you miss it that much, I'll take you down every day, but I won't promise to stay."

"What are you going to do?"

"I don't know, but one sure thing I'm not going to spend the whole day sitting in Westmore's office."

"Why don't you join the country club and learn to play golf?"

"Well, I'll tell you this much, sitting around a board room all day isn't going to get us in any country club."

"You and I could sit on the *steps* of the country club and they wouldn't ask us in if it rained kangaroos. If that's what you're thinking."

"Nan, we don't have to have a fight over this. If you want to go, I'll take you down in my car. And I'll bring you back in the afternoon."

"I can walk down to Market Street and take the trolley, and I can take the trolley home, thanks just the same."

So it came about that for a few weeks Nan Brosnan every morning boarded the trolley, spent four or five hours at Westmore & Company's office, and took the trolley home. She went stubbornly, hoping that with the renewal of the habit the zest would return. But without Marietta it was not fun. It was only business. Work. And often there were stretches of hours at a time when nothing happened that was of interest to her financially. The men who once had made casual conversation now no longer chatted with her in that way they had of talking about the market while never taking their eyes off the board. Now they would bid her the time of day, but without Marietta she was left alone. Marietta was not very pretty; the most that could be said for her was that she was vivacious and had good legs. But whatever she had to offer, in the board room it was what had impelled the men to stop for a chat.

On a Friday afternoon Nan Brosnan made up her mind to discontinue her visits to Westmore & Company. She got off the trolley and walked up the hill to Oak Road. The garage was empty, and she let herself in the front door. She was tired, and some of her weariness was caused by apprehension. Marietta had not stopped being cross with her. Her decision to abandon the trips to Westmore's was a victory for Marietta, but nothing pleased Marietta.

In the livingroom Nan took off her shoes and started to go to the kitchen, but she made only one step and the rug slipped away. For the briefest moment she had a sense of exhilaration while both feet were in the air, and even at the very moment that her leg was breaking the pain was slower in coming than her understanding of what was happening to her. The pain came fully and strong and she forced herself to look at her leg, just above the ankle, where blood was coming. "Mother Mary, Mother of Jesus, let me die," she said. "Get me out of here." Her prayer was not answered.

THE NOTHING MACHINE

Her dress and the modified beehive coiffure deceived no one about her age, and were not meant to. It was a comparatively simple matter to fix the important dates of her career and of her life: her class in college, so many years as a copywriter and copy chief, so many years with one agency as account executive, so many years as vice-president of one firm and then another. She did not claim to be forty or forty-five, but her record spoke for itself and her chic proclaimed her determination to quit only when she was ready and not one minute before. The only thing was—more and more she liked to have Monday and Tuesday and Wednesday evenings to herself, to whip up her own dinner, to read a while, to work if she felt like it, to watch what the competitive accounts were doing on television, to take a warm bath in a tub of scented water and go to bed at a time of her own choosing. All she had she had worked for, fought for, fought dirty for when she'd had to. She had gone through those years when they said terrible things about her, and she had known they were saying them; but now that was past, and she was up there where they had to respect her—or be respectful to her—and they gave her plaques now, and wanted her name on committees. "Oh,

Judy's tough all right," they said. "But she had to be, to get where she did in this rat-race. There aren't many men around that started the same time she did."

Judith Huffacker waved a pink-gloved hand at the chairman of the board. He raised his hat and shook it in farewell, and then was hurried along by the passengers behind him. That was that, and she turned to the man at her side. "Where can I take you?"

"Well, I was going to suggest *I* take you to dinner. It's a little late, but some place like the Oak Room. How would that suit you?"

"No. No thanks. I've had a long day, but I'll drop you anywhere you say."

"Oh, come on. Have dinner with me. I don't want to go back to Detroit and admit I couldn't talk the famous Judith Huffacker into a dinner."

"Admit it to whom?"

"Any of the guys you know and I know."

"Like who, for instance?"

"Well—Jim Noble. Ed Furthman. Stanley Kitzmiller. You want me to name some more?"

"Production men. Don't you know any advertising men?"

"Sure, but I thought you'd be more interested in your impression on production men. You're aces with them."

"I'm glad to hear that."

"The ad men, of course, but that goes without saying."

"Not always, you may be sure. All right, let's go to the Oak Room."

When they were under way he said, "This your car?"

"Yes, are you impressed?"

"Naturally. I'm always impressed when people spend

their own money when they don't have to. You could have had the use of one of our cars, couldn't you? Don't you rate that executive-car deal? I'm sure you do."

"Yes."

"And it takes a certain amount of guts to drive around in a foreign car when you're working with an American manufacturer."

"You put it correctly. I'm working with them, not for them. I've worked with a lot of them, don't forget, and if your company doesn't like my taste in cars, if that's going to make the difference, they can either get me fired or take their business elsewhere."

"Nobody'd fire you at this stage."

"They wouldn't call it that, but that's what it would be."

"Do you mind if I call you Judith?"

"No, I don't mind. What do I call you?"

"Van," he said. "At the plant they call me B.B., but my outside friends call me Van."

"What is B.B. for?"

"Benjamin Brewster Vandermeer is the full handle. Now I can ask you, who was Huffacker?"

"He was my second husband."

"Oh, you were married twice? I didn't realize that. Are you divorced?"

"Twice. But Huffacker's dead. He died some time after we were divorced. I kept on using his name because I'd had three names in ten years and it was getting to be confusing."

"Have you any children?"

"I have a daughter, married and living in Omaha, Nebraska. I have two grandchildren. And I own a Mercedes-Benz."

"I don't want to sound oversensitive, but do you resent my asking you these questions?"

"Well, resent isn't the word exactly. Or maybe it is. I've spent so many years working with men, and with some success, working on equal terms. I don't like it when a man asks me the kind of questions he wouldn't ask another man. If you came to my house for a social visit it'd be different, but we've been together since nine o'clock this morning, talking some pretty technical stuff and all the give and take of a business conference. But as soon as we get alone together, you want to know about my sex life."

"You're absolutely right."

"Well, give up, because you're not going to find out."

"Oh, that isn't what I meant. When I said you were absolutely right I meant you were right to be annoyed. But you're kind of a legend, you know. You must be aware of that."

"Fully. I've read enough about myself to know that. And I've heard enough, too. The kind of stuff that *Fortune* can hint at but wouldn't dare come out and say it."

"Well, I can take the hint. Let's just be a couple of guys that haven't had anything to eat all day, and are hungry and irritable. All right?"

"Fine."

"*I've* been married twice and *I* have two grandchildren. Now we're even, okay? I don't own a Mercedes-Benz, but I think they make a hell of an automobile. Now we've traded information just about fact for fact."

She wished she had not consented to have dinner with this man. All day he had been easy to work with because he had been brisk and efficient and bloodless. He had the right answers in his mind or readily available in his batch of papers, and it was not his job to relate his facts to the field of theory in which she functioned. At the airport he could have left her for a few minutes and in that brief time been lost in the crowd. She regretted that just that had not happened, so that she would now be on her way to her comfortable apartment and a warm, fragrant bath. She had had to change her mind about him too often: from a nothing-machine, with his quick mind and attaché case, to a lonesome out-of-towner, to one of the Detroit boys who gossiped about her, to a man who could express himself in sarcastic terms that compelled her respect. She very nearly told him she had decided to drop him at the Plaza, but the words she uttered were in a conciliatory tone: "You don't get to New York very often?"

"About once a month," he said. "Our department has a dinner at the University Club, usually on the second Monday. But I go back to Detroit the same night if I can."

"Oh, yes. I knew about those dinners. We have them, too, but I don't always have to go," she said.

"I suppose they do some good. For my part, they have a dubious value. I don't get home till around two o'clock in the morning and I like my sleep. But departmental dinners must be worth it or the company'd do away with them."

"They can be a bore, all right," she said.

"I don't need the inspirational presence of my fellow man," he said. "I can perform just as well over the telephone and the teletype, and those big martinis they serve at the University Club, they certainly do promote frank discussions. Here we are."

At the table he said, "They all seem to know you here, customers *and* waiters."

"I've been coming here a long time," she said.

"I'll tell you one thing. Whether you like it or not, you didn't get that reception because you were vice-president of an ad agency. That was for a good-looking woman. Shall we order?"

It was unexpectedly smart of him to have noticed the quality of the reception, but he was not making it easier for her to like him. He put his elbows on the table and clasped his hands and looked about the room. "All these people that I've never seen before and probably never will again. I don't suppose I'll see you again, either. At least not for a year."

"I guess not. You're originally from the Middle West, aren't you?"

"Hell, that's written all over me. Yes, I've lived in Wisconsin, Illinois, Indiana, Ohio, and Michigan. I was born Wisconsin. My father was a preacher, that's why we moved around so much. I graduated from Purdue and got a job near Indianapolis . . . Oh, here's somebody I don't want to see." He raised his water glass in front of his face, but he had been seen and recognized.

"Hyuh, there, Van. Do you remember me? Charley Canning?" The newcomer was in his middle fifties, dressed with expensive care by no tailor on this side of the Atlantic. He seemed sure of his welcome and had his hand out.

"Oh, hello there."

"*Hello* there? Have I changed that much, or have you got a lousy memory? Charley *Canning,* from Humphreysville. Or maybe I'm wrong. You *are* Benjamin Vandermeer?"

"Yes, and I lived in Humphreysville, but I can't seem to place you."

"Well, for Christ's sake, don't crack your brains trying. You know damn well who I am, but maybe you have your reasons for wishing I didn't remember you. Good day, sir." Canning stared angrily at Vandermeer and at Judith Huffacker, then went on his way.

"Why did you do that? He seemed all right, and he knew you were doing it deliberately."

He nodded. "I did it deliberately."

"But why? He doesn't know why you did it."

"No, and he wouldn't understand if I told him," he said. "I haven't seen that fellow in thirty years. If I told *you* why I snubbed him you probably wouldn't understand either . . . I didn't order any wine. Are you used to having wine with your dinner?"

"Forget about the wine, and stop being evasive. I want to know why you disliked that man so. If it's not too personal."

"It isn't personal, in the sense of his doing something to me. Consciously, deliberately doing something to me." He looked at her quickly. "All right, I'll tell you.

"I went to live in Humphreysville, my first job after I graduated from Purdue. It's a little town about fifteen miles from Indianapolis, population about twelve-fourteen hundred, and I was assistant county engineer. A kind of a maid-of-all-work and utility outfielder. Highways. Water supply. Anything that was on a blueprint or you looked at through a transit. I liked it. I got twelve hundred a year, and that was twelve hundred more than a lot of my classmates were making. And I liked the town, the people. It was like going back home, to any of the other Middle Western towns I'd lived in. And like most Middle Western towns, especially Indiana, they were crazy about basketball, so when the high school coach had to quit, I took over the team. I'd played at Purdue and they knew that.

"Well, we had a pretty good season. Won sixteen and lost eight and came in second in the county league. And at the end of the season they had the usual banquet. My boys, and letter men from other years and a few leading citizens. Small. If we'd won the county league it would have

(251)

been bigger, but they always had a team banquet regardless of how they came out. The basement of the Presbyterian church, which was used for a lot of community get-togethers because they had a kitchen and plenty of chairs et cetera. We had the high school principal give out the little miniature basketballs, silver. I still have mine at home. And it was a very nice sociable gathering. A lot of kidding among ourselves, replaying some of the games we lost, and recalling funny incidents that happened on our trips. And the whole thing broke up around nine-thirty, quarter of ten, because the boys had dates and the place where they hung out closed at eleven.

"But instead of that, eight of my boys and their dates all got into cars—not *their* cars. They didn't have cars, with one or two exceptions. There were cars waiting outside for them. And they all drove off to a roadhouse down near Indianapolis, where this fellow you just saw gave them another kind of a party. Got them all liquored up, and some of them had never taken a drink before, and when they got home that night some of them were sick, and the girls were crying, and the parents raised holy hell, and the whole town was in an uproar the next day. And that's why I don't like Canning."

"Was anybody hurt?"

"You mean drunken driving? No, nothing like that."

"What did you do?"

"How do you mean?"

"Well, about Canning?"

He shrugged his shoulders. "Nothing. Oh, I could have gone and had it out with him and most likely he would have ended up on the floor. That was what I felt like doing, I'll admit that. But if I didn't know my own boys better than that, that I'd been seeing every day and three-four nights a week for four months. And if they wanted to sneak off and go to a roadhouse with a fellow like Canning, maybe *I* didn't know *them* so well, either. No, I didn't do anything. But as soon as the first job came along, I left Humphreysville and I've never gone back since. A fellow like Canning, he probably got a big laugh out of seeing a bunch of kids get drunk. Canning was a rich guy. His father owned the hardware store and was agent for Deering and Delaval and companies like that. This fellow was a Dartmouth graduate, Phi Psi, I think he was. I wouldn't have accomplished anything by mopping up the floor with him, although I admit I was strongly tempted."

"Yes," she said.

He laughed. "Tonight, too. Here in the Plaza Hotel, New York City, I wanted to give him a punch in the nose. That would have been something, explaining that to the New York police. Thirty years later. You would have had to tell your friends you were out with a lunatic, all these people that know you."

"Yes, they'd have thought you were a lunatic. But I don't."

"Well, that's good. I'm glad to hear that."

They talked no more about Canning or Indiana or anything so remote as thirty years ago. He paid the bill and walked with her to her car and they shook hands. "Let me know if you're coming to Detroit," he said. "My wife and I'd be glad to have you stay with us."

"I'll do that, Van," she said. The lie was not as bad as some she had told. It was the most harmless lie imaginable. At home, comfortable at last in her lavender-scented bath, she thought of lies and of truth, and of a life she had not spent with a man who could be so unforgiving of a little thing that had happened thirty years ago. Humphreysville, Indiana. Good God!

PAT COLLINS

Now they are both getting close to seventy, and when they
see each other on the street Whit Hofman and Pat Collins
bid each other the time of day and pass on without stopping
for conversation. It may be that in Whit Hofman's greeting
there is a little more hearty cordiality than in Pat Collins's
greeting to him; it may be that in Pat Collins's words and
smile there is a wistfulness that is all he has left of thirty
years of a dwindling hope.

The town is full of young people who never knew
that for about three years—1925, 1926, 1927—Whit Hofman's favorite companion was none other than Pat Collins.
Not only do they not know of the once close relationship;
today they would not believe it. But then it is hard to believe, with only the present evidence to go on. Today Pat
Collins still has his own garage, but it is hardly more than a
filling station and tire repair business on the edge of town,
patronized by the people of the neighborhood and not situated on a traffic artery of any importance. He always has
some young man helping out, but he does most of the
work himself. Hard work it is, too. He hires young men out
of high school—out of prison, sometimes—but the young
men don't stay. They never stay. They like Pat Collins, and

they say so, but they don't want to work at night, and Pat Collins's twenty-four-hour service is what keeps him going. Twenty-four hours, seven days a week, the only garage in town that says it and means it. A man stuck for gas, a man with a flat and no spare, a man skidded into a ditch—they all know that if they phone Pat Collins he will get there in his truck and if necessary tow them away. Some of the motorists are embarrassed: people who never patronize Pat Collins except in emergencies; people who knew him back in the days when he was Whit Hofman's favorite companion. They embarrass themselves; he does not say or do anything to embarrass them except one thing: he charges them fair prices when he could hold them up, and to some of those people who knew him long ago that is the most embarrassing thing he could do. "Twelve dollars, Pat? You could have charged me more than that."

"Twelve dollars," he says. And there were plenty of times when he could have asked fifty dollars for twelve dollars' worth of service—when the woman in the stalled car was not the wife of the driver.

Now, to the younger ones, he has become a local symbol of misfortune ("All I could do was call Pat Collins") and at the same time a symbol of dependability ("Luckily I thought of Pat Collins"). It is mean work; the interrupted sleep, the frequently bad weather, the drunks and the shocked and the guilty-minded. But it is the one service he offers that makes the difference between a profit and breaking even.

"Hello, Pat," Whit Hofman will say, when they meet on Main Street.

"Hyuh, Whit," Pat Collins will say.

Never more than that, but never less . . .

Aloysius Aquinas Collins came to town in 1923 because he had heard it was a good place to be, a rich town for its size. Big coal interests to start with, but good diversification as well: a steel mill, a couple of iron foundries, the railway car shops, shoe factories, silk mills, half a dozen breweries, four meat packing plants and, to the south, prosperous farmers. Among the rich there were two Rolls-Royces, a dozen or more Pierce-Arrows, a couple of dozen Cadillacs, and maybe a dozen each of Lincolns, Marmons, Packards. It was a spending town; the Pierce-Arrow families bought small roadsters for their children and the women were beginning to drive their own cars. The Rolls-Royces and Pierce-Arrows were in Philadelphia territory, and the franchises for the other big cars were already spoken for, but Pat Collins was willing to start as a dealer for one of the many makes in the large field between Ford-Dodge and Cadillac-Packard, one of the newer, lesser known makes. It was easy to get a franchise for one of those makes, and he decided to take his time.

Of professional experience in the automobile game he had none. He was not yet thirty, and he had behind him two years at Villanova, fifteen months as a shore duty ensign, four years as a salesman of men's hats at which he made pretty good money but from which he got nothing else but stretches of boredom between days of remorse following salesmen's parties in hotels. His wife Madge had lost her early illusions, but she loved him and partly blamed life on the road for what was happening to him. "Get into something else," she would say, "or honest to God, Pat, I'm going to take the children and pull out."

"It's easy enough to talk about getting another job," he would say.

"I don't care what it is, just as long as you're not away

(256)

five days a week. Drive a taxi, if you have to."

When she happened to mention driving a taxi she touched upon the only major interest he had outside the routine of his life: from the early days of Dario Resta and the brothers Chevrolet he had been crazy about automobiles, all automobiles and everything about them. He would walk or take the "L" from home in West Philadelphia to the area near City Hall, and wander about, stopping in front of the hotels and clubs and private residences and theaters and the Academy of Music, staring at the limousines and town cars, engaging in conversation with the chauffeurs; and then he would walk up North Broad Street, Automobile Row, and because he was a nice-looking kid, the floor salesmen would sometimes let him sit in the cars on display. He collected all the manufacturers' brochures and read all the advertisements in the newspapers. Closer to home he would stand for hours, studying the sporty roadsters and phaetons outside the Penn fraternity houses; big Simplexes with searchlights on the running-boards, Fiats and Renaults and Hispanos and Blitzen-Benzes. He was nice-looking and he had nice manners, and when he would hold the door open for one of the fraternity men they would sometimes give him a nickel and say, "Will you keep your eye on my car, sonny?"

"Can I sit in it, please?"

"Well, if you promise not to blow the horn."

He passed the horn-blowing stage quickly. Sometimes the fraternity men would come out to put up the top when there was a sudden shower, and find that Aloysius Aquinas Collins had somehow done it alone. For this service he wanted no reward but a ride home, on the front seat. On his side of the room he shared with his older brother he had magazine and rotogravure pictures of fine cars pinned to the walls. The nuns at school complained that instead of paying attention, he was continually drawing pictures of automobiles, automobiles. The nuns did not know how good the drawings were; they only cared that one so bright could waste so much time, and their complaints to his parents made it impossible for Aloysius to convince Mr. and Mrs. Collins that after he got his high school diploma, he wanted to get a job on Automobile Row. The parents sent him to Villanova, and after sophomore year took him out because the priests told them they were wasting their money, but out of spite his father refused to let him take a job in the auto business. Collins got him a job in the ship-yards, and when the country entered the war, Aloysius joined the Navy and eventually was commissioned. He married Madge Ruddy, became a hat salesman, and rented half of a two-family house in Upper Darby.

Gibbsville was on his sales route, and it first came to his special notice because his Gibbsville customer bought more hats in his high-priced line than any other store of comparable size. He thus discovered that it was a spending town, and that the actual population figures were deceptive; it was surrounded by a lot of much smaller towns whose citizens shopped in Gibbsville. He began to add a day to his normal visits to Gibbsville, to make a study of the automobile business there, and when he came into a small legacy from his aunt, he easily persuaded Madge to put in her own five thousand dollars, and he bought Cunningham's Garage, on Railroad Avenue, Gibbsville.

Cunningham's was badly run down and had lost money for its previous two owners, but it was the oldest garage in town. The established automobile men were not afraid of competition from the newcomer, Collins, who knew nobody to speak of and did not even have a dealer's franchise. They thought he was out of his mind when he began spending money in sprucing up the place. They also thought, and said, that he was getting pretty big for his britches in choosing to rent a house on Lantenengo Street. The proprietor of Cunningham's old garage then proceeded to outrage the established dealers by stealing Walt Michaels' best mechanic, Joe Ricci. Regardless of what the dealers might do to each other in the competition to clinch a sale, one thing you did not do was entice away a man's best mechanic. Walt Michaels, who had the Oldsmobile franchise, paid a call on the new fellow.

A. A. Collins, owner and proprietor, as his sign said, of Collins Motor Company, was in his office when he saw Michaels get out of his car. He went out to greet Michaels, his hand outstretched. "Hello, Mr. Michaels, I'm Pat Collins," he said.

"I know who you are. I just came down to tell you what I think of you."

"Not much, I guess, judging by—"

"Not much is right."

"Smoke a cigar?" said Pat Collins.

Michaels slapped at the cigar and knocked it to the ground. Pat Collins picked it up and looked at it. "I guess that's why they wrap them in tinfoil." He rubbed the dirt off the cigar and put it back in his pocket.

"Don't you want to fight?" said Michaels.

"What for? You have a right to be sore at me, in a way. But when you have a good mechanic like Joe, you ought to be willing to pay him what he's worth."

"Well, I never thought I'd see an Irishman back out of a fight. But with you I guess that's typical. A sneaky Irish son of a bitch."

"Now just a minute, Michaels. Go easy."

"I said it. A sneaky Irish son of a bitch."

"Yeah, I was right the first time," said Collins. He hit Michaels in the stomach with his left hand, and as Michaels crumpled, Collins hit him on the chin with his right hand. Michaels went down, and Collins stood over him, waiting for him to get up. Michaels started to raise himself with both hands on the ground, calling obscene names, but while his hands were still on the ground Collins stuck the foil-wrapped cigar deep in his mouth. Three or four men who stopped to look at the fight burst into laughter, and Michaels, his breath shut off, fell back on the ground.

"Change your mind about the cigar, Michaels?" said Collins.

"I'll send my son down to see you," said Michaels, getting to his feet.

"All right. What does *he* smoke?"

"He's as big as you are."

"Then I'll use a tire iron on him. Now get out of here, and quick."

Michaels, dusting himself off, saw Joe Ricci among the spectators. He pointed at him with his hat. "You, you ginny bastard, you stole tools off of me."

Ricci, who had a screwdriver in his hand, rushed at Michaels and might have stabbed him, but Collins swung him away.

"Calling me a thief, the son of a bitch, I'll kill him," said Ricci. "I'll *kill* him."

"Go on, Michaels. Beat it," said Collins.

Michaels got in his car and put it in gear, and as he was about to drive away Collins called to him: "Hey, Michaels, shall I fill her up?"

The episode, the kind that men liked to embellish in the retelling, made Pat Collins universally unpopular among the dealers, but it made him known to a wider public. It brought him an important visitor.

The Mercer phaeton pulled up at Pat Collins's gas pump and Collins, in his office, jumped up from his desk, and without putting on his coat, went out to the curb. "Can I help you?" he said.

"Fill her up, will you, please?" said the driver. He was a handsome man, about Collins's age, wearing a brown Homburg and a coonskin coat. Pat Collins knew who he was—Whit Hofman, probably the richest young man in the town—because he knew the car. He was conscious of Hofman's curiosity, but he went on pumping the gasoline. He hung up the hose and said, "You didn't need much. That'll cost you thirty-six cents, Mr. Hofman. Wouldn't you rather I sent you a bill?"

"Well, all right. But don't I get a cigar, a new customer? At least that's what I hear."

The two men laughed. "Sure, have a cigar," said Collins, handing him one. Hofman looked at it.

"Tinfoil, all right. You sure this isn't the same one you gave Walt Michaels?"

"It might be. See if it has any teeth marks on it," said Collins.

"Well, I guess Walt had it coming to him. He's a kind of a sorehead."

"You know him?"

"Of course. Known him all my life, he's always lived here. He's not a bad fellow, Mr. Collins, but you took Joe away from him, and Joe's a hell of a good mechanic. I'd be sore, too, I guess."

"Well, when you come looking for a fight, you ought to be more sure of what you're up against. Either that, or be ready to take a beating. I only hit him twice."

"When I was a boy you wouldn't have knocked him down that easily. When I was a kid, Walt Michaels was a good athlete, but he's put away a lot of beer since then." Hofman looked at Collins. "Do you like beer?"

"I like the beer you get around here. It's better than we get in Philly."

"Put on your coat and let's drink some beer," said Hofman. "Or are you busy?"

"Not that busy," said Collins.

They drove to a saloon in one of the neighboring towns, and Collins was surprised to see that no one was surprised to see the young millionaire, with his Mercer and his coonskin coat. The men drinking at the bar—workingmen taking a day off, they appeared to be—were neither cordial nor hostile to Hofman. "Hello, Paul," said Hofman. "Brought you a new customer."

"I need all I can get," said the proprietor. "Where will you want to sit? In the back room?"

"I guess so. This is Mr. Collins, just opened a new garage. Mr. Collins, Mr. Paul Unitas, sometimes called Unitas States of America."

"Pleased to meet you," said Paul, shaking hands.

"Same here," said Collins.

"How's the beer?" said Hofman.

Paul shook his head. "They're around. They stopped two truckloads this morning."

"Who stopped them? The state police?" said Hofman.

"No, this time it was enforcement agents. New ones."

Hofman laughed. "You don't have to worry about Mr. Collins. I'll vouch for him."

"Well, if you say so, Whit. What'll you have?"

"The beer's no good?"

"Slop. Have rye. It's pretty good. I cut it myself."

"Well, if you say rye, that's what we'll have. Okay, Collins?"

"Sure."

Hofman was an affable man, an interested listener and a hearty laugher. It was dark when they left the saloon; Collins had told Hofman a great deal about himself, and Hofman drove Collins home in the Mercer. "I can offer you some Canadian Club," said Collins.

"Thanks just the same, but we're going out to dinner and I have to change. Ask me again sometime. Nice to've seen you, Pat."

"Same to you, Whit. Enjoyable afternoon," said Collins.

In the house Collins kissed Madge's cheek. "Whew! Out drinking with college boys?" she said.

"I'll drink with that college boy any time. That's Whit Hofman."

"How on earth—"

She listened with increasing eagerness while he told her the events of the afternoon. "Maybe you could sell him a car, if you had a good franchise," she said.

"I'm not going to try to sell him anything but Aloysius Aquinas Collins, Esquire. And anyway, I like him."

"You can like people and still sell them a car."

"Well, I'm never going to try to make a sale there. He came to see me out of curiosity, but we hit it off right away. He's a swell fellow."

"Pat?"

"What?"

"Remember why we moved here."

"Listen, it's only ha' past six and I'm home. This guy came to see me, Madge."

"A rich fellow with nothing better to do," she said.

"Oh, for God's sake. You say remember why we moved here. To have a home. But *you* remember why I wanted to live on this street. To meet people like Whit Hofman."

"But not to spend the whole afternoon in some hunky saloon. Were there any women there?"

"A dozen of them, all walking around naked. What have you got for supper?"

"For *dinner,* we have veal cutlets. But Pat, remember what we are. We're not society people. What's she like, his wife?"

"How would I know? I wouldn't know her if I saw her. Unless she was driving that car."

They had a two weeks' wait before Whit Hofman again had the urge for Pat Collins's company. This time Hofman took him to the country club, and they sat in the smoking-room with a bottle of Scotch on the table. "Do you play squash?" said Hofman.

"Play it? I thought you ate it. No, I used to play handball."

"Well, it's kind of handball with a racquet. It's damn near the only exercise I get in the winter, at least until we go South. If you were a good handball player, you'd learn squash in no time."

"Where? At the Y.M.?"

"Here. We have a court here," said Hofman. He got up and pointed through the French window. "See that little house down there, to the right of the first fairway? That's the squash court."

"I was a caddy one summer."

"Oh, you play golf?"

"I've never had a club in my hand since then."

"How would you like to join here? I'll be glad to put

you up and we'll find somebody to second you. Does your wife play tennis or golf?"

"No, she's not an athlete. How much would it cost to join?"

"Uh, family membership, you and your wife and children under twenty-one. They just raised it. Initiation, seventy-five dollars. Annual dues, thirty-five for a family membership."

"Do you think I could get in? We don't know many people that belong."

"Well, Walt Michaels doesn't belong. Can you think of anyone else that might blackball you? Because if you can't, I think I could probably get you in at the next meeting. Technically, I'm not supposed to put you up, because I'm on the admissions committee, but that's no problem."

Any hesitancy Pat Collins might have had immediately vanished at mention of the name Walt Michaels. "Well, I'd sure like to belong."

"I'll take care of it. Let's have a drink on it," said Whit Hofman.

"We're Catholics, you know."

"That's all right. We take Catholics. Not all, but some. And those we don't take wouldn't get in if they were Presbyterian or anything else."

"Jews?"

"We have two. One is a doctor, married to a Gentile. He claims he isn't a Jew, but he is. The other is the wife of a Gentile. Otherwise, no. I understand they're starting their own club, I'm not sure where it'll be."

"Well, as long as you know we're Catholics."

"I knew that, Pat," said Hofman. "But I respect you for bringing it up."

Madge Collins was upset about the country club. "It

isn't only what you have to pay to get in. It's meals, and spending money on clothes. I haven't bought anything new since we moved here."

"As the Dodge people say, 'It isn't the initial cost, it's the upkeep.' But Madge, I told you before, those are the kind of people that're gonna be worth our while. I'll make a lot of connections at the country club, and in the meantime, I'll get a franchise. So far I didn't spend a nickel on advertising. Well, this is gonna be the best kind of advertising. The Cadillac dealer is the only other dealer in the country club, and I won't compete with him."

"Everything going out, very little coming in," she said.

"Stop worrying, everything's gonna be hunky-dory."

On the morning after the next meeting of the club admissions committee Whit Hofman telephoned Pat Collins. "Congratulations to the newest member of the Lantenengo Country Club. It was a cinch. You'll get a notice and a bill, and as soon as you send your cheque you and Mrs. Collins can start using the club, although there's no golf or tennis now. However, there's a dance next Friday, and we'd like you and your wife to have dinner with us. Wear your Tuck. My wife is going to phone Mrs. Collins some time today."

In her two years as stock girl and saleslady at Oppenheim, Collins—"my cousins," Pat called them—Madge had learned a thing or two about values, and she had style sense. The evening dress she bought for the Hofman dinner and club dance was severely simple, black, and Pat thought it looked too old for her. "Wait till you see it on," she said. She changed the shoulder straps and substituted thin black cord, making her shoulders, chest, and back completely bare and giving an illusion of a deeper décolletage than was actually the case. She had a good figure and a lovely complexion, and when he saw her ready to leave for the party, he was startled. "It's not too old for you any more. Maybe it's too young."

"I wish I had some jewelry," she said.

"You have. I can see them."

"Oh—oh, stop. It's not immodest. You can't see anything unless you stoop over and look down."

"Unless you happen to be over five foot five, and most men are."

"Do you want me to wear a shawl? I have a nice old shawl of Grandma's. As soon as we start making money the one thing I want is a good fur coat. That's all I want, and I can get one wholesale."

"Get one for me, while you're at it. But for now, let's get a move on. Dinner is eight-thirty and we're the guests of honor."

"Guests of honor! Just think of it, Pat. I haven't been so excited since our wedding. I hope I don't do anything wrong."

"Just watch Mrs. Hofman. I don't even know who else'll be there, but it's time we were finding out."

"Per-*fume!* I didn't put on any per*fume.* I'll be right down."

She was excited and she had youth and health, but she also had a squarish face with a strong jawline that gave her a look of maturity and dignity. Her hair was reddish brown, her eyes grey-green. It was a face full of contrasts, especially from repose to animation, and with the men— beginning with Whit Hofman—she was an instant success.

The Hofmans had invited three other couples besides the Collinses. Custom forbade having liquor bottles or cocktail shakers on the table at club dances, and Whit Hofman kept a shaker and a bottle on the floor beside him.

The men were drinking straight whiskey, the women drank orange blossoms. There was no bar, and the Hofman party sat at the table and had their drinks until nine o'clock, when Hofman's wife signalled the steward to start serving. Chincoteagues were served first, and before the soup, Whit Hofman asked Madge Collins to dance. He was feeling good, and here he was king. His fortune was respected by men twice his age, and among the men and women who were more nearly his contemporaries he was genuinely well liked for a number of reasons: his unfailingly good manners, no matter how far in drink he might get; his affability, which drew upon his good manners when bores and toadies and the envious and the weak made their assaults; his emanations of strength, which were physically and tangibly demonstrated in his expertness at games as well as in the slightly more subtle self-reminders of his friends that he *was* Whit Hofman and *did have* all that money. He had a good war record, beginning with enlistment as a private in the National Guard for Mexican Border service, and including a field commission, a wound chevron, and a Croix de Guerre with palm during his A.E.F. service. He was overweight, but he could afford bespoke tailors and he cared about clothes; tonight he was wearing a dinner jacket with a white waistcoat and a satin butterfly tie. Madge Ruddy Collins had never known anyone quite like him, and her first mistake was to believe that his high spirits had something special to do with her. At this stage she had no way of knowing that later on, when he danced with his fat old second cousin, he would be just as much fun.

"Well, how do you like your club?" he said.

"My club? Oh—*this* club. Oh, it's beautiful. Pat and I certainly do thank you."

"Very glad to do it. I hope you're going to take up golf. More and more women are. Girl I just spoke to, Mrs.

Dick Richards, she won the second flight this year, and she only started playing last spring."

"Does your wife play?"

"She plays pretty well, and could be a lot better. She's going to have a lot of lessons when we go South. That's the thing to do. As soon as you develop a fault, have a lesson right away, before it becomes a habit. I'm going to have Pat playing squash before we leave."

"Oh."

"He said he was a handball player, so squash ought to come easy to him. Of course it's a much more strenuous game than golf."

"It is?"

He said something in reply to a question from a man dancing by. The man laughed, and Whit Hofman laughed. "That's Johnny King," said Hofman. "You haven't met the Kings, have you?"

"No," said Madge. "She's pretty. Beautifully gowned."

"Oh, that's not his wife. She isn't here tonight. That's Mary-Louise Johnson, from Scranton. There's a whole delegation from Scranton here tonight. They all came down for Buz McKee's birthday party. That's the big table over in the corner. Well, I'm getting the high sign, I guess we'd better go back to our table. Thank you, Madge. A pleasure."

"Oh, to me, too," she said.

In due course every man in the Hofman party danced with every woman, the duty rounds. Pat Collins was the last to dance with Madge on the duty rounds. "You having a good time?" he said.

"Oh, *am* I?" she said.

"How do you like Whit?"

"He's a real gentleman, I'm crazy about him. I like him the best. Do you like her, his wife?"

"I guess so. In a way yes, and in a way no."

"Me too. She'd rather be with those people from Scranton."

"What people from Scranton?"

"At the big table. They're here to attend a birthday party for Buzzie McKee."

"Jesus, you're learning fast."

"I found that out from Whit. The blonde in the beaded white, that's Mary-Louise Johnson, dancing with Johnny King. They're dancing every dance together."

"Together is right. Take a can-opener to pry them apart."

"His wife is away," said Madge. "Where did Whit go?"

Pat turned to look at their table. "I don't know. Oh, there he is, dancing with some fat lady."

"I don't admire his taste."

"Say, you took a real shine to Whit," said Pat Collins.

"Well, he's a real gentleman, but he isn't a bit forward. Now where's he going? . . . Oh, I guess he wanted to wish Buzzie McKee a happy birthday. Well, let's sit down."

The chair at her left remained vacant while Hofman continued his visit to the McKee table. On Madge's right was a lawyer named Joe Chapin, who had something to do with the admissions committee; polite enough, but for Madge very hard to talk to. At the moment he was in conversation with the woman on his right, and Madge Collins felt completely alone. A minute passed, two minutes, and her solitude passed to uneasiness to anger. Whit Hofman made his way back to the table, and when he sat down she said, trying to keep the irritation out of her tone, "That wasn't very polite."

"I'm terribly sorry. I thought you and Joe—"

"Oh, *him*. Well, I'll forgive you if you dance this dance with me."

"Why of course," said Hofman.

They got up again, and as they danced she closed her eyes, pretending to an ecstasy she did not altogether feel. They got through eighteen bars of "Bambalina," and the music stopped. "Oh, hell," she said. "I'll let you have the next."

"Fine," he said. She took his arm, holding it so that her hand clenched his right biceps, and giving it a final squeeze as they sat down.

"Would you like some more coffee?" he said. "If not, I'm afraid we're going to have to let them take the table away."

"Why?"

"That's what they do. Ten o'clock, tables have to be cleared out, to make room for the dancing. You know, quite a few people have dinner at home, then come to the dance."

"What are they? Cheap skates?"

"Oh, I don't know about that. No, hardly that."

"But if *you* wanted to keep the table, they'd let you."

"Oh, I wouldn't do that, Madge. They really need the room."

"Then where do we go?"

"Wherever we like. Probably the smoking-room. But from now on we just sort of—circulate."

"You mean your dinner is over?"

"Yes, that's about it. We're on our own."

"I don't want to go home. I want to dance with you some more."

"Who said anything about going home? The fun is just about to begin."

"I had fun before. I'm not very good with strangers."

"You're not a stranger. You're a member of the club, duly launched. Let's go out to the smoking-room and I'll get you a drink. How would you like a Stinger?"

"What is it? Never mind telling me. I'll have one."

"If you've never had one, be careful. It could be your downfall. Very cool to the taste, but packs a wallop. Sneaks up on you."

"Good. Let's have one." She rose and quickly took his unoffered arm, and they went to the smoking-room, which was already more than half filled.

At eleven o'clock she was drunk. She would dance with no one but Whit Hofman, and when she danced with him she tried to excite him, and succeeded. "You're hot stuff, Madge," he said.

"Why what do you *mean?*"

"The question is, what do *you* mean?"

"I don't know what you're *talking* about," she said, sing-song.

"The hell you don't," he said. "Shall we go for a stroll?"

"Where to?"

"My car's around back of the caddyhouse."

"Do you think we ought to?"

"No, but either that or let's sit down."

"All right, let's sit down. I'm getting kind of woozy, anyhow."

"Don't drink any more Stingers. I told you they were dangerous. Maybe you ought to have some coffee. Maybe I ought to, too. Come on, we'll get some coffee." He led her to a corner of the smoking-room, where she could prop herself against the wall. He left her, and in the hallway to the kitchen he encountered Pat Collins on his way from the locker-room.

"Say, Pat, if I were you—well, Madge had a couple of Stingers and I don't think they agree with her."

"Is she sick?"

"No, but I'm afraid she's quite tight."

"I better take her home?"

"*You* know. Your first night here. There'll be others much worse off, but she's the one they'll talk about. The maid'll get her wrap, and you can ease her out so nobody'll notice. I'll say your goodnights for you."

"Well, gee, Whit—I'm sorry. I certainly apologize."

"Perfectly all right, Pat. No harm done, but she's ready for beddy-bye. I'll call you in a day or two."

There was no confusing suggestion with command, and Pat obeyed Hofman. He got his own coat and Madge's, and when Madge saw her coat she likewise recognized authority.

They were less than a mile from the club when she said, "I'm gonna be sick."

He stopped the car. "All right, *be* sick."

When she got back in the car she said, "Leave the windows down, I need the fresh air."

He got her to bed. His anger was so great that he did not trust himself to speak to her, and she mistook his silence for pity. She kept muttering that she was sorry, sorry, and went to sleep. Much later he fell asleep, awoke before six, dressed and left the house before he had to speak to her. He had his breakfast in an all-night restaurant, bought the morning newspapers, and opened the garage. He needed to think, and not so much about punishing Madge as about restoring himself to good standing in the eyes of the Hofmans. He had caught Kitty Hofman's cold appraisal of Madge on the dance floor; he had known, too, that he had failed to make a good impression on Kitty, who was in a sour mood for having to give up the Buz McKee dinner. He rejected his first plan to send Kitty flowers and a humorous note. Tomorrow or the next day Madge could send the flowers and a thank-you note, which he would make sure contained no reference to her getting tight or any other apologetic implication. The important thing was to repair any damage to his relationship with Whit Hofman, and after a while he concluded that aside from Madge's thank-you note to both Hofmans, the wiser course was to wait for Whit to call him.

He had a long wait.

Immediately after Christmas the Hofmans went to Florida. They returned for two weeks in late March, closed their house, and took off on a trip around the world. Consequently the Collinses did not see the Hofmans for nearly a year. It was a year that was bad for the Collins marriage, but good for the Collins Motor Company. Pat Collins got the Chrysler franchise, and the car practically sold itself. Women and the young took to it from the start, and the Collins Motor Company had trouble keeping up with the orders. The bright new car and the bright new Irishman were interchangeably associated in the minds of the citizens, and Pat and Madge Collins were getting somewhere on their own, without the suspended sponsorship of Whit Hofman. But at home Pat and Madge had never quite got back to what they had been before she jeopardized his relationship with Whit Hofman. He had counted so much on Hofman's approval that the threat of losing it had given him a big scare, and it would not be far-fetched to say that the designers of the Chrysler "70" saved the Collins marriage.

Now they were busy, Pat with his golf when he could take the time off from his work—which he did frequently; and Madge with the game of bridge, which she learned adequately well. In the absence of the Whit Hofmans the social life of the country club was left without an outstanding couple to be the leaders, although several couples tried to fill the gap. In the locker-room one afternoon, drinking gin and ginger ale with the members of his foursome, Pat Collins heard one of the men say, "You know who we all miss? Whit. The club isn't the same without him." Pat looked up as at a newly discovered truth, and for the first time he realized that he liked Whit Hofman better than any man he had ever known. It had remained for someone else to put the thought into words, and casual enough words they were to express what Pat Collins had felt from the first day in Paul Unitas's saloon. Like nearly everyone else in the club the Collinses had had a postcard or two from the Hofmans; Honolulu, Shanghai, Bangkok, St. Andrew's, St. Cloud. The Hofmans' closer friends had had letters, but the Collinses were pleased to have had a postcard, signed "Kitty and Whit"—in Whit's handwriting.

"When does he get back, does anyone know?" said Pat.

"Middle of October," said the original speaker. "You know Whit. He wouldn't miss the football season, not the meat of it anyway."

"About a month away," said Pat Collins. "Well, I can thank him for the most enjoyable summer I ever had. He got me in here, you know. I was practically a stranger."

" 'A stranger in a strange land,' but not any more, Pat."

"Thank you. You fellows have been damn nice to me." He meant the sentiment, but the depth of it belonged to his affection for Whit Hofman. He had his shower and dressed, and joined Madge on the terrace. "Do you want to stay here for dinner?"

"We have nothing at home," she said.

"Then we'll eat here," he said. "Did you know the Hofmans are getting back about four weeks from now?"

"I knew it."

"Why didn't you tell me?"

"I didn't know you wanted to know, or I would have. Why, are you thinking of hiring a brass band? One postcard."

"What did you expect? As I remember, you didn't keep it any secret when we got it."

"You were the one that was more pleased than I was."

"Oh, all right. Let's go eat."

They failed to be invited to the smaller parties in honor of the returning voyagers, but they went to a Dutch Treat dinner for the Hofmans before the club dance. Two changes in the Hofmans were instantly noticeable: Whit was as brown as a Hawaiian, and Kitty was pregnant. She received the members of the dinner party sitting down. She had lost one child through miscarriage. Whit stood beside her, and when it came the Collinses' turn he greeted Pat and Madge by nickname and first name. Not so Kitty. "Oh, hel*lo*. Mrs. *Col*lins. *Nice* of you to come. Hello, Mr. Collins." Then, seeing the man next in line she called out: "Bob-bee! Bobby, where were you Tuesday? You were supposed to be at the Ogdens', you false friend. I thought you'd be at the boat."

The Collinses moved on, and Madge said, "We shouldn't have come."

"Why not? She doesn't have to like us."

"She didn't have to be so snooty, either."

"Bobby Hermann is one of their best friends."

"I'm damn sure we're not."

"Oh, for God's sake."

"Oh, for God's sake yourself," she said.

The year had done a lot for Madge in such matters as her poise and the widening of her acquaintance among club members. But it was not until eleven or so that Whit Hofman cut in on her. "How've you been?" he said.

(*276*)

"Lonely without you," she said.

"That's nice to hear. I wish you meant it."

"You're pretending to think I don't," she said. "But I thought of you every day. And every night. Especially every night."

"How many Stingers have you had?"

"That's a nasty thing to say. I haven't had any. I've never had one since that night. So we'll change the subject. Are you going to stay home a while?"

"Looks that way. Kitty's having the baby in January."

"Sooner than that, I thought."

"No, the doctor says January."

"Which do you want? A boy, or a girl?"

"Both, but not at the same time."

"Well, you always get what you want, so I'm told."

"That's a new one on me."

"Well, you can *have* anything you want, put it that way."

"No, not even that."

"What do you want that you haven't got?"

"A son, or a daughter."

"Well, you're getting that, one or the other. What else?"

"Right now, nothing else."

"I don't believe anybody's ever that contented."

"Well, what do *you* want, for instance?"

"You," she said.

"Why? You have a nice guy. Kids. And I hear Pat's the busiest car dealer in town."

"Those are things I have. You asked me what I wanted."

"You don't beat about the bush, do you, Madge? You get right to the point."

"I've been in love with you for almost a year."

"Madge, you haven't been in love with me at all. Maybe you're not in love with Pat, but you're certainly not in love with me. You couldn't be."

"About a month ago I heard you were coming home, and I had it all planned out how I was going to be when I saw you. But I was wrong. I couldn't feel this way for a whole year and then start pretending I didn't. You asked me how I was, and I came right out with it, the truth."

"Well, Madge, I'm not in love with you. You're damn attractive and all that, but I'm not in *love* with you."

"I know that. But answer me one question, as truthful as I am with you. Are you in love with your wife?"

"Of course I am."

"I'll tell you something, Whit. You're not. With her. With me. Or maybe with anybody."

"Now really, that *is* a nasty thing to say."

"People love you, Whit, but you don't love them back."

"I'm afraid I don't like this conversation. Shall we go back and have a drink?"

"Yes."

They moved toward the smoking-room. "Why did you say that, Madge? What makes you think it?"

"You really want me to tell you? Remember, the truth hurts, and I had a whole year to think about this."

"What the hell, tell me."

"It's not you, it's the town. There's nobody here bigger than you. They all love you, but you don't love them."

"I love this town and the people in it and everything about it. Don't you think I could live anywhere I wanted to? Why do you think I came back here? I can live anywhere in the God damn world. Jesus, you certainly have that one figured wrong. For a minute you almost had me worried."

(278)

He danced with her no more that night, and if he could avoid speaking to her or getting close to her, he did so. When she got home, past three o'clock, she gave Pat Collins a very good time; loveless but exceedingly pleasurable. Then she lay in her bed until morning, unable to understand herself, puzzled by forces that had never been mysterious to her.

The Hofman baby was born on schedule, a six-pound boy, but the reports from the mother's bedside were not especially happy. Kitty had had a long and difficult time, and one report, corroborated only by constant repetition, was that she had thrown a clock, or a flower vase, or a water tumbler, or all of them, at Whit at the start of her labor. It was said, and perfunctorily denied, that a group of nurses and orderlies stood outside her hospital room, listening fascinatedly to the obscene names she called him, names that the gossips would not utter but knew how to spell. Whatever the basis in fact, the rumors of hurled bric-a-brac and invective seemed to be partially confirmed when Kitty Hofman came home from the hospital. The infant was left in the care of a nurse, and Kitty went to every party, drinking steadily and chain-smoking, saying little and watching everything. She had a look of determination, as though she had just made up her mind about something, but the look and decision were not followed up by action. She would stay at the parties until she had had enough, then she would get her wrap and say goodnight to her hostess, without any word or sign to Whit, and it would be up to him to discover she was leaving and follow her out.

Their friends wondered how long Whit Hofman would take that kind of behavior, but no one—least of all Pat Collins—was so tactless, or bold, as to suggest to Whit that there *was* any behavior. It was Whit, finally, who talked.

He was now seeing Pat Collins nearly every day, and

on some days more than once. He knew as much about automobiles as Pat Collins, and he was comfortable in Pat's office. He had made the garage one of his ports of call in his daytime rounds—his office every morning at ten, the barber's, the bank, the broker's, his lawyer, lunch at the Gibbsville Club, a game of pool after lunch, a visit with Pat Collins that sometimes continued with a couple of games of squash at the country club. On a day some six weeks after the birth of his son Whit dropped in on Pat, hung up his coat and hat, and took a chair.

"Don't let me interrupt you," he said.

"Just signing some time-sheets," said Pat Collins.

Whit lit a cigarette and put his feet up on the windowsill. "It's about time you had those windows washed," he said.

"I know. Miss Muldowney says if I'm trying to save money, that's the wrong way. Burns up more electricity. Well, there we are. Another day, another dollar. How's the stock market?"

"Stay out of it. Everything's too high."

"I'm not ready to go in it yet. Later. Little by little I'm paying back Madge, the money she put in the business."

"You ought to incorporate and give her stock."

"First I want to give her back her money, with interest."

"Speaking of Madge, Pat. Do you remember when your children were born?"

"Sure. That wasn't so long ago."

"What is Dennis, about six?"

"Dennis is six, and Peggy's four. I guess Dennis is the same in years that your boy is in weeks. How is he, Pop?"

"He's fine. At least I guess he's fine. I wouldn't know how to tell, this is all new to me."

"But you're not worried about him? You sound dubious."

"Not about him. The doctor says he's beginning to gain weight and so forth. Kitty is something else again, and that's what I want to ask you about. You knew she didn't have a very easy time of it."

"Yes, you told me that."

"How was Madge, with her children?"

"I'll have to think back," said Pat. "Let me see. With Dennis, the first, we had a couple false alarms and had the doctor come to the house one time at four o'clock in the morning. He was sore as hell. It was only gas pains, and as soon as she got rid of the gas, okay. The real time, she was in labor about three hours, I guess. About three. Dennis weighed seven and a quarter. With Peggy, she took longer. Started having pains around eight o'clock in the morning, but the baby wasn't all the way out till three-four in the afternoon. She had a much harder time with the second, although it was a smaller baby. Six and a half, I think."

"What about her, uh, mental state? Was she depressed or anything like that?"

"No, not a bit. Anything but."

"But you haven't had any more children, and I thought Catholics didn't believe in birth control."

"Well, I'll tell you, Whit, although I wouldn't tell most Protestants. I don't agree with the Church on that, and neither does Madge. If that's the criterion, we're not very good Catholics, but I can't help that. We had two children when we could only afford one, and now I don't think we'll ever have any more. Two's enough."

"But for financial reasons, not because of the effect on Madge."

"Mainly financial reasons. Even if we could afford it,

though, Madge doesn't want any more. She wants to enjoy life while she's young."

"I see," said Whit Hofman. The conversation had reached a point where utter frankness or a change of the subject was inevitable, and Whit Hofman retreated from candor. It then was up to Pat Collins to break the silence.

"It's none of my business, Whit," he began. "But—"

"No, it isn't, Pat. I don't mean to be rude, but if I said any more about Kitty, I'd sound like a crybaby. Not to mention the fact that it goes against the grain. I've said too much already."

"I know how you feel. But nothing you say gets out of this office, so don't let that worry you. I don't tell Madge everything I know. Or do. She made some pretty good guesses, and we came close to busting up. When I was on the road, peddling hats and caps, I knew a sure lay in damn near every town between Philly and Binghamton, New York. Not that I got laid every night—but I didn't miss many Thursdays. Thursday nights we knew we were going home Friday, salesmen. You don't make any calls on Friday, the clients are all busy. So, somebody'd bring out a quart."

"Did you know a sure lay in this town?"

"Did I! Did you ever know a broad named Helene Holman?"

"I should say I did."

"Well, her," said Pat Collins.

"You don't see her now, though, do you?"

"Is that any of your business, Whit?"

"Touché. I wasn't really asking out of curiosity. More, uh, incredibility. *Incredulity.* In other words, I've always thought you behaved yourself here, since you've been living here."

"I have. And anyway, I understand the Holman dame is private property. At least I always see her riding around with the big bootlegger, Charney."

"Ed Charney. Yes, she's out of circulation for the present, so my friends tell me."

"Yes, and you couldn't get away with a God damn thing. You're too well known."

"So far I haven't tried to get away with anything," said Whit Hofman. "How would you feel about a little strenuous exercise?"

Pat Collins looked up at the clock. "I don't think any ripe prospect is coming in in the next twenty minutes. Two games?"

"Enough to get up a sweat."

They drove to the country club in two cars, obviating the continuance of conversation and giving each man the opportunity to think his own thoughts. They played squash for an hour or so, took long hot showers, and cooled out at the locker-room table with gin and ginger ale. "I could lie right down on that floor and go to sleep," said Whit. "You're getting better, or maybe I'm getting worse. Next year I'm not going to give you a handicap."

"I may get good enough to take you at golf, but not this game. You always know where the ball's going to be, and I have to lose time guessing." They were the only members in the locker-room. They could hear occasional sounds from the kitchen of the steward and his staff having supper, a few dozen feet and a whole generation of prosperity away. The walls of the room were lined with steel lockers, with two islands of lockers back-to-back in the center of the room, hempen matting in the passageways, a rather feeble ceiling lamp above the table where their drinks rested. It was an arcane atmosphere, like some goat-room in an odd lodge, with a lingering dankness traceable to their recent hot showers and to the dozens of golf shoes and plus-fours and last summer's shirts stored and forgotten in the lockers. Whit, in his shorts and shirt, and Pat, in his B.V.D.'s, pleasantly tired from their exercise and additionally numbed by the gin and ginger ales, were in that state of euphorious relaxation that a million men ten million times have called the best part of the game, any game. They were by no means drunk, nor were they exhausted, but once again they were back at the point of utter frankness or retreat from it that they had reached in Pat's office, only now the surrounding circumstances were different.

"Why don't you get it off your chest, Whit?"

Whit Hofman, without looking up, blew the ash off his cigarette. "Funny, I was just thinking the same thing," he said. He reached for the gin bottle and spiked Pat's and his own drinks. "I have too damn many cousins in this town. If I confided in any of them they'd call a family conference, which is the last thing I want." He scraped his cigarette against the ash tray, and with his eyes on the operation said, "Kitty hates me. She hates me, and I'm not sure why."

"Have you got a clear conscience?"

"No," said Whit. "That is, *I* haven't. When we were in Siam, on our trip, Kitty got an attack of dysentery and stayed in the hotel for a couple of days. I, uh, took advantage of that to slip off with an American newspaper fellow for some of the local nookie. So I haven't got a clear conscience, but Kitty doesn't know that. Positively. I don't think it's that. I *know* it isn't that. It's something—I don't know where it began, or when. We didn't have any fights or anything like that. Just one day it was there, and I hadn't noticed it before."

"Pregnant."

"Oh, yes. But past the stage where she was throwing up. Taking it very easy, because she didn't want to lose this baby. But a wall between us. No, not a wall. Just a way of looking at me, as if I'd changed appearance and she was fascinated, but not fascinated because she *liked* my new appearance. 'What's this strange animal?' That kind of look. No fights, though. Not even any serious arguments. Oh, I got sore at her for trying to smuggle in a ring I bought her in Cairo. I was filling out the customs declaration and I had the damn thing all filled out and signed, then I remembered the ring. I asked her what about it, and she said she wasn't going to declare it. She was going to wear it in with the stone turned around so that it'd look like a guard for her engagement ring. So pointless. The ring wasn't *that* valuable. The duty was about a hundred and fifty dollars. An amethyst, with a kind of a scarab design. Do you know that an amethyst is supposed to sober you up?"

"I never heard that."

"Yeah. The magical power, but it doesn't work, I can tell you. Anyway, I gave her hell because if you try to pull a fast one on the customs inspectors and they catch you, they make you wait, they confiscate your luggage, and I'm told that for the rest of your life, whenever you re-enter the country, they go through everything with a fine tooth comb. And incidentally, an uncle of Jimmy Malloy's was expediting our landing, and he would have got into trouble, no doubt. Dr. Malloy's brother-in-law, has something to do with the immigration people. So I had to get new forms and fill out the whole God damn thing all over again. But that was our only quarrel of any consequence. It did make me wonder a little, why she wanted to save a hundred and fifty when it wasn't even her money."

They sipped their drinks.

"The day she went to the hospital," Whit Hofman continued, "it was very cold, and I bundled her up warm. She laughed at me and said we weren't going to the North Pole. Not a nice laugh. Then when we got to the hospital the nurse helped her change into a hospital gown, but didn't put her to bed. She sat up in a chair, and I put a blanket over her feet, asked her if she wanted anything to read. She said she did. Could I get her a history of the Hofman family? Well, there *is* one, but I knew damn well she didn't want it. She was just being disagreeable, but that was understandable under the circumstances. Then I sat down, and she told me I didn't have to wait around. I said I knew I didn't have to, but was doing it because I wanted to. Then she said, 'God damn it, don't you know when I'm trying to get rid of you?' and threw her cigarette lighter at me. Unfortunately the nurse picked that exact moment to come in the room, and the lighter hit her in the teat. I don't know what came over Kitty. 'Get that son of a bitch out of here,' and a lot more on the same order. So the nurse told me I'd better go, and I did." He paused. "Kitty had an awful time, no doubt about it. I was there when they brought the baby in to show her. She looked at it, didn't register any feeling whatsoever, and then turned her face away and shut her eyes. I have never seen her look at the baby the way you'd expect a mother to. I've never seen her pick him up out of his crib just to hold him. Naturally she's never nursed him. She probably hasn't enough milk, so I have no objection to that, but along with hating me she seems to hate the baby. Dr. English says that will pass, but I know better. She has no damn use for me *or* the child." He paused again. "The Christ-awful thing is, I don't know what the hell I *did*."

"I agree with Dr. English. It'll pass," said Pat Collins. "Women today, they aren't as simple as they used to be, fifty or a hundred years ago. They drive cars and play golf. Smoke and drink, do a lot of the same things men do."

"My mother rode horseback and played tennis. She didn't smoke that I know of, but she drank. Not to excess, but wine with dinner. She died when I was eight, so I don't really know an awful lot about her. My father died while I was still in prep school. From then on I guess you'd say I was brought up by my uncle and the housekeeper and my uncle's butler. I have an older brother in the foreign service, but he's too close to me in age to have had much to do with bringing me up. He was a freshman when our father died."

"I didn't know you had a brother."

"I saw him in Rome. He's in the embassy there. Both glad to see each other, but he thinks I'm a country bumpkin, which I am. And since I don't speak French or Italian, and he has a little bit of an English accent, you might say we don't even speak the same language. He married a Boston girl and you should have seen her with Kitty. Every time the Italian men flocked around Kitty, Howard's wife would act as an interpreter, although the Italians all spoke English. But I don't think that has anything to do with why Kitty developed this hatred for me. Howard's wife disapproved of me just as heartily as she did Kitty. We were all pretty glad to see the last of each other. Howard's wife has twice as much money as he has, so he doesn't exactly rule the roost, but in every marriage one of the two has more money than the other. That's not what's eating Kitty." He sipped his drink. "I've been thinking if we moved away from here. Someone told me that this town is wrong for me."

"They're crazy."

"Well, it's bothered me ever since. This, uh, person

said that my friends liked me but I didn't like them back."

"That *is* crap."

"As a matter of fact, the person didn't say like. She said love. Meaning that as long as I lived here, I wouldn't be able to love anybody. But I've always loved Kitty, and I certainly love this town. I don't know what more I can do to prove it."

"As far as Kitty's concerned, you're going to have to wait a while. Some women take longer than others getting their machinery back in place after a baby."

Whit Hofman shook his head. "Dr. English tells me Kitty's machinery is okay. And whatever it is, it started before the machinery got out of place. It's me, but what in the name of Christ is it? It's getting late, Pat. Would you have dinner with me here?"

"If you'll square me with Madge. It *is* late. I'm due home now."

"You want me to speak to her, now?"

"We both can."

There was a telephone in the hall off the locker-room and Pat put in the call.

"I knew that's where you'd be," said Madge. "You could just as easily called two hours ago."

"I'm going to put Whit on," said Pat, and did so.

"Madge, I take all the blame, but it'll be at least an hour before Pat could be home. We're still in our underwear. So could you spare him for dinner?"

"Your wish is our command," said Madge.

Whit turned to Pat. "She hung up. What do you do now?"

"We call Heinie and order up a couple of steaks," said Pat.

It was not only that the two men saw each other so fre-

quently; it was Pat's availability, to share meals, to take
little trips, that annoyed Madge. "You don't have to suck
up to Whit Hofman," she would say. "Not any more."

"I'm glad I don't."

This colloquy in the Collins household resembled
one in the Hofmans'. "Not that it matters to me, but how
can you spend so much time with that Pat Collins person?"
said Kitty.

"What's wrong with Pat? He's good company."

"Because your other friends refuse to yes you."

"That shows how little you know about Pat Collins,"
he said. "You don't seem to realize that he had hard going
for a while, but he never asked me for any help of any
kind."

"Saving you for something big, probably."

"No. I doubt if he'll ever ask me for anything. When
he needed money to expand, he didn't even go to our bank,
let alone ask me for help. And I would have been glad to
put money in his business. Would have been a good investment."

"Oh, I don't care. Do as you please. I'm just amused to
watch this beautiful friendship between you two. And by
the way, maybe he never asked you for anything, but did he
ever refuse anything you offered him? For instance, the
club."

"He would have made it."

"Has he made the Gibbsville Club?"

"As far as I know, he's not interested."

"Try him."

"Hell, if I ask him, he'll say yes."

"Exactly my point. His way is so much cagier. He's
always there when you want him, and naturally you're going to feel obligated to him. You'll want to pay him back

for always being there, so he gets more out of you that way than if he'd asked for favors. He knows that."

"It's funny how *you* know things like that, Kitty."

She fell angrily silent. He had met her at a party just after the war, when he was still in uniform and with two or three other officers was having a lengthy celebration in New York. Whit, a first lieutenant in the 103d Engineers, 28th Division, met a first lieutenant in the 102d Engineers, 27th Division, who had with him a girl from New Rochelle. She was not a beauty, but Whit was immediately attracted to her, and she to him. "This man is only the 102d and I'm the 103d. He's only the 27th and I'm the 28th," said Whit. "Why don't you move up a grade?"

She laughed. "Why not? I *want* to get up in the world."

He made frequent trips to New York to see her. She was going to a commercial art school, living at home with her family but able to spend many nights in New York. Her father was a perfectly respectable layout man in an advertising agency, who commuted from New Rochelle and escaped from his wife by spending all the time he could in sailing small boats. His wife was a fat and disagreeable woman who had tried but failed to dominate her husband and her daughter, and regarded her husband as a nincompoop and her daughter as a wild and wilful girl who was headed for no good. One spring day Kitty and Whit drove to Greenwich, Connecticut, and were married. They then drove to New Rochelle, the first and only time Whit Hofman ever saw his wife's parents. Two days later the newly married couple sailed for Europe, and they did not put in an appearance in Gibbsville, Pennsylvania, until the autumn. It was all very unconventional and it led to considerable speculation as to the kind of person Whit Hofman had married, especially among the mothers of nubile girls. But a *fait accompli* was a *fait accompli,* and Whit Hofman was Whit Hofman, and the girls and their mothers had to make the best of it, whatever that turned out to be.

In certain respects it turned out quite well. The town, and indeed the entire nation, was ready to have some fun. There was a considerable amount of second-generation money around, and manners and customs would never revert to those of 1914. Kitty Hofman and the Lantenengo Country Club appeared almost simultaneously in Gibbsville; both were new and novel and had the backing of the Hofman family. Kitty made herself agreeable to Whit's men friends and made no effort in the direction of the young women. They had to make themselves agreeable to her, and since their alternative was self-inflicted ostracism, Kitty was established without getting entangled in social debts to any of the young women. A less determined, less independent young woman could not have achieved it, but Gibbsville was full of less determined, less independent young women whom Whit Hofman had not married. And at least Whit had not singled out one of their number to the exclusion of all the others, a mildly comforting and unifying thought. He had to marry somebody, so better this nobody with her invisible family in a New York suburb than a Gibbsville girl who would have to suffer as the object of harmonious envy.

Kitty did nothing deliberately to antagonize the young women—unless to outdress them could be so considered, and her taste in clothes was far too individualistic for her new acquaintances. She attended their ladies' luncheons, always leaving before the bridge game began. She played in the Tuesday golf tournaments. She precisely returned all invitations. And she made no close friendships. But she actively disliked Madge Collins.

From the beginning she knew, as women know better than men know, that she was not going to like that woman. Even before Madge got up to dance with Whit and made her extraordinary, possessive, off-in-dreamland impression with her closed eyes, Kitty Hofman abandoned herself to the luxury of loathing another woman. Madge's black dress was sound, so much so that Kitty accurately guessed that Madge had had some experience in women's wear. But from there on every judgment Kitty made was unfavorable. Madge's prettiness was literally natural: her good figure was natural, her amazing skin was natural, her reddish brown hair, her teeth, her bright eyes, her inviting mouth, were gifts of Nature. (Kitty used a great deal of makeup and dyed her blond hair a lighter shade of blond.) Kitty, in the first minutes of her first meeting with Madge, ticketed her as a pretty parlor-maid; when she got up to dance with Whit she ticketed her as a whore, and with no evidence to the contrary, Madge so remained. Kitty's judgments were not based on facts or influenced by considerations of fairness, then or ever, although she could be extremely realistic in her observations. (Her father, she early knew, was an ineffectual man, a coward who worked hard to protect his job and fled to the waters of Long Island Sound to avoid the occasions of quarrels with her mother.) Kitty, with her firmly middle-class background, had no trouble in imagining the background of Madge and Pat Collins, and the Collinses provided her with her first opportunity to assert herself as a Hofman. (She had not been wasting her first years in Gibbsville; her indifferent manner masked a shrewd study of individuals and their standing in the community.) Kitty, who had not been able comfortably to integrate herself into the established order, now rapidly assumed her position as Whit's wife because as Mrs. Whit Hofman she could look down on and crack down on

Madge Collins. (By a closely related coincidence she also became a harsher judge of her husband at the very moment that she began to exercise the privileges of her marital status.) Kitty's obsessive hatred of the hick from West Philadelphia, as she called Madge Collins, was quick in its onset and showed every sign of being chronic. The other young women of the country club set did not fail to notice, and it amused them to get a rise out of Kitty Hofman merely by mentioning Madge Collins's name.

But the former Madge Ruddy was at least as intuitive as Kitty Hofman. Parlor-maid, whore, saleslady at Oppenheim, Collins—the real and imagined things she was or that Kitty Hofman chose to think she was—Madge was only a trifle slower in placing Kitty. Madge knew a lady when she saw one, and Kitty Hofman was not it. In the first days of her acquaintance with Kitty she would willingly enough have suspended her judgments if Kitty had been moderately friendly, but since that was not to be the case, Madge cheerfully collected her private store of evidence that Kitty Hofman was a phony. She was a phony aristocrat, a synthetic woman, from her dyed hair to her boyish hips to her no doubt tinted toenails. Madge, accustomed all her life to the West Philadelphia twang, had never waited on a lady who pronounced third *thade* and idea *ideer*. "Get a look at her little titties," Madge would say, when Kitty appeared in an evening dress that had two unjoined panels down the front. "She looks like she forgot to take her hair out of the curlers," said Madge of one of Kitty's coiffures. And, of Kitty's slow gait, "She walks like she was constipated." The animosity left Madge free to love Kitty's husband without the restraint that loyalty to a friend might have invoked. As for disloyalty to Pat Collins, he was aware of none, and did he not all but love Whit too?

Thus it was that behind the friendly relationship of

Pat Collins and Whit Hofman a more intense, unfriendly relationship flourished between Madge Collins and Kitty Hofman. The extremes of feeling were not unlike an individual's range of capacity for love and hate, or, as Madge put it, "I hate her as much as you like him, and that's going some." Madge Collins, of course, with equal accuracy could have said: "I hate her as much as I love him, and *that's* going some." The two men arrived at a pact of silence where their wives were concerned, a working protocol that was slightly more to Whit's advantage, since in avoiding mention of Madge he was guarding against a slip that would incriminate Madge. He wanted no such slip to occur; he needed Pat's friendship, and he neither needed nor wanted Madge's love. Indeed, as time passed and the pact of silence grew stronger, Whit Hofman's feeling for Madge was sterilized. By the end of 1925 he would not have offered to take her out to his parked car, and when circumstances had them briefly alone together they either did not speak at all or their conversation was so commonplace that a suspicious eavesdropper would have convicted them of adultery on the theory that two such vital persons could not be so indifferent to each other's physical presence. One evening at a picnic-swimming party at someone's farm—this, in the summer of '26—Madge had had enough of the cold water in the dam and was on her way to the tent that was being used as the ladies' dressing-room. In the darkness she collided with a man on his way from the men's tent. "Who is it? I'm sorry," she said.

"Whit Hofman. Who is this?"

"Madge."

"Hello. You giving up?"

"That water's too cold for me."

"Did Pat get back?"

"From Philly? No. He's spending the night. It's funny talking and I can't really see you. Where are you?"

"I'm right here."

She reached out a hand and touched him. "I'm not going to throw myself at you, but here we are."

"Don't start anything, Madge."

"I said I wasn't going to throw myself at you. You have to make the next move. But you're human."

"I'm human, but you picked a lousy place, and time."

"Is that all that's stopping you? I'll go home now and wait for you, if you say the word. Why don't you like me?"

"I do like you."

"Prove it. I'm all alone, the children are with Pat's mother. I have my car, and I'll leave now if you say."

"No. You know all the reasons."

"Sure I do. Sure I do."

"Can you get back to the tent all right? You can see where it is, can't you? Where the kerosene lamp is, on the pole."

"I can see it all right."

"Then you'd better go, Madge, because my good resolutions are weakening."

"Are they? Let me feel. Why, you are human!"

"Cut it out," he said, and walked away from her toward the lights and people at the dam.

She changed into her dress and rejoined the throng at the dam. It was a good-sized party, somewhat disorganized among smaller groups of swimmers, drinkers, eaters of corn on the cob, and a mixed quartet accompanied by a young man on banjo-uke. Heavy clouds hid the moon, and the only light came from a couple of small bonfires. When Madge returned to the party she moved from one group to another, eventually staying longest with the singers and the banjo-uke player. "Larry, do you know 'Ukulele Lady'?"

"Sure," he said. He began playing it, and Madge sang a solo of two choruses. Her thin true voice was just right for the sad, inconclusive little song, and when she finished singing she stood shyly smiling in the momentary total silence. But then there was a spontaneous, delayed burst of applause, and she sat down. The darkness, the fires, the previously disorganized character of the party, and Madge's voice and the words—"maybe she'll find somebody else/ bye and bye"—all contributed to a minor triumph and, quite accidentally, brought the party together in a sentimental climax. "More! More! . . . I didn't know you were a singer . . . Encore! Encore!" But Madge's instinct made her refuse to sing again.

For a minute or two the party was rather quiet, and Kitty had a whispered conversation with the ukulele player. He strummed a few introductory chords until the members of the party gave him their attention, whereupon he began to play "Yaaka hula hickey dula," and Kitty Hofman, in her bare feet and a Paisley print dress, went into the dance. It was a slow hula, done without words and with only the movements of her hips and the ritualistic language of her fingers and arms—only vaguely understood in this group— in synchronous motion with the music. The spectators put on the knowing smiles of the semi-sophisticated as Kitty moved her hips, but before the dance and the tune were halfway finished they stopped their nervous laughter and were caught by the performance. It hardly mattered that they could not understand the language of the physical gestures or that the women as much as the men were being seduced by the dance. The women could understand the movements because the movements were formal and native to themselves, but the element of seductiveness was as real for them as for the men because the men's responsiveness —taking the form of absolute quiet—was like a held breath, and throughout the group men and women felt the need to touch each other by the hand, hands reaching for the nearest hand. And apart from the physical spell produced by the circumstances and the dance, there was the comprehension by the women and by some of the men that the dance was a direct reply to Madge's small bid for popularity. As such the dance was an obliterating victory for Kitty. Madge's plaintive solo was completely forgotten. As the dance ended Kitty put her hands to her lips, kissed them and extended them to the audience as in a benediction, bowed low, and returned to the picnic bench that now became a throne. The applause was a mixture of hand clapping, of women's voices calling out "Lovely! Adorable!" and men shouting "Yowie! Some more, some more!" But Kitty, equally as well as Madge, knew when to quit. "I learned it when Whit and I were in Hawaii. Where else?" she said.

Madge Collins went to Kitty to congratulate her. "That was swell, Kitty."

"Oh, thanks. Did you think so? Of course *I* can't *sing,*" said Kitty.

"You—don't—have—to—when—you—can—shake —that—thing," said Bobby Hermann, whose hesitant enunciation became slower when he drank. "You—got—any —more—hidden—talents—like—that—one—up—your— sleeve?"

"Not up her sleeve," said Madge, and walked away.

"Hey—that's—a—good—one. Not—up—her—sleeve. Not—up—your—sleeve—eh—Kitty?"

In the continuing murmur of admiration for the dance no one—no one but Madge Collins—noticed that Whit

Hofman had not added his compliments to those of the multitude. In that respect Kitty's victory was doubled, for Madge now knew that Kitty had intended the exhibition as a private gesture of contempt for Whit as well as a less subtle chastening of Madge herself. Madge sat on a circular grass-mat cushion beside Whit.

"She's a real expert," said Madge. "I didn't know she could do the hula."

"Uh-huh. Learned it in Honolulu."

"On the beach at Waikiki."

"On the beach at Waikiki," said Whit.

"Well, she didn't forget it," said Madge. "Is it hard to learn?"

"Pretty hard, I guess. It's something like the deaf-and-dumb language. One thing means the moon, another thing means home, another means lonesome, and so forth and so on."

"Maybe I could get her to teach me how to say what *I* want to say."

"What's that?" said Whit.

"Madge is going home, lonesome, and wishes Whit would be there."

"When are you leaving?"

"Just about now."

"Say in an hour or so? You're all alone?"

"Yes. What will you tell *her?*"

"Whatever I tell her, she'll guess where I am. She's a bitch, but she's not a fool."

"She's a bitch, all right. But maybe you're a fool," said Madge. "No, Whit. Not tonight. Any other time, but not tonight."

"Whatever you say, but you have nothing to fear from her. You or Pat. Take my word for it, you haven't. She's

(*298*)

watching us now, and she knows we're talking about her. All right, I'll tell you what's behind this exhibition tonight."

"You don't have to."

"Well I hope you don't think I'd let you risk it if I weren't positive about her."

"I did wonder, but I'm so crazy about you."

"When we were in Honolulu that time, I caught her with another guy. I'd been out playing golf, and I came back to the hotel in time to see this guy leaving our room. She didn't deny it, and I guessed right away who it was. A naval officer. I hadn't got a good look at him, but I let her think I had and she admitted it. The question was, what was I going to do about it? Did I want to divorce her, and ruin the naval officer's career? Did I want to come back here without her? That was where she knew she had me. I *didn't* want to come back here without her. This is my town, you know. We've been here ever since there was a town, and it's the only place I ever want to live. I've told you that." He paused. "Well, you don't know her, the hold she had on me, and I don't fully understand it myself. There are a lot of damn nice girls in town I might have married, and you'd think that feeling that way about the town, I'd marry a Gibbsville girl. But how was I ever to know that I was marrying the girl and not her mother, and in some cases her father? And that the girl wasn't marrying me but my father's money and my uncle's money. Kitty didn't know any of that when I asked her to marry me. She'd never heard of Gibbsville. In fact she wasn't very sure where Pennsylvania was. And I was a guy just out of the army, liked a good time, and presumably enjoying myself before I seriously began looking for a job. The first time Kitty really knew I didn't have to work for a living was when I gave her her engagement ring. I remember what she said. She looked at it and then looked at me and said, 'Is there more where this came from?' So give her her due. She didn't marry me for my money, and that was somewhat of a novelty. Are you listening?"

"Sure," said Madge.

"That afternoon in the hotel she said, 'Look, you can kick me out and pay me off, but I tried to have a child for you, which I didn't want, and this is the first time I've gone to bed with another man, since we've been married.' It was a good argument, but of course the real point was that I didn't want to go home without a wife, and have everybody guessing why. I allowed myself the great pleasure of giving her a slap in the face, and she said she guessed she had it coming to her, and then I was so God damned ashamed of myself—I'd never hit a woman before—that *I* ended up apologizing to *her*. Oh, I told her we were taking the next boat out of Honolulu, and if she was ever unfaithful to me again I'd make it very tough for her. But the fact of the matter is, her only punishment was a slap in the face, and that was with my open hand. We went to various places —Australia, Japan, the Philippines, China—and I got her pregnant."

"Yes. But what was behind this hula tonight?"

"I'd forgotten she knew how to do it. The whole subject of Honolulu, and ukuleles, hulas—we've never mentioned any of it, neither of us. But when she stood up there tonight, partly it was to do something better than you—"

"And she did."

"Well, she tried. And partly it was to insult me in a way that only I would understand. Things have been going very badly between us, we hardly ever speak a civil word when we're alone. She's convinced herself that you and I are having an affair—"

"Well, let's."

"Yes, let's. But I wish we could do it without—well, what the hell? Pat's supposed to be able to take care of himself."

"I have a few scores to settle there, too."

"Not since I've known him."

"Maybe not, but there were enough before you knew him. I used to be sick with jealousy, Monday to Friday, Monday to Friday, knowing he was probably screwing some chippy in Allentown or Wilkes-Barre. I was still jealous, even after we moved here. But not after I met you. From then on I didn't care what he did, who he screwed. Whenever I thought of him with another woman I'd think of me with you. But why isn't Kitty going to make any trouble? What have you got on her, besides the navy officer?"

"This is going to sound very cold-blooded."

"All right."

"And it's possible I could be wrong."

"Yes, but go on."

"Well—Kitty's gotten used to being Mrs. W. S. Hofman. She likes everything about it but me—and the baby. It's got her, Madge, and she can never have it anywhere else, or with anybody else."

"I could have told you that the first time I ever laid eyes on her."

"I had to find it out for myself."

There is one law for the rich, and another law for the richer. The frequent appearances of Whit Hofman with Madge Collins were treated not so much as a scandal as the exercise of a privilege of a man who was uniquely entitled to such privileges. To mollify their sense of good order the country club set could tell themselves that Whit was

with Pat as often as he was with Madge, and that the
three were often together as a congenial trio. The more
kindly disposed made the excuse that Whit was putting
up with a great deal from Kitty, and since Pat Collins
obviously did not object to Whit's hours alone with Madge,
what right had anyone else to complain? The excuse made
by the less kindly was that if there was anything *wrong*
in the Whit-Madge friendship, Kitty Hofman would be
the first to kick up a fuss; therefore there was nothing
scandalous in the relationship.

The thing most wrong in the relationship was the
destructive effect on Madge Collins, who had been brought
up in a strict Catholic atmosphere, who in nearly thirty
years had had sexual intercourse with one man, and who
now was having intercourse with two, often with both
in the same day. The early excitement of a sexual feast
continued through three or four months and a couple
of narrow escapes; but the necessary lies to Pat and the
secondary status of the man she preferred became incon-
venient, then annoying, then irritating. She withheld nothing
from Whit, she gave only what was necessary to Pat, but
when she was in the company of both men—playing golf, at
a movie, at a football game—she indulged in a nervous
masquerade as the contented wife and the sympathetic
friend, experiencing relief only when she could be alone with
one of the men. Or with neither. The shame she suffered with
her Catholic conscience was no greater than the shame of
another sort: to be with both men and sit in self-enforced
silence while the man she loved was so easily, coolly making
a fool of the man to whom she was married. The amiable,
totally unsuspecting fool would have had her sympathy in
different circumstances, and she would have hated the character of the lover; but Pat's complacency was more hateful to

her than Whit's arrogance. The complacency, she knew, was real; and Whit's arrogance vanished in the humility of his passion as soon as she would let him make love to her. There was proficiency of a selfish kind in Pat's lovemaking; he had never been so gentle or grateful as Whit. From what she could learn of Kitty Hofman it would have been neatly suitable if Pat had become Kitty's lover, but two such similar persons were never attracted to each other. They had, emotionally, everything in common; none of the essential friction of personality. Neither was equipped with the fear of losing the other.

It was this fear that helped produce the circumstances leading to the end of Madge's affair with Whit Hofman. "Every time I see you I love you again, even though I've been loving you all along," she told Whit. Only when she was alone with him—riding in his car, playing golf, sitting with him while waiting for Pat to join them, sitting with him after Pat had left them—could she forget the increasingly insistent irritations of her position. Publicly she was, as Whit told her, "carrying it off very well," but the nagging of her Catholic conscience and the rigidity of her middle-class training were with her more than she was with Whit, and when the stimulation of the early excitement had passed, she was left with that conscience, that training, and this new fear.

The affair, in terms of hours in a bed together, was a haphazard one, too dependent on Pat's unpredictable and impulsive absences. Sometimes he would telephone her from the garage late in the afternoon, and tell her he was driving to Philadelphia and would not be home until past midnight. On such occasions, if she could not get word to Whit at his office or at one of the two clubs, the free evening would be wasted. Other times they would make love on country roads, and three times they had gone to hotels in Philadelphia. It seldom happened that Whit, in a moment of urgently wanting to be with her, could be with her within the hour, and it was on just such occasions, when she was taking a foolish chance, that they had their two narrow escapes in her own house. "You can never get away when I want you to," said Whit—which was a truth and a lie.

"Be reasonable," she said, and knew that the first excitement had progressed to complaint. Any time, anywhere, anything had been exciting in the beginning; now it was a bed in a hotel and a whole night together, with a good leisurely breakfast, that he wanted. They were in a second phase, or he was; and for her, fear had begun. It told on her disposition, so that she was sometimes snappish when alone with Whit. Now it was her turn to say they could not be together when she wanted him, and again it was a truth and a lie of exaggeration. They began to have quarrels, and to Whit this was not only an annoyance but a sign that they were getting in much deeper than he intended. For he had not deceived her as to the depth or permanence of their relationship. It was true that he had permitted her to deceive herself, but she was no child. She had had to supply her own declarations of the love she wanted him to feel; they had not been forthcoming from him, and when there were opportunities that almost demanded a declaration of his love, he was silent or noncommittal. The nature of their affair—intimacy accompanied by intrigue—was such as to require extra opportunities for candor. They were closer than if they had been free and innocent, but Whit would not use their intimacy even to make casual pretense of love. "I can't even wring it out of you," she said.

"What?"

"That you love me. You never say it."

"You can't expect to *wring* it out of anyone."

"A woman wants to hear it, once in a while."

"Well, don't try to wring it out of me."

He knew—and she knew almost as soon as he—that his refusal to put their affair on a higher, romantic love plane was quite likely to force her to put an end to the affair. And now that she was becoming demanding and disagreeable, he could deliberately provoke her into final action or let his stubbornness get the same result. It could not be said that she bored him; she was too exciting for that. But the very fact that she could be exciting added to his annoyance and irritation. He began to dislike that hold she had on him, and the day arrived when he recognized in himself the same basic weakness for Madge that he had had for Kitty. And to a lesser degree the same thing had been true of all the women he had ever known. But pursuing that thought, he recalled that Madge was the only one who had ever charged him with the inability to love. Now he had the provocation that would end the affair, and he had it more or less in the words of her accusation.

"You still won't say it," she said to him one night.

"That I love you?"

"That you love me."

"No, I won't say it, and you ought to know why."

"That's plain as day. You won't say it because you don't."

"Not *don't. Can't,*" he said. "You told me yourself, a long time ago. That people love me and I can't love them. I'm beginning to think that's true."

"It's true all right. I was hoping I could get you to change, but you didn't."

"I used to know a guy that could take a car apart and

put it together again, but he couldn't drive. He never could learn to drive."

"What's that got to do with us?"

"Don't you see? Think a minute."

"I get it."

"So when you ask me to love you, you're asking the impossible. I'm just made that way, that's all."

"This sounds like a farewell speech. You got me to go to a hotel with you, have one last thing together, and then announce that we're through. Is that it?"

"No, not as long as you don't expect something you never expected in the first place."

"That's good, that is. You'll let me go on taking all the risks, but don't ask anything in return. I guess I don't love you *that* much, Mr. Hofman." She got out of bed. "What are you going to do?"

"I'm getting out of this dump, I promise you that. I'm going home."

"I'm sorry, Madge."

"Whit, you're not even sorry for yourself. But I can make up for it. I'm sorry for you. Do you know what I'm going to do?"

"What?"

"I'm going home and tell Pat the whole story. If he wants to kick me out, all he has to do is say so."

"Why the hell do you want to do that?"

"You wouldn't understand it."

"Is it some Catholic thing?"

"Yes! I'm surprised you guessed it. I don't have to tell him. That's not it. But I'll confess it to him instead of a priest, and whatever he wants me to do, I'll do it. Penance."

"No, I don't understand it."

"No, I guess you don't."

"You're going to take a chance of wrecking your home, your marriage?"

"I'm not very brave. I don't think it is much of a chance, but if he kicks me out, I can go back to Oppenheim, Collins. I have a charge account there now." She laughed.

"Don't do it, Madge. Don't go."

"Whit, I've been watching you and waiting for something like this to happen. I didn't know what I was going to do, but when the time came I knew right away."

"Then you really loved Pat all along, not me."

"Nope. God help me, I love you and that's the one thing I won't tell Pat. There I'll have to lie."

It was assumed, when Pat Collins began neglecting his business and spending so much time in Dick Boylan's speakeasy, that Whit Hofman would come to his rescue. But whether or not Whit had offered to help Pat Collins, nobody could long go on helping a man who refused to help himself. He lost his two salesmen and his bookkeeper, and his Chrysler franchise was taken over by Walt Michaels, who rehired Joe Ricci at decent wages. For a while Pat Collins had a fifty-dollar-a-week drawing account as a salesman at the Cadillac dealer's, but that stopped when people stopped buying Cadillacs, and Pat's next job, in charge of the hat department in a haberdashery, lasted only as long as the haberdashery. As a Cadillac salesman and head of the hat department Pat Collins paid less attention to business than to pill pool, playing a game called Harrigan from one o'clock in the afternoon till suppertime, but during those hours he was at least staying out of the speakeasy. At suppertime he would have a Western sandwich at the Greek's, then go to Dick Boylan's, a quiet back room on the second story of a business building, patronized by doctors and lawyers and merchants in the neighborhood and by recent Yale and Princeton graduates and near-graduates. It was all he saw, in those days, of his friends from the country club crowd.

Dick Boylan's speakeasy was unique in that it was the only place of its kind that sold nothing but hard liquor. When a man wanted a sandwich and beer, he had to send out for it; if he wanted beer without a sandwich, Boylan told him to go some place else for it; but such requests were made only by strangers and by them not more than once. Dick Boylan was the proprietor, and in no sense the bartender; there were tables and chairs, but no bar in his place, and Boylan wore a suit of clothes and a fedora hat at all times, and always seemed to be on the go. He would put a bottle on the table, and when the drinkers had taken what they wanted he would hold up the bottle and estimate the number of drinks that had been poured from it and announce how much was owed him. "This here table owes me eight and a half," he would say, leaving the bookkeeping to the customers. "Or I'll have one with you and make it an even nine." Sometimes he would not be around to open up for the morning customers, and they would get the key from under the stairway linoleum, unlock the door, help themselves, and leave the money where Dick would find it. They could also leave chits when they were short of cash. If a man cheated on his chits, or owed too much money, or drank badly, he was not told so in so many words; he would knock on the door, the peephole was opened, and Boylan would say, "We're closed," and the statement was intended and taken to mean that the man was forever barred, with no further discussion of the matter.

Pat Collins was at Dick Boylan's every night after Madge

made her true confession. Until then he had visited the place infrequently, and then, as a rule, in the company of Whit Hofman. The shabby austerity of Dick Boylan's and Boylan's high-handed crudities did not detract from the stern respectability of the place. No woman was allowed to set foot in Boylan's, and among the brotherhood of hard drinkers it was believed—erroneously—that all conversations at Boylan's were privileged, not to be repeated outside. "What's said in here is Masonic," Boylan claimed. "I find a man blabbing what he hears—he's out." Boylan had been known to bar a customer for merely mentioning the names of fellow drinkers. "I run a san'tuary for men that need their booze," said Boylan. "If they was in that Gibbsville Club every time they needed a steam, the whole town'd know it." It was a profitable sanctuary, with almost no overhead and, because of the influence of the clientele, a minimum of police graft. Pat Collins's visits with Whit Hofman had occurred on occasions when one or the other had a hangover, and Boylan's was a quick walk from Pat's garage. At night Whit Hofman preferred to do his drinking in more elegant surroundings, and Pat Collins told himself that he was sure he would not run into Whit at Boylan's. But he lied to himself; he *wanted* to run into Whit.

At first he wanted a fight, even though he knew he would be the loser. He would be giving twenty pounds to a man who appeared soft but was in deceptively good shape, who managed to get in some physical exercise nearly every day of his life and whose eight years of prep school and college football, three years of army service, and a lifetime of good food and medical care had given him resources that would be valuable in a real fight. Pat Collins knew he did not have a quick punch that would keep

Whit down; Whit Hofman was not Walt Michaels. Whit Hofman, in fact, was Whit Hofman, with more on his side than his physical strength. Although he had never seen Whit in a fight, Pat had gone with him to many football games and observed Whit's keen and knowing interest in the niceties of line play. ("Watch that son of a bitch, the right guard for Lehigh. He's spilling two men on every play.") And Whit Hofman's way of telling about a battle during one of his rare reminiscences of the War ("They were awful damn close, but I didn't lob the God damn pineapple. I *threw* it. The hell with what they taught us back in Hancock.") was evidence that he would play for keeps, and enjoy the playing. Pat admitted that if he had really wanted a fight with Whit Hofman, he could have it for the asking. Then what *did* he want? The question had a ready answer: he wanted the impossible, to confide his perplexed anger in the one man on earth who would least like to hear it. He refused to solidify his wish into words, but he tormented himself with the hope that he could be back on the same old terms of companionship with the man who was responsible for his misery. Every night he went to Dick Boylan's, and waited with a bottle on the table.

Dick Boylan was accustomed to the company of hard drinkers, and when a man suddenly became a nightly, hours-long customer, Boylan was not surprised. He had seen the same thing happen too often for his curiosity to be aroused, and sooner or later he would be given a hint of the reason for the customer's problem. At first he dismissed the notion that in Pat Collins's case the problem was money; Collins was selling cars as fast as he could get delivery. The problem, therefore, was probably a woman, and since Collins was a nightly visitor, the woman was at home—his wife. It all came down to one of two things: money, or a woman. It never occurred to Dick Boylan—or, for that matter, to Pat Collins—that Pat's problem was the loss of a friend. Consequently Dick Boylan looked for, and found, all the evidence he needed to support his theory that Collins was having wife troubles. For example, men who were having money troubles would get phone calls from their wives, telling them to get home for supper. But the men who were having wife trouble, although they sometimes got calls from women, seldom got calls from their wives. Pat Collins's wife never called him. Never. And he never called her.

It was confusing to Dick Boylan to hear that Pat Collins's business was on the rocks. Whit Hofman did not let his friends' businesses go on the rocks. And then Boylan understood it all. A long forgotten, overheard remark about Whit Hofman and Madge Collins came back to him, and it was all as plain as day. Thereafter he watched Pat Collins more carefully; the amount he drank, the cordiality of his relations with the country clubbers, the neatness of his appearance, and the state of his mind and legs when at last he would say goodnight. He had nothing against Pat Collins, but he did not like him. Dick Boylan was more comfortable with non-Irishmen; they were neither Irish-to-Irish over-friendly, nor Irish-to-Irish condescending, and when Pat Collins turned out to be so preoccupied with his problems that he failed to be over-friendly or condescending, Dick Boylan put him down for an unsociable fellow, hardly an Irishman at all, but certainly not one of the others. Pat Collins did not fit in anywhere, although he got on well enough with the rest of the customers. Indeed, the brotherhood of hard drinkers were more inclined to welcome his company than Collins was to seek theirs. Two or three men coming in together would go to Pat's table instead of starting a table of their own and inviting him to join them. It was a distinction that Dick Boylan noticed without comprehending it, possibly because as an Irishman he was immune to what the non-Irish called Irish charm. But it was not Irish charm that made Pat Collins welcome in the brotherhood; it was their sense of kinship with a man who was slipping faster than they were slipping, and who in a manner of speaking was taking someone else's turn in the downward line, thus postponing by months or years the next man's ultimate, inevitable arrival at the bottom. They welcomed this volunteer, and they hoped he would be with them a long while. They were an odd lot, with little in common except an inability to stand success or the lack of it. There were the medical men, Brady and Williams; Brady, who one day in his early forties stopped in the middle of an operation and had to let his assistant take over, and never performed surgery again; Williams, who at thirty-two was already a better doctor than his father, but who was oppressed by his father's reputation. Lawyer Parsons, whose wife had made him run for Congress because her father had been a congressman, and who had then fallen hopelessly in love with the wife of a congressman from Montana. Lawyer Strickland, much in demand as a high school commencement speaker, but somewhat shaky on the Rules of Evidence. Jeweler Linklighter, chess player without a worthy opponent since the death of the local rabbi. Hardware Merchant Stump, Eastern Pennsylvania trapshooting champion until an overload exploded and blinded one eye. Teddy Stokes, Princeton '25, gymnast, Triangle Club heroine and solo dancer, whose father was paying blackmail to the father of an altar boy. Sterling Agnew, Yale ex-'22, Sheff, a remittance man from New York whose father owned coal lands, and who was a part-time lover of Kitty Hofman's. George W. Shuttleworth,

Yale '91, well-to-do widower and gentleman author, currently at work on a biography of Nathaniel Hawthorne which was begun in 1892. Percy Keene, music teacher specializing in band instruments, and husband of a Christian Science practitioner. Lewis M. Rutledge, former captain of the Amherst golf team and assistant manager of the local branch of a New York brokerage house, who had passed on to Agnew the information that Kitty Hofman was accommodating if you caught her at the right moment. Miles Lassiter, ex-cavalry officer, ex-lieutenant of the State Constabulary, partner in the Schneider & Lassiter Detective & Protective Company, industrial patrolmen, payroll guards, private investigators, who was on his word of honor never again to bring a loaded revolver into Boylan's. Any and at some times all these gentlemen were to be found at Boylan's on any given night, and they constituted a clientele that Dick Boylan regarded as his regulars, quite apart from the daytime regulars who came in for a quick steam, drank it, paid, and quickly departed. Half a dozen of the real regulars were also daytime regulars, but Boylan said—over and over again—that in the daytime he ran a first-aid station; the sanctuary did not open till suppertime. (The sanctuary designation originated with George Shuttleworth; the first-aid station, with Dr. Calvin K. Brady, a Presbyterian and therefore excluded from Boylan's generalities regarding the Irish.)

For nearly three years these men sustained Pat Collins in his need for companionship, increasingly so as he came to know their problems. And know them he did, for in the stunned silence that followed Madge's true confession he took on the manner of the reliable listener, and little by little, bottle by bottle, the members of the brotherhood imparted their stories even as Whit Hofman had

done on the afternoon of the first meeting of Whit and
Pat. In exchange the members of the brotherhood helped
Pat Collins with their tacit sympathy, that avoided mention
of the latest indication of cumulative disaster. With a
hesitant delicacy they would wait until he chose, if he chose,
to speak of the loss of his business, the loss of his jobs, the
changes of home address away from the western part of
town to the northeastern, where the air was always a bit
polluted from the steel mill, the gas house, the abattoir, and
where there was always some noise, of which the worst was
the squealing of hogs in the slaughterhouse.

"I hope you won't mind if I say this, Pat," said
George Shuttleworth one night. "But it seems to me you
take adversity very calmly, considering the first thing I ever
heard about you."

"What was that, George?"

"I believe you administered a sound thrashing to
Mr. Herb Michaels, shortly after you moved to town."

"Oh, that. Yes. Well, I'm laughing on the other side of
my face now. I shouldn't have done that."

"But you're glad you did. I hope. Think of how you'd
feel now if you hadn't. True, he owns the business you
built up, but at least you have the memory of seeing him
on the ground. And a cigar in his mouth, wasn't it? I
always enjoyed that touch. I believe Nathaniel would have
enjoyed it."

"Who?"

"Nathaniel Hawthorne. Most generally regarded as a
gloomy writer, but where you find irony you'll find a sense
of humor. I couldn't interest you in reading Hawthorne,
could I?"

"Didn't he write *The Scarlet Letter?*"

"Indeed he did, indeed so."

"I think I read that in college."

"Oh, I hadn't realized you were a college man. Where?"

"Villanova."

"Oh, yes."

"It's a Catholic college near Philly."

"Yes, it must be on the Main Line."

"It is."

"Did you study for the priesthood?"

"No, just the regular college course. I flunked out sophomore year."

"How interesting that a Catholic college should include *The Scarlet Letter*. Did you have a good teacher? I wonder what his name was."

"Brother Callistus, I think. Maybe it was Brother Adrian."

"I must look them up. I thought I knew all the Hawthorne authorities. Callistus, and Adrian. No other names?"

"That's what they went by."

"I'm always on the lookout for new material on Nathaniel. One of these days I've just got to stop revising and pack my book off to a publisher, that's all there is to it. Stand or fall on what I've done—and then I suppose a week after I publish, along will come someone with conclusions that make me seem fearfully out of date. It's a terrifying decision for me to make after nearly thirty years. I don't see how I can face it."

"Why don't you call this Volume One?"

"Extraordinary. I thought of that very thing. In fact, in 1912 I made a new start with just that in mind, but after three years I went back to my earlier plan, a single volume. But perhaps I could publish in the next year or two, and later on bring out new editions, say every five years. Possibly ten. I'd hoped to be ready for the Hawthorne

(315)

Centenary in 1904, but I got hopelessly bogged down in the allegories and I didn't dare rush into print with what I had then. It wouldn't have been fair to me or to Nathaniel, although I suppose it'd make precious little difference to him."

"You never know."

"That's just it, Pat. He's very real to me, you know, although he passed away on May eighteenth or nineteenth in 'sixty-four. There's some question as to whether it was the eighteenth or the nineteenth. But he's very real to me. Very."

This gentle fanatic, quietly drinking himself into a stupor three nights a week, driven home in a taxi with a standing order, and reappearing punctually at eight-thirty after a night's absence, became Pat Collins's favorite companion among the brotherhood. George was in his early fifties, childless, with a full head of snowy white hair brushed down tight on one side. As he spoke he moved his hand slowly across his thatch, as though still training it. Whatever he said seemed to be in answer to a question, a studied reply on which he would be marked as in an examination, and he consequently presented the manner, looking straight ahead and far away, of a conscientious student who was sure of his facts but anxious to present them with care. To Pat Collins the mystery was how had George Shuttleworth come to discover whiskey, until well along in their friendship he learned that George had begun drinking at Yale and had never stopped. Alcohol had killed his wife in her middle forties—she was the same age as George—and Boylan's brotherhood had taken the place of the drinking bouts George had previously indulged in with her. "The Gibbsville Club is no place for me in the evening," said George. "Games, games, games. If it isn't bridge in the card room, it's pool in the billiard room. Why do men feel they have to be so strenuous—and I include bridge. The veins stand out in their foreheads, and when they finish a hand there's always one of them to heave a great sigh of relief. That's what I mean by strenuous. And the worst of it is that with two or possibly three exceptions, I used to beat them all consistently, and I never had any veins stand out in *my* forehead."

As the unlikely friendship flourished, the older man, by the strength of his passivity, subtly influenced and then dominated Pat Collins's own behavior. George Shuttleworth never tried to advise or instruct his younger friend or anyone else; but he had made a life for himself that seemed attractive to the confused, disillusioned younger man. Ambition, aggressiveness seemed worthless to Pat Collins. They had got him nowhere; they had in fact tricked him as his wife and his most admired friend had tricked him, as though Madge and Whit had given him a garage to get him out of the way. He was in no condition for violent action, and George Shuttleworth, the least violent of men, became his guide in this latter-day acceptance of defeat. In spite of the friendship, George Shuttleworth remained on an impersonal basis with Pat Collins; they never discussed Madge at all, never mentioned her name, and as a consequence Pat's meetings with his friend did not become an opportunity for self-pity.

The time then came—no day, no night, no month, no dramatic moment but only a time—when George Shuttleworth had taken Whit's place in Pat Collins's need of a man to admire. And soon thereafter another time came when Pat Collins was healed, no longer harassed by the wish or the fear that he would encounter Whit. It was a small town, but the routines of lives in small towns can be restrictive.

A woman can say, "I haven't been downtown since last month," although downtown may be no more than four or five blocks away. And there were dozens of men and women who had been born in the town, Pat's early acquaintances in the town, who never in their lives had seen the street in the northeastern section where Pat and Madge now lived. ("Broad Street? I never knew we had a Broad Street in Gibbsville.") There were men and women from Broad Street liberated by the cheap automobile, who would take a ride out Lantenengo Street on a Sunday afternoon, stare at the houses of the rich, but who could not say with certainty that one house belonged to a brewer and another to a coal operator. Who has to know the town as a whole? A physician. The driver of a meat-market delivery truck. A police officer. The fire chief. A newspaper reporter. A taxi driver. A town large enough to be called a town is a complex of neighborhoods, invariably within well-defined limits of economic character; and the men of the neighborhoods, freer to move outside, create or follow the boundaries of their working activities—and return to their neighborhoods for the nights of delight and anguish with their own. Nothing strange, then, but only abrupt, when Pat Collins ceased to see Whit Hofman; and nothing remarkable, either, that three years could be added to the life of Pat Collins, hiding all afternoon in a poolroom, clinging night after night to a glass.

"What did you want to tell me this for?" he had said.

"Because I thought it was right," she had said.

"Right, you say?"

"To tell you, yes," she said.

He stood up and pulled off his belt and folded it double.

(318)

"Is that what you're gonna do, Pat?"

"Something to show him the next time," he said.

"There'll be no next time. You're the only one'll see what you did to me."

"That's not what I'm doing it for."

"What for, then?"

"It's what you deserve. They used to stone women like you, stone them to death."

"Do that, then. Kill me, but not the strap. Really kill me, but don't do that, Pat. That's ugly. Have the courage to kill me, and I'll die. But don't do that with the strap, please."

"What a faker, what a bluffer you are."

"No," she said. She went to the bureau drawer and took out his revolver and handed it to him. "I made an act of contrition."

"An act of contrition."

"Yes, and there was enough talk, enough gossip. You'll get off," she said.

"Put the gun away," he said.

She dropped the revolver on a chair cushion. "You put it away. Put it in your pocket, Pat. I'll use it on you if you start beating me with the strap."

"Keep your voice down, the children'll hear," he said.

"They'll hear if you beat me."

"You and your act of contrition. Take off your clothes."

"You hit me with that strap and I'll scream."

"Take your clothes off, I said."

She removed her dress and slip, and stood in brassiere and girdle.

"Everything," he said.

She watched his eyes, took off the remaining garments, and folded her arms against her breasts.

He went to her, bent down, and spat on her belly.

"You're dirty," he said. "You're a dirty woman. Somebody spit on you, you dirty woman. The spit's rolling down your belly. No, I won't hit you."

She slowly reached down, picked up the slip and covered herself with it. "Are you through with me?"

He laughed. "Am I through with you? Am *I* through with you."

He left the house and was gone a week before she again heard from him. He stayed in town, but he ate only breakfast at home. "Is this the way it's going to be?" she said. "I have to make up a story for the children."

"You ought to be good at that."

"Just so I know," she said. "Do you want to see their report cards?"

"No."

"It's no use taking it out on them. What you do to me, I don't care, but they're not in this. They think you're cross with them."

"Don't tell me what to do. The children. You down here, with them sleeping upstairs. Don't you tell me what to do."

"All right, I won't," she said. "I'll tell them you're working nights, you can't come home for dinner. They'll see through it, but I have to give them some story."

"You'll make it a good one, of that I'm sure."

In calmer days he had maintained a balance between strict parenthood and good humor toward the children, but now he could not overcome the guilt of loathing their mother that plagued him whenever he saw the question behind their eyes. They were waiting to be told something, and all he could tell them was that it was time for them to be off to school, to be off to Mass, always time for them to go away and take their unanswerable, unphrased questions with them.

Their mother told them that he was very busy at the garage, that he had things on his mind, but in a year he had lost them. There was more finality to the loss than would have been so if he had always treated them with indifference, and he hated Madge the more because she could not and he could not absolve him of his guilt.

One night in Boylan's speakeasy George Shuttleworth, out of a momentary silence, said: "What are you going to do now, Pat?"

"Nothing. I have no place to go."

"Oh, you misunderstood me. I'm sorry. I meant now that Overton's has closed."

"That was over a month ago. I don't know, George. I haven't found anything, but I guess something will turn up. I was thinking of going on the road again. I used to be a pretty good hat salesman, wholesale, and when I was with Overton I told the traveling men to let me know if they heard of anything."

"But you don't care anything about hats."

"Well, I don't, but I can't pick and choose. I can't support a family shooting pool."

"Isn't there something in the automobile line? A man ought to work at the job he likes best. We have only the one life, Pat. The one time in this vale of tears."

"Right now the automobile business is a vale of tears. I hear Herb Michaels isn't having it any too easy, and I could only move four new Cadillacs in fourteen months."

"Suppose you had your own garage today. Could you make money, knowing as much as you do?"

"Well, they say prosperity is just around the corner."

"I don't believe it for a minute."

"I don't either, not in the coal regions. A man to make

a living in the automobile business today, in this part of the country, he'd be better off without a dealer's franchise. Second-hand cars, and service and repairs. New rubber. Accessories. Batteries. All that. The people that own cars have to get them serviced, but the people that need cars in their jobs, they're not buying new cars. Who is?"

"I don't know. I've never owned a car. Never learned to drive one."

"You ought to. Then when you go looking for material for your book, you'd save a lot of steps."

"Heavens no," said George Shuttleworth. "You're referring to trips to Salem? New England? Why it takes me two or three days of walking before I achieve the proper Nineteenth Century mood. My late lamented owned a car and employed a chauffeur. A huge, lumbering Pierce-Arrow she kept for twelve years. I got rid of it after she died. It had twelve thousand miles on the speedometer, a thousand miles for each year."

"Oh, they were lovely cars. Was it a limousine?"

"Yes, a limousine, although I believe they called it a Berliner. The driver was well protected. Windows on the front doors. I got rid of him, too. I got rid of him *first*. Good pay. Apartment over the garage. Free meals. New livery every second year. And a hundred dollars at Christmas. But my wife's gasoline bills, I happened to compare them with bills for the hospital ambulance when I was on the board. Just curiosity. Well, sir, if those bills were any indication, my wife's car used up more gasoline than the ambulance, although I don't suppose it all found its way into our tank. But she defended him. Said he always kept the car looking so nice. He did, at that. He had precious little else to occupy his time. I believe he's gone back to Belguim. He was the only Belgian in town, and my wife was very sympathetic toward the Belgians."

"Took his savings and—"

"His plunder," said George Shuttleworth. "Let's not waste any more time talking about him, Pat. You know, of course, that I'm quite rich."

"Yes, that wouldn't be hard to guess. That house and all."

"The house, yes, the house. Spotless, not a speck of dust anywhere. It's like a museum. I have a housekeeper, Mrs. Frazier. Scotch. Conscientious to a degree, but she's made a whole career of keeping my house antiseptically clean, like an operating surgery. So much so, that she makes me feel that I'm in the way. So I'm getting out of the way for a while. I'm going away."

"Going down South?"

"No, I'm not going South. I'm going abroad, Pat. I haven't been since before the War, and I'm not really running away from Mrs. Frazier and her feather dusters. I have a serious purpose in taking this trip. It has to do with my book. You knew that Nathaniel spent seven years abroad. Perhaps you didn't. Seven years, from 1853 to 1860."

"You want to see what inspired him," said Pat.

"No, no! Quite the contrary. He'd done all his best work by then. I want to see how it spoiled him, living abroad. There were other distractions. The Civil War. His daughter's illness. But I must find out for myself whether European life spoiled Nathaniel *or* did he flee to Europe when he'd exhausted his talent. That may turn out to be my greatest contribution to the study of Hawthorne. I can see quite clearly how my discoveries might cause me to scrap everything I've done so far and have to start all over again. I've already written to a great many scholars, and they've expressed keen interest."

"Well, I'll be sorry to see you go, George. I'll miss our evenings. When do you leave?"

"In the *Mauretania*, the seventh of next month. Oh, when I decide to act, nothing stops me," said George Shuttleworth. "I want to give you a going-away present, Pat."

"It should be the other way around. You're the one that's leaving."

"If you wish to give me some memento, that's very kind of you. But what I have in mind, I've been thinking about it for some time. Not an impulse of the moment. How much would it cost to set you up in a business such as you describe?"

"Are you serious, George?"

"Dead serious."

"A small garage, repairing all makes. No dealership. Gas, oil, tires, accessories. There's an old stable near where I live. A neighbor of mine uses it to garage his car in. You want to go on my note, is that it?"

"No, I don't want to go on your note. I'll lend you the money myself, without interest."

"Using mostly second-hand equipment, which I know where to buy here and there, that kind of a setup would run anywhere from five to ten thousand dollars. Atlantic, Gulf, one of those companies put in the pump and help with the tank. Oil. Tools I'd have to buy myself. Air pump. Plumbing would be a big item, and I'd need a pit to work in. Anywhere between five and ten thousand. You can always pick up a light truck cheap and turn it into a tow-car."

George Shuttleworth was smiling. "That's the way I like to hear you talk, Pat. Show some enthusiasm for something. What's your bank?"

"The Citizens, it was. I don't have any at the moment."

"Tomorrow, sometime before three o'clock, I'll deposit ten thousand dollars in your name, and you can begin to draw on it immediately."

"There ought to be some papers drawn up."

"My cheque is all the papers we'll need."

"George?"

"Now, now! No speech, none of that. I spend that much every year, just to have a house with sparkling chandeliers."

"Well then, two words. Thank you."

"You're very welcome."

"George?"

"Yes, Pat."

"I'm sorry, but you'll have to excuse me. I—I can't sit here, George. You see why? Please excuse me."

"You go take a good long walk, Pat. That's what you do."

He walked through the two crowds of men and women leaving the movie houses at the end of the first show. He spoke to no one.

"You're home early," said Madge. "Are you all right?"

"I'm all right."

"You look sort of peak-ed."

"Where are the children?"

"They're out Halloweening. They finished their home work."

"I'm starting a new business."

"You are? What?"

"I'm opening a new garage."

"Where?"

"In the neighborhood."

"Well—that's good, I guess. Takes money, but it'd be a waste of time to ask you where you got it."

"It'd be a waste of time."

"Did you have your supper?"

"I ate something. I'm going to bed. I have to get up early. I have to go around and look for a lot of stuff."

"Can I do anything?"

"No. Just wake me up when the children get up."

"All right. Goodnight."

"Goodnight."

"And good luck, Pat."

"No. No, Madge. Don't, don't—"

"All right. I'm sorry," she said quietly. Then, uncontrolled, "Pat, for God's sake! Please?"

"No, Madge. I ask you."

She covered her face with her hands. "Please, please, please, please, please."

But he went upstairs without her. He could not let her spoil this, he could not let her spoil George Shuttleworth even by knowing about him.

"Hello, Pat."

"Hyuh, Whit."

Never more than that, but never less.

THE PROFESSORS

Free tea and cookies were served every afternoon at five in the Faculty Club. Locally, among the older teachers and those already living on their pensions, the repast was known as the appetite-spoiler: a man who had not been able to put aside much money during his active career could come to the Faculty Club—the F.C.—and stuff himself with tea that was half milk but at least was warm, and with chocolate Hydroxes, and when he went home to supper he was not as hungry as he might have been otherwise. All the men who depended upon the F.C. teas to keep their food budgets in order had an understanding about that, and some of them had become very adept at picking up four cookies with one hand while holding cup and saucer with the other. There were those who stacked the cookies, like poker chips, and there were some who could scoop them off the tray, using their thumbs to slide the cookies back into the palms of their hands. In either case the men would take their tea and biscuits and seat themselves in their accustomed places and devour the first batch in silence, washing it down with the tea in somewhat of a hurry, in order to go back for a second cup and another polite handful before Arthur, the club waiter, would start removing the tea things at half past five.

Arthur had a rude name for these members: tea customers, he called them, although tea was not the word he used. "Two, three lumps of sugar in every cup, and all them sweet crackers," he would say. "It's hardly any wonder they don't have any teeth left. But I rackon most of them don' get to sink their teeth into many sirloins." Arthur had been with the club for forty years and through three university administrations, and was no more in awe of a Nobel Prize winner than of the freshmen's basketball coach. At half past five on the dot he would take away the hot water and the carton of teabags and what was left of the biscuits, and if a professor asked for one more cup of tea Arthur had ways of handling him, depending on the degree of his dislike of the professor. "Sorry, sir, it's after ha' past. Club rule," a refusal; or "Well, I guess I could let you have another cup but I could get myself into trouble." In the latter case the professor would usually give up. There was only one club member who got special privileges from Arthur: Ernest Pangborn, soon-to-retire professor of Romance Languages, who in all his years on the faculty had never had the senior yearbook dedicated to him. But every afternoon, at about five-twenty-seven Arthur would start staring at Ernest Pangborn until he got his attention, and Arthur would point with his forefinger to the carton of teabags and then look up at the Seth Thomas clock, and Pangborn would get to his feet in time to be served the last cup of tea, his third, and only for Professor Pangborn would Arthur open a fresh box of cookies.

"Ernest, you have a drag with Arthur. How do you rate it?" The man who spoke in archaic collegiate slang was Jack Veech, Mathematics Department, a full professor and a few years younger than Ernest Pangborn.

"I'm sure I don't know, and it's probably just as well I don't."

"Why? Why do you say that?"

"Why do I say it? I say it because it's what I mean, Jack. And I mean it because whatever it is that got me in Arthur's good graces, he isn't self-conscious about it and neither am I. But if I knew what it was, I'd think of it whenever I saw Arthur and in all probability I'd have referred to it. Or been at such pains not to refer to it that it would have been just as awkward for both of us. I don't believe in being too analytical about what makes some people like me, those who do, I used to be *very* analytical about what made people *dis*like me, but I gave that up. They just do. And when there's no overt reason for it, when it's instinctive, or acquired through association, I'm not going to be able to change it. And for quite a long time I haven't wanted to. A few people like me, and those few I place on the side of love. Some others dislike me, and that can be equally mysterious. Not baffling, though. From my earlier investigations I can easily recall standing, as it were, outside myself and disliking me. When I was a young man, for example, I was occasionally complimented by young women on my profile. That, of course, was forty years ago. But when I studied my profile I saw a well-shaped head, a fairly good nose, but a rather insolent young man. Insolent, and sensual, and surprisingly cruel at least potentially. That was my appearance, which some young ladies admired, and which I sincerely did not."

"I only *asked* you how you got your drag with Arthur."

"I know, and I apologize for the disquisition. My excuse is that the opportunity doesn't come very often. Would you like to have, as they say, equal time? I'll ask you a leading question. Why do you think Arthur is less fond of you than he is of me?"

"I don't know, and I couldn't care less."

"No, Jack, you must care a *little*, and not only because

Arthur Dayton looks out for me. You observed that he does, and the fact irritated you."

"You claim you don't know why he likes you. Therefore I can claim I don't know why he doesn't like the rest of us."

"I don't know the answer to either question. I was only offering you the chance to theorize, which I know you like to do."

"Not on such matters."

"Well, true. It's not the kind of thing a first-class mind ought to be concerned with. Very trivial. Very, very, very, very trivial."

"Is that sarcasm, Ernest?"

"No, not really, Jack. I do concern myself with trivial matters, that in your field would be—well, obstacles. I've often thought, as I gazed at your blackboard after one of your lectures, all that clear thinking, unimpeded by trivial things, and none of it having any meaning for me except that my friend Jack Veech makes a very sloppy *phi*. Your *phi* and your *psi* are written in such haste that if I were one of your students I'd be confused."

"It isn't my Greek letters that confuse them."

"Of course not. But I'm not one of your students, and I'm sure if I were—"

"You wouldn't last very long."

"I was about to say, I wouldn't last very long. In fact I didn't go that high in mathematics. I fulfilled those requirements—how did I? After solid I took a year of physics. I guess that was it. I never had to take trigonometry. Now I doubt if I could pass high school algebra."

"You might be able to. They don't use *phi* or *psi* in it to distract you, in case the teacher didn't make them pretty."

"Oh, now, Jack, you're not going to be peevish about that, surely."

"I've seen *your* handwriting, in English, and it's nothing to brag about."

"It's legible, though, Jack. Small, but legible. I formed the habit of writing small to save paper, years ago. But my letters are clear, easy to read."

"Under a magnifying glass."

"Well, no one can say that about your hand. Large, sweeping, flourishing, you might say. Isn't it odd that—"

"That what?"

"Oh, we've had enough of this conversation. I think I'll amble homeward." Ernest Pangborn had come close to remarking how odd it was that he, a tall man, should have such small handwriting, while Veech, who was short, wrote a large, sweeping, flourishing hand.

Pangborn did indeed amble homeward, with a gait that all newcomers to the university were likely to attribute to alcohol and first-year medical students to the onset of locomotor ataxia. Neither opinion was correct; Pangborn could not afford liquor, and his coordination and reflexes were in good condition, but in another day the women students, seeing Pangborn's walk, would say, "Truckin' on down." Veech, on the contrary, walked like a midshipman, one of the lower-class midshipmen who had recently been braced.

But Jack Veech's hatred to Ernest Pangborn was not caused by the difference in height or even by an instinctive dislike of the sort mentioned by Pangborn. The hatred went back to the early days of their acquaintance and Veech's second year on the campus. It was a large university, with a large faculty, and newcomers on the instructor and assistant professor levels often found that they were meeting only the men and women in their field and their neighbors in faculty housing accommodations, houses and apartments for the married teachers, smaller apartments and single rooms for the unmarried. Among such a large faculty there were those who had independent incomes, and they lived where they chose. Men like Jack Veech had more or less to take what was assigned to them, in order of seniority in the teaching profession. It was through this circumstance that Jack Veech made the acquaintance of Ernest Pangborn.

It was in the very early Thirties, and Maizie and Ernest Pangborn were still able to hang on to their house. Maizie had a little money of her own, Ernest Pangborn a little less, which together enabled them to have the house and to travel abroad. They then lived on a scale that was higher than that of full professors and as a sort of punishment for their conspicuous extravagance Ernest was given extra chores. One of the chores was to serve on a committee that assigned living quarters to new teachers, and in the course of determining seniority, Ernest discovered that there was a one-year gap in John Philip Veech's academic history. A whole year was unaccounted for.

A couple of weeks before college was to open, Ernest Pangborn saw John P. Veech on the campus. "Veech, I'm Pangborn. Interested in a Coke?"

"Why, yes. Thanks very much," said Veech.

They took a table in the cafeteria and Veech waited for Pangborn to begin.

"I'm on a committee that decides who is going to live where," said Pangborn. "It's a dull dreary task, and the only thing that keeps it from being duller is to try to be conscientious about it. And I noticed that according to seniority, which is what we go by, two new men get their choice of rooms in West Hostetter before you do. But they're not entitled to that seniority. They're both younger than you, and they took their bachelors' and masters' a year after you did.

You graduated in '26, I believe. Master's in '28. Taught for two years, but in the academic year '30-'31 you apparently vanished from the face of the earth. It couldn't have been a sabbatical, but if it was a leave of absence, you're entitled to first choice of what's left in West Hostetter. There's a corner room left, and as far as I can see, you've got more right to it than the other two. But the record doesn't say what happened to '30-'31. If you were on leave, I suggest you correct the record and then you can have the corner room."

"I wasn't on leave that year," said Veech. "I stopped teaching because I was ill."

"Well, couldn't you have that put on the record? It isn't there now, and if you were ill I think you're entitled to have it so stated, even if it wasn't an actual leave of absence."

"Why should you bother about it if I don't?" said Veech.

Pangborn took the rebuff in silence, drank the rest of his Coke and said, "You may be sure I never will again," and left Veech.

The rudeness was of such a pointless kind that Pangborn did not speak of it to Maizie, therefore to no one, until at a faculty cocktail party he overheard Veech saying, "I've never been sick a day in my life. I have a system of exercises that I do every day, no matter where I am. On shipboard. Even on trains. It's ridiculous for men to let themselves get out of shape. Toxicity affects the brain and nobody can tell me otherwise."

At home that evening Ernest Pangborn said to his wife, "How do you like John Veech?"

"John Veech. Mathematics. The one that looks like an overgrown jockey."

"If you weren't from Kentucky you'd say an overgrown

coxswain. Yes, what do you think of him?"

"Just a quick impression, just right off like that?" She snapped her fingers.

"Yes."

"A man I wouldn't trust. Maybe the soul of honor, as upright as they come, but not a man I would trust. Why?"

"He's a liar." He then told her why he thought so. "His home town is Duluth. I think I'll write to Don Marshall."

"And you give Don my love and tell him he's still my second favorite Beta, even if he didn't think to send us a Christmas card last Christmas."

When Don Marshall's letter arrived a couple of weeks later Pangborn said nothing to Maizie, but something made her think of Veech and she said, "Honey'd you ever hear from Don? Don Marshall? About Mr. Veech?"

"Yes, I heard from him. Veech is a liar, all right. And this is a pretty darn nice university."

"Well, you always said *that*, honey. This little old cow college, you always loved and revered it. Why now specially?"

"Because they gave John Veech a second chance."

"Second chance? Was he here before?"

"No, never here. Michigan. They let him resign. He was arrested in Detroit, contributing to the delinquency of a minor. Found guilty, served several months and got time off for good behavior. Don said it didn't surprise anyone in Duluth."

"He must be awful good scholastically."

"He is, or so I'm told. But I'm darn proud of this old place."

In a year or so Veech got married and at regular intervals became the father of sons, three in number, who were well-disciplined reproductions of Veech. They marched to the model school in the Teachers College, took prizes in junior sports, won merit badges in the Scouts, and stayed out of trouble. Some faculty mothers envied Nadine Veech, who had a husband that was not too damned busy to do his share in raising the three boys; some faculty fathers, in self-defense, referred to the Veech boys as the Junior R.O.T.C. And yet when Vernon, the youngest of the Veech boys, ran away and was missing for two days, the university community suspended all criticism of the manner in which Jack Veech was raising his sons. The concern and sympathy were genuine, and upon Vernon's being restored to his parents the other fathers and mothers, as though by universal agreement, forbade their children to tease the Veech child. He had been discovered, cold and hungry, in an abandoned henhouse on a farm not twenty miles from the campus. He was thirteen years old.

It was one of the many, many times that Ernest Pangborn missed Maizie. If she had been alive he could have talked it out with her, and one silly-seeming comment might have shown him what to do. And if not a frivolous remark, it might be a couple of lines from her favorites, Elinor Wylie, Edna St. Vincent Millay. He knew so well that she would love to be able to say

> I shall stop fighting and escape
> Into a little house I'll build.

or, from Millay, "Standing beside some tumbled shed" or "And I upon the floor will lie/and think how bad I've been." Wylie and Millay she knew as she knew Wodehouse and Bolton and Porter and Berlin, and certain sections of the Book of Common Prayer, including the words that had been said over her in April of that year in the University Chapel.

There would be nothing profound in her comments on the fugitive Vernon Veech, for in her childlessness she was diffident where the problems of parents were concerned, and sensitive to the unuttered disappointment of her husband. He could invent the impossible dialog: "Maybe I ought to go see Veech," he would say.

"If you think you *ought* to, but not just because they got the whole football squad out looking for Vernon. Maybe you'd be better off with the football players. We're such strangers maybe Jack Veech'd order you off his porch."

In the end, though, he went to call on Veech and Nadine.

"Oh—Ernest. Come in," said Veech.

"I won't stay."

"Much rather have you come here than tie up the phone. I wish people would have sense enough not to call us up. They're so damned inconsiderate."

"Their intentions are good, Jack. Some of them just don't think."

"They have nothing to think with, especially the women. Not that the men aren't just as bad. I never realized how many stupid people there are at this place. Oversized Ag school is what it is."

"I'm sorry but I can't agree with you on that, but I know you're upset, understandably. Just say hello to Nadine for me, and if I can help in any way, do call me."

"I just got finished telling you, we want to keep the line clear. But I'll tell Nadine you were here."

"Yes, do, but *don't* call this an oversized Ag school. You don't mean that, Jack. You of all people."

"Did you come here to start an argument? I never meant anything more in all my life."

"Goodnight, Jack," said Pangborn.

After Vernon Veech's adventure quieted down, the boy's father one evening called on Ernest Pangborn in his rooms in East Hostetter. "You've got this place fixed up pretty nicely. You sold your house when Maizie died. You must have got a pretty good price for it, the way the real estate situation is."

"Well, there were mortgages to be taken care of, and the government has that ceiling business. But I wanted to get out of the house. All this, my books and this furniture, I had in my study. The bedroom furniture I left behind, with everything else. I'd like to go away for a year. I have a sabbatical coming and the people in Main Hall will let me go any time I like, but I have difficulty making plans. It's easier just to stay on. How would you like a cup of coffee? I have this little electric thing."

"Never drink it at night, thanks. But you go ahead and have one."

"I will later. I get along with a lot less sleep than I used to." Pangborn was willing to continue the small talk as long as Veech wished to, but Veech was now ready.

"I said something the other night at my house, when you came to see us. You know what I have reference to."

"Yes. I know."

"Since then I've been thinking. You said to me, 'You didn't mean that. You of all people.' Why me of all people?"

"Oh, you *didn't* come here to explain your remark. You want *me* to explain *mine*."

"If you mean did I come here to apologize, I don't make a habit of apologizing."

"Well, it's a habit you could form, to use when necessary."

"And I don't see why I'd apologize to you anyway."

"No, I guess you don't. You could apologize to me for

saying what you did about a place that I happen to love. But that hasn't occurred to you, so—don't apologize, whatever you do."

"I won't. You can be sure of that. But you still haven't told me what you meant by 'you of all people.' "

"Are you bluffing, Jack?"

Veech looked at Pangborn. "Bluffing?" He uttered the word, but only as an echo, not as angry protest.

"You have no feeling of gratitude for this place?"

"Oh," said Veech. "You're referring to something that happened in Detroit? How did you find out?"

"Not from Main Hall, I assure you. And I assure you, I've never spoken of it to anyone now living."

"All the years since, that I've been making up for that, that I've been living a decent life. Those years don't mean anything?"

"They do indeed mean something. They mean that this oversized Ag school showed good judgment. But even if you hadn't vindicated them, I'd love the place because it gave you a second chance. Were you accepted anywhere else, Jack?"

"No, I wasn't."

"Then go on home and do something nice for Vernon."

"I've been very nice to Vernon."

"Then by God you've learned *something* here. I didn't think you had."

"Gratitude doesn't go on forever," said Veech.

"Yes it does. Phony humility doesn't go on forever, but that only sickens people anyway. Gratitude is something else."

"I ought to be grateful to you for keeping quiet?"

"Oh, Lord, you have no understanding of it, or of me. Tell me, how were you nice to Vernon?"

"How was I nice to him? Different ways. I bought him a new bike. I'm letting him go to camp next summer."

"Then you are grateful, aren't you? You're grateful to your son for not dying, for not making more trouble."

"When it comes to raising a family I guess I know more about that than you do."

"That's not the crushing remark you intended it to be, Jack, honestly it isn't," said Pangborn.

"Well, goodbye, Mr. Chips," said Veech. He rose and left, and Ernest Pangborn laughed more heartily than he had in many months. Veech's parting remark could have and should have made him sadder, but Veech had no way of knowing that through outrageous accident he had spoken the name that Maizie used when she wanted to deflate Pangborn. "You're being Chipsy," she would say, and it would cover quaintness, pomposity, prolixity, eccentricities of dress, penny-watching, and even hand-holding during lectures by visiting notables. He went to the door and shouted down the stair-well. "Hey, Jack?"

"What?"

"Touché."

"What'd you say?"

"Never mind," said Pangborn, and returned to his rooms.

Thereafter he often sought the company of Jack Veech, knowing that Veech despised him for doing so, but caring little what Veech felt. He was sure that to Veech he was an ineffectual turner of the other cheek, too ready to forgive, a slob. But when he caught himself in the act of being Chipsy he would know that it was time to bask in the light of the cold, hard intelligence of Jack Veech, and Veech never let him down. Veech could be relied upon to say at least one thing during a conversation that would be so down-to-earth, or pragmatic, or unconsciously cruel that it had the double effect of exposure to a fresh point of view, and, immediately, a reaffirmation by Pangborn of his own point of view. He used Veech because he could not change him, and then he found that he did not want to change him. An association that had really begun with a name, if not a voice, from the grave, now continued because Veech had become a medium. A medium, a confessor, a messenger. Then Pangborn began to notice that as they grew older he was seeing more of Veech than of any other member of the faculty, and that their encounters, their conversations, were not all of his own maneuvering; some of them, then more and more of them, came about through an effort on the part of Veech. Pangborn would be walking across campus and Veech would join him; Pangborn would take his accustomed chair in the Faculty Club, and the chair next to him would be taken by Veech. Only once during that time did Veech depart from the severity of his manner toward Pangborn, but that exception was enough to give Pangborn another look at the man. "Well, we finally got the last of the boys off to college," said Veech one afternoon at the F.C.

"Vernon?" said Pangborn.

"Yes. He started at Kenyon yesterday."

"You sent all three to Kenyon. You didn't go there."

"No, but Nadine's father did, and he's paying the bills. You don't think I could send three sons to a place like that? I don't know how I'd have managed to send them through here, even allowing for free tuition and having them live at home. Well, with Vernon and Victor at Kenyon and Vance in the army, our food bills won't be so high. Nadine said to me yesterday, next Sunday we ought to have a steak and eat it all by ourselves. A nice choice cut just big enough for the two of us. I'm looking forward to it. Then I can start paying some bills. Who knows? I may be able to save some money."

"I always thought you had some."

"My family had some, but I was cut off. Didn't you find that out when you were finding out everything else about me?"

"No."

"I haven't been to Duluth since 1930. My father paid for my lawyers, and he allowed my mother to give me five hundred dollars when I got out of prison. But only on condition I never go back to Duluth. No, I haven't any money. And neither has Nadine. *Her* family weren't giving any money to a jailbird."

"I never knew any of this, Jack."

"Well, you weren't supposed to. I didn't go around broadcasting it, you can be sure of that."

It was another look at the man and at the life he and his wife had led for more than twenty years, close to twenty-five. And Ernest Pangborn did not know what to say. A compliment would be rejected, and a word of pity would be unthinkable. Indeed, the compliment was being paid to Pangborn; Veech honored him with his confidence and accorded him honor more subtly, more truly, by asking no further assurances of his silence. Pangborn did not know what to say, knew there was nothing to say, and while he was thinking he became conscious of Arthur, who was making his end-of-tea-time signals.

"Let me have your cup," said Ernest Pangborn. He picked up Veech's cup and saucer and carried them with his own to the tea table. "For Professor Veech and me, please, Arthur."

Arthur looked up at the clock. "Well—all right," he said.

A SHORT WALK
FROM THE STATION

On a Friday evening in February this year Francis King
dozed off just after his train left the 30th Street Station, and
he would have slept all the way to Paoli had it not been for
Joe Dybert. Joe Dybert shook him gently. "Wake up,
Francis," said Joe Dybert. "Show momma the blue."

"Huh? . . . Oh. Oh, hello, Joe. We here?" said Francis King.

"Think you can make it? What'd you have for lunch,
boy?" said Joe Dybert.

The two men left the station together, walking in step
but without conversation until they reached the street. "Give
you a ride up the hill?"

"No thanks," said Francis King. "See you tomorrow."

"Tomorrow's Saturday. You won't see *me* tomorrow."

"What did *you* have for lunch? We're going to your
house for dinner tomorrow night. Drive carefully, Mr. Dybert. Drive carefully." Francis King turned up the collar of
his topcoat and put on his gloves, but now that he was
alone the thought of walking up the short incline to Cardiff
Road sickened him. It was only a short walk, three blocks,
and the times he had made it automatically surely numbered
well up in the thousands; nevertheless his legs weighed a
ton. He had no sensation of dizziness, he felt no pain. It

was just that he wanted to stand there a couple of minutes.

Friends of his and their wives waved to him and tapped their horns in goodnight salute, all knowing that Francis King never accepted the offer of a lift in the evening. "Forget something, Francis?" said one such friend, on foot and not waiting for an answer.

"Just trying to think," said Francis King, and it was the truth: he was trying to understand the leaden immobility of his legs. He knew he could walk only so far—to Arlington Drive, which was at the bottom of the incline. He knew he could get that far, that his legs would let him get that far, but not beyond. And then, in shame and embarrassment, he saw the truth: it was not the short incline to Cardiff Road that was so formidable; it was the thought of once more, for the many-thousandth time, walking past Lydia Brown's shop with his eyes averted, pretending the shop did not exist, pretending there was no Lydia Brown.

The Tack Room was hideously expensive. Lydia Brown's prices for everything were really out of this world. You could get cashmere things much cheaper almost anywhere on Chestnut Street, and the horse things she still carried—to justify the original name of the shop—cost less on Walnut Street. The presents for men were higher than in the New York stores, the children's things were ridiculously overpriced. But Lydia Brown's friends went on buying from her whenever they could, partly out of admiration for her courage, partly because her old friends approved of the appearance of her shop and the way she kept it up in among the cluster of real estate offices, liquor stores, drug stores, hairdressers' salons in the vicinity of the station. The Tack Room was a convenient and pleasant place to drop in for a cigarette, a cup of coffee in the mid-morning, a cup of tea in the afternoon. Old friends could borrow an umbrella there, leave their bundles there, make a telephone call. The field-stone and white trim house was inviting. And if the mounting block at the curb got in the way of off-side car doors, what were a few scratches nowadays, when every anonymous parking attendant did worse than scratch your door? All her old friends wanted Lyd Brown to stay in business, and she always took it with a smile when they kidded her about overcharging them for chutney and English biscuits and Italian leather and Swedish woodwork. Sometimes in the Philadelphia shops a salesperson would say, "We don't carry that any more. The only place I can think of where you might find it is Lydia Brown's store, the Tack Room, you know?" Everything in the Tack Room was the best.

Francis King made straight for the Tack Room, and climbing the three steps from the sidewalk level did not tax his strength. The shop was brightly lighted by three frosted globes hanging from the ceiling, but as he entered he saw no one. Then, from a room at the rear of the store, Lydia Brown came forth.

"Hello, Francis," she said. "Is there something the matter?"

He nodded. "I don't know what it is. I just want to sit down a minute."

"Would you like a glass of water? Brandy? Can I call a doctor?"

"I just want to sit down a minute. It isn't anything. Not a heart attack."

"I'll get you a brandy," she said.

He sat down and opened his coat, took off his hat and gloves and put them on a display table. She brought him a pony of brandy from the back room, and as he took a sip she lowered the Venetian blinds at all the windows. "I was about ready to close up anyway," she said, and stood in front of him with her arms folded and looked down at him over the rims of her glasses.

"If you could see yourself," he said.

"You didn't look so hot when you came in. What did you have for lunch?"

"You're the second one asked me that. I fell asleep on the train, and Joe Dybert asked me the same question. I had oyster stew, apple pie, and two cups of coffee. What I've had for lunch every Friday for thirty years, with time out for the war. What did *you* have for lunch, Lyd?"

"A chicken sandwich and a glass of milk. Why?"

"I don't know. I just thought I'd ask you. *You* asked *me.*"

She took a chair facing him and lit a cigarette. "Nobody would believe it, that the first conversation we have after all these years consists of what we had for lunch."

"Well, I guess after all these years that's just about all we have to talk about."

"You have a point. How are you feeling?"

"Much better, thanks. I'll leave, don't worry."

"Don't hurry. I have nothing to do till seven."

"And then what do you do?"

"What?"

"I'm not just being inquisitive. I've often wondered what you do when you're not being a business woman."

"Terribly nice of you, Francis. I'm touched."

"You have a nice store," he said.

"I like it."

"You must do pretty well."

"Pretty well. I had the best Christmas since I opened the shop."

"Good."

"Rose helped," said Lydia Brown.

"You don't have to tell me that. I'm the one that pays the bills. Why the smile?"

"The only communication we ever have, your name at the bottom of a check. Francis D. B. King. Francis D. B. King. I remember I used to write Mr. and Mrs. Francis D. B. King, to see how it would look. Lydia B. King. Mrs. Francis D. B. King. Mrs. F. D. B. King. L. B. K. I guess every girl that ever lived did that."

"I did it too. I wrote Mrs. Francis D. B. King with you in mind."

"You did, really?"

"Sure. And Lydia B. King, and Lydia King. I don't remember writing L. B. K., but possibly I did."

"I just can't imagine you being so sentimental. Romantic."

"You forget," said Francis King.

"Do I, indeed? I—for*get*. What an unearthly nerve you have, to say a thing like that. The one thing I've never had a chance to do was forget. Do you realize that every morning, when I'm opening up my shop, for close to thirty years I see you walking past here on your way to the train. You've never looked in, not even looked in this direction. But I'm the one that forgets? You don't even see the shop."

"I've always known it was here. During the war I remember I'd be at my battle station, pitch dark in the early morning, and I'd think of how it was at home. I'd think of all the houses in the neighborhood, all the stores. And I always thought of your shop."

"I was hoping you'd be killed in the war."

"What?"

"You find that hard to believe?"

"I find it impossible to believe. By the time the war started it was already a good ten years since we'd had our quarrel. It was one thing to stop speaking to me, but to hate me enough to want me killed, ten years later! I never did anything that bad, Lydia."

"You did to me, Francis. You as good as killed me. Look at me. What am I? Close to sixty years old, no chance of ever having children and I love children. An apartment over my shop instead of a nice home of my own."

"That part isn't hard to understand, being bitter. But hating me enough to want me killed. Do you know, if I'd known that I might have obliged you."

"Oh, come, Francis."

"Oh, yes. When I went out to the Pacific I arranged all my affairs. Made my will, provided for Rose and the children. I put everything in order, so to speak. But I couldn't undo what I'd done to you. I guess it's very seldom a man is so completely in the wrong that there's nothing he can do, absolutely nothing. But I didn't realize you hated me that much."

"Oh, yes."

"And do you now?"

"Right now? This minute? No." She looked away, reflectively. "When you came in here you looked as though you might fall over dead right here."

"That would have been awkward."

"Yes, it would have been. But you asked me a question. Do I hate you now? And the answer is no."

"Why not?"

"You must figure that out for yourself, Francis."

"Because you don't feel anything. Is that why?"

"Yes."

"I looked so nearly dead that you couldn't hate me any more? Is that it?"

"Yes."

"How do I look now?"

"Oh, you're all right now, I suppose."

"Therefore you ought to be hating me again."

She shook her head. "No. Nothing. Absolutely nothing. I'll never hate you again."

Her face was suddenly bright and beautiful, her eyes as blue as her cashmere slip-on and as bright as her necklace of pearls. "Lydia," he said.

"What?"

"Would it be all right if I stopped in again, once in a while?"

"No."

"Never?"

"Never," she said. "I really don't want to see you again, Francis."

"I see," he said. "Well—thanks for the brandy." He rose and picked up his hat and gloves.

"Would you like me to call you a taxi?" she said.

"No thanks," he said.

She held the door open for him, and after he passed through it he heard the spring lock. Even before he reached Arlington Drive she had turned out the lights in her shop, and it was very dark going up to Cardiff Road. Dark and cold, and the wind was strong.

SUNDAY MORNING

Marge Fairbanks had her second cup of coffee and third cigarette, then she put on her zippered arctics and polo coat and went back to the garage. On an impulse that she did not immediately recognize as defiant she started the Fiat, and she was well on her way to the village before she even wondered what had made her take the little car. Her car—that is, the car she was supposed to use—was the station wagon. In the Fairbanks household the station wagon seldom got to the station. It got everywhere else, but hardly ever to the station. Oh, no. The car that was driven to the station every morning, five days a week, and left there in the sun and rain and snow, was the Fiat, the little car that she loved but almost never got a chance to drive. The once bright little Fiat, with its stunning grey paint job and white-wall tires, and its maneuverability and park-ability. She had chosen it and had contributed four hundred dollars toward its purchase, but a month after they bought it Allan expropriated it, and now it was referred to as *his* car. Her car was the Chevy, the station wagon, that was twice as old and twice as big as the Fiat; that needed new floor mats; that got a washing once or twice in the spring and once or twice in the summer; that she tried to keep clean inside but could not seem to, what with dog hair, bobby pins, candy wrappers, matchbooks, Kleenex, comic books, pencil stubs, and the rest of the accumulation of strange articles, souvenirs of family activity and car pool. The inside of the Fiat was not spotlessly clean, but at least it was not disorderly, and the upholstery of the driver's seat was the only place that showed wear.

She passed the Catholic church and waved to Patty O'Brien in her four-year-old mink and her white gloves, but obviously Patty did not recognize her in the Fiat. On a weekday Patty would have waved automatically at the Chevy. Patty, and Kevin, and the O'Brien twins, trying not to be late for the nine o'clock Mass. Marge Fairbanks wondered who felt worse this morning, Patty or Kevin. They must have had to get up at seven-thirty, to be all dressed up and shaved and the children given their breakfast and made to look presentable. The O'Briens' car was nowhere to be seen, although it was probably parked somewhere near; but how had Kevin gotten his car, or had they all come to Mass in a taxi? The Fairbankses had driven the O'Briens home from Ethel Canning's party, somewhere around four o'clock, having persuaded Patty and Kevin that if they were picked up by the police, someone would lose his or her license. With the hangovers they must have, the O'Briens were still risky drivers, but the police never stopped anyone on Sunday morning. Come to think of it, Marge Fairbanks could not remember when she had seen a policeman this early on Sunday morning. A little later, yes, when all the churches would be holding services, but not at this hour.

She pulled up in front of Mr. Goldstein's store and got out. In this weather Goldstein kept the Sunday papers inside. In the summertime the papers were piled on boards in front of the store and you helped yourself, but on a sloppy day like this—rain, snow, gusts of wind—you had to go inside. Goldstein was standing behind the cigar counter.

"Good morning," said Marge Fairbanks.

"No papers," said Goldstein.

"What's the matter? A strike?" she said.

"Don't ask me, all I know is that they didn't deliver. You can have the advance stuff, but the news and sports sections you'll have to come back later."

"Have you any idea how soon they'll be here?"

"Don't ask *me*, Mrs. Fairbanks. Maybe an hour, maybe two hours."

"What do you mean, don't ask *you*? Who else *shall* I ask, if not you? You know I have to drive four miles in and four miles back."

"Lady, don't take it out on me," said Goldstein. "I ain't responsible *how* many miles you drive."

She left the store and got in the car. She was busy lighting a cigarette when there was a startling horn blast behind her. She looked in the mirror and said, "Oh, go to hell," and then recognized the car, Ralph Shipstead's Cadillac. He got out and walked to the Fiat.

"I just told you to go to hell," she said. "Don't you know it's Sunday morning, blowing your horn like that?"

"Jesus, do I know it's Sunday morning. Move over."

"No I won't. Get in the other side, if you want to."

He did so. "You haven't got another cigarette, have you?"

"Yes," she said. "Here."

"I came out without any."

"Well, Goldstein sells them. No papers, by the way."

"I know. I was around earlier and I went back to the house and then I came out without any cigarettes. I must have left them on—I don't know where I could have left them . . . *I* know, I was wearing a different coat. How do you feel?"

"I feel all right. I didn't have much to drink. I never do."

"Well, your boy Allan made up for it. Not to mention ten others. I saw Kevin O'Brien a few minutes ago, trying to park his car. He had a space big enough to park a trailer truck, but he couldn't make it today."

"He had his own car?"

"That's right, you gave them a ride home. Yes, he had his own car. They must have had to take a taxi to Ethel's."

"That was my guess, too. I saw them going into church."

"Then he finally got it parked. Are you going to wait around for the papers?"

"No, I have to go back and get breakfast for Allan."

"No hurry about that, is there?"

"No, but then I have to take the children to Sunday School."

"Thank God ours are away at school. Let's go for a ride."

"I can't. Finish your cigarette and then you have to get out."

"You don't go for me, do you, Marge?"

"Not really, I guess."

"Have you got somebody else—I don't mean Allan."

"No, but you don't think I'd tell you if I had."

"You might. I can't figure you."

"You don't know me. You've only been here a short time."

"Oh, it doesn't usually take me long."

"That's the trouble with you, if you don't mind my saying so. You find yourself irresistible."

"Well, at least you're giving me some plain talk, instead of that housewife routine. I know there's more there than just the housewife, but this is the first time you've ever really talked."

"There's nothing there for you, Ralph, so don't waste your time."

"You're really letting me have it, aren't you? What are you sore about? You're usually very polite and so forth."

"I hate to have people blow their horns at me."

"Mm. That's not it, but I see I'm doing myself no good. You going to be at the club this afternoon?"

"We might. I don't know."

"There's a football game on TV, and the reception's very good at the club. Bunch of us are going to be there. Few drinks. Maybe get up a pool. If you're lucky you might win a buck. I came away with two hundred dollars last week. A hat pool, based on the total score. All luck. You don't have to know anything about football."

"I never win."

"You might this time."

"Heavy *double entendre*."

"Well, what the hell, Marge? The way you said 'I never win.' That sounded like *double entendre*."

"Goodbye, Ralph."

"Thanks for the cigarette," he said.

She headed for home, thinking of her encounter with Ralph Shipstead. He was a loathsome man, who decorated his person with expensive haberdashery and surrounded himself with luxury, but never seemed quite dressed or established. It was not merely a matter of taste in his clothes or in the gadgeted house he had built, with its elaborate high-fi and heated pool and pitch-and-putt golf course. Nor was it that the money for it all had come to him. It was a more positive thing, that he belonged elsewhere, that he should

(353)

not have made money with his cleverness but with his muscles. If a pro football player could have made his kind of money, it would have seemed all right; but his money, she knew, had come from shrewd deals involving depletions and depreciations and dodges. At this moment he wanted her, and it excited her to think that in her present frame of mind he could almost have her. Almost.

She left the village behind her and began the slower drive along the narrow, twisting roads to her house. In a few minutes she was on Monument Road, more than a mile from her house but always when the car was once on Monument Road she would say to herself, "Practically home." She said it now, and she remembered that it was just about here less than an hour ago she had first sensed the involuntary act of defiance that she had made in taking the Fiat. She slowed down until the little car almost stalled, and she was angry with herself for abusing the engine. She stopped the car and switched off the engine, and she immediately understood this unusual act: she was delaying as long as possible her return to her house, and if anyone came along she would wave them on. She would not even offer a lame excuse. "Just go on and don't bother me," she would say—knowing that she would say nothing of the kind. But no one was likely to bother her at this hour. Between here and her house there were only the Martins, who never got their Sunday papers until after church; and the Greens, who always ate Sunday lunch at the club. What else did anyone want to know about the Martins and the Greens? She could tell them. Would anyone be interested to learn that Nannie Martin was thinking of changing to Presbyterian? Would the *Herald Tribune* send a reporter to interview Dixie Green if they knew that Dixie had once had a date with the gentleman who now sat in the White House?

She did not want to go home. The children would be up, messing around the kitchen, impatient because she had taken those few extra minutes to chat with Ralph Shipstead. And Allan would be in bed. Not really asleep, but not ready to get up. She knew how he would look when she went in to ask him if he wanted his breakfast: he would have his arms wrapped around a pillow and his pajamas would be drawn tight across his shoulder blades. Two hours ago he had made love to her and it had been all right. Oftener than not he made love to her on Sunday morning, and it was usually all right. Better than when he made love to her when they got home from a party like Ethel Canning's. After twelve years she had convinced him that she simply did not like to be made love to when he was tight. It had not actually taken twelve years to convince him of that. Twelve years was what they had been married. Five years was what it had taken her to convince him that alcohol did not make him a lover, and she conceded that in that respect he was considerate, even docile. Oh, in a lot of things he was considerate, when he was considerate. He was not mean, he was good about money, he was almost unquestionably faithful to her. By comparison he was a very good husband, and by comparison the children were dreams. But what was *she*, Marge Fairbanks? A secure wife, yes, and a conscientious mother, yes. But what else? But she, she, she? What was she, apart from husband and children, apart from Ralph Shipstead's mechanical lechery for her? And worst of all, what did she want, what could she be, other than what she had and what she was? Was this all? Was it worth it?

The drizzle on the windshield reminded her of tears, and she waited for the thought to bring the tears, but they did not come. She was not even that unhappy. She began to feel foolish and oddly conspicuous on this empty road. She sighed, and then turned the switch and pushed the starter button. The little car tried, but the engine would not start. She looked at the fuel gauge and the needle pointed to the far left. The son of a bitch! He hadn't even bothered to get gas.

She put the keys in her pocket and got out of the car, and as she began the homeward walk she kicked the front tire. It hurt her toe, and now she *could* cry, a little.

THE SUN-DODGERS

Back in the long nighttime of the Twenties and Thirties, when so many of the people I knew had jobs that made them sun-dodgers, Jack Pyne was known derisively as a mystery man. He was even called *the* mystery man, but it was not said in a way that would make you want to meet him or to inquire into the reason for calling him that. We all have our secrets, and Jack Pyne undoubtedly had his, but when he was referred to as a mystery man it was a term of contempt. In our set it was universally known that Jack Pyne made his living by peddling gossip to the Broadway columnists. They paid him no money, but Jack Pyne always had some chorus girls or bit players who paid him twenty-five dollars a week to get their names in the papers. The chatter writers would mention his clients in return for his acting as a spy or a messenger boy or procurer. You would be surprised to learn the names of some of the girls who once were clients of Jack Pyne. You might even be shocked and incredulous.

When business was good Jack Pyne sometimes had three or four clients, some of them paying him more than twenty-five dollars a week, and when business was exceptionally good Jack Pyne might have four individual clients, a second-rate night club, and a Broadway show. The night club seldom paid him any cash, but he was on the cuff there for meals and, within reason, free drinks for newspaper men. There were occasional periods when Jack Pyne probably had an income of close to two hundred dollars a week from the chorus girls and a hundred and fifty dollars a week as press agent for a musical comedy, in addition to the food and liquor he got free from the night clubs. It was in that way that he got the nickname of mystery man. "Who's Jack Pyne hustling for a buck now? The mystery man," someone once said. "Jack Pyne, the man of mystery."

We had favorite joints and favorite tables in the joints, and in the course of a single night, any night, we would move from a favorite table in one joint to a favorite table in one or two other joints, more or less according to a schedule. Jack Pyne always knew where we could be found at any hour between eleven P.M. and six o'clock in the morning. In our group there were, among the regulars, four or five newspaper men, a Broadway doctor, a Broadway attorney, one or two lyric-writers, a playwright, two or three press agents, a bookmaker, a detective from the Broadway Squad, sometimes a Catholic priest, a vaudeville actor turned sketch writer, a salesman for a meat packer, a minor poet, a real estate speculator, a radio announcer. At no time were all these men together at the same table, but they were the regulars of our group. There were other groups: the mobster group, the song-writing and music-publishing group, the gamblers, the minor hoods, and in the course of a night we might be visited briefly by members of the other groups, with the exception of the minor hoods. They kept to themselves because they did not want to go anywhere near a newspaper man; they did not want to be seen talking to a newspaper man. As a group, a class, they were the cruelest, stupidest, most evil men I have ever known, and I was afraid of them. I was not afraid of the big shots; they, with their new importance and power, generally behaved themselves in public, but the smallies, as we called the minor hoods, were unpredictable, reckless, and we knew the stories about them and their savagery. They were not all young men; some of them were in their forties and fifties, and I had a theory that the reason the older ones survived was that they had been out of circulation, in prison, and thus invulnerable to the high mortality rate among smallies.. It was not only a theory I had; some of them had been in prison before Prohibition went into effect and came out to find that highjacking and gang warfare paid better than armed robbery and felonious assault, and not only paid better but were safer in that prosecution had become more difficult and the mobs retained cleverer attorneys. A man who had gone to prison for homicide in 1916 and was released in ten years would discover that in his absence an almost ideal situation had been created. If he could make a connection with an established mob he might easily make a living on a standby basis, with nothing to do but remain on call until the mob had some punishment to dole out. And if the punishment involved murdering a member of an opposition mob, the legal authorities often could not or would not make an arrest. The smallies were killing each other off in private mob warfare, and if you noticed that one of the familiar faces was missing from the smallies' table, you could usually guess why. But you had to guess, most of the time. I didn't know many of them by name, although I knew them by sight, and even when their bodies were found in Bushwick or in Dutchess County, the newspaper photographs did not identify them for me. One man with half his face shot away and curled up in the back of a sedan looks much the same as another man who died in the same circumstances. A man

(359)

who had been soaked with gasoline as well as stabbed or shot might be the missing face from the smallies' table, but I could only guess.

When the tabloids came out with stories and pictures of a mobster's murder the regulars at our table postponed discussion of it, but we could not help looking at the smallies' table to see how they were taking it. Sometimes their table would be vacant, which usually meant that one or more of the smallies had been picked up by the police and the others were in hiding. The big shots were always at their own table, gabbing away as though nothing had happened, and probably from their point of view nothing had; the murder we were reading about had been ordered weeks before, and the actual killing was old hat to the big shots. This was New York, not Chicago, and it has never ceased to amaze me how few of the real big shots got killed. But of course there is the old saying that generals die in bed, too.

If we often stole glances at the smallies' table, they in turn spent a lot of time staring at us. Plainly they resented us and our presence; obviously they thought we did not belong in the same joints that they frequented—and in a way they were right, but we were sun-dodgers and had no place else to go. If they had had their way they could easily have got rid of us, and without working us over. I know I would not have gone to a joint after being warned off by a couple of those hoods. They had a neat trick of pushing a man to the sidewalk, laying his leg across the curbstone, and jumping on it. No guns, no knives, no acid. They had a hundred other tricks, too, to maim or cripple people, of either sex, who got in their way. But the big shots' visits to our table gave us a sort of *laissez-passer*, which, though it increased the smallies' resentment of our presence, protected us from abuse. I must qualify that statement a little bit: they would not have abused the detective from the Broadway Squad. *He* abused *them*, sometimes beat them up just to keep in practice. But he was a special case, a terrifying man with fist and boot, and not really one of our group. Two things were always, always said of Tommy Callaghan: he was a law unto himself, and he led a charmed life. He has been written about in articles and in fiction, and I think there was even a movie that was more or less based on his career. His attitude and policy were expressed very simply. "I hate hoods," he would say, and he made no distinction between the big shots and the smallies. One of the biggest of the big shots always had to tip his hat to Tommy Callaghan, no matter where they ran into each other; at the fights in the Garden, at the race track, or in a hotel lobby. But this is not a repetition of the legend of Tommy Callaghan. In this chronicle he plays a minor part, and having introduced him I will go on until I need him later in the story.

However, since I have been rambling along with digressions where I felt like making them, I want to put in a warning to those readers who may still retain an impression of those days and those people that may be charming, but has nothing to do with the truth. Broadway really was not populated by benevolent bookmakers who gave all their money to the Salvation Army, and bootleggers who were always looking around for a paraplegic newsboy who needed surgery, and crapshooters who used their tees and miss-outs—crooked dice—in order to finance a chapel. There is something about the words rogue and rascal that brings a smile to the eyes of people who never spent any time with rogues and rascals. And I have never been able to accept the paradox of the prostitute who was faithful to one man. The big shots and the smallies that I saw—and I saw dozens of them—were unprincipled, sadistic, murderous bullies; often sexually perverted, diseased, sometimes drug addicts, and stingy. The women were just as bad, except when they were worse. The picture of a band of jolly Robin Hoods on Times Square is all wrong and not very romantic to those who knew that perhaps the most spectacular gambler of them all was nothing but a shylock—a usurer—and a fixer. And now back to Jack Pyne.

The joint that usually was our last stop before going home was a place called The Leisure Club, Fiftieth Street near Eighth Avenue, on the second story. It had several things to recommend it: it stayed open until nine o'clock in the morning; it was considered neutral territory by the important mob leaders; the booze was basically good liquor that had been cut only once; and it was not expensive. The Leisure offered no entertainment more elaborate than a colored piano player who also sang dirty songs. His name was Teeth, the only thing he would answer to. He played quite good piano, in spite of not having eighty-eight notes to work with. It was a studio piano, and he had to be inventive to do right by Youmans and Gershwin and Kern on an abbreviated keyboard. The dirty songs were the work of anonymous composers, and they were the same dirty songs that could be heard in little joints all over town, or parodies of songs by Cole Porter and Noel Coward. It was rather high-class stuff for a joint like The Leisure, most of it too subtle for the big shots and the smallies, but their girl friends liked it.

The Leisure had not caught on with the Park Avenue-Junior League-Squadron A crowd, probably because they would be flocking to Harlem at just about the same hour that The Leisure was showing signs of action. In any event, The Leisure was strictly a Broadway joint, not for post-debutantes or squash players. It was for show people, newspaper men, various kinds of hustlers, and mobsters, in addition to the regulars whom I have already mentioned. Since for most of the customers it was the last place before going home, it was usually well filled, with no new male faces from night to night. There were, of course, new girls from the musical comedies and other night clubs, and women who had come in from out of town; but some of these girls and women soon became steady customers too.

At The Leisure our group gathered at a booth in the middle of a row of booths. When we were more than nine in number the waiters would put a table against the booth table as an extension, but that seldom was necessary. We hardly ever numbered fewer than five or more than nine, and eight was the most comfortable; four on each side of the table and two at the open end. I describe the seating arrangements because I never saw anyone make room for Jack Pyne. If he joined our table, he had to sit at the open end. And I never heard anyone actually ask him to sit down.

He would come in, say a few words to the hatcheck girl, and head for our table. "Hello, there, you muggs," he would say.

Somebody would say, "Jack," and the others would nod—or not nod. There was one fellow, a newspaper reporter, who would be a bit more loquacious. "Why, hello there, Jack. We were just talking about you."

"Oh, yeah? What'd you say?"

"Just saying what a great fellow you were. We just got finished taking a vote."

"Come off it."

"On the level. We're raising a little purse to send you on a trip. Where would you rather go, Jack? Devil's Island? You speak French, don't you, Jack?"

"Lay off, lay off, you muggs."

There was no insult he would not take, whether it concerned his honesty, his morals, his manhood, his appearance, or his methods of earning a living. The newspaper reporter who suggested Devil's Island (and who had first called him a mystery man) would mention an extraordinary sexual perversion and suddenly say, "What's it like, Jack? I hear that's what you go for." Always, when they were making a fool of him, he would pretend to think they were kidding him, as though they would only kid a man they were fond of. But it was all insulting, often straight-factual, and finally not very funny. We all had a crack at insulting Jack Pyne, but he was so totally lacking in self-respect and so completely unable or unwilling to make any kind of retort that we finally did lay off, and he became a bore. I think we began to hate him then. He was a bore, and a terribly cheap individual, and because we had given up the mean sport of insulting him, he convinced himself that he was one of the boys.

We all read the same newspapers and heard the same gossip, and that went for Jack Pyne. He had the same information we had out of the newspapers, but now he had opinions as well. He was one of the boys, and he would hold forth on politics and sports and other topics of the day, and I've never known anyone who could be so consistently wrong about everything. We would sit in glassy-eyed silence while he told us what he thought was going to happen at City Hall or the Polo Grounds or the Garden. And why. If there were only four or five of us at the table we would fiddle with matchbooks, make rings on the table with our highball glasses, and neither look at Jack nor say a word to him. Then when he had said his say we would resume talking, but not about the topic Jack had just discussed. We would not agree with him, we would not contradict him; we would simply ignore all he had said. Almost literally we were giving him the freeze. When our group was larger, when there were so many of us that the waiter added the extra table, Jack Pyne was no problem. The larger group always meant that one of the Broadway columnists was present, and Jack Pyne knew better than to interrupt their monologs. The Broadway columnists were his gods, his heroes—and his bread and butter.

You may wonder why we put up with Jack Pyne. The answer is easy: in the beginning he had been a pathetic clown, and later there was no way to get rid of him. And I guess we were not very selective on the late shift. The meat salesman was no Wilson Mizner, the radio announcer no Oliver Herford, the Broadway doctor no James Abbott MacNeill Whistler. We did not pretend to be the Algonquin Round Table, and there was no test of wit that a man had to pass to be welcome in our group. We were brought together by the circumstances of our jobs and their unconventional hours, and the attraction of convivial drinking. The married men among us never brought their wives, and the rest of us rarely brought a girl. Our conversation would have bored women, and women would have inhibited our conversation. From this distance I could not repeat one of our conversations, not so much because the talk was rough—although it was that—as because it was so immediately topical. It was lively, but evanescent, and the interruptions by Jack Pyne only gave us a chance to get our breath.

Then one night—say around four o'clock in the morning—the character of our meetings began to change. It was not something we noticed at the time, but I know now that the change began when one of the smallies came to our table and said to Jack Pyne, "Hey, Pincus, I want to talk to you." Jack got up and followed the gangster to an empty table. They talked for five minutes or so, and Jack came back to our table and the gangster returned to his group.

"Who's your friend, Jack?" said the newspaper reporter. "I don't remember seeing him before. Don't want to see him again, either."

"I went to school with him. We grew up together," said Jack Pyne.

"He didn't look as if he went to school very long."

"No. I knew him in sixth grade. Seventh grade. Around then," said Jack Pyne.

"He's been away?"

"I'll say he has. He was doing five to ten up the river. He only got out about a month ago."

"What was the rap, Jack?"

"Why, I guess it was felonious assault. I didn't ask him, but I remember hearing about it. I think he was up twice. I don't know. I don't know for sure."

"He knew you. He made you the minute you came in tonight."

"Yeah. Yeah, I guess he did. I guess he was kind of expecting me."

"What has he, got some little broad he wants you to get her picture in the paper?"

"I didn't say that, did I?" said Jack Pyne.

"You didn't say anything, but that's a pretty good guess, isn't it? Your fame has spread far and wide, Jack. You're getting somewhere. Who's the broad? We'll find out, so don't be coy."

"Ella Haggerty. She's in the Carroll show."

"Mixed up with a hood like that? She does better than that, Jack."

"Not now she doesn't, and she better not. He's stuck on her."

"She doesn't need you to get her picture in the paper. I know Ella. You guys know Ella Haggerty."

Some of us did, and some of us didn't.

"I know her myself," said Jack Pyne. "She recommended me. She told Ernie to hire me, and Ernie said he went to school with me."

"Small world. What's Ernie's last name?"

"Black, he goes by. Ernie Black. It used to be Schwartz."

"Well, what the hell? Mine used to be Vanderbilt, but Buckley's easier to remember. I'll tell you something, Jack. Your friend Ernie, whether it's Black or Schwartz, he's got himself a very expensive lady friend."

"I know that."

"You know whose girl she was for a couple of years."

"I know."

"And where he had her living and all that? Those fur coats and diamonds."

"I been to her apartment. I know all that," said Jack Pyne.

"You know all that. Then what's she doing with some smallie like this Ernie Black? You don't go from J. Richard Hammersmith to some cheap hood just out of stir."

"She did."

"She did, but you better find out why, and you better get your money in advance. The way I see it, Jack, you've got nothing but trouble ahead of you. This coffee-and-cakes mobster, he hasn't got enough dough to keep her in bath salts. So he's going to have to get big all of a sudden, and how do you get big in his racket? You know as well as I do. From where he is, you start by killing somebody. That's the only way to make a fast big score. Homicide."

"I know, I know," said Jack Pyne.

"And even then you don't get rich, unless you happen

to kill somebody very big. And if you kill somebody very big, you end up very dead. Jack, you ought to get out of this contract as quickly and as gracefully as you can."

"I can't," said Pyne. "I made a contract."

"Then leave town."

"Sure. Where would I go? My show closed Saturday and I got expenses."

"Well, if you don't want to take my advice, that's up to you," said Buckley.

"Who's the banker tonight?" said Jack Pyne.

"I am," I said.

Jack tossed me a five-dollar bill. "I had two drinks. Give me three bucks change."

I did so, and he left.

"You know," said Buckley. "I wouldn't be surprised if I accomplished something tonight. I think we finally got rid of the mystery man."

"Is that what you were doing?" I said.

"Sure. Everything I said was true, but Pyne hadn't looked at it that way. It just needed me to point out certain disadvantages."

Buckley was entirely correct. Days, then weeks, then years passed, and no more was seen of Jack Pyne. It was as though the sewer had swallowed him up. Our group, I have said, changed in character, and I may be putting too much emphasis on the effect Jack Pyne's disappearance produced. But there is no use denying the coincidence that the only time we were visited by one of the smallies, one of our number disappeared. We didn't talk about the coincidence, but one of the smallies had invaded our territory despite the implied protection we enjoyed from the big shots.

Several months after Jack Pyne vanished a body was fished out of the East River. It was identified as Ernie Black,

né Schwartz, and the mutilations indicated to police that
Black had been tortured in gangster fashion. I advanced the
theory that we might soon be welcoming Jack Pyne back to
the fold, but I was wrong. Wherever he had gone, he liked
it better than The Leisure, and not long after that The
Leisure itself was raided and permanently closed. We had
to find a new late spot, and in so doing we lost some of our
group and recruited some newcomers. Then I changed jobs
and got married and moved to Great Neck, and began leading a very different life from the one I had known.

That was more than thirty years ago. We have grandchildren now, and my wife and I last year bought a little
house near Phoenix, Arizona. I have my retirement pay, a
few securities, and an unsteady income from my writing. I
occasionally sell a piece to a magazine and I have written
two books, one of which did well as a paperback. Our two
daughters are married and living in the East, and until
about a month ago it looked as though we had it made.
We liked Arizona; the climate suited us, we made new
friends, we had no money worries, the future looked good.
So did the past. Our new friends seemed to be entertained
by my reminiscences of the old days, and now and then I
could convert my reminiscences into an honest buck. For
instance, I wrote a story about Ella Haggerty that I sold
as fiction but was almost straight fact. Ella married a clar-
inet player in 1930 or '31 and shortly after that dropped
out of sight. The piano player from The Leisure, the man
known as Teeth, went to Paris, France, during the depression and became a great hit. He was married briefly to an
English lady of title, and after World War II he was
awarded the Medal of Resistance, which must have amused
him as much as it did me. I had a letter from him in 1939.
He was thinking of writing his memoirs even then, and he

particularly called my attention to his new name—Les Dents. "It sounds like 'let's dance' if you pronounce it English style but I talk mostly French these days," he wrote. Only one of the former big shots is still alive. He is living, I believe, in Hot Springs, Arkansas. My friend Buckley, the newspaper reporter, was killed in the War. He and another correspondent, riding in a jeep in Italy, hit a land mine. His old paper established the Buckley Scholarship at a school of journalism, a memorial he would object to as he hated the very word journalism. My friends of the old days who have survived are in the minority, and Madge and I have our aches and pains as well as the obituary pages to remind us of the passage of time, but things were going all right until last month, when one afternoon Madge came to my workroom and said a man wanted to see me. "Who is he?" I said.

"I didn't ask him his name, but he wanted to make sure you had worked on the old New York *World*."

"Probably a touch," I said.

I went out to our tiny patio, and a man got up to greet me. He was wearing a white sombrero, the kind that costs about seventy-five dollars, and a gabardine coat and trousers that in the West they call a stockman's suit. "You don't remember me?"

"I'm afraid I don't," I said.

"Well, I shouldn't have expected you to. It's a long, long time," he said. Then, suddenly, he said: "Jack Pyne."

"Jack Pyne," I repeated. *"Jack Pyne?"*

"You think I was dead?"

"As a matter of fact I did," I said.

"Now you recognize me?"

"Yes, of course," I said. "Sit down. What can I get you to drink?"

"Not a thing," he said. "I just happened to hear in a

roundabout way that you were living out here, so I took it in my head to look you up. I bought your book. You must be coining money. I see it every place I go. Airports. Drug stores. You coulda cut me in." He smiled to show he was joking. "I reccanized Ella Haggerty, and I said to my wife, I said I introduced him to her."

"But you didn't," I said.

"I know I didn't, but it impressed the hell out of my missus. Like we took a trip over to Europe a couple of years ago, and did you ever hear of the famous entertainer, Les Dents? You know who that is?"

"Yes. Teeth, from the old Leisure Club."

"Oh, you knew that. Well, he remembered me right off. I was twenty pounds lighter then. Good old Teeth. He sat and talked with the wife and I for a couple hours, and all those French people and the international set, they couldn't figure out who we were."

"What are you doing now, Jack?"

"Well, I got a couple of things going for me. Different things. I got my money all invested in various enterprises. I only live about ten miles from here. You ought to come and take a look at my place. You have a car, don't you? Or I could send one for you."

"We have a car," I said. "But, Jack, what ever happened to you? You just disappeared into thin air."

"You mean way back? Oh, I just took it into my head one night, what was I wasting my time sitting around those night spots. So I sold my business—"

"What business?"

He shook his head somewhat pityingly. "Jack Pyne. I had one of the first if not *the* first really successful public relations concerns. You know, your memory ain't as good as it ought to be. I noticed a couple things in your book. Sure it was fiction, but you sure did take a lot of liberties.

I mean, didn't you know Ella was my girl? I kept that dame for three years. She cost me a fortune. Maybe you were afraid I'd sue you for libel, but that's not the way I operate. I told my wife, I said this book was about an old girl friend of mine. That was before I read the book, and then she asked me which one was me and I said I guess you were afraid I'd sue you for libel. I wouldn't take an old friend into court. You ought to know me better than that."

"Well, I'll put you in my next book."

"No, don't do that. You don't have to make amends. But you and your wife come out and have dinner at my house and I'd like to straighten you out on those days. You remember Pete Buckley?"

"Sure."

"Always pestering me to meet Ella, but I said to him one night, I was glad to help him out any time he needed a send-in with one of those underworld characters. I knew them all. But it was one thing to tell my mob friends a guy was all right, and a very different story to introduce a thirty-five-dollar-a-week police reporter to my girl. I sent them a cheque when they had that memorial for Pete. Very sarcastic when he made his load, but a great newspaper man when he was sober. Great. No doubt about it." He stood up. "Old pal, I gotta see a couple executives downtown, but you and I are going to have a lot of fun together, cutting up the old touches. Right?"

We have not gone to his house, although we have heard it is one of the showplaces. But we see him a great deal. A great deal. He has found out where we are and he knows when we'll be home. It is a sad thing after so many years to have a house you love seem to turn into a night club table. Suddenly I miss Pete Buckley, too.

(372)

THINGS YOU
REALLY WANT

It was Friday, and because it was Friday, promptly at three o'clock the doorman announced that Mr. Miles's station wagon was at the door, and Mrs. Miles's personal maid told the doorman that They would be right down. And in a very few minutes They *were* down: Elsie Miles in her blue windowpane tweed cape and black beret; George Miles in his trench coat with hood and his Tyrolean hat. The motor was running; the heater was functioning. The doorman, Jim, saw to it that the wicker hamper and Mrs. Miles's Noah bag, her small black suitcase, and Mr. Miles's old cowhide and new pigskin attaché cases were nicely arranged on the floor of the station wagon.

"You didn't forget anything?" said George Miles.

"No," said Elsie Miles.

"Well, Jim, we're off," said George Miles.

"Have a nice weekend," said Jim.

George Miles pointed to a double-parked car just ahead. "One of our doctors left his motor running," he said.

"Yes sir, he does that," said Jim. "They all got something on their minds."

"Don't you think you'd better turn it off? Leaving a car unattended, with the motor running."

"He'll only give me a bawling-out," said Jim.

"Next time a police car comes around, just point to the doctor's Pontiac. You don't have to say anything. Just point. They'll take the hint. I think it's outrageous."

"Dangerous, all right," said Jim. "I guess you can pull out now, Mr. Miles. Nothing coming."

"So long, Jim," said George Miles.

"Goodbye, Jim," said Elsie Miles.

"Nice weekend," said Jim.

The next westbound street was two blocks north, and George Miles drove to it in silence. There he was stopped by a traffic light. "Doctors of all people ought to observe the rules," he said.

"No, there's no excuse for it," said Elsie Miles.

"What?"

"I said there was no excuse for it, the way that car was parked."

"Absolutely no excuse," said George Miles. "Aside from all the obvious dangers. Car running away. Some kid stealing it. And filling the air with carbon monoxide. It's the attitude of these doctors."

"Hey, station wagon. Get the lead out!" The driver of the car behind blew his horn and yelled, and Elsie Miles giggled.

"The light's changed," she said.

"Christ, *I* know it," said George Miles.

He did not again speak to her. They crossed Manhattan Island and the George Washington Bridge and more than half the width of New Jersey without saying a word.

"I forgot something," he said.

"You did? What?" she said.

"Aren't you going to gloat over it? *I* forgot something, instead of you?"

"I'm not going to gloat. What did you forget? Is it important enough to go back for?"

"It's important, but I'll be damned if I go back for it," he said. "It's my medicine."

"Your pills? Well then of course we'll go back. I'll drive if you want me to."

"Forget it."

"Not at all forget it. Let's watch for a pay station and the next one we see, we can stop and call the apartment and have Roger bring it out in the other car."

"I let him go home after lunch."

"Then let's just call him at home. He only lives out in Jackson Heights. Dear knows it won't kill him to work a few extra hours. You pay him enough."

"The company pays him."

"Well, then, he *gets* paid enough, whoever pays him."

"Oh, Roger puts in plenty of extra time," he said. "I have a more sensible idea."

"What?"

"When we get to Stroudsburg I'll stop in a doctor's office and get him to give me a prescription. It's just nitroglycerin. If he wants additional information he can phone Jack Cushman."

"Yes, I must say that makes more sense." She looked at him in the late afternoon light. "Do you feel all right?"

"Elsie, I wouldn't be at the wheel if I felt some kind of an attack coming on. I feel fine except that I feel embarrassed. I pride myself on not forgetting things, and I forgot the most important thing I own. Anyway, the most important when I need it."

"There's something I've been meaning to do, and when we get back Monday I'm going to do it," she said.

"What's that?"

"I'm going to ask Jack Cushman to write out a prescription for me. Your pills. And I'm going to carry it with me all the time, wherever we go."

"This is the first time I ever forgot them."

"I didn't intend that as any criticism of you, George. I'm going to ask Jack for two prescriptions. I'm going to have one filled, and carry the pills with me. And I'll save the other prescription."

"All right," he said.

The doctor in Stroudsburg was not in his office, but when he heard that the transient patient was George R. Miles he cut short his supper and arrived at the office in fifteen minutes. He was familiar with the kind of pills George R. Miles had left behind, but to be on the safe side he telephoned Dr. Cushman. "I've had the pleasure of meeting Dr. Cushman, but perhaps you'd better speak to him first," said Dr. Reeber.

"Jack, I'm sorry to trouble you, but I came away without my dynamite pills. I'm in Dr. Reeber's office, in Stroudsburg, P-A. I'm okay, but I didn't want to go up in the woods without the pills. Dr. Reeber is right here. I'll put him on."

Dr. Reeber was a study in dignified restraint, with the great John Cushman at the other end of the line, and George R. Miles in his office. He wrote out the prescription while talking with Cushman. "Thank you, Dr. Cushman. Pleasure talking to you again." Reeber tore the prescription off the blank and handed it to George R. Miles.

"How much do I owe you, Doctor?"

"Nothing. I wouldn't charge you anything—"

"Now, now, now, now, now, Doctor. I took you away from your supper, not to mention two long distance calls. I insist."

"Well—ten dollars."

"Ridiculous," said George Miles. "Make it a hundred dollars and send me a bill." He gave his address.

"Very well, Mr. Miles. I'll send you a bill," said Dr. Reeber. "You and Mrs. Miles on your way up to your camp?"

"Yes, we go there every weekend we possibly can."

"I've hunted over your land. I got a deer there last fall."

"Well, there're plenty of them."

"Yes, Senator Rossbach is a friend of mine."

"Oh, is Karl a friend of yours? You must get him to bring you up there when the trout season opens. You tell him I said to bring you, and be sure and stop in at the cabin. I've had to curtail my fishing and gunning the last couple of years, ever since I sprained my ankle. But we're there nearly every weekend that the roads are clear, October right through June. Then of course we go to the seashore. Well, Dr. Reeber, thank you very much, and don't forget about that bill."

"I'll say goodbye to Mrs. Miles," said the doctor.

Another half hour was wasted in having the prescription filled and in chatter with the pharmacist, who had immediately recognized the name of Reeber's patient. "That'll be fourteen dollars," said the pharmacist. "Be glad to send you a bill, if you like, Mr. Miles."

"Whatever you say," said George Miles. "Send it to the camp, or my New York address."

"Well, I guess you pay your bills from New York," said the pharmacist. "We'll open an account for you, with the address on the prescription."

"Thank you. Goodnight."

"Come in again," said the pharmacist.

Once more they were under way. "It's nice to be known," said Elsie.

"It has its advantages sometimes," he said. "As long as you remember it's the almighty dollar and not your own personal charm."

"Don't be so cynical, George."

"It's not cynical. It's just being realistic. You weren't in there to see Dr. Reeber when he was talking to Jack Cushman. You could see the wheels going around in his head. Apparently he's met Jack Cushman, without making much of an impression. But this time he has me in his office with him, and the next time he meets Jack you can bet he's going to mention tonight's little consultation."

"Other doctors worship Jack Cushman."

"Of course they do. I admire Jack, too. But let's face it, Elsie, I couldn't have got Jack on the phone so quickly if I'd been Joe Blow from Kokomo. Jack knows who I am, don't forget. Just as I know who Jack is and where he stands in his profession. He wouldn't be my doctor if he were just another Reeber."

"George, for all you know, Dr. Reeber may be hiding his light under a bushel."

"For all I know, but *you* don't believe that. Not for a minute, not for a fraction of a second."

"Well—maybe he was over-polite, but this must have been a big day for him. You as a patient, and having a conversation with the great John Cushman. Are you getting hungry?"

"Yes, and I'm looking forward to my four ounces of bourbon. I may even have five ounces. What have we got in the hamper?"

"You'll see when we get there."

"You always say that."

"You always ask the question," she said.

(*378*)

The caretaker had left everything ready for their arrival; logs and kindling in the fireplaces, ice cubes in the bucket, night lights on in cellar and hallways. "Otto never forgets a thing," said George Miles. "I think when I step down I'll make him chairman of the board."

"Well, if you do, I hope you can sneak me into the first meeting."

"Listen, Otto has such dignity that he could almost carry it off. Put him in a good suit, spend a few dollars in the barber shop. We have men on the board that don't look the part one bit more than Otto does. I suppose I could take him to one meeting and introduce him as the man from Krupp's and get away with it. But that will never happen."

"Why not?"

"Because Otto wouldn't do it. No matter how much I offered to pay him, he wouldn't sacrifice his dignity. In fact, he'd probably tell me to go to hell. When you're as good as Otto, you *can* tell people to go to hell. *I* can't tell people to go to hell, but Otto Lichtenwalner can. Do you realize that all Otto really needs is a hatchet?"

"And a gun."

"No, he doesn't need a gun. With a hatchet or an axe he can make a bow and arrows, with a bow he can start a fire. He can build lean-tos wherever he's going to need them. He can converse in two languages. He can have a well-balanced diet without poisoning himself. Salt-free, too."

"Don't start envying Otto. You go through this about once a year, usually when something's gone wrong at the office. What is it now?"

"Nothing special. Will you have your drink now, or when supper's ready?"

"You have yours and I'll get mine later. You can set the table, if you like," she said.

"That's one thing Otto does forget."

"Deliberately, I think."

"A subtle way of telling us to go to hell. Probably considers it woman's work."

George Miles set the table in the large room, which was furnished in cedar and oaken chairs and sofas, Navajo rugs and animal trophies. He lit the fire, poured a drink, and in five minutes of heat from the blaze he fell asleep with the empty glass in his hand.

She let him sleep for an hour. She had her own drink and a couple of cigarettes. She blew some smoke from the second cigarette under his nostrils, and he opened his eyes. He smiled. "Up to your old tricks," he said. "That'll always wake me. You could have a brass band in here, and I'd sleep through it. But one whiff of cigarette smoke. How long was I out?"

"Just over an hour, I think. About an hour."

"I needed that."

"I know you did, but now come and have supper. Go wash your face and don't go back to sleep, George."

"I could just close my eyes and not move till eight o'clock tomorrow morning."

"And be stiff as a board the whole weekend. Anyway, I'm hungry, so come on, please. Up, up."

"The chairman of the board as stiff as a board. Did I do any talking?" He rose and stretched, went to the kitchen and doused his face in cold water.

"The usual muttering. Why, did you dream?"

"Something about that doctor in Stroudsburg. He was telling me to go to hell and I wanted to hit him, but when I swung at him he drove away in an empty car. An empty car. I knew he was in the car, but I couldn't see him. Nobody was at the wheel."

"It makes more sense than most of your dreams."

"They make a lot of sense, but I can't put them into words. I forget them as soon as I begin to wake up." He laughed. "Then Jim, the doorman, he began telling me to go to hell. I thought at first it was Otto, but then I realized it was Jim."

"Put some more cold water on your face and come have your supper," she said.

"Oh, squab. Good," he said. "We haven't had that for a long time. Tomorrow let's take a walk down to the lower dam and see what the ice did to the footbridge. Last year, remember, the ice broke it in two."

"Was it last year?" she said.

"No, you're right. It was the year before. *No*, Elsie, I'm right. It was last year."

"I guess it *was* last year."

"Oh, yes. It was definitely last year. Do you want me to prove it to you?"

"I take your word for it," she said.

"It was last year because I wanted to go to work and fix it myself, but I was having to take it easy."

"On account of your sprained ankle," she said. "Why did you have to tell Dr. Reeber you had a sprained ankle?"

"How did you know I told him that?"

"He mentioned it when he was saying goodbye to me. You were putting on your coat."

"Well, why not tell him I had a sprained ankle? That's what I tell everybody."

"That's all right to tell people that don't know any better, but Dr. Reeber is a *doctor*. He *prescribed* for you. He knows you haven't got a sprained ankle."

"I might have a sprained ankle too, as well as a cardiac condition. There's no law of nature that says you can't have both."

"It's so unnecessary, making up stories. Eisenhower had that big operation. Ill-etis. Ill-eyetis. And Johnson, the Vice-President, everybody knows he has a heart condition. Even Kennedy, as young as he is, he was in the hospital for a year."

"That was his back. Elsie, let me handle my own illnesses. Let me decide how much my stockholders should know and shouldn't know. I'm perfectly willing to step down when I reach sixty, and not a word of complaint from me. If they started rooting out all the board chairmen that are in worse shape than I am, you'd see a real industrial revolution in this country."

"I don't know anything about that, George. All I know is you go to extremes to try to prove how healthy you are. Coming here every weekend—does Jack Cushman prescribe that? The long drive, in all kinds of weather?"

"Hap McTaggart drives down to Southampton every weekend, just about the same distance. And he's out there banging away at ducks. Playing poker for high stakes. And the food and the booze he puts away! Yet *he* has a cardiac condition."

"Maybe Rose McTaggart doesn't care what happens to *her* husband."

"Well, if you put it that way I guess I can't argue with you. And maybe if I were married to Rose, I'd just as soon conk out in a duck blind. Maybe that's what Hap's doing, I don't know. But *I'm* not. I take very good care of myself. I don't overdo. And coming here weekends, just the two of us, I figure another fifteen months before I step down. These weekends and two long vacations, enough rest and relaxation from tension."

"Then hereafter don't bring two attaché cases full of business papers."

"Only one full of business papers. The other, the old one, that has other things in it."

"I can imagine what other things. The George R. Miles Foundation. The Phi Gamma Delta scholarship."

"Those things relax me. Some men like mystery stories. They bore the pants off of me . . . How many of these little birds did you cook?"

"Two."

"I could eat another. See? My appetite's fine. Elsie, I think you're the one that needs to relax."

"Only when we come here. I'm relaxed the rest of the week."

"Well, another year and a half, fifteen months, and we can both relax at the same time. I want to go to Hong Kong. I want to go to Hong Kong, and I want to spend three weeks in Scotland. I'd like to spend all fall at Ann Arbor, just watching the team develop. Get to know the individual players. Like to see more of the grandchildren. And I want to read up on the Civil War. Not just the battles. I want to decide for myself what the economic factors were. For instance, did you ever know that there was a hell of a ruckus outside of the Somerset Club? The Somerset Club, in *Boston*, because some of the members objected to a parade going by, and they pulled down the shades. That's Boston, mind you. A parade of soldiers on their way to fight the Confederates. They say it was worse than the time the old Union Club displayed a Union Jack during a St. Patrick's Day parade. I want to look into all these things, things I never had time for. You'd enjoy Hong Kong, wouldn't you?"

"Of course I would."

"And seeing more of the grandchildren. And with a name like Stewart, you'd enjoy Scotland. Maybe we ought to use your maiden name while we're there. If we were

Spanish, you know, our kids would be called Miles y Stewart. Not the letter *e*. The letter y, Spanish for *and*. Miles and Stewart."

"I know," she said.

"Do you want help with the dishes?"

"No thanks, not tonight."

"You sure?"

"Positive," she said. She stood up and looked at him. "Do you know what I wish you *would* do for me?"

"What?"

She looked at him again, and knew she could not say what she had intended to say. "Buy me something."

"You mean something in particular?"

"Yes."

"What?"

"A nice pin, with a ruby in it."

He laughed. "Got it all picked out, eh?"

"Yes," she said.

"All right," he said. "I don't see why not. There aren't many things you really want, are there?"

"Not many," she said.

TWO TURTLEDOVES

O'Brien rose from his chair, folded his newspaper, took off his glasses and reached for a bottle of rye, saying, "The same?"

"The same it'll be," said Kane. "Don't hardly seem worth staying open."

"Oh, we'd a good crowd earlier," said O'Brien, filling a shot glass. "A lot of them went home to watch the midnight Mass on TV."

Kane grinned. "Why don't you have your own set on? You'd of kept them here."

"That I won't have. One or two suggested it, but a saloon is no place to be watching Mass."

"I was only joking," said Kane.

"Why's it you're not home watching?" said O'Brien.

"Christmas Eve's no different to any other in my line of work," said Kane. "I just come from a lady's apartment over on the Boulevard. One of her kids dropped a whole wad of wrapping paper, thick heavy stuff, down the bowl. There was water half an inch deep all over the bathroom floor."

"How would she know your home phone number?"

"I got an answering service."

"Oh, sure. I never thought of that."

"Wait'll she sees her bill," said Kane.

"You're gonna give it to her good?"

"She can afford it. One of them apartments with three bathrooms, over on the Boulevard."

"I can remember when there was only private houses there. The Park Avenue of Jersey City."

"Not that I minded going out. The wife has her two sisters and their husbands to our place. Trimming the tree. Trimming the *tree!* You should see the size of the tree. It's no more than thirty inches high and it ain't even wood. Some kind of a plastic proposition. You could trim it in ten minutes' work. But you've a nice tree, Bob."

"Not as big as some I had in years past, but it's a nice spruce."

"Who trimmed it for you?"

"The day fellows. It's been up over a week."

"It's over a week since I was in."

"Drink up and have one," said O'Brien, with the rye bottle poised.

"Well, bein's it's Christmas. Merry Christmas, Bob."

"The same to you and many of them, John. I think I'll have one myself," said O'Brien.

"This is an occasion."

"I think I'll close up early. I was expecting some of the lads from the post office, but it don't look like they're coming after all."

"It don't always pay to be accommodating."

"Oh, I wasn't only waiting for them," said O'Brien. He lowered his voice. "I got a man and a woman in the back room in one of the booths. They been there since before ten o'clock."

"You'd think they'd go to a hotel."

"Oh, there's none of that. I won't have that in my place. These are just a man and woman in their forties, sitting there and talking and looking at one another."

"Do you know them?"

"I seen him come in once in a while. She's a stranger to me. He come in a little before ten and went straight back to the back room, and then a few minutes later she drove up in a taxi. Nobody here knew her or him. And now they been sitting and talking for over three hours. Well, just about three hours. There's nothing going on. They ain't even sitting on the same side of the table, and a couple times I went in and they weren't even talking."

"Well, you're accommodating *them*. Does it pay?"

"You mean are they spending? Well, they got a bottle of good Scotch on the table, and they bit quite a hole out of it, and take a look at this." O'Brien reached in his vest pocket and held up a neatly folded fifty-dollar bill. "For Christmas, he says, but it ain't for Christmas. It's for leaving them be."

"Nobody around here gives fifty-dollar bills to saloon-keepers," said Kane. "You don't know what he does for a living?"

"He looks like some kind of a professional man. A lawyer, maybe, or a doctor. A professional man, though."

"A politician?"

O'Brien grinned. "Oho, no. Is there a politician I don't know?"

"Maybe mixed up in one of the rackets?"

"I thought of that, but other times when he come in he didn't seem to be acquainted with the racket guys. He never spoke to them and they never had anything to say to him."

"A man of mystery."

"Not even that. I size him up for a professional man, and him and her wanted to be together on Christmas Eve."

"Where was the taxi from?" said Kane. "From around here?"

"I didn't take notice to that, I was too busy. I just happened to see her get out and come right in. I guess she paid the driver before she got out."

"Very likely gave him a bill and told him to keep the change," said Kane.

"Very likely."

"You aroused my curiosity. Is it all right if I go back and have a look at them?"

"If you want to. But now don't interfere with them or anything like that. He gave me the fifty bucks."

"Listen, I won't bother them. I just want to have a look."

Kane sauntered to the back room and returned in a minute or so, shaking his head. "Never saw him or her before in me whole life. But I think she's getting a crying jag on."

"No," said O'Brien. "She looked that way two hours ago. It's no jag."

"A married woman and he wants her to leave her husband," said Kane.

"Maybe."

"Two people that promised to meet each other every Christmas Eve."

"Maybe that. I don't know."

"Or maybe they never seen one another before this afternoon and he's on the make."

"That I don't believe."

"Me either, but anything's possible. Maybe they used to be husband and wife."

"Yes, that I thought of. One of them married again but one not."

"I got a brother a detective in Paterson, but my wife says I should of been the detective and him the plumber . . . She's no hooker."

"No, I can spot them. This woman's no hooker."

"I didn't think so, either. Anyway, a hooker'd have a room to take him to."

"One look'd tell you she was no hooker."

"Does he have a car? You could tell something from that if he had a car."

"I never seen him get out of a car. He only come in here about a half dozen times before."

"She looks as if a Cadillac wouldn't be too much for her."

"A Cadillac or one of them," said O'Brien.

"The funny thing to me is a woman like her coming here on Christmas Eve. Not that I'm knockin' the place, Bob."

"You don't have to apologize. I got no illusions."

"I'm pretty convinced that she's the married one, but how did she get away from her family for all Christmas Eve?"

"Well, you had to fix somebody's toilet on Christmas Eve."

"How do you mean that, Bob?"

"Oh, hell, I don't know. You know what let's do? Let's just leave them be."

"All right," said Kane. He studied O'Brien. "You taking umbrage, Bob?"

"I'm not taking anything, but they're not bothering nobody, so you and me have a drink and then I think I'll close up."

"Close up, then," said Kane. "I can pay for me own drinks." He pulled his leather cap down squarely on his head and went out.

O'Brien put on his glasses, picked up his newspaper, and returned to his chair at the end of the bar.

WINTER DANCE

When the big Packard Twin-Six came rumbling into view
it was an exciting sight to the boy. The radiator and hood
had a leather cover that was streaked with ice. Strapped to
the spare tires at the rear of the car was a long-handled
shovel, crusted with snow. Icicles hung from the fenders,
and the running-boards carried an extra thickness of frozen
slush. All the side curtains were securely in place. The windshield was solid ice except for an arc, directly in front of
the chauffeur, which the manually operated wiper had kept
partially clear. The heavy car moved slowly as the tire
chains bit into the snow. You could not see the spokes of
the artillery wheels; they were hidden by a disc of ice and
snow. But the big car had made it, as it nearly always made
it in spite of the winter in the mountains. Now, moving
slowly along South Main Street, the car made the boy think
of those trains in the far West that were drawn by two and
three locomotives up and through the mountain passes.
There was something triumphant and majestic now in the
way the big Packard eased its way along South Main. Here
it was safe and sound, the dignified winner over fifteen miles
of narrow, winding mountain roads and the hazards that
winter could put in its way.

The boy watched the Packard until it came to a stop

ten feet from the curb but as close as it could get to Winkleman, the furrier's.

"There goes your girl, Ted."

"Aw, shut up," said the boy.

"She's stopping at Winkleman's. Why don't you go in
and price his coonskins? He has a coonskin in the window."

"And a card on it saying three hundred dollars," said
the boy.

"Well, ask him if he's got any for less."

"In front of her?" said the boy.

"Okay. I was only trying to be helpful."

"We could take a walk down and have a *look* at the
coat," said the boy.

"And wait till she comes out? She may be all day. Go
on in and try it on."

"Winkleman knows I'm not in the market for a coonskin," said the boy.

"Listen, for Christ's sake, Ted. This is your best
chance to talk to her. You know where she's probably going
from there."

"I know."

"You want to talk to her, don't you?"

"Sure," said the boy.

"And not with the older crowd."

"Yes," said the boy.

"Well, you won't be able to get her away from the
older crowd. Even if you cut in on her, they won't let you
get two steps with her."

"Shall we take a walk down to Winkleman's?" said the
boy.

"Give her a few seconds to get out of the car and inside
of the store."

"That's a good idea. We'll wait till she gets inside,"

said the boy. "But then I don't know what to say."

"Just strike up a conversation."

"That's easier said than done," said the boy. "Think of something."

"Well, just casually sidle up to her and say, 'Oh, hello, Natalie. Going to the tea dance?' And she'll say, 'Yes, are you?' "

"End of conversation," said the boy.

"Not necessarily. Ask her where she's staying tonight."

"I know where she's staying, and anyway, she'll think it's kind of fresh. It's none of my business where she's staying," said the boy.

"Well, have you got some money with you?"

"Dollar and forty, forty-five cents."

"That's enough. Ask her if she wants a hot chocolate. She just had a cold ride, and I'll bet she'd welcome a hot chocolate."

"*I've* never asked her to have a hot chocolate."

"What if you haven't? You have to start sometime, you dumb bastard. I'll bet she'd give anything for a hot chocolate. That's a cold ride, believe you me. And even if she says no, at least she'll give you credit for being considerate. My sister Kit, I've heard her say a hundred times, next to a good dancer, if a boy's considerate."

"She's liable to think I'm too young to buy her a hot chocolate. She's at least twenty."

"You have a dollar and forty cents. A hot chocolate will set you back fifteen cents. She knows fifteen cents won't break you. Maybe she won't even think of that, if she *wants* a hot chocolate. She's probably half frozen."

"No. They have one of those charcoal heaters, and sixty-five robes. It's as warm in her car as Mrs. Hofman's limousine."

(393)

"How do you know?"

"Because last year she gave us all a ride home from tobogganing."

"Natalie?"

"Well, not Mrs. *Hofman*. Huh. Fancy that, Mrs. Hofman giving us a ride in her limousine. I'd like to see *that*."

"Well, she's inside. Now's your chance."

"I wish it was some other store," said the boy. "I don't like to go barging in Winkleman's. That's a woman's store."

"He has a man's raccoon coat in the window. And who else is going to buy a raccoon if we don't? Not my *father*. Not *your* father. Maybe Winkleman will think you're getting one for a Christmas present. *I* am, but not this year."

"Oh, I'm getting one, next year or the year after," said the boy.

"Well, then you have a good excuse."

"The only trouble is, Winkleman will start waiting on us, and then how do I get to strike up a conversation with *her*? 'What can I do for you, boys?' And then I barge over and ask her if she wants a hot chocolate. Boy, will she see through that. She'll know we followed her in, and she'll be sore as hell."

"She'll be so busy she won't pay any attention till you speak to her. Didn't you ever go shopping with a woman?"

"Oh, you know so much about everything, you make me sick."

"You're the one that makes me sick. What's the worst she can do? Chop off your head and put it on a pikestaff? The positively worst she can do is say, 'No thank you, Ted. I do not wish a hot chocolate.'"

"If I thought for sure she wanted a hot chocolate," said the boy. "Maybe she's not going to stay in there very long. By the time we get there maybe she'll be just leaving.

Nobody gets to the tea dance before six. She's spending the night at Margery Hill's. If they all left at half past five, they'll be at the club around six. If she has to change her dress, that'll take her at least a half an hour. Five o'clock. I'm trying to dope out whether she's going to be in Winkleman's long enough. And anyway, maybe she's going some place else besides Winkleman's. I don't think Winkleman's is such a good idea. I'll bet she has other places to go. No, she wouldn't have time for a hot chocolate."

"Well, you're right. She's leaving Winkleman's. Let's see where she goes."

The girl in her six-buckle arctics came out of the fur shop, stepped into the snowbank and got in her car. The boy and his friend watched the big Packard moving slowly southward and turning west into Lantenengo Street. They did not speak until the car was out of sight.

"Well, you're fifteen cents ahead. Buy *me* a hot chocolate."

"You just had one," said the boy.

"I could polish off another."

"Oh, all right. Then what? Shall we start for the club?"

"Christ, it's only twenty after four."

"I have to pick up the kid sister. The old man wouldn't let me have the car unless I dragged her. *They* want to get there *early*. They *always* want to get there early."

"Yeah, they don't want to miss anything. What's there to miss before six o'clock? But what do *you* want to get there early for?"

"Because my damn kid sister wants to, and my old man said I had to," said the boy. "And I have to dance the first dance with her, and if she's left in the lurch I have to dance with her, and when she's ready to go home *we* have to go home. God damn it I wish I had my own car."

"I'm getting one when I graduate. I don't know whether I want a Ford or a Dodge."

"New or second-hand?"

"Brand-new."

"The Dodge costs more, but around here you need a Ford for the hills," said the boy.

"Yeah, but I wouldn't use it much around here. I'd use it mostly in the summer, and the Vineyard's practically all flat."

"I never thought of that," said the boy. "Well, I guess we ought to get started."

"Where's your car?"

"Henderson's Garage. The old man left it there to get new chains put on. Finish your hot chocolate. You'll get plenty at the club, free."

"It'll have skin on it. Christ, I hate skin on hot chocolate. It makes me puke."

"You're so delicate," said the boy.

"Well, do you like it?"

"No," said the boy. "But I have sense enough to drink tea."

The orchestra was playing "Rose of the Rio Grande," a fine fox trot with a melody that could just as easily have had a lyric about China, and the next tune *was* about Chinese—"Limehouse Blues." The band was just getting started, and trying to fill the dance floor.

"Stop trying to lead," said the boy.

"Oh, you stop being so bossy," said his sister. "Why are you so grouchy? Because your girl isn't here? Well, here she comes."

"Where?"

"In the vestibule. All the older crowd. Margery Hill has a new hat. Oh, isn't that becoming?"

" 'Oh, isn't that becoming?' You sound like Mother."

"And you sound like the Terrible-Tempered Mr. Bangs. Oh, hello, Ralph. Are you cutting in on my adorable brother? Teddy, dear, will you relinquish me?"

"Thanks for the dance," said the boy. He joined the stag line and lit a cigarette.

"Got a butt?"

"Hello, Jonesy. Sure," said the boy, offering a pack.

"Your girl's here. Just got here a minute ago."

"Oh, crack wise," said the boy, and turned away. Presently the fellows from the older crowd gathered in the vestibule, waiting for the girls to come downstairs from the ladies' dressing-room.

"Hello, Teddy," said Ross Dreiber.

"Hello, Ross," said the boy.

"Why aren't you out there tripping the light fantastic? Looking them over?"

"Just looking them over."

"Any new talent? I see your sister. She fourteen?"

"Fifteen."

"Fifteen. Well, I'll be out of college by the time she's allowed to go to proms. But she certainly has sprung up since last summer."

"Sure has."

"What have you got? Two more years?"

"One more after this," said the boy.

"Then where?"

"Lafayette, I guess. Maybe Princeton."

"Well, when you get ready to go, if you decide on Lafayette, I'd be glad to write a letter to our chapter there. You know you can't go wrong with Deke, anywhere. What was your father?"

"Theta Delt."

"Well, I have nothing to say against Theta Delt. They're a keen organization. But take a look at Deke before you shake hands. And think twice about Princeton, boy. I know a lot of good eggs were awfully disappointed they went to Princeton. Take my word for it. But of course it all depends on the man."

"Yeah. Sure."

"Have you got another butt on you? . . . Omars! My brand! Deke for you, boy. You even smoke the right cigarettes."

The boy held a match to Dreiber's cigarette.

"Hello, Teddy."

He turned. "Hello, Nat," he said.

"Finish your cigarette, Ross. I'll dance with Teddy. Or are you waiting for somebody?"

"No, I'm not waiting for anybody. But do you mean it?"

"Of course I do. Come on," she said.

"Probably get about two steps," said the boy.

"Well, then let's walk down to the other end of the room and start from there. Shall we?"

"Fine," said the boy.

She took his arm and they marched to the far end of the room. She greeted friends along the way, but said nothing to the boy. Then she held up her arms and said, "All right?" and they began to dance. He was good, and he had self-confidence because he was good. She was good, and she liked dancing with him. There was no need to talk, and at this end of the room people got out of their way. They got all through two choruses of "Stumbling" before the music stopped. "Oh, that was grand," she said. She applauded with him.

"Shall we sit down?" said the boy.

"Well, I think I'd better find our crowd."

"Don't do that, Nat. Please?" said the boy.

"No, Teddy. I must, really," she said. "Cut in later."

"Couldn't we just sit down a minute?"

She shook her head. "You know they'll only kid you."

"Oh, you know that?"

"Uh-huh. They kid me too, don't forget."

"They do? Who does?"

"Oh, my crowd. Same as your crowd kids you."

"You're not sore at me because they kid you?"

"Of course not. And don't you be embarrassed, either."

"You know it's all my fault, Nat," said the boy.

She hesitated. "You mean on account of the postcard?"

"I showed it to everybody. I shouldn't have."

"Well, if I felt like sending a friend of mine a post-card," she said.

"But I went around bragging about it, and showing it to everybody."

"Well, if you wanted to. I don't even remember what I said on the card."

" 'You would love it here. Lots of good trout fishing. Have gone on two pack trips. See you at Christmas. Natalie.' And a picture of the ranch."

"I remember," she said. "Not very incriminating, was it? Will you take me over to their table now, Teddy?"

"And your word of honor you're not annoyed with me."

"Only if you let them embarrass you," she said.

"Nat?"

"What?"

"I don't have to say it, do I? You know, don't you? You do know?"

She nodded. "Give me your arm," she said.

THE WOMEN OF
MADISON AVENUE

Mrs. Dabner walked boldly if not bravely up Madison Avenue, thinking of how she would look to someone in a bus. How often, when she came to New York, she would be in a Madison Avenue bus and see a woman like herself—nice-looking, well-dressed, late-thirtyish, early-fortyish—and wonder what the woman was doing, where she was bound, what she was thinking. "I'll bet I know a lot of people you know," she would say to that woman. "I'll bet we could sit down together and inside of five minutes—why, we might even be related."

There were always so many attractive women on Madison Avenue after lunch. They would come in pairs from the restaurants in the upper Fifties and the Sixties, say a few words of farewell at the Madison Avenue corner, and go their separate ways, the one on her way to the hairdresser or to finish her shopping, the other deciding to walk home. So many of them were so attractive, and Ethel Dabner liked to look at them from her seat in the bus. But today she was walking, and inside one of those buses, looking at her, possibly thinking how attractive *she* was, might be the one woman in New York who had good reason to hate her. Ethel Dabner did not like people to hate her, and if she could ever sit down and have a sensible talk with Laura

Howell she could make Laura realize that she really had no reason to hate her. But how long since anyone had been able to sit down and have a sensible talk with Laura Howell?

Ethel Dabner turned her head to look at a crowded bus, but what was the use of looking for a woman she had never seen?

At Sixty-fourth Street she left Madison Avenue and was glad to leave it, with its crowded buses and all those women, one of whom could have been Laura Howell. She let herself in the ground-floor apartment and was relieved, though not surprised, to find that she was alone. Half past three, he had said, and that was half an hour away, but sometimes he was early and invariably he was punctual. "I may even be a little late today," he had said. "I don't know how long this meeting'll last, but if I'm still in there at ha' past three I'll get word to you."

"You'll get word to me? How will you get word to me? You can't tell your secretary to call me and say you'll be late."

"No, but . . ."

"But what?"

"Well, I was thinking," he said. "I can tell Miss Bowen to call this number and have her say that Mr. Howell would be late for his appointment with Mr. Jenkins."

"Who's Mr. Jenkins?"

"There is no Mr. Jenkins, but you're Mr. Jenkins's secretary. Do you see? You'll answer, and Miss Bowen will think you're Mr. Jenkins's secretary."

" 'Tisn't worth the bother. You just get here when you can."

"Well, just so you understand I may be a little late."

"Honey, I understand. All you have to do is tell me you'll be a little late."

He was so careful, so elaborate, so—as he put it—ready for any and all contingencies. The simple thing, to meet her in her hotel, was too simple for him. "I could run into sixty-five thousand people in your hotel," he had said. "I could just be *seen* there, without knowing who saw me." And so there was this apartment, rented by his bachelor son who was now in the army. "I told Robbie I'd keep it for him while he was away, for when he got leave."

"Who do you think you're kidding? Doesn't he know you want it for yourself?"

"If he wants to guess, but he's on my side."

"One of these days we'll be there and the door'll fly open and there'll be your son and a half dozen of his G.I. buddies."

"No. He'll have a little problem of getting the key. I took care of *that* contingency."

"What's to prevent someone seeing me leave the apartment? Did you take care of that contingency?"

"How many people do you know in New York?"

"Half the girls I went to school with and a lot of their husbands. First *and* second husbands, if it comes to that."

"All right. You're in town for a visit. Couldn't you be calling on someone on East Sixty-fourth Street? Someone they don't know?"

"I guess I could. I guess so."

It was a strange apartment for such goings-on. From the beginning she had felt as though they had invaded the dormitory rooms of a sophisticated undergraduate. There were a few college souvenirs: an initiation paddle marked D.K.E., some group photographs, some pewter mugs and silver trophies; but the pictures on the walls were esoteric moderns, the statuettes unidentifiable forms in ebony and aluminum, and hanging above the fireplace a small collec-

tion of Polynesian stringed instruments. In the bathroom
there was an explicit drawing of a nude, that seemed to
have been cut rather than drawn, the lines were so sharp,
and the nakedness of the woman offended Ethel Dabner.
It was a *map* of a woman, without mystery, without charm,
without warmth or even sensuality, and she hated the drawing and the German who had made it, so much so that she
based her dislike of her lover's son on the fact that he would
own such a picture.

She hung her street clothes in Robbie's closet, in
among the plastic-covered civilian suits and the treed shoes.
She put on his kimono and went to the kitchen and filled a
bucket with ice cubes from the nearly empty refrigerator.
Burt would want a Scotch and soda when he arrived, and
now she had nothing to do but wait.

If he had been his usual punctual self he would be here
now; it was half past three. But in spite of having been fore-
warned, she was annoyed to find that at three-thirty-two he
had not arrived. He was two minutes late, and she had had
to fish in her purse for glasses in order to read the time on
her wristwatch. Her watch, her rings, her bracelet, her necklace lay on the coffee table, and she thought of taking them
to the bathroom and leaving them on the glass shelf, where
they would be all together in one place when she was ready
to put them on again. But she had no desire to go back to
the bathroom; she had a desire *not* to go back to the bathroom and that nasty drawing.

Every little sound she made was distinct in the silence
of the apartment, but in a little while the outside street noise
began to break up into individual sounds, notably the sounds
of the buses starting and stopping. There were the other
sounds, too, but her ear kept going back to the special
sounds of the buses, and she thought of the women on the

buses, looking out at the women who walked, the attractive, well-dressed women who had decided to walk home after a pleasant, happy lunch with a woman friend. What would she be thinking about, the attractive woman who was walking home? How nice it was to have Jane Jones for a friend? How well Jane looked? She would walk up Madison Avenue, this woman, with a little smile on her face because she was thinking of her friend Jane Jones, and that was one of the things that would make her attractive, that smile of appreciation for her friend. People in the buses would look out at her and think what an attractive woman she was, a woman other women could trust.

Fourteen minutes to four, and the telephone rang. "Hello," she said, then, remembering: "Mr. Jenkins' office."

There was a loud laugh at the other end. "It's me," he said. "I just broke up the meeting. I told those bastards we had to wind it up by quarter to four, so I'll be right there, honey."

"Well, you just hurry, d'you hear?" she said.

"Listen, I'm just as eager as you are," he said.

"I didn't mean that," she said. "I'm just tired of sitting here all by myself in this apartment."

"Shouldn't take me but twenty minutes," he said.

"All right," she said, and hung up.

So sure of himself, so sure of her, whichever it was, she hated it. She hated what he took for granted, that she wanted and needed him, was as eager as he was. And now she found that a decision had been made for her; he had not made it, she had not made it, but it was there and only needed to be acted upon. She got all dressed again and satisfied herself that anyone seeing her from the bus would consider her very attractive and nice. She took the nasty picture down from the bathroom wall and put it face down on the floor and stamped on it. She next put the apartment key on the coffee table near the ice bucket, and for the last time she left the apartment.

In the bus she got a seat next to the window and at Sixtieth or maybe it was Sixty-first Street an attractive, nice-looking woman walking up Madison happened to look in the window and catch her eye. Ethel Dabner smiled and bowed, and the nice-looking woman smiled back.

YOU DON'T REMEMBER ME

The question was sometimes asked about Stan Wigmore:
"Has he any money of his own?" It was a mean question,
because the people who asked it were generally well aware
that Stan Wigmore had some money of his own, but not
very much, and nowhere near as much as Dee Wigmore.
You would hear the question after Stan had been in some
escapade or was more offensive than usual, and it was
not so much a query for information as a criticism and a
protest. The comparative financial status of Stan Wigmore
and of Dee was his most vulnerable aspect, and it provided
comfort for those who had been recently shocked or offended by him.

It was, therefore, highly irregular for Mary Chorpenning to have replied to Jack Spangler when he asked the usual
question. The scene was the beach club; the time, about
two o'clock one Sunday afternoon in the early part of the
summer. Stan Wigmore, alone, wearing a Hong Kong pajama suit and Paisley scarf, no socks, and highly polished
alligator loafers, had a plate of food in one hand and a tall
iced coffee in the other, and he was looking around for a
place to sit. After a quick and rather expert appraisal of the
crowd he went to a table where there were four young
people and two vacant chairs. He asked if he could sit with

them, and they nodded. He did not attempt to make conversation with the young people. He ate his food and sipped his iced coffee, taking quick looks at the other tables and out at the ocean while ministering to his appetite. The young people remained silent as he hurried through his lunch, wiped his mouth with a paper napkin, lit a cigarette and departed. The moment he left the young people's table they relaxed into the frenetic weariness that is their current mode; in the minutes, fewer than ten, that he had been with them they had sat stiffly, watching him raise fork to mouth as though observing some new and alien custom.

Wigmore, cigarette in hand, walked up to the top of the dune, speaking to no one on the way, and slowly but uninterruptedly scanned the bathers on the beach who had not come up for lunch. He saw, or did not see, what or whom he was looking for, then abruptly he turned his back to the ocean and walked rapidly away in the direction of the club entrance, out and down the road to a hulking new Bentley saloon.

The group about the umbrella table watched him drive off in the big green car, and Jack Spangler was the first to speak. "Stanley M-for-Martin Wigmore," said Spangler. "Has he any money of his own?"

"Well, he has enough so he doesn't have to go on living with Dee," said Mary Chorpenning.

"He has? I didn't realize that," said Spangler. "When did that happen?"

"He always did have," said Mary Chorpenning.

"Now how the hell would you know a thing like that?"

"*You* must have known it at one time. He was never starving."

"Oh, that's different," said Spangler. "I thought you were trying to say he had some secret fortune of his own."

"Not at all. But enough to live on," said Mary Chorpenning.

"To live on. The subsistence level. But not Bentleys. No ninety-dollar shoes," said Spangler. "You're not telling us anything new, Mary, but I'm curious to know why you're defending him all of a sudden."

"I'm not defending him. Only making a statement of fact. Stan Wigmore has always had some money of his own," said Mary Chorpenning.

"And about thirty million dollars of Barlow money via Dee," said Spangler. "And he needs every cent of it to get away with what he gets away with."

"Well, now, why? What's he done now?" said Agnes Lamb.

"Who do you suppose he was looking for so casually a minute ago?" said Spangler.

"I don't know," said Agnes Lamb. "I've been away."

"I'm almost afraid to mention it in front of Mary," said Spangler. "Mary seems to be on some defensive kick about him. So you tell her, Mary."

"The Maclyn girl," said Mary Chorpenning.

"Kitty Maclyn?"

"That's what they say," said Mary.

"But she's only about seventeen, isn't she? Isn't she at Miss Curry's?" said Agnes Lamb.

"No, I think she's at college somewhere. She's eighteen or nineteen," said Mary.

"Still a lot less than half his age," said Agnes. "Well, I didn't know anything about that. Is it something new?"

"I don't know," said Mary. "Jack probably knows."

"I understand it's not new, but it's certainly out in the open now," said Spangler.

"To what extent?" said Agnes Lamb. "Does Dee know?"

"Of course she knows," said Spangler. "But she always *has* looked the other way."

"Well, let's get down to cases. Is it an *affair?*"

"Everybody seems to think so," said Spangler.

"Well, the thing I always want to know is, where do they go? But then where does anyone go? Lots of places, I suppose, or else whenever I come down here I wouldn't always seem to hear of some new pairing off."

"You're so pious, Agnes," said Spangler. "Where did *you* go when you were still married to Jim and seeing Pete?"

"That was ages ago, and I wouldn't tell you anyway. But you can be very sure Stan Wigmore and Kitty Maclyn aren't going there."

"Somebody's house," said Spangler. "Well, that's probably where Wigmore and Kitty go."

"Not your house, Jack?" said Agnes.

"No, not my house. In the first place, I wouldn't be so disloyal to Dee. And in the second place, I'm not doing any favors for Stanley Wigmore if I can help it. I've let my house be used for assignation purposes, but for friends only. Not that I haven't got a pretty good idea whose house Wigmore could borrow."

"Don't look at *me,*" said Mary Chorpenning.

"I wasn't thinking of you, dear. I just happened to take that moment to study your pearls. Are those the ones that your aunt paid so much for and they turned color?"

"Yes. They're the real ones. Now worth about five hundred," said Mary.

"And what was it your aunt paid for them?"

"Oh, heavens. I think it was thirty thousand."

"Was it because she was acid?"

"That's what made them change color, but real pearls aren't worth anything anyway," said Mary.

"Let's not change the subject," said Agnes Lamb.

"What does George Maclyn say about all this? Kay—I wouldn't expect her to come up out of her highball glass. But when I used to know George years ago, when he and Kay were first married, no daughter of his would dare have anything to do with a married man. Do you remember, Mary? What was it we used to call him?"

"George? Uh—Father, wasn't it?"

"No, no. It wasn't Father. *The Vicar.* We used to call him The Vicar."

"Oh, you don't have to tell me anything about George," said Spangler. "I went to Allen-Stevenson with him for three years. I used to get him in boxing."

"You boxed?" said Mary Chorpenning.

"We had to, and he was just as nasty-mean-cruel as he could be. If Kay's gassed half the time, I can fully understand why. She's married to a mean, sadistic—"

"Then what's he doing letting his eighteen-year-old daughter play around with someone like Stan Wigmore?" said Agnes Lamb.

"I don't really think they're playing around," said Mary Chorpenning.

"Here we go again," said Spangler.

"Maybe they are, I don't know, but I just don't think so," said Mary.

"Well, of course the whole thing's all news to me, but it just isn't like Stan Wigmore to—and none of these kids have Platonic affairs, so I'm told. I was never sure about my own, but thank heaven they're both married and I *guess* settled down."

"Mary, Mary, watch this," said Spangler, nervously excited. He lowered his voice and spoke to Agnes Lamb. "Coming up the boardwalk. Kitty Maclyn. Now don't just stop talking, for heaven's sake, but watch."

The girl was quite tall, her blond hair worn almost at shoulder length and swinging as she walked. She had on a white blouse, left unbuttoned except over her middle, and her narrow blue pants were a tight fit. Her shoes were flats of leather with thongs between her bare toes. She was carrying a long cigarette in her right hand, which she held at arm's length behind her. She was fearfully self-conscious and arrogantly affected in manner and clothes, and she defied the world to deny that she was beautiful.

"Good Lord, that's Kitty Maclyn?" said Agnes Lamb.

"That's our Kitty," said Spangler.

"I never thought I'd feel sorry for Dee Barlow," said Agnes Lamb.

The girl went to the table at which Wigmore had eaten his hasty lunch. She sat in the very chair he had been sitting in.

"I wish we could hear what they're saying," said Agnes Lamb. "Who are the others?"

"The boy with the khaki pants is Mike Raymond, next to him, Amy Compton. The boy in the blazer is I don't know who, and the other girl is Carmelita Dougherty," said Spangler. "And that ought to make you feel a hundred."

The Maclyn girl and the others exchanged no greetings but immediately began a conversation, in which all but the boy in the blazer participated. The Maclyn girl sat with her legs stretched out under the table and moved her body back and forth in a rocking motion. She smoked her cigarette and looked at the top of the table rather than at her friends while talking. The Raymond boy put his arm around her shoulder, and she reached back and gently removed it and in a continuous motion smoothed her back hair, fondly, sensually. She dinched her cigarette in a glass ash tray and again in a continuous motion picked up the Raymond boy's wrist and squinted at his watch. She got up and left her friends and started back toward the entrance, but as she reached the Spangler table she halted.

"Hello, Mrs. Chorpenning. Hello, Mr. Spangler. Hello, Mrs. Lamb. You don't remember me, but I'm Kitty Maclyn." She put out her hand.

"Of course I remember you, Kitty. How are your mother and father?" said Agnes Lamb.

"Very well, thank you. Are you down for the summer?"

"No, just till the first of August."

"Mummy would love to see you, I'm sure," said the girl. Then a second's awkwardness, and she said: "Well, nice to've seen you again, Mrs. Lamb. Mrs. Chorpenning. Mr. Spangler." She went on her way.

"*She* is *gorgeous*," said Agnes Lamb.

"Isn't she?" said Mary Chorpenning.

"Perfectly lovely," said Agnes Lamb.

"Are you *crying?*" said Spangler.

"Oh—shut—up," said Agnes Lamb.

YOUR FAH NEEFAH NEEFACE

This woman, when she was about nineteen or twenty, had a stunt that she and her brother would play, usually in a railroad station or on a train or in a hotel lobby. I saw them work the stunt under the clock at the Biltmore in the days when that meeting-place was a C-shaped arrangement of benches, and I remember it so well because it was the first time I ever saw the stunt and the first time I ever saw her or her brother. It was more than thirty years ago.

She was sitting there, quite erect, her legs crossed, smoking a cigarette and obviously, like everyone else, waiting to meet someone. She was wearing a beret sort of hat that matched her suit, and it was easy to tell by the way she smoked her cigarette that she had handled many of them in her short life. I remember thinking that I would like to hear her talk; she was so self-possessed and good-humored in her study of the young men and young women who were keeping dates at the clock. The drag she took on her cigarette was a long one; the smoke kept coming from her nostrils long after you thought it was all gone. She was terribly pretty, with a straight little nose and lively light blue eyes.

Presently a young man came up the stairs in no great

hurry. He was wearing a black topcoat with a velvet collar and carrying a derby hat. He was tall, but not outstandingly so, and he had tightly curled blond hair—a 150-pound crew type, he was. He reached the meeting-place, scanned the faces of the people who were seated there, and then turned away to face the stairs. He watched the men and women coming up the stairs, but after a minute or so he turned his head and looked back at the girl, frowned as though puzzled, then again faced the incoming people. He did that several times, and I began to think that this was a young man on a blind date who had not been given a full or accurate description of his girl. She meanwhile was paying no attention to him.

Finally he went directly to the girl, and in a firm voice that everyone under the clock could hear he said, "Are you by any chance Sallie Brown?"

"I am, but what's it to you?" she said.

"Do you know who I am?" he said.

"No."

"You don't recognize me at all?"

"Never saw you in my whole life."

"Yes you did, Sallie. Look carefully," he said.

"I'm sorry, but I'm quite positive I've never seen you before."

"Asbury Park. Think a minute."

"I've been to Asbury Park, but so've a lot of people. Why should I remember you?"

"Sallie. It's Jack. I'm *Jack*."

"Jack? Jack Who? . . . No! My brother! You—you're Jack? Oh, darling, darling!" She stood up and looked at the people near her and said to them, rather helplessly, "This is my brother. My *brother*. I haven't seen him since —oh, darling. Oh, this is so wonderful." She put her arms around him and kissed him. "Oh, where have you *been?* Where have they been keeping you? Are you all right?"

"I'm all right. What about you?"

"Oh, let's go somewhere. We have so much to talk about." She smiled at all the other young men and women, then took her brother's arm and they went down the stairs and out, leaving all of us with the happy experience to think about and to tell and re-tell. The girl I was meeting arrived ten or fifteen minutes after Sallie and Jack Brown departed, and when we were in the taxi on our way to a cocktail party I related what I had seen. The girl waited until I finished the story and then said, "Was this Sallie Brown blond? About my height? And was her brother a blond too, with curly hair cut short?"

"Exactly," I said. "Do you know them?"

"Sure. The only part of the story that's true is that they are brother and sister. The rest is an act. Her name is Sallie Collins and his name is Johnny Collins. They're from Chicago. They're very good."

"Good? I'll say they're good. They fooled me and everybody else."

"They always do. People cry, and sometimes they clap as if they were at the theater. Sallie and Johnny Collins, from Chicago. Did you ever hear of the Spitbacks?"

"No. Spitbacks?"

"It's a sort of a club in Chicago. You have to be kicked out of school to be a Spitback, and Johnny's been kicked out of at least two."

"And what about her?"

"She's eligible. She was two years behind me at Farmington."

"What was she kicked out for?"

"Oh, I don't know. Smoking, I think. She wasn't there

(415)

very long. Now she's going to school in Greenwich, I think. Johnny's a runner downtown."

"What other tricks do they do?"

"Whatever comes into their heads, but they're famous for the long-lost-brother-and-sister one. They have it down pat. Did she look at the other people as much as to say, 'I can't believe it, it's like a dream'?"

"Yes."

"They can't do it as much as they used to. All their friends know about it and they've told so many people. Of course it annoys some people."

"What other *kind* of thing do they do?"

"Oh—I don't know. Nothing mean. Not practical jokes, if that's what you're thinking of."

"I'd like to meet her sometime. And him. They seem like fun," I said.

I never did meet Johnny. He was drowned somewhere in Northern Michigan a year or so after I was a member of their audience at the Biltmore, and when I finally met Sallie she was married and living in New Canaan; about thirty years old, still very pretty; but instinctively I refrained from immediately recalling to her the once famous long-lost-brother stunt. I do not mean to say that she seemed to be mourning Johnny after ten years. But fun was not a word that came quickly to mind when I was introduced to her. If I had never seen her before or known about her stunts I would have said that *her* idea of fun would be the winning of the Connecticut State Women's Golf Championship. Women who like golf and play it well do seem to move more deliberately than, for instance, women who play good tennis, and my guess that golf was her game was hardly brilliant, since I knew that her husband was a 4-handicap player.

"Where are you staying?" she said, at dinner.

"At the Randalls'."

"Oh, do you sail?"

"No, Tom and I grew up together in Pennsylvania."

"Well, you're going to have a lot of time to yourself this weekend, aren't you? Tom and Rebecca will be at Rye, won't they?"

"I don't mind," I said. "I brought along some work, and Rebecca's the kind of hostess that leaves you to your own devices."

"Work? What kind of work?"

"Textiles."

"Well, that must be a very profitable business these days, isn't it? Isn't the Army ordering millions of uniforms?"

"I don't know."

"You're not in that kind of textiles?"

"Yes, I am. But I'm not allowed to answer any questions about the Army."

"I would like to be a spy."

"You'd make a good one," I said.

"Do you think so? What makes you think I would?"

"Because the first time I ever saw you . . ." I then had been in her company for more than an hour, and felt better about recalling the incident at the Biltmore.

"How nice of you to remember that," she said, and smiled. "I wonder why you did?"

"Well, you were very pretty. Still are. But the whole performance was so expert. Professional. You could probably be a very good spy."

"No. That was all Johnny. All those things we used to do, Johnny thought them up. He was the brains of the team. I was the foil. Like the girl in tights that magicians always have. Anybody could have done it with Johnny masterminding . . . Would you like to come here for lunch Sunday? I happen to know that Rebecca's without a cook, so you're going to have to go to the club, otherwise. Unless of course you have another invitation."

I said I would love to come to lunch Sunday, and she thereupon engaged in conversation with the gentleman on her left. I was surprised to find on Sunday that she and I were lunching alone. We had cold soup, then were served crab flakes and some vegetables, and when the maid was gone Sallie took a piece of paper from the pocket of her blouse. "This is the clock at the Biltmore that day. This is where I was sitting. Here is where you were sitting. If I'm not mistaken, you were wearing a grey suit and you sat with your overcoat folded over your lap. You needed a haircut."

"By God, you're absolutely right."

"You had a watch on a chain, and you kept taking it out of your pocket, and putting it back."

"I don't remember that, but probably. The girl I was meeting was pretty late. Incidentally, went to Farmington with you. Laura Pratt."

"Oh, goodness. Laura. If she'd been on time you never would have seen the long-lost-brother-and-sister act. She hated me at Farmington, but I see her once in a while now. She lives in Litchfield, as I suppose you know. But have I convinced you that I remembered you as well as you remembered me?"

"It's the greatest compliment I ever had in my life."

"No. You were good-looking and still are, but what I chiefly remembered was that I was hoping you'd try to pick me up. Then I was just a little bit annoyed that you didn't try. God, that was forever ago, wasn't it?"

"Just about," I said. "How come you didn't say anything at dinner the other night?"

"I'm not sure. Selfish, I guess. That was *my* evening. I wanted you to do all the remembering, and I guess I wanted to hear you talk about Johnny."

"He drowned," I said. "In Michigan."

"Yes, but *I* didn't tell you that. How did you know?"

"I saw it in the paper at the time."

"Rebecca told me you were getting a divorce. Does that upset you? Not her telling me, but breaking up with your wife."

"It isn't the pleasantest experience in the world," I said.

"I suppose not. It never is. I was married before I married my present husband, you know."

"No, I didn't know."

"It lasted a year. He was Johnny's best friend, but other than that we had nothing in common. Not that a married couple have to have too much in common, but they ought to have something else besides loving the same person, in this case my brother. Hugh, my first husband, was what Johnny used to call one of his stooges, just like me. But somehow it isn't very attractive for a *man* to be another man's stooge. It's all right for a sister to be a stooge, but not another man, and almost the minute Johnny died I suddenly realized that without Johnny, Hugh was nothing. As a threesome we had a lot of fun together, really a lot of fun. And with Hugh I could have sex. I don't think there was any of that in my feeling for Johnny, although there may have been. If there was, I certainly managed to keep it under control and never even thought about it. I didn't know much about those things, but once or twice I vaguely suspected that if either of us had any of that feeling for Johnny, it was Hugh. But I'm sure he didn't know it either."

"So you divorced Hugh and married Tatnall."

"Divorced Hugh and married Bill Tatnall. All because you were afraid to pick me up and ditch Laura Pratt."

"But I could have become one of Johnny's stooges, too," I said. "I probably would have."

"No. Johnny's stooges all had to be people he'd known all his life, like me or Hugh, or Jim Danzig."

"Who is Jim Danzig?"

"Jim Danzig was the boy in the canoe with Johnny when it overturned. I don't like to talk about poor Jim. He blamed himself for the accident and he's become a hopeless alcoholic, at thirty-two, mind you."

"Why did he blame himself? Did he have any reason to?"

"Well—he was in the canoe, and they were both a little tight. It was at night and they'd been to a party at the Danzigs' cabin and decided to row across the lake to our cabin, instead of driving eight or nine miles. A mile across the lake, eight and a half miles by car. One of those crazy ideas you get when you're tight. Johnny would have been home in fifteen minutes by car, but they started out in the canoe, heading for the lights on our landing. I guess there was some kind of horseplay and the canoe overturned, and Jim couldn't find Johnny. He kept calling him but he didn't get any answer, and he couldn't right the canoe, although Jim was almost as good a boatman as Johnny—when sober. But they'd had an awful lot to drink, and it was pitch dark. No moon. And finally Jim floated and swam ashore and then for a while was lost in the woods. It was after Labor Day and most of the cabins were boarded up for the winter, and Jim in his bare feet, all cut and bleeding by the time he got to the Danzigs' cabin, and a little out of his head in addition to all he'd had to drink. I think they had to dynamite to recover Johnny's body. I wasn't there and I'm glad I wasn't.

From the reports it must have been pretty horrible, and even now I'd rather not think about it."

"Then don't," I said.

"No, let's change the subject," she said.

"All right. Then you married Tatnall."

"Married Bill Tatnall a year and a half after Hugh and I were divorced. Two children. Betty, and Johnny, ages six and four. You haven't mentioned any children. Did you have any?"

"No."

"Children hold so many marriages together," she said.

"Yours?"

"Of course mine. I wouldn't have said that otherwise, would I? How often do you see the Randalls?"

"Oh, maybe once or twice a year."

"Did they know you were coming here for lunch?"

"No," I said. "They left very early this morning, before I was up."

"That explains it, why you don't know about Bill and me. Well, when you tell them you were here today, don't be surprised if they give you that tut-tut look. Naughty-naughty. Bill and I raise a lot of eyebrows hereabouts. Next year it'll be some other couple, but at the moment it's Bill and I."

"Who's the transgressor? You, or your husband?"

"It's the marriage, more so than Bill or I individually. In a community like this, or maybe any suburban or small-town community, they don't seem to mind adultery if they can blame one person or the other. The husband or the wife has to be the guilty party, but not both."

"I don't agree with you," I said. "I think that when a marriage is in trouble people take sides, one side or the other, and they mind a great deal."

"Yes, they want the marriage to break up and they want to be able to blame one or the other. But when the marriage doesn't break up, when people can't fix the blame on one person, they're deprived of their scandal. They feel cheated out of something, and they're outraged, horrified, that people like Bill and I go on living together. They really hate me for putting up with Bill's chasing, and they hate Bill for letting me get away with whatever I get away with. Bill and I ought to be in the divorce courts, fighting like cats and dogs. Custody fights, fights about alimony."

"But you and your husband have what is commonly called an arrangement?" I said.

"It would seem that way, although actually we haven't. At least not a spoken one. You see, we don't even care that much about each other. He just goes his way, and I go mine."

"You mean to say you never had a discussion about it? The first time he found out you were unfaithful to him, or he was unfaithful to you? You didn't have any discussion at all?"

"Why is that so incredible?" she said. "Let's have our coffee out on the porch."

I followed her out to the flagstone terrace and its iron-and-glass furniture. She poured the coffee and resumed speaking. "I guessed that Bill had another girl. It wasn't hard to guess. He left me severely alone. Then I guessed he had another, and since I hadn't made a fuss about the first one I certainly wasn't going to make a fuss about the second. Or the third."

"Then I gather you began to have gentlemen friends of your own."

"I did. And I guess Bill thought I'd been so nice about his peccadillos that he decided to be just as nice about mine."

"But without any discussion. You simply tacitly agreed not to live together as man and wife?"

"You're trying to make me say what you want me to say, that somehow we did have a discussion, a quarrel, a fight ending in an arrangement. Well, I won't say it."

"Then there's something a lot deeper that I guess I'd better not go into."

"I won't deny that, not for a minute."

"Was it sexual incompatibility?"

"You can call it that. But that isn't as deep as you seem to think it was. A lot of men and women, husbands and wives, are sexually incompatible. This was deeper, and worse. Worse because Bill is a yellow coward. He never dared come out and say what he was thinking."

"Which was?"

"He got angry with me one time and said that my brother Johnny'd been a sinister influence. That's as much as he'd actually say. That Johnny'd been a sinister influence. He didn't dare accuse me—and Johnny—of what he really meant. Why didn't he dare? Because he didn't want to admit that his wife had been guilty of incest. It wasn't really so much that incest was bad as that it had happened to his own wife. Someone, one of Bill's lady friends, had planted that little idea in his thick skull, and he believed it. Now he fully believes it, but I don't care."

"A question that naturally comes to my mind," I said, "is why are you telling me all this?"

"Because you saw us together without knowing us. You saw Johnny and me doing the long-lost-brother act. How did we seem to you?"

"I thought you were genuine. I fell for it."

"But then Laura Pratt told you it was an act. What did you think then?"

"I thought you were charming. Fun."

"That's what I hoped you thought. That's what *we* thought we were, Johnny and I. We thought we were absolutely charming—and fun. Maybe we weren't charming, but we *were* fun. And that's all we were. And now people have ruined that for us. For me, at least. Johnny never knew people thought he had a sinister influence over me. Or me over him, for that matter. But aren't people darling? Aren't they lovely? They've managed to ruin all the fun Johnny and I had together all those years. Just think, I was married twice and had two children before I began to grow up. I didn't really start to grow up till my own husband made me realize what people had been thinking, *and* saying, about Johnny and me. If that's growing up, you can have it."

"Not everybody thought that about you and Johnny."

"It's enough that anybody did. And it's foolish to think that only one or two thought it," she said. "We did so many things for fun, Johnny and I. Harmless jokes that hurt nobody and that we thought were uproariously funny. Some of them I don't ever think of any more because of the interpretation people put on them . . . We had one that was the opposite of the long-lost-brother. The newlyweds. Did you ever hear of our newlyweds?"

"No," I said.

"It came about by accident. We were driving East and had to spend the night in some little town in Pennsylvania. The car broke down and we went to the local hotel and when we went to register the clerk just took it for granted that we were husband and wife. Johnny caught on right away and he whispered to the clerk, loud enough for me to hear, that we were newlyweds but that I was shy and wanted separate rooms. So we got our separate rooms, and you should have seen the hotel people stare at us that night in the dining-room and the next morning at breakfast. We laughed for a whole day about that and then we used to do the same trick every time we had to drive anywhere overnight. Didn't hurt anybody."

"What else did you do?"

"Oh, lots of things. And not only tricks. We both adored Fred and Adele Astaire, and we copied their dancing. Not as good, of course, but everybody always guessed who we were imitating. We won a couple of prizes at parties. Johnny was really quite good. 'I lahv, yourfah, neeface. Your fah, neefah, neeface.' " She suddenly began to cry and I sat still.

That was twenty years ago. I don't believe that anything that happened to her since then made much difference to Sallie, but even if it did, that's the way I remember her and always will.

MODERN LIBRARY GIANTS

A series of sturdily bound and handsomely printed, full-sized library editions of books formerly available only in expensive sets. These volumes contain from 600 to 1,400 pages each.

THE MODERN LIBRARY GIANTS REPRESENT A
SELECTION OF THE WORLD'S GREATEST BOOKS